NEVER AGAIN!

Also by Harold Weisberg

Whitewash: The Report on the Warren Report
Whitewash II: The FBI-Secret Service Coverup
Photographic Whitewash: Suppressed Kennedy Assassination Pictures
Whitewash IV: JFK Top Secret Assassination Transcript
Oswald in New Orleans: Case for Conspiracy with the CIA
Post Mortem: JFK Assassination Coverup Smashed
Martin Luther King: The Assassination (Formerly titled *Frame-Up*)
Selections from Whitewash
Case Open

Never Again!

The Government Conspiracy
in the JFK Assassination

Harold Weisberg

Carroll & Graf Publishers/Richard Gallen
New York

First edition 1995

Carroll & Graf Publishers, Inc.
260 Fifth Avenue
New York, NY 10001

Library of Congress Cataloging-in-Publication Data is available.

ISBN: 0-7867-0206-0

Manufactured in the United States of America

10   9   8   7   6   5   4   3   2   1

Contents

Contents

Preface

THE UNITED STATES GOVERNMENT CONCEIVED AND EXECUTED AT LEAST one John F. Kennedy assassination conspiracy.

This conspiracy extended into and involved the White House.

The proof presented for the first time in this book is the result of thirteen prolonged and costly lawsuits I filed under the Freedom of Information Act (FOIA) against various government components: the Department of Justice and the Federal Bureau of Investigation (FBI) and including the Central Intelligence Agency (CIA) and the National Archives.[1]

Some of these lawsuits were precedential. One led to the Congressional amending of the FOIA to open FBI, CIA, and related files.

Is there a smoking gun in these records?

Yes. In fact there are many.

But this book does not charge that the government conspired to kill JFK.[2]

Not *that* smoking gun.

For the first time anywhere, based on fact and evidence, not theory, this book assembles and documents indications that some members in the higher echelons of the military may have been involved in such a conspiracy.

---

[1] These lawsuits are listed by their federal district court for the District of Columbia case numbers along with some of the appeals to the circuit court for the District of Columbia in the bibliography. Also several suits for records relating to the assassination of Martin Luther King, Jr., are listed. The withheld records disclosed to me as a result of the FOIA lawsuits total about .33 million pages. Ultimately all such records, along with my own work, will be available as a permanent public archive at Hood College in Frederick, Maryland. These lawsuits are listed in the bibliography.

[2] See especially chapter 2, "Dirty Linen."

It proves, without any question at all remaining, upon examination of these once-secret official records, that there was an immediate and highest-level conspiracy created to see to it that the crime itself was not investigated and thus, that it would be impossible to investigate and solve at a later date.

That is how Lee Harvey Oswald came to be accused immediately of being the lone assassin. This, too, is a smoking gun. There are others.

How immediate was this conspiracy?

It was conceived within hours of the crime, and within two days, it was recorded in these once-secret records. The conspiracy was put on paper as soon as it was known that Oswald had been killed by Jack Ruby. This meant there would be no trial. Now it was possible for the government to see to it—and it did—that no one else would be charged. Having no trial meant that it would not be necessary to present a case of Oswald's guilt beyond a reasonable doubt before a jury. It also meant that the alleged evidence did not have to be produced publicly and subjected to cross-examination, John Henry Wigmore's wonderful engine for establishing truth. And it meant that no defense counsel would be presenting evidence that questioned, refuted, or destroyed the government's case.

That there was no real case against Oswald is established in my six previous books on the JFK assassination.[3] That the alleged medical evidence could *not* have convicted Oswald but *does prove that there existed a conspiracy* to assassinate is proven, I believe overwhelmingly, in this book.

On how high of a level was this government conspiracy? Virtually the very highest possible, with Attorney General Robert Kennedy immobilized as he was by the great tragedy.

The very first step was taken by FBI Director J. Edgar Hoover. He ordained Oswald the lone assassin and declared there was no conspiracy the evening of the very day of the assassination, Friday, November 22, 1963.[4]

[3] *Whitewash: The Report on the Warren Report* (1965); *Whitewash II: The FBI-Secret Service Coverup* (1966); *Photographic Whitewash* (1967); *Oswald in New Orleans* (1967); *Whitewash IV* (1974); and *Post Mortem* (1975). *Martin Luther King: The Assassination* (1993) formerly *Frame-Up* (1969, 1971).

[4] 62–109060, Not Recorded, [Cartha] DeLoach to [John P.] Mohr, 6/464. Original in a "94"-classification file, number illegible. This is a memorandum intended for Director J. Edgar Hoover covering the interview he gave

Nicholas de B. Katzenbach was the Department of Justice's number two man as the deputy attorney general. He was also the acting attorney general when Robert Kennedy was not there. Katzenbach then was the man in charge of the Department of Justice.

He formulated the conspiracy, on paper, as soon as he knew that Oswald was dead and that there would be no trial. He put it in a memorandum to presidential assistant Bill Moyers, his official channel to President Lyndon Baines Johnson.[5]

Katzenbach discussed his schemes with J. Edgar Hoover that Sunday afternoon, November 24, and got Hoover's approval.[6] There being no secretary or typist available on Sunday, Katzenbach drafted his plan in longhand. He had it typed and distributed early the next morning, Monday, November 25.[7]

---

author William Manchester. But *nobody* inside the FBI *ever* addressed Hoover by name. What was intended for him was addressed to the writer's immediate superior who, in turn, forwarded it to his superior until it reached, in those days, Hoover's deputy and closest friend, Clyde Tolson. He decided whether or not to forward it to Hoover's office. A "Not Recorded" serial is a duplicate filing, one that is not the "Record" or "Recorded" copy.

The "94"-file classification is ostensibly for "Research Matters" only, but in fact it was a catchall political file. It held copies of Hoover's writings and correspondence, the FBI's files on the media, on its lobbying, leaking, and propaganda, and on other matters that seemed delicate enough to justify hiding them in a manner that would frustrate a normal search. Normal searches held that "Research Matters" were not what was being sought. I have never had any FOIA request for records filed as "94" met. In my experience the FBI and its Department of Justice counsel just have refused such requests and always have gotten away with it, whether under appeal or in court. File number 62–109060 is the FBIHQ's main JFK assassination file. It should not be confused with 62–109090, its main liaison with the Warren Commission file.

[5] The Department of Justice file copy is from its file 129–11. It had been kept in a file by Howard P. Willens, a Department of Justice lawyer loaned to the Warren Commission and its liaison with his actual employer, the Department of Justice, until May 21, 1965. I also have a copy of Katzenbach's handwritten draft of this memo, obtained from the Department's Criminal Division. The FBIHQ file copy is from its general JFK assassination file, 62–109060, in which it is part of Serial 1399.

[6] This is also a part of FBIHQ 62–109060–1399, with copies directed only to six of the most powerful FBI officials none lower in rank than assistant director.

[7] Dallas FBI file 89–43–393. See chapter 2, "Dirty Linen," for these and other related records in greater detail and for documentation.

My documentation of this is complete; it includes Katzenbach's handwritten draft of his Sunday memo to Moyers and the FBI head-quarters (FBIHQ) internal memo acknowledging that Katzenbach and Hoover did conspire, (that word, naturally, never used) against solv-ing the crime or letting it be solved—against even investigating it at all.[8]

In late 1993, in compliance with the special law enacted to require the disclosure of still undisclosed records relating to the JFK assassi-nation and its investigations, the government began making a vast quantity of records available at the National Archives. The volume was so great, some estimates stating that a million pages were being disclosed, that for all practical purposes there was and remains de facto denial to most Americans. The cost is prohibitive and few have the space for the several hundred file cabinets required to hold them. The media, however, praised the government for its openness. The CIA meanwhile disclosed a considerable volume of pages it had withheld. The FBI disclosed nothing at all. And those who did exam-ine what was disclosed reported that a large percentage of those records had been revealed many years earlier and were not new. But the government was extoled for its *openness*.

Basking in their praise the government retrieved from the Lyndon B. Johnson Library in Austin, Texas, transcripts of Johnson's phone calls totaling about six hundred pages. This library, like all presiden-tial libraries, is part of the National Archives. The government also made available duplicates of some of the tape recordings themselves. A few attracted great attention when aired on TV and radio. Contrary to the impression given the public, the disclosed transcripts were selected with some care. All were not disclosed, nor by far were all the tapes heard.

What was disclosed—and I have copies of what was—*includes no indication of any kind of the three Johnson phone conversations concerning the Hoover-Katzenbach conspiracy not to investigate the crime itself!* Not Moyers's call to Johnson, not Johnson's immediate call to Hoover, and not his call to Katzenbach placed as soon as he

---

[8] Johnson's activities, transportation, movements, and phone calls for Sun-day, November 24, 1963, were obtained at my suggestion from the LBJ Library by my friend Dr. Gerald Ginocchio, Professor of Sociology at Wof-ford College, Spartanburg, South Carolina.

had spoken to Hoover. Also not disclosed was Johnson's call made early the night of the day of the assassination that, according to Hoover's Warren Commission testimony, directed him to investigate and report on the crime.

Some members of the media did refer to this Katzenbach memo, but then immediately explained it away as merely reflecting fear of a disastrous war as a result of the assassination.

A never ending fear?

What is stated as policy in the memo was the practice beginning then, and to this day, one that has not been changed or ended.

It was not a disclosure, much as the media heralded it as what it was not, new information. I published it almost two decades earlier, in my 1974 book, *Whitewash IV*, with a facsimile reproduction of a staff memo on Chairman Earl Warren's first meeting with his Commission staff on January 20, 1964.

Without realizing that Johnson had hornswoggled him into tears, the staff listened while Warren told them that he took the job, knowing full well that he should not, to prevent getting "the country into a war which could cost 40 million lives" (*Whitewash IV*, page 24). If any such possibility had been believed to exist, it ended before the Commission held any hearings, most likely earlier, by the time it was appointed, seven days after the assassination. By then nothing at all had happened.

In its treatment of the Katzenbach memo that articulated the conspiracy against investigating the crime itself, the unending conspiracy, the media again made itself apologist for errant officialdom rather than to serve its traditional role of exposing official miscreants.

What walks like a duck, talks like a duck, and looks like a duck is not a duck to our media, which have yet to report that the crime itself was never officially investigated!

And thus, until now, in this book, this conspiracy was left unexposed.

There have been many allegations of a wide assortment of conspiracies, but not one is proven. They are theories. Virtually all are untenable when examined alongside the vast available volume of once-secret records.

Not a single one of the many authors of the many popular conspiracy theories that are presented as "solutions" to the JFK assassination has come to examine the approximately .25 million pages of JFK assassination records I obtained as the result of those FOIA successful lawsuits. They all know that I have made these records available to others writing in the field. Those authors who have some knowledge of these facts merely ignore what is inconsistent with what they want to believe. If they did, they could not have promulgated the theories they present as fact.

The wilder the theory presented, the more attractive it was to the proliferative, irresponsible talk shows that seek sensation. Over the years these theories have confused and misled the general public, turned the major media off even more, and had the effect of protecting those who failed the nation in that time of crisis and since then.

Beginning with my first book, which was completed in mid-February 1965 and is based entirely on the Warren Report and its appended twenty-six volumes of evidence, my work is entirely factual and comes from the records of the official investigations. After completing my first book, which was the first on the Warren Report, I started a systematic examination of the Commission's records at the National Archives. When the Freedom of Information Act was promulgated, I began efforts to obtain counsel to sue for the withheld records. When I could obtain counsel, I began a series of suits.[9]

This book, my seventh on the subject, was inspired by the first of two lengthy articles in the *Journal of the American Medical Association (JAMA)*. It was published in May of 1992. *Never Again!* draws on those articles, comparing them with the *official* records I obtained through the lawsuits and with the *official* assassination information I had published earlier. What *JAMA* published is based exclusively on the statements made to its editor, Dr. George D. Lundberg, and his reporter, Dennis L. Breo, by two of the autopsy prosectors, Dr. James J. Humes and Dr. J. Thornton Boswell. Both are pathologists, as is Lundberg. The third prosector present at the autopsy, Dr. Pierre Finck, refused to be interviewed by *JAMA*. Later he agreed.

---

[9] I filed Civil Action (CA) 70–2569 against the National Archives as my own lawyer. As a result the archives was required to take clear and comprehensible photographs of the President's shirt collar and tie and let me examine them. But inviolation of its own regulations it refused me copies. See page 244–47 for other views I got from the FBI.

This book, for the first time, shows how the conspiracy was implemented, beginning with the instant refusal of the FBI to investigate the crime itself. The FBI even refused to accept free copies of clear photographs of the President being killed![10] I found this and similar evidence in the FBI's Dallas records that they had kept secret even from FBI headquarters! Washington's first knowledge of these records[11] was when Dallas FBI produced them—and others like them—to process for disclosure to me in a lawsuit.[12]

Whether or not the new President was involved in this conspiracy—and the reason to believe that he in fact was is credible and again official—his assistant Bill Moyers was at the very least knowing and silent. Katzenbach's typed memo of Monday morning was rushed to Moyers. However, the Secret Service logs of Johnson's phone conversations and travel that Sunday indicate that at what was virtually the first possible moment LBJ was free Moyers phoned him. They spoke briefly. Johnson then phoned Hoover first and then Katzenbach, all within a quarter of an hour.[13]

Early the next morning all hell broke loose behind the scenes in Washington over Katzenbach's proposal for the appointment of a presidential commission of the most eminent officials.[14] Before the

[10] See *Post Mortem*, pages 247, 318, 323, and 613. The National Archives's photographer told me that the FBI had employed all its remarkable skill in order to make the copies provided to the Commission to be unclear and as professionally incompetent as any he ever had seen.

[11] See chapter 2, "Dirty Linen" for FBI 89–43–493.

[12] CA 78–0322, later combined with CA 78–0420, a similar lawsuit seeking all of the New Orleans FBI office's JFK assassination records. This particular Dallas record is in its main JFK assassination file. Its number is 89–43. This document is Serial 493. See chapter 2, "Dirty Linen."

[13] See footnote 8.

[14] Katzenbach's proposal that LBJ appoint a presidential commission to investigate the assassination involved double-crossing and triple-crossing as LBJ and Katzenbach were assuring Hoover that LBJ did not approve of it while he in fact was putting it in place. And Johnson was involved with the FBI's successful effort to talk the *Washington Post* out of endorsing the appointment of a presidential commission. Very early on Monday morning there had been a leak to the *Post* of the recommendation that a commission be appointed. The *Post* liked the idea. There then was a leak to the FBI that it favored a commission. Cartha DeLoach, who then was in charge of the FBI's lobbying, leaking, propaganda, and at least some aspects of its usually polite blackmailing, misrepresented Johnson's position to the *Post* and persuaded it to cancel its planned endorsement of the appointment of

week was out, that, too, became another part of this conspiracy with the appointment and empowering of what came to be known as the "Warren Commission" after its chairman, the then Supreme Court Chief Justice Earl Warren.

Hoover did not give orders to the Commission. He did control what it dared do, even what it dared think of doing, with the Byzantine manipulations of which he was the preeminent master in our Byzantium on the Potomac. He did this before the Commission was able to assemble its staff.[15]

The Commission was appointed November 29, 1963. The first of Hoover's leaks by means of which he controlled what the Commission would dare do appeared between December 2 and 5. Later on December 5, in an executive session that the Commission classified as TOP SECRET, Katzenbach assured it that only the FBI could have done the leaking because it alone had what was leaked.[16] The

a presidential commission. Johnson's other manipulations included leading Richard B. Russell, a respected conservative leader of the southern Democrats, to believe that he would not be appointed to the Commission and then appointed him nonetheless, as Russell told the author. It was Russell's belief that Johnson appointed him to the Commission to prevent Russell from leading the Senate opposition to civil-rights legislation.

It is the author's belief that Johnson selected the Commission's members for their reputations, standing, and political following. That Russell was a member of the Warren Commission assured that Russell's conservative and southern supporters would not publicly disagree with whatever the Commission concluded. The major sources supporting this view are the author's interview of Russell and their correspondence and FBIHQ JFK assassination records, duplicate copies of which are filed in the author's subject files. Until his death, which he knew was imminent, Russell encouraged the author's inquiry into the Warren Commission and its conclusions. Insofar as this relationship was recorded by Russell and his staff, it is also reflected in the deposit of Russell's records at the University of Georgia, Athens, Georgia.

[15] See chapter 2, "Dirty Linen," especially quotations from the transcript of the Commission's executive session of January 22, 1964. See also the full texts of this transcript and that of the executive session of five days later, both published in facsimile in *Whitewash IV*, pages 36 ff. and in *Post Mortem* pages 475 ff.

[16] Here and throughout the author draws on a simply enormous volume of records much too numerous and voluminous for him to even try to list. Duplicate copies made from the originals in what he describes as his "subject" files. There is one, for example, on this particular leak by the FBI.

Through FOIA actions I obtained copies of all but one of these executive session transcripts. They are Byzantine in content and in their reflection of

TOP SECRET Commission executive session transcripts I obtained and published include the Commission's January 22, 1964, confession of living in terror of what Hoover was up to and could do to it (*Post Mortem*, pages 475 ff.).

Obtaining and publishing these transcripts was anything but easily accomplished. Forcing disclosure of the official records kept secret required that I file thirteen separate Freedom of Information Act lawsuits[17] once it had become clear that the government had no intention of abiding by the law. Most of these entailed at least one trip to the federal court of appeals for the District of Columbia. One case

---

the Commission members' attitudes, actions, perceptions of their function and of the problems they faced, particularly from Hoover and the FBI. Here are just two of the numerous illustrations provided by Gerald Ford.

The missing executive session transcript was withheld under the feigned need to protect the privacy of Norman Redlich. He was then next in rank on the Commission's staff to its general counsel, J. Lee Rankin. Rankin had been solicitor general of the United States in the Department of Justice, the official who represents the department before the Supreme Court. From several hundred pages of records that the author obtained from the National Archives outside that particular FOIA lawsuit, he is without doubt that the actual reason for withholding this one transcript is to protect the reputation of former President Gerald Ford. (Confirmed by its later release). At that executive session Ford sought to accomplish what a weird collection of political extremists and virulent racists had failed to accomplish: getting Redlich, a Jew, fired for what he was not, a "red." For more on Ford's little-known record as a member of the Warren Commission and the means by which he was able to become our only unelected president, see *Whitewash IV*, index, page 219. Again, with official records only, it is proven beyond any doubt that in the hearing of the Senate Judiciary Committee considering his appointment to be vice president, which is unprecedented in our history, Ford swore falsely. *Whitewash IV* first states this on page 11 and goes on to prove it with added detail. Ford's false swearing includes his statement that in his commercializing of his Warren Commission work in his book, *Portrait of the Assassin* (New York: Simon & Schuster, 1965), he had used only what the Commission published.

In fact he stole and *mis*used the Commission's TOP SECRET executive session transcript of January 27, 1964. He then edited it, and in other ways doctored and altered the transcript, presenting his major changes in what was said and meant as having been in the original when they were not. See the word-for-word comparison prepared for this author by Paul Hoch of Berkeley, California, printed in *Whitewash IV*, pages 124–30. Ford was an FBI informer on the Commission's secrets. This is the subject of a separate file in the author's FBI record files.

[17] These lawsuits are listed in the bibliography.

got to the Supreme Court, where in failing, it became an exceptional success with what it brought about after the Court refused to accept the case. In 1974 Congress amended the investigative files exemption of the act, with this particular lawsuit cited as proof that amending was needed to accomplish the purposes of the act. This is what opened FBI, CIA, and similar files to FOIA access. As a result, I was able to compel the disclosure of this great volume of records.

It was Senator Edward Kennedy who saw to it that the legislative history is complete and unequivocal (*Congressional Record*, May 30, 1967, page S 9336) in reflecting that this lawsuit persuaded the Senate to amend the investigative files exemption to open those records to FOIA access. After the FOIA was enacted and before its effective date (July 4, 1967), I tried to get the American Civil Liberties Union (ACLU) to represent me in my efforts to obtain withheld information. I took a well-known ACLU lawyer from one of Washington's most prestigious law firms to the National Archives several times and showed him Warren Commission evidence that meant the exact opposite of what the Commission had concluded. He was visibly shaken. He then referred me to another lawyer. When I met with this second ACLU lawyer, I discovered that he would not represent me in FOIA litigation but as a criminal lawyer would when (as they anticipated) the FBI came after me for what I was doing.

Looking back over the more than a third of the life of the United States of America I have lived through and recalling what I can of what I have learned and observed in my lifetime that includes experience as a reporter, an investigative reporter, a United States Senate investigator, editor, and a professional wartime intelligence analyst, it is not remarkable that the FBI took no overt steps against me.

It did, however, resort to a sick assortment of dirty tricks that at this writing seem not to have ended. These include papering its officials and others in government, including the Department of Justice, whose lawyers defended the government in my FOIA lawsuits, with an assortment of half-truths, exaggerations, misrepresentations, and slanderous outright lies about my wife and me. These were intended to portray me as a "red" and an enemy of the government.[18]

---

[18] See chapter 2, "Dirty Linen." There is a large collection of such prejudicial, defamatory, dishonest, and false records in the author's subject file.

These papers became part of the FBI's campaign to frustrate the FOIA and to deny me those records that as a matter of law I was entitled to have. Obtaining the records I did get, which is very far from all the FBI has that are relevant, would have been impossible had not my friend Jim Lesar represented me when he knew I could not pay him.

In part because of the position in which my prior experience and work in the field put me and in part because I believe that the FOIA made me surrogate for the people, over the decades I've responded to probably thousands of requests from the media on the subject. As the media prepared for the twenty-fifth anniversary of the assassination in 1988, these requests were more voluminous. Over the decades, from supermarket tabloids to *The New York Times* and the *Washington Post*, reporters and editors have checked facts with me, as has TV and radio. To a lesser degree, book-publishing and magazine fact checkers also consulted me.

In court the government's campaign to keep FOIA information from me included false swearing that did on not infrequent occasions constitute the felony of perjury. For false swearing to be perjury the sworn lie must be material. Virtually all these FBI lies related to its denial of having the records I had requested and identified. This is material in FOIA litigation. And it could mean that the government lawyers, who presented this perjury to the courts, committed the crime of subornation of perjury.

Not a single one of the judges to whom, under oath and thus myself subject to the penalties of perjury, I charged perjury by the FBI had the slightest interest. Not one made the most rudimentary effort to learn the truth. Not one addressed the question. Not one charged me with perjury.

This is but one of the many means by which these FOIA efforts to bring JFK assassination facts and the truth to light were officially obstructed. My effort began with my requests of the FBI under the FOIA being ignored.

In Civil Action 75–1996 I proved that the FBI alone of all agencies in the government had ignored more than two dozen of my FOIA requests. With this undenied in the court record, a Ralph Nader litigation group called it to the attention of the United States Judiciary Committee's Subcommittee on Oversight of the Freedom of Information Act at its (published) hearings on September 15 and 16, October 6, and November 10, 1977.

The subcommittee's chairman, then Senator James Abourezk, asked at the outset: "Is the FBI a government unto itself" and whether the FBI "must" abide by the law (hearings, page 138). He followed this with the record I had made in court, including the FBI records that "approved" the stated policy not even to "acknowledge" my requests that under the law were to have been responded to within ten days (hearings, page 139). Quinlan J. Shea, then the Justice Department's conscientious appeals office director, testified: "Mr. Chairman, if you are looking for a Department of Justice representative to defend that sort of practice in 1969, 1970, or any other time, I am not going to do it" (hearings, page 140).

The FBI's then-assistant director in charge of its FOIA branch, Allen McCreight, was mute during the department's testimony cited above (hearings, pages 126 ff.). He did not promise to abide by the law.

William G. Shaffer, then deputy assistant attorney general, Civil Division, which handled FOIA litigation for the department, and Mrs. Lynne Zusman, who headed its FOIA litigation section, did respond. Shaffer described my FOIA efforts as "of unique historical importance." He admitted I did "have reason to complain about the way [I] was treated in the past." He then promised that "we in the Civil Division are going to try to do something to straighten out all those cases" (hearings, page 140).

The "something" the Civil Division promised to do consisted of organizing a "get Weisberg" crew of six of its lawyers, so described by one of them to Jim Lesar. When all six, plus a couple of other department and FBI lawyers, were present at the hearings in my CA 77–2155 and all were defeated, the "something" switched to perjury and other obstructions.

Compelling the disclosure of about .33 million pages of these once-secret documents was not easy. It was enormously costly, monetarily as well as in the amount of time I could not use writing and making other use of the records as I obtained them. But in leading to the amending of the act, to the disclosures I was able to compel and put to use in my books—in making them forever available to anyone with any interest in them—it was worth that time and to me that is not an inconsiderable cost.

What is remarkable is that I was able to do what I have done, which would not have been possible in any other country in the world. What is further remarkable is that, beginning in 1972, I was fortunate enough to survive many serious medical problems that are not uncommonly fatal. These medical problems did, however, come to preclude my effective use of the sixty file cabinets of these formerly secret records.

Then, in May of 1992, the American Medical Association came to my rescue with its know-nothing campaign to support the conclusions of the Warren Report and defend the JFK autopsy pathologists whose actual record is not possible to defend on fact or with truth. The absolutely incredible thing the AMA did in several issues of its prestigious *Journal* simplifies into the insistence that the JFK autopsy pathologists were correct in 1963 merely because in 1992 they insisted that they were and that nothing else makes any difference. This provided a skeleton that could be fleshed out with a minimum of searches for information in the formerly secret official records and with the information I had earlier brought to light and published— materials that were readily available to the pathologists and to *JAMA*.

Over the years my work has grown into a rather large study of how the basic institutions of our society work—or fail to work—in those times of great stress and since then. The major media are one of our basic institutions. Among medical publications *JAMA*'s influence and importance are unique. What it did in those several issues symbolizes the abdication of and other failings of the major media.

JAMA is just the latest of consequences of this successful official conspiracy I have sought to recall and retrieve from this probably unprecedented mass of once-secret official information. I will tell a full story of how this conspiracy was carried out, and the environment in which it was, to make it comprehensible and to leave it without reasonable question.

Even in a very long book it is not possible to include all information. One example of this omission is the files I have established relating to Hoover's and the FBI's leaking, the means by which they asserted control. Control is the name of Hoover's and the FBI's game.

This successful conspiracy did have the effect of seeing to it that those who plotted and assassinated would not be brought to justice then or in the future. In not investigating the crime itself, the government, chiefly Hoover and his FBI, also assured that there would be no leads for others. In conspiring so that the crime could not be solved, the government in effect protected a coup d'état.

Assassinating President Kennedy meant we would automatically have Lyndon Johnson as president.

No two men believe in and have identical policies. These men differed widely in personality and on some major issues, particularly in foreign affairs. Once Johnson assumed the presidency, he did change some of Kennedy's national policies. One example of this was his abandonment of Kennedy's stated policy that the United States would not recognize any military dictatorship that overthrew a democratically elected government. Juan Bosch was elected President of the Dominican Republic. The Dominican military revolted and threw Bosch out. Johnson sent the Marines and the Navy in support of the revolting Dominican military, and a president acceptable to the Dominican military was installed.

There is controversy over whether Kennedy intended withdrawing from Vietnam, our intrusion into the affairs of another country that began with the Eisenhower-Nixon administration. When I interviewed one of Kennedy's generals, James P. Gavin, in June, 1967, when we were both at the annual convention of the American Booksellers Association in Washington, D.C., he told me that Kennedy had called him and other generals into his office and discussed Vietnam with them.

"What can I do to persuade you that Vietnam is a political problem and that political problems are not susceptible to military solutions?" Kennedy said in his approach to Gavin and the other generals.

Gavin was certain that Kennedy intended to withdraw from Vietnam after the coming election, and he approved of that policy.[19]

Whatever the purposes of the assassination, major policy changes were inevitable and they ensued.

So it is to make as comprehensible as is possible and as full an account as is possible in this book that I can draw upon what can

---

[19] This interview was broadcast on the syndicated radio book-and-author program *Author's Roundtable*.

make for an understanding of how the government conspiracy not to solve the crime could and did achieve success. It was not possible to use all such records or to include all the people involved. I hope here I have made the most informative use of the records possible.

This conspiracy was an unprecedented event in our history—at least in our more recent history.

But never before in our history was there a law that says the people have the right to know what their government does. No other country as far as I know has this right established in law for its people.

Although bureaucrats and those who control government may not agree, the FOIA can make for better, more honest, more responsive, and more responsible government. It makes possible the rectification of error not perceived by those in authority who err.[20]

It is my experience with and under the law that just about all bureaucrats detest it and that all presidential administrations abominate, inhibit, and nullify it with policies inimical to the law and executive orders proscribing and limiting it.

But to a degree that in retrospect I regard as both inadequate and satisfactory, it did work. I did obtain these records, and with good fortune I have been able to draft this book that I hope enables us to learn and perhaps in the future may be valued. It can be if it does no more than help perfect the historical record of this unprecedented government conspiracy—and of the great crime it protected.

---

[20] Perhaps the most anti-American evil ended by the democratic means of exposing it that was made possible by use of the FOIA is the FBI's police-state abuse to which it gave the Orwellian name of "Counterintelligence Program" or "Cointelpro." We are indebted to Carl Stern, NBC-TV News legal correspondent in Washington, whose FOIA efforts brought it to light. Stern had expressed an interest in the law when I first used it, discussed it with me, and asked me to discuss my experiences with NBC counsel, which I did.

Then, when the act was amended in 1974, Stern filed for and obtained FBI Cointelpro records. It was then immediately apparent that this "program" had nothing at all to do with counterintelligence and that the name was only a cover for intrusions into the lives and affairs of Americans who, for various reasons, usually political, the FBI did not like. Lives were ruined by it, as were careers, including those of the famous as well as the little-known. The program involved violence; the husband of a well-known actress claimed that the FBI's probe drove his wife to suicide.

Santayana warned us that if we do not learn from our past we are doomed to relive it.

There was no joy, no elation for me in finding proof of an official JFK assassination conspiracy in the official records so long denied to me. There is none in writing it. There is a feeling of responsibility, of unpleasant obligation and duty, and there is the satisfaction, perhaps the reward, of meeting a citizen's debt.

If I had been willing to charge the government with conspiracy when the proof was not available, beginning in 1965, I could have, in the words of one editor, become "rich and famous." If I had been willing in 1966, after accumulating more than one hundred international rejections for *Whitewash* without a single adverse editorial comment, I could have had another chance at it. A major publisher wrote me that if I would reorganize the book into charging a government conspiracy it would be "an extraordinary, important book" they'd be glad to publish.[21] He asked that I go to New York and confer "with one of the most impressive legal minds," with a "lawyer of liberal persuasion and utterly fearless." Then I'd be on my way.

I found this fearless pillar of wisdom to be most concerned about my making what he described as very serious charges against the Commission's lawyers with mere "misrepresentation." If he'd read the book with an open mind, he would have known they lied their heads off.

The book he wanted would have lacked credibility because no proof of any conspiracy was then available. Without the proof, I refused to state it as so.

If the first book on the Warren Commission had said more than the evidence made available by that Commission justified, it would have been flogged mercilessly, and justifiably. While some criticism of the Commission was inevitable, for LBJ's purposes it would have been helpful for the first book about the Commission to lack credibility, to appear to be extreme, and to receive the criticism irresponsibility warrants. *Whitewash*'s history justified my decision. While it did

---

[21] In the author's files.

not bring me wealth, it was the first and has become the basic book on the Commission. From the time it appeared, and for the twenty-seven years before *JAMA*'s political adventuring with the assassination, its facts and its conclusions have been available in the bookstores to those who want them.

The famous publisher's offer is what made me decide that I should publish the book unchanged. Copies were in major newspaper offices less than a fortnight after my conference with that legal eminence. In the more than two and a half decades since then, no single error in it has been called to my attention, and no person mentioned in it has complained about unfairness or inaccuracy.

Giangiacomo Feltrinelli, of Milan, then the western world's most radical publisher, translated and published *Whitewash* in early 1967 as *Chi ha ucciso Kennedy? Le prove della congiure.* He then asked me to write "a clear indictment" that would be a "tremendous j'accuse'," meaning to "cut and slash" the government, based on a theory he was sure I had.[22]

I was still no more willing to be irresponsible and to theorize official criminality, or without proof, to write such a book.

I began to gather the proof after the FOIA investigative-files exemption was amended over my earlier lawsuit. It was a major disappointment to me that the major media, which had failed to meet its obligations in the JFK assassination and the official investigations that followed, ignored this rare validation of Andrew Jackson's proud boast that this is a nation in which one determined man can become a majority. Not one single story reported that the Congress amended the act because of an unknown with no influence at all.

The first, and the only, mention of this event (of one determined man becoming a majority) was on January 17, 1978, in an unusual lawsuit I had filed. In it I asked the court to delay the release of what the FBI referred to as its "general" releases of JFK assassination records until it had provided me with copies. In this way I could respond to media inquiries and prevent the misuse of these disclosures as a "media event" in support of the FBI's position on the JFK assassination.

That was a man-bites-dog story: the critic who wrote the first book

[22] Letter to author from Giangiacomo Feltrinelli.

on the Warren Report asks for a temporary order to delay the disclosure of assassination records. *Washington Post* reporter George Lardner was in the courtroom. Lardner heard Judge Gerhard Gesell say
in his decision, in the words Lardner used in his story published the
next morning, "It is apparent that no consideration whatsoever" was
given to provisions of the FOIA that distinguish between commercial
benefit and serving the public interest [my purpose], and no consideration at all was given to my "poor health and indigency." Gesell
ordered that this first vast installment of the greater volume of records
that were to follow be given to me "with all reasonable dispatch."
They were.

That "poor health" then became my major problem. A series
of complications following successful surgeries left me with limited
mobility: able to walk only short distances, able to use the basement
stairs only a few times a day, and unable to stand still before file
cabinets other than momentarily. I had the need to keep my legs
elevated when not walking, and beginning more than three years
before I began to write this book, my cardiologist ordered me not to
lift more than fifteen pounds. Consequently, receiving such a mass
of files posed serious problems for me.

Rae Barrett of Sharon, Vermont, organized and inventoried these
records in four long rows of file cabinets in our basement. I was
quite fortunate to have her efficient help. Before returning to Sharon
to care for ill family members, she also did most of the record
searching to be used in my FOIA lawsuits, and she assisted in the
preparation to take the depositions of a number of FBI agents deposed in those lawsuits. She more than anyone else, through her
considerable, efficient, and intelligent effort in establishing these files,
is responsible for the access to them that I and others who use
them enjoy.

These sixty file cabinets of records will be, in time, a free, permanent, and public archive at Hood College in Frederick, Maryland. In
time the school plans to make these records available to other institutions through imaging techniques.

Jim Lesar is the other indispensable contributor to my efforts.
Before Jim took the District of Columbia bar examinations, he did
the appeals briefing in the case over which the Congress amended
the investigative-files exemption in 1974. For this and for much else

we are all in his debt. When I obtained the until-then TOP SECRET
Warren Commission executive session transcript in 1974 and could
not pay for its publication, he borrowed the money with which I
then was able to publish *Whitewash IV*, of which he is the coauthor.

Perhaps the most unusual of our many shared experiences was
when he was James Earl Ray's counsel and I was the investigator
for the case in which the man accused of assassinating Martin Luther
King, Jr., sought the trial he never had. I did the investigating for
the habeas corpus proceeding, and Jim did the briefing. As a result
Ray was granted an evidentiary hearing to determine whether or not
he would be granted a trial. I did the investigating for those two
weeks of hearings in Memphis in 1974 and located the witnesses;
Jim presented them and their testimony to the court. We actually
exculpated Ray, only to have Federal District Court Judge Robert R.
MacRae hold that on what was before him, guilt or innocence, was
immaterial. He continued to deny Ray a trial. As in the JFK case
the only official candidate for assassin was convicted without any
trial. We were subjected to many pressures. Even Jim's mail from
the Supreme Court of the United States was crudely opened before
being given to him. I was threatened overtly in the presence of a
witness by the state's assistant attorney general, Henry Haile.

Over these many long years that now seem even longer than they
were, many, many good and caring people, more by far than I can
remember, helped me in arranging for my appearances and providing
transportation and housing for me. Some helped by obtaining information for me. There are many more than I now can remember. To
mention and thank some and not others—inevitable when there are
so very many—would be unfair. I hope that they read this and understand that I do appreciate what they did, from south to north and into
Canada, from coast-to-coast, and from Australia and New Zealand to
the former iron curtain in Europe.

Two dear friends to whom for years I have been particularly indebted for their many acts of kindness and for their assistance are
Dr. David R. Wrone, Professor of History of the University of Wisconsin at Stevens Point, and Dr. Gerald McKnight, Professor of History at Hood College. Over the many years of our cherished
friendships, their extensive help, personal and professional, has meant
much and continues to do so. Jerry is a neighbor, and particularly

during the years of my illnesses and its limitations, there was no personal need we had for which he did not take the time from his own busy days to meet. Professionally he and Dave Wrone for years have been more than merely helpful. When Dave read the first few drafts of this book, he began retyping them on his computer. This was particularly difficult work because when I type I must keep my legs elevated, and with the typewriter to one side, my hunt-and-peck typing is full of errors and my handwriting is close to illegible. Without him this book might never have been presentable enough to show to a publisher.

Wrone and McKnight teach courses on the politics of assassination—not as whodunits—but as government and political science studies. Wrone is coauthor with DeLloyd Guth of the only professional bibliography in the field (*The Assassination of John F. Kennedy*. Westport, CT.: Greenwood Press, 1980). McKnight at the time of this writing has just completed the manuscript of a book on Dr. Martin Luther King, Jr.'s last major project, the Poor People's Campaign, a project that he did not live to lead. He is also the author of several scholarly studies published by *The South Atlantic Quarterly* on the FBI's domestic-intelligence intrusions into the sanitation-workers' strike, which King was in Memphis to support when he was assassinated, and on a group of young Memphis-area blacks who called themselves, provocatively, The Invaders, after a then popular TV program. Wrone and McKnight are the only two professional historians who are true experts on the assassinations.

When Rae Barrett had to return to her family, there was much I was not able to do because for practical purposes I do not have access to those four rows of file cabinets and the innumerable boxes in our basement. My dear friend of many years, Richard Gallen of New York City, with great thoughtfulness and kindness made it possible for Helen Wilson, of Owings, Maryland, to help me into her senior year at Hood College, particularly with filing and refiling records needed for this book.

Without my wife, Lillian Stone Weisberg, my work would not have been possible. In dedicating my first book to her and making no other dedications since, I intended and still intend to dedicate all my work to her. Without her many sacrifices and the great amount of time she has devoted so effectively to so many of my work's aspects, I could not have done it. She corrected my many typographical errors and others in the book manuscripts for which she was also in effect typesetter, proofreader, and indexer. She corrected and retyped those innumerable FOIA lawsuit affidavits, some of which are, with their attachments, book-length. In all they take up several file drawers. Into her eightieth year when most of us look for ease and less work of any kind, she handles most of the details of our tiny publishing enterprise. And through my troubles she has been so much more than a wife, from the moment of the assassination until now. She has been, in every sense, indispensible to my work.

Although it becomes obvious in this book I nonetheless articulate my back-handed indebtedness to the American Medical Association and its *Journal*, the famed *JAMA* of medicine, and to the nation's organized doctors and their know-nothing attempt to rewrite our history and the actualities of the great tragedy of the assassination.

Dr. George Lundberg, *JAMA*'s editor, and his writer Dennis Breo, who became Lundberg's hired gun, did not soil the propaganda in defense of the indefensible Warren Report and of the autopsy pathologists (whose indefensible incompetence in forensic medicine will mark them forever in our history) with as little as a single officially established fact about the assassination other than when mentioned accidentally by the autopsy pathologists. For the most part those people I refer to as *JAMA*'s gang of four pretend that their ignorance is in fact omniscience, that there are no facts relevant to the assassination other than what the two pathologists spoke of in their *JAMA* interviews.

My work has proven that our basic institutions failed us. Ignorant intrusion into the intense political controversy over the JFK assassination and its investigations makes *JAMA* the unavoidable symbol of the major media and their failures, something many governmental agencies and the courts did as well with their post-assassination failures and abdication of responsibility.

The use of words like "lie," as I am well aware, is generally frowned upon. But as Ecclesiastes says, there is a time and a place for everything. There are times when understatement is appropriate. This is a time when understatement is *not* appropriate.

The AMA and its *Journal* intruded into the intense controversy over the assassination of President Kennedy and its investigations without the most perfunctory attempt to learn the established truth. Instead they decided to support the thoroughly discredited official accounts of both the crime and its official investigations and to accept the words of the autopsy prosectors who also had been discredited thoroughly and officially. That means they began with the *intent* to lie.

This applies to the prosectors as well, more so because what they told Lundberg and Breo is proven to be false by their sworn testimony and by many other means. Unless they were perjurers under oath thirty years ago, they *were* liars to Lundberg and Breo in 1992.

When this relates to that most subversive of crimes, the assassination of a president, the official investigations of it, and to the involvement of these pathologists, the matter hardly could be more serious, the offenses hardly greater. Forthrightness with the reader and with history require that such offenses not be glossed over.

This is a long book because I sought to address each and every one of *JAMA*'s distortions, misrepresentations, and outright lies, of which there are many.

It is a long book because of the abundance of documentary and evidentiary riches, unknown or only very little-known, I have accumulated over three decades of arduous and sometimes pioneering work. The knowledge I acquired in the course of my work enables me to try to put it all in context; to try to assemble for history enough of the relevant information required for an all-encompassing understanding of this complex and strongly controversial subject so important to the nation; and to include information on what the government did and did not do.

It is long because it is essential for context and for the full understanding of all the failures that individually and collectively endanger our system or freedom through self-government. This has never been done before, with fact and with official proof.

These considerations more than any others compelled me to make the not inconsiderable effort this book represents for an aging, ailing, and infirm man in his eighties.

This book means much to me, more perhaps than it would mean

to most, because I am the first member of my family ever born into freedom.

In no other country could this have been possible.

Is this not a tribute to our country?

Because the government conspiracy that I bring to light *is* a danger to our system, it is my hope that I have, in the words of another writer, gone where no man has been, and what is more important, in her words, left a path for others.

I had hoped to do that with my first book, and to a degree, I did.

I hope again that I have done this.

"Let justice be done though heaven should fall."

—an old Latin proverb

Foreword

"AN ELEMENTARY PRINCIPLE OF GOOD JOURNALISM [IS] THE REQUIRE-ment to examine a subject in its entirety and seek out the point of view of the other side."

These are the words of the lead editorial in one of the nation's leading newspapers, the *Washington Post*, of August 15, 1992. They were addressed to those who for nonpartisan political reasons distorted, misrepresented, and were untruthful in espousing an inflexible preconception without regard to the readily available facts. The *Post* also criticized "sly formulation" that "stops short" of telling an outright lie.

These wise words state the intent of this book, "to examine a subject in its entirety and to present the other side's point of view." And in so doing, I will make a record of and call to public attention the departures from this traditional standard of American "good journalism" by the *Journal of the American Medical Association* in its May 27, 1992, and later articles on the assassination of President John F. Kennedy.

That issue featured two articles by *JAMA*'s "At Large" reporter, Dennis L. Breo, based on interviews by *JAMA*'s editor, Dr. George D. Lundberg, a pathologist, of two of the three military pathologists who performed the autopsy on the body of President Kennedy at the Naval Hospital, Bethesda, the night of Friday, November 22, 1963. They are James J. Humes and J. Thornton Boswell.

JAMA did not "examine" the "subject in its entirety," and it did not "seek out the point of view of the other side." Examining this entire subject requires that it be presented in context, with all that is relevant and available examined with it, including "opposing viewpoints." It requires also that the word of any one person not be blindly accepted as truth without an effort to determine whether or not it is true—and that what is not proven to be true not be presented as truth. Otherwise, instead of journalism, there is propaganda.

"[I]n its entirety" is a quintessential requirement where there is controversy, as there was and will be surrounding the JFK assassination and the autopsy performed on his body.

If we do not examine the subject "in its entirety," we get what John Godfrey Saxe (1816-1887) described decades ago in his poem "The Wise Men and the Elephant." Six wise men, all blind, were take for the first time to an elephant. One of the wise men felt a leg. He announced he was touching a mighty oak. A second, who grasped the wriggling tail, disputed the first, proclaiming it was a snake. And none of the six, for all their wisdom, identified an elephant.

This was what happened when Lundberg restricted himself in questioning these two pathologists, without speaking to anyone else who was present and without regard to "the other side" that was readily available to him. *Humes and Boswell said only what it suited them to say.* Breo, who wrote the articles, then used what suited him and Lundberg to use.

This book, the ignored "other side," examines the subject "in its entirety," using what was readily available to Humes and Boswell and to Lundberg and Breo, along with what they said, what *JAMA* published, and what Lundberg said about what he published. The information in this book, ignored by this quartet, is all *official* information. It is in the records of "the President's Commission on the Assassination of President John F. Kennedy," better known as the Warren Commission, after its chairman, the Chief Justice of the Supreme Court, Earl Warren, and in the records of the executive agencies of the federal government.

I hope the reader will not perceive a mighty oak or a snake, but a complete elephant.

There is widespread confusion, misrepresentation, and outright lying about "withheld" official JFK assassination records. No one contributed more to this situation, which encouraged additional withholdings of these records, than Oliver Stone. In the course of promoting himself and his movie-in-production, *JFK*, his crass commercialization of the assassination, he said, with considerable public attention, anything at all that seemed likely to get him and his movie attention. He lied from the very beginning, claiming, from the profundity of his ignorance and indifference to fact, that "all" Warren Commission records were withheld when in fact 98 percent of them were not. He also alleged that an undescribed "entire" official record was withheld when I alone had .25 million pages of it without having all that had been disclosed.

Typical of those who seek and get attention with such startling charges, Stone had no interest in looking at them or in asking for copies of them. He knew I had them and that I give all writers free and unsupervised access to these records. But neither Stone nor his staff researchers nor virtually all others who have written books advancing unproven and unprovable conspiracy theories as solutions has come to do any research. Stone's propaganda prevented the immediate vote in the House of Representatives to disclose the withheld records of its former Select Committee on Assassinations.

The movie was greeted with a widespread demand for the disclosure of withheld records. It led people to believe these records hold a smoking gun. *They do not!* It then would have been politically hazardous for any Representative to oppose disclosure of those records. All that was required was a simple resolution of the House alone. The Senate would not have been involved, and the President's signature was not called for. And if Stone had kept his flapping mouth closed, popular demand was so great such a resolution could have been passed overnight. But having promoted both himself and his movie by making ignorant and false claims for months and being unwilling to forgo the benefit of movie-ticket sales or to the personal publicity on which he thrives, Stone demanded at the hearing before which he testified, that "all" official records be disclosed.

This required that all the committees with jurisdiction in each house of Congress hold hearings. After this each house would agree on a single bill, with all the conflicting views reconciled. Then the conferees of both houses would agree on a single bill, again reconciling differences. And finally both houses would agree on the bill that emerges from the conference.

A bill then passed by the Senate and the House required the signature of President George Bush who had been the CIA director and who had already announced his opposition to any such bill. As had the CIA he had headed. Ultimately this is what happened, but it caused two years of delay. It then made the greater mass of records more difficult for individual researchers to digest.

Despite the misinformation concerning the ill-conceived and misdirected campaign for the disclosure of "all" withheld JFK assassination records, so many of which had in fact been disclosed and ignored, the fact is not diminished that a great volume of formerly withheld records are, and for years, have been publicly available.

On one side stand *JAMA* and all the other Warren Commission supporters, including its counsels, some of whom have become prominent (and our only unelected president, who is the only living Commission member), and on the other side are those who substitute conspiracy theories of their own weaving for reality. All abuse the truth and deceive the people while confusing them, each side foreclosing any possibility of an honest and impartial official effort to establish the truth about the crime and its investigations.

It is not possible to write responsibly about the JFK assassination or its investigation without knowledge and use of what records *are* publicly available. It is spectacularly irresponsible for *JAMA*'s ex cathedra pronouncements to be made entirely oblivious to and ignorant of this great volume of publicly available information.

The Warren Commission's life ended officially on the day it issued its 912-page Report, September 27, 1964. Some of the staff kept on working to publish the Commission's appendix. It consists of twenty-six large volumes, running an estimated ten million words. The first fifteen volumes are transcripts of the testimony taken by the Commission. The other eleven consist of the Commission's exhibits.

When the Commission's records were transferred to the National Archives, their volume was estimated at two hundred cubic feet, including the containers that held them. Subsequently other materials were placed in this archive by the executive agencies. The last published estimate of the extent of these records that are not publicly available is only 2 percent of the entire archive.

Readers are entitled to know, I believe, more about those who write on controversial subjects than is usually encapsulated on the dust jackets of books.

I am the first member of my family *ever* born into freedom.

I believe that we all are born, in poet Robert Frost's words from "Stopping by Woods on a Snowy Evening," with "promises to keep and miles to go before [we] sleep." Each of us decides for himself whether or not he does have promises to keep, and if so, whether or not he keeps them or how he keeps them.

Those who are born into freedom are also born with the obligation of helping to preserve this inherited freedom. Freedom did not come to us automatically, and it is not preserved automatically. Its preservation requires effort, sometimes struggle, and sometimes the struggle is difficult and costly.

Freedoms are like muscles. If they are not used, they atrophy and are lost.

I regard those who in my youth were commonly referred to as our Founding Fathers as the greatest political thinkers the world has ever produced. They are more than *our* Founding Fathers. They introduced an entirely new concept of freedom through representative self-government. This is both our inheritance at birth and an obligation imposed upon us at birth. The obligation is to seek to defend and preserve the freedom we inherited, the freedom implicit in our Declaration of Independence and in our Constitution.

Governments, by their nature and resulting from the desire of those who govern to continue to govern as they see fit, can and do endanger freedom. In order for our system of freedom through self-government to function as our Founding Fathers intended, citizens must participate in government, and by their participation, defend and preserve it. Abdication of this responsibility endangers our freedom.

In our more recent history candidates for president select as their running mates those who can appeal to a different segment of the electorate. Thus our presidents and vice presidents often have different policies and beliefs.

But were this not true, it is true that no two human beings see in the same way and think exactly alike on all issues and policies. No matter how broad may be the areas of their agreement, there also are always areas of broad disagreement.

When we vote, we choose presidents, not vice presidents.

When a president is assassinated we are denied the president we elected, the one whom we chose from among all others.

A presidential assassination thus has the effect of an American coup détat. It is American in form because it means, as it has meant historically, that someone else becomes the head of state, and because it means uniquely that our vice president automatically becomes the president. There are no options, no substitutions. The Constitution prescribes the succession.

John F. Kennedy chose Lyndon B. Johnson to be his vice president.

And once Johnson assumed power, there were changes in policy.

The most hotly disputed of these policy changes was our Vietnam policy. I am certain that JFK did plan and had begun preparing for a change in Vietnam policy. As I wrote earlier, James P. Gavin, one of JFK's army generals, told me when I interviewed him in June 1967 that JFK had called Gavin and other generals in and told them that Vietnam was a political, not a military problem. JFK stated that American policy should be not to recognize any military dictatorship that overthrew an elected government.

Under JFK's successor Lyndon B. Johnson, this policy was radically altered. In 1965, when the Army of the Dominican Republic overthrew that country's first freely elected government headed by Juan Bosch, Lyndon Johnson recognized the military dictatorship. He also assisted it to the extent of sending the Navy and the Marines there.

Whatever may have been the intent of the JFK assassination, it was followed by changes in national policy.

The evidence ignored or misrepresented in the official investigations of the JFK assassination leaves no question that it was the end product of a conspiracy. Using the official evidence, I published proof of conspiracy in six books on the JFK assassination. No serious error and fewer than a dozen minor ones have been attributed to all six texts.

Unlike the authors of most of the well-known books on the subject—books that invent conspiracy theories and then present them as solutions—I do not espouse any conspiracy theory, not in any of my books. My books are entirely factual.

Conspiracy is a matter of fact, not of theory.

Proving that the assassination was a conspiracy, however, does not identify who conspired. As will be seen with official documents I obtained under the FOIA, some never before published, because the crime itself was never investigated officially and was never officially intended to be investigated, there are no leads for private persons to follow to identify the assassins. Those books that assume but do not prove that there was a conspiracy and that identify, generally or by name, the alleged assassins are works of fiction.

On the simplest basis, if a crime is beyond the capability of any one person, it is a conspiracy. No marksman, not the world's best shots, not the master riflemen that the National Rifle Association (NRA) provided for the Warren Commission's tests, has ever been able to duplicate the shooting skill attributed to Lee Harvey Oswald, the officially ordained assassin who was a "rather poor" shot in the evaluation of the Marine Corps in which he served.

There were two sets of tests for the Commission at the Army's Edgewood Arsenal proving grounds in Aberdeen, Maryland. One, under greatly improved conditions, failed to duplicate the accuracy of Oswald's alleged shooting within the time permitted, from 4.6 to 6.5 seconds.

The second set of shooting tests was supposed to establish whether or not what came to be known as "the single-bullet theory" was possible. This subtheory of the official theory, invented by Commission assistant counsel Arlen Specter, now a United States Senator, requires that a single bullet of the alleged manufacture enter the back of the President's neck, exit the front of his neck, then enter the body of Texas Governor John F. Connally (who was in the jump seat of the Presidential limousine on the President's side) under his right armpit, smashing four inches of Connally's fifth rib before emerging from under his right nipple to enter the dorsal side of his right hand, wreaking havoc with his right wrist bones, and then once entering his left thigh, and after penetrating more or less parallel with its surface for several inches, just to come to rest there.

The test of this theory used masonite and animal bones to replicate human bones, and it used gelatin blocks as a substitute for human tissue.

It was so well-known that the alleged bullet did not have the penetrating power required by this theory that the experts at Aberdeen did not even try. Instead the supposed duplication was addressed by dividing the parts of the bizarre theory of the magical bullet into separate sections in separate tests and then making "computations" to compute, not prove, whether one of those bullets had that much power. If the answer had not been known from the beginning, it would have been a simple matter to line up the right thicknesses of masonite and gelatin, etc., and fire a bullet at them. *This was never done!*

This is not all the Commission theorized. Its entire Report is but a theory. Its defenders, like Lundberg, Breo, Humes, and Boswell, denounce private persons who say there was a conspiracy as mere theorists. They lack the integrity to admit that what they themselves defend is no more than a theory. Even the FBI and the Secret Service do not agree with the Warren Report. Their disagreement is over this single-bullet theory.

But don't look for this in the Warren Report or in its twenty-six volume appendix. The Commission knew the fallacy of the single-bullet theory not later than December 9, 1963, the day it received an FBI special report. In neither the Warren Report nor its appendix did the Commission publish the FBI's conclusions. But in *Whitewash* I published in facsimile those portions of the FBI special report relating to the shooting. My source was the Commission's own files. Not a single newspaper or magazine picked this up from my book.

What led to the instant popular disbelief in the Warren Report is typified by these two illustrations. The newspapers failed the country, and the people were not satisfied with what they reported. And the Report is based on what most people not only could not believe but knew to be impossible.

Despite the vast differences among all of us who criticize the Warren Report, we are lumped together as "critics." But we do not have the same beliefs, and we have not reached the same conclusions.

Because *Whitewash* was the first on the subject, I was among the first to discuss any aspect of the broader subject of the assassination on radio and TV talk shows. From what was reflected by these large audiences,* I believe that at least half of the people did not believe

* When the author appeared on Jack McKinney's excellent radio show on Philadelphia's WCAU, the machine that counted all incoming calls re-

the Warren Report before my book appeared. Other critics take credit for generating this disbelief, unfortunately with inaccurate and baseless information.

Some, like Mark Lane, whose first book was out of date before it appeared, wanted it believed that they had done all the work. These people who sought above all else to promote themselves and their books were just as misinformative as the Warren Report and its apologists.

Many people were confused by the theories other authors made attractive through disregard for truth or fact. There were those who believed that as long as the government was criticized, it made no difference at all whether the criticism was truthful or not. Along with this confusion grew disenchantment with the government.

This is one of the reasons I was troubled when appearing before collegiate audiences. Truth required that I state and document a case against the government in which it lied to the people, misled them, and misinformed them. It disturbed me that the truth I offered was bleak and depressing to those young minds. So I thought of something positive or encouraging for these young and still formative people to whom I told the disturbing truth.

I evolved another truth: There is no other country in the world in which I could have survived doing what I did and continue to do. In the Soviet Union I would have been fortunate only to be condemned to a psychiatric institution. In Great Britain and in any of the Commonwealth of Nations with their Official Secrets acts, I would have been charged and jailed. In the countries with dictatorships of the right the authoritarians would have done whatever their whims dictated, and I would have suffered severely if in fact I survived. Our unique Freedom of Information Act is the most American of laws because it makes it a legislated right of the people to know what their government does and has done.

Despite its failings our governmental system, the system devised by those great political thinkers of the 1700s, remains the best and the freest system of self-government yet devised by mankind. It is therefore necessary to criticize failures and transgressions because

---

ported that some *17,000* callers got only busy signals and so did not get through.

that is the only means by which errors can be corrected. So, strive to keep them honest.

To examine this "subject in its entirety" and to meet the *Post*'s standards require a broad examination of JFK's autopsy, not an examination as limited as *JAMA*'s was in interviewing only two of the prosectors. It requires an examination of the atmosphere and environment in which the autopsy was performed, reported, and testified to. Other information that is relevant to the autopsy must also be examined. There was readily available long before *JAMA*'s articles a vast volume of official information on the assassination and its investigations that it should have examined.

This information falls into two broad classifications: that of the Commission and that of the executive agencies. The Commission's information consists of what it used, what it did not use, and what it misused. The executive agencies' information consists of what it let the Commission have and what it kept secret from the Commission. There is also, of course, information that these agencies have succeeded in keeping secret. Only this last segment was not available to Humes, Boswell, Lundberg, and Breo or to anyone else.

But what was readily available is a simply enormous volume of information. All four ignored it. Not a word, written or spoken, acknowledges its existence.

If Humes or Boswell ever intended anything other than the self-defense presented for them by Lundberg and *JAMA*, there is no indication. It is apparent that both knew they would not be asked any embarrassing questions. It also is apparent that if they had not known this, they would not have agreed to be interviewed.

If they were to protest that they did not have the time or the energy to examine the records that were available, .25 million pages with me alone, located less than an hour away from Boswell, always available to them was what I did with some of this information, particularly as it relates to them and their autopsy.

At the least both men knew of the beginning of my work, and unless they ignored the books I sent them, they knew they failed. They certainly knew that a book with the title *Post Mortem* focused on them and their work.

* * *

If this were a work directed primarily toward scholars, it would suffice to include many more notes than there are pages, referring to the innumerable documents I obtained in those many FOIA lawsuits that took so many years and precluded so much other work. I could refer to the Warren Report's many pertinent pages and to more pages from its twenty-six volumes of appendix, all used in my books. If I did this, I would need only paraphrase or summarize what these official sources contain, including what is pertinent from Humes's, Boswell's and Finck's testimony. With the documents I had not obtained by the time I published my books, I could have done this, too.

But there was an alternative that seemed better to me: to use lengthy excerpts from what I had published in which I had drawn on and cited these official sources, to put them together in a context, and to give them meanings only a subject expert can.

I began by reviewing what I had published for the citations they held as well as for the content and meaning of what I had written. I made copies of the appropriate pages so as not to have so many books to keep referring to. But before I had finished, it occurred to me that there were advantages to this offbeat use of what I had published so many years ago. Yet I was uneasy about departing from traditional practice.

That is until I read the *Washington Post* editorial quoted earlier. The simple directness of its words, "the elementary principle ... [being] the requirement to examine a subject in its entirety," decided it for me. "[I]n its entirety" includes in context. Context when addressing what Lundberg and *JAMA* perpetrated is quite broad, especially because what they perpetrated includes political and historical fraud. It encompasses what Lundberg's responsibilities as an editor and as a pathologist were when he played political games with our history. More than twenty thousand strangers have written to tell me that they suffer still from this great tragedy with which our government was less than honest in its dealings and in telling us about. Today, perhaps, half of these letters are from deeply troubled younger Americans. They write to me or telephone me, saying they had not been born when JFK was assassinated, or how young they were then and how, despite their youth and immaturity, they were moved by it then. They are moved by it now out of their dissatisfaction with how the government consigned the popular President to history with the dubious epitaph, as I called it twenty-seven years ago, of the inadequate, incomplete, and dishonest official "investigation" that was not a real investigation at all.

This book is for them. With my books not normally stocked in bookstores, they do not know how to get them. Their understanding, and this goes again to that succinct and excellent definition of good journalism by the *Washington Post*, requires, I think, the "entirety" that can come from reading what I have written, not just from reading the citations.

As *JAMA*'s editor and moreover because he is also a pathologist, Lundberg had the responsibility, when addressing his captive audience of the nation's doctors, of seeing to it that *he* examined the "subject in its entirety." He did not. Instead he cast himself and the prestigious publication he edits in the invidious role of apologist for errant government. He limited himself entirely to what Humes and Boswell told him, more likely to only those parts he preferred. He then assumed that they were the world's first two perfect humans, that they had made no mistake. Next came the assumption that they had remembered all there was to remember and had remembered it with complete fidelity, and of course, that they were only honest and complete in what they told him.

The other viewpoint as I published it years ago was all drawn together for him. He did not have to read those 912 pages of the Warren Report or the 10,000,000 words of its testimony and exhibits; he did not have the need to read those .25 million pages of records I obtained through all those FOIA lawsuits and the Commission files in the National Archives.

In using selections of what I have published that are relevant to his daring to address the JFK autopsy for his audience in particular without regard for both its "entirety" and the "other side," I provide the reader and history with this entirety that Lundberg ignored. Whether from ignorance or from mendacity, he did do that. And, in that, I believe, for what he undertook to do, to reach the nation's doctors, other *JAMA* readers, and the millions of people reached through his propagandist press conference, he did worse, much worse, than fail to meet his responsibilities. He deceived and misled his vast audience and did that with unprofessionalism and dishonesty.

There is not a word in this book that was not readily available to him. There is not a single document quoted of which he could not have had a copy. Most of those people who use my records are people with whom I do not agree, but neither I nor anyone else has the right to censor what others write. Then, too, there seems to me to be little point in referring people to sources not readily available to them just for the sake of impressing scholars, who love lengthy citations and endless notes. That my books have withstood time's testing and close scrutiny from the government and those who support its "solution" to "the crime of the century" make them even more dependable sources.

The publishing histories of the three books that followed *Whitewash* contain far fewer rejections from editors. None of the three found a home until I made a success of *Whitewash* in publishing it myself. The first of these, Edward Jay Epstein's *Inquest*, a work of pseudo-scholarship based on a stupid and baseless conjecture, was publishable because it praised the FBI and condemned Warren and his Commission. The second, Mark Lane's *Rush to Judgment*, was contracted in England. It became a success in the United States not by its content, which by the time it was published held nothing new. It succeeded because of the United States publisher's recognition of the commercial potential of the subject. This led to an enormous and successful advertising and public relations effort.

The third, Sylvia Meagher's magnificent *Accessories after the Fact*, gave the Bobbs, Merrill editor, who had failed to persuade that corporation to publish *Whitewash* two years earlier, the argument that it could still make the profit it had declined with *Whitewash* by publishing her great work.

In the course of going from publisher to publisher with the manuscript of *Whitewash*, I reached David McKay and Company. "I'm Harold Weisberg," I told the receptionist. "May I please see the managing editor?" To my surprise a voice came over the partitions that divided up the space, saying "Send him in."

A man rose from his desk in the cubicle, introduced himself as Howard Cady, and asked, "Are you the Harold Weisberg of the Paris case?"

"I am," I replied, surprised even to hear of the Paris case, which had been kept secret. "How do you know about the Paris case?"

"I was in headquarters," he said, referring to the Office of Strategic Services (OSS) headquarters. "Everyone in headquarters knew about it. We were all impressed by it." ("The Paris case," as it was known in OSS, was called that after the sergeant in charge of an OSS World War II detail that had been framed by the military police. They had lost all their appeals and were in a military prison when I was asked to look into it. Six months later they were free.)

After chatting about that affair from twenty-two years earlier for a short while, we talked about *Whitewash*. He accepted the manuscript saying he liked the idea. To him *Whitewash* was similar to what I had done in the Paris case, giving the existing official records their true meaning.

When I visited their offices once again, he returned the manuscript to me with regret. He had been unable to overcome the strong opposition of the publisher's wife to publishing a solid and factually correct refutation of the official "solution" to the JFK assassination even though it was the spectacular "crime of the century" about which no book had yet appeared.

Another of those extra-duty assignments in which the proper component had not succeeded involves a different and later aspect of my work on the JFK assassination. The OSS got that assignment from the White House. It was assigned to X–2 or counterintelligence. Counterintelligence asked me to help when they had so far failed and only forty-eight hours remained before the deadline given by the White House.

The simplest solution was to seek the most obvious source.

During World War II our government had taken over about a dozen ships owned by a Scandinavian on the grounds that he and the ships served the Nazis. He denied it, and encouraged by inactivity of our government his lawyers had gone to court with a demand for their return or payment for them. Somehow the agencies responsible for the seizure of these ships had lost the records. It cost the government fifty cents and a half-day of my time to provide the information to the White House before the time permitted by the court expired.

I took a cab, then twenty cents for that distance, gave the driver a 25 percent tip, and went to the third floor of the branch of the

District National Bank on the south side of G Street, Northwest, between 14th and 15th streets. With office space scarce from wartime's expanded needs, our government had rented that space for the storage of such records. Within a couple of hours I located the records and made notes since these were pre-Xerox days. I spent another twenty-five cents to get back to my office—faster than I could by hoofing it.

Back in my office I phoned X–2 with a summary of what the existing records proved. I told them where those records were and what proof they held. This mislabelled DEAD file held all the proof necessary to support the validity of taking those ships. They had been in the service of the Nazis. It included proof of ownership of the ships and records of their use by the enemy.

Consistent with the thinking of the early British philosopher William of Ockham to seek the simplest solution and with the point of Edgar Allan Poe's ''The Purloined Letter'' not to overlook the obvious, the deposit of mostly DEAD files on the third floor of that District National Bank building is the first—and the only—place I looked.

The cost to the government was negligible, but the benefit was enormous because it was faced with the choice of releasing those ships to serve Hitler again or paying for them, a large sum for those days.

Aside from the fifty cents in cash I spent, it cost the government a half-day of my time. As an enlisted man I was paid fifty dollars a month. OSS added an allowance for food and quarters.

Before I completed my next assignment, OSS promoted me to corporal. The next assignment required some travel. I held the lowest possible military rank, and it was my job, alone and unassisted, in the words of the Warren Commission. I was given a car and a driver, and the way the OSS worked, the private was the boss and his chauffeur was a first lieutenant.

These two recollections, of the special wartime, high-pressure job done for the White House that was so easy and of my having, as a private, an official car of my own and a first lieutenant as a personal chauffeur, serve to illustrate a truism. It is that there need be no relationship between what something costs and what it is worth.

This truism is applicable to official and private investigations of the JFK assassination and what has been written about both, including Lundberg's extravaganza.

These two recollections also illustrate that at least in those days there were some skills not taught in colleges and universities.

They are developed through experience. There were no courses to teach me how to go about investigating Nazi cartels, for example. I learned how by doing it.

Lawyers are not taught how to investigate in law school, and most of them never learn how in the course of their professional lives.

The Commission's lawyers, eminently qualified as lawyers but not as investigators, were utterly lost when they had the need to investigate. None stood up to the FBI when there were questions about the FBI's investigations for the Commission.

With Lundberg and Breo writing much more than could be said about the autopsy and the information it could yield, they were taking the word of these same lawyers. This is another reason—for them and for me—to examine the "subject in its entirety."

In my lawsuit for the JFK assassination records of the FBI's Dallas and New Orleans offices, Civil Actions 78–0322 and 78–0420, combined, the FBI actually told that court that I know more about the JFK assassination than anyone in its employ!

And if this is not far-out enough, in my Civil Action 75–1996 for records relating to the assassination of Martin Luther King, Jr., the Department of Justice persuaded the judge sitting on that case to have *me* serve as *the department's* consultant in *my* case against *it*!

The knowledge required to be able to write and publish seven books on our political assassinations, the work that entailed, and the additional knowledge acquired in doing so are also credentials.

To me the assassination of any president is the most subversive crime possible in a society like ours. It negates our political system, our freedom through self-government. It nullifies the expressed will of the people. It turns elections meaningless. It requires that those who can make a correct and accurate record of the facts of the assassination do so. We must write of what the government did and did not do, of what it did and did not tell the people about this most subversive of crimes and its official investigations.

Recently I had to rethink what I could do to continue to be productive in this field. The advent of serious illnesses have handicapped me and limited what I am able to do. With the knowledge I have acquired from my work, including the knowledge I obtained from those many FOIA lawsuits and the unprecedented, great volume of previously withheld relevant records, I decided that what was best suited to my limitations was to try to perfect the historical record for which this "subject in its entirety" is so significant.

In the work required to prepare this analysis of the truly exceptional thing the AMA did in becoming a political partisan in this controversial subject and to muster enough of the relevant official evidence to enable me to meet the principle of good journalism according to the *Washington Post* editorial, I have intended and tried to examine the "subject in its entirety."

It is my hope that it can reach as many Americans as possible. But if that is not its fate, it is a record for our history, and it is another of my efforts to keep those promises of Robert Frost's poem before I sleep.

After this book was written, the Congress passed a law to satisfy that "widespread demand for the disclosure of withheld records" relating to the JFK assassination inspired mostly by Oliver Stone's movie. Two presidents, Bush and Clinton, were required by that law to appoint an independent board, with the power of subpoena, to see to it that this was done, that there be the fullest disclosure possible. Bush did nothing at all. Clinton did nothing for too long. But, finally, as this book is about to be published, the board Clinton did appoint is staffed and beginning its work. It is the Assassination Records Review Board. It is officed at 200 E Street, Northwest, Second Floor, Washington, DC 20530. Its telephone number is (202) 724–0088. Its facsimile number is (202) 724–0457. All disclosed JFK assassination records are available at the new, modern, and large branch of the National Archives on the campus of the University of Maryland at College Park, a Washington suburb.

Chapter 1

An Introduction

IN ALL THE LONG HISTORY OF POWERFUL AND INFLUENTIAL PERSONS AND forces going out of their way to defend the Report of the President's Commission of the Assassination of President John F. Kennedy, none is as surprising, as unusual, or as improper as that by the American Medical Association.

Announcing its support at a press conference in New York City on May 19, 1992, the AMA intended to publicize the May 27 issue of its prestigious *Journal*, one of the most important if not the most important medical publications in the world.

Although the *Journal*'s editor, Dr. George Lundberg, distributed advance copies of the articles, by an embargo the media were prohibited from using them for a week. So the media were limited to using what Lundberg said of what was in those articles.

And what he said was shockingly inaccurate and false. It was overtly political. It was propaganda, not medical news. It made the national association of doctors a partisan in the lingering controversy over that assassination and its official investigations.

When the President was shot at about 12:30 P.M. local time in Dallas, Texas, on November 22, 1963, he was rushed to Parkland Memorial Hospital. He was in fact dead at the moment of the shooting because a large part of the right side of his head, including much of that hemisphere of the brain, had exploded and was missing.

The Dallas doctors did all that was possible before pronouncing him dead. That was delayed so a priest could administer last rites.

It then was not a federal crime to kill a president, although it was to kill a postman. Therefore the only applicable law regarding murder was Texas law. Under Texas law it was required that an autopsy be performed on the body of the victim in Texas.

1

While the autopsy or postmortem examination of the body is to determine the medical cause of death, it is not limited to that. What it involves also includes examination of the vital organs and establishing any medical facts relating to the crime.

The competent and respected Dallas county coroner, Dr. Earl Rose, was prevented from performing the autopsy. The Secret Service kidnapped the casketed corpse, rushing it to Love Field inside the city of Dallas and onto the presidential airplane, *Air Force One*, to be taken to Washington. Departure was delayed slightly until Sarah Hughes, federal judge for whose appointment Vice President Lyndon Baines Johnson had been responsible, came to swear him to the oath of office.

Almost as soon as the plane was airborne, Admiral George G. Burkley, physician to the President, conferred with Mrs. Jacqueline Kennedy, and on his recommendation she decided to have the autopsy performed at the Naval Hospital in Bethesda, just north of Washington.

After *Air Force One* landed at Bolling Field, an Air Force base just southeast of Washington, the casket was transferred into a Naval ambulance and taken in a motorcade to Bethesda.

There the hospital's two ranking pathologists, Commander James J. Humes and Commander J. Thornton Boswell, had been assigned to make the autopsy examination. They asked Lieutenant Colonel Pierre Finck, chief of the Wounds Ballistic Branch of the Armed Forces Institute of Pathology at the Army's Walter Reed Hospital, to join them. He did at about 8:30 P.M., after the examination had began.

All three were eminently qualified as hospital pathologists, but none had any real experience in *forensic* pathology—and that is what is required in a murder investigation.

Few elements of evidence are more significant in a murder investigation than the report of the forensic pathologists. These three were just not up to that.

Whether or not other factors or forces or influences were involved, the report on the autopsy performed on the President was bad, atrociously bad.

It was so incredibly bad that I, a layman with no medical experience or knowledge, was able to pinpoint most of what was wrong with it in *Whitewash*, which was completed only three months after the twenty-six volumes of appendix published in support of the Warren Report were first available, in November 1964.

Later I published six additional books on the JFK assassination and its investigations. My 1975 book, *Post Mortem*, extensively documents what I regarded as relevant to the botched autopsy.

The Warren Commission's "solution" to the crime—*and what is little understood is that its "solution" is only a theory*—is that Lee Harvey Oswald, alone and unassisted, fired three bullets within 5.6 seconds from a 6.5 mm Mannlicher-Carcano carbine left over from World War II from the easternmost window on the sixth floor of the Texas School Book Depository building, where he worked. The first of three bullets entered the back of President Kennedy's neck, exited its front, then entered Texas Governor John F. Connally's chest under his right armpit, smashing four inches of his fifth rib before exiting under his right nipple, after which it shattered his right wrist before coming to rest in his left thigh, having penetrated it for about two inches, parallel to his thigh bone. The second bullet missed the motorcade entirely, striking the curve of the upper surface of a curbstone at the opposite end of Dealey Plaza and inflicting a minor wound on the face of a bystander, James T. Tague, with a spray of concrete from the impact. The third bullet entered the back of the President's head and exploded out of its right side, taking pieces of scalp, of skull bone, and much of the tissue of the right half of the brain with it.

The FBI and the Secret Service never agreed to the Commission's theorized solution.

Each organization was just as determined to hold that there had not been any conspiracy, that Oswald was the lone assassin. But each also knew that the career the Commission invented for its first shot was absolutely impossible.

The FBI's instant theory, and again it is only a theory, is that the first bullet hit the President only, inflicting all his nonfatal wounds; that the second hit Connally and no one else; and that the third was the fatal shot to the President's head.

The Secret Service agrees with the FBI's theory. I have seen no record of either agency changing its adherence to this theory.

Both agencies just ignored the wounding of Jim Tague.

The Commission began with the FBI's theory, which it got from the FBI, but soon realized that it could not ignore Tague's wound, so it adopted the "solution" of its assistant counsel, Arlen Specter, that the first bullet was supermagical.

Both agencies and the Commission, as well as the AMA, ignore the fact that nobody in the entire world has been able to duplicate the fantastic shooting attributed to the duffer Oswald.

As I wrote earlier, the Commission got the best shots the National Rifle Association could provide. Under vastly easier conditions they were unsuccessful in their attempts to duplicate the shooting attributed to Oswald.

With 912 pages for its Report, the Commission found no space for this definitive testing of the theory it presented to the nation as fact, as its solution to the most terrible and subversive of crimes.

Profound in his ignorance, which is the kindest comment Lundberg's intrusion into the assassination controversy permits, he proclaimed the correctness of the Warren Commission's theorized conclusions and told the world that his interviews of the two autopsy pathologists prove them.

Lundberg actually said that because Humes and Boswell say they were right, they *were* right, and nothing else makes any difference.

This he said in his own name, in that of the American Medical Association, and in that of its *Journal.*

Lundberg quotes Humes and Boswell as currently insisting that the single-bullet theory is not a theory, but is an established fact. To do this, he had to ignore all the great amount of *official* information that proves it is not a fact. That information is at least as authoritative as the two pathologists.

As an editor and as a pathologist it is wrong for Lundberg to ignore all the available official information relating to the so-called investigations and all the readily available facts relevant to the assassination and its investigations.

Personally or professionally he could not, with honest intentions, arrange for the largest audience possible, ignoring all this information and pretending it does not exist, and state to this great audience that the Warren Report is correct because—and *only* because—Humes and Boswell repeated to him some of what they told the Warren Commission twenty-eight years earlier!

His proclamation that Humes and Boswell prove they were correct twenty-eight years ago by the mere repetition to him of what they had said is absurd. They offer no evidence; he presents no evidence; and some of the supermarket tabloids would not go for the ridiculousness he published in *JAMA*. An uncritical media assisted him in this monstrous fraud perpetrated on the country.

Even if Lundberg were entirely ignorant of anything at all about the assassination other than what Humes and Boswell repeated to him, he should have had enough common sense to realize that their saying they were right does not prove they were *proven* right.

If he had followed the traditional standards of forensic pathology, he should have said nothing and formed no opinions, without first consulting any other relevant information available. Out of all the great amount of factual, official information that was available, a forensic pathologist would have had more than a passing interest in testing.

Of the tests (the results of which were public and readily available in great quantity), he should have looked immediately for the reenactment test to determine whether or not the shooting was within the capability of a man who had not handled a rifle in years and had been a lousy shot. If he had met this absolutely minimum investigative requirement, he would have known that the best shots in the country, under greatly improved conditions, had found it impossible to duplicate the feat attributed to Oswald.

If he had consulted only the Commission's records available in the National Archives, he would have found the FBI's disbelief of the magic-bullet theory recorded in various ways. He would have begun with the Commission's first numbered record, Commission Document 1, the five-volume report LBJ ordered the FBI to make as soon as he returned to Washington from Dallas on November 22, 1963.

If he had consulted the well-known factual literature, he would have seen the relevant FBI statements reprinted in facsimile in my *Whitewash: The Report on the Warren Report*, on page 195. This still-available book is the standard source of the basic material for researchers on the subject.

If he knew anything at all about the facts of the crime and the most basic conclusion of the Warren Report—and neither the fact that he interviewed the autopsy pathologists nor that he staged his very successful press conference indicates that he has any such factual knowledge or interest at all—he certainly would have known that the Commission's own tests proved that the shooting it theorized in order to reach its lone-assassin, nonconspiracy conclusion in fact proved that there had been a conspiracy. This is because that shooting was proven to be impossible for any one person.

With this "Elementary, my dear Watson" fact beyond question, Sherlock Lundberg ignored it, or worse, was ignorant of it.

And with so many more of *the available official records* proving the same thing, there is the obvious question for any legitimate Sherlock: How could the presidential Commission, most of whose investigating was done for it by the FBI, conclude the opposite?

In assessing what Lundberg did, which means what he used the *Journal of the American Medical Association* for, with or without the approval of the AMA, it is necessary to understand how the official records he ignored answer this basic question.

We shall do what Lundberg should have done and did not do: Examine a definitive selection of the official dirty linen of the JFK assassination.

The records of the Commission, of the Department of Justice, and of its FBI that were once withheld—records for which officialdom expected perpetual secrecy and were generated before there was the FOIA—are painfully clear: The crime itself was never investigated officially and was never intended to be investigated officially.

This is our evidence of a time when the government was supposed to investigate the most serious and subversive of crimes, the assassination of a president!

That I and the authors of the books that followed mine did not wind up in mental wards or gulags and that we have no Official Secrets Act does not mean there was no official opposition to criticism of the official solutions to the JFK assassination. There were leaks and staged official actions that were designed to convey the notion that nothing was being hidden. This was the opposite of the truth.

The Federal Bureau of Investigation, which dominated the Commission from the moment of its appointment, larded its records with the most prejudicial allegations against us. These ranged from distortions of fact to overt fabrications. It then found its own ways of getting this misinformation and disinformation circulated in secret, where it counted.

The CIA was more successful in withholding its relevant records.

But both agencies did all they could to frustrate publication of books critical of the Warren Report. This extended to efforts to ruin the books after they were published. Several such FBI efforts against me had the opposite effect.

The FBI did not eschew blackmail. It planned to blackmail those who criticized the Warren Report, those who wrote it, and even the members of the Commission itself. While this police-state abusiveness was more modest than that of some foreign states, in principle it was similar.

There was modest criticism of the FBI in the Warren Report, but the FBI would not abide it. No matter how justified it was, the FBI regarded none as justified—especially when the criticism was of its founding director, J. Edgar Hoover.

Its preparations for blackmail are hidden from the files it disclosed under compulsion, but it let one slip out that I regard as a damage-control tickler. It will be directly quoted later.

All of the FBI's internal JFK assassination records that I've seen—and through lawsuits brought under the Freedom of Information Act, I've gotten about .25 million pages of them—are laced with defamatory references to those of us who dared criticize the Warren Report, which, to the FBI, also meant criticizing it.

Each time our names were mentioned in these records, which the FBI believed nobody would ever see, there are slurs and characterizations that were intended to influence all the apparatchiks who saw those records, namely Hoover.

The FBI knew I was not and had never been a Communist, but it never missed an opportunity to suggest that I had been one and still was. Its most effective dirty trick of this nature was a complete fabrication. It was inspired by a White House request for information on seven of us who had written critically about the Report. What the

Harold Weisberg

FBI sent the White House effectively killed any interest, if there had been any, in learning what the criticisms were.

Coinciding with official effort to convince the country that the government had hidden nothing about the JFK assassination, Marvin Watson, a special assistant to LBJ, asked the FBI for information, in the words of its November 8, 1966, response, "regarding the authors of books dealing with the assassination of President Kennedy." The FBI attached a "summary memoranda setting forth pertinent information contained in FBI files concerning" seven of us (FBIHQ File 62–109060–4250).

The memorandum on me, headed by the title of my first book and my name, was classified SECRET. Under this claim to secrecy three paragraphs are redacted. Of the six that remain, all include outright lies, complete fabrications, distortions, and misrepresentations save for the last. The last says, in full, "Weisberg has no known arrest record." That was and remains true. That alone.

One paragraph that I will quote in full typifies the police-state practice of the FBI when it wants to influence others in the government:

In 1956, it was alleged that Weisberg had an annual celebration of the Russian Revolution. This celebration involved a picnic at his residence and was attended by twenty-five to thirty unknown people. It was believed this affair was in commemoration of the Russian Revolution inasmuch as it was held on the day when the Communists celebrate all over the world.

When I saw this record for the first time about twenty years after the letter was written, I could not recall any time we had twenty-five to thirty guests. My wife finally figured out what it was.

Our "residence" then was a small farm. We raised poultry. My wife and I won state and national first prizes for raising, cooking, and barbecuing chickens.

I had my own breeding flocks, then uncommon, and hatched my own eggs; and when I learned that this was attractive to children, who even in the country never saw eggs hatch or just-hatched chicks or waterfowl, I arranged for all the eggs to hatch on weekends, so the children, not in school, would enjoy what once was common, but had become rare. It delighted them and their parents.

Dear friends, Jack and Vicki Frankel, were visiting us one weekend and saw the delight of the area children when they came with their parents. Jack was with the Jewish Welfare Board. His responsibilities included looking out for the interests of Washington-area Jewish military personnel. He asked to bring his people with their children up after the Jewish High Holidays, and for some years he did.

The Jewish High Holidays *never* coincide with the November Russian Revolution. They usually begin in September.

When one of our friends from the University of Maryland agriculture faculty visited the farm, he told me, "We've gotta steal this idea from you!" And so the University of Maryland replicated my idea in Wheaton, Maryland, a Washington suburb, and called it "Old MacDonald's Farm."

After receiving this and similar fabrications, the White House had no further interest in books critical of the Warren Report. Of course this was what the FBI wanted.

Pleased with the results of its poison-pen, the FBI made further distribution of its venom. From the records I received, the FBI's propaganda extended to higher officials of the Department of Justice, to those who represented the government in my FOIA litigation, and even to the Senate Intelligence Committee. In the Senate, fortunately, when Barry Goldwater was chairman, he placed a correction in that committee's records.

This type of treatment of the truth raises obvious questions about the dependability of FBI investigations and its reports provided to the White House and to the Commission. Before anyone can honestly and responsibly offer an opinion in support of the Warren Commission, he should have an understanding of this and other similar information that could have influenced the Commission's conclusions.

The FBI was long on clichés, especially those preferred by Hoover. Its most common description of my books was that they were "vitriolic and diabolical."

My first recollection of its use was in a July 13, 1967, memorandum reporting that I had requested a copy of an FBI press release. Although the FOIA was then the law of the land, and under that law it was required to provide me with a copy—and this was a *press*

release not some arcane secret—it was recommended that "no acknowledgment should be made" and that I not be sent that press
release.

This request of mine was a matter of such moment in the FBI that
its top brass received copies of it and recorded their approval by
affixing their marks. (The serial number of this 62–109060 record is
not legible. It is from the 140th section or volume of that large file.)

When the same decision was made on April 1, 1969, it was costly
to the FBI. In 1977 I filed another FOIA lawsuit for other withheld
assassination records and received about sixty thousand pages without
charge under court compulsion. Although the FBI tied me up in it
and other lawsuits for more than a decade, it also wasted a decade
of its own time. (Not Recorded in 62–109060. In the FBI's filing
system the "Record" copy is the one always indexed. Those "Not
Recorded" are duplicate copies placed in other files.) In the end I
received about .33 million pages.

No matter how wrong the FBI was, it portrayed itself as always
absolutely right. Hoover in particular was never admittedly wrong,
as he not uncommonly was. The Rube Goldberg contraptions that
were created to tell him he was right when he was very wrong
are ludicrous.

He made mistakes in his testimony to the Warren Commission,
and he fractured the language instinctively. When the FBI got the
transcript of his testimony, it put a crew of its top-flight apparatchiks
to work cleaning it up.

It was quite an operation. Five supervisors and five of the rank of
assistant director or higher were involved in what was often a rewriting of what Hoover actually said.

When they had it all in everyday English and with sentences that
had a beginning and an end, and the errors were corrected, Alan H.
Belmont, the number three man wrote the number two man, Clyde
Tolson, and attached a copy of the Hoover testimony that they
wanted published rather than the stenographic transcript of what he'd
actually said.

Nobody inside the FBI ever addressed Hoover by name from any
record I've seen!

Because Hoover was always right no matter how wrong he was, Belmont placed all the blame on the court reporter in his May 19, 1964, memo to Tolson:

Attached is a copy of the transcript of the Director's testimony before the President's Commission on the Assassination of President Kennedy. This transcript has been examined for accuracy, including misspellings and typographical [sic] errors on the part of the court reporter. It is noted that apparently the court reporter did not record the Director's testimony accurately in some instances. We have made as few changes as possible, in order to preserve the intent and accuracy of the Director's testimony.

This testimony was gone over by Messrs. Mohr, Malley, Branigan, M. A. Jones, Gheesling Rogge, and me, on a word-by-word basis. In addition, Assistant Directors Sullivan, Rosen, DeLoach, and Conrad have read the testimony and furnished their suggestions.

It is planned that I will personally go over these changes with Mr. Rankin of the Commission.

What this memo does not state is that the court reporter "missed" some of what Hoover said because the file actually includes new "testimony" that was inserted for publication as though Hoover had said it.

Hoover wanted all those who counted to him—in and out of the FBI and in the Commission in particular—to understand that he was on top of everything. He was not above making an ostentatious show of his knowledge. In his Commission testimony (5H105) he volunteered that people were wondering why Oswald had not shot at the President as the limousine approached the Book Depository on Houston Street, before turning left onto Elm, where Kennedy was assassinated. Hoover's answer to his own question was that "there were some trees" in the way. In fact, as I pointed out in my first book, Houston was the one street that no trees lined.

The FBI was so anxious to know what was said about its performance in the JFK assassination investigation that it monitored radio and TV broadcasts. This included my appearance on a Washington radio station on September 13, 1966, as the FBI report of that same

day noted, beginning at 2:10 P.M. (62–109060, Not Recorded). After
reporting some of my criticisms, this report states:

> Weisberg commented that one question which is still unan-
> swered was volunteered by Mr. Hoover.
> 'Why didn't the assassin shoot prior to the car turning left off
> of Houston Street?' Weisberg commented that Mr. Hoover an-
> swered this by saying: 'There were trees in the way'; however,
> according to Weisberg, there are no trees on Houston Street. [This
> and related records are from the FBI's liaison with the Warren
> Commission headquarters file, 62–109090. This particular record
> is Serial 169. Other relevant records are in that file at that point.]

Since the FBI had my book, it also knew that I had published a
Secret Service picture showing not so much as a twig on Houston
Street (*Whitewash*, page 201).

So, with Hoover so obviously wrong, how did the FBI stroke him
and tell him how right he was? It said: "Weisberg is completely off-
base on this point. The motorcade as it turned left off of Houston
Street entered a park, [where there were trees] that did block the
view of the motorcade prior to entering the park. The Director's
testimony is accurate."

The initials of all the FBI's big shots were affixed. When it came
to Hoover being right no matter how wrong he was, nothing was
too absurd or ridiculous. He and all his top associates had to be
satisfied, placated.

For anyone to make any responsible, factual, or honest comment on
the accuracy of the Warren Report almost three decades after it was
issued, it is essential to know the information that then was secret
and since was rescued from its official hiding places.

It is necessary to understand that the FBI was in de facto control,
and why. Without some understanding of this I believe there is no
real context for evaluating the Warren Report or Lundberg's adventuring into his defense of that Report and of the autopsy pathologists
he interviewed.

This is not a flat world, although to Lundberg it is. His position
in saying that those pathologists were right only because they say

they were right is a neat duplication of Hoover being right in saying there were trees when there were no trees to interfere with the shooting.

The pathologists and their autopsy report do not stand alone. There was an enormous amount of relevant and available official information necessary for Lundberg to be familiar with before he launched his adventure. Some of it will be used here to evaluate what he did—and what he did not—do and say.

Chapter 2

Dirty Linen

I BELIEVE THAT THE GOVERNMENT NEVER INVESTIGATED THE CRIME IT-self and never intended to, this having begun with J. Edgar Hoover's instant vision of a lone-nut assassin virtually the moment he learned of the assassination. I believe that the government engaged in a propaganda campaign initially to make this preconception appear to be credible and then to refute legitimate criticism of the preordained official "solution." I believe that Lundberg and the *JAMA* came to the government's rescue when the government itself could not and dared not respond to Oliver Stone's widely popular movie *JFK*. To begin my proof, I turn to some of the most extraordinary official records created by the government when it never expected me or anyone else to be able to compel it to disgorge these unprecedented secrets.

Examination of the hundreds of thousands of pages of FBI records I obtained by FOIA lawsuits leaves it without question that in political cases (and the FBI's definition of "political" is quite broad) the name of the FBI's game is control. Only an understanding of Hoover's unique reasoning makes it clear why what most would regard as run-of-the-mill criminal cases have political aspects to the FBI.

From the outset there was never a time the FBI did not, one way or another, have de facto control over all the official investigations, including those of the Warren Commission and of the Secret Service. Before long Hoover had the Secret Service effectively out of the government's investigation even though it, and it alone, is responsible for the protection of presidents.

In the JFK case Hoover's need to control included the fact that the FBI's effective, decades-long self-promotion created a myth that it was on top of everything criminal. Hoover, I believe, simply could

15

not abide having it believed that a president could be assassinated and his FBI not prevent it.

The fact is that, although he was able to hide it, he was really hysterical as soon as he knew the President had been killed.

My friend Dr. David Wrone, Professor of History at the University of Wisconsin at Stevens Point, put the case of Hoover's hysteria together from my FOIA documents. Hoover's hysteria went unobserved outside the FBI, and nobody inside the FBI ever reported it.

But it was not hysteria that prompted Hoover to the illegal action of moving into the case when he had no jurisdiction, as he did virtually the minute of the crime and as he later boasted to William Manchester.

The Kennedy family sanctioned Manchester's sort of authorized account of the assassination. It ended in controversy, but he did produce the book, *The Death of a President* (New York: Harper & Row, 1967).

Through the intercession of Cartha DeLoach, then the number four man in the FBI hierarchy, Manchester got to interview Hoover. That came to pass beginning at 10:10 A.M., June 4, 1964, in Hoover's office (62–1009060, Not Recorded; original in 94–42768).

Aside from making it clear that he never suspected any assassin other than Oswald, without confederates, Hoover was quite explicit that without jurisdiction he had controlled the case.

DeLoach, nominally head of what the FBI called its Crime Records Division, was in fact in charge of its propaganda, leaking, lobbying, and other activities not on its organizational chart.

As was the custom, after the Manchester interview, DeLoach prepared a memo for Hoover covering it. In the FBI's unique practices he did not address his memo to Hoover. DeLoach addressed this memo of more than seven single-spaced, typewritten pages to John P. Mohr, whose title then was assistant to the director. But even Mohr could not address Hoover directly. He routed it to Hoover's longtime friend, Associate Director Clyde Tolson.

It was FBI practice for those through whose hands these memos passed to initial them, sometimes adding comments or recommendations. This particular memo—the original of which is in one of those DeLoach files the FBI has always refused to search for me, a "94" classification file—was provided to me from the FBI's main JFK assassination file, 62–109060, in which it is not the "Record" copy. The "Record" copy is hidden in the "94" classification file.

(In the FBI's file classifications, "94" is "Research Matters." The FBI has deceived the courts in my FOIA lawsuits into believing that this classification is limited to "Research Matters" and outside the disclosure requirements of the FOIA. The FBI's field offices, having no use for the classifications "80 Laboratory Research Matters," use that file classification for similarly hiding from search and required disclosures. The field offices file the information they get from FBIHQ lab in their relevant main case files.)

On a single page of this lengthy memo covering what transpired at the Manchester interview, DeLoach stated that on three different occasions Hoover told Manchester that he had entered the case without any legal authority to do so.

In a sentence referring to Hoover's second call on the afternoon of the assassination to Robert Kennedy, brother and attorney general, DeLoach wrote that Hoover "once again told him [Kennedy] that the FBI was moving into the investigation. The Director advised Manchester that the FBI took this action despite the fact that there was no law making it a Federal violation to assassinate the President."

The fourth paragraph on this second page begins, "The Director told Manchester that the FBI immediately entered the case, despite nonjurisdiction . . ." In the same paragraph, referring to a conversation with the new President, DeLoach wrote, "The Director stated [to Manchester] he advised the President that the FBI had already entered the case." This third repetition of the FBI's involvement refers to what Hoover told LBJ when LBJ phoned him about 7:25 P.M., not long after he had reached his office after returning from Dallas.

Beginning with DeLoach's flourished "D" and including Tolson's "T" that looks more like a checkmark and falling below all other initials, the crabbed "OK. H" is scrawled, meaning approvals are noted.

The rest of this great volume of records that I secured under the FOIA and those records from the Warren Commission, some of which I also had to sue to obtain, confirm that the FBI did dominate all investigations.

The FBI's control of all investigations continued legally once LBJ asked Hoover to investigate and report the findings of its investigation to him. Presidents may legally request the FBI to make investigations of crimes that are not violations of federal law, as Hoover informed the Commission (5H98).

When the New Orleans Secret Service investigation led it to the Jones Printing Company, the printer of the Fair Play for Cuba Committee handbills Oswald had distributed, and the Secret Service was on the verge of learning, as I later learned, that it was not Oswald who picked up those handbills, the New Orleans FBI at once contacted FBIHQ. The FBI *immediately* leaned on the Secret Service headquarters and *immediately* the New Orleans Secret Service was ordered to desist. For all practical purposes, that ended the Secret Service investigation of the JFK assassination—the moment it was about to learn that the man the FBI ordained the "lone" and unassisted assassin was not alone and did have at least one associate who picked up a print job for him.

When the Dallas FBI Oswald case agent, James P. Hosty, Jr., in an emotional moment early on the afternoon of the assassination, blurted out to Lieutenant Jack Revill of Dallas police intelligence that the FBI knew Oswald had the potential but did not believe he would do anything like kill the President, Chief Jesse Curry directed Revill to prepare an affidavit stating this under oath. This information reached the press. Hoover then ordered that Curry be made to apologize on live TV, coast-to-coast, and Curry, humbly and on nationwide TV did apologize—*for telling the truth.*

The FBI was able to suppress this truth for thirteen years. Then, when the retirement of J. Gordon Shanklin, Dallas FBI special agent-in-charge, was secure, the truth was leaked to the *Dallas Times Herald*, the more conservative of the city's two daily newspapers. Leaked by someone inside the Dallas FBI office, it resulted in a belated and phony FBI investigation of the FBI. This self-investigation could not avoid confirming the fact that had been suppressed in the FBIHQ and field-office files, but had existed in other hidden and undisclosed records: Oswald had threatened bombings of the FBI's Dallas office, of the Dallas police headquarters, or of both. The reported recollections of Dallas FBI employees differed. The FBI's investigation of itself thus made it impossible to level any charges against anyone involved in suppressing this truthful basis for Hosty's excited confession to Revill.

About two weeks before the assassination Oswald left a threatening note for Hosty in an unsealed envelope, which led to its being read before Hosty got it. Shanklin had no choice but to inform FBIHQ, and as soon as Oswald was killed by Jack Ruby, FBIHQ ordered Shanklin to have that note destroyed. Shanklin gave the same order to Hosty. As Hosty later testified in an investigation by the House of Representatives Oversight Committee, he tore it up and flushed it down the toilet.

Knowing the truth, Hoover first ordered that Curry make a public apology for telling the truth in which he said that he and his policemen had made a mistake. Then, once Curry humiliated himself and his police department as publicly as possible, Hoover ordered the severing of all FBI relations with the Dallas police. This extended even to training the police.

For scholars of the future I have made a separate file of duplicates of the disclosed records of this FBI self-investigation by its inspector general. These records are scattered in the disclosed files in which they appear in the order in which they were filed, not as a separate file. In and of itself, this is a Byzantine story of one of the most Byzantine of agencies headed by the most Byzantine of dictators in our Byzantium on the Potomac.

It is most remarkable that brutal as the FBI's assertion of raw power was, no inkling of its employment was ever complained about or even leaked by those dominated and controlled by it. Not by the Secret Service, not by the Dallas police, and not even by the Warren Commission or by any of its staff. The staff learned of it when the members, in secret, confessed awareness of the fact that the FBI was controlling it and what it dared do during an executive session on the evening of January 22, 1964. The staff was barred from the executive sessions, and the transcripts were classified TOP SECRET even though the Commission had no authority to classify anything.

The Commission ordered the January 22 transcript destroyed. When I learned that the stenotypist's tape escaped the memory hole and that it was hidden in the Commission's files, I was able to compel its transcription and disclosure to me under the FOIA. I published this transcript in facsimile in *Post Mortem* (page 475 ff.).

I published a related transcript of the executive session of five days later, also in facsimile, in *Whitewash IV* along with other formerly suppressed and relevant records.

Hoover and his top echelon of skilled political operators, particularly DeLoach, first tried to prevent the appointment of the Commission. Failing in that, they controlled appointments, such as the chairman's general counsel. Hoover did not like Chairman/Chief Justice Earl Warren's choice for general counsel, a Justice Department lawyer from the Criminal Division, Warren Olney. Through Commission member Gerald Ford, then House minority leader, Hoover got his way. This is established in other Commission executive session transcripts that I obtained under the compulsion of the FOIA.

The FBI had no fear of J. Lee Rankin with whom, for the eight years he was the solicitor general of the United States, the lawyer who takes the Justice Department's cases to the Supreme Court, it had satisfactory relations. Rankin became the Commission's general counsel, the man who actually ran it.

No less Byzantine was the Commission's origin.

In varying degrees an enormous number of books pretending to solve the unsolved crime using conspiracy theories represent Jack Ruby, who killed Lee Harvey Oswald on live TV the morning of Sunday, November 24, 1963—and in the Dallas police headquarters building at that—as the avenger, the silencer for organized crime or other sinister forces. This is especially true of those "mafia" fantasies that hold virtually no mention of and no understanding at all of the crime itself, like John F. Davis's *Mafia Kingfish*, and David E. Scheim's *Contract on America*.

But Ruby's real service was to the federal and local governments: With Oswald being the lone candidate as assassin for both local and federal authorities, killing Oswald eliminated any trial and thus any working of our system of justice to determine who committed the aptly called "crime of the century." No trial meant that the government would not be embarrassed by having a jury find that there really was no case at all with which to convict Oswald alone.

The first, and it appears to have been the instant, appreciation of this great boon from Ruby's pistol, in all the records I have examined, was by the man then running the Department of Justice in Robert Kennedy's absence. Nicholas de B. Katzenbach's official title was deputy attorney general. Usually the deputy is in day-to-day control of the department and at least in theory of its many components, like the FBI.

It took some ten years for the department's Criminal Division to get around to its FOIA response to me, but ultimately it did. And lo! there in its main JFK assassination file (129–11) are two different versions of the memo Katzenbach addressed to LBJ through his liaison, Bill Moyers, a top presidential assistant.

One version is his handwritten draft of that Sunday when he had no typing or secretarial help. The other is the typed version.

The fact that Katzenbach drafted this memo in which he pressed his major policy recommendation on LBJ as soon as he realized that with a dead Oswald there would be no trial is further established by an FBI memo found in its main assassination file (62–109060), in which it is part of Serial 1399. (The FBI serializes its records not when they are created, but in the order in which they reach its general files. The serial number does not reflect time with any precision at all.)

This record is on the Katzenbach memo. It was bucked upward for Hoover by Assistant Director Courtney A. Evans to the bureaucrat immediately above him, Alan H. Belmont. (Evans was FBI liaison with the Department of Justice.)

Written early on the morning of the first working day after the assassination, Monday, November 25, Evans wrote that "Katzenbach handed to me this morning the attached memorandum which he has sent to Bill Moyers, who will be the principal assistant to President Johnson in the White House. Katzenbach said that this memorandum was prepared by him after his discussion with the Director yesterday."

"Yesterday" is when Ruby killed Oswald.

The policy Katzenbach urged on the new President begins with:

1. The public must be satisfied that Oswald was the assassin; that he did not have confederates who are still at large; and that the evidence was such that he would have been convicted at trial.

The penultimate paragraph begins as follows: "The only other step would be the appointment of a Presidential Commission of unimpeachable personnel to review and examine the evidence and to announce its conclusions.''

Although Katzenbach employs quiet words in an unsensational way, what he actually urged on the President is that it become his policy and the national policy not to investigate the crime itself and that he appoint eminences on whose names and reputations he could trade to rubber-stamp this deliberate refusal to make any real investigation.

The FBI was so opposed to the appointment of a presidential commission, to its not having official control of the case, it was even suspicious of any LBJ advisers who agreed with it. Consider, Abe Fortas, then a prominent lawyer in private practice and a friend of LBJ, who was later appointed to the Supreme Court by Johnson.

In a November 27, 1963, memo that Evans addressed to Belmont, but was clearly intended for Hoover, Evans wrote, following his report on Katzenbach's activities and what he had said:

> As a sidelight, Katzenbach said he had learned on an extremely confidential basis that Abe Fortas, the Washington lawyer, had been in touch with President Johnson and had argued against the idea of having a Presidential Commission look into the Kennedy assassination. Fortas's argument to Johnson was that for the President to announce such a commission would merely suggest that there was evidence of something [*sic*] other than Oswald alone killing Kennedy and thus build up public speculation. Fortas' second argument was that the formation of such a commission would cause a reflection on the FBI. Fortas, of course, is no friend of the Bureau and there would appear to be some obvious underhand motive in his using us in his argument, although we do not know what this is.

Tolson, DeLoach, and two others in the top FBI echelon merely initialed this memo, but Hoover, after affixing many vertical lines for marginal emphasis to sentences and paragraphs of the memo, wrote of Evans's suspicions, ''Certainly something sinister here. H.''

Katzenbach was busy working both sides of his proposal beginning early on the day it was typed.

In an FBI memo dated two days later, unusual in that it is on plain paper with no author or addressee or subject matter indicated,

Belmont, along with still other reports of what fast-foot Katzenbach was doing and saying, concludes: "Katzenbach is now visiting with the Chief Justice to ask him for the President if he will head this Commission."

If Katzenbach told the FBI what argument persuaded Warren to take the assignment, I have seen no FBI record reporting it.

However, Warren did tell his Commission staff at his first meeting with them, on January 20, 1964 (*Whitewash IV*, pages 24–25). Assistant Counsel Melvin A. Eisenberg's memo on what Warren said states: "When the position was first offered to him he declined it, on the principle that Supreme Court Justices should not take this kind of role. . . ."

What persuaded Warren to do what he knew was wrong, in Eisenberg's words, was some rumors, "if not quenched, could conceivably lead the country into a war which could cost 40 million lives."

Could there be a better reason, in Byzantium on the Potomac, for the chief justice to preside over a commission that concluded that there had been no conspiracy than if he did not, it "could cost 40 million lives"? Could there be a more persuasive reason for concluding that there had not been any conspiracy, foreign or domestic?

As of the moment Belmont wrote this memo, he had the draft of the statement the White House had already prepared to release announcing the formation of the Commission, even when it did not yet have the chairman's agreement.

At the time Katzenbach put his plot against our system of freedom through self-government on paper, that Sunday afternoon, November 24, less time had passed than what constitutes a working day for most federal employees. Even though the FBI did work after the end of the working day and on weekends, it had not been possible even to begin a real investigation in the two days between the assassination and Oswald's murder.

Not that the FBI ever intended to investigate the crime itself. It only wanted to get away with ordaining Oswald the lone-nut assassin.

In his 7:25 P.M. phone call to Hoover on November 22, LBJ ordered the FBI to make a full investigation and then report to him. By the time Katzenbach drafted this memo, nothing like a real investigation had been possible, regardless of the manpower assigned to it by the FBI or the diligence and competence with which the agents worked.

The FBI did complete its interpretation of what LBJ ordered of it rapidly. It also leaked it before it was delivered to the Commission, on December 9, 1963. Its first of many leaks of which I have records was carried out a week before the Commission first saw, and then was stunned by, what the FBI did, in five fancy volumes. The first volume is the text of its report. The last is its report on Ruby. The others are its alleged evidence.

The FBI's supposedly definitive report on its investigation of the assassination of a president is an atrocity and a disgrace. It is no more than a virulent diatribe against Oswald. Only an agency knowing that the entire bureaucracy of government lives in terror of it would even have dared such a travesty.

It is available to those who would like to read it in the FBI's public reading room and at the National Archives, where it is identified as Commission Document 1 (CD1).

In reading this supposedly definitive investigative report, there is no way to know how many shots were fired or even how many wounds the President had.

There is an elaborate index, but it has no entries for anyone with the illusion that he can learn something about the crime from the vaunted FBI's report on it that was to have raised and answered all questions.

As the report itself is a diatribe against Oswald, so is even the index a diatribe against Oswald.

This poisoning of national and world opinion against Oswald was the FBI's carefully hidden but known intention. This is revealed in the one passage Katzenbach edited out of his handwritten draft of his memo to LBJ through Moyers. It refers to this "definitive" report not as an exhaustive report on the crime itself but as a report on Oswald, referring to it as "a thorough FBI report on Oswald."

It is not often that a writer can look back on his work after several decades and see that he was prescient—or has as much reason to be as unhappy about it. My first books were titled *Whitewash*. There were four to this series. These books are distinguished by their sub-titles. The second alleges an FBI "cover-up" in its subtitle. This was the official intent from the very beginning, and they did it, all of them.

There was much double-talk and double-dealing over Katzenbach's recommendation of what became the Warren Commission. This is set forth in many additional relevant records scattered throughout those disclosed to me under court compulsion. Even LBJ was involved in double-crossing; while he was assuring Hoover that he would not appoint a presidential commission, LBJ was busily engaged in preparing for and in empowering his commission.

After completing all the preliminaries, having the law researched and the empowering papers drafted, Johnson announced his commission and its members four days after he got Katzenbach's memo, on November 29.

It may be that Johnson had in mind Katzenbach's proposal of a presidential commission before he got the memorandum. The Secret Service logs of his activities suggest this. Its "Activity" sheet, compiled from handwritten records of his movements, visits, and phone calls, records a phone call to him from Bill Moyers at 8:50 P.M. Sunday, November 24. Five minutes later LBJ phoned Hoover. This "Activity" sheet's next entry is a 9:00 P.M. call to Katzenbach, but the handwritten phone logs give the time as 8:57.

From the time Secretary of State Dean Rusk, Under Secretary of State George Ball, and Secretary of Defense Robert S. McNamara departed at 3:35 P.M., with the exception of two phone conversations with national-security adviser, McGeorge Bundy, the second at 5:30 P.M., all other entries are social, conversations for the extending of sympathies and expressions of thanks or kindnesses.

So, while these three consecutive phone conversations, from Moyers and then to Hoover and to Katzenbach—the only ones not social—may have been for other purposes, it does seem probable that Moyers informed LBJ of what he was told by Katzenbach, after which LBJ phoned Hoover and then Katzenbach, with discussion of and agreement with what Katzenbach had proposed being the subject of these conversations.

Early the next morning, Monday, November 25, when the FBI got its copy of Katzenbach's memorandum, and before 10 A.M., the time posted on one of this series of long-suppressed FBI internal records, it was busy lobbying the *Washington Post* in a successful effort to kill the *Post*'s planned editorial endorsement of the appointment of such a presidential commission.

Simultaneously—and even earlier—with no indication of any directive from Washington headquarters, on the local operating level, the FBI's street agents knew exactly what was expected of them, as did their supervisors.

This, I believe, in some ways, is more Byzantine, much more dangerous, than if the FBI's malfeasances had been ordered by or in the name of its unquestioned dictator, Hoover.

Two of the examples of this activity on the local level come from the Dallas FBI files I obtained in Civil Action 78–0322 in federal district court in Washington. These are records the Dallas FBI did not even send to headquarters.

Chapter 3

What a Stench!

ONLY MOMENTS AFTER THE 12:30 P.M. FRIDAY SHOOTING OF THE PRESI-dent and the Governor, from the internal evidence after the President's death was announced and before Oswald was accused, identified, and charged, Sergeant H. C. Sherrill, of the nearby Richardson, Texas, Police Department, phoned the Dallas FBI office with a tip. In the words of "lead" Investigative Clerk Robert G. Renfro prepared for Shanklin, the Richardson police believed "Jimmy George Robinson and members of the National States Rights Party [NSRP] should be considered possible suspects" because of their demonstrated "strong feelings against" JFK.

The NSRP was a minuscule ultraright racist gang begun by Jesse B. Stoner, who had found the Ku Klux Klan to be too liberal for him. Robinson also had a record of racist violence.

On the clerical end this lead was handled promptly. A search of the FBI's Dallas indices led to the posting of not fewer than five citations to different Dallas office files. One was to a civil-rights file; one was to a "100"-classification file, designated for "Subversive Matter [Individual]; Internal Security [Organizations]; Domestic Security Investigations"; one was a "105"-classification file, like the "100s", a "security-related classification," for "Foreign Counterintelligence" that included "individuals and organizations" with a "Nationalistic Tendency" and some "Internal Security" records; one was of a "157" classification, also "security-related," for "Extremist Matters" and "Civil Unrest;" and one that is unclear seems to have been for violations of the Voorhis Act. In addition there is a reference to a three-by-five card index, and there is an illegible entry.

Although there exist these records pertinent to Robinson and the NSRP reflecting the FBI's knowledge of reasons that could qualify

27

them as suspects in the assassination, there is no indication that the citations posted were checked. No notations indicate this, and there are no other notations on any attachment. Instead there is written, below the last of these citations: "Not necessary to cover as true subject located."

The initials of the FBI agent who so summarily dismissed the lead from the nearby police department are only partly legible. The first is clearly a "J" and the last is as clearly an "H," but the middle initial can only be guessed at. It does not appear to be the middle initial of any of the six Dallas agents and of the one supervisor whose names began with "H" listed as the staff on the day of the assassination.

In accord with standard practice this "lead" has a rubber stamp with boxes for noting whether the record was searched, indexed, serialized, and/or filed. Above the stamp the file identification and the serial number of the record within that file are posted, in this instance 89-43-84. This conspiracy "lead" memo was completely processed and was filed on the date stamped on the center of the form, November 22, 1963, or the day of the assassination.

This means that whether or not the agent or supervisor who "memory-holed" this lead knew Oswald's name, which he did not include in his notation, Robinson's record was processed completely and was filed—*before Oswald was charged with killing the President!*

Oswald was not charged until after midnight, not until November 23.

But before any real investigation was made or even possible, or before any real case against Oswald could have been built, the FBI was eliminating consideration of the possibility that there had been a conspiracy.

At the very least the FBI should have tried to determine whether or not Oswald had any connection with the NSRP and/or Robinson or with any other possible conspirators.

While there are no indications that this was ordered by FBIHQ, it seems that any supervisor or street agent would not refuse to follow any lead that could have led to establishing the existence of a conspiracy against JFK without first having reason to believe that the nonconspiracy investigation is what Hoover and headquarters wanted.

Consistent with this, bright and early on Monday, November 25, the first normal working day after the assassination, Walter Bent, sales service manager of the Dallas Eastman Kodak film-processing division, phoned the Dallas FBI office with a tip. Special Agent Milton L. Newsom's memo to Shanklin, written immediately, informed Shanklin that Bent had invited the FBI to examine motion and still pictures of the assassination taken by Charles Bronson, an engineer, that, according to Bronson, showed both the assassination and the building from which the FBI said all the shots had been fired.

Newsom took another agent, Emory E. Horton, with him to Eastman Kodak. Once they returned, Newsom sent Shanklin a memo about their examination of Bronson's film (89–43–518, 493).

Sure enough, in Newsom's words, Bronson's "film did depict the President's car at the precise time the shots were fired."

Yet, even for free, Newsom did not want prints of the 35mm slides of superior quality taken with Bronson's Leica. "The pictures were not sufficiently clear for identification purposes," Newsom wrote.

Bronson's 8mm film taken with his good Keystone camera? In Newsom's words, it "failed to show the building from which the shots were fired."

Armed with these two FBI reports that I had obtained in court and that FBIHQ had never seen, my friends Gary Mack, then of KFJZ-FM, Forth Worth, and Earl Golz, then an investigative reporter for the *Dallas Morning News,* called Bronson. The FBI reports were news to him, and he was quite willing for them to see his films.

There were ninety-two individual frames or individual pictures of the very window the FBI deemed "the sniper's nest."

They were taken moments before the shooting, and Oswald was not visible in the window, even though in the FBI's reenactment of the assembling of the rifle that allegedly was brought into the building unassembled, it took the FBI, not the duffer Oswald, six minutes to do the reassembling.

Bronson, in return for protecting his rights, beginning with copyrighting his film, allowed the paper to use his photos. It devoted about two-thirds of its Sunday, November 26, 1978, front page and three full pages inside to the reproduction of Bronson's stills and frames and to related stories.

Eight millimeters is only a little more than a quarter of an inch.

Bronson's eight millimeter film was of such superior quality that one frame, published on the front page under a banner headline, was enlarged to almost nine inches in width. It includes views of the crowd awaiting the motorcade, a block of Houston Street, and that empty window, clear even after printing it on newspaper stock.

"Bronson's still photographs of the motorcade were crisp and clear," the *News* said in the caption.

That the President had been hit and his position and that of the other occupants of the limousine, essential information in the investigation and reconstruction of the shooting that lacked it thanks to the FBI, is recorded in a published picture also quite clear.

So also are dozens of witnesses to the assassination. For the purpose of "identifying" them and their locations, Bronson's pictures are excellent. This, too, was important information in any real investigation, again information the FBI and the Commission did not have.

There are many people clearly visible in and identifiable from Bronson's pictures who were not interviewed by the FBI and were not used as witnesses.

It is not easy to exaggerate the value of Bronson's stills and movies in any real investigation, had one been intended. Nor would Newsom, with Horton's assent, have made up such cockamamie excuses for refusing to accept the offered copies. The reason the FBI avoided collecting these and many other known pictures is that the photographs could have jeopardized its preconceived "solution"—a solution reached before any investigation was possible.

The Commission used the eight millimeter amateur movies taken by Dallas clothing manufacturer Abraham Zapruder. The FBI and the Commission could hardly ignore Zapruder's films.

Exclusive rights to Zapruder's film were bought by the old *Life* magazine. It got the rights to use or not to use it, in practice the latter more often than the former. What it used, it used sensationally, but only in support of the official story.

Because of this sensational use of Zapruder's film, it could not be ignored, although at first the FBI actually pretended it had no value at all.

Zapruder's pictures were taken from the opposite or north side of Elm Street. From that perspective it shows views of the victims, their expressions, the reflection of injuries, and the positions of their bodies. Bronson's pictures were of great value because, taken from the other side, they were 35mm in size and capable of greater enlargement.

But the FBI avoided great numbers of known films that, more than four years later, it was forced to tabulate, this tabulation disclosed to me by compulsion of the federal court.

This tabulation, in an evidence envelope known as an "FD 340," was filed on January 11, 1968, by Special Agent F. F. John, with this description on the envelope: "List of alleged photos pertinent to assassination and pertinent comments re each of those accounted for" [DL 89–43–1A271].

The last words were meant to cover its ass because the FBI knew very well that all were not "accounted for." So glaring was the FBI's avoidance of pictures known to exist that I published a book on it, *Photographic Whitewash: Suppressed Kennedy Assassination Pictures,* early in 1967, seven months before this list was prepared.

In retrospect, twenty-eight years after I titled my first book *Whitewash* and referred to the cover-up in the subtitle of the second book, based on what I have learned from the records I obtained later in my FOIA lawsuits, it is apparent that I understated the facts. The reality is that even more important evidence was suppressed.

Few things are more important in a murder-by-gunshot investigation than the autopsy, and of the autopsy few items are more important than the autopsy X rays and photographs of the autopsy.

The autopsy was performed in Bethesda, Maryland, at the Naval Hospital. That is in the territory of the FBI's Baltimore office. It and all FBI field offices have scattered through their territory resident agencies, or suboffices. Of those of the Baltimore field office, the closest was at Hyattsville, a few miles to the east of Bethesda. Two of its agents, James W. Sibert and Francis X. O'Neill, were ordered into the case at 3 P.M., or three hours before *Air Force One* landed at Bolling Field. They were assigned to the case when the FBI was involved in it illegally. (Their report on the autopsy is published in facsimile in *Post Mortem* on pages 532–38.) They awaited the plane before it landed and were part of the motorcade to the Naval Hospital. There they helped remove the body from the casket and remained with it along with the Secret Service agents, who never left it, until the body was turned over to the morticians.

As the Baltimore field office told FBIHQ and as Alex Rosen, head of the General Investigative Division, told Hoover through Alan Belmont, on November 26, 1963:

> The Secret Service has advised our Baltimore office that the photographs and X-rays of the President's body would be available to us through Secret Service Headquarters, Washington.

Under "ACTION RECOMMENDED" Rosen recommended no action at all:

> It is not recommended that we request these photographs and X-rays through the Secret Service at this time as it does not appear that we shall have need of this material.

He added that if they changed their minds they could get it later (62–109060–426).

The FBI later also declined a copy of the autopsy report itself.

It thus did not have—had not even seen—the photographs, X rays, or autopsy report when it prepared its supposedly all-inclusive and definitive report. When it was slightly embarrassed later because it did not have this important evidence, its internal justification was that it had deferred to the wishes of the Kennedy family. This is false; no record reflects any family wish that specific evidence not be used in the investigation. Rosen stated the real truth—the FBI did not want them.

(Were it not so deadly serious, this particular one of the FBI's endless lies might be amusing as well as what it is—disgusting. It was Alex Rosen himself who was meanspirited and small-minded enough to blame the victim's family, the Kennedys, for the FBI's deliberate negligence. This can be found in his memo to Hoover that he addressed to Belmont on December 17, 1963, only three weeks after he had said the FBI should ignore the autopsy's best evidence, the pictures. The memo itself also reports the Commission's request for twenty additional copies of its five-volume report, copies it already had on hand. Then Allen Dulles, the fired CIA director, who was, to the silence of the media, appointed to the Warren Commission and who leaked its secrets to frustrate it, leaked to the FBI's liaison with the CIA, Special Agent Sam Papich, that "Rankin is considering an investigative staff to conduct additional investigations [and] will consider relations between various federal agencies to see if there are defects. . . ." The petty recommendation that Rosen made follows: "In this light, it may be well [*sic*] to give Rankin only ten additional copies of their report at this time."

(Rosen's lie that held the Kennedy family victim for the transgression he personally had recommended only three weeks earlier was formulated in discussing the Commission's interest "in the medical reports." Rosen wrote, "[T]he medical report from the U.S. Naval Hospital at Bethesda was not in the possession of the Bureau and had not been included inasmuch as the President's family had indicated a desire the report be kept confidential.")

Medical pictures showing where the wounds were on the President's body and the nature of those wounds were what the FBI had no need for? How could the FBI possibly account for those wounds with complete accuracy and dependability without being able to locate them precisely? Without examining these pictures, it would be impossible. This was particularly true of the path of the nonfatal wound that had to have been traced through the body and never was. The FBI was free to conjecture and contrive, which is exactly what it did!

The Commission did the same in its Report in which a grossly inaccurate location of this very wound is absolutely indispensable to the Report. Had the Commission located that wound accurately, it could have never issued its lone-assassin Report. This is the wound about which Pathologist J. Thornton Boswell first conned the *Baltimore Sun*'s Richard Levine, then the Associated Press and *The New York Times*, and more recently *JAMA* and its editor, George D. Lundberg.

All of this was made possible by the FBI's refusal of the autopsy pictures when they were offered it.

There are many similar illustrations in the hundreds of thousands of once-withheld pages of its records the FBI was compelled to disclose.

These preceding illustrations are enough to make it beyond question that the crime itself was never investigated and was never intended to be investigated.

But there is also the official conclusion that Oswald acted entirely alone, that there had not been any conspiracy. This is a matter carefully avoided in all records. But not entirely.

There are some things that absolutely must be reported to any director, to Hoover, in particular. Cartha DeLoach had to report a conference with columnist Jack Anderson to Hoover, as he did in his memo addressed to Tolson on April 4, 1967 (62-1090060-5075).

Anderson, of the syndicated Washington Merry-Go-Round column, had gone to New Orleans and interviewed District Attorney Jim Garrison. Garrison charged that there had been a conspiracy in the JFK assassination. The sole living party to his alleged conspiracy was the respected Clay Shaw. What Garrison told Anderson impressed him very much. Anderson discussed this with LBJ's press secretary, George Christian, and Christian, who also suspected there had been a conspiracy and said so, told him to speak to the FBI. So Anderson saw DeLoach at 11:55 A.M. on April 4.

After recounting what Anderson had told him and immediately after the above references to what Christian said about his own suspicion that there had been a conspiracy, DeLoach wrote:

> In this connection, Marvin Watson [a top LBJ assistant] called me late last night and stated that the President had told him in an off moment that he was now convinced that there was a plot in connection with the assassination. Watson stated the President felt that the CIA had something to do with this plot. Watson requested any further information we could furnish in this connection would be most appreciated by him and the President.

DeLoach concluded his memo by referring to what information the FBI had given the White House that led the President to believe that there had been a conspiracy which placed him in office. The initials of only DeLoach and Tolson appear on this memo. However, Hoover made numerous vertical lines in the margins and on both sides of the statement of the President's belief that there had existed a conspiracy to assassinate. These are glimpses, mere peeks, at the FBI's dirty linen.

Shaw was acquitted by a New Orleans jury, but books theorizing conspiracies and the showing of the Zapruder film on coast-to-coast TV triggered increased public interest. This led to the creation of the House Select Committee on Assassinations (HSCA).

Some abuses by the FBI and CIA had already been exposed by the Senate's temporary Church Committee that would become its permanent committee on intelligence. The Church Committee was a public-relations disaster for the FBI. The HSCA could be one, too. And, indirectly, I was responsible for a major public-relations disaster for the FBI.

The investigative-files exemption of the FOIA was amended by the Congress in 1974, to become effective in 1975. In one of my earlier FOIA lawsuits, in which I sought the nonsecret FBI records on the scientific testing in its JFK assassination investigation, the FBI had succeeded in rewriting the law when it was before a judge not unfriendly to it, John J. Sirica, later of Watergate fame, by means of false representations to him. That lawsuit, which I lost all the way to the Supreme Court because of the FBI's false swearing, was cited in the debates on the 1974 amending of the act as requiring an amendment to make the files of the FBI, CIA, and similar agencies accessible under the act. It was Senator Edward Kennedy, then chairman of the Judiciary Committee's FOIA Subcommittee, who saw to it that the legislative history would be explicit and unequivocal on this point.

After the amendment became effective, a series of efforts by a number of people brought to light the FBI's police-state acts against those it just did not like, for political or other reasons. None of the FBI's victims had committed an illegal act.

As I mentioned earlier, the FBI had an Orwellian name for its vendetta, calling it a "Counterintelligence Program" or "Cointelpro," in abbreviation. It had nothing at all to do with counterintelligence. It was a campaign to hurt those people the FBI did not like, using any means necessary. There were bombings and deaths, along with less serious offenses.

After the House Committee's life ended, my friend Mark Allen and I filed separate FOIA requests for the information the FBI had given it. Complications following arterial surgery prevented my filing suit when the FBI did not comply. Allen did file suit. The House of

Representatives entered the suit to claim both correctly and successfully that its records and the records of its committees are not within
the disclosure requirements of the act. The court agreed and directed
that the FBI disclose only its own records that were not within any
of the act's exemptions and not to disclose *any* information at all
that originated with the HSCA. It, therefore, is certain that no FBI
record disclosed to Allen other than those originating with the HSCA.

Although it has steadfastly denied retaining any JFK assassination
ticklers in several of my FOIA lawsuits, in the Mark Allen case the
FBI disgorged simply enormous ticklers. One of these ticklers is
headed simply "The Federal Bureau of Investigation." It has no
description of its purpose. By content it is what I regard as a damage-
control tickler. It is undated, but again by content it lists under three
broad headings what, in its relations with the Warren Commission,
could be hurtful to the FBI before any Congressional investigation.

It is an extraordinary record of improper acts that range from
preparations to blackmail to acknowledgment that the FBI opposed
and impeded the Warren Commission and in fact had not conducted
any real investigation of the JFK assassination at all. The most pictur-
esque of the latter is "[Alex] Rosen's characterization of [the] FBI
'standing with pockets open waiting for evidence to drop in.' "

This record makes clear what had been hidden from the internal
investigation when the destruction of Oswald's note threatening
bombings that had been left for Special Agent James Hosty, Jr., was
ordered by FBIHQ as soon as it knew that Oswald was dead and
there would be no trial. Under "Lee Harvey Oswald" there is this
entry: "Hosty note destruction: handling by Bureau on Nov. 24 and
effect in subsequent days." Of all incongruous headings, under "Assistance to Warren Commission," along with reflections of opposition to and impending the Commission, it says, "Destruction of
Hosty note: implications."

Some *assistance* to the Warren Commission *that* was.

"Handling" is Orwellian FBI language for the ordered destruction
of that note that would have been so important.

These items that can relate only to preparations for blackmail are
also listed: "Preparation of dossiers on staff and members" of the
Commission; "Preparation of dossiers on WC staff *after* the Report
was out," with "Sept. 24," hand-lettered above this entry. [That was

not the date the Report was released. It was the date that page proofs became available inside the government.]

And reflecting what the FBI did to those who criticized the Report after it was published, it reports the "subsequent preparation of sex dossiers on critics of probe."

It regularly refers to the existence of records it was required under the law to have disclosed to me and were kept secret. This is to say that the FBI is and was lawless under the law requiring it to make its nonexempt records available.

That the FBI did compile and did use information to blackmail in itself is not really new. What is new is that it is documented by the FBI itself, not by its critics.

What is truly remarkable in this document that was never expected to be seen by others outside the FBI is the confession that it interfered with, and in all possible ways, impeded the Warren Commission and that it never really investigated or ever intended to investigate the JFK assassination itself. Many entries I do not quote here relate to the various, really multitudinous, ways in which the FBI itself discloses this among other acts and failures that seriously could be embarrassing to it if it were faced with a genuine investigation, one the HSCA itself never intended to make. That committee really dedicated itself to debunking the critics, of whom I alone was never mentioned at any hearings, and to supporting the official "solution" to the greatest degree possible. They slapped a few official wrists with featherweight taps to give the false and misleading impression that the committee had conducted an impartial investigation in which it sought the answers it never had sought and allocated blame it never had mentioned.

So, important as autopsies are in general in cases of murder by gunshot and important as the Navy's autopsy on President Kennedy was in that supposed investigation, it is not the autopsy alone that is of great importance. It does not stand alone in any independent inquiry into what the government did and did not do when the President was assassinated in broad daylight on the streets of a large American city.

It is not possible to make any fair and independent assessment of the Kennedy autopsy without regard to the other information relating to the crime and to its supposed official investigation.

Yet this is what the experienced pathologist did, a man who had spent a decade as a military pathologist and who is editor of the *Journal of the American Medical Association.*

In his interviews with two of the three pathologists who performed the autopsy, he ignored entirely the great mass of relevant information that was readily available to him and limited himself entirely to what these men, who he was supposedly investigating independently, had to say about their autopsy and their report on it.

As we shall see, whether or not he had any inkling of the fundamental information that could not be ignored in any honest assessment of the work of these pathologists, he reflected both ignorance of it and the intent to ignore it if it did exist.

What Lundberg evolved in his cheap imitation of an investigation, what Breo wrote to influence *JAMA*'s readers, particularly those in the medical profession, and what Lundberg sought to do in the carefully controlled and staged press conference to influence the rest of the world boils down to what is an anathema to and the exact opposite of what is required of forensic pathology: The autopsy pathologists were right because and only because they say they were right!

For no other reason!

Not a single one!

What malodorous official linen!

Yet it exudes only the merest whiff of the stench of which the entire stack of once-secret records reek!

And those I have are surely far from all!

Here is but a small sample of how the official mind set about seeing to it that the terrible crime itself was not investigated (with the inevitable result that it could not be in the future), and by using only a few of the many records obtained through those many FOIA lawsuits, of how, from the moment those history-altering shots were fired in Dealey Plaza, this crime in fact was never investigated.

The most obvious of the many questions raised is can the official investigations be trusted at all or in any part?

Another of the significant questions raised relates to Lundberg's managed and controlled media-event intrusion into the national concern over the assassination and its official investigations.

Could Lundberg, as a pathologist or as an editor, ignore all of this information that was readily available to him (if he had wanted it) and pretend it did not exist?

Whether out of ignorance or with intent, he did ignore all records and their clear meaning.

If he acted out of ignorance, then the best that can be said of him is that he was not qualified to conduct these interviews or offer any opinions on the autopsy and its prosectors.

If he pretended that none of this evidence existed, while knowing that it did or having reason to believe that it did, then in plain words, he was deliberately dishonest and exploited his position and the prestige enjoyed by the American Medical Association and its *Journal* for wrongful political and propagandist ends.

Either way, whichever is true—and one or the other must be—he has done an enormous disservice.

To the still-sorrowing nation, to efforts to recover the faith and hope lost as a result of the assassination and its unacceptable investigations.

To our society and to the integrity of its system of self-government.

To the AMA and its *Journal*.

To his professions, which he also failed in other ways as we shall see. To himself, his personal and professional reputations.

To the media which he imposed on, deceived, misinformed, and misled.

To our history.

To the truth, the bedrock of a representative society if it is to function.

There will be no question of fact remaining once we have examined what he published and what he said to so vast an audience.

The only lingering question may be why.

If it can be said at all that he examined the autopsy, and he did not at all, but if he could, could he have done that honestly, without questioning the claims made by the autopsy pathologists that they were not ordered to make any changes in their report and that they were not limited by higher military authority in what postmortem examinations they could make? The truth was published long ago and documented in *Post Mortem*.

The autopsy pathologists claimed in their interviews that they were not given any such orders and Lundberg rubber-stamped this.

Their claims are false, as will be proven by the prosectors' own earlier sworn testimony.

As we will also see, he did examine the autopsy surgeons in a vacuum, seemingly without any knowledge at all of their previous testimony, which was public, published, and available to him.

This briefest glimpse of the dirty linen of Byzantium on the Potomac indicates the magnitude and significance of what Lundberg, Breo, and *JAMA* ignore and/or pretend does not exist.

It also gives perspective and context to what they did and did not do.

Chapter 4

What Did *JAMA* Do and How Did *JAMA* Do It? And Why?

To those not well informed on the JFK assassination, and this includes the media, Lundberg and *JAMA* seemed to be independent and impartial. They were not.

Their successful propagandist operation began with a carefully controlled and orchestrated press conference. It took place not in Chicago, where they are officed, but in New York, the major-media center, especially of TV.

The *JAMA* issue containing Breo's articles was to be published on May 27. The press conference was a week earlier, on May 19. Reprints of the articles were distributed. In boldface type on the lower right-hand corner of the cover, the following was printed: "All contents of this advance copy of the *Journal of the American Medical Association* are embargoed for release at 3:00 P.M. Central time on the day before the issue date."

Removing the embargo at 4 P.M. Eastern time on the day before the issue date made it possible for the articles to attract additional attention in the morning papers of the issue date and on the evening TV news of the night before.

Embargoing every word in the articles for a week after the press conference served to make it impossible for the media to find and then to write about anything wrong in what the autopsists had said and in what Breo had written. It also limited the initial stories to what had been said at the press conference by Lundberg.

Humes and Boswell refused to attend the press conference even though they were in the country. They refused to face any questions. The third autopsy pathologist, Army Lieutenant Colonel Pierre Finck, had retired to his native Switzerland. He refused *JAMA*'s request to be interviewed or to appear at the press conference.

41

None of the reporting I read, saw, or heard found this at all unusual; that with the *JAMA* articles presented as a defense of them, the doctors declined to appear at the press conference and not having appeared, refused to respond to any questions. .

If unjustly attacked, most of us want to be heard, want to be able to address those charges against us personally, not by proxy; want to leave it without question that we are not afraid and have nothing to hide, nothing to avoid being asked about. But not Humes, Boswell, or Finck.

So, while the coverage of the press conference quoted what the reporters said Humes and Boswell had said, it was not really that at all. It was a contrived defense of them in which Lundberg and Breo asked cream puff questions and then used what it pleased them to use of their questions and the answers they got, which avoided the basic questions that had long been raised about their autopsy—and their performances in the greatest, the most dramatic, the most challenging moments of their personal and professional lives.

The doctors did not say a word in their own defense about what had been said about them nor did they address their accusers and the allegedly false and unfair criticisms that have been leveled at them. This is not natural.

But it was treated by the media as though the accused *had* been there in person and *had personally* defended themselves. From one end of the country to the other, the papers gave their readers the understanding that the *doctors* held the press conference and that they had personally responded to questions asked of them there, even though buried in some stories there was mention of their having absented themselves.

In *The New York Times* of May 20, Dr. Lawrence K. Altman's story began with the fiction that at this press conference, "[b]reaking a 28-year silence, the two pathologists who performed the autopsy on President John F. Kennedy have affirmed their original findings . . ." The headline also gives a false impression: "Doctors Affirm Kennedy Autopsy Report."

The *San Francisco Chronicle* used the *Times*'s story in its issue that day and again gave its readers to understand that these fearless pathologists had held the press conference to defend themselves and their work in person. Its main headline reads: "JFK Doctors Back

Warren Commission." The subhead puts them there in person: "They say a bullet from lone gunman killed him." (This is what they did say, although it was not possible for them to prove it in their autopsy, and their autopsy report does not establish it.)

That day's *Washington Post* headline: "2 JFK Autopsy Pathologists Defend Conclusion on Fatal Bullet."

And the *Los Angeles Times*: "Autopsy Doctors Say 1 Gunman Killed Kennedy." Reporter John J. Goldman's story begins: "NEW YORK. Two pathologists who conducted the autopsy of President John F. Kennedy broke almost three decades of silence Tuesday to make public their conclusion that he was struck by two bullets from a single high-velocity rifle fired by a lone assassin." They did not break their nonexisting silence that day, and of course, they were not there to do it, as Goldman said they were.

Beth J. Harpaz's story for the Associated Press, used by many of the country's papers, gives the impression that Humes and Boswell were there in person, while not saying that they were, in quoting Lundberg as quoting them. It uses the present tense in the first paragraph of the lead to suggest their presence along with two of the Dallas doctors: "Two doctors who tried to revive the mortally wounded President John F. Kennedy and two others who performed the autopsy are certain he was shot twice from behind by a lone gunman, as the Warren Commission concluded."

As an experienced pathologist, Lundberg should have known this autopsy did not and could not have proven this thesis.

United Press International, the second largest news syndicate, distributed to its many clients Arthur Spiegelman's story for use the next day, a Wednesday. Those who read only its opening paragraph had no choice but to believe that the missing pathologists were at the press conference: "Two doctors who performed the autopsy on President John F. Kennedy broke a 28-year silence Tuesday to say the president was killed by two bullets . . ."

Those who read only the beginning of Tom Friend's story in *USA Today* would not have had any reason even to suspect that the pathologists and four of the Dallas doctors did not appear at the press conference and that Friend's story did not quote what they said there:

President John F. Kennedy was killed by two bullets fired from
a high-powered rifle from behind, say the pathologists who did
the autopsy.

In their only interviews since JFK died in 1963, the pathologists
and four doctors who treated him have no doubts the Warren
Commission conclusions are correct.

And what, pray, did the mavens of the media expect of the autopsy
pathologists, other than to, in Altman's words, "affirm their original findings"?

Would they have "broken 28 years of silence," as they near the
ends of their lives, to tell the world that they had been inadequate
for the task they faced; or had been incompetent; or had made serious
mistakes; or had been under military pressure not to make a full,
complete, and dependable postmortem examination?

The little boy of the fairy tale had enough common sense and
honesty to tell the emperor that he was not garbed in magnificent
raiment, but was naked. Yet, in all the media so overwhelmed by
what Lundberg said, among all the editorial writers, there was not
one with the common sense to ask what else could be expected of
the autopsy surgeons, but that they would insist that they had done
well when quite obviously the opposite is true?

Could even a reasonably intelligent child have expected them to
say that they had made possible the perpetration of an enormous
official fraud when that most subversive of crimes was investigated
and to break "28 years of silence" to do that, and with that, to
consign themselves to the trash heaps of history?

Neither the Associated Press nor anyone else had any question
when Lundberg boasted that he was using *JAMA* to end "the talk
of conspiracy" in the JFK assassination because, "as a professional
publication devoted to scientific research [it] had a very good chance,
perhaps the best chance, of setting to rest the talk of conspiracy" in
the JFK assassination.

This is a proper function for the official publication of the American Medical Association?

Out of all the reporting on this May 19 *JAMA* press conference
that I saw, heard, and read, not a single reporter asked the obvious
question: Was Lundberg neutral?

That he was not neutral came out in his response to a question that was asked of him on the following morning's Fox-TV newscast.

Lark McCarthy asked him, "Why did the pathologists agree to talk to you?"

Lundberg replied, "Well, for starters, we're friends and have been for a long time."

In these stories JAMA did not report medical news. Its boast at the top of its table of contents (page 2709) is that its mission is "to promote the science and art of medicine and the betterment of public health." The only science and art it promoted in Breo's articles is the science and art of propaganda.

Back in their offices after Lundberg's press conference, their deadlines close and rushing closer, reporters had a few minutes to read their notes, listen to their tapes, or read what Breo wrote—which they were not permitted to use—about Lundberg's interviews.

But they could ask no questions about the articles, the press conference, or what the pathologists were quoted as having said.

They were without the means of doing any meaningful checking of any of Lundberg's statements. If they had the means, they did not have the time. They had to have their stories done almost immediately for the evening TV or radio news or the next morning's papers.

But if there had been time, the media could have checked the obvious—what Humes and Boswell had testified to before the Warren Commission—but most if not all of that testimony was not readily available.

A few of the media had obtained copies of the twenty-six large volumes of testimony and exhibits the Warren Commission published in 1964, twenty-eight years earlier. But for the few whose employers had bought those volumes, there is little likelihood that they were not in dead storage or long discarded. Besides the length and technical nature of the testimony of the autopsy surgeons precluded any careful reading of it before the stories had to be filed and TV commentaries taped and ready to air.

What this meant is that all were entirely limited to what Lundberg said at his press conference.

His press conference was in New York City where TV is centered, not in Washington, where the Warren Commission was and where news of its work originated. The Warren Commission was a Washington story, not a New York story, and it was a story almost three decades old. With no experienced reporters who had covered the Warren Commission still reporting in 1992, Lundberg, whether or not by design, had arranged for this carefully controlled and managed press conference to be held in New York, where in the media there were no subject experts.

Even for Washington reporters acquiring the knowledge was in itself a full-time job. They did not have the time for it, and the media had no interest in making the necessary investment. Some may have had sources they trusted, mostly among former Commission assistant counsels. Over the years some reporters asked critics for information or for their opinions. Some had skimmed FBI records when they were disclosed, but that skimming was perforce hasty and skimpy. It lasted only when there were stories in prospect, and that was for a few days only after the releases.

None had heard Humes, Boswell, Finck, or the Dallas doctors testify because the Commission took its testimony in closed sessions. It then classified all its transcripts—*of what was to be published verbatim*—TOP SECRET. And all were kept TOP SECRET by the Commission (which in fact lacked any authority for any classifying at all) until the transcripts were to be set in type. Because the Government Printing Office is not permitted to set anything classified TOP SECRET in type, in order to have the type set for publication, the classification was reduced to CONFIDENTIAL, and that restriction was removed on publication.

Not content with this extraordinary control over what did not qualify for any degree of classification and with having barred the press from its hearings and testimony, the Commission permitted little time for reporters to master its 912-page Report when it was released. It prepared the first chapter of this Report so that it could serve as a combination summary and press release. The Associated Press, which serves most of the nation's media, did not even pretend to prepare its own summary of the Report. It put on the wire for all its clients this first chapter of the Report, and that first chapter became their main if not the only story.

This means that for most Americans the story they read about the

Warren Report when it was published was what the Warren Commission wanted them to read.

The Commission saw to it that nothing else was reasonably possible for most of the media.

(Having seen how effective this method was, the FBI did pretty much the same thing with its JFK assassination releases of December 1977 and January 1988. Disclosing close to one hundred thousand pages, it separated them roughly in half and permitted the media to read copies in the FBI's reading room or to buy copies, which very few did. As a result most of what might have been newsworthy in what the FBI released never got any attention at all. There were stories for that hectic first day, prepared in great haste and under difficult conditions. There were fewer stories the second, and in a few days there were no more stories at all.)

In its Report the Commission used only what it wanted of the testimony and exhibits and ignored what did not suit it. The Report, therefore, is a selective, one-sided account.

What the Commission published in support of its Report totaled an estimated ten million words, in twenty-six large volumes. The press had four days to master all of that uncollated information before the release date, an obvious impossibility.

The Commission arranged it so that its Report could be assessed and written about only on the Commission's terms. Reporters had nothing with which to compare what the Report said to determine whether it was accurate, fair, and complete. At that time and later, when the testimony and exhibits were released, there were no experts of the subject matter to whom reporters could turn for information or checking. By the time they had mastered the Report, there was no media interest in it.

If any reporter had read and remembered the 912-page Report when it was issued, or if he knew anyone who had, he still was not in a position to be able to make any independent judgment about what the Commission did. And by then the Commission had ceased to exist, so there was no Commission to be asked any questions.

It is a safe assumption, borne out by what they wrote, that there were no reporters at Lundberg's press conference who were in a position to know whether what Lundberg said concerning what Breo had written of what the autopsists had said is exactly what they originally testified to before the Warren Commission. In effect, after all the hoopla to attract reporters to his press conference, Lundberg had arranged it so they had no choice but to take his word for what he said.

And as we shall see, there are radical differences between what was testified to under oath and what appeared in *JAMA*.

Whatever was in Lundberg's mind, whatever he intended, in fact, like the Warren Commission and the FBI before him, he managed the news.

If he had not been able to do this, he would have had a monumental fiasco on his hands.

As we shall see, some of these doctors either lied to Lundberg or earlier swore falsely when under oath. And not by any means did they do this only once and by accident.

My, what that would have done to Lundberg's press conference!

What it would have done to his already printed issue of *JAMA*!

To Lundberg's reputation!

To the doctors and to their reputations!

And what it would have done to the credibility of the Warren Report itself!

Chapter 5

AMA as Flack

JAMA IS THE *JOURNAL OF THE AMERICAN MEDICAL ASSOCIATION*. IT IS the nation's, if not the world's, most prestigious medical publication. It is "usually," as the *San Francisco Examiner* noted in its May 24, 1992, editorial, "thanking" *JAMA* for its May 19 press conference, "devoted to scientific news" of interest to American doctors who care for America's health.

Its press conference was, however, staged like a political event.

This meant also that all the media could use was what was said by Dr. George D. Lundberg. Lundberg produced no one else at the press conference to be questioned by the media reporters or to appear on TV screens. It was Lundberg's event. He used it to tell the world that, in the words of Dr. Lawrence K. Altman in the May 20 *New York Times,* "the interviews were the result of a seven-year effort to 'help calm the ardor of the honest conspiracy theorists who have simply not had access to the facts.' "

The first interviews were of Drs. James J. Humes and J. Thornton Boswell, the Navy pathologists who performed the autopsy on President John F. Kennedy. They had been assisted in the autopsy by Lieutenant Colonel Pierre Finck, chief of the Army's Wounds Ballistics Branch at Walter Reed Hospital. In the second article, the interviews were of four Dallas doctors who went through the motions of trying to save the obviously dead president. There were many more than four doctors involved in Dallas.

The person closest to a forensic expert on the firearms injuries involved in the autopsy, Colonel Finck, had retired to his native Switzerland and "refused" to be interviewed. His "refusal" was, as will become clear, a boon to *JAMA* in its politicizing of medical "news." Later he did agree to an interview.

What the press was permitted to use of these two articles was limited to what Lundberg used at the press conference, and he limited what he used to what supported the conclusions of the Warren Commission.

Writing for all the world as though Humes and Boswell were at the press conference, Beth J. Harpaz wrote in an Associated Press story that Humes and Boswell both said, "The conspiracy buffs have totally ignored this scientific fact, and everything else is hogwash."

The alleged "central fact" was "that President Kennedy was struck from above and behind by the fatal shot."

There was more than one shot, and each and every shot was "central" in the autopsy, as certainly, pathologist that he is, Lundberg knew.

Lundberg had previously said, "I think the nonavailability of information has contributed greatly to people wondering. We're trying to put an end to the wonderment."

"Nonavailability of information?" All but what the autopsy pathologists said is "hogwash"? This is the "scientific" approach, "scientific" news?

Not only was there not a single new alleged fact, Humes and Boswell were not even present at the press conference to hear what they were said to have said. Uncomplainingly *The New York Times* and other publications printed their pictures, credited to Breo. Consistent with a major public-relations campaign orchestrated by a skilled public-relations agency, Breo took a number of informal, flattering pictures of Humes and Boswell, dressed casually, smiling, and so *JAMA* could provide different pictures to different media elements. They looked like anyone's grandfathers.

With the no-show stars and with the *JAMA* issue embargoed until after they went to press, the magazines were limited to what had already appeared in the papers and to what had been all over radio and TV. But two different pictures, one of each man, did make it into *People* magazine's June 8 story.

Lundberg and *JAMA* orchestrated a major propagandist event under controlled conditions, and Lundberg repeated to the world what had been published twenty-eight years earlier by the Warren Commission, without even the suggestion of proof or having made an independent scientific study of the criticism of the conclusions of the Warren

Report. He characterized all such criticism as "hogwash" by "conspiracy buffs." This is the stereotyped falsehood that all criticism of the Warren Report and of the Humes, Boswell, and Finck autopsy was and is trivial, and that it was made up by those for whom it was a hobby.

In fact, only a few months prior to this press conference, the Warren Report had been reprinted commercially and was available in bookstores in a hardback reprint of the official version for considerably less than the going rate for hardback books of that size.

Lundberg should have known that in what he produced at his super-duper, controlled, politicized press conference and in his *JAMA* there was not a single word not already published. Yet he, without comment by the media, attributed his spectacular issue to ending "the nonavailability of information" about the autopsy, about which he had not a single new word to say.

Of those who have written factually about the JFK assassination and its investigations and of the autopsy, in particular, I alone published much more information about the autopsy than the Warren Commission included in its Report or its appended twenty-six large volumes of alleged evidence.

There is no theorizing of any kind in any of my seven books on the JFK assassination and its investigations, and they include official information suppressed by the Warren Report. Some of this formerly suppressed official information appears elsewhere in this book.

For correctly understanding what Lundberg and *JAMA* were really up to, it should be understood that *even the FBI and the Secret Service do not and have never agreed with the basic conclusions of the Warren Commission*, as will be set forth in what follows.

This is not news to at least Humes and Boswell. I reproduced the FBI's accounting of the assassination in facsimile in my first book, *Whitewash: The Report on the Warren Report*. On May 24, 1966, I sent each a copy of this book, calling to their attention the chapters addressing the medical evidence. I asked each for "an opportunity to discuss" this medical evidence with him, "alone or together."

Neither ever responded.

Before quoting my letter to Boswell sent six months later there is, to give it context, what was headlined on papers nationwide from Lundberg's adventure, what he told the world: These two and the four Dallas doctors had spoken to him for his *JAMA* issue for the first time in public since the assassination. For Lundberg and for *JAMA* they were, Lundberg said, for the first time breaking their "twenty-eight years of silence."

Universally these alleged decades of silence were featured. It did have human-interest appeal. It was both emotional and sensational.

Consistent with Lundberg's purposes, with what he published in *JAMA*, with what Breo wrote, and with what Lundberg made available to the media, without any opportunity for reporters to question those he quoted, *there is not a word of truth in it.*

None of the doctors was ever silent other than before the Warren Commission. Not a single one! Not the autopsy pathologists and not the Dallas doctors, of whom there were more than the four Breo interviewed.

If Lundberg and Breo did not know this, they were ignorant and without qualification for what they wrote and published. If they did know this, then they lied.

If the media, particularly the major papers and syndicates, had consulted their own morgues, or libraries, they would have known that *JAMA* and its editor were lying to them and through them to the world at a time when there was renewed criticism of the official "solution."

That no major syndicate or paper resorted to the traditional journalistic practice of consulting the record is consistent with major-media reporting of both the assassination and its investigations.

So what is the truth, and why the lie?

The first wave of factual criticism began with the publication of the first of my *Whitewash* books for general distribution on May 7, 1966. A limited edition had been published on August 17, 1965. On May 24 I sent copies of the book to both Humes and Boswell and sought an interview with them to discuss the alleged medical evidence and my disproval of their representation of it.

They were silent only briefly, until Boswell, and others with whom he was in contact, saw an opportunity to pull a Lundberg.

Richard Levine was then a reporter for the *Baltimore Sun*. Before he got interested in the JFK assassination, at the request of *Sun* staffers, I'd gone to Baltimore for several Sunday meetings with those wanting to learn what the other than official account of the assassination was.

We met in the home of Art Geiselman, Jr., an investigative reporter. Separately Levine interviewed me about another in a series of the government's orchestrated moves designed to respond to public criticism of its handling of the JFK assassination. It seemed to be preserving all the vital evidence, like the autopsy photographs and X rays, while in fact assuring that authentic scholars would be forever denied any chance of studying them in the context of what was known about the assassination. His article, published on November 4, 1966, quotes me as describing "the government's announcement as an effort by the government under pressure 'to give the impression it has nothing to hide while it is hiding things.' "

Levine's interest, as he made clear in a series of late-night and early-morning phone calls after the end of his day's work, was in sensation. After reading *Whitewash*, he fixed on the autopsy as the center of his interest. He then decided to seek an interview with Boswell.

Levine's manifestation of interest coincided in time with the interests of the White House, only some of which are reported in the previous chapter, and those of the FBI, both of which I learned about years later from previously suppressed official documents among the .25 million pages of which I received as the result of a series of lawsuits against the government under the Freedom of Information Act.

What is little understood is that from almost the moment those shots were fired in Dallas, the official investigations were propagandist rather than real. There never was any real investigation of the crime itself, and none was ever intended, from the level of the FBI street agent in Dallas to the highest echelons of the Department of Justice and its FBI, and likewise by the Warren Commission itself or by the LBJ White House. The White House was sensitive to the fact that only this assassination made Johnson president, that his legitimacy could be questioned, then and in history, if the official investigation was not full and complete, if it was found to be wanting in any way, and if it did not get and warrant popular acceptance.

Boswell went public—*twenty-eight years ago*—the exact opposite of Lundberg's statement that achieved sensational international attention. His going public coincided with the propagandist interests of the White House and of the executive agencies.

My December 1, 1966, letter to Boswell was written after the *Sun* published Levine's interview, to which it refers. What I told him, beginning with the first sentence, is what Levine told me of what Boswell had told him in a less than honest effort to explain away his failure to respond to my May 24 letter:

Dear Dr. Boswell:

It has been reported to me, I hope erroneously, that your failure to respond to my letter of six months ago, with which I enclosed a copy of my book, *Whitewash: The Report on the Warren Report*, was due to pique because I had not consulted you in advance of its publication.

A writer attempting to consult all of the 552 people listed as Commission witnesses and the countless thousands of others in the printed evidence in 27 such massive volumes could never in a lifetime complete a book.

It is my belief that the autopsy of an assassinated president should be a model of completeness, precision, specification, fact, and accuracy. It is my belief that when a body such as the President's Commission, with a staff of men of such outstanding qualifications, takes testimony from medical experts enjoying the high position and respected status you and your colleagues have earned, all of us, including writers, are entitled to assume and expect that the Commission and its witnesses approached their unhappy responsibilities with unlimited dedication to completeness and truthfulness.

Are you suggesting I should have expected your testimony would be inadequate, incomplete, or inaccurate, that the Commission desired this, that the requirements imposed on a pathologist by science and law cannot be met except with the prodding assistance of a writer?

The Commission and the medical experts made their own record. All will have to stand on it.

As always happens with this subject, whenever official persons make statements, they raise more questions than they answer. This is true of your statements to the *Baltimore Sun*, broadcast widely by the Associated Press.

As in the past, I shall make no effort to force myself upon you or Dr. Humes, no effort to entice you to say anything you do not want to say. Whether or not you elect to see me and answer questions is entirely your decision. My original offer stands: I will make a tape recording and provide you with a copy.

I cannot avoid noting for the present and for history that you and Dr. Humes decline or refuse to see those you have reason to believe seriously question the autopsy and the testimony on it while, for example, seeing Fletcher Knebel, a Commission defender. I note also that you granted an interview to the *Baltimore Sun* when it was first apparent to you that the reporter had no knowledge of the subject matter at all and had as his sole purpose eliciting from you what you ultimately said, that you erred in the official autopsy chart.

My new book, *Whitewash II*, will soon be available. This time I shall not send you copies. But I do want you to know that among the things I say and prove in it is that the President got an autopsy unworthy of a Bowery bum.

Yours truly,
Harold Weisberg

As this letter reports, rather than those alleged twenty-eight years of silence purported by Lundberg and *JAMA*, the pathologist had also agreed to be interviewed by Fletcher Knebel for a popular mass-circulation magazine of the day. *Look* sold about seven million copies an issue, and its stories, like Knebel's interview of Boswell, frequently were the basis of nationwide newspaper stories.

And as I also told Boswell, he clearly exploited Levine's unprofessional desire to obtain a major, international sensation to justify himself—by boasting of his own alleged carelessness in the autopsy.

I do not know whether Boswell was entirely alone in his exploitation of Levine and the possibilities he saw in the interview for defending himself and the Warren Report. The indications are that he reported his success to those who shared his interest with Levine the moment Levine left his Bethesda, Maryland, office.

Before Levine could get back to his *Sun* office in Baltimore, Boswell was being interviewed by the Associated Press. He told the Associated Press precisely what he had told Levine, which Levine had accepted uncritically.

Levine was outraged. He fumed at me over the phone, saying that I had double-crossed him by telling the Associated Press what Boswell had told him. That he was outraged was understandable. He was scooped on his own sensation. But I had nothing to do with it and did not know about it until Levine called. Before the morning's papers could appear, it was a TV and radio news sensation.

May I be forgiven in history for not recognizing that Levine was scoop-minded; for not realizing that his true interests and purposes were not the same as those of the other *Baltimore Sun* reporters who invited me to meet with them; that all he wanted was a sensation. In not recognizing this, I became involuntarily an adjunct of the government's propagandist campaign to put down all criticism of the official solution.

The Associated Press gave Boswell and his explanation a big international play.

Levine still had his scoop. The *Sun* played up his story as the major one of the day, with a large banner headline across the entire top of the front page and with a total of eighty-eight column inches of space, a significant amount of space for the *Sun*.

The banner headline, in large black type, read: "Kennedy X-Ray Data Release Backed." Under it, two columns wide, was the beginning of Boswell's twenty-eight years of silence, a three-tiered headline in large black italics: "Pathologist Who Made Examination Defends Commission Version." The headline atop the continuation of Levine's story, six columns wide, read: "Bethesda Pathologist Who Examined Kennedy Backs Release of X-Ray Data."

That pathologist, Boswell, sure was silent, commencing two years after his twenty-eight years of silence supposedly began when, aside from the international attention provided by the Associated Press, he had all this attention, about a hundred inches of type, counting the banner headline, in the largest paper in his own state.

This silence was so great that one can read Levine's story and wonder why Lundberg got so excited about repeating the thrust of it, which with a few unfactual embellishments is exactly what Lundberg did.

The headlines tell the story.

The two-column headline in the 1966 *Baltimore Sun* said that Boswell "Defends Commission."

This was the identical headline treatment of Lundberg's 1992 promotional press conference.

Over Altman's story in 1992, *The New York Times* had "Doctors Affirm Kennedy Autopsy Report."

The *Washington Post*'s headline was "2 JFK Autopsy Pathologists Defend Conclusion on Fatal Bullet."

The *Baltimore Sun*'s headline over the Harpaz story was "JFK Doctors Back Lone-Gunman View."

That same story was headlined in the *Los Angeles Daily News* as "Kennedy Autopsy Doctors Back Lone-Assassin Finding."

Goldman's story in the *Los Angeles Times* was headlined: "Autopsy Doctors Say 1 Gunman Killed Kennedy."

Over the Reuters story the *San Francisco Chronicle* placed this headline: "JFK Death: AMA Backs Warren Panel View." The headline on the inside was "Lone Gunman Shot JFK, AMA Says."

The *San Francisco Examiner* used the Altman story that had been syndicated by *The New York Times*, with the headline, "JFK Doctors Back Warren Commission," and the subhead, "They say a bullet from lone gunman killed him."

Whether or not out of ignorance, and there is nothing in what Lundberg said or published that reflects his having any knowledge of anything at all other than of Oliver Stone's movie *JFK*, Lundberg pulled a fast one. He repeated what Boswell had said two years into that "silence" of his and represented it as though it was new.

In fact *JAMA* itself had published pretty much the same account in its January 4, 1964, issue. It then said that what it published was the "unofficial finding of a team of pathologists who performed" the autopsy!

What was new, as we shall see, was the exaggerated emphasis on what was *not* new, Oliver Stone's portrayal of the doctors in his movie *JFK*. It angered them and Lundberg, and apparently it persuaded the doctors to agree to be interviewed.

What is missing from Lundberg's charges is that criticism of the autopsy and of the Warren Commission Report is not, as he said, limited to those he castigated as "conspiracy theorists."

Months before the first of my *Whitewash* books went into general distribution, the Commission, in general, and the pathologists, in particular, were thoroughly criticized by a panel of experts at the annual meeting of the American Academy of Forensic Sciences, held that year in Chicago. Aside from the lengthier account published by the academy, *Medical Tribune* for Wednesday, March 23, 1966, reported strong criticism from the prosectors' peers under the headline: "Forensic Panelists Hit Inquiry on Assassination."

Criticisms of Humes, Boswell, and Finck included the doctors' "lack of understanding of forensic problems." Cited also were their "errors in judgment."

Lundberg, *JAMA*, and the American Medical Association then began by palming off an ancient rehash as something new. They expanded this to include false representation. The legitimate news is obscured.

What was ignored in Levine's story is Boswell's confession of error. "Boswell himself," Levine wrote, "contributed to the controversy with a sketch he made during the autopsy indicating that the President had been shot lower in the back than the wound described in the Warren Report. Yesterday he said that the error did not seem significant at the time, since he assumed that the wound photographs would be available."

Before the Warren Commission Humes testified that he *knew* the photographs and the X rays would *not* be available, and none of the three prosectors "corrected" this alleged "error," one that will interest us more since Lundberg misused it in *JAMA*.

In its rewrite of the story it syndicated for morning papers, the Associated Press angled this story in 1966 differently. As it appeared in the *Washington Star*, under the headline, "Doctor at Kennedy Autopsy Explains Sketch Controversy," that story begins: "A doctor who helped perform the autopsy . . . said today he made a diagram error in a hasty 'worksheet' sketch which was not drawn for the final autopsy report. . . . Boswell said the diagram showed that the bullet wound was in the President's back. Actually, he said, the wound was at the base of the neck. . . . Boswell said the diagram was . . . not intended to be exact. . . ."

Not a single one of these statements is true.

It was not made in haste, it was not "drawn" by Boswell, and it not only *was* for "the final autopsy," it was attached to it and was published as part of it by the Commission.

I have held that original in my hands, and I published a copy of it in *Post Mortem*, after I rescued it from its official hiding place. Unlike the news media, I published it in full. Rather than a "hasty" sketch, it is a mimeographed, official, part-of-the-autopsy form prepared by and used by the Navy, with the heading of AUTOPSY. It has an outline of the body, front and back views, with lines for posting the indicated information needed, about three dozen such lines for noting size, weight, color, and similar information about parts of the body.

All Boswell had to do to post the location of that wound was to make a mark, a dot or a small circle, where the wound was. The body is drawn on the form.

Most incredible of all his misstatements is that *any* part of *any* autopsy is "not intended to be exact." An autopsy is intended to be a work of precision to the greatest degree humans are capable of it. When the autopsy is of the victim of a crime of violence, especially a murder, the greatest exactness, obviously, is required.

Boswell rambled on to the Associated Press with many other misstatements, like "the sole purpose" of the body chart, was to indicate " 'right, left, front, back—things like that.' "

The form he used—was required to use—gives the lie to this demeaning untruth.

I have examined other autopsies. For purpose of comparison I cite the protocols on the examinations of Martin Luther King, Jr., Dallas Policeman J. D. Tippit, and Lee Harvey Oswald. Each had such charts as part of the final report.

What no reporter, and neither Lundberg nor Breo seems to have asked Boswell, is if he made an error, why did it take him more than three years to correct it and why did he not correct it when he testified to the Warren Commission?

If that was an error, why did he not, when he had the opportunity, correct it before it was published in the Warren Report? He and Finck were both asked if they had anything to say after they heard Humes's testimony, and neither said anything about this body-chart "error."

Boswell's lies are of the quality of his forensic pathology—atrocious. But he and Lundberg were lucky because the media have always been unquestioning in their support of the official government line on the assassination.

Humes used the rudimentary notes Boswell had made on this chart when writing the autopsy protocol. How could he have used it without perceiving this alleged error. If he did not miss it, how could he not have corrected it?

All the autopsy papers, except for the protocol, were completed before Oswald was charged. *Nobody* had been charged when the body was turned over to the morticians. So, as of the time the chart was annotated and marked up, Boswell et al. had reason to believe first that it would have to be used in the trial of anyone accused and then after Oswald was charged, early the next morning, that it would be used in the prosecution of Oswald and if not used by the prosecutor, certainly it would have been used by defense counsel.

It was not until after Oswald was killed, two days later, that Boswell's posting of the location of this wound with absolute exactness on that body chart became a problem—when it was for all practical purposes impossible for him to change.

Why else would Humes have had to resort to the entirely unacceptable method of having a Naval artist draw a sketch—from Humes's verbal description yet!—to show this wound at the base of the neck, when he had the official autopsy diagram to locate it?

If any informed questions had been leveled at Boswell in all the many interviews that he granted, which are now referred to as his twenty-eight years of silence—beginning with Levine, including the two that immediately followed his, and through others, like the Josiah Thompson interview in 1967, up to 1990 and 1992, when two friends of mine interviewed him—Boswell would have been turned into Humpty Dumpty by his lie.

But that would not have been helpful to the continued acceptance of the Report.

Chapter 6

Twenty-eight Years of Silence

JOSIAH THOMPSON'S ACCOUNT OF HIS JANUARY 10, 1967, interview with Boswell appears scattered through the eighteen pages of his *Six Seconds in Dallas*, in which he takes Boswell at face value, unquestioningly. Apparently Thompson asked Boswell no questions about his body-chart marking of that bullet hole because he wrote instead, "When the press pointed this fact [that his marking of the hole is inches lower than in the official account] out to Commander Boswell, he replied that the sketch was only meant to be a rough mark location and that he had mistakenly placed the back wound too low" [*Six Seconds in Dallas*. New York: Bernard Geis Associates, 1967, page 48].

That satisfied Thompson, too. He was then Professor of Philosophy at Haverford College, in suburban Philadelphia, with a specialty in the Danish philosopher, Sören Kierkegaard. Thompson's personal philosophy then does not appear to have included asking pointed questions.

He since abandoned the halls of ivy to become a successful private eye in the San Francisco area, and presumably, he has learned that not all responses, especially to embarrassing questions, can be assumed to be truthful.

The 1990 interview that Boswell granted was to a professional policeman, who was then working for the writer who would conduct the 1991 interview and was working on his second book on the JFK assassination.

These interviews do not indicate that Boswell was ever confronted with the fact that his explanation of hasty error is not reasonable.

Humes and Finck were less silent than Boswell.

Humes's most spectacular "silences" were on coast-to-coast TV.

CBS-TV did a series of four hour-long specials on the JFK assassination that aired in June, 1968. I published excerpts from these transcripts in *Post Mortem* (pages 39–41).

A decade later he was a star witness before the House Select Committee on Assassinations (JFK volume, pages 323–32). On September 7, 1978, his testimony was telecast live and featured on newscasts.

Finck was a witness in the unsuccessful Jim Garrison prosecution of respected New Orleans businessman and writer Clay Shaw. TV cameras were not allowed in the courtroom, but the press was there and large parts of his testimony were reprinted verbatim around the world. As is usual, it was taken down by a court reporter, and the transcript is available. I am among those who have it.

It is not easy to believe that despite his longtime friendship with the prosectors Lundberg was entirely ignorant of their very public careers and their widely published statements. But if he had been that ignorant, Lundberg had the obligation to know what he was talking about. He had the responsibility of not using the respected medical association and its respected *Journal* to rewrite our tragic history with a pack of obvious lies.

Without question this is what he did. Because he is a professional pathologist with a decade of experience in the military alone, it ought to be a safe assumption that he knows the pathology business, knows that it requires extreme accuracy and the greatest care, and knows that glib explanations of any departure from these requirements are not tolerable.

Lundberg particularly ignored the report of the panel convoked of the most eminent experts by the Department of Justice in secret. This report was readily available to him from the department or in my book *Post Mortem*, in which I reproduced it in facsimile. That report is specific in stating that the panel found serious and significant errors in the autopsy with regard to both admitted wounds: (1) to the head, the entry point of which the panel found was *four inches higher on the head than stated in the autopsy report*; and (2) with regard to the nonfatal wound that the protocol states struck no bones, while the panel said the X rays disclose five fragments!

*　　　*　　　*

Of all the many officially perpetrated outrages and indecencies that taint officialdom's attempts at explaining away all the deficiencies in the medical evidence of the assassination—and that only begins with Humes, Boswell, and Finck—none besmirches the nation more than the monstrous lie that it was all the doing of the Kennedy family, that *it* wanted the evidence hidden and suppressed. Boswell hinted at this in saying that he expected the autopsy pictures to be available, thus suggesting that they were not available. And that is, as I have proved and published in *Post Mortem*, a lie.

The Navy has, as all authorities and jurisdictions have, a form for authorization of autopsies. One for JFK was executed, but the Warren Commission elected not to publish this authorization in its Report. Aside from many references to it in *Post Mortem*, I also reproduce it in facsimile on page 507.

It is not that the Commission somehow had overlooked the authorization. My copy is from its files. But with *only* ten million words available, it had no space for this autopsy authorization. That would have taken half a page away from what it published in those twenty-six volumes of appendices. It had to reserve the space in its 912-page Report for what it considered was *really* important, page after page of arcane FBI science proving that the pubic hairs found on Oswald's blanket were Oswald's.

The unpublished authorization is in the name of the widow; the authorizing signature is that of the brother and attorney general of the United States, Robert Kennedy.

Aside from authorizing all that is in general necessary in any autopsy, specifically including "the preservation and study of all tissues that may be removed," the form has a space for specifying any limitations. This wording on the form follows: "This authority shall be limited only by the conditions expressly stated below."

Not a word appears between this and Robert Kennedy's signature. *The family imposed no restrictions at all!*

This abominable official indecency of falsely blaming the victimized family for all of the many suppressions, for which it was not responsible, was so offensive to me that I devoted an entire chapter to it in *Post Mortem*, "Hades, Not Camelot" (pages 289–301).

Howard Willens, a Department of Justice lawyer on loan to the Commission and doing the Commission's dirty work, actually *sought*

Robert Kennedy's approval for the Report it had not yet written—in June when it had yet to interview most of its witnesses!

The autopsy and what related to it, along with all the other medical evidence, was the area of the Commission's work of which Arlen Specter was in charge. Nobody on the Commission staff wrote more memos covering his own ass than Specter.

Contrary to all the official myths about the suppression of the autopsy X-ray films, Specter assumed they would be available to the Commission. There was nothing in the world to keep the Commission from using the films at its hearings and not publishing them. There was, in fact, every reason to do just that.

Before the Commission was very far into its work, on May 12, 1964, Specter wrote a memo on the subject of the "Examination of Autopsy photographs and X-rays of President Kennedy."

Its first sentence begins: "When the autopsy photographs and X-rays are examined . . ." He then itemized what should be done when they were examined. He assumed they would be examined, the norm.

Earlier, on April 16, he wrote a memo on the remaining work in his area. Item two is "Obtain further medical evidence," and under that (a) is "Photographs and X-rays of the autopsy should be examined . . ."

Two weeks later, on April 30, he wrote, "It is indispensable that we obtain the photographs and X-rays." He took four paragraphs to explain why.

One of his reasons was the assumption that it would "confirm" the Humes-Boswell-Finck testimony.

And, as he concluded, he had learned that the films would be available if the Commission decided it needed to see them.

When the body and casket left the Naval Hospital, the Secret Service took, among other things, the X rays and the photographs, the latter not yet processed. The man in direct charge of the Secret Service was a lawyer with the rank of inspector, Thomas J. Kelley. Kelley told Specter that Robert Kennedy did not "decline to make them available, but only wanted to be satisfied that they were really necessary." Specter then suggested "that the Commission transmit to the Attorney General its reasons for wanting the films" and give "assurances that they will be viewed only by the absolute minimum number of people ... with the films not to become a part of the Commission's records."

It did not happen often with the upwardly mobile Specter, but in this he was spinning his wheels. The Commission did not level with him. In some areas this is not at all surprising; much as it boasted of its staff, it also did not trust the staff with everything. Its executive sessions were without any staff present, with the exception of Rankin, their honcho, who really ran it all. And the Commission did expect permanent secrecy for those transcripts it classified TOP SECRET, though it did not have authority to classify anything.

What Rankin kept secret from Specter is that they had the pictures quite early. I learned this when I got access to the transcript of their January 21, 1964, session, court-assisted, so to speak.

John Sherman Cooper, respected Republican Senator from Kentucky, and John J. McCloy, who had an exceptional and varied career, from government service to international banking, were kicking around ideas that could be helpful in that very early day in the Commission's life. McCloy turned from Cooper to Rankin, and this ensued:

> **Mr. McCloy.** Let me ask you about this raw material business that is here. What does it consist of? Does it consist of the raw material of the autopsy? They talk about the colored photographs of the President's body—do we have that?
> **Mr. Rankin.** Yes, it is part of it, a small part of it
> **Mr. McCloy.** Are they here?
> **Mr. Rankin.** Yes. . . . [*Whitewash IV*, page 133]

While Specter, the Commission's assistant counsel in charge of the medical evidence, was campaigning for the Commission to examine this evidence, in deepest secrecy, the Commission did have it and from its records never told him!

In 1974 I published that page from the transcript in facsimile in *Whitewash IV*, and it remains almost entirely unknown.

And considering all the actual silence of those twenty-eight years, few people are more reprehensible than those who had this knowledge and remained silent. As a result they caused the victimized family to be blamed for the suppression of the autopsy films and its "raw material," for which the Commission alone is responsible.

The Commission was denied nothing it needed or wanted. If all of those who had personal knowledge of this are not already dead, before long all will be, there will be no one left who can tell the truth.

But that illegally TOP SECRET transcript does!

Chapter 7

The Muck That Was Not Raked

TWENTY-SIX YEARS LATER BOSWELL CHEWED THE SAME RANCID CUD. *JAMA* was as delighted with it in 1992 as the Associated Press and the *Sun* had been in 1966, all having that same major interest, defending the indefensible Warren Report. Uncritically the major popular media regarded it as a defense of the accuracy of the Report when Boswell told them that he had made a little error in his haste in allegedly mislocating the President's nonfatal bullet wound by four or five inches and placing it on his back rather than in the base of his neck. Wonderful! In an autopsy in a criminal case wherein accuracy is vital to any possible solution of the crime, in this, the major crime of our era, the pathologists were "careless," and the major media hailed this as meaning that all was well because alleged carelessness meant the autopsy remained strictly dependable.

If this was incredible then, that no element of the major media raised any questions, but instead joined in to endorse it as proof of official probity, how much more incredible is it that *JAMA*'s editor, twenty-six years later, treats it in an identical way?

JAMA did seek media attention for its lie, beginning with its press release and again for its press conference. Its release begins by emphasizing that "Humes and Boswell agreed to talk with *JAMA* about their four-hour autopsy of Kennedy—their first public discussion of the case—because the interview was to appear in a peer-oriented, scientific journal."

While those of us not privy to what was in the minds of *JAMA*'s editor and its national reporter, there can be no doubt at all that Humes and Boswell knew better.

We are left to wonder why they elected to be interviewed by a pathologist who they knew was professionally better equipped to doubt what they said than most reporters were. It is not possible to avoid the suspicion that before saying a single word on the record to Lundberg and Breo, they had dependable assurances that whatever they said would be accepted and repeated without any questions. Otherwise they would have been absolutely insane to say a word for publication, especially in publication aimed at their peers and certain to attain considerable national attention.

My purpose in emphasizing Boswell's public interviews is to indicate that rather than never once having spoken in public, as *JAMA* stated, he did speak in public when Boswell and Humes thought it could serve their interests and when they had no choice. As recently as Harrison Edward Livingstone's *1992* book, Boswell did agree to be interviewed and was interviewed. (I have not listed all the known interviews of both doctors.)

JAMA exploited an emotionally attractive, human-interest approach to launch its campaign to defend the Warren Commission and Lundberg's friends, the autopsy pathologists.

Breo's second article was dramatized in *JAMA*'s press conference with this headline, "DALLAS PHYSICIANS SUPPORT AUTOPSY, DENOUNCE CONSPIRACY THEORY BY EX-COLLEAGUE."

As with the autopsy pathologists *JAMA* jerked at the heartstrings still again in flacking for greater attendance at its press conference when it said of the four Dallas doctors interviewed and quoted that they, too, "broke their 28-year silence."

There were some fifteen Dallas doctors engaged in the futile effort to save the President. *JAMA* interviewed only four. How or why they were selected is not known. However, again from recollection, which can always be imperfect, almost none of them had been silent. (Crenshaw, then a resident, had been silent.)

The four selected for this part of the *JAMA* propaganda in support of the Warren Report are, in the order in which *JAMA* names them, surgeons Malcolm Perry and Charles J. Carrico (then a resident), M. T. "Pepper" Jenkins, chief of anesthesiology, and Charles Baxter, also a surgeon.

Some, particularly Malcolm Perry, were pressured into silence by the Commission's then-assistant counsel, Arlen Specter. Others were pressured by the Secret Service. But still they talked sometimes to the major newspapers and a large number of TV and radio stations in Dallas.

They also responded to out-of-town reporters. Ben Bradlee, Jr., of the *Boston Globe*, assisted by Harrison Livingstone, who later wrote two books titled *High Treason*, not only questioned them at length, but with their permission taped the interviews, of which I have copies. Some of these doctors were interviewed on radio, as I reported in quoting them in my books.

Two of *JAMA*'s four Dallas doctors agreed to interviews with me in 1972, along with a third not included among *JAMA*'s interviewees because he did not agree with what *JAMA* said then. None asked for confidentiality, none complained about my publishing what they told me, and I corresponded later with them.

There was a nationally telecast veritable parade of them when the PBS program *Frontline* (June 15, 1988) got access to the autopsy pictures and X rays at the National Archives for the Dallas doctors. They were photographed when they emerged from their examination, their words were recorded, and they were seen and heard from coast-to-coast, in this twenty-fifth anniversary program.

Ten years earlier they had been called to testify before the House Select Committee on Assassinations, and like Humes, were seen and heard coast-to-coast, with their testimony then published by the committee.

What makes *JAMA*'s falsification of the public record more ridiculous and less pardonable is that it did not have to say that either the autopsy pathologists or any of the Dallas doctors had been silent in order to achieve the widespread public and major-media attention *JAMA* could expect from publishing Breo's account of Lundberg's interviews.

There is absolutely no question at all about it: *JAMA* did lie. Why it lied we do not know. Whether out of ignorance or with the intent to lie, this alone, and at the very least, disqualifies it.

It was inevitable that most of the media and certainly *The New York Times* had the "twenty-eight-years of silence" lie brought to their attention. It published this as the fourth of four "corrections," in the June 9 issue:

An article on May 20 about the autopsy of President John F. Kennedy included an erroneous reference from the *Journal of the American Medical Association* to the history of statements by the doctors who performed the autopsy and others who treated him in the emergency room. Some of them spoke previously in public about the matter; they were not breaking a 28 year silence.

To the *Times* this was but another speck for the dustbin of history. It made no interpretation of its "discovery." Inadequate, really shameful as it is, it still exceeds all of the media of which I know, from coast-to-coast, which made no "correction."

We have had great newspapers, to be distinguished from those that are rich or powerful or influential, of which there is no shortage. They were great newspapers because their publishers, editors, and reporters were great. They did not accept official dishonesties; they hated and exposed them. Where they saw corruption, they saw a target, saw the need of the people to know. They were not part of the muck. In that day, almost a century ago, they "raked" the muck and came to be known as "muckrakers."

The Pulitzer Prize is named for and in honor of one such publisher, Joseph Pulitzer.

We now have more muck and fewer to rake it.

Chapter 8

Truth Forever on the Scaffold, Wrong Forever on the Throne

JAMA SAYS THAT LUNDBERG INTERVIEWED HUMES AND BOSWELL OVER a two-day period. What Breo used in his article hardly represents two days of interviews. It therefore represents a culling of those interviews and selective use of only a portion of what was said in his article.

In his writing, which is the opposite of "scientific research" and is blindly one-sided, Breo skips around and repeats what was of most interest to him and to Lundberg. In my critique that follows, instead of skipping around in the article, I have tried to compare the Lundberg interviews, to the degree Breo used them, as well as what Lundberg said about them at the New York City press conference and later in his many interviews, with the official records, the facts and the truth. I also keep all of their comments on each subject together so I can quote them by subject matter, and then I compare them with the facts and the truth, what Lundberg stated was "nonavailable."

This record, I am confident, will speak for itself!

Like their lawyers as well as the members of the Warren Commission who, lacking the restraints and inhibitions of our adversary system of justice, and were, in their absence, unable to restrain and regulate themselves, so also, from his total and overwhelming ignorance of the established facts of the JFK assassination and its investigations, was Lundberg unable to restrain himself when the press asked none of the questions crying out to be asked. Common sense alone, and that required no knowledge of the established fact, should have told the reporters that Lundberg was dumping on them what was entirely impossible.

Take, for example, this pontification from his imagined Olympus: "I can state without concern or question that President Kennedy was struck and killed by two, and only two bullets, fired from one high-velocity rifle" [Quoted from the Reuters report in the *San Francisco Examiner*, May 19, 1992].

JFK was not killed by *two* bullets. Only one was fatal. As a pathologist, Lundberg should have known that, in general, one of the purposes of an autopsy is to establish which one bullet did cause death. In the JFK case it was so obvious that no autopsy was required to prove it.

There is no way that this autopsy could have proved (or not proved) that each of these two bullets was fatal or that both were "fired from one high-velocity rifle."

It is just plain false for Lundberg to describe the Mannlicher-Carcano rifle from which, in the official story, all bullets were fired as being of "high-velocity." With a muzzle velocity of about 2100 feet per second, these bullets were of only medium to low-velocity for a rifle. That is what Robert A. Frazier, the FBI's expert, testified to the Warren Commission. It published his testimony. Moreover it is nearly impossible for wounds to pinpoint the velocity of the bullets that caused them. In addition the design of the bullet or bullets, which Lundberg did not once mention, is an important factor in the character of the wounds caused.

Quoting further from the Reuters dispatch, Lundberg next said, "The eyewitness accounts and the scientific evidence are indisputable" in his account of the careers of the two bullets. *Lundberg did not cite a single eyewitness in his press conference.* Breo mentioned none in his article. Lundberg did not ask a single question about any eyewitness.

Nor did he, in his press conference or in what he published in *JAMA*, refer to any of the great volume of "scientific evidence" that was readily available. It was available in what the FBI chose to let the Commission have. What the Commission did not publish was in its files that have been available at the National Archives since 1965. It was also available in the court records in two of my lawsuits against the FBI.

I have always provided access to my records to others. The documents have always been available from me, and once disclosed to me, they are accessible in the FBI's public reading room.

The transcripts of the testimony of these FBI laboratory agents are part of the court records. They have always been available from the clerk of the court as well as from me and from my lawyer.

Breo puffs Lundberg up a bit: "*JAMA*'s Lundberg, a stickler for detail, poses some questions that remain official mysteries."

He then states one of these supposed "official mysteries" in the subheading of what follows in his story, in boldface type, "Who ordered the autopsy?" He then repeats these same words in the first sentences of the text, "Who ordered the autopsy?"

To begin with, as certainly Lundberg, as a professional pathologist and as a pathologist for a decade in the military, knew very well, this is the wrong question. The autopsy was required by law as well as by the Navy's regulations.

What he really meant was who authorized it. And that is neither a secret nor a mystery. The authorization was signed by Robert Kennedy, then the attorney general as well as a surviving brother.

This shows that Lundberg is "a stickler for detail"?

This shows that Lundberg "poses some questions that remain official mysteries"?

Of all the questions that could be asked about the autopsy, of all the many criticisms of the autopsy by professionals, including the American Academy of Forensic Sciences, *these* alone are of such great importance that Breo uses them to tell *JAMA*'s readers how important and how wise and well-informed his boss is?

Breo then quoted answers to this question from the transcripts of Lundberg's interviews:

'It must have been Jackie Kennedy,' says Humes. 'She made the request through Admiral Burkley.' Boswell says, 'It must have been Robert Kennedy. He was acting on behalf of the family.' Lundberg counters ["Counters"? Some "interview"!], 'Well, we have a lot of "must haves" but no answer.' Humes says, 'Well, George, I hope you're not saying that we shouldn't have done the autopsy! My orders came from Ed Kenney, the surgeon general of the Navy. The President's personal physician, Admiral Burkley, was standing beside me at the autopsy table . . .' Lundberg concludes, 'OK, there were verbal OKs all over the place.' Boswell adds, 'Captain Stover [the medical center's commanding officer] was thorough, and I'm sure he had someone complete the paperwork.'

Boswell was correct, but Lundberg, who knew nothing at all, knew better. His concept of conducting interviews was to argue his uninformed and incorrect beliefs.

He did not know that the autopsy had been properly authorized and ordered, therefore it had not been. Reality for some reason seemed to be what he believed it to be, without having bothered to learn the truth, as he could have by a simple letter or phone call to the Navy's FOIA office. But then he had only seven years in which to prepare, from the time he got that seven-year justify-the-Warren-Report and my-old-chums itch.

There was nothing else at all about the autopsy and what relates to it that he had the time to learn in those seven years, as will be apparent.

So that Breo can be evaluated, we must consider what he wrote about two matters that have been intensely controversial for years: (1) what happened to JFK's brain; and (2) the forensic qualifications of the Humes and Boswell. His treatment of them will also provide a means of determining how much the words of all four principals can be accepted.

Toward the end of his article, Breo asked, "What happened to the brain?" He then wrote, "Boswell says, 'I believe that it was buried with the body.' Humes says, 'I don't know, but I do know that I personally handed it over to Admiral Burkley and that he told me that the family intended to bury it with the body. I believe Admiral Burkley.'"

All should have known not only that this was not true, but that it was impossible. Humes and Boswell should have known this from what they had said in their own autopsy report. Lundberg and Breo should have known because they should have read the autopsy report, the basis of Lundberg's interviews and of Breo's article.

Humes wrote the autopsy report in longhand. It was retyped, and the retyped copy is the one filed as official. (I published the rewritten holograph of this report in facsimile in *Post Mortem* on pages 509–23.) The Commission's copy was provided by the Secret Service almost a month later, under the date of December 20, 1963. The Commission filed it as one of its numbered documents, or as Commission Document 77, and in its file of "Key Persons," under "Kennedy, John F. 4–1."

On page 4 of the typed copy, page 8 of Humes's handwritten "original" (the quotation marks will be explained later; see *Post Mortem*, page 516), Humes wrote, "The brain is removed and preserved for further study following formalin fixation." The next-to-the-last sentence in the text of Humes's report is: "A supplemental report will be submitted following more detailed examination of the brain and of microscopic sections" [*Post Mortem*, page 523].

Humes's March 16, 1964, testimony to the Warren Commission (2H347 ff.), with Boswell and Finck present and testifying after he did, included his explanation of the need for this formalin fixation. His testimony also included his explanation for the delay caused by this fixation: "This delay necessitated by, primarily, our desire to have the brain better fixed with formaldehyde before we proceeded further with the examination of the brain which is a standard means of approach to study of the brain. The brain, in fresh state, does not lend itself well to examination" [2H355].

Humes asked to be able to refer to "the second portion" (the supplemental report) of his autopsy report. It was entered into the record as Exhibit 391. (It is the last exhibit in 16H987–98.) It was dated December 6, 1964.

But the President was buried on November 25, twelve days earlier than the date Humes completed his study of the fixed brain and handed in his report.

Humes and Boswell certainly knew very well that they had the brain in their possession, soaking in the formaldehyde solution, when the President was buried.

When interviewed by Lundberg, they therefore knew that it was not possible for "the family" to "bury it with the body" [Humes's words], or that "it was buried with the body" [Boswell's words].

According to the February 1, 1965, "personal" notes Finck made at the request of Brigadier General J. M. Blum, director of the Armed Forces Institute of Pathology, the brain was still at the Naval Hospital on November 29 because Humes phoned him that day to tell him that the three prosectors "would ... examine the brain" at the Naval Hospital.

At this point in his article Breo reported on another controversy. He began:

> Boswell concludes, 'In hindsight, we might have called in a civilian pathologist like Russell Fisher, who was right next door in Baltimore. [Fisher then was Maryland's chief medical examiner, and expert in forensic pathology and the author of basic texts in that specialty.] We didn't need him to confirm our findings, but it might have removed the doubts about military control.' Humes says, 'Russell was a friend and we easily could have asked him to come in to help, but we had no problem in determining the cause of death.'

While there were questions about only military pathologists being involved in the autopsy examination, that was not the major criticism. Lundberg should have, as a pathologist himself, recognized that Humes was being misleading. The real problem was that neither Humes, Boswell, nor Finck was experienced in *forensic* pathology, the minimal requirement of a full, complete, and competent autopsy examination. Lundberg let them pretend that they had the requisite *forensic pathology* experience when not one of the three did. Their Warren Commission testimony, which was under oath, makes it without question that none of them did.

Although I know of no single newspaper, magazine, or radio or TV newscast that picked it up and used it, United Press International provided its international clients with precisely this well-known criticism as soon as Lundberg had staged his Hollywood-on-Madison Avenue exploit. The story was filed from Wichita, Kansas, where "the annual Western Conference on Civil and Criminal Procedures" was being held. United Press International's report begins, "An internationally recognized forensic pathologist called 'absurd' conclusions regarding the assassination of President John F. Kennedy drawn in an article in the *Journal of the American Medical Association*" [Undated wire-service teletype copy sent me].

That statement was credited to Dr. Cyril Wecht, the former head of the American Academy of Forensic Sciences. He is a medical doctor, a lawyer, and a longtime Professor of Medical-law at Duquesne University in Pittsburgh. For years he was also the chief medical examiner for Allegheny County and its coroner. He has been not only a practicing forensic pathologist for decades: he has also taught it for decades to those who become forensic pathologists. He is, without question, one of the country's foremost forensic pathologists.

He told United Press International, "You must remember, Humes and Boswell had never done medical-legal autopsies in their careers. It was really inept." United Press International also reported that he "questioned Lundberg's qualifications to draw any conclusions based only on his interview with the physicians. The whole thing is a farce, really. He [Lundberg] has not studied the autopsy materials [as we have just seen]. He is not a fully formally trained board-certified forensic pathologist. I'm not sure he would be qualified to testify in a court of law."

Wecht also said that Lundberg's and *JAMA*'s purpose was to make "the American public believe that some kind of true investigative study has been done afresh. And there is nothing new here."

What Breo wrote and Lundberg published depends on Humes's and Boswell's word and that alone. The *JAMA* article reflected no interest in or effort to confirm what they had said. That would have focused interest on what they had said and what Lundberg had published so uncritically, especially on two controversial matters. Lundberg devoted close to 10 percent of Breo's article to the first of them, which is that Humes destroyed some original autopsy records. My exposé of this event reached many people who did not have my book because the first public attention to it was when I used it in 1966 on a New York City TV show. Humes not only destroyed original records of it—he then certified that he had destroyed "certain preliminary draft notes" otherwise undescribed (*Post Mortem*, page 524).

So, when by accident, it became apparent to me that what I had been led to believe by WNEW-TV would be a segment of the *Allen Burke Show* that would be like a book-and-author show had in fact been booby-trapped in advance, I prepared to defend myself and my book in just the few moments before the cameras rolled. I thought about what I had published that was closest to being entirely indefensible by government partisans. I decided to use Humes's certification of his having destroyed some of the original autopsy records and the Warren Commission's unquestioning acceptance of it.

I had gotten to the WNEW-TV studios a bit early and was able to observe the show being taped. It had a professional Arab, Mohammed Mehdi, saying that there is no such thing as anti-Semitism—there is only anti-gentilism by Jews. In the working-class audience there were four people who were conspicuous. They were carefully well-dressed. They were soon mixing it up with Mehdi, and in so doing, they identified themselves as lawyers.

What, I wondered, were those four doing in that audience?

The most obvious explanation was that they were there for me and by accident were there for this earlier segment of Mehdi with his pro-Arab and anti-Semitic propaganda.

So, at the first possible moment, once I was on the show, I showed Humes's certification, which I had printed in facsimile. Later I was able to ask Humes's four defenders at the studio to justify his actions. They could not. The intensity of the controversy and the audience's reaction to it led the show's producers to let the cameras roll. Instead of a single segment of a show they wound up with a show that ran for more than two hours and got the highest ratings that station had ever earned for that time slot.

WNEW-TV aired the show Saturday night, ending after 2 A.M. on a Sunday morning. My phone started ringing then, and it rang so constantly I never got back to bed.

On Monday one bookstore sold out of its three hundred copies of *Whitewash: The Report on the Warren Report* before the day was over. One wholesaler reordered the book three times that week. By the end of the week it had to be reprinted.

The major media could not have been unaware of this enormous attention or of the use I'd made of Humes's destruction of original autopsy records.

On the day I got the first one hundred copies of the book from the printer, I sent copies to each of the then more numerous New York City newspapers. *The New York Times* kept asking for additional free copies. When, after getting a dozen, they asked again, I made them pay for the thirteenth. I go into this because the major media are a central part of the entirety of the subject matter to which the *Washington Post* referred. All the New York major media and some of lesser importance received copies, and not one mentioned the book or its contents. The *Times* then had a section on its book review pages for "Books Received." It did not mention getting *Whitewash*.

Fred Graham, a lawyer, was the paper's legal correspondent at its Washington bureau. He was assigned to review it and the book that followed it, Edward Jay Epstein's *Inquest*. Graham told me that *Whitewash* had come between him and his wife because the only time they had to read it was in bed and her reading it kept him from reading it. They were both that interested in it. But, in his review, he faulted the book for being "painstaking and overwhelming."

Later Graham became CBS News's legal correspondent in its Washington bureau. He then did a study for the Twentieth Century Fund on the freedom of the press. Graham was still with the *Times*, and when in violation of the letter of agreement between the representative of the estate of President Kennedy and the General Services Administration, of which the National Archives was part, a urologist, John Lattimer, whose prejudices were known in advance, was granted exclusive access to the autopsy material, including the pictures and X rays, he gave Fred Graham an exclusive on his interpretation of the meaning of what he examined. The letter of agreement limited access to those materials to official investigators, pathologists, and radiologists. Lattimer was a urologist, not a pathologist. From the first drumbeat of anti-JFK propaganda since the assassination, that surely is one part of President Kennedy's anatomy about which there was no question. Lattimer's interpretation endorsed the Warren Report.

The FBI prepared the four lawyers at the WNEW-TV show to confront and try to ruin me and my book.

In 1974 Congress amended the FOIA to make the FBI, CIA, and similar agencies' files accessible under it, subject to certain specific exemptions. These amendments became effective in 1975. I then requested of the FBI all of its records on me. It took years for the incomplete compliance to be delivered. In those records I learned what had happened at the show. It is not what most Americans expect of either their TV stations or their FBI.

Paul Noble, the producer, had asked the FBI to provide special agents to confront me. The New York office turned him down. Noble accepted their alternative: He "was furnished all public source material which refuted criticism placed on the FBI or the Warren Commission . . ." [62–109060–4151].

In New York this memo to FBIHQ is filed 66–3476. Files of the "66" classification are for "Administrative Matters," known internally as "Admats." In practice they are used for other purposes. In particular, "66" files are used to hide the FBI's surveillances.

This memo to headquarters also stated that a sound tape had been provided to the FBI four days before the show aired. FBIHQ knew what was on the show before it was aired from this six page, single-spaced memo.

This cozy arrangement the FBI had with WNEW-TV is not uncommon, and it is not limited to TV and radio. It includes book publishing, the print press, and not such a small number of reporters.

(One well-known reporter for a Washington paper that no longer exists was virtually an FBI adjunct. He informed on fellow reporters, and for such services he had no trouble reaching DeLoach and others in the upper echelon. The FBI paid back him and the paper with exclusive stories.)

It took years of constant effort for me to obtain the records that include this documentation on the FBI's role.

This, too, is part of a full canvas, that "entirety" that the AMA and its *JAMA* fit into, that makes the whole picture of the autopsy clearer and more meaningful.

At FBIHQ my FOIA requests were filed in its "100" file classification, in 100–351938. According to the FBI's public list of its file classifications, this "100" file classification is for "Subversive Matter" on individuals and on "Domestic Security Investigations."

Unlike the print press, which ignored what I had aired on WNEW-TV for the first time anywhere, this FBI New York memo, never expected to be seen by others outside the FBI, did tell FBIHQ of me:

He spoke of the autopsy ... How the first records were destroyed by the Chief Medical Examiner. He also stated that the Naval examinations did not wholly agree with the findings of the doctors in Dallas who tried to save the President's life on the day he was assasined [*sic*]. He explained that the doctors in Dallas had stated in their reports that there was a wound in the neck area of the President indicating a possibility of a person firing from another position than that position of OSWALD'S.

Convoluted, understated, and a little modified, but close enough. It stated that I said that some autopsy records were destroyed. It does not say that I showed Humes's certification.

After my work Lundberg did not dare ignore the fact that Humes had his private little bonfire, and in his recreation room at that.

This very unusual thing, the destruction of records relating to the autopsy examination of *a president* who had been assassinated is not mentioned in the Warren Report.

And yet the Warren Commission had not entirely ignored it. It merely suppressed it from its Report, from the section of the Report for which now-Senator Arlen Specter was responsible.

Except for what Humes is quoted as saying about his autopsy protocol, which we will address later, what follows is all that Breo used of what Humes had said:

Humes spent most of Saturday, November 23, drafting the autopsy report. In the process, he burned his autopsy notes, but not really. 'This is the criticism I keep hearing over and over again,' he says, 'that I burned my notes and that this means there must have been a conspiracy. Well, it's true that I burned my original notes because they were stained with the President's blood, and I did not want them to become a collector's item, but I burned them *after* I had copied verbatim in my own handwriting the entire contents. I make no apology for this, but I will explain my reason:

'One of my assignments had been to escort foreign Navy officers around US bases. Along the way, we'd always try to show the foreign officers slices of Americana. On one of these trips, we saw an exhibit that purported to be the chair on which President Abraham Lincoln sat when he was shot at Ford's Theater. There were stains on the back of the chair that were reported to be from Lincoln's blood. I was appalled at this type of display, though I later learned that the stains were from Macassar, a hair preparation of the day that inspired the antimacassar doily, and not from Lincoln's blood. In any event, when I saw that my own notes were stained with Kennedy's blood, I vowed that this type of revolting object would not fall into the wrong hands. I burned the notes that night in my fireplace.'

Admiral Burkley wanted the autopsy report by midnight Sunday, November 24, and early Sunday morning Humes returned to the Naval medical school to go over his handwritten report with Drs. Boswell and Finck. The three pathologists met in the office of Adm. C. B. Galloway, the commanding officer of the National Naval Medical Center. While talking, they were called to watch a nearby TV set—Jack Ruby had just shot Lee Harvey Oswald in Dallas. Returning to their report, the three experts had no trouble agreeing on the facts of their autopsy. The report, 'A63–272,' was the 272nd autopsy performed that year at the hospital. The admiral's secretary typed the handwritten report into six pages. Humes says, 'Our conclusions have stood the test of time. The cause of death is given as 'gunshot wound, head.' The summary, as published in the 1964 Warren Commission report, reads as follows: . . .

That night, Humes hand-delivered the autopsy report, signed by Humes, Boswell, and Finck, to Admiral Burkley at the White House. On December 6, 1963, Humes alone submitted to Burkley his supplementary report, writing in the final summary: 'This supplementary report covers in more detail the extensive degree of cerebral trauma in this case. However, neither this portion of the examination nor the microscopic examinations alter the previously submitted report or add significant details to the cause of death.'

Shortly afterward, Humes turned over everything from the autopsy to Admiral Burkley—bullet fragments, microscopic slides, paraffin blocks of tissue, undeveloped film, X rays—and the preserved, unsectioned President's brain. 'Burkley said he wanted everything,' Humes says, 'and he came out to Bethesda to get it. I gave it to him all in one package. What was left at Bethesda? Zero. I didn't make a copy of anything. Frankly, I was glad to be out from under the responsibility. Admiral Burkley gave me a receipt for the autopsy materials, including the brain. It was my understanding that all the autopsy materials except the brain would be placed in the National Archives. He told me that the family wanted to inter the brain with the President's body. I don't know what happened to the brain, but I do know that Admiral Burkley was an honorable man.

The medical autopsy of President John F. Kennedy was concluded. The conspiracy autopsies had yet to begin [pages 279–2800].

In the first sentence quoted, Breo wrote that Humes had said that he burned his notes on Saturday, November 23, 1963:

> Humes spent most of Saturday, November 23, drafting the autopsy report. In the process, he burned his autopsy notes, but not really. . . . 'I burned my original notes because they were stained with the President's blood, and I did not want them to become a collector's item, but I burned them *after* I had copied verbatim in my own handwriting the entire contents.'

Humes's reason then follows, that he had mistakenly believed a century after Lincoln was assassinated that stains he saw on the back of a chair that Lincoln had used were of Lincoln's blood. It turns out that what Humes imagined was not so. Those stains were "from Macassar," a hair preparation of the day.

Even though Humes knew he had been wrong in what he imagined, he still says he thought that his notes with the President's blood on them might "fall into the wrong hands," of someone who would make appalling use of the blood, so "I burned the notes that night in my fireplace." There is no equivocation here. Humes said that he burned those notes Saturday night.

Saturday was the day after JFK was assassinated and the day before Jack Ruby killed Lee Harvey Oswald.

What Humes did not say, or if he did, Lundberg or Breo or both decided not to say, is that his little bonfire of original evidence was in his recreation room.

Humes did not burn those notes that night.

It makes no sense at all to conjecture that any such records could "fall into the wrong hands." And Humes knew very well that autopsy records are kept strictly private except when used in court. To evaluate his explanation for his destruction of evidence, and that without any question at all is what it was, it makes no difference whether the records would remain with the Navy or be given to the family. Neither was about to give them away or leak them. Moreover, he said he knew that he was going to give everything to Admiral

George Burkley, the President's physician at the White House. Humes also knew that the White House was so concerned about anything at all getting out that the Secret Service took his pictures and X rays, without even permitting the pictures to be developed or used in the autopsy.

Can he *really* have had any such concern when he surrendered without protest all those bloody color pictures to the Secret Service?

What about the President's blood that was surely on so many sheets and surgical gowns and cloths? Did he have them gathered up and destroyed?

Did he collect all the instruments used so no improper use could be made of them?

No, it is only unreasonable to suspect that the dried presidential blood on his notes had a chance of getting into the "wrong hands." From the available evidence this is a cock-and-bull story he made up. And made up late, at that, long after the autopsy.

That he would or had any reason to suspect that the Secret Service detail in charge of presidential protection or the Navy admiral who was the President's personal physician would do any such ghoulish thing defames them, and it defames Humes for making such a false and defamatory record.

Humes also said that before destroying his "notes" he copied "verbatim in my own handwriting the entire contents," so that no information was lost.

What else did Humes say in his 1992 version of those 1963 events other than that after copying his autopsy notes "verbatim," he burned them to prevent any improper use of them?

With the passage of time and the accumulation of years, memories can and do fail, recollections can become confused or incorrect, and even when intending the best, we can make mistakes. However, what Humes and his associates were involved in was the most important, the most dramatic, the most shattering single event of their lifetimes. They were involved, and they did have a great responsibility. A few minor errors can be understood.

Yet knowing how long Lundberg had pressed them to agree to be interviewed for publication in the *Journal*, they had an additional responsibility to check the official records if they were not absolutely certain of their recollections. Humes and Boswell clearly did not do that. They also did not tell Lundberg that their recollections might be unclear or flawed. In everything quoted, they are unequivocal and explicit.

Breo did no checking of any kind at all. He shirked his responsibility as a writer.

An editor's responsibilities include assuring himself that what he publishes is true, accurate, and on controversial subjects, fair. Lundberg wore two hats because he was also the interviewer whose interviews were converted into major articles in the prestigious publication he also edits. An editor does not meet his responsibility any more than a writer does by refusing to do any checking of facts.

Those two hats Lundberg wore were dunce caps.

There is no question about his dual responsibility as the interviewer, who controlled what questions would be asked and thus what information would be adduced, and as the editor, whose responsibility was to insure that what he published was true and accurate.

Perhaps all involved were irresponsible and had no interest in being responsible. Perhaps there were other reasons, but if there were, then the offenses are more serious than that of mere irresponsibility.

Whatever may explain or account for the statements quoted in this chapter, if they were all that is questionable or not true—as they most certainly are not—then they alone would assure "Wrong Forever on the Throne."

There was and there is a record, quite an extensive record that all four, Humes and Boswell and Lundberg and Breo, should have consulted before a word was put on paper for publication anywhere, especially in the *Journal of the American Medical Association.*

What they did not do is in the next chapter.

We will compare the quotations in this chapter with the available record, most of which is the official record and all of which these four men pretended did not exist.

Chapter 9

The Record That Speaks for Itself

ON MONDAY, MARCH 16, 1964, JAMES J. HUMES, J. THORTON BOS-
well, and Pierre Finck appeared before the Warren Commission
(2H347–384). The Commission took the major testimony about the
autopsy from Humes. After he testified, Boswell and then Finck gave
testimony. All were under oath. Specter asked them, in words he
addressed to Boswell, "Do you have anything that you would like
to add by way of elaboration or modification . . .?" Boswell replied,
"None" (2H375). Specter then asked Finck, "So do you have anything you would like to add to what he [Humes] said?" and "Or
would you like to modify his testimony in any way?"

Finck's answer to both questions was "No" (2H381).

Their answers mean that Boswell and Finck endorsed every word
in Humes's testimony, of which they heard, and had no questions of
any kind about what Humes swore to under oath. If they disagreed
with anything Humes testified to or believed he had been less than
fully complete or fully honest, they did not indicate it. When they
had the obligation to record any disagreement or to provide any
omission, correction, or amplification, they did not.

What interests us at this point is their under-oath agreement with
Humes's testimony about when he burned the autopsy notes and why.

In the order in which Humes is quoted on this in the preceding
chapter, he told Lundberg and *JAMA* that:

> He drafted the autopsy report on Saturday, November 23, 1963;
> while drafting the report he burned his notes;
> ' "because they were stained with the President's blood" '; but
> he did not burn his notes until after he made a verbatim handwrit-
> ten copy of them;

early the next morning, Sunday, he returned to the Naval medical school to go over his report with Boswell and Finck.

They met and conferred on the autopsy-report draft that morning, Sunday, in the office of Admiral C. B. Galloway, the commanding officer of the entire naval medical installation at
Bethesda, the National Naval Medical Center.

While conferring in Galloway's office, Ruby's shooting of Oswald was on TV, and they then and there learned about that
shooting;

after watching what was on TV, they 'had no trouble agreeing
on the facts' in this handwritten draft of the autopsy report;

they signed the typed copy prepared by Admiral Galloway's
secretary;

Humes delivered the typed copies they all had signed to Admiral
Burkley that night;

On December 6 Humes delivered a copy of their supplementary
autopsy report to Admiral Burkley;

this included 'bullet fragments, microscopic slides, paraffin
blocks of tissue . . . Xrays and' the brain;

that Burkley went out to Bethesda to obtain this evidence;
Humes had made no copies of what he gave Burkley;

but he did get a receipt from Burkley for all this evidence that
included the brain.

Virtually none of this stacks up. Virtually all of it is proven wrong
by the well and publicly known official evidence and in my earliest books.

This means that if any of these four had checked, Humes likely
would not have risked lying, and if any of the reporters had checked
their morgues, they could have learned the truth.

But nobody cared about checking anything that Humes said and
JAMA published.

The simplest of these many falsehoods to dispose of is Humes's
false claim that shortly after December 6 he had given Burkley "bullet fragments" and "X rays." The night of November 22 the FBI
and Secret Service took the "bullet fragments" and "X rays." Dated
receipts that I have obtained and published cover this. Humes never
had them to give to Burkley.

To illustrate how well and how publicly known the information
on this subject is, and how, if Lundberg had behaved like an editor,

he would not have made political partisans of the American Medical Association and its *Journal,* I cite from my *Post Mortem* only the textual references to these receipts and to my facsimile reproduction of them (pages 102, 250–51, 270–72, 274, 277, 279, 527, 534, 546–47).

I also point out another lie by Humes: that he got a receipt for the X rays, photographs, and bullet fragments. A Navy corpsman typed up the receipts for the X rays and photographs. The Secret Service gave its signed receipt for them to Captain J. H. Stover, commanding officer of the medical school, not to Humes. Photographer John Stringer, radiologist John H. Ebersole, and Secret Service Agent Roy Kellerman acknowledged the receipt in writing (*Post Mortem*, pages 546–47).

When the surgeons removed the bullet fragments from the President's head, FBI Special Agents James W. Sibert and Francis X. O'Neill received them. The receipt Sibert signed (*Post Mortem*, page 266) was given to Admiral Burkley. When Burkley decided to give what he had to the Secret Service for safekeeping, its agent in charge of the White House detail, known as its "Protective Research Service," Robert I. Bouck, itemized what Burkley gave him in a receipt dated November 26, 1963. It includes the earlier receipt from the Secret Service.

The Commission suppressed the Bouck receipt from its printed volumes, but it is found in Number 371 (CD371) of the Commission files. It was supposed to have been included in Commission Exhibit (CE) 397, but its omission is without explanation. I brought it to light and published it in *Post Mortem* on page 527.

The footnote I added is relevant to the "entirety" that is the requirement of good journalism, to the care that writers and editors ought to exercise when they deal with matters of great national interest and concern, and it is relevant to the credibility of the Warren Report that Humes, Boswell, and Lundberg endorsed and claimed to have established. Other mentions of the receipt occur in *Post Mortem*, but I here quote this footnote only because it states the disturbing facts with brevity:

The Commission failed to publish this receipt even though it is supposed to be part of CE 397. The reason is obvious: Had it been published, questions would immediately have arisen as to why none of the items included in the list are a part of the Commission's [published] evidence. That the Commission did not obtain these items, readily available to it, is proof that it did not seek the most basic evidence of the crime. The Navy death certificate alone is destructive of the entire official solution to that crime. . . .

We address this death certificate separately below. But just imagine, Humes turned in their autopsy protocol without reference to, or quotation from, this death certificate, which the President's own physician, Admiral Burkley, executed!

And imagine further what it means when in fact the Commission not only had this death certificate and suppressed it from its Report— the Report that all four men and the American Medical Association through its *Journal* told the world is beyond question the absolute truth—when it had 912 pages of space in its Report and 10,000,000 words in its appended 26 volumes of testimony and exhibits!

It is, of course, commentary on our media as well as on the Commission and its apologists that none reported this.

And what kind of pathologist is *JAMA*'s editor when he ignored this fact?

When I published this in 1975, the media entirely ignored the fact that, among other things, the Commission had and suppressed the official certificate of death.

A separate question is how the media could have ignored what is so accurate in the footnote: The death certificate alone destroys the official solution to this great crime. How could they also not have reported why and how (as we soon will do) the "solution" is destroyed by the death certificate?

Perhaps this is as good a point as any to remind the reader that in Lundberg's interview, as quoted by Breo, Humes said that all that has been written that does not agree with him and the official solution is "hogwash."

This is the simplest to disprove of the many claims Humes made. Keeping in mind Humes's account of his destruction of his original autopsy notes, here is the actual record of what Humes destroyed, when he destroyed it, and why.

As we have seen, Boswell began his alleged "twenty-eight years of silence" with several published interviews. Of all inappropriate days, on November 24, 1966—the third anniversary of their recording in their autopsy protocol—the *Baltimore Sun*'s Levine interviewed him. Here is what he wrote about what Boswell had told him:

> He said that Dr. Humes told him, after arriving home, that he decided to write the 'protocol,' or final report, immediately after the autopsy, and did so early in the morning from notes taken at the autopsy and from his recollections.
>
> Later that day, November 22, Dr. Humes and Dr. Boswell went over the rough draft and completed the protocol in its final term.
>
> Before this, an incident took place that had created much controversy. Dr. Humes destroyed 'certain preliminary draft notes' by burning them in his fire place.
>
> Dr. Boswell said that all original notes were preserved, as far as he knows, and were turned over to the National Archives. He said the things that were burned were copies of the protocol as they were revised.

Before Humes had said anything publicly about what he destroyed, Boswell said that Humes had not in fact destroyed his "notes." Boswell also said that to the best of his knowledge "all original notes were preserved" and that they "were [eventually] turned over to the National Archives."

In this Boswell is supported by a number of receipts I have. The most convenient one to cite is the Bouck receipt of November 26 itemizing what he got from Burkley: "One copy of autopsy report and notes of the examining doctor which is described in letter of transmittal Nov. 25, 1963, by Dr. Galloway."

This letter of transmittal, which I published in *Post Mortem* in facsimile on page 526, says, "1. Transmitted herewith by hand is the sole remaining copy (number 8) of the completed protocol in the case of John F. Kennedy. Attached are the work papers used by the prosecutor and his assistants. 2. This command holds no additional documents in connection with this case." [Years later when I made an FOIA request of the Naval Hospital, I was told by letter that it had turned in everything and retained not a single scrap of paper relating to the JFK autopsy. If they had not, they would have violated Navy regulations.]

Admiral Galloway did not say he was forwarding *copies* of Humes's notes. He referred to them as "the work papers" Humes used in preparing the protocol. This is to say, the originals. And this is what Boswell told Levine, that "the things that were burned were copies of the protocol as they were revised."

However, *Humes did not destroy his notes* after making a "verbatim" handwritten copy of them! And, Boswell knew this. Yet, from what Breo wrote and Lundberg published of the joint interview of both Humes and Boswell, there is no indication of the truth.

Humes did testify before the House Select Committee on Assassinations the afternoon of September 6, 1978. His testimony is in the first volume of that committee's hearings on the JFK assassination, where it takes up nine pages beginning on page 323. This represents a very brief testimony, exceptionally brief considering that Humes was the chief autopsy prosecutor. This brevity provides one measure of that committee's lack of interest in trying to establish the facts of the assassination.

G. Robert Blakey was the committee's general counsel after its shakedown and staff changes. He had been a Department of Justice lawyer specializing in organized crime. Blakey began each public hearing with what he termed a "narration" of the testimony to be taken. In these narrations he cited what various critics had said or written. The hearings that followed were devoted to debunking, disproving, and ridiculing those critics.

In all those many hours Blakey avoided mention of only one critic, an aging and infirm man—me. But I did not avoid him. For many newspapers I was the source for most of the stories that were critical of what he was up to, most importantly *The New York Times* and the *Washington Post*. And I was not anonymous.

After his narrative on Humes, Blakey turned the questioning over to one of his younger assistants, Gary T. Cornwell. Cornwell's questions, relating to the drafting of the autopsy protocol, are on page 330, of the committee's report and considering what I had published in *Post Mortem* alone, copies of which the committee had gotten from me, his questions were hardly adequate.

Cornwell asked Humes, 'You finally began to write the autopsy report at what time?'

Humes's response is: 'It was decided that three people couldn't write the report simultaneously, so I assumed the responsibility for writing the report, which I began about eleven o'clock in the evening of Saturday, November 23, having wrestled with it for four, five, or six hours in the afternoon, and worked on it until three or four o'clock in the morning of Sunday the 24th.'

Cornwell started to ask Humes if he had notes relating to the location of a wound, and Humes interrupted him to answer a question Cornwell had not asked: ''I had the draft notes which we had prepared in the autopsy room, which I copied.''

Cornwell's questioning ended with this exchange:

'First, the notes are no longer in existence, is that correct?'

Humes replied, 'The original notes, which were stained with the blood of our late President, I felt, were inappropriate to retain to turn in to anyone in that condition. I felt that people with some peculiar ideas about the value of that type of material, they might fall into their hands. I sat down and word for word copied what I had on fresh paper.'

'And then you destroyed them?' Cornwell asked

'Destroyed the ones that were stained with the President's blood,' Humes answered.

And there the whole thing died an utterly unnatural death. The committee knew the truth from what it had gotten from me, and even being the Keystone Kops that they were, they should have been able to read the Commission's records that I had read, copied, and drawn upon.

When Humes testified before the Commission and was questioned by Specter, he had no real interest in what Humes destroyed, or even that he had destroyed anything at all. His questioning was as perfunctory as Cornwell's. Reading the testimony in the printed volume makes the destruction of evidence in a criminal investigation, in an autopsy report, in the investigation of the assassination of a president, appear to be as normal as day turning into night.

Here's how I covered Specter and Humes:

He was shown Exhibit 397 and asked to identify it. 'These are various notes in longhand, or copies, rather, of various notes in longhand made by myself, in part, during the performance of the examination of the late President, and in part after the examination when I was preparing to have a typewritten report made' (2H372). This was not the case, and Humes finally conceded it. There was but a single page containing twenty-five words of notes of his conversation with Doctor Perry, fifteen pages of a rough draft of the autopsy report, two charts not in Humes's handwriting, and two certifications (17H29–48). Both certifications are dated November 24, 1963.

The first certification is by Humes and countersigned by the commanding officer of the Naval Medical School. It states that 'all working papers associated with' the autopsy 'have remained in my personal custody at all times' and were turned over to his superior with the handwritten draft. The second certified that he had 'burned certain preliminary draft notes' relating to the autopsy.

If the Commission had any questions about the burning of any kind of historic papers, especially undescribed 'preliminary draft notes,' the transcript does not reveal it (2H373).

Humes described two charts as follows: 'notes actually made in the room in which the examination was taking place, I notice now that the handwriting in some instances is not my own, and it is either that of Commander Boswell or [Lt.] Colonel Finck.' He was asked if he reviewed 'all the markings on those papers and (noted) them to be present when you completed the autopsy report?' He replied, 'Yes, sir,' adding that all the papers had been at all times 'in my personal custody' [*Whitewash*, page 183].

Specter did not even bother to ask Humes why he destroyed anything at all. For a former assistant district attorney, Specter should have known to ask Humes that question and many others, none of which were outside of either his legal training or his experience. What he omitted he omitted deliberately and knowingly.

In the next chapter I will repeat some of what was available to them in *Post Mortem* about what medical evidence disappeared; what Humes really burned and perhaps why; what was supposed to be in the Commission's files and isn't; and was to have been published in its exhibits and wasn't—all related to Lundberg's adventure in rewriting our history in the name of the American Medical Association.

All of this was the work and the unique responsibility of Arlen Specter. His more recent claim to international fame was to wrap himself securely in his senatorial immunity and libel diminutive Professor Anita Hill by accusing her—on coast-to-coast TV—of being a felon, a perjurer. Perjury is false swearing to what is material. Subornation of perjury is inducing one to commit perjury. I believe that Specter's record on the Commission edges toward these felonies, and I am without any doubt at all, as I have published without a peep from him, that he was not honest in his Commission work.

When on the Commission he lived by those two basic rules of the FBI—first cover the Bureau's ass and then cover your own. He did this in his questioning of Humes when Humes was under oath, and he did it in what he wrote in the Commission's Report and what he omitted from that Report.

In time I located *some* of what the Commission had quite literally hidden. It was misfiled where no one would ever think of looking for it—misfiled with the copy that was sent to the Government Printing Office for *printing—and the notes were not printed!*

These notes were in Specter's hands when he questioned Humes, as the testimony establishes. In his questioning, Spector identified them by both their Commission file and exhibit numbers!

For his autopsy report Humes used a pad of white paper with light blue lines that do not show up when photocopied. I published, from a Xerox made from the original, his existing handwritten version of his autopsy protocol, his notes of his phone conversation with Dr. Perry, the originals of his certifications countersigned by Burkley, and other documents.

What Humes really destroyed is as he testified in secret—the first draft of his autopsy report!

Humes swore, before all the controversy was raised in *Whitewash,* that he did not write the first draft until Sunday morning, November 24. He fails to state when "later" was, but he testified, under oath, remember, that he "later revised" it and that the copy he held in his hand was the revision. This leads to a question: What could have happened Sunday morning that could have led Humes to revise his autopsy protocol?

The reason is obvious to those familiar with the basic facts of the JFK assassination.

Jack Ruby shot and killed Lee Harvey Oswald that morning.

In doing this, Ruby also saw to it that with Oswald being the only official candidate for assassin, there would be no trial. And with no trial Humes and company would not be called to testify in public, under oath, and subject to the penalties of perjury.

Thus Humes was assured that neither he nor his autopsy protocol would be subject to the rigors of the American judicial system; that no defense counsel would be going over it with care, looking for what he could use for the defense. Without fear of being pressed, Humes was able to say just about anything he—or others—wanted said.

In partial summary, Humes was explicit when he was under oath before the Warren Commission that what he burned was the first draft of his protocol, *not his notes.*

While we have no way of knowing why Humes lied, despite his partial truthfulness when he was under oath before the Commission, of all the possible explanations none seems more probable than that when he prepared his original autopsy protocol he knew that there would be a trial and examinations of all of them as well as of their protocol. He would be subject to close and very public scrutiny. But once Oswald had been shot, there would be no trial and thus no cross-examination. This meant that information in the original protocol that could have jeopardized the government's instant decision, could now be removed.

Chapter 10

"The Least Secret Autopsy in the History of the World" —James J. Humes

IT SEEMED INCREDIBLE THAT WHEN A PRESIDENT IS ASSASSINATED THE government would keep so much about the crime secret. Secrecy assured that people would have the obvious suspicions, that the secrecy was necessary to hide the government's involvement in the crime. Some of this secrecy—but not all—can be attributed to an unimaginable and permeating government paranoia. One example is in what Commission chairman United States Chief Justice Earl Warren told his staff at his first conference with them, on January 20, 1964, as explanation of why he took the job, when as chief justice, he should not have. If he did not, President Johnson convinced him, and if he did not "quench" the rumors of a conspiracy, that it "could conceivably lead the country into a war which could cost 40 million lives."

This if there had been *no* conspiracy?

Two staff members wrote memoranda for the record. I quote from that made by Melvin Eisenberg. After I dug it out, I published it in *Whitewash* IV on page 26. On the facing page is the memo of the other staff member, number-three man on the staff, Howard Willens, a Department of Justice lawyer on loan to the Commission. He wrote of what Warren said, that "the President was very concerned regarding the international repercussions of the assassination." He recorded this, a meaningless paraphrase, for possible later cover-the-ass self-justification. Instead of writing what Warren had said, he later could claim that what he wrote meant the same thing anyway.

How paranoid was the Commission? It classified as TOP SECRET all the stenographic transcripts of all the testimony it took, testimony that it was to have published!

It held that classification until printing, too!

That the Commission lacked the legal right to classify anything did not prevent it from doing so.

There was to have been a *public* trial. Would the government have dared withhold that from the defense, with all the risks and other hazards with which that would have been fraught? Withholding such information, available under the court's "discovery" procedures, could have gotten the case thrown out of court. What a scandal the withholding and the dismissal would have been!

It clearly was not within the National Archives guidelines for withholding or within the 1966 FOIA exemptions, so there was no basis for those suppressions. But if this had not been true, why should any of it have been withheld anyway—for any reason at all—when it would have been required to have been produced at the public trial?

When the Commission's records were first available at the National Archives, I was there daily before the doors opened. Day after day for months I plodded through boxes of files. My major interest was in what is called "the body of the crime," particularly the medical evidence, and of this the autopsy records most of all.

The files held astoundingly little about the crime itself. They were overloaded with the wildest rumors and with the FBI's indulgence of its political preconceptions. It actually titled most of its JFK assassination records as relating to Cuba. And most of the rest as relating to the USSR.

When it became clear that either the archives did not have the nitty-gritty or if it did, it was not going to let me see it, I started seeking some of the Naval Hospital records from the Secret Service. I knew the Secret Service had gotten some of them.

Impossible as it seems, the Commission apparently did not have—and it makes no mention of it in its Report—the official certificate of death. There is no record I've seen reflecting any interest in this or any effort to obtain it by any of the Commission's surviving lawyers, Specter especially, before or after the Report was published.

How could the Commission have conducted anything that could reasonably be called an investigation without the certificate of death or all the other Naval Hospital autopsy records of any kind?

In *Post Mortem*'s chapter 9 I recounted the official gutting of the Commission's JFK autopsy file, its J.F.K. 4–1 file, by confessing:

... [I]t did surprise me to find there was nothing of any consequence in the 'J.F.K. 4–1' file. If anywhere, I did believe, certainly here there would be some information of significance, some knowledge about the murder, how it was accomplished, what was learned at the autopsy, some of the missing evidence and records.

The staff of the archive was going over this tremendous accumulation and preparing more of it to be released. I delayed requesting copies of every paper in the autopsy file until the last minute. Just stop and think of the situation at the end of 1967, four years after the murder, three after its 'solution.' The world was rampant with dissatisfaction about the inadequate and insufficient Report on the assassination (and this is certainly an understatement of the reality), but the federal government was still keeping vast stores of files secret! In this case, apparently, secrecy was maintained by assigning less than a corporal's guard to do the actual work of making it available. With all the millions of federal employees, *a single* man of the two assigned to the archive to go over these files and prepare them for 'release'! This was not his only responsibility—it is one added to an already full schedule of work. In between the other, full-time duties, he did this. The wonder is not that it took so long but that he was able to accomplish anything. In practice, this amounts to a different kind of suppression.

In reality, what it actually means is that, aside from what has been denied under the 'guidelines'—which gives each agency that was the source of the defunct Commission's documents the right to suppress what it wants suppressed—great gobs of files were suppressed by the designed malfunction of bureaucracy—by simply not putting the manpower on it. On a subject like this, with the national honor and integrity involved, with Macbethian scandals openly bruited, the government quietly and effectively gave validity to these hasty beliefs by delaying what it dared not forcibly suppress. It hoped, with each passing day, that somehow that awful pile of dirt swept under the too-small rug would just go away, just be forgotten. Its clear wish was that, with the popular President securely buried, with the passing of time, people would forget how he got buried, lose interest in his murder and the phony, official explanation of it in that contrived Report. . . .

First, I was promised this autopsy file, then I was denied it, then I was promised all but two documents. This was a total of four pages, or a minute of Xeroxing. Of course, I was assured there was no suppression, no violation of regulations. Finally, I got what I was told was all but those special four pages that had to be denied so there could be 'orderly processing.' These were then promised by September 15 and were not then available.

I completed the writing of this book while I waited for two withheld documents from the 'J.F.K. 4–1' file, for four sheets of paper to appear from the file on the presidential autopsy of four years earlier. Save for a single sheet, the few pages of what is filed under 'J.F.K. 4–1' add nothing to what was already available and known to me and in my own files. There are the same mistakes I found in other files. What was missing, what should be there and is *not—what is required to be there*—had been gutted. Here is *everything* in that file:

The brief covering letter of December 20, 1963, with which James J. Rowley, chief of the Secret Service, sent Rankin a copy of the autopsy protocol. This is not an original copy, of which there were eight. An original copy was too good for the archive, too good for the Commission. This, at the very best, is a third generation copy. Some of it is completely illegible. In addition it has, at some step in the repeated photocopying of photocopies, been reduced in size. But it is supposed to be one of the original eight copies and it should be marked as from the 77th file, 'Clinical Records of Autopsy.' It is not. Every copy made from what Rowley sent the Commission on December 20 should also show this number if, properly, they come from this source.

An even more remote copy of allegedly the same document, the presidential autopsy protocol, contains notations not on any of the more than half-dozen copies of this allegedly single version, and an attachment I had not seen elsewhere. It has a source indicated, and that source cannot possibly be the right one, else the list of files is wrong. It is marked as coming from 'CR362a', or part 'a' of File 362. Now, on page 28 of the list of these files there appears this description of File 362, which is identified as 'three envelopes' coming from 'AG Texas': 'Travis Kirk's letter 437.'

In its infinite wisdom, the Report spares us the identification of 'Travis Kirk's letter 437,' in quotation marks in the listing, and the blessing of revelation is denied us. However, it is not likely that, with whatever significance can be read into the mystery we must here abandon, 'Travis Kirk's letter 437' could not have included a copy of the autopsy, nor could 'AG Texas' have originated it, estimable as the services of the Hon. Waggoner Carr were.

The autopsy authorization *is* in CR362a, from which I had obtained a copy. For years the archives had insisted it had no copy of it. The most reasonable explanation appears to have been its withholding from all the autopsy files or its destruction at some later date, with a copy having by some accident been in papers from the Texas investigation under Carr.

But the authorization is *not* with any of the *federal* autopsy papers or files in the archives. Several years later I saw the original.

This set of the autopsy report is the only one of the many I have seen that has a copy of what, in the original or an original copy, should be in this file, and in photocopy, attached to every copy. It is of a generation so remote, so illegible—so indistinct where it is not illegible—that I cannot make out the identification of the government form or be certain of some of the printing on it [pages 100–101].

After an itemization of other extensive suppression from a very large FBI report in which there was duplication of some of the records in this gutted J.F.K. 4–1 file, chapter 9 from *Post Mortem* continues:

Also in 'J.F.K. 4–1' is a Xerox of a 'certified copy' of what is politely called the 'inquest' held in Dallas. In it Justice of the Peace Theran Ward 'certified' that particular proceeding was consummated almost two weeks prior to the assassination! It contains this language: 'Witness my hand, officially, this 10th day of November A. D. 1963.'

How careful everyone was to be precise, to assure accuracy and completeness when this president was murdered!

There is a copy of Secret Service Agent Elmer Moore's report of December 12 in which that Service found other than the Commission, that from the autopsy report, the Zapruder movie, and other evidence later misinterpreted by the Commission, all that could be concluded about the trajectory was that it was 'to the rear and above the level of the President,' hardly indicating a trajectory to the 66-foot-high sixth-floor window. This report contains a number of other things not supporting the official account.

A single page—the fifth—of the FBI supplemental report of January 9 is Xeroxed and filed here. It is originally File 107.

Illegible, remote-generation copies of Specter's two March 12, 1964, reports of his interviews with the autopsy doctors and Sibert and O'Neill are included. They are so pale and close to illegible that their purpose cannot be serious. Because the remainder of the document is so much paler, the correction of the single word previously referred to, that says the President's rear nonfatal wound was in the 'back,' is more visible here.

An equally illegible, equally pale copy of an uninformative press release dated March 16 says only that four members of the Commission, listed, heard the three autopsy doctors testify.

Finally, there is a letter from J. Edgar Hoover to Rankin, dated March 18, answering negatively an inquiry by Melvin Eisenberg about several possible scientific tests.

And that (save for the four withheld pages) is the entire content of the entire 'autopsy file' of the President's Commission on the Assassination of President Kennedy!

It is not a file, it is a frivolity.

It does not contain what is essential. It contains not a single reference to any effort to obtain what was not spoon-fed the Commission by the federal police. More, it contains no single clue that the Commission of eminences, on their own or under prodding, ever, in any way, did anything to get the missing data that it should have had—could not have discharged its responsibilities without having [pages 104–5].

No record in this autopsy file indicates some of its contents were withheld under law or regulations. What is missing was just removed.

In the very last sentence of his article Breo proclaims that those who do not agree with the official mythology of the JFK assassination are "ignorant of the essential facts." Were this true, how better to explain that than by attributing it to the denial or suppression of essential facts by the government.

And that "scientific evidence" Humes and Boswell "developed during their autopsy" *JAMA* says it "proves the 1964 Warren Commission conclusions that Kennedy was killed by a lone assassin, Lee Harvey Oswald." Had Humes and Boswell developed even a suspicion of this in an autopsy fifteen hundred miles away, ignoring the proof that for most of us is required in making such statements, they would indeed have been magicians. That "scientific evidence" is not in their protocol. Their protocol expresses their opinions or interpretation of their alleged "scientific evidence."

(For more of what was suppressed by *all* official investigations, see the Afterword.)

Chapter 11

Into and Partly Out of the Memory Hole

IN HIS FIRST CERTIFICATION HUMES SAID HE "OFFICIALLY TRANSMITTED all other papers related to this report to higher authority." In the second he said that "no papers relating to this case remain in my possession." This certification says that Humes delivered his "autopsy notes" to his commanding officer. Typed below Humes's certification is, "Received above working papers this date. J. H. Stover, Commanding Officer, U.S. Naval Medical Center." Stover did sign it. It even is timed. It says Humes handed in his notes at 5 P.M.

So what Humes certified is that *after* his rec room fire he handed everything he had, every scrap of paper relating to the autopsy, to his commanding officer. In addition to the rewritten version of the autopsy report draft, he still did have and he did give Captain Stover his "autopsy notes."

The Commission did not publish the official copies of these certifications. It published a version of them. I found the originals hidden where no one would ever look for them in the Commission files. They have identical handwritten endorsements that read: "Accepted and approved this date George G. Burkley, Rear Adm MC USN Physician to the President."

Humes did not keep any papers relating to this autopsy. And as we have seen from Admiral Galloway's covering letter to Burkley of the next day, Monday, November 25, 1963, he gave Burkley the last or "sole remaining copy (number eight) of the completed protocol in the case of John F. Kennedy," *along with* "the work papers used by the prosector and his assistant." Galloway concluded, "This command holds no additional documents in connection with this case." So, in addition to the fact that Humes turned in his notes,

103

they are included in what the Navy gave Burkley, described as the "working papers."

Before going into a tracing of the history of "memory-holing" of vital information about the assassination and what that means and says about its official investigations, there is still another receipt to which for the first time anywhere Humes referred in his *JAMA* interview. Breo quotes Humes directly as saying, " 'Admiral Burkley gave me a receipt for the autopsy materials, including the brain' " [page 2800].

There is no record of any receipt to Humes from Burkley in any of the records. There is *no receipt of any kind* that says it is for the brain. No receipt even uses that word, "brain."

If Burkley had given such a receipt to Humes it could not have been before Humes completed his supplementary autopsy report on December 6, 1963.

The government kept secret a series of records relating to the transfer made on April 26, 1965, of all autopsy materials to the National Archives, until under the FOIA I compelled their disclosure to me. The list of what was included in this transfer seems to be complete. It includes the original of Humes' certification of burning his draft and the receipts previously mentioned. *It does not include Humes's other certification, of handing in his notes and Stover's acknowledgment of receipt of them.* It makes no reference to the brain, and it includes no reference to any receipt given for that brain or to the transfer of any "notes."

In fact, the X rays taken at the Bethesda Naval Hospital disclose that the left half of the brain was intact and undamaged, according to the report of the panel of experts appointed to study the films by the Department of Justice.

This transfer was seven months after the Commission ceased to have any official life, since it then had delivered its Report to LBJ and made it public. In form the transfer is from Burkley to Mrs. Evelyn Lincoln, formerly JFK's personal secretary. In fact the Secret Service held the listed materials for Burkley. The acknowledgment of receipt Mrs. Lincoln wrote at the bottom of this memorandum reads: "Received April 26, 1965, in Room 409, National Archives, Washington, DC., from Dr. Burkley and Robert Bouck."

Bouck prepared his previously cited November 26, 1963, receipt for what he acknowledged receiving from Burkley on that day. It appears to include all the documents and objects, other than tissue in various forms, that as of that date the Navy had not given Burkley. That was ten days before Humes completed his supplementary autopsy report that included them. The copy of Bouck's receipt that I obtained from the Commission's files in the National Archives has only one of its many items marked: "One copy of autopsy report and notes of the examining doctor which is described in letter of transmittal Nov. 25, 1963, by Dr. Galloway." The marks added by hand are vertical lines drawn on each side of this quoted item that acknowledged receipt of Humes's "notes."

The Commission file copy of Galloway's letter included this:

1. Transmitted herewith by hand is the sole remaining copy (number eight) of the completed protocol in the case of John F. Kennedy. Attached are the work papers used by the prosector and his assistant. 2. This command holds no additional documents in connection with this case.

Galloway did deliver to Burkley, and Burkley did turn over to the Secret Service Humes's notes that Humes told Lundberg he had destroyed. "Work papers used by" Humes and Boswell cannot have included any copies; Galloway and Bouck both referred to the *original* notes.

The National Archives initially withheld these transferred records from me, and under FOIA compulsion it was the National Archives that made copies of some for me that I later published in *Post Mortem*. Until the archives learned that my writing was critical of the government's record in the JFK assassination, it could not have been more cooperative in observing traditional norms of scholarship and research. Once it was apparent that I was severely critical of the government's record, its attitude changed.

When, for example, I began my very long and costly quest for the nonsecret results of the nonsecret FBI laboratory tests of ballistics and related evidence and asked the archives for access to those records, the man then in charge, Marion Johnson, both an archivist and a lawyer, immediately reported this to the FBI lab. The FBI disclosed its lab's memo on this to me under the FOIA. That memo also disclosed how the FBI told Johnson to try to fob me off.

After I established my willingness to sue, from time to time the archives decided to let me have quietly what could attract more attention if given to me only in court and under FOIA compulsion. There was always the chance, although it happened remarkably few times, that a reporter would be in the courtroom.

Even so, the archives never provided me with a copy of Humes's notes, something it should have had in the Commission's files.

No copies of Humes's notes exist in the records that the FBI and the Secret Service disclosed to me.

Thus there lingers the mystery about Humes's autopsy notes. He lied to Lundberg by saying that he had destroyed his notes because they held traces of JFK's blood. Humes handed in the notes to Admiral Galloway. Admiral Galloway had them hand-delivered to Burkley. Burkley was not called as a witness by the Warren Commission, strange as that is. The White House detail of the Secret Service had Humes's notes from the very first. This is recorded in Bouck's November 26, 1963, memo.

So we have a very real mystery: What happened to the notes made during the autopsy performed on President Kennedy?

Solving this mystery was the responsibility of the Warren Commission. It did not. It instead pretended that there was no such mystery, making no mention of it in its 1964 Report.

When Specter took Humes's testimony, with Boswell and Finck present, along with some members of the Commission, this ensued:

> **Mr. Specter.** 'Now, Doctor Humes, I hand you a group of documents which have been marked as Commission Exhibit Number 397 and ask you if you can identify what they are?'
> **Commander Humes.** 'Certainly. These are various notes in longhand, or copies rather of various notes in longhand, *made by myself in part during the performance of the examination of the late President,* [Emphasis added] and in part after the examination when I was preparing to have a typewritten report made' [2H372].

Note the "made by myself" and "during" the autopsy examination. This means that, as of the day of his testimony, he had in his hands the *only* autopsy notes that had *any* reason to have blood on them and that they were notes he, personally, made. He made those notes when Oswald was alive, the night of November 22, 1963, and everybody expected him to be tried in public. And Humes did not burn them!

Shortly thereafter Specter asked, "Are there any notes which you made at that time which are not included in this group of notes?"

Commander Humes. 'In the privacy of my own home, early in the morning of Sunday, November 24th, I made a draft of this report, which I later revised, and of which this represented the revision. That draft I personally burned in the fireplace of my recreation room.'

Here it is important to pay close attention to what Humes testified to and what it means. Asked what else he had in his hands, other than the notes he made *during* the autopsy examination, he identified those pages as his *second* "draft" of his autopsy report. *In addition to his autopsy notes!* After he completed his "revision" of the first draft, what did he burn? "That [i.e., the first] draft I personally burned in the fireplace of my recreation room."

Or, Humes burned the draft of his protocol that he wrote *before* Oswald was shot—and he burned that and nothing else.

This then ensued:

Mr. Specter. 'May the record show that Exhibit Number 397 is the identical document which has been previously identified as Commission File Number 371 for our internal purposes.... And do the next fifteen sheets represent the rough draft which was later copied into the autopsy report which has hitherto been identified with an exhibit number?'

Commander Humes. 'That is correct, sir.'

While Specter said "copied into the autopsy report," it in fact *was* that autopsy report. It was typed, word for word, and was *not* "copied into."

The Commission's Report has no section on the autopsy. It reprints the autopsy protocols, Exhibits 387 and 391, in two separate volumes of the appendix. The supplemental report is the last thing in Volume

16, pages 987–89. The earlier report, the autopsy report itself, is part of Exhibit 397 in Volume 17, pages 29–48.

This testimony was under oath. Humes is explicit; he burned the first draft of his protocol, not his notes; and when he testified, he had his notes made during the autopsy examination in his hands.

Humes was also under oath when he testified before the House Committee on Assassinations. After the narration by general counsel G. Robert Blakey, he was questioned by assistant counsel Gary T. Cornwell. Humes had told him that the prosectors had decided that "three people couldn't write the report simultaneously, so [he] assumed the responsibility for writing the report, which [he] began about eleven o'clock in the evening of Saturday, November 23, . . . and worked on it until three or four o'clock in the morning of Sunday the 24th'' [JFK Volume I, page 330].

Cornwell asked if he had "any notes or records at that point as to the exact location of the—" when, although Cornwell clearly had something else in mind, Humes interrupted him to testify, "I had the draft notes which we had prepared in the autopsy room, which I copied."

Cornwell first returned to the question Humes had interrupted and then asked, "[T]he notes are no longer in existence . . .?" Humes replied:

> The original notes, which were stained with the blood of our late President, I felt, were inappropriate to retain to turn into anyone in that condition. I felt that people with some peculiar ideas about the value of that type of material, they might fall into their hands. I sat down and word for word copied what I had on fresh paper.

"And then you destroyed them?" Cornwell repeated. Humes responded, "Destroyed the ones that were stained with the President's blood."

No interest at all in the destruction of evidence.

Or, in the alleged copies not existing, either.

If not an experienced prosecutor like Specter, Cornwell was a lawyer. He was regarded by the members of that committee and its dominating general counsel, G. Robert Blakey, as qualified to act as the committee's counsel in its public hearings that were broadcast coast-to-coast on TV and radio and covered by experienced Washington reporters.

Whatever his qualifications as a lawyer, Cornwell was not qualified to conduct that hearing if his preparations for it did not include familiarity with the Warren Commission's record. Yet he took testimony that directly contradicted the same man's testimony before the Warren Commission. Before the House Humes swore under the penalties of perjury that he had destroyed his notes because they were bloody, the same fairy tale with which he later conned the all too-willing Lundberg. But before Specter and the Warren Commission, where he was also subject to the penalties of perjury, Humes swore that what he destroyed was the first draft of his autopsy report and that he *then* held those very notes in his hands.

The Warren Commission's failure to publish Humes's notes was, in and of itself, a gross betrayal of national trust as well as a deliberate refusal to make the investigation ordered and expected of it. Based on prior experiences, I believe that the reason they were not published is because if they had been the Commission would not have been able to formalize its lone-assassin theory imposed upon it by FBI Director J. Edgar Hoover. Hoover had already gone public with it before the Commission was fully organized, boxing in the Commission.

(Because the matter was "material," the legal requirement for false swearing to be perjury, and because Humes swore in direct contradiction of himself, his swearing seems to be perjury.)

(For additional proof of Humes's false swearing to what was most material, his contacts with Dr. Malcolm Perry in Dallas, see the Afterword. The sworn-to information in it was kept secret until after this book was written.)

Chapter 12

To Set the Record Straight?

IN THE SPRING OF 1966, I BEGAN THE WORK ON *POST MORTEM* THAT would last almost a decade. The information from it in the preceding chapter is from the first of its three parts.

Its second part is devoted entirely to the panel of experts that the Department of Justice appointed in secrecy to evaluate and report on the autopsy protocol and the kept-secret pictures and X rays taken during the autopsy. There was no public knowledge of this secret panel or its secret report until it served the government's interest to disclose it. This is how it happened.

New Orleans District Attorney Jim Garrison had charged a prominent local businessman and author, Clay Shaw, with being part of a conspiracy to kill President Kennedy. Garrison filed suit in a local Washington, D. C., court to have the autopsy and other related evidence presented to the jury that would try Shaw. Judge Charles Halleck held a hearing in the lawsuit on the Friday in January 1969 before the Monday on which the New Orleans jury impaneling would begin.

I was the first person outside the government to see this report because I was an expert witness for Garrison's Washington lawyer, my friend Bernard "Bud" Fensterwald, Jr.

Quite improperly, the kind of dirty trick the government can get away with, the government had withheld this report and the motion it would argue, all the while planning to hand them to us in the courtroom the morning of the hearing, when it would be impossible to check or to analyze.

The night before the court date I met with Bud and his then-partner, William Ohlhausen, as well as Bud's associate who had not yet taken the District of Columbia bar examinations, Jim Lesar. (Jim later handled most of my many FOIA lawsuits.)

It was only then that we learned what the government had planned to surprise us with in court the next morning. The only reason it failed was because someone, who was deeply offended by the government's serious improprieties, had leaked a copy to Bud after the end of the working day. We had only the one set of legal arguments and the one of the panel report and related records. (All are in the appendix to part 2 of *Post Mortem,* pages 565 ff.)

In the morning we were met by Numa Bertel, an assistant New Orleans district attorney, and by a true eminence of forensic pathology, Dr. Cyril Wecht, Garrison's other expert witness. I gave Wecht our sole copy of that secret panel report with my annotations and explained briefly what it did, how it did it, where it was flawed and vulnerable, and how we could use it. His testimony was masterful, and it was on that basis that Garrison. Halleck ordered that the autopsy records and other official evidence Garrison sought, like the rifle, be made available to the Shaw jury. The government had its appeal ready and filed it immediately.

For his part the paranoid Garrison, having just won his lawsuit but not yet knowing it, announced that he was withdrawing from his *successful* effort to get this evidence shown to his jury because it was all, in his sick imagination, part of a CIA plot to wreck his "investigation"! And he did, blowing the only opportunity ever to have this basic evidence in the JFK case examined by experts and by lawyers before an impartial jury that had no government connections.

The CIA had no need to try to wreck Garrison's case, if it had that intent, because, as it turned out, he had no case at all. The jury returned with an unanimous "not guilty" verdict in less than an hour. And it was a jury that believed there had been a conspiracy to assassinate JFK.

The report of the Department of Justice's secretly convoked panel says it confirmed the autopsy protocol. But in fact, as is clear beyond any question at all, what it could not have avoided and included in its report utterly destroys the protocol.

Part 3 of *Post Mortem,* its longest part, includes some of the withheld evidence I was able to obtain by various means, none improper. The second and third of its fourteen chapters resume the account of my quest for the suppressed and destroyed autopsy evidence referred to in the preceding chapter of this book. They here are quoted as from a single chapter. The first of these two chapters explains how and why the autopsy came to be performed in a military hospital, with threats of court-martial to anyone who uttered a word about it. In the course of bringing to light some of what is not in the Warren Report and its twenty-six volumes of appendix, it also goes into some of the sycophantic literature, books in uncritical, unquestioning support of the Report.

Here again I use what was readily and publicly available to the *JAMA* gang of four if they had had any interest in full and honest reporting rather than propaganda only. At the same time this added use of *Post Mortem* also serves to draw together for the reader and for history what information was readily available relating to what this cabal was up to and thus compares what they concocted with the established facts of the assassination and its investigation.

The quotation below from *Post Mortem* begins with reference to Admiral George Burkley and explains why it was necessary to quote from the often undependable books by William Manchester and Jim Bishop, who had access to records and information denied those who did not support the official story. This included access to Burkley, who was not only the President's own physician but also the only medical man who was in both the Dallas emergency room and the Bethesda autopsy room. This should have made him a mandatory witness before the Warren Commission, but it didn't.

To quote William Manchester *(The Death of a President)* in a work like this is to cast swine before pearls. His is a work of unrivaled inaccuracy. Were Pulitzer or Nobel prizes to be awarded for conspicuous inaccuracy, Manchester would be without peer. Only were bad taste to enter into the weighing could he have a rival, Jim Bishop *(The Day Kennedy Was Shot)*.

In an era of commissioned and rewritten and simplified history, there is, unfortunately, no other choice, the assassinated President's physician not having been a witness before the successor President's Commission that brought us this definitive study, this Report to ask and answer all questions, this last word on how the President was cut down and all that is relevant to it, including how his corpse fell into the hands and under the scalpels of the military.

It is to Admiral George B. Burkley that *all* that is missing was delivered, *all* that was withheld from the Warren Commission was funneled.

Some of that is still missing. Some I have recaptured. And some makes no sense.

Burkley was a ranking military man and a ranking medical man.

Could there be better reasons for *not* calling him as a witness? Or a better one for giving him all that did not reach the Commission?

Or, one might ask, a better reason for wondering about the military and the autopsy, the military and a possible conspiracy? It is my resurrection of the first of those suppressed Burkley papers that I removed from the first part of this book for further effort. It and the results are here for the first time reported.

Not, I emphasize, found *anywhere or in any form in the Commission's* files, Report, or interests. Not even in its 'TOP SECRET' executive sessions, which I do have, from which even its staff was banned and denied access to the transcripts.

Thus it is that we are bankrupted into dependence upon Bishop and Manchester. So the reader can, after four years, better estimate that literary nightmare in which Washington became a rewritten Camelot, Manchester's [following] paragraphs are included:

The clutch of men standing around her emptied glass after glass, and in the staff cabin Kilduff was setting something of a record. Mac was drinking gin and tonic as though it were going out of style. He later calculated that between Dallas and Washington he consumed nearly two-thirds of a bottle of gin. Like the Abbe Sieyes, who regarded the Reign of Terror as something to live through, each of them was trying to survive the hideous ride, and if liquor would help they wanted it. Liquor didn't help. It didn't do anything. Nothing testifies more persuasively to the passengers' trauma than their astonishing immunity to alcohol. O'Donnell's instinct had been correct; in time of stress, when emotions have been ravaged and shredded, spirits are usually medicinal. Up in the control cabin Colonel Swindal, who couldn't touch anything now, was promising himself a tall jigger when he reached his MATS office at Andrews. He would keep that promise—and discover that it was like drinking tap water. Kilduff, having downed more than enough to anesthetize him, gave up in despair. He was still cold sober. And when

Ben Bradlee met Mrs. Kennedy and her escorts at Bethesda
Naval Hospital, he was outraged; from their conduct he assumed that no one had sense enough to give them something
to drink.

The decision to move to Bethesda was made by her. Dr.
Burkley, kneeling in the aisle, explained that because the
President had been murdered there would have to be an
autopsy. "Security reasons," he said, required that the hospital be military. The option lay between Bethesda and Walter Reed.

'Of course, the President was in the Navy,' he said softly.
'Of course,' said Jacqueline Kennedy. 'Bethesda.' It was
then that Godfrey left to place his exasperating call stipulat-
ing an ambulance.

'I'll stay with the President until he is back at the White
House,' Burkley promised, and he, too, left. (*The Death of a
President.* New York: Harper & Row, 1967, [pages 349–50].)

As befits Camelot, these are the one-name characters incompletely identified (and not Manchester's closest buddies):

Malcolm ["Mac"] Kilduff was assistant press secretary.

Kenneth O'Donnell was appointments secretary.

Colonel James Swindal was pilot of the President's 707, then
called *Air Force One.*

Brigadier General Godfrey McHugh was then the President's
Air Force Aide.

Andrews refers to the military airfield at Washington, Andrews
Air Force Base.

In Bishop's also-rancid rendering, here is how the same goose
fat comes out [*The Day Kennedy Was Shot.* New York: Funk &
Wagnalls, 1968, pages 274–75]:

General [Chester] Clifton asked Andrews to have a forklift
ready to carry the casket down the rear exit ... He also
phoned the Army's Walter Reed Hospital and said that the
autopsy would be performed there.

Dr. Burkley, standing alone, noticed that Mrs. Kennedy
was alone. He approached and, rather than bend down to
speak to her, dropped to his knees. It was a comical attitude
for the dignified admiral. He was at eye level with her and
said: "It's going to be necessary to take the President to a

hospital before he goes to the White House.'' She was in a
trance-like state, but the young lady came out of it quickly.
''Why?'' she said. The tone was sharp because she had had
her fill of hospitals and their cast-iron rules.

Burkley looked like a supplicant at prayer. ''The doctors
must remove the bullet,'' he said. ''The authorities must
know the type. It becomes evidence.'' Mrs. Kennedy could
understand the situation. The admiral did not use the word
autopsy, which entails evisceration and the removal of the
brain and other organs. She asked where the bullet could be
removed. Burkley said he had no preference although he
had. He was a United States Navy admiral, and Kennedy
had been a Navy lieutenant. ''For security reasons it should
be a military hospital,'' he said.

Mrs. Kennedy was prompted to say the right word.
''Bethesda,'' she said. The admiral was satisfied. He got off
his knees and went forward to the communications shack to
alert the Naval Hospital . . .

By all available versions, there was no doubt that, after the
corpse was removed illegally and with Washington's raw power
alone, none but some military establishment was ever considered
for the performance of the autopsy.

From these accounts we have agreement on two things that are
significant and may account for the inability of the Commission to
reach an acceptable conclusion (or at least provided it with a phony
basis for telling itself it could conclude only as it did). There was
never any question but that, for no reason whatsoever, no need of
any kind, the autopsy would be at a military hospital. It seems that
Admiral Burkley was responsible for the choice of Bethesda, where
only what could not and should not ever have happened anywhere
is exactly what did [*Post Mortem*, pages 239–41].

(This is still another reason why Burkley should have been called
as a witness by the Commission. He was not only the one medical
person who was in both the Dallas emergency room and the Bethesda
autopsy room, he is the one who arranged for the autopsy to be at
the Navy medical installation at Bethesda.)

There is another and potentially perhaps more significant consistency. To avoid the possibility of misleading the reader and mak-

ing what may not be an accurate record, it is necessary to return to the opening thought of this chapter, the undependability of the sources. Manchester, in particular, has accomplished the close to impossible, the absolute perfection in inaccuracy under conditions that make this accomplishment the very apotheosis of egregiousness. He was permitted, through Kennedy influence, to sit in on the Commission's secret sessions—and all but one were completely secret, one, when it was meaningless, partly open. He also had a private office, taxpayer-provided, in the National Archives, complete with cot. From the evidence of his book, he used it for no more than a pad and a base for the sleaziest plagiarism. Of what he reports, the one thing that can be accepted without qualm is that the President was dead. That conclusion did not require access to the secret, a taxpayer-provided private office in the archives, and Kennedy sponsorship. Bishop's concept of history and reporting is the ultimate in contempt for the reader and his intelligence. His work is the most commercially acceptable of literary scrimshaw.

Saying this is *not* to say that nothing they report *can* be truthful. If their record in some things is close enough to suggest they had identical sources or that there was copying, where there is accord it also can betoken that one confirms the other. Thus, without assuming it to be dependable, but recognizing if it is, there should be consideration of their consistency.

Burkley said the purpose of the autopsy was to remove and identify a bullet. Burkley was in the Dallas emergency room, saw, knew what had been observed, understood, and believed probable there. The nature and magnitude of the damage to the head eliminated all possibilities but one, that whatever caused it had exploded. There thus could be no expectation of recovering a bullet from the head.

Officialdom thus is hoist on its own evidentiary petard. Its explanation of the lack of mention of any wound in the back is that the body was not turned over in Dallas. Thus, the sole point from which a bullet *could* be recovered, from all official knowledge as of the time of the flight back to Washington, had to be of the wound in the *front* of the neck, meaning that this was a wound of entry.

With Oswald allegedly behind the President shooting at him, he could not, simultaneously, have been in the front. All contemporaneous accounts of this front-neck wound attributed it to a shot from the front. Officials did contort themselves to try and explain

Harold Weisberg

how Oswald could have hit the one target simultaneously from two opposite sides.

Long after completion of the autopsy, at the time of the December 5 official 'reconstruction' of the crime in Dallas, we have this explanation given to Joseph A. Loftus, whose story appears in *The New York Times* of the next day:

> One question was how the President could have received a bullet in the front . . . after his car had passed the building . . . One explanation from a competent source was that the President had turned to his right to wave and was struck at that moment.

'Competent source' here is one of the traditional euphemisms for an official who would not permit the use of his name. There were *no* others with any knowledge of the official reconstruction.

Dr. Humes is then quoted as saying 'he had been forbidden to talk,' which is [an] understatement of the truth.

What follows is partial explanation of how the knowledge could be controlled, how the press could have been foreclosed from any independent investigation. [The article continues:]

> Most private citizens who had cooperated with newsmen reporting the crime have refused to give further help after being interviewed by agents of the Federal Bureau of Investigation.
>
> So did all local officials.
>
> One high officer said he wished he could answer questions 'because it would save us a lot of work.'

So thoroughly did the FBI close *every* mouth that even the Secret Service was immediately frozen out, as I reported in *Whitewash II*.

This front-neck wound, never described as anything other than an unmistakable wound of entry until Arlen Specter went to work on it and the experts, is the rock on which the official 'solution' must founder, hence attention is called to these agreeing sources, that the purpose of the autopsy as explained to the distraught widow was to recover a bullet for identification, when the only possible point from which a bullet could be recovered was the front of the neck.

If we assume what it may not be safe to assume, that these literary schmalz-men are accurate, that Burkley swung the deal for Bethesda; and if we assume what without any question is true, that once the President was murdered, there was no question of 'security,' what grist for the conspiracy mill! An admiral talked the widow into the naval establishment in which everything wrong *did* happen and nothing right was possible—where the solution to this monstrous crime was immediately made close to an impossibility!

Need one know more to fret about the possibility of a military conspiracy?

Especially when the military then and there prevented the most essential examinations from being made?

Even more, when all those present were threatened with retaliation if they ever said a word?

Here, perhaps, there is a concept of 'security' but what a monstrous conspiracy that would have to conjure! Can this be possible—can this be conceived—in the United States of America in 1963?

On the point of 'security,' one of the knee-jerk irrationalities that have dominated American life for so many years, Burkley himself supports Manchester and Bishop. There is, dear reader, a Burkley file, and there is a Burkley report on these tragic events, written five days after Dallas. The original of his report is not in that file. Nor is a copy of it, with all those Xeroxes working overtime. What is filed is a retyped copy, seemingly edited, and that by a person not familiar with the White House, its personnel or operations. One clue is that '*Air Force One*' appears as '*Air Force "1."* '

As retyped, Burkley's is a nine-page statement. The rest of the Commission's once-secret Burkley file consists of thirty-four pages on which there is casual mention of his name, most often as riding in the ambulance to the hospital. There is *no* report of *any* interrogation of the President's physician by the Commission, Secret Service, or FBI. Only in retrospect, with an understanding that the purpose of the entire 'investigation' was to *avoid* fact and knowledge, can there be sense in the avoidance of questioning of the one medical man who had been in the Dallas emergency room and the Navy autopsy room—the *one* medical man present at *all* medical examinations of the corpse.

And thus it is that the nine-page statement by the President's own physician is the one source that reports least of a medical nature. From it one can assume that the real cause of death was complications following the ingrowth of a toenail. Those of a more conspiratorial bent might from it assume that the real cause of death was a tainted oyster, à la Harding.

Of what Burkley saw at the Dallas hospital? This is all save for a few words on the fruitless treatment?

> I immediately entered the room, went to the head of the table and viewed the President. It was evident that death was imminent and that he was in a hopeless condition (page 2).

Hence the basis for wondering whether oysters or toenails was the immediate cause of death. There is no mention of the visible wounds, the exploded head.

Here is the medical man most directly responsible for the President's health; he was there, at the crucial place, at the 'head of the table,' and he 'viewed the President.' What better reason for saying nothing about what he saw when, by the time he prepared this statement, that was already a swirling controversy? Of course, as the reader should also remember from part 1, by the time Burkley wrote this, the only man accused of the crime was safely dead, so why louse up this nice clean 'solution' with factual and detailed medical observation?

Now, this is not to suggest that the dashing admiral did not do his duty as he saw it, through Rudolf Friml's eyes.

On Mrs. Kennedy's 'desire to be in the room' where the Dallas doctors were working over the corpse. Burkley felt it was 'so right' for her to be in it rather than at the door to it that:

> I overrode the protests of some of the people in the room and brought Mrs. Kennedy inside the door where she stood, and with my arms protecting her, she momentarily rested her head on my shoulder (page 3).

Loyal servant, 'protecting' the poor widow from the great danger to her person from all those doctors, Secret Service, and FBI agents? From whom else could he have been 'protecting' her?

The admiral, from his own statement, was not without regard for his medico-legal responsibilities, for he describes what happened after the casket had been taken out of the emergency room:

> At this point I again examined the room, and they had cleaned the room. The roses which had been in the car with the President were in the wastebasket, however, and two roses which had broken off were lying on the floor. I picked them up and put them in my pocket . . . (page 5).

Thus, from two examinations of the room, the evidence rescued for the solution of the crime of the century, the character of which is completely undescribed by the man who 'viewed the head,' is, with the sensitivity of the poetic soul, not the roses from the wastebasket but two that had broken off. Concluding this paragraph, the admiral says that on the way to the plane:

> I then reached into my pocket and took out the roses I had gotten from the floor and gave them to Mrs. Kennedy stating what they were. She took them, put them in her jacket pocket, smiled, and thanked me (page 5).

Entirely consistent is the admiral's contributions to understanding of the crime from his observations at the Naval Hospital and in its autopsy room:

> The body was taken to the mortuary where I met it and observed the transfer to the table. The examination was performed by Commander Humes and members of his staff. Also present were Admiral Kenn[e]y, Admiral Galloway, and Captain Canada. General McHugh had remained in the vicinity of the President constantly throughout this time (page 7).

If the admiral provides no help in resolving possible conflict between tainted oysters, a possible complication from an ingrown toenail, and perhaps a black curse as the cause of death, it is not because he was unaware of the true nature of the real responsibilities of the physician to the President:

> I made numerous trips to the 17th floor for reassurance to those in that area—

(Reassurance? Was some magical power about to restore
life?)

> —and to supply them with some idea of the contemplated
> departure time. On one of these occasions, Mrs Kennedy
> spoke to me in the bedroom of the suite expressing her
> appreciation which was greatly valued by me and which I
> will long remember. The body of the President was fully
> clothed in a blue suit, white shirt, tie, socks, and shoes. His
> hair was combed in the usual fashion and his appearance in
> the casket gave no evidence of the injury he had received
> (pages 7–8).

This is one of the places in Burkley's statement that leads to
the belief it was edited. I have omitted nothing from this direct
quotation, beginning with 'the body was taken to the mortuary.'
The President goes, in this account, right from autopsy-table dissection to restoration of the body to 'usual fashion and appearance,' from the medical nakedness to beautiful, funeral garb, with
nothing in between save the visits to Mrs. Kennedy's tower room.

It would be a deception to lead the reader to believe Admiral
Burkley was incompetent in either career, medicine or military,
much as this, the only statement from him in the Warren Commission's file on him, indicates that he filled no more than a handle-
polishing, musical-comedy role in real life. There is every reason
to hold the contrary view, that as admiral and as doctor, George
G. Burkley knew his business. That this is the only statement from
him in the Commission's file can hardly be blamed on him. He
did not conduct the investigation, did not run the FBI or Secret
Service.

Unfortunately, because the President's physician was also a military man, it does tend to fuel conspiratorial suspicions. On how
the corpse got to the Naval Hospital, where the impossible did
happen, Burkley is not inconsistent with Manchester and Bishop,
both of whom can always use shoring up on what they present as
fact. He is just missing some of the details:

> During the course of the flight, determination of the imme-
> diate action on arrival in Washington was made to assure
> complete compliance with Mrs. Kennedy's wishes. I spoke
> to her while kneeling on the floor so I would be on the
> level of her face rather than leaning forward, and expressed

complete desire of all of us and especially of myself to comply with her wishes, stating that it was necessary that the President be taken to a hospital prior to going to the White House. She questioned why and I stated it must be determined, if possible, the type of bullet used and compare this with future material found. I stated frankly that I had no preference, that it could be any hospital, but that I did feel, if possible, it should be a military hospital for security reasons. The question was answered by her stating that she wanted the President taken to Bethesda Naval Hospital ... (page 6).

Viewed in the light of history, this limited representation of the many medico-legal purposes of an autopsy to identifying of a bullet is not without interest, nor is this senseless preoccupation with 'security' for a President already assassinated. What is interesting is the total absence of any fact about the evidence of the crime so well known to the President's own physician long before he wrote this 'report' which, assuredly, is without serious purposes. Unless one considers schmalz and mythology, sticky goo and that Camelot jazz, serious and of purpose when a president is murdered.

What Burkley knew—what was until now suppressed—is hardly encompassed by any designation as modest as 'national scandal.' It is in one of a series of items of evidence denied the Warren Commission itself that, after long effort, I was able to get.

Yes, dear reader and doubting Thomases, there *is* evidence that *was* denied the presidential Commission itself. Every one of the numerous items of this suppressed evidence that, after so many years, I have been able to obtain is exactly what every investigator, every lawyer, knows he must have. So the withholding from the Commission could not have been pulled off by the executive agencies without the complicity of the Commission and its staff. There is no reason not to wonder whether, in fact, someone on that body did not let it be known that it would be better for such unequivocal evidence not to reach the Commission.

There is no doubt about the Commission's duties and responsibilities, and there is unanimity in description of them and its power and authority. The language of Executive Order Number 11130 creating it directs and authorizes it 'to evaluate all the facts and circumstances' (R471). The White House release is almost identical, 'to study and report upon all facts and circumstances'

(R472). The opening paragraph of the Foreword of the Report (ix) concludes: 'The President directed the Commission to evaluate all the facts and circumstances surrounding the assassination . . .' And in Public Law 88–202 (R473–4), the Congress gave it all necessary powers. The first, that of subpoena, was given to the Commission or any authorized member 'requiring the attendance and testimony of witnesses and the production of any evidence that relates to any matter under investigation by the Commission.'

The Commission and its staff could not have been prevented from having this suppressed evidence had they desired it. But had this Commission had what will follow, it could never have issued the Report it was so clearly understood it would write before it began its work, before it made any investigation, as the preinvestigation outline in part 1 so abundantly illustrates [*Post Mortem,* pages 241–45].

[This refers to pages 111–12, which states that the Commission's early outline of its work included the conclusions it would reach *before it began its investigation,* and to a facsimile reproduction of this outline on pages 467–72 of *Post Mortem.*]

There is no reason not to pinpoint the primary responsibility. For the medical evidence, it is that of a man who is no stranger, that former and present prosecutor, Arlen Specter, an ambitious man well-schooled in the evidentiary requirements of murder investigations and prosecutions.

What I am about to disclose was *not* in the Commission's files. I have every still-existing paper of every one of all the appropriate files from which I shall quote, the production of which was, for me, at great effort and cost. I also have written assurances that here the official files are more like Mother Hubbard's than Earl Warren's—bare.

In the face of this suppression, there were may difficulties to be overcome in making it possible to persuade the production of the missing evidence. I could not steal from hidden, locked safes, nor could I club recalcitrant public officials into proper behavior. Persuasion was my only possible means.

One problem was the law. Until July 4, 1967, under then-existing law, the government could invoke any kind of fancied excuse, with no requirement to disclose it, allege what was then called 'good cause' or 'the national interest,' and send citizens packing. Then a new law, Public Law 89–487, was enacted.** It was signed by President Johnson a year to the day before its effective date. Even that President could not have been more glowing in his rhetorical exultation over the freedoms to be bestowed by this law which his and the successor administration began flaunting at the moment of self-glorification and have without end thereafter.

I really believed the National Archives was the repository of the most sacred objects in our national heritage and that it was run by scholars with nonpolitical, scholarly purposes and interests and for the benefit of the people. I was trusting—and foolish—enough to say so on coast-to-coast TV.

Following earlier verbal efforts, on May 23, 1966, when only *Whitewash* and a little-known other book (Sylvan Fox's *The Unanswered Questions About President Kennedy's Assassination*) had been published, I began a systematic written effort to gain access to all the 'autopsy or medical papers of any kind or description.' The file of subsequent correspondence is thicker by far than the manuscript of a large book.

And this is exclusive of court papers. In one suit, Civil Action Number 2569–70, the lower-court papers alone also are much longer than a long book.

[This is my FOIA suit for the results of the FBI's nonsecret testing over which the FOIA was amended in 1974 to open FBI, CIA, and similar files to FOIA requests.]

Even letters do make a kind of record for history, as some officials came to realize. Court records can and do document, and in this case it is of government falsification of the most incredible kind.

At first I believed the policy of the National Archives was to be helpful, genuinely helpful, and that what its staff could not provide just did not exist. It was a short honeymoon.

There is no longer room for doubt about the intended dishonesty of the Commission's Report as well as of its record. The Report is internally inconsistent. It is in violent disagreement with the

[**This footnote identifies the act pursuant to this law as the Freedom of Information Act, 5 U. S. C. 552.]

testimony upon which it is based. That testimony also contradicts itself, as it does its alleged documentary substantiation. And the most vital documentation, as I soon learned, was missing.

I knew the most important evidence, by any standard, from legal to literary, was suppressed and that, as soon as the material in the archives was accessible, I had superabundant confirmation.

Or, I knew from the first this was not a wild-goose chase. The only questions were, had it all been destroyed and could I get any or all of it?

There were many conferences, including with the archivists and their top assistants, as well as Marion Johnson, the man in immediate charge of this archive. They produced what can be expected from such conferences when suppression is the official policy, nothing but polite stalling and outright lies. Before long it was taking months to get answers to simple requests. Today some remain unanswered after more than four years.

Then, as I began to ferret through the unpublished files, interesting, important unpublished evidence came to light. Initially it had been expected that none of the Commission's files would be public. The political intolerability of this decision was apparent to the pros where it was not to the eminences, and the pros saw to it that under careful control some of the files would be available. This was not the most publicized fact in government. It was, in fact, little-known.

To this day, the existence of these autopsy notes is denied, although every source stipulates their existence, from Dr. Humes's Commission testimony to that of Dr. Finck in New Orleans (he expanded knowledge in admitting that *all* the autopsy doctors had made notes and he had turned in his before leaving) to Admiral Galloway's covering letter with which he sent them to the White House, and to Dr. Burkley's receipt for them from the Secret Service.

But after years of trying, and I mean 'years' literally, I have finally obtained some of this missing evidence. *After* July 6, 1966, certification by the archivist, then Dr. Robert H. Bahmer, that it was not in the Commission's files—*not one item of it.*

My first direct effort with the Secret Service also was on May 23, 1966. It drew no response from Director James J. Rowley. After a little more than a year, I renewed the correspondence, this time invoking the attorney general's executive order. Rowley insisted that 'the Secret Service never did withhold any evidence' from the Commission, subsequently amplified in a manner that can explain the absence from the Commission's files of what the Secret Service did have and the Commission should have: '. . . all the information available to the Secret Service relating to the assassination of President Kennedy was made available to the Warren Commission and its staff.' Based on those items of suppressed evidence where I can make an evaluation, I am prepared to believe that the Commission, or, more likely, some of the staff, declined to have what it did not use and was not in its files, not that Rowley hid it from them.

It was at this point that Thomas J. Kelley, by then promoted to assistant director in charge of Protective Research Service, took over the correspondence that grew to an extensive file.

Inherently writers make judgments, whether or not so realizing or intending. I prefer to make mine explicit. The Secret Service was part of a cover-up, the specific charge of my second book. It was silent when it should not have been, and it remains silent when the course of honor and really dedicated public service requires that it and its personnel speak out. However, when the pressures of the unprecedented situation, which would have required that a relatively minor agency set itself publicly against a clear federal policy determination as a substitute for fact and truth, and the adverse effects on employment and careers that would have been inevitable are considered, the silences can be understood, whether or not one agrees with the fact or the motivation. In various ways I did receive expressions of the deepest misgivings held by some of the agents through their relatives and friends.

The first thing I went after really made no great difference, but it had the advantage of letting the Secret Service know the act of coughing up need not be painful. A missing one of the original copies of the autopsy protocol thus was added to those estimated three hundred cubic feet. It was a redundancy, but it was also a precedent.

The first thing of real substance I was able to get, that which I first added to part 1 and then removed for further investigations, is Admiral Burkley's copies of the still-existing autopsy papers. These are the originals. The terrible blots on them include the President's body fluids. They are here reproduced from Xeroxes, not the color photographs I have. That the President bled once is too much. It is not necessary to show his blood.

However, when, finally, the Secret Service produced these papers, it did not come up with all of them. It, the Commission and Specter all managed the same omission, the first two pages of the

file, CD 371. One is the November 26, 1963, receipt the Secret
Service gave Admiral Burkley for eleven itemized pieces of evidence. The second is a November 25 letter from Admiral Galloway to Admiral Burkley. Reason for the remarkable consistency
in what is missing is not hard to find: Almost without exception,
the items were not in the Commission's files, in some cases are
still missing, and all raised substantial doubts about both the autopsy and the integrity with which it was performed and reported.

Of all these things, despite his contrary assurance that Exhibit
397 'is the identical document which has been previously identified as Commission Number 371' in the evidence Specter included
only a copy of the holograph of the autopsy, one of the typed
copies of it, the two November 24 certifications by Dr. Humes,
the body chart, and what with typical vagueness is made to appear
as something separate, the head sketch previously referred to. *This
is all,* as Volume 17 of the Warren Report shows.

The rest, 'memory-holed.'

I can now clear up a perhaps minor mystery. Regardless of
when he did it, and I emphasize that this is one of the many
points at which one must question Finck's evasiveness, that head
sketch is on the reverse side of the *original* of the body chart.
These forms are one long sheet of paper. It would thus seem to
be a sketch he made at the autopsy bench. And bearing on the
number of sheets of notes, that is but a *single* sheet. The *only* one
ever produced.

Two of the articles still missing need not greatly concern those
whose interest is establishing the truth about what happened and
exploring the nature of the investigation in its various forms. They
do, however, limn the thoughtful care with which everything was
preserved for investigation, for posterity. I have verbal and written
assurances that they have disappeared. They are the first item,
'One piece of bronze colored material inadvertently broken in
transit from casket in which body was brought from Dallas,' and
the fourth, 'One receipt dated Nov. 22, for bed sheet, surgical
drapes, and shroud used to cover body in transit.'

Why these things were permitted to disappear, why the name
of the maker of this November 22 receipt was avoided by Robert
Inman Bouck in preparing the receipt he gave Burkley, may remain among the minor continuing mysteries, none of which, I
hope all can agree, can be regarded as acceptable when the assassination of a president is 'investigated.'

At that time in 1967 other of the receipted evidence also was missing, I was likewise assured. In time I have been able to inspire sufficient official diligence to retrieve them from the memory-hole file that in this case did not bottom in an incinerator. We shall address them after considering this first resurrection.

It is the official White House copy of what the Commission designated as its File 371. The first thing in it, this Burkley receipt to Bouck, was omitted—meaning suppressed. Regardless of who did it, and that we have no way of knowing, the responsibility is Specter's. If, as is customary in such cases, the file the members were given is identical with what was published in the hearings, then the members did not know of this itemization of evidence in the Burkley receipt, although a copy was in the Commission's files, where I found it in early 1966. It is *not* in Exhibit 397, was *not* published by the Commission.

Examination of the listing provides immediate and obvious explanation for this omission, which must be regarded as not accidental but *deliberate. The first seven items were not in the Commission's files.* Of the others, parts of only three are, and the fourth was hidden.

Item two is described as 'One letter—Certificate of Death of John F. Kennedy—State of Texas—dated Nov. 22, 1963.' We have already examined a Texas certificate of death, part of an 'inquest' dated ten days before the assassination. But there is no such *letter.* And should it not be asked, how can an official inquiry into this death have published that verbal monstrosity of all those volumes without including *any* certificate of death?

There were at least two. The other, also missing, is the sixth item, 'An original and six pink copies of Certificate of Death (Nav. Med. N)' [*sic*].

In each case we shall come to a good reason, if 'good' is the word, for each omission.

Item three does not begin to describe what it covers, for in the end I also fished it out. The description read: 'One carbon of letter dated November 26 from Commanding Officer, U.S. Naval Medical School, concerning law and regulations regarding confidential nature of the events.' This threat of court-martial if those at the autopsy spoke to anyone is all-inclusive. It makes no exception for official investigations. So it includes orders not to talk to official investigators, under threat of court-martial if anyone does.

The fifth item covers and will be part of a scandal that will not rest in perpetuity. Phrased with inept bureaucratic evasiveness, it reads: 'One receipt dated Nov. 22, 1963, regarding a carton of photographic film undeveloped except for X rays, delivered to PRS for safekeeping.' This is the receipt Roy Kellerman gave for what was represented as, but was not, all the film. Ultimately I got this receipt, too. It is sufficient to prove that the missing X rays were not given to the Secret Service. 'PRS' is the 'Protective Research Service' of the Secret Service, the presidential-protection section.

How reminiscent that 'safekeeping' is of the biblical maiden's lament in the Song of Solomon: 'My mother's children made me the keeper of the vineyards, but mine own vineyard have I not kept.'

Seventh item is: 'One receipt from FBI for missile recovered during the examination of the body.' There is no evidence of or testimony about the recovery of a 'missile.'

The Commission did have an edited version of the eighth item, described as 'One letter from University of Texas South West Medical School including report from Dr. [Kemp] Clark and summary of their findings of treatment and examination of the President in the Dallas County Hospital. Said letter of transmittal states that three carbon copies have been retained in that area.' [*sic*].

That edited version is in CD 392. It is in the Report as the first thing in Appendix VIII, the so-called medical appendix (pages 516–46). Because it is reproduced in facsimile, it is surprising that the diligent press did not note as I immediately did (*Whitewash,* page 168) that the 'covering letter' is no such thing as published but is, rather, two paragraphs, entirely unidentified and unsigned, and without subtlety cut out of something also not identified. Even the size of the typing is different from that of the following two pages headed SUMMARY.

Next is 'One copy of autopsy report and notes of the examining doctor which is described in letter of transmittal Nov. 25, 1963 by Dr. Galloway.'

That letter by Admiral Galloway is the second page of CD 371. It is not as described and, naturally, was also not published or included in that 'identical' Exhibit 397.

For some reason, an unknown somebody marked both margins at this item on the original. Perhaps because it includes what is missing still, 'notes of the examining doctor.'

'Transmittal letter and seven copies of the above item (autopsy report)', the next listing, also is missing, although at least some of the copies had to have reached somebody.

And the last is that suppressed authorization for the autopsy signed by Robert Kennedy that I had earlier obtained. All but a single misfiled copy, the one I did find, had been destroyed or removed or suppressed from every one of the many 'autopsy' files, although the initial requirement of any autopsy.

Of the many existing self-descriptions of the official investigation as at best a fraud and at worst a conspiracy, this is one of the most damning, the first itemization of the best official evidence of the crime, most of it withheld from the Commission, which *did* know of its existence and made *no* effort to obtain and consider it, permitting it—*knowingly* permitting it—to be suppressed. And what of that evidence? Not one item in the list without taint and almost all missing—suppressed until after I spent years of the most disagreeable labor, persisting, arguing, and ultimately, threatening legal action, some of it was finally given to me.

Can there be a more frightening self-description of that of which officialdom is capable? And of all the stifled voices, muted for undisturbed employment, or perhaps, from fear—is not this silence an awful crime in itself?

With this the official record when a president is murdered, of what is officialdom not capable? Who can expect to enjoy any rights, can consider he can live without any fear of what officials can do to him? [*Post Mortem,* pages 245–51]

Chapter 13

If It Isn't Written Down, It Wasn't Done

THE NARRATIVE ACCOUNT OF MY INVESTIGATION, WHAT IT DISCLOSED and of official impediments it had to overcome, continues in the next chapter of *Post Mortem.* Here again it contains information that two of *JAMA*'s gang of four were well aware of and withheld from the two who were not aware of it.

Today the destruction of the autopsy protocol should be considered in the light of the expert opinion of Mrs. Elizabeth Neichter, experienced professional medical records consultant. At the time I wrote *Post Mortem,* I did not have this expertise available to me. She said, "the rule of thumb for all medical records is—if it isn't written down it wasn't done" and "it is unacceptable to revise originals . . . or to destroy them for any reason."

Despite this standard Humes et al. did destroy the original of the autopsy protocol, did revise it at least twice, changing its meaning, as we shall see, all with official approval. Could anything more strongly suggest a military conspiracy, with executive-agency involvement? In all the years of my inquiry into the assassination, that I think is not unfairly described as intensive, in all the hundreds of thousands of pages of withheld official records I rescued from their official oblivion, there is not a single explanation for the destruction of the autopsy protocol, no claim to any legitimate need for it. Yet it was done.

The *Post Mortem* narrative continues:

As delivered to the archives with a covering letter by Rowley, what I had decided to investigate further is described as:

Handwritten notes by Dr. J. J. Humes which include the holographic draft of the autopsy report; the autopsy description sheet;

133

two certificates dated November 24 by Dr. Humes (Commission Exhibit 397); and the official autopsy report (Commission Exhibit 387).

The self-serving comment that follows is both accurate and deceptive:

> Copies of these documents, as you know, were furnished to the President's Commission on the Assassination of President Kennedy and are Commission exhibits which have been widely reproduced.

Had it been Rowley's intention to persuade scholars of the future that it would be a waste of time even to look at these seeming duplications of the published, he could not have phrased it better. But, the very opening sentence of his letter makes all of this false and dishonest. It refers to 'the following *original documents* . . .' (emphasis added), and the Commission *never* had copies of these 'original documents,' which are *different* from the copies the Commission did have, those made from *copies*, not the originals.

I had no trouble getting a Xerox of what Rowley then gave the archives under my persistent prodding. But it was some time before, by accident, I located the actual originals. Had I not been lulled by Rowley's clever phrasing, this would not have been the case, for what was added to his attached receipt should have led me to it.

For some reason not immediately apparent, this required two *different* receipts. And, again without explanation, the receipts for this imperishable national treasure are not signed by the archivist or his numerous top assistants who do act in his name, nor are they signed by the man in immediate charge of this archive, Marion Johnson. For this purpose, the lowest man on the bureaucratic totem pole, John F. Simmons, known as 'Mike,' Johnson's friendly and conscientious assistant, was used. No title is included. Neither receipt even says 'National Archives.'

The first is on a Secret Service letterhead form used for communications to be filed by their file identification—not Rowley's letterhead. The second is a carbon copy of another receipt.

The first reads, 'Received from the United States Secret Service the following material—Commission Exhibit #387,' followed by this, indented: '(A) Original Autopsy Protocol dated 22 November 1963 signed by Cmdr. J. J. Humes—standard Form 503, six (6) pages. Countersigned by Cmdr. J. Thornton Boswell and Lt. Col. Pierre A. Finck' [*sic*]. (The supplemental autopsy report, forwarded by the Navy December 6, was not included.)

The second, a two-page work of propaganda and rather carefully drawn, not an objective receipt, was copied for me with 1–5/8 inches of the top of each page missing. (The same amount of copying was eliminated from Rowley's letter and the first receipt.) The bottom of what seems to be the seven capital letters possibly spelling RECEIPT barely shows at the top of the first. [Now about what was supplied to me:]

With regard to '(A),' that is *not* 'the original holographic draft of the Autopsy Protocol' for, as consultation with the cited source shows, it is the original of the *revision* of the 'draft' (2H373).

This misrepresentation may give even more point to the totally unnecessary fate of the original, the sworn word of then-Commander Humes from the same paragraph: 'That draft I personally burned in the fireplace of my recreation room.'

From Specter's and the Commission members' total lack of interest or reaction, no question being asked, no eyebrow raised—no consternation or concern—the proper place for the autopsy protocol of an assassinated President is a 'recreation room,' not a hospital, and the proper disposition is Orwell's, to be 'personally burned' by the prosecutor. Sure as hell, *that* burned draft, the *original* that was *not* destroyed until it was known that there would be *no* trial, Oswald also having been put away, is not going to be quoted now by some devil like me loving scripture!

The reader might want to consider why some unnamed bureaucrat had to lie. Why any lie is necessary or acceptable about anything connected with the assassination of a president or its investigation.

(In this, Simmons is innocent, for the nature of his multitudinous duties precluded his having made the study of this verbal enormity that I have. That cannot be true of the writer of this false, propagandizing 'receipt')

This is not the only lie—should one mince words on such a subject?—in this paragraph. The parenthetical conclusion is deliberately false. It is not '*these* sixteen (16) pages' that are on 'pages 29 through 44, Volume XVII' of the hearings. Had they been, the international uproar would still be echoing after seven years. Shortly the difference will become apparent.

Nor is '(B)' not similarly false. This is *not* the same 'Original Autopsy Descriptive Sheet' that is 'on pages 45 and 46, Volume

XVII' of the hearings. The words 'autopsy descriptive sheet' are *not* on page 373 or anywhere else in Humes's testimony. Nor can these possibly be that for which I had for so long made repeated requests, *all* of the 'notes actually made in the room where the examination was taking place.' We have not only [Lieutenant] Colonel Finck's sworn word that he, personally, made notes and handed them in before he left and that all three doctors made notes on pieces of paper. Moreover, on the page prior to that cited in the deceptive argument, hardly appropriate in what is guised as no more than a 'receipt,' Humes had sworn, in describing what he held in his hand, *not* an 'autopsy descriptive sheet' nor 'Form NMS Path,' both being headings on that required Navy Medical Service form, nor did he cite the identification of the autopsy by the number that appears on it, 'A 63 #272.' He could not identify it by the name of the President, for this autopsy was performed with such tender care, with such regard for precision, history, and the legal aspects of medicine, that the blanks required to be filled in for a number of entries, including name, date, and hour expired, diagnosis and physical description, are all blank.

Humes's under-oath description of what he held, what was then and there placed into evidence, is 'these are various notes in long-hand, or copies, rather, of various notes in longhand made by myself, in part during the performance of the examination of the late President and in part after the examination when I was preparing to have a typewritten report made.'

However his cited testimony from page 373 is interpreted—and it is hardly the function of simply a receipt to make interpretations—it cannot be limited to this autopsy descriptive sheet, for in the testimony he describes handwriting that 'in some instances is not my own.' Humes is blessed (as I see it) with a distinctive, backhand style, and *none* of the entries—these áre not notes but entries on a form—is in his handwriting.

Besides, Boswell told reporter Richard Levine that he had filled out this form. From the original I now have, it is easily discernible that two different implements were used, one by Finck and one by Boswell. In neither case is it by Humes, so *any* notes he made 'during the performance of the examination of the late President' *are not here—or anywhere else.*

The archivist of the United States, the custodian of the most precious documents in our national heritage, kept busy writing lies to me and arguing. Instead he should have been searching the files and demanding those he did not have from those who did, which is his official responsibility. I decided to do what had not been done: Compare this lie, earlier written to me, that these are all the notes and those to the holding of which Humes swore, with the finished report itself, to see if it has descriptions or measurements not in this autopsy descriptive sheet. To assure true impartiality, I asked Howard Roffman, a brilliant young student, then in high school and writing his own book on this assassination, to make this comparison for me. He found, as I was confident had to be the case, what is required for even a lousy pretense of medico-legal science such as this, much more than is noted on this single sheet. (The second side holds only four brief notations and five measurements, all related to only the head.)

From my own checking in 1964, I knew the autopsy report held facts not contained *anywhere* in any of the published evidence. As soon as the twenty-six volumes became available, my wife and I had made a word-by-word comparison of the fifteen pages of holograph with the typed autopsy report and had found substantive changes, *some to diametric opposites.* So I knew in advance what Howard's study would show. What surprised me is the extent, much greater even than I had expected.

What I asked of Howard was much work. He compared everything available: the two versions of the autopsy report; the notes printed in CE397, said to be all the notes, whereas none are properly described as notes and none meet Finck's New Orleans descriptions of those all the doctors made; and the reports of the two panels made public by the Department of Justice so long after they were completed and when the government was in distress. These two panels, of course, conducted their studies long after the Report was issued and from the existing evidence only. The 1968 panel report included an inventory of what it examined. Both panels are silent on the contradictions and omissions. This silence is a remarkable self-exposure and a self-condemnation, an attack on the integrity of both panels and of the Department of Justice that no writer, using passionate language, can approximate.

Howard's factual listing is fifteen single-spaced typewritten pages. To make this study and comparison, he isolated every single statement of fact in the typed autopsy report. He then sought for each fact, or even an approximation of it, in each of the other sources, the so-called notes. This leaning over backwards is an effort to be as fair as possible by including all that any carping critic might later complain [was omitted]. However, it is obvious, with only these so-called notes as sources, unless some notes had been destroyed at some point, there could have been no other sources for the two much later panels to draw upon.

Howard's study shows a statement of a total of eighty-eight facts. Of these, *only twenty-four are in the 'notes.' Sixty-four statements of facts in the autopsy report are not in any of these 'notes'!*

Because this is the autopsy of a president, because the credibility of the official Report on his assassination, that of all the Commission and its staff, the Department of Justice, all those medico-legal eminences, and indeed, of the military, too, hangs on this alone, let me express these shocking figures in two other ways. Of the 'facts' stated in the autopsy report, *almost three out of four have no existing source.* The percentage is just under 73–72.7 percent.

Or, putting it the other way, of what is represented as fact in this autopsy report, only *one in four exists in any existing written source!*

It can, of course, be argued that some of the doctors might have remembered the color of the President's eyes and hair. This cannot be true in most cases, for of these unrecorded sixty-four facts, fifty include or are solely of physical characteristics. Most of these are of parts of the body and their condition. Often they relate to the bullet wounds.

And of these, the startling number of fifteen involve numbers and figures. These are essentials it just cannot be believed the doctors carried in their heads. Many of these are of measurements referring directly to the wounds—their size, their distances from other parts of the body.

This is complex data, often of minute measurements, and those had to have been the most emotional days in the lives of all the doctors. They simply could not have carried all this in their heads.

And more incredible still, a third of this number is of cases where figures are used *that conflict with the final autopsy report!* These range from what Howard, more tolerant than I, regards as possible 'minor misquoting'—I regard *no* error in this autopsy as tolerable—to the size of the missing piece of scalp. The figure of the report, 13 cm, exists *nowhere* in *any* notes and actually appears to be in contradiction to what is recorded in them.

This is but a brief summary of the great labor Howard undertook for me, countless hours of detailed work.

No matter how generously one regards it, no matter how much apologists may prefer to discount, I do not believe that reasonable men can conceive that three-quarters of the fact of anything as complicated as the autopsy performed on a human body, especially that of a president, can possibly have been reported except from written notes.

They no longer exist.

The destruction of such records of any murder, particularly the assassination of a president, and false swearing about it or them, are criminal. When the government that has to be the prosecutor and alone can make the charges is itself criminally responsible, neither charging nor prosecution is likely. However, I have repeatedly invited those I accuse to file charges against me and seek a judicial determination of fact. None has—or will.

'(C)' is relatively innocuous—that is, compared with the foregoing only. It is sufficiently serious to deceive in this affair. It is undoubtedly true that, as Humes certified, he had turned in to Captain J. H. Stover everything he had not already destroyed. Stover's countersigning means no more than that Humes had done this. It does not mean that neither he nor his command nor the Navy then had no other records. Somebody had the missing X rays. Again this is not identical with what is 'on page 47, Volume XVII' of the hearings. There is no deviation. '(D)' is identically represented as exactly what is 'on page 48.' Whoever cooked up this deliberate deceit sought to hide behind the use of 'portrayed.' That is a semantic 'Emperor's clothes' for there is a vital difference, a difference not simply that Humes and the Commission had Xeroxes, whereas what I had finally forced out of suppression in secret files are the originals.

The difference is what was added, *by Admiral Burkley, by hand, to each.**

The Warren Report and Burkley's notations cannot coexist. It is impossible.

Thus, this Commission, all of its members were lawyers, including the Chief Justice, and its competent, large legal staff, dominated and headed by the former solicitor general of the United States, the government's lawyer, went out of their way to accept what should not have been accepted in the most blighted backland jerkwater court: secondhand evidence when

*See *Post Mortem* page 262. What distinguishes this and what follows from all other copies of all versions in all files and published—what was so carefully suppressed—is Burkley's personal, handwritten approval.

the originals were available, were known to be available, and could have been obtained for a phone call.

There is no other reason for avoiding the originals, no other reason for their being hidden, none for its taking so much dogged effort to obtain them.

Now that I do have them—color pictures and Xeroxes, both made from originals—let us consider them in the sequence of the longer receipt. Let us see what they say, understand what this means.

First is the original of Humes's rewritten draft of the autopsy report, the closest thing to the original, that having been burned, not in innocence but *after* it was known that, with the only accused himself assassinated, there would be no court in which any evidence had to be produced and subjected to cross-examination.

Admiral Burkley countersigned and approved the handwritten autopsy report, as he also approved the retyped version. To be certain that there was no question, he initialed the first page, 'GGB,' as he did the last. Humes, it will be remembered, personally delivered everything to Burkley, and Burkley had been with the body when it was being treated and examined in Dallas and during the autopsy in Bethesda, the one medical man in the world and, except for a few Secret Service men, the *only* man in the world of whom this is true.

The *substantive* changes, changes of fact, not opinion—not all of those made after Oswald was killed but only those made in what was not removed from the draft that was burned—are incredible and *all*, we now for the first time know, were *approved by the President's own physician!* The unknown, the conjectured and invented, none of which belong in a medico-legal document, least of all in the autopsy report on a president, they also were approved. To cite what in context is minor but in fact is major, the first page is typical. Where, in his version, Humes had the car 'moving at approximately twenty miles per hour,' something neither he nor anyone else knew or could know and twice as fast as it was, that was crossed out and changed to 'moving at a slow rate of speed,' something none of the signatories had any way of knowing and certainly not by their own observation. Also unknown to the signatories, the last sentence began with an argument, not fact: 'Three shots were heard and the President fell face down to the floor of the vehicle.' This was completely false, a fabrication. The 'correction' was no less an invention, an invention entirely consistent with every argument and change in the autopsy, to make it seem that all the shots had come from the back and that the accused Oswald was the lone assassin. After this change, the autopsy report reads: "Three shots were heard and the President fell *forward*' [Emphasis added].

He did not.

'Puncture' in describing the nonfatal bullet wound means entrance. It had been used repeatedly in what survived the recreation room burning. In every case but one, it was removed, including those cases where, without doubt, it was meant. One example is on page 4, a point on which the entire autopsy, the entire 'solution' to the crime and the Warren Report itself all hang. The last full sentence, in describing what has come to be known as the rear, nonfatal wound, said to have been in the neck, the description of 'a 7×4 mm oval puncture wound,' with the elimination of 'puncture,' became 'a 7×4 mm wound.'

On page 7, in a single sentence where there are *seven changes of fact about the head wound,* the description 'puncture' is *twice* eliminated, although in later testimony it was, with Specter's deftness in the absence of any adversary, reintroduced. In one of these cases nothing replaced it; in the other, a word that is anything but synonymous, 'lacerated.' And, on pages 8 and 9, 'puncture' is stricken through, replaced by nothing on page 8 and by 'occipital,' which is entirely different, on page 9.

On the other side of the same coin, where the wound that it was later decided, contrary to the existing evidence, had to be an exit wound or there could be no single-assassin, nonconspiracy Report, the qualification 'presumably' was inserted on pages 8, 9, and 10.

Other factual changes are to *opposites.* One of the most readily comprehended is on page 5, where 'left' was changed to 'right.' On page 14, where the rear wound was related to the plane of the body and thus not dependent upon what was un-

known, the position of the body, the change was to what
amounts to a deliberate, unscientific and unwarranted attempt
to frame the accused and the solution. As altered, this reads:
'The projectiles were fired from a point behind and somewhat
above the level of the deceased.' Without knowing the position
of the body in three different ways, this could not be said. Was
the President at the time of each shot vertical, bolt erect? Was
he turned in either direction from at right angles to the length
of the car? Or, was he, while erect in a vertical plane as compared with the car or the seat, leaning to either side?

At best, these changes reflect such uncertainty as to disqualify
the autopsy report in its entirety. At worst, they are, because
agreed to by so many, a deliberate conspiracy to frame the then-
dead accused, to corrupt history, and to vindicate any assassin
or assassins.

But what is most incredible of all in this rewriting of fact to
ordain falsehood as truth is a failure by all. Neither Admiral
Galloway, who dominated and ordered changes made, nor Admiral Burkley, who was everywhere and approved, nor any of
the three surgeons themselves caught the one slip-up. *Five* medical military officers are involved in this, each culpably.

In a single place they neglected to murder truth. In a single
place an accurate description of a wound remained. And say
what they now may or will, it is an uncontested fact that all
five did agree on it. It is the one vital fact to escape that recreation room assassination of the medical truth.

The fourth paragraph of the holographic autopsy report
begins:

> Dr. Perry noted the massive wound of the head and second
> *puncture* wound of the low anterior neck in approximately
> the midline [Emphasis added].

This is entirely in accord with everything, fact and all the initial
medical statements, *all* of which had the President shot in the
front of the neck.

There is *no* change here in the *holograph.* Nobody, at any
time—Humes or anyone else—noted *any* alteration here in what
he wrote on his blue-lined, white, letter-sized pad.

But somebody in the military's butcher shop of history at Bethesda did eliminate this truth before the report was typed. In the typed version, the word 'puncture' was eliminated. In its stead there appears 'much smaller.' The dramatic representation, that the Dallas doctors said the President had been shot from the *front,* fell victim to those in the military determined to rewrite what happened when the President was gunned down in cold blood in broad daylight on the streets of a major American city.

If we today cannot pinpoint what person did this, absent confession, there is no possibility of doubt about where it was done. All the evidence is that Humes turned in his draft to his superiors at Bethesda, and that all of this was supervised by the commander of that military installation, Admiral Galloway.

And this, too, was verified by another admiral, the President's personal physician. Burkley approved the original truth saying that the President's wound in the front of the neck was caused by a shot from the front, and he approved the mysterious change which attempts to hide this fact.

I have no doubt that Humes intended to change this. I do not know if he was ordered to, and, if so, by whom. But my first accusation of perjury, in *Whitewash,* is on this point and to this day remains undisputed.

The day *after* the autopsy examination, Humes called Perry twice. The Report acknowledges but a single call. Perry personally confirmed to me when I interviewed him that he had received two calls from Humes, both the same day. He had, prior to these calls, scheduled a press conference.

Perry is a man deserving of both pity and sympathy. He is friendly, personable, conscientious, and, without doubt, dedicated to his calling and justifiably proud of his skill in it. A bizarre touch in what he told me is that, although he knew the President to be irreversibly dead the moment he saw him, when he performed the surgical process then called a 'tracheotomy' and since retitled 'tracheostomy' he made it in the most cosmetic manner. Instead of the usual vertical incision, he made a transverse one, a cut from side to side. His purpose—and he had, he told me, done this several hundred times—was so that, upon healing, the incision would be made invisible by the natural folds of the skin.

But he was forced into perjurious testimony by national policy, his personal situation, and above all, by Arlen Specter.

As I have repeatedly charged, including in public appearances in Philadelphia announced to and covered by the press, Specter suborned perjury, a crime.

Knowing full well that Perry and the other quoted Dallas doctors had said immediately that the President had been shot from
the front—and that Oswald could not possibly have fired that shot,
proving there had been a conspiracy—Specter pretended to the
Commission that the TV tapes and radio recordings were not available (3H377 ff.). And he pretended there was no printed press at
all in the United States! In an embarrassed, bumbling, and hesitant
effort to circumvent this obstacle to the writing of the Report of
the predetermined conclusions, he said, for all the world, as though
he, not Perry, were the witness:

> We have been trying diligently to get the tape recordings
> of the television interviews, and we were unsuccessful . . .
> our efforts at CBS, NBC, and ABC and everywhere includ-
> ing New York, Dallas, and other cities were to no avail . . .
> The problem is they have not yet catalogued all the footage
> they have . . .

Picture of the American electronic media come apart, unable
to operate!

It is Specter's picture, not the reality, as I discovered later in
ransacking the files on this point, too. One inventory of one Dallas
station alone is more than one hundred pages long. And restricting
this solely to Dallas and TV, only one station, located outside of
Dallas, KTVT-TV, had no video tape. Three others in that area,
WFAA, WBAP, and KRLD, *all* offered to duplicate for the Commission *all* of their tapes. This is set forth in elaborate detail in
one of a number of Commission files on this subject, Number
962, which also suggests that the Commission had delayed its
inquiry for inventories, and so late, that some were about to be
erased for reuse.

Specter was not under oath, so he did not commit perjury. But
he lied in telling the members of the Commission that 'the problem
is they have not yet catalogued all the footage.' (And suppose,
were cataloguing the real question, that all but one of the stations
had catalogued, or 99 percent of the footage had been catalogued,
'*all* the footage' still would not have been, would it?) But the
Commission's needs and purposes did not require 'catalogues';
they required Perry's words, and they *then* were readily available,
including in the Commission's own files.

This is the way Specter 'gandy-danced' his way past the disaster
Perry presented. Before the Commission, he led Humes into testi-

fying to making but a *single* 'redundant' phone call to Perry (2H371). Questioned twice and separately (6H16 and 3H380, the earlier testimony in the later volume), Perry told Specter of *two*. He said of the second of these two calls Humes placed to him that 'he told me, of course, that he could not talk to me about any of it and asked that I keep it in confidence, which I did' and 'he advised me that he could not discuss with me the findings of the necropsy.' On all counts, according to other and probative testimony and what Perry told me, this is false.

There was no legal need for secrecy; only an urgent need for public information that was truthful. The entire world was in turmoil. Humes *did* 'discuss' with Perry 'the findings,' based on which, as Perry later told me, he knew the wound officially described as in the back of the President's neck was actually in his back. And, although he said he did not tell anyone, Perry had to and he did.

He did have an announced and scheduled press conference on the medical evidence for that very day, undoubtedly the real purpose of Humes's call. Had it been for information, he would have telephoned Perry the night before, while he was examining the body and could check it, not after the body had been surrendered and long after the embalming and reconstruction had been completed and the corpse was in the White House.

It is Dr. Kemp Clark who first pulled the plug on this perjury (6H23):

> Dr. Perry stated that he had talked to the Bethesda Naval Hospital on two occasions that morning and that he knew what the autopsy findings had shown and that he did not wish to be questioned by the press as he had been advised by Bethesda to confine his remarks to what he knew from having examined the President, and suggested that the major part of this press conference be conducted by me [*Post Mortem*, pages 252–60].

[Humes, under oath, had testified to only a single, late morning phone call to Perry. Perry and Dr. Kemp Clark, under oath, testified to two calls from Humes. Specter conducted the questionings before the Commission. He made no effort to reconcile the two versions, both under oath, and no member of the Commission did. Specter and all the Commissioners were lawyers and knew the significance of the contradiction in terms of the rest of Humes's testimony. William Manchester's semi-official *The Death of a President,* a work distinguished by its author's lack of interest in evidence and fact about the crime while devoting himself and his book to the tinsel as well as to the schmalz, gives the lie on this to Humes and significantly, to the charade he and Specter played.]

Bethesda's physicians had heard reports of Mac Perry's medical briefing of the press . . . an entrance wound in the throat. . . . They were positive that Perry had seen an exit wound. . . . Humes telephoned Perry in Dallas shortly after midnight. . . . [*The Death of a President.* New York: Harper & Row, 1967, pages 423–24]. Having already told the world that the President had been shot from the front, could Perry the next day say the opposite? Or can anyone blame him for going on an unannounced vacation— translation: into attempted hiding?

Clark, also under oath, named two other witnesses to this conversation. Need it be added that Specter and the Commission had no interest and questioned neither these two nor any others about it? These were the hospital administrator and Dr. George T. Shires, *both* of whom *Specter* interviewed on other matters.

So, especially with the reports that only one bullet was expected to be recovered from the body, and that possible only from the wound in the front of the neck, there is great point in Burkley's affirmation of Humes's quotation of Perry's statement that the anterior neck wound, which he did see clearly and through which he made the tracheostomy incision, was caused by a shot from the front.

It is doubtful if there ever has been any proceeding of the importance of this assassination investigation in which there was as much perjury, except for the Reichstag fire trial. And there the falsely accused was acquitted, not killed.

The difference between the original autopsy descriptive sheet that had been suppressed until I forced it out—that had never been seen by the Commission—is a difference that, were the official conclusions at all tenable, would in itself entirely destroy them.

The reader will recall that when I first published a copy of the Commission's copy, this exposure and reporter Richard Levine's needling led to the fantasyland 'explanation' that Boswell had merely been a bit careless in marking the back wound, never for a moment dreaming that in the autopsy of a president there is any need for care or accuracy. (What better qualification for a Navy chief of pathology?)

The wound *was* in the *back,* not the neck, as all official observers testified. Only when Specter went to work to rescript the assassination into a fake solution consistent with the official predetermination of what would be called truth and fact was there ever any question. Until then all the evidence was of a back wound. This includes Specter's own suppressed notes of his own interviews with the autopsy witnesses before their testimony.

Now we know that Admiral Burkley placed it there, too. And Burkley certainly knew. For the moment we shall restrict ourselves to this first rescue from oblivion. In the lower left-hand corner of the front of the form he wrote, 'Verified GGBurkley,' all run together.

He did not just initial it. He did not just sign his name. He used a word that cannot be fudged as Boswell fooled the press. The meaning of 'verified' is not subject to argument. Webster could not be more precise and limiting:

1. To prove to be true; to conform; substantiate. 2. To check or test the accuracy or exactness of. 3. To authenticate; specif., *Law,* to confirm or substantiate by oath or proof; also to add a verification ...

Those who instinctively grasp at evidentiary straws to support the official mythology would do well to restrain themselves, for there will be more on this point in what follows. I here make this comment so that those who think they see invisible straws and grab at them do not imagine that a medical man who rises to be an admiral in the Navy and physician to the President does not know the meaning of simple words and here, for no reason at all, just got 'careless' and threw in an extra and a wrong word.

Burkley's additions to both of the originals of the certifications are word for word identical.

The one that says Humes turned in 'all working papers associated with' the autopsy, including the 'autopsy notes,' at 5 P.M., Burkley endorsed with 'Accepted and approved this date,' signing it with his full name, 'George G. Burkley,' and as 'Rear Adm MC USN Physician to the President.'*

*Cites page 526 of *Post Mortem,* on which this is reproduced from the original in facsimile. Galloway's words are, ''Transmitted herewith by hand is the sole remaining copy (number eight) of the completed protocol in the case of John F. Kennedy. Attached are the work papers used by the prosector and his assistant.''

This constitutes Burkley's certification that those now-missing autopsy notes at that moment did exist and, when added to the receipt and letter so carefully omitted by Specter in publishing File 371 as Exhibit 397, were in his possession. That receipt, the item marked in both margins and the only item in it marked in any way, reads, 'One copy of autopsy report and notes of the examining doctor which is described in letter of transmittal Nov. 25, 1963 by Dr. Galloway.' And the next day Burkley gave all these items to the Secret Service, which gave him the receipt from which I have quoted.

When Burkley noted 'accepted and approved' to Humes's other certification, what he actually did is mind-boggling. This admiral 'accepted and approved' what Humes admitted, 'that I have destroyed by burning' his first draft of the autopsy report on the President!**

Aside from what I have already established beyond peradventure, that this revision and conflagration was not until *after* Humes and everyone else knew that nobody would have to face examination of his records and cross-examination by defense counsel in a trial of Oswald, by then safely murdered, can anyone conceive of any *good* reason for the destruction of *any* record in a crime of this nature? Or its acceptance and approval by the President's physician—an admiral?

When the nature of the changes now known to have been made are considered, and with the until-now suppressed confirmation that the Commission's medical evidence in its entirety is dubious and in all essential elements false, can even the most tolerant put any but the most disturbing interpretation on, first, the unpunished destruction of imperishable, irreplaceable evidence by a man qualified in forensic pathology and, second, the unhesitating acceptance and approval by the physician to the President himself?

When all the experts were military men, when all civilians were kept out of the autopsy room by military guard, when the military destroyed the evidence and the military approved the

---

**Cites page 523 of *Post Mortem*, on which this is reproduced from the original in facsimile.

destruction of the evidence, and when this new evidence proves the testimony about the wounds was perjurious, criminal, and all of this criminality, this false swearing, was also by the military, is not a question of some kind of military conspiracy unavoidable?

And must I not again ask, is there anything like this in our history or that of any other land considering itself free and civilized? [*Post Mortem,* pages 260–62]

Chapter 14

JAMA's Four

HUMES AND BOSWELL WERE VERY SENSITIVE TO SUGGESTIONS THAT what they could say and do was subject to military control. That this was said in Oliver Stone's movie *JFK* was, according to Breo, why they agreed to the interviews, having refused Lundberg's requests for seven years: "To set the record straight, they agreed to relive for *JAMA* their act of Friday, November 22, 1963."

Breo quoted Humes as saying, "I was in charge of the autopsy—period. Nobody tried to interfere—make that perfectly clear."

At another point, where he recounted the beginning of the autopsy examination, what Breo wrote has this heading: "Humes was in total charge." Humes said, "There was no interference with our autopsy, and there was no conspiracy to suppress the findings."

Boswell said, "Nobody tried to interfere and we were able to focus on the matter at hand." Boswell also said, "We documented our findings in spades. It's all there in the records. And Jim is not the kind of guy anybody pushes around."

Referring to having seen a photographer outside the morgue before the body arrived, Humes said, of the man in uniform he asked to get rid of the photographer, "The man who said he was some general representing the military section of the District of Columbia . . ." Under the heading "No generals in the morgue," *JAMA* continued, "As the general remained *outside* [his emphasis]." Major General Philip C. Wehle, commanding general of the Army's Military District of Washington, was very much *in* the autopsy room.

In a paragraph that Breo began by saying that while Admiral Burkley "stood by their side, a team of 10" began what turned into a four-hour autopsy examination, he quoted Humes as saying, "I was

in charge from start to finish and there was no interference—zero.''
He then listed his assistants of all ranks and functions.

In this same section of his article, headed, ''No generals in the
morgue,'' Breo quoted Humes as saying, ''Nobody made any decisions in the morgue except ME [emphasis *JAMA*'s]. Nobody distracted or influenced me in any way, shape or form.''

A reference to top brass leads into what they said to deprecate
Finck:

> He [Humes] dispels another myth—that the morgue was con-
> trolled by generals and other brass in uniform. 'The President's
> military aides from the Air Force, Army, and Navy were all pres-
> ent,' Humes says, 'and they were all in dress uniforms, but they
> were not generals and their influence on the autopsy was zero.
> The only other high-ranking officer was Admiral Burkley and he
> left shortly after the autopsy began to join Jackie and Bobby
> Kennedy upstairs.'

He forgot to mention Admiral Galloway, who remained throughout
the autopsy. Or, how he could have gotten messages allegedly from
the Kennedys via Burkley if Burkley did not return? The FBI report
on the autopsy from its two agents who were there, Francis X.
O'Neill and James W. Sibert, list both Galloway and Burkley as
''attending'' the autopsy.

Although Humes said they were ''not generals,'' JFK's air aide,
Godfrey McHugh, was a general, and he remained with the body
from the time it was placed on *Air Force One*.

The alleged ''myth'' is misstated. It was not that the top brass
controlled the morgue. It was that they controlled the autopsy and
what the autopsy report said.

Breo, quoting Humes and Boswell, explained how Finck came to
be involved. Humes said that at ''about'' the time he first got inside
the hospital late that afternoon, ''I also received a phone call from
Dr. Bruce Smith, the deputy director of the Armed Forces Institute
of Pathology [AFIP], offering me whatever help I might need. Bruce
was a friend and I thanked him saying I would call later if I
needed help.''

Breo continued:

While Humes was preparing for his dinner party ... Boswell had been at the hospital going over autopsy slides with pathology residents. He recalls, 'Early in the afternoon we received a call from Dr. Bruce Smith from AFIP, saying, 'The President's body is on its way to Bethesda for an autopsy.' I argued, 'That's stupid. The autopsy should be done at AFIP' [which was located five miles away at the Walter Reed Army Medical Center]. After all, the AFIP was the apex of military pathology and, perhaps, world pathology. I was told 'That's the way it is. Admiral Burkley, the [President's personal physician] wants Bethesda.' Apparently Admiral Burkley called the AFIP from *Air Force One* en route from Dallas.'

With the decision by Mrs. Kennedy that the autopsy be at Bethesda, as Burkley had hinted strongly to her, not made until about 4 P.M., if Dr. Smith phoned Bethesda "*early* in the afternoon," is that more fuel for believing there had been a military conspiracy. Adding to this is that the AFIP told Boswell that Burkley "wants Bethesda." Was that before he got Mrs. Kennedy to designate Bethesda?

Two pages later Breo returned to AFIP and to Finck by quoting Humes as having phoned Dr. Smith after he saw the body. Then Smith "decided to make available Dr. Pierre A. Finck, who was AFIP's expert in ballistics." (Finck's expertise was in fact *wounds* ballistics, not ballistics. He headed the Wounds Ballistics Branch there.) "I had never before met Dr. Finck, who arrived about 9:15 P.M."

"Finck, a shy, retiring man who had been educated in Europe, was an army colonel ..." The words are Breo's. He gave no source for making a milquetoast of Finck.

After several more pages Breo returned to Finck again and to the reason for deprecating him. Under the heading, "The Garrison prosecution," he wrote:

The next confirmation (allegedly of the autopsy protocol) came in 1969 in New Orleans when Pierre Finck was subpoenaed to testify at the trial of Clay Shaw, as part of District Attorney Jim Garrison's conspiracy prosecution. Shaw, of course, was acquitted, and until the publication of this interview, Finck's testimony is the only *public* [*JAMA*'s emphasis] airing of the expert medical opinions on the assassination.

Like all those years of alleged silence hoked up still again, this is an incredible error, made more mysterious in what follows immediately—if one is conspiracy-minded. *Finck was not a prosecution witness! He was the witness of the Shaw defense!*

As at the very least Boswell has to have known from what Breo continued with, nothing omitted:

> Boswell says, 'A careful reading of the entire transcript of Dr. Finck's testimony shows that he held tightly to the facts of our autopsy and supported its conclusions. However, Pierre was a meek and mild man who had been trained abroad, not in the United States. He was very 'brass conscious,' and he thought that generals were out of this world. At Bethesda, Finck was out of his element—an Army colonel in a Navy hospital—and he apparently mistook the President's military aides and other military personnel for generals. During the trial, Garrison was able to exploit Pierre's misperceptions about the scene to give the impression that it was controlled by generals. Jim [Humes] and I state categorically that there was no interference with our autopsy. The patient was extraordinary, the autopsy was ordinary, or at least as ordinary as it could be under the circumstances.' Boswell knows because he, too, was in New Orleans in 1969 at the request of the U.S. Justice Department. 'The Justice Department was so convinced that Garrison was on a fishing expedition in his prosecution of Clay Shaw,' Boswell says, 'that it summoned me to New Orleans to refute Finck's testimony, if necessary. It turned out that it wasn't necessary.' It now appears, Boswell adds, that filmmaker Oliver Stone may have taken Finck's mistaken perceptions about the alleged military presence in the morgue, as detailed in the transcript of the trial, and used it as the sole basis for the mistaken autopsy scenes in his movie *JFK*. Humes calls the movie scenes 'absolutely false and ridiculous,' but we are getting ahead of the story.

Boswell misrepresents Finck's testimony. I possess and have read the lengthy stenographic transcript. I have an entire chapter on his New Orleans testimony in *Post Mortem* (pages 230–38). I wrote a book on New Orleans and its relationship to the Kennedy assassination, *Oswald in New Orleans*. While it is true that Finck undertook to stick with the conclusions of the protocol, for Humes to say that he "held tightly to the facts of our autopsy and supported its conclusions" distorts it seriously.

Boswell, to whom Finck was a stranger, now has him "meek" and "very 'brass conscious,' " suggesting that he was intimidated by or was afraid of "brass." A man who rose to lieutenant colonel afraid of "brass"? So "meek" he, a lieutenant colonel, could not recognize a general when he saw one? As in: "He apparently mistook the President's military aides and other military personnel for generals"? Navy corpsmen were generals to this Army lieutenant colonel?

Finck's testimony will speak for itself to us soon, but here, according to Boswell, "During the trial, Garrison was able to exploit Pierre's misperceptions about the scene to give the impression that it was controlled by generals."

First of all, Garrison is not the one "to exploit" Finck's alleged "misperceptions." He did not cross-examine Finck. An assistant, Alvin Oser, later a judge, who handled most of the courtroom work, cross-examined Finck.

And what Oser found of use in his questioning of Finck in 1969, *is what Finck himself put in a memorandum to his boss four years earlier!*

That Boswell was in New Orleans for the trial "at the request of the U.S. Justice Department" is remarkable for several reasons. The department pretended publicly that it had a hands-off policy on Garrison and his case. But here it was lining up expert witnesses for the defense and, wonder of wonders, "to refute Finck's testimony"— *which was for the defense!*

But what was the federal government, particularly its Department of Justice, up to by this secret intrusion into a state prosecution? Why the department did that we'll never know, but that it did does suggest that it had a serious interest in defeating a prosecution based on the allegation that there had a been a conspiracy to kill JFK.

Breo et al. are again wrong, their norm, with Boswell's conjecture that "Stone may have taken Finck's mistaken perceptions about the alleged military presence in the morgue, as detailed in the transcript of the trial, and used it as the sole basis for the mistaken autopsy scenes in his movie . . ." How little they knew and how disinterested they were in being factual is still surprising considering their project.

Stone has no need of fact. He made it up to suit himself. What he did not make up himself Garrison had already made up for him in his book, *On the Trail of the Assassins,* Stone's major source.

Two months before Stone started shooting his film, when I learned he was basing his movie largely on Garrison's book, I wrote him in detail, attaching proof and offering more if he wanted it, warning him that he would be producing a "fraud and a travesty" if he trusted Garrison's book. Stone was indifferent.

We'll come to Finck, the *real* Finck, not this phony two-dimensional man invented by these four, when they knew he had refused to come to the United States and join in their interviews and thus would not dispute what they said about him. Finck was, in New Orleans, however, anything but "a meek and mild man." He argued with the judge and continued to argue with him even when cautioned!

Chapter 15

Specter's Bastard

OF ALL THE ASPECTS OF THE FRAUD TOUTED AS THE INVESTIGATION OF that assassination by the major media, probably the most transparently fraudulent, the most obviously and knowingly corrupt and dishonest is Arlen Specter's bastard, his single-bullet theory. Without that theory the government could not have avoided the simply overwhelming proof that the crime was the end product of a conspiracy.

This nonfatal shot is all-controlling because the truth it establishes is that here had been the conspiracy to assassinate JFK. Then and since the government and its apologists have insisted there had not been. A conspiracy was really beyond question at the autopsy table, too.

Humes' attitude then and in 1992 is apparent in what he told Lundberg and Breo:

'We also noted damage to the neck muscles, trachea, and pleura, but there was no bullet. It was bothering me very greatly, like nothing you can imagine, that we could find neither the second bullet nor its exit track. 'J' and I both knew that bullets can do funny things in the body, and we thought it might have been deflected down to the extremities. We X-rayed the entire body, but did not find a bullet.' The autopsy was also criticized because the pathologists did not dissect the President's neck to track the second bullet. Humes says bluntly, 'Dissecting the neck was totally unnecessary and would have been criminal. By midnight, we decided it was time to quit speculating about the second bullet, and I am very comfortable with this decision. It is true that we were influenced by the fact that we knew Jackie Kennedy was waiting upstairs to accompany the body to the White House and that Admiral Burkley wanted us to hurry as much as possible. By

157

midnight, our task was done—it was perfectly obvious what had
killed the man. The second bullet was important, but not of overriding importance. We knew we would find the explanation sooner
or later.' The explanation came sooner, the next morning at 7:30,
when Humes called Dallas to talk to Dr. Malcolm Perry, the surgeon who had performed the tracheostomy. 'The light came on
when I talked to Dr. Perry,' Humes says. 'Of course, the bullet
had exited through the neck.'

Throughout the interview, as Breo reported it, Humes boasted of
his skill in forensic pathology and in examining bullet wounds. He
actually said this "second bullet was important, but not of overriding
importance" when that wound could prove that there had been a
conspiracy to kill the President.

The cause of death was ghastly obvious: that large part of the
head had been blown away.

It required no autopsy to establish that.

What else in the world was the autopsy to establish when the
cause of death was not a question? If the fatal and the nonfatal
wounds did not come from the same place, they could not have come
from the same rifle, and if they came from different rifles, obviously
there was more than one assassin. That alone means there had been
a conspiracy.

And if the bullet (assuming that one only caused the nonfatal
injuries, another matter to have been established in the autopsy examination) had been deflected, as from a bone inside the body, then the
trajectory back to the point of origin could not be projected by means
of the wounds.

Although Humes, Boswell, and Finck say that no bone was struck
inside the President's body, the X rays that they had taken *and exam-*
ined at the autopsy prove that the bone was struck. As we shall see,
later in their own left-handed way, they admit this. The Department
of Justice panel also attested to this while pretending to support the
autopsy report.

Humes says bluntly, "Dissecting the neck was totally unnecessary
and would have been criminal."

"Totally unnecessary" when without dissection there was no way
of establishing the path of that bullet through the body? "Totally

unnecessary'' when the path could only be conjectured, as they did conjecture it in their report (as it turns out, inaccurately)? ''Totally unnecessary'' when Humes could not probe the wound to establish its path, but found the probe blocked?

''Criminal'' to do his duty? ''Criminal'' to conform with the standards of forensic medicine and to the specific instructions of the AFIP on autopsies that dictated what they were required to do?

What these four cover-up artists really said here is that Humes had been ''bothered'' so ''greatly'' because ''we could find neither the second bullet nor its exit track.'' So they avoided the one means by which they had of learning and establishing the fact they refused to dissect the neck, although their responsibilities as prosectors required them to dissect.

In this short direct quotation from *JAMA* there are other untrue statements. As we have seen, they did not ''X-ray the entire body,'' as they said, ''down to the extremities.'' As we have also seen, what Humes referred to as ''the explanation'' of the career of this ''second bullet'' did not come first to him ''the next morning'' when he phoned Perry in Dallas. He was, as he swore to the Commission, ''somewhat certain'' of it as soon as he laid eyes on the corpse that a tracheostomy had been performed. Admiral Burkley was there to let him know if Humes had asked. So were a number of others who were in the hospital, to his knowledge, and had been in Parkland Memorial Hospital in Dallas. The Secret Service agents were in the emergency room and saw the tracheostomy performed. One has to wonder why, especially because he believed on first sight that it had been done, he did not ask those at hand whether he was correct in believing that it had been performed.

Breo's first mention of the nonfatal bullet follows:

Humes emphasizes that his autopsy found that the other bullet that struck Kennedy, the so-called 'magic bullet' that was the first to hit Kennedy and that also hit Texas Gov. John Connally, was also fired from above and behind. He says, 'There was an 'abrasion collar' where this bullet entered at the base of the President's neck, and this scorching and splitting of the skin from the heat and scraping generated by the entering bullet is proof that it entered from behind. Unfortunately, at the time of the autopsy, the tracheotomy ... obliterated the exit wound through the front of his neck near the Adam's apple.'

This is the same Humes who in several ways testified to the Commission that he believed immediately that there had been a tracheotomy. The same Humes who boasted that the Department of Justice panel supported his work when, on this very point of whether the bullet hole had been "obliterated," in fact it said there was no obliteration, that Perry's incision had *not* obliterated the bullet hole. Perry cut away no tissue at all. He made only a straight, horizontal incision.

On page 9 of its report (*Post Mortem,* page 588) the panel, interpreting the autopsy photographs it identified by number on the preceding page, wrote that "at the site of the tracheostomy incision in the front of the neck, there can be identified the upper half of the circumference of a circular cutaneous wound, the appearance of which is characteristic of that of the exit wound of a bullet."

This panel stated that despite the incision a bullet hole is visible in the pictures. It should have been more visible to the prosectors. The panel report does not state why it was concluded that this was an exit wound. It does not state that the Dallas doctors repeatedly described it as an entrance wound.

Humes makes no reference to what is shown on the tissue he removed from the site of the wound for testing during the autopsy or to the results of any examination or testing of this tissue. The government did not produce it for the examination by the doctors who were permitted to scrutinize the autopsy pictures, X rays, and other materials. It also is not mentioned in the Department of Justice report. This does not mean that the tissue removed for precisely this testing confirmed what Humes and Boswell said it reflects.

Breo quoted the summary of the autopsy report. With regard to this nonfatal bullet he repeated, without questioning or checking, or apparently without consulting Humes or Boswell about it: "As far as can be ascertained, this missile struck no bony structures in its path through the body."

This is not what Humes and Boswell wrote in another of their official reports that was kept secret.

In 1966 a controversy began with the attention given to the publication of *Whitewash* and was accelerated by the later publications of

Edward J. Epstein's and Mark Lane's books. The government made a big show about hiding nothing. On October 31 an executive order transferred to the National Archives all the records the FBI had that had been "considered by" the Commission. The next day, November 1, in strict secrecy Humes, Boswell, the radiologist, and the photographer "inspected" the films at the archives. Ten days later, on November 10, they signed a report that does not identify its author or authors. This was kept secret until, along with the panel report of the Department of Justice and yet another secret report of the prosectors, it was released to the Washington, D. C., court in the Garrison case.

Later the three prosectors filed another secret report that is undated. The disclosed copy is a poor one, and the dates of their signing are not clear. This report, as I noted when I published it in facsimile, abounds in "contradictions of the autopsy report." It is in *Post Mortem* on pages 575–79. What at this point is relevant is what they said on next to the last page, under *"NO OTHER WOUNDS"*:

> The X-ray films established that there were small metallic fragments in the head. However, careful examination at the autopsy and the photographs and X-rays taken during the autopsy, reveal no evidence of a bullet or of a major portion of a bullet in the body of the President . . .

What this peculiar language must mean, and as the second panel confirmed, is that there were indeed *minor* "portions of a bullet" in the President's body, a negation of the official solution. The trio of prosectors not only did not say how many minor fragments there were—they did not say that they had insisted in their autopsy protocol that there had been no fragments in the body. Striking bone could cause fragmentation. Any fragmentation in the part of the body of which they spoke meant the end of the Warren Report.

The report of the Department of Justice panel of experts on pages 3 and 4 quotes this same language from the autopsy report without comment. Later, under the heading *"Examination of X-ray films,"* and on page 13, this report states under *"Neck Region,"* without any further identification of the part of that region to which it refers, that "several metallic fragments are present in this region."

These were the most eminent of experts, albeit from institutions that received money from the federal government, and they failed to make any mention of how in the world these undescribed "metallic" fragments (which they could easily have measured and described) got inside the President's body. They did not say whether any bones showed any signs of bullet impact, one way in which metallic fragments could have been deposited. The only possible way metallic fragments could have been deposited was upon the impact of Commission Exhibit 399 on Kennedy's bone. This alone destroys the Report.

The amount of metal missing from this bullet, CE399, after all the many fragments it is acknowledged to have deposited in Governor Connally's body, is so close to its original weight that even if what is virtually postage-stamp weight is attributed to those fragments in the President's body, their additional weight makes it weigh too much. That, too, destroys the Report and the integrity of all the individuals involved in it.

Even more damning, the official account ignores other pieces of metal in three parts of Governor Connally's body. The total weight of these fragments exceeded the weight loss attributed to CE399 (assuming it lost any at all). The Commission's hocus-pocus "solution" ignores the weight of all the metal that doctors in Parkland Memorial Hospital washed out of Connally's wrist wound. It also ignores all the metal that remained in his thigh and in his chest. The wrist, thigh, and chest metal fragments alone weighed far more than that one bullet could have lost.

Dr. George T. Shires testified that the X rays show a fragment in Connally's chest. Specter did not have Shires called to Washington to testify before the Commission. Before the Commission Perry testified he had decided not to remove the fragment from Connally's thigh.

In an honest investigation, and in any honest report on that investigation, *either* of these fragments is enough to destroy the Report based on Specter's invention of the magical single-bullet theory.

Specter's part of the Report includes his questioning of all the doctors, in and from Dallas, and the three prosectors. The Report states that this one bullet, Exhibit 399, caused all the nonfatal wounds on both victims (his single-bullet theory) and that the doctors, after examining the bullet, all agreed that it was possible.

The truth is precisely the opposite. *All the doctors said it was not possible.*

It could *not* have "literally shattered" Connally's fifth rib and "smashed" his right wrist, emerging unscathed—the thrust of Robert Frazier's cited testimony.

Even Humes, contrary to what *JAMA* quoted him as saying, testified that this single-bullet theory is "most unlikely" and "extremely unlikely." Boswell and Finck, both under oath then and there, affirmed Humes's testimony.

So Humes and Boswell said in the autopsy report also signed by Finck that this bullet did not strike any bone; in but the first of their two reports for the Department of Justice, they said the exact opposite: that it did not deposit any "major" fragments. And having cited the Department of Justice report of its panel of experts as validating their autopsy report, it turns out that those experts also found bullet fragments in the President's body when any fragments at all invalidate the autopsy report and Warren Report itself. Lundberg and Breo disregarded what was readily and publicly available, one of the reasons I throughout cite my earlier books.

And thus they have Humes boasting that "our conclusions have stood the test of time," when in fact he personally refuted them in his November 1, 1966, secret report for the Department of Justice.

They quoted him also with regard to this bullet as saying:

> The second bullet was more of a puzzle. 'If we made a mistake,' Humes says, 'it was in not calling Dallas before we started the autopsy. Our information from Parkland Hospital in Dallas before we started the autopsy was zero. If only we had seen the President's clothes, tracking the second bullet would have been a piece of cake, but we didn't have the clothes. In hindsight, we could have saved ourselves a lot of trouble if we had known that the doctors at Parkland performed a tracheostomy in an attempt to save the President's life and that this procedure obliterated the exit wound of the bullet that entered at the base of the neck.'

The Dr. Perry business and the truth about the clothing are worthy of the separate attention they get in our next chapters, as we further examine the nonfatal shot Humes said was not all that important.

Chapter 16

The Nitty-gritty

THE JFK AUTOPSY REPORT WAS WRITTEN BEFORE IT WAS KNOWN THAT there would be no trial, when the only official suspect had not yet been killed, but it was revised as soon as it was known that Oswald had been shot and killed. This is what lends particular importance to Humes's untoward burning of his original draft of the autopsy report. As drafted, it was intended to survive rigorous examination and cross-examination, but it was rewritten to conform with the changed situation.

Under the heading "The original 1963 autopsy report" the following is quoted in *JAMA*'s article:

'It is our opinion that the deceased died as a result of two perforating gunshot wounds inflicted by high-velocity projectiles fired by a person or persons unknown. The projectiles were fired from a point behind and somewhat above the level of the deceased. The observations and available information do not permit a satisfactory estimate as to the sequence of the two wounds.

'The fatal missile entered the skull above and to the right of the external occipital protuberance. A portion of the projectile traversed the cranial cavity in a posterior-anterior direction (see lateral skull roentgenograms), depositing minute particles along its path. A portion of the projectile made its exit through the parietal bone on the right, carrying with it portions of cerebrum, skull, and scalp. The two wounds of the skull combined with the force of the missile produced extensive fragmentation of the skull, laceration of the superior sagittal sinus, and of the right cerebral hemisphere.

'The other missile entered the right superior posterior thorax above the scapula and traversed the soft tissues of the suprascapular and supraclavicular portions of the base of the right side of

165

the neck. The missile produced contusions of the right apical parietal pleura and of the apical portion of the right upper lobe of the
lung. The missile contused the strap muscles of the right side of
the neck, damaged the trachea, and made its exit through the
anterior surface of the neck. As far as can be ascertained, this
missile struck no bony structures on its path through the body.

'In addition, it is our opinion that the wound of the skull produced such extensive damage to the brain as to preclude the possibility of the deceased surviving this injury.

'A supplementary report will be submitted following more detailed examinations of the brian and microscopic sections. However it is not anticipated that these examinations will alter the
findings.'

Humes and Boswell were quite wrong in describing the bullets
used as of "high-velocity." Those old War World II bullets were,
when fresh and new, of medium-to low-medium velocity, according
to the FBI's Warren Commission testimony.

Here the autopsy report does not limit the shooting to any one
person. It says that the bullets were fired "by a person or persons."

Under the heading "Fatal wound 'blatantly obvious,'" Breo
wrote:

> The pathologists found two wounds from a high-velocity missile
> that would later be matched to the military-jacketed bullets fired
> from above and behind the President by Lee Harvey Oswald. The
> fatal shot entered the back of the President's skull and exploded
> away almost a 6-inch section on the right side of his head; the
> second bullet entered at the base of his neck, but its exit track
> was not immediately apparent.

Then, when Breo again quoted them on both wounds, he wrote
this about the head wounds, to which he refers in the singular, an
odd choice for a medical journal:

> 'The fatal wound was blatantly obvious,' Humes recalls. 'The
> entrance wound was elliptical, 15 millimeters long and 6 millime-
> ters wide, and located 2.5 centimeters to the right and slightly
> above the external occipital protuberance. The inside of the skull
> displayed the characteristic beveled appearance. The X rays dis-
> closed fine dustlike metallic fragments from back to front where

the bullet traversed the head before creating an explosive exit wound on the right temporal-parietal area. These fragments were not grossly visible. Two small fragments of bullet were recovered from inside the skull—it blew out 13 centimeters of skull bone and skin—that we did not even have to use a saw to remove the skullcap. We peeled the scalp back, and the calvarium crumbled in my hands from the fracture lines, which went off in all directions. We made an incision high in the spinal cord and removed the brain, which was preserved in formalin. Two-thirds of the right cerebrum had been blown away.

'After the brain was removed, we looked more closely at the wound, and noted that the inside of the rear of the skull bone was absolutely intact and beveled and that there could be no question from whence cometh that bullet—from rear to front. When we received the two missing fragments of the President's skull and were able to piece together two-thirds of the deficit at the right front of the head, we saw the same pattern on the outer table of the skull—a bullet that traveled from rear to front. Every theorist who says the bullet came from the front has ignored this critical irrefutable diagnostic fact. We did everything within the means of reasonable people to record with X rays and photos what we saw.'

In the penultimate sentence above, Humes departed from medico-legal standards, as he did in his examination and report on his examination, and assumed, without ever seeking or considering any other evidence, that there was only one bullet fired at the head. The official investigations all began with the same presumption and all failed to investigate the obvious indication of another bullet that appears in the X rays Humes mentioned.

This presumption, which permeates everything in *JAMA* and in the official investigations, is what Breo began with:

There are two and only two physicians who know exactly what happened—and didn't happen—during their autopsy of President John F. Kennedy on the night of November 22, 1963, at the Naval Medical Center in Bethesda, Md. The two, former US Navy pathologists James Joseph Humes, MD, and J. Thornton Boswell, MD, convened last month in a Florida hotel for two days of extraordinary interviews with *JAMA* editor George D. Lundberg, MD.

Bullets came from above and behind

The scientific evidence they documented during their autopsy provides irrefutable proof that President Kennedy was struck by only two bullets that came from above and behind from a high-velocity weapon that caused the fatal wounds. This autopsy proof, combined with the bullet and rifle evidence found at the scene of the crime, and the subsequent detailed documentation of a six-month investigation involving the enormous resources of the local, state, and federal law enforcement agencies, proves the 1964 Warren Commission conclusion that Kennedy was killed by a lone assassin, Lee Harvey Oswald.

In the very first sentence Breo and Lundberg got carried away with themselves and their adventures in rewriting our history. Finck, obviously, and a number of other "physicians" were present, several with the rank of admiral, and who knew what occurred. And, as we have seen, it is not true that Humes and Boswell "for the only time ... publicly discusses their famous case."

Under the heading "Irrefutable evidence," Breo quoted Lundberg on his pleasure at getting the interviews and Humes on his alleged lack of interest in the controversy over his autopsy:

Lundberg says, 'I am extremely pleased that, finally, we are able to have published in the peer-reviewed literature the actual findings of what took place at the autopsy table on November 22, 1963. I completely believe that this information, as personally given by Jim [Humes] and "J" [Boswell], is scientifically sound and in my judgement, proves irrefutable evidence that President Kennedy was killed by only two bullets that struck him from above and behind and that caused fatal high-velocity wounds.'

Humes concludes, 'I really have not had much ongoing interest in the autopsy. We did what we had to do in 1963, and we did it right....'

With all the intense, national and international controversy about and involving that autopsy; with all the books and articles so critical of it, some charging him with being an accessory in crimes; with all the nutty theories, many so unfair to him; with the international attention to the Garrison fiasco and to what was attributed to him through it; and with Oliver Stone's movie so incensing him, Humes did not have ''much ongoing interest in the autopsy''? This is not easy to believe!

Chapter 17

The Gritty

In *WHITEWASH* I BUILT UP THE TWO INTERRELATED FINAL CHAPTERS, "The Number of Shots" (pages 155 ff.) and "The Doctors and the Autopsy" (pages 167 ff.). I wrote:

> For reasons never explained, if the question was ever asked, the autopsy report was not released by the government until it appeared in the Report. This was more than ten months after the assassination. At that time it was smothered, as was almost everybody and everything, in the tremendous mass of the Report. The autopsy is not mentioned in the first chapter, titled 'Summary and Conclusions,' which also served as a press release. It is barely mentioned in the chapter on the assassination, the shortest chapter, and is itself one of the shortest chapter sections in the entire Report. About a page is devoted to it (R59–60), including information not related to the autopsy itself. . . .
>
> When the President's body reached Bethesda at 7:35 P.M. the night of the assassination, all was in readiness. X rays and photographs were taken immediately. Pathological examination was begun at about 8 P.M. It was concluded about 11 P.M. The autopsy disclosed two wounds in the President's head. One, presumed of entrance, was one-fourth by five-eighths of an inch in size. According to the Report, it was about an inch to the right and slightly above the bony protrusion at the center of the lower part of the back of the skull. The other, presumed of exit, was about five inches in diameter. It was difficult to measure accurately because of the multiple crisscross fractures radiating from it. Some of the missing pieces of the skull were returned from Dallas during the autopsy. They accounted for about three-quarters of the missing skull. Thirty to forty 'dustlike fragments of metal' were revealed by the X rays of the head, 'with a sizeable metal fragment lying just above the right eye.' The FBI was given 'two small, irregu-

larly shaped fragments' that were recovered [*Whitewash,* pages 178–79].

The description "dustlike" does not appear in the autopsy protocol.

In the existing holograph, the one Humes composed at the time of his conflagration of evidence in his recreation room fireplace, under the heading "MISSILE WOUNDS," he had written originally that the X rays disclosed "minute fragments" in the head. This was changed before typing, when the holograph was altered, to "minute particles."

How "minute" these "particles" were Humes did not say until he testified before the Commission. It was there that for the first time he gave their number, thirty to forty, and described them as "dustlike" (2H353).

The section of the Report on 'The Autopsy' fails to locate this, the fatal wound, with precision. It is described in the printed version of the autopsy in the Appendix (R538–46) in highly technical language. [Lt.] Colonel Finck prepared a chart illustrating it, part of Exhibit 397 (17H64), which also does not appear in the Report. The closest thing to a location (R86) is a quotation from Commander Humes in the discussion of 'The President's Head Wounds' (R86). The words there used are 'a large defect in the upper right side of the skull' (R86). This section is described in the 'The Autopsy' as the place where the wounds are discussed fully. They are not.

There are photographs of Exhibits 385 and 386 in the Appendix of this book. Both are 'artist's conceptions' prepared at the Naval Medical Center. Exhibit 385 is a view of the right side of the President's head. It shows no head wound; Exhibit 386, which portrays the President as hairless, is a rear view and represents only that portion of this fatal injury. These two exhibits (16H977) are also excluded from the Report, as is Exhibit 388 (16H984), another 'artist's conception,' which does show the right side of the President's head. Unlike Exhibits 385 and 386, which depict the head erect, this one portrays it bent forward, almost on the chest. It shows a hairline and the wound the Report says was of entrance. This wound is several inches above the hairline. Secret Service Agent Kellerman, present at the autopsy, located this wound as 'in the hairline' (2H81) [*Whitewash,* page 179].

It is perhaps even more important in 1992, after all the attention to the autopsy created by *JAMA*, to understand that the failure of the Report to locate the alleged point of entry of the fatal wound with precision and to describe it clearly and comprehensively is not mere carelessness or sloppiness. As became clear in later official reviews of the autopsy materials, which confirm what I reported in *Post Mortem* in 1975 (part 2), the prosectors and the Report locate this alleged point of entry incorrectly—much lower on the back of the head than the autopsy film itself establishes.

JAMA, Humes, Boswell, Finck do no better with their allegedly nonfatal wound in 1992 than the prosectors and the Report did in 1964. They were guilty of the same inaccuracies I cited in 1965, serious errors that were later magnified as more information became available:

> Throughout the Report are references to the President's 'neck' wound, also in rare unguarded moments referred to as a 'back' wound. In this section the Report employs language more representative of the artist's conception, a wound 'near the base of the back of President Kennedy's neck, slightly to the right of his spine.' At the referred to 'full discussion' (R87–92), the same language is used, with the addition of technical language, 'approximately 5½ inches (14 centimeters) from the tip of the right shoulder joint and approximately the same distance below the tip of the right mastoid process . . .' This would not exactly locate the bullet hole unless all the President's dimensions, especially the length of this neck, were known.
>
> 'The doctors traced the course of the bullet through the body and as information was received from Parkland, concluded that the bullet had emerged from the front portion of the President's neck that had been cut away by the tracheotomy at Parkland.'
>
> This language is worthy of comment because it is typical of the skill with words utilized throughout the Report to give an impression of things the Commission cannot state as fact. The path of this bullet was not followed; it was projected. Humes testified, 'Attempts to probe in the vicinity of this wound were unsuccessful without fear of making a false passage' (2H361). According to Secret Service Agent Kellerman, Finck did the probing (2H93) . . . from the hole that was in his shoulder, and with a probe, and we were standing right along side of him, he is probing inside the shoulder with his instrument and I said, "Colonel, where did it go?" He said "There are no lanes for an outlet

of the entry in this man's shoulder.'' ' 'Tracing,' therefore, would hardly seem the most appropriate word. It was 'concluded' that the bullet exited from the front of the neck. It was neither traced there nor proved.

Information was not received from Parkland Hospital, in the sense implied here, of the voluntary passage of information from Dallas. It was sought, [but not until] after the examination was completed [as we have seen].

The 'portion of the President's neck that had been cut away by the tracheotomy at Parkland' is described in the autopsy report as a 'tracheotomy incision' (R541) [*Whitewash,* page 179].

The authors of the Report knew very well that *no* ''portion'' of the President's neck ''had been cut away.'' This is a deliberate misrepresentation, one designed to make the incredible autopsy report appear to be credible.

Perry, who made the incision, explained it to me. Reacting automatically, although he knew that the President was dead, he made the tracheotomy slit from side to side, to coincide with the creases in the skin. As he looked back on it years later, he realized that this was odd, an automatic reaction prompted by cosmetic concerns. This was so that on healing it would not be conspicuous and would appear to be another crease in the skin. But *he cut away nothing at all. He removed no tissue at all.* He made the cut as fast as he could and then inserted the proper tubes.

It is unfortunate that, in a Report on such a major event in United States history, language has to be used to distort and misrepresent and even to state untruths. A number of instances have been cited. It is no more justifiable than the willingness of the Commission to accept incontrovertibly false sworn statements or its capacity to avoid asking the right questions.

A possibly major conflict to testimony about the most material kind of fact relates to the autopsy itself. Dr. Humes testified (2H361–2) that he 'had the impression' when he saw the anterior neck wound that a tracheotomy had been performed [*Whitewash,* page 180].

That is not at all what Humes told Lundberg and Breo: ''It was bothering me very much that we could not find the second bullet nor its exit track.''

"The explanation," Breo's words, "came sooner, the next morning at 7:30 when Humes called Dallas to talk to Dr. Perry, the surgeon who had performed the tracheotomy . . ." Humes also told Lundberg and Breo, "If we made a mistake," Humes said, "it was in not calling Dallas before we started the autopsy."

If we were "somewhat certain" and had the "impression" that there had been a tracheotomy in Dallas, it was not a mere "mistake" not to have phoned Perry. Bethesda was full of doctors who could have placed the call for Humes. (See also the Afterword.)

Why Humes was not honest we do not know. What we do know is that there is an enormous difference between his alleged complete bewilderment at the autopsy because he could not find the "exit track" of this bullet, what he told Lundberg, and his belief as soon as he saw the body that there had been a tracheotomy, strengthened by his additional testimony that he was "somewhat certain" of it.

This was not Humes's only misrepresentation of his "call" to Perry and of what he and Perry said:

'To ascertain that point, I called on the telephone Dr. Malcolm Perry and discussed with him the situation of the President's neck when he first examined the President and asked him had he in fact done a tracheotomy which was somewhat redundant because I was somewhat certain he had.' Perry confirmed that he had made the incision at the point of the wound. When asked by Assistant Counsel Specter when the conversation occurred, Humes replied, 'I had that conversation Saturday morning, sir,' the day after the assassination and the autopsy. Although Specter knew of two phone calls to Perry from Humes, later in the hearing he asked, 'And at the time of your conversation with Dr. Perry did you tell Dr. Perry anything about your observations or conclusions?' Humes's reply was, 'No, sir; I did not.' The next words in the transcript are, '(a short recess was taken)' (2H371).

'That conversation,' according to Dr. Perry, was two conversations, with Humes initiating both. His account of the first conversation is substantially in accord with Humes's. Of the second he said, 'He subsequently called back—at that time he told me, of course, that he could not talk to me about any of it and asked that I keep it in confidence, which I did . . .' (6H16). By the time Dr. Perry got before a second Commission hearing, in Washington, he said he could not remember the times of the conversations but gave the same account of them. His words in describing Humes's caution on this occasion were, 'He advised me that he could not discuss with me the findings of necropsy,' or autopsy, postmortem examination (3H380).

Contradictory testimony, also under oath, was given by Dr. Kemp Clark, who reported a request from Dr. Perry following the phone conversations with Bethesda.

'Dr. Perry stated that he had talked to the Bethesda Naval Hospital on two occasions that morning and that he knew what the autopsy findings had shown and that he did not wish to be questioned by the press, as he had been asked by Bethesda to confine his remarks to what he knew from having examined the President, and suggested that the major part of this press conference be conducted by me.' Dr. Clark thought two others, whom he named, were witnesses to this conversation (6H23).

Both the questioning and the answering during Dr. Perry's appearance in Washington were characterized by an indirection and evasiveness that was not short of professional. Exactly what he told the news media, a major part of the testimony, was never made clear. The circumlocution was elaborate. He spoke of news stories, the contents of which, were never revealed . . . [*Whitewash,* page 180].

(This vagueness was contrived by Specter. There never was any doubt about what Perry had said about that wound in the front of the President's neck. On three separate occasions in response to questions from reporters, Perry had said it was an entrance wound, *a wound from the front, not from the back.*)

The surgeons could not probe the so-called posterior neck wound. Humes had no doubt that the anterior incision was from a tracheotomy. With no missile, from the very beginning of the autopsy, the experts were baffled. Yet at no time during the examination of no less a person than the President of the United States was the telephone call made. It was not made at the comparatively early hour of 11 P.M. when the postmortem study had been completed. It was not made until the next day, and then it was repeated.

In the phone conversation, Humes learned that before the tracheotomy the wound was about a fifth of an inch in diameter. His note (17H29) reads, 'size, 3-5 mm.' His autopsy report gives the dimensions of the 'exit' wound as 'a 7×4 millimeter oval wound

... 14 cm (or 5½ inches) from the tip of the right acromion process' (R540). The entrance wound, then, was larger than the exit wound in a gunshot injury in which no bones were struck. All the testimony indicates this would be quite an abnormal reversal of the usual relationship. After this bullet exited the front of the President's neck, it made a much larger hole in the Governor's back if, as the Report wants believed, it did strike the Governor. Connally's entrance wound was more than twice the diameter of the presumed exit wound. The President was only about four feet behind the Governor.

There are too many questions about the autopsy, the autopsy report, and the manner in which both were handled by the Commission and in the Report itself. None should exist. This was not a Bowery bum; this was the President of the United States. Similarly, the Report should not be vague on the precise location of the President's wounds, especially with what it almost always termed his 'neck' wound, but sometimes referred to as a back wound or one near the base of the back of his neck. The latter description is accurate, but without meaning. Was it above or below the base of the neck? The difference is vital in the Commission's reconstruction of the crime. The unvarying evasiveness is in itself highly suspicious.

The President's entire body was X-rayed and a number of photograph's were taken before the examination began [*Whitewash*, page 181].

Humes told the Warren Commission that they had X-rayed the entire body, and he told Lundberg and Breo that because they both "knew that bullets can do funny things in the body, and we thought it might have been deflected down to the extremities," they had "X-rayed the entire body."

Humes and Boswell also claimed repeatedly that their work was "confirmed" by the Department of Justice panel of experts. That panel's once-secret report is printed in facsimile in *Post Mortem* on pages 580–95. It stays that Humes and Boswell did *not* X-ray "the extremities."

During the examination, additional X rays and photographs were made (2H349). All were given immediately to the Secret Service. The pictures were not available for use during the examination.

Neither the pictures nor the X rays were available for subsequent
use in the preparation of the artist's representations.

*With this elaborate photographic record, why should there ever
have been any question about the exact location of each wound?*
These pictures were not offered for the Commission's record.
Why? When the entire 'solution' of the crime hinged upon reconstructions in which the number of shots and the location of wounds
were vital and the angle of declination was important, why should
testimony have depended upon recollections and secondhand
sketches based on recollections? Even the autopsy surgeons testified without benefit of any of this unquestioned data. For unexplained reasons, they even anticipated this!

'When appraised of the necessity for our appearance before this
Commission, we did not know whether or not the photographs
which we had made would be available to the Commission. So,
to assist in making our testimony more understandable to the Commission members, we decided to have made drawings, schematic
drawings, of the situation as we saw it, as we recorded it and as
we recall it. These drawings were made under my supervision and
that of Dr. Boswell by Mr. (H.A.) Rydberg ... a medical illustrator in our command at Naval Medical School' (2H349–50).

Why should Humes have believed the pictures would *not* be
available to the Commission? Was this Commission not to have
access to everything? It could have, for it had the power of subpoena to overcome recalcitrance. He was, for some reason, so
certain that the Naval Medical authorities went to some trouble to
prepare these mock-ups [*Whitewash*, page 181].

(This is elaborate faking to obscure the deliberateness with which
the Commission kept the ''best evidence'' from the official record.
There was nothing to prevent the Commission from using the photographs and X rays as evidence without making them public. Moreover, from his situation, Humes was certain that his testimony would
be required. It obviously required the autopsy protocol to be in
evidence.)

Throughout his testimony, Humes repeatedly referred to the
greater desirability of the pictures. For example, '... the photographs would be more accurate as to the precise location ...'
(2H369); '... photographs are far superior to my humble verbal
description ...' (2H371), 'the pictures would show more accu-

rately and in more detail the character of the wounds as depicted particularly in 385 and 386 and in 388–A . . .' The chairman asked him, '. . . if we had the pictures here . . . would it cause you to change any of the testimony you have given?' (2H372). What was Humes to say except that his testimony was correct? That is what he did, but he qualified it, saying, 'To the best of my recollection, Mr. Chief Justice, it would not.'

Commission member McCloy wanted to know if any pictures of the President had been taken in Dallas. None were. Congressman Ford wanted to know what kind of pictures. Humes told him both black-and-white and color, never examined by personnel at Bethesda. Specter affirmed the undeveloped negatives had been given to the Secret Service. Humes stated, 'The photographs were taken for the record and for other purposes.' And at that point discussion of the pictures ended. If they were taken 'for the record and for other purposes,' these hearings certainly met both descriptions. At no point is there any indication why they were not used. The absence of the best available evidence was regarded by the Commission as a perfectly natural thing (2H372). How good Humes's best recollection may have been will soon be apparent [*Whitewash*, page 182].

(The truth, as I learned from the formerly TOP SECRET Warren Commission executive-session transcripts, is that Rankin told the members on January 21, 1964, that they did have these photographs. I published that page of the transcript in facsimile on page 133 of *Whitewash IV*. When Commission member McCloy asked "about the color photographs of the President's body—do we have them?" Rankin told him "yes" two times, each time digressing into what McCloy had not asked him about. He ultimately succeeded in getting the matter of the Commission's possession of the autopsy photographs dropped.)

In describing the manner in which the illustrator worked (he told the illustrator, 'to a certain extent from memory and to a certain extent from the written record' [2H370]), Humes expressed satisfaction with their accuracy. Asked, 'And proportion?' he replied:

'Commander Humes. "I must state these drawings are in part schematic. The artist had but a brief period of some two days to prepare these. He had no photographs from which to work, and had to work under our description, verbal description, of what we had observed.''

'**Mr. Specter.** ''Would it be helpful to the artist, in redefining the drawings if that should become necessary, to have available to him the photographs or X rays of the President?''

'**Commander Humes.** ''If it were necessary to have them absolutely true to scale, I think it would be virtually impossible for him to do this without the photographs.''

'**Mr. Specter.** ''And what is the reason for the necessity for having the photographs?''

'**Commander Humes.** ''I think that it would be most difficult to transmit into physical measurements the—by word—exact situation as it was seen by the naked eye. The photographs were—there is no problem of scale there because the wounds, if they are changed in size or changed in size and proportion to the structures of the body and so forth, when we attempt to give a description of these findings, it is the bony prominences, I cannot, which we used as points of references, I cannot transmit completely to the illustrator where they were situated'' ' [*Whitewash,* page 182].

(Having asked the necessary question, why are autopsy photographs necessary, and gotten this convoluted nonreponse, Specter had covered himself.)

'**Mr. Specter.** ''Is the taking of photographs and X rays routine or is this something out of the ordinary?''

'**Commander Humes.** ''No, sir, this is quite routine in cases of this sort of violent death in our training. In the field of forensic pathology we have found that the photographs and X rays are of most value, the X rays particularly in finding missiles which have a way of going in different directions sometimes, and particularly as documentary evidence these are considered invaluable in the field of forensic pathology'' ' (2H350).

Is it conceivable that what is routine in the field of forensic pathology was too good for the President of the United States or for the Commission that was to have and give the final word on his assassination? [*Whitewash,* pages 182–83].

As we have seen, and as Specter knew because he wrote the memo on it to the Commission, Robert Kennedy did not deny the Commission access to anything at all. As we have also seen, despite contrary public pretense in their top secret executive session their general counsel told the members that they had the autopsy pictures.

Unless informed, there was no reason for Humes and Boswell to wonder about having the pictures and X rays to use in their testimony. This is the norm. Unless they had been given to understand they would not be using the films in their testimony, they would have assumed they would be following normal procedures. Their substitution of an artist's inaccurate, secondhand conceptions for the real evidence, for tracings even, means that they had reason to believe that they would not be using the films in their testimony. There was no other reason for them to prepare the inadequate, inaccurate, and unacceptable sketches as a substitute.

After Humes divested himself of this burden, the Commission turned to the autopsy report.... Specter asked Humes about a change on page 14 of the handwritten draft, and he explained it as intended for clarification. There were no further questions about these changes (2H373). There certainly should have been. [They relate to the wounds.]

One change Humes did not see fit to make was the part of his autopsy report on the President of the United States based upon a *Washington Post* story of November 23, 1963. It said, 'Three shots were heard' and quoted a Dallas photographer as having seen 'a rifle barrel disappearing into a window on an *upper floor*' of the Depository.

Compared with this report about the rifle on the 'upper floor' and the 'three shots,' the clarification becomes interesting. The rough draft stated the projectiles were fired from 'a point behind and somewhat (illegible word) above a horizontal line to the vertical junction of the body at the moment of impact.' As altered, the last part reads, 'a point behind and somewhat above the level of the deceased.' The final version, clearly allowed placing the sources of the shots on a more 'upper floor' than the original [*Whitewash,* page 183].

To make these comments Humes had to know the exact position of the President's body at the time of bullet impact as well as the direction in which his head faced. Had he been facing to his right, obviously, an untenable opinion, then this shot would have to have come from a point other than the Depository building, from east or south of it, depending on how his head was positioned. And if he had been looking upward, then the imagined source of the shot would have to have been much lower. Humes couldn't have known at the time.

The speed of the car was changed from 'approximately twenty miles an hour' to 'a slow rate of speed.' The incorrect statement that the President 'fell face downward to the floor of the vehicle' was replaced by the word 'forward.'

Dr. Perry's description of the anterior neck wound, that very critical question of exit or entrance, was described as a 'puncture wound' in the handwritten draft. The final copy reads 'much smaller wound.' This is a change of fact and is not subject to the hocus-pocus about the news media not providing their tapes. It is the bugaboo the Commission avoided so obviously in the Perry interrogation. It is what Humes said Perry told him over the phone.

The posterior wound, which the Commission said was of entrance, was described on page 4 with the word 'puncture,' meaning the same thing, in the handwritten draft, from which the word 'puncture' was then stricken. Is it possible the autopsy surgeons had doubts? But on page 2, where Dr. Humes did no editing, the information Dr. Perry conveyed to him is: 'Dr. Perry noted the massive wound of the head and a second, *puncture wound,* of the low anterior neck in approximately the midline . . .'

On the seventh handwritten page, the last ten lines contain six changes in the description of the head wound. These include the alteration of the President's lower or 'entrance' wound as described from 'puncture' in the draft to 'lacerated' in the final copy. In the description of its location, the words 'tangential to the scalp' were deleted. 'In the underlying bone is a corresponding puncture wound . . .' is in the original, but the word 'puncture' was deleted in the final copy. On the eighth handwritten page, the word 'puncture,' relating to this same head wound, was again deleted. This is what the Report describes as the entrance wound on the fatal bullet. Humes eliminated these descriptions of the wound as of that character in the final version.

Of the massive wound the Commission said was of exit, Humes did also in the draft referring to one of the pieces of retrieved skull. But in the final copy he made it read 'presumably' a 'wound of exit.' On the ninth handwritten page, he again altered the description of the smaller head wound by deleting the word 'puncture.' Here he also weakened his description of the President's rear 'neck' wound, adding 'presumably' before 'of entry.' The anterior neck wound which he had described as 'of exit' got the same addition, 'presumably,' in front of it.

Such major substantive changes between the second draft and the final form of the autopsy cannot be regarded as editing. They changed the content. What might there not have been in the version Humes burned? There remains the question that was of no interest to the Commission: Why? Could the first draft not have been turned over with the 'notes'? *Should* they not have been? Had Humes the authority or right to destroy *any* records of any kind?

The two charts appended to the draft of the autopsy report and authenticated as 'notes made in the room where the examination was taking place' were not included in the autopsy report printed in the Report . . . [*Whitewash,* pages 183–84].

It is a wretchedly bad and terribly botched autopsy, inaccurate, incompetent, and incomplete, and a dishonest protocol that could not be admitted into court evidence if there was any opposition to it.

Restricting ourselves to what Humes and Boswell told Lundberg and Breo and to what they had in their report, one of the medico-legal horrors is their locating the wound in the head as "to the right and slightly above the occiput."

First of all, this pretense at locating it does no such thing. Humes and Boswell were in a position to measure the wound and fix its precise location. They should have, but they did not. Then there is that major, glaring factual error I discovered in the Department of Justice panel's report, noted above, in which Humes et al. placed the entry of the fatal head wound bullet four inches lower on the head than it was.

This is the same panel report Humes claimed "confirms" their protocol "until hell freezes over." In fact the opposite is true. That panel absolutely demolished the autopsy protocol. That panel identified a simply enormous factual error in addition to having provided the correct location for what Humes and Boswell said (and still insist upon) was the wound's location.

Under the panel's reading of the X rays that Humes had taken, on page 11 of its report, it states the wound referred to as of entrance was "approximately 100 mm *above* the external occipital protuberance"! (Emphasis added.) That is *four inches!*

And see how reminiscent the panel's location of the wound is of the original language Humes had used in his revised holograph of the autopsy report. In it Humes had written that this wound was "a puncture wound tangential to the surface of the scalp," and then he had eliminated all those meaningful words, and replaced them with the single essentially meaningless word "lacerated."

Then, too, Humes and Boswell are further damned by their protocol. The trajectory track of the bullet that made the wound clearly contradicts their statement. If the official story were true, with the point of impact four inches lower, then it cannot be true with that impact four inches higher.

When Humes and Boswell said, with regard to the nonfatal wound, that its "exit track was not immediately apparent," they were actually saying that it was *never* apparent. At best they guessed.

There was nothing to keep them from tracing this track, and they were required to do it in the autopsy because it is the norm and a legal requirement.

Absent some compelling proof that the dustlike fragments went from back to front, this is no more certain than that they went from front to back. Humes's statement is a bald assertion, not fact, and it certainly is not forensic pathology. It was the prosectors' obligation to establish the direction the particles went, to the degree humanly possible, not merely conjecture it because that is what officialdom wanted in order to sustain the lone-assassin theory.

The day of Lundberg's press conference George Lardner of the *Washington Post* phoned me to ask for comments on the *JAMA* stories. He read to me what he wanted me to comment on.

I told Lardner that it is impossible for full-jacketed and hardened military ammunition, the only kind used in the crime according to the official accounts, to break into forty dustlike particles and for them to be concentrated in so small an area of the brain. And I got no complaint, denial, refutation, or protest from *JAMA,* from any of its four, or from anyone else.

Under the terms of the Geneva Convention convened after World War I to outlaw the use of dumdum and dumdumlike bullets in warfare, the lead alloy of military bullets was hardened significantly, and most had thick, hardened copper-alloy jackets. While copper may not have been used in all, all did conform to the convention on humanitarian warfare.

The bullets Oswald was said to have used are about an inch long and a tiny fraction more than a quarter of an inch in diameter. It is not a particularly big bullet, and much of its bulk is of copper alloy that does not tend to fragment into such tiny particles. Those thirty to forty dustlike particles have to have come from the lead-alloy core. They could not be deposited unless the core jacket was missing and then missing in a way that would not influence the flight path of these bits, that were as tiny as dust and of relatively very little energy. Unlikely as this seems, it is a virtual impossibility for that hardened, full-jacketed military ammunition to have deposited anything like those thirty to forty dustlike particles and to have clustered them in tissue as soft as human brain.

There is no question that there existed these thirty to forty particles—particles so tiny Humes himself described them as like dust—and that they were in the head on a front-to-back as well as back-to-front axis.

They could not have come from the American manufactured bullets for the World War II Italian Mannlicher-Carcano rifle. And that alone means that even if Oswald were an assassin, he was not alone because this deposit of ultrafine particles means there was another shooter other than Oswald.

And that means there was a conspiracy.

Chapter 18

"Truth Is Our Only Client"
—Chief Justice Earl Warren

THE COMMISSION'S ASSISTANT COUNSELS WERE THE ONES WHO DID THE real work, taking the depositions of the witnesses (when outside of Washington done mostly without the presence of any Commission member and when in Washington mostly done with only a few members present). They had no opposing counsel to keep them straight and honest. They served their client, and it was not truth. It was the government that paid them, and instinctively—without orders—and I am certain there were no such orders—they did what they knew was expected of them.

There were no *public* hearings, no hearings at which the press and public could be present, no opportunity for what leaps from the printed page to be known and objected to. As a result, testimony that would inevitably lead to expressions of outrage was lost in the vast volume of those ten million words disclosed at a single moment. Nobody in the media was going to read that many words in time to inform the people about their meaning, and no media organization was about to make the enormous investment that would have meant. The way it worked out, the Report having been issued two months earlier than the testimony and greeted by the media as the unquestionable truth, what media perusal there was of the testimony and exhibits was in seeking confirmation of what the media already had printed and said in support of the Report.

The only adverse comment I recall from the issuance of the Report and its appended volumes was a leak from the FBI. Hoover sought vengeance for the slight criticism of his FBI by the Commission, a criticism so mild it can be compared to smiting his wrist with a feather.

I have sympathy for the witnesses, especially those who testified to,

or it was known in advance would testify to, shots other than the predetermined three of the official preconception that became the instant official "solution." Not one of them was led into a straight account of
having seen what was not in accord with this official preconception.
And all were in some way abused by the assistant counsels. This is
particularly true of those who said they saw the impact of other bullets
or said they saw persons other than Oswald in the Texas School Book
Depository's (TSBD) windows. I went into this in some detail, so
strong was the impression it made on me, in my second book, *Whitewash II,* published in late 1966.

Mrs. Donald Baker, nee Virginia Rachley, testified to seeing the
impact of a bullet on Elm Street, outside the TSBD building, that
had to have come from the west, from the general area of that grassy
knoll. After I wrote this, there was not a word of complaint from
Wesley J. Liebeler when we confronted one another on a talk show
in Los Angeles. Liebeler, an assistant counsel, questioned Mrs. Baker
before the Commission.

> In this it is consistent with what Assistant Counsel Wesley
> Liebeler did to the witnesses and what they said and could have
> said. That hard-working legal tornado, assuming he did not stop
> for lunch or the usual requirements of nature, wound up the testi-
> mony of six witnesses, if Mrs. Baker is included, in four and a
> half hours. . . .
> On Liebeler's surgically sharp examination of Mrs. Baker need
> more be said than that, when she testified to having seen some-
> thing, presumably a bullet, strike the road near the Depository
> building, Liebeler showed her not a picture taken from where she
> had stood or near it, of which there was no shortage, but one
> taken from the opposite end of the street and looking uphill, from
> far away; a confusing picture that destroyed perspective, did not
> show where she was standing or the part of the street that she
> said had been struck? In even the Commission's abysmally poor
> photography, this picture is in a class by itself for improper expo-
> sure, fuzziness, and general lack of clarity or meaning [*Whitewash
> II,* page 131].

The Commission had an abundance of surveyor's plats. It had
aerial photographs. Liebeler had shown her "an aerial photograph
already in evidence, Exhibit 354" (16H949). Liebeler put into her

testimony this wretchedly bad picture as "Baker Exhibit No. 1," and to make the record for history of the utter dishonesty of all of this, I included in *Whitewash II*'s appendix one of the Commission's clear aerial photographs (page 247) and one of its surveyor's plats (page 246).

There is much more like this, much more that I have published, especially in my first two books. As in *Whitewash II*, what David Belin, an assistant counsel, did to the married teen-agers, Mr. and Mrs. Arnold Rowland. The FBI interviewed these kids *five times* in an effort associated with Belin's to discredit them merely because Rowland said he had seen another man, not Oswald, in a TSBD window just before the assassination [*Whitewash II*, pages 82–87, 92]. Rowland's memory was so fantastic that he told Belin how to check the time when he saw this man by repeating what he said he heard broadcast on a police radio from a parked police motorcycle. Belin did not bother to check the Commission's transcripts of the police radio broadcasts, which have the time included periodically. I did, and precisely what Rowland said he heard is in the transcripts. Among those who confirmed his observation was the wife of a deputy sheriff.

Even Abraham Zapruder, who took the eight millimeter movie that showed the President being killed and that was used later by the Commission as a time clock, volunteered testimony that proved the Commission wrong in one of its most basic conclusions, that the President could not have been struck before frame 210. Liebeler was silent on hearing this unexpected testimony during that session of his that took place the month after the Commission had planned to issue its Report without having interviewed any of these many witnesses.

In *Whitewash* I wrote about one of his many destructions of the official theory that was alchemized into supposed fact:

The middle of the three large road signs on the north side of Elm Street was between Zapruder and the President for about 20 frames, from about 205 to 225. Because of the downward grade to the underpass, at the beginning of the sequence, only part of the President's head is still visible over the top of this sign. The Commission's entire case is predicated upon the assumption that the first shot could not have been fired prior to frame 210, for that is the portion of the film in which, even on a still day, the President first became a clear shot from the sixth-floor window.

Zapruder was explaining how he took his pictures. 'I was shooting through a telephoto lens ... and as it (the presidential car) reached about—I imagine it was around here—I heard the first shot and I saw the President lean over and grab himself ...' (7H571). Lawyers know very well that such words as 'here' in testimony relating to a location reflect nothing on the printed page. When they want the testimony clear, they ask the witness to identify the spot meant by 'here.' Zapruder was not asked to explain where 'here' was. *But the startling meaning of Zapruder's testimony is this: He saw the first shot hit the President! He described the President's reaction to it. Had the President been obscured by the sign, Zapruder could have seen none of this. Therefore, the President was hit prior to frame 210, prior to frame 205, the last one that shows the top of his head* [*Whitewash,* page 47].

Zapruder had a graphic means of recalling another disproof of what the Commission had been determined to prove. As he testified to Liebeler, he heard a bullet going over his shoulder, or being shot from that grassy knoll on the edge of which he stood when taking his pictures. Zapruder's observation is included in the handwritten memo by the Dallas Secret Service agent who, the night of the assassination, forwarded a print of Zapruder's movie to his Washington headquarters with his memo.

Zapruder's volunteering of personal-knowledge disproof of the Commission's preconclusion was not wanted. So he was shown the prints of frames other than those he was testifying to, and said, "This is before—this shouldn't be there—the shot wasn't fired, was it? You can't tell from here?" Liebeler ignored him.

There was virtually no end to the witnesses who disputed or disproved the Commission's predetermined "solution." Here were mostly everyday people, who had no ax to grind, merely testifying to what they swore they had seen, and they were abused by these assistant-counsel representatives of federal power.

This particular part of our recapturing of the known and established facts of the assassination is an indictment of Specter and the investigation in 1963 and of *JAMA* today. Despite the availability of much additional evidence that was officially ignored, *JAMA* ignored it, too.

So I limit myself still again to what was published, at least some of which Humes and Boswell had or which they all would have had with ease.

What we address is what Humes regarded as relatively unimportant and not in any event of "overriding" importance, Specter's magic bullet that caused so many wounds and emerged unscathed from Governor Connally.

The man who found that bullet, Commission Exhibit 399, when he saw it roll out from underneath the mattress on a hospital gurney outside the emergency room was the Parkland's senior engineer, Darrell C. Tomlinson. What follows is from *Whitewash*:

> Contrary to the already quoted testimony of Tomlinson, who discovered this bullet, during the testimony of Dr. Shaw [chief of thoracic surgery at Parkland], Assistant Counsel Specter said, '... for the record, that in the depositions which have been taken in Parkland Hospital, that we have ascertained, and those depositions are part of the overall records, that is the bullet which came from the stretcher of Governor Connally' (4H112) [*Whitewash*, page 171].

This is what Specter cited as I reported in *Whitewash*. It included direct quotation of what Tomlinson *actually* swore to before Specter when Specter deposed him in Dallas, *not* before the Commission, on March 20, 1964, in Parkland Hospital:

> Darrell C. Tomlinson was senior engineer at Parkland Memorial Hospital. He was one of the early witnesses, testifying March 20, 1964 (6H128 ff.). He had been sent to convert the operating-room elevator from automatic to manual control and to operate it. He found an unidentified stretcher on this elevator. This was a hospital, not an emergency or ambulance type, stretcher. It was high and had wheels. The practice of the operating room was to push the stretchers into an elevator going down to the emergency-room level where someone on that floor would remove them.
>
> Tomlinson did not know where this stretcher came from (6H134). It is inferred that this was the Connally stretcher from the testimony of an orderly, R. J. Jimison (6H125–8), who helped transfer the Governor to an operating table and then put that stretcher on the elevator. To Jimison there was nothing unusual about this stretcher, and in particular he did not notice a bullet on

it. When Tomlinson got on this elevator, at a time he cannot say,
but some time after the arrival of the motorcade, he pushed a
stretcher off the elevator, into the hall, and attended to a number
of other duties involving trips with the elevator, at least one involving a time lag while waiting for a technician to get blood
[*Whitewash,* pages 161–62].

What follows, quoted from *Whitewash* and undenied by Specter
or anyone else since it was published, is his "proof" that the magical
bullet, Exhibit 399, "came from Connally's stretcher." What is
quoted next comes from one deposition, the most important of them:

When pressed in an unsuccessful effort to get him to identify
one particular stretcher—not as the Governor's, but as the one he
removed from the elevator—Tomlinson went out of his way to
make clear his belief that anything could have happened to that
stretcher, 'I don't know how many people went through . . . I
don't know anything about what could have happened to them
between the time I was gone, and I made several trips before I
discovered the bullet . . .' (6H132–3). The strongest commitment
Tomlinson made was that the bullet *could* have come from the
stretcher he found in the elevator. Tomlinson even insisted he did
not have personal knowledge of where the elevator stretcher came
from (6H134).

When an intern or doctor went to the men's room, he pushed
a stretcher blocking the door out of his way. On leaving the men's
room, he left the stretcher where it then was. When Tomlinson
pushed this stretcher against the wall, 'I bumped the wall, and a
spent cartridge or bullet rolled out that had apparently been lodged
under the edge of the mat' (6H130). There was no question asked
about the unusual location of the bullet, under the mattress. Instead, Tomlinson was pushed and wheedled with the sole purpose
of getting him to make a positive identification of the stretcher.
Tomlinson insisted he was not going to say anything that was not
truthful, that being questioned by various agents as he had been
and giving sworn, recorded testimony were unusual to him, and
'I am going to tell you all I can, and I'm not going to tell you
something I can't lay down and sleep at night with either.'

This bullet, taken from the floor after having been jarred out
presumably from underneath a mattress of an unidentified
stretcher, is the one the Report describes as 'found on Governor
Connally's stretcher.' The testimony makes clear it is only a pre-

sumption that either of those stretchers was the one on which the Governor had been. Both could have been in no way related to the assassination. The Commission did establish that neither had held the President [*Whitewash,* page 162].

This is the "proof" Specter told the Commission it had in its depositions—the "proof" provided by the man, who having found that bullet, swore he'd not be able to sleep at night if he testified to what Specter wanted him to testify. And so with no less magic than is imparted to the bullet, it appears in the Report that this is the bullet "that was found on Governor Connally's stretcher."

Without regard to where in the hospital any stretchers might have been prior to the arrival of the motorcade or to what uses they had been put, there was so much confusion that the President and the Governor were entered upon the records incorrectly. These records show eight admissions during that short interval (6H150; 21H156).

It is the Commission's belief that this bullet fell out of Governor Connally's body through his trousers, which had only the one hole, the point of entry of the thigh wound; was completely undetected in the emergency room during examination, unnoticed during transportation to the operating room, undetected when the Governor was lifted off the stretcher, after he was lifted off the stretcher, and as the stretcher was rolled out of the operating room and while it was on the elevator; unnoticed after it was in the hall for some time, including by a doctor who moved it, and at some point in some mysterious way it got underneath the mattress. Also, the Report asks for belief that the bullet, in making its own way out of the Governor's thigh, was able to fall uphill.

If that is not enough, this reconstruction deals with a bullet that made a single hole, a small one at the point of entrance. It penetrated about three inches into the Governor's thigh and deposited in the thighbone or femur a fragment that to this day remains there. This bullet, a little over an inch long, then wormed its way back to the hole it had made in entering and emerged far enough so that, under the right circumstances, it would be in a position to fall uphill. The exact distance of this buried fragment from the point of entry is neither stated nor approximated in the Report. It was neither asked nor volunteered in the extensive and repetitious examinations of all the doctors directly and indirectly involved [*Whitewash,* pages 162–63].

Dr. Perry explained to me why this supposed bullet hole was undetected when Connally was first examined before he was moved into
the operating room. The hole in Connally's thigh was so small it
could not have been made by a bullet. Perry closely examined that
hole because he was an arterial surgeon, and the other doctors wanted
to be certain that if they had to remove the fragment, its proximity
to the femoral artery would not endanger Connally.

So here's how Specter handled Perry:

One by one the doctors were called before the Commission's
staff and subjected to great persuasion in an effort to get them
either to retract their initial medical opinions that the anterior neck
wound was one of entrance, or to say it could have been either
an entrance or an exit wound. One of the devices used by the
Commission's questioners was to state a hypothetical question
based in part, or seemingly based in part, on the unpublished
autopsy report. With this hypothesis the doctors were in a position
to make the kind of response the Commission so desperately
wanted. In formulating this question, however, the interrogators
may have taken advantage of the doctor. One of the assumptions
the doctors were asked to make had to do with the type of bullet,
which was but a presumption. Another was that the projectile was
of 'high-velocity.' None of the doctors qualified himself as a ballistics expert, and some were careful to point out that they were
not. The testimony of the FBI firearms expert Robert A. Frazier,
previously quoted, was that the presumed bullet was not a high-
velocity bullet.

Special pressure was applied to Dr. Malcolm Perry. It was un-
dignified and abusive. Putting him in the middle of nonsense about
the unavailability of tape recordings of his interviews, promising
to send him copies of his statements, and getting him to promise
he would reply in a letter, not under oath, was neither fair nor
responsible. None of this or any of the related proceedings is
reflected in the Report.

When the runaround began to annoy even members of the Commission, Congressman Ford asked if all the news media had not
made tape recordings of their interviews with the doctors, as, of
course, radio and TV had. In a largely incoherent manner Perry
replied 'This was one of the things I was mad about, Mr. Ford. . . .
I know there were recordings made, but who made them I don't
know' (3H375). Later the subject was resumed with as much

avoidance of the available clippings from the papers. The reason given for the unavailability of the tapes is that in four months, by the time of the doctor's appearance, the media had not catalogued them. However, Dr. Perry was not shown the newspaper accounts, either.

The delicacy of this question is illustrated by the circumspection with which it was handled. Dulles suggested to the lawyers 'If you feel it is feasible, you send to the doctor the accounts of his press conference or conferences,' and to the doctor, 'If you are willing sir, you could send us a letter . . . pointing out where you are inaccurately quoted . . . Is that feasible?' [*Whitewash,* pages 169–70]

So the Commission *knew* there had been a press conference! And all members and their legal staff knew that the White House transcribes and distributes the stenographic transcripts of its press conferences. Yet they pretended that no direct quotation of what Perry said was available to them!

Specter portrayed our major media as being so crippled or incompetent they could not function or retrieve their coverage of one of the most significant events in our country's history. All Specter had to do was to get a clerk to phone the Library of Congress and ask for the newspapers for November 23, 1963, that it had. A messenger would have been in Specter's office promptly with what he had asked for. I know because the Library of Congress rendered me that kind of service when Specter was a toddler, and I was not an important person at all on the Senate staff.

The tapes were not Specter's most obvious source. It is unlikely that Specter did not have personal knowledge of what Perry had told the press just from reading it in the *Philadelphia Inquirer,* the major paper in the city where he lived and worked. Or in The New York *Times*, if like so many people out of New York City, he read the *Times*. Or simply out of an interest in the unprecedented crime.

Here, because this bullet and its known history are so important in the autopsy and in the protocol, it is worth remembering that Humes included in the protocol some of what his morning paper, the *Washington Post* published the day after the assassination, November 23. What the trio of military pathologists included in the protocol that was approved by higher military authority was not of their knowledge, and certainly is not appropriate to either the heading on the inside pages of the typed protocol "Pathological Examination Report" or to the typed heading under which it appears, "Clinical Summary." It says:

Three shots were heard and the President fell forward [changed from 'face downward to the floor of the vehicle'] bleeding from the head. (Governor Connally was seriously wounded by the same gunfire.) According to newspaper reports (*Washington Post*, November 23, 1963), Bob Jackson, a *Dallas Times Herald* photographer, said he looked around as he heard the shots and saw a rifle barrel disappearing into a window on an upper floor of the nearby Texas School Book Depository building.

The Navy, either the Humes team or Admiral Galloway, improved upon what Jackson was actually quoted as saying. What the Navy inserted that is *not* in the *Post*'s story is the word "three." The Post story does not quote Jackson as saying he heard "three" shots.

This "improvement" was not by Humes. It does not appear in his holograph (*Post Mortem*, page 510).

This is Navy top medical brass altering the direct quotation in Humes's protocol of a newspaper story, which has no business being in an autopsy protocol to begin with, to make the news report say what it did not say because that would make it support the official preconception already fixed and in place.

Surely Spector had heard of the famous *New York Times*, the "newspaper of record," with that fantastic index? The *Times*'s November 23, 1963, coverage was extensive, beginning with its entire front page. It had articles on *seven* inside pages, including all of page 2, set in what for the *Times* is large type. Page 2, with its wider columns, totaled only five across the page.

If Specter suddenly had not developed a nincompoop's limitations, he would have found on page 2 near the top:

Later in the afternoon [i.e., after a brief announcement by the White House press aide with the party, Malcolm Kilduff] Dr. Malcolm Perry, an attending surgeon, and Dr. Kemp Clark, chief of neurosurgery at Parkland Hospital, gave more details. Mr. Ken-

nedy was hit by a bullet in the throat, just below the Adam's apple,
they said. This wound had the appearance of a bullet's entry.

The next paragraph Specter would not have found attractive, not
any more than Humes et al. would have, because it quotes the Dallas
doctors as saying the head wound could have been caused by two
bullets, not only one.

In 1963 the two most important wire services were the Associated
Press and United Press International. The *Dallas Times Herald,* despite having its own reporters on the story, carried a condensed version of United Press International's November 22 story in its Sunday
edition, the 24th. Its fourth paragraph reads: "Staff doctors at Parkland Hospital in Dallas said only that the sniper's bullet pierced the
midsection of the front part of his neck and emerged from the top
of his skull."

It then quotes "White House sources as saying they understood
the President was shot in front of his neck." The White House had
this in its files from November 22, 1963.

Specter was not going to trouble the White House press office.
Perish the thought!

But *if* he had, the one thing that would not have been overlooked
is the very first news conference transcript of the LBJ administration,
November 22, 1963, at 3:16 P.M. Central time. It is nine legal-sized
pages long. Wayne Hawks of the White House press office presented
the transcript of Perry and Clark, and they answered questions. On
the second page Perry said he performed the tracheotomy that from
time to time Humes pretended he knew nothing about. Thus *all* the
media had that information, and if Humes read or heard any reporting, *any* reporting at all, he would have had reason to be "'somewhat certain" about that tracheotomy.

Of the neck wound, in response to a question (on page 4 of the
White House transcript), Perry said it was "a bullet hole almost in
the midline." He not only repeated this when asked, but also demonstrated it on his own neck.

Asked again (page 5), "Where was the entrance wound?" Perry
responded, "There was an entrance wound in the neck."

Asked still again (page 6), "Doctor, describe the entrance wound.
You think from the front in the throat?" Perry responded, "The

wound appeared to be an entrance wound in the front of the neck; yes, that is correct.''

Is there any wonder, as reported above, that on the next day, Saturday, November 23, Perry told Kemp Clark that he knew what Bethesda was going to say from having spoken to Humes and wanted not to answer questions, just to disappear, and to become unavailable to the press? And, quite obviously, whichever of Humes's contradictory versions is accepted, it wasn't anything like what Perry said of their conversation(s), and the only way in the world that Perry could have known was from Humes.

About a half-dozen of the Dallas doctors testified that they believed this anterior neck wound was of entrance. At least two nurses also did. They are Diana Hamilton Bowron and Margaret M. Henchcliffe. It is they who cut the President's shirt and tie out of Carrico's way, and it is they who had, with the possible exception of Dr. Charles Carrico, the best view of this wound.

Even Boswell told Levine in the *Baltimore Sun*, ''The pathologists had already been told the probable extent of the injuries and what had been done by the physicians'' in Dallas [*Post Mortem*, page 37]. They thus did know before Humes saw the corpse that Perry had performed the tracheotomy.

Even the two FBI agents at the autopsy, Sibert and O'Neill, knew that the tracheotomy had been performed, and their only source had to have been one of the pathologists. In their report, where they recounted the removal of the body from the casket, they said, ''It is also apparent that a tracheotomy had been performed'' [*Post Mortem*, page 534].

It is apparent that just about everyone involved knew immediately that Perry had performed a tracheotomy, and that he and others had told the world that the anterior neck wound was one of entrance. This, as Manchester, the semi-official insider with access to these people reported, is what really got Humes to phone Dallas, to cut off talk of a front-entrance wound. And Perry went into hiding so the press could not question him further.

Specter is not a ninny. He had to have known all about what Perry and a number of other Dallas doctors had already said, and he had to have known that the malarkey he fed the Commission and Perry was ridiculous. But, in the totality of the secrecy in which the Commission functioned, he was able to pull it off. The Commission, thanks to a major media that had abdicated their responsibility when the Commission published, got away with murder.

I found Perry to be only slightly reticent on some details, the touchier ones, but he was inclined toward honesty and forthrightness. He had this past forced upon him and he was aware of it. But, again returning to what was available to the *JAMA* four, this is what I wrote in *Post Mortem*:

I left on a long trip to a number of cities, including Dallas. There, on the morning of December 1, 1971, I interviewed three Parkland Hospital doctors then available who had taken part in the emergency treatment of the President.

I had interviewed Perry on an earlier trip. To the credit of all, despite the fact that my views had been well-publicized and, in fact, had been repeated on local television just a few days earlier, not one objected to being interviewed. All the interviews were in their offices in the attached school of medicine. Before summarizing these interviews and in fairness to these men, I remind the reader of the unenviable position in which all had been placed and of the pressures, already detailed, to which all had been subjected.

In confidence I respect, one I will not name told me of a first-person account by a Navy doctor present at the autopsy, a fact hidden in all records.

It was deer season in Texas. Some of those I interviewed outside the hospital had just returned from trips to hunting country, some were about to leave. Perry had sought deer and antelope the previous week. He and his family are fond of the meat. Hunting is a form of exercise he enjoys. They had not had good luck. His eleven-year-old son had the only chance at a deer, a bad shot, so they bagged none.

This led us into a discussion of hunting, rifles, ammunition, and the effects of various kinds of ammunition, designed for different purposes. As with many men who really enjoy hunting, Perry is an expert on ammunition. In common with many hunters and gun hobbyists, he handloads his own ammunition. In connection with this writing and that on the King's assassination, I have made a study of rifles and ammunition, have consulted various experts, standard literature, and criminalists, and I believe that Perry is much more expert in these areas than most doctors in other parts of the country. It has been my opinion that there are few cities in the country in which the assassination could have been committed where the witnesses could have been as helpful to any sincere investigation because of their knowledge of wounds, weaponry, and ammunition [*Post Mortem,* pages 374–75].

(All experienced hunters develop some knowledge of how different kinds of bullets work. It is the basis for the ammunition they select when hunting.)

This, too, is a secret in the official investigations. Neither the commission nor the FBI was interested. Their interests lay in the other direction, in hiding. Perry's amateur expertise is one of these secrets, through no fault of his.

Most of this is Arlen Specter's fault. I found Dallas officials who developed an intense personal dislike for him and the manner of his 'investigation.' Specter knew what to do to keep what he wanted out of the official evidence. One new example of this is Allan Sweatt, then chief criminal deputy in the sheriff's office. Sweatt was responsible for the immediate taking of statements from eyewitnesses. He handled all the pictures immediately known about. But Sweatt was not a witness before the Commission, and was not the subject of any FBI interrogation in the Commission's evidence. Specter used Sweatt's polygraph room to conduct the Ruby lie-detector test. He used polygraph 'experts' whose credentials were considered dubious in Dallas. The first thing Specter did was to chase Sweatt, an authentic expert from his own office. Sweatt was not present when Ruby was questioned.

So, if there are inadequacies and errors in the testimony of the doctors and if, as I believe, in some cases it crossed the line into criminality, the responsibility is Specter's. The doctors deserve sympathy and sympathetic understanding of the position in which all had been put. All were under inordinate pressure. Perry is but one example. He is but one of the many with technical knowledge valuable (if not, indeed, essential) to any thorough and honest investigation whose expertise was hidden from the members of the Commission and its record, secret and published [*Post Mortem,* pages 375–76].

(What is omitted here, my interview with Dr. Charles Carrico, appears in the coming chapter, with nothing omitted either here or there.)

When I left Room D614A and walked across the hall, Perry was in.

He is a warm, friendly man, inclined to smile pleasantly while talking, with what appears to be justified pride in his and his institutions's professional accomplishments. While he remembered me and my belief that the official account of the assassination is wrong, he was not reluctant to be interviewed. His recollections of the great events in which he had been caught up are, and for the rest of his life will be, sharp. From my interviews with him, I am without doubt that, had he not been subjected to powerful and improper pressures, there would have been no word he would have said that would not have been completely dependable.

From time to time embarrassment showed. He began defensively going back to the anterior neck wound. He does not deny telling the press that it was one of entrance. He does say that he has been given a tape of one of his interviews in which he hedged the statement by saying it was, to a degree, conjectural. Most doctors, under those circumstances, great urgency, the President as the patient, and without even having turned the body over, would have said something like 'appeared to be' in describing the wound as one of entrance. While superficially maintaining the position in which Specter put him under oath, of saying he did not really know whether the wound was of entrance or exit, Perry readily admits that Humes correctly understood him to describe it as a wound of entrance. He also admits that federal agents showed him and the other doctors the autopsy report *before* their testimony [*Post Mortem,* page 377].

The evidence is simply overwhelming: from Humes through Specter they all knew the truth. Aside from his other sources, Humes knew from Perry that Perry had identified the anterior neck wound as one of entrance. Without doubt Perry told Humes on the first of Humes's calls to him, the only one mentioned by Specter and the Report, although the Commission's own evidence is that there was more than one call from Humes to Perry. (See also the Afterword.)

What could have been the purpose of any other call Humes made to Perry *before* beginning to draft his autopsy report?

The only possible explanation, one that tells us why Specter and the Commission and their Report ignore Humes's second call to Perry, is what Dr. Kemp Clark, chief of surgery and Perry's superior, testified to. Specter, pretending that Humes made only one call to

Perry, asked him when he testified before the Commission, "Did you tell Dr. Perry anything about your observations and conclusions?" Humes replied, "No, sir."

This, according to the transcript of the testimony, was followed by the taking of a recess.

Perry himself testified that on the second call Humes told him what the autopsy report was going to say "and asked that I keep it in confidence," which I did."

Perry also informed his superior, Kemp Clark. He asked Clark to help him keep his knowledge from Humes confidential. As Clark himself testified:

'Dr. Perry stated that he had talked to the Bethesda Naval Hospital on two occasions that morning, and he knew what the autopsy findings had shown and that he did not wish to be questioned by the press' about it. So he asked Clark that, with a press conference pending, most of that press conference "be conducted by" him.

Perry then made himself scarce.

All of this, all from the official evidence, is here quoted again from a single page (180) of *Whitewash,* where it has always been available to anyone, including Lundberg. And I emphasize still again that in 1966 I sent both Humes and Boswell copies of that book.

The reader is reminded that this autopsy report was kept secret from all others, especially the press, until it was published in the Report at the end of September, 1964. The quotations from *Post Mortem* continue:

As I led [Perry] over the events and his participation, what he did and the sequence, he recalled that he first looked at the wound, then asked a nurse for a 'trake' (short for tracheotomy) tray, wiped off the wound, saw a ring of bruising around it, and started cutting. In describing the appearance of the wound and the ring of bruising, he used the words 'as they always are.' Pretending not to notice the significance of this important fact he had let bubble out, I retraced the whole procedure with him again. When he had repeated the same words, I asked him if he had ever been asked about the ringed bruise around the wound in the front of the neck. The question told the experienced hunter and the experienced surgeon exactly what he had admitted, one description of an entrance wound. He blushed and improvised the explanation that there was blood around the wound. I did not further embarrass him by pressing him, for we both knew he had seen the wound clearly. He had *twice* said he had wiped the blood off and *had* seen the wound clearly, if briefly, before cutting.

The official presentation, and that of an unofficial apologist to whom we shall come, would have us believe that bruising is a characteristic of entrance wounds only. This is not the case. The reader should not be deceived on this or by Perry's admission that there was bruising. Exit wounds also can show bruising. One difference is that exit wounds do not have to show bruising. That in this case, there was bruising by itself need not be taken as an expression of Perry's professional opinion that it was a wound of entrance. The definitive answer is in those words he twice used, quoted directly above *'as they always are.'* It is *entrance* wounds *only* that *always* are of this description. Thus Perry had said again and in a different way that this was a shot from the front. In context, this also is the only possible meaning of what Carrico had said. [This is included in the coming chapter.]

In the official version, the President's nonfatal and all of Connally's wounds were caused by the same bullet. We discussed them, Perry was called in on the Connally surgery 'by the boss' because he is an expert on arterial injury. When the other doctors noted the location of the thigh wound, they feared the possibility of proximity to an artery. One would never know this from Specter's questioning of any of the doctors or from any of the reports of federal agents. There is no reason to believe it is because of the reluctance of the doctors to speak freely.

Because of the reason for which he had been called in, Perry made careful observations of that wound as he made his examination. The hole was much too small for a bullet to have caused it. He said that from his examination of the X rays, the fragment was relatively flat and could not have been deposited by a whole bullet that then backed out. He showed me with his fingers that the fragment was less than a half-inch under the skin and that it had gone about three to three and a half inches after penetration. This near-the-skin trajectory alone is more than enough to invalidate the entire official story. Because he saw no danger to any artery, Perry did not remove this fragment. This, he said, is the usual practice. He volunteered that, had the fragment been there from an unremembered childhood accident, it would have presented no hazard to Connally. I asked, had there been such a childhood accident, would it not have left a scar? Perry said the fragment was so thin it need not have [*Post Mortem,* pages 377–78).

Specter deposed all Connally's surgeons, some twice—once in Dallas and again before the Commission, like Perry. To the best of my recollections, he did not once ask any of these surgeons to testify to the size of the wound of entry on Connally's thigh. If he had, the whole false case for his single-bullet mythology would have perished instantly on this simple and obvious point, that the wound was too small to have been made by the entire, "pristine" bullet, as it appears to be at the end of its fabulous career, at rest in the National Archives.

Gradually, as we discussed his observations, Perry came to realize that he was providing a professional destruction of the official story. So, when we were discussing the Connally thigh wound, I reminded him that the official police account, written at the time of the crime and quoting the doctors, has said the same thing, that this wound had been caused by a fragment.

He then volunteered on this point that the X rays showed fragmentation in Connally's wrist. When I quoted Shaw's and Gregory's testimonies that there was more metal in the wrist than can be accounted for as missing from Bullet 399, Perry nodded his head in agreement [*Post Mortem,* page 378].

This is reported in detail in *Whitewash,* in chapters "The Number of Shots" and "The Doctors and the Autopsy," pages 155–87.

In addition to the bullet fragments that Perry reports are visible in Connally's wrist X rays, a considerable number of unknown sized fragments were washed away as the wound was cleansed. Still others were recovered by the medical personnel and turned over to a Texas Ranger by a nurse. Those fragments were later given to the FBI. There is public disagreement about whether what the FBI gave the Commission is all the Rangers gave the FBI.

There was the thigh fragment. There was the one Dr. Shires testified remained in Connally's chest, shown in the chest X ray. And there were what the Commission, in the area of its work of which Specter was in charge, somehow managed not to report: that there were also fragments in President Kennedy's body. All these fragments can total, from the official record, only about a grain and a half and must have come from the magic bullet. In troy apothecaries' weight, *it takes 480 grains to make one ounce!* A truly minute amount of metal for all those fragments.

Connally's surgeons disputed Specter's fantasy in their testified-to disagreement with it in the previously cited source. They agreed that more metal had been in Connally's wrist alone than is missing from Bullet 399, which they examined. Dr. Robert R. Shaw alone testified that more than twice what is missing from 399 is in the wrist (*Whitewash,* page 174).

> Perry was not unwilling to express criticism of the autopsy doctors. Humes had told Specter that the bruise on the President's pleura might have been caused by Perry's surgery. Perry was affronted by the suggestion. He said they never cause such bruising in tracheotomies in adults and are exceedingly careful to avoid it in the smaller bodies of children. When Perry learned of this bruising, he had wondered if the cause was fragmentation. If he then had no way of knowing it, on the basis of my 'new evidence,' that today does seem to be the most reasonable explanation [*Post Mortem,* page 378].

As reported above, the very X rays that Humes et al. had taken during the autopsy reveal fragments in the very area of JFK's body that Humes said was bruised by a surgical ineptness he (contrary to the evidence) attributed to Perry.

This confirms Perry's belief that the pleura bruise was from fragmentation.

This evidence was not disclosed officially until 1969, and it was not publicly available until I published it in *Post Mortem,* in 1975.

Could the Commission and Specter have had a better reason for not having the autopsy film *available to them* to use as the basis for taking testimony from its own medical experts?

> The autopsy doctors were wrong in attributing the chest incisions to subcutaneous emphysema. The way Perry said this, it was

as though he were saying, 'Any child should know that.' Perry, personally, had asked for these incisions. They were a 'closed chorostomy.' This is irrelevant except as a professional opinion on the competence of the Bethesda doctors.

Having learned what Specter suppressed, that Perry is an amateur expert in ammunition, I discussed other evidence that Specter suppressed, the pattern of fine fragmentation in the right front of the President's head as disclosed without explanation in the panel report. Perry was without doubt that this could not have been caused by a jacketed, military bullet. The reader should remember that, under the terms of the Geneva Convention, military ammunition is encased in a hardened jacket for 'humanitarian' reasons, to prevent just this kind of fragmentation in human bodies. Military ammunition is designed to avoid explosion of the bullet in the body, for a clean transiting of the body. This is not the cause with hunting or 'varminting' ammunition, that is, a bullet designed for the human killing of pests or undesirable animals.

Perry's opinion is that the fine fragmentation and its pattern in the right front of the head alone could be the end of the Warren Report. As he thought about this 'new evidence' on the wounds, Perry said that, from his experience, the panel description of the pattern of fragmentation is consistent with what he would expect from a 'varminting' round. It is the opposite of the behavior of a military round, which is supposed to prevent this.

To illustrate his point, which is not his alone, Perry described the explosion of a varminting bullet on a recent hunt, when he had shot a prairie dog. The damage in each case was similar. The inference is that the massive damage to the President's head could have been caused by an entering bullet. Other amateur experts, like Dr. Richard Bernabei, had already told me this.

All his colleagues hold the highest opinion of the county coroner, Dr. Earl Rose, who was avoided with such official diligence that his name is not once mentioned in the testimony. Rose objected vigorously to the kidnapping of the corpse. It was his responsibility, under the only obtaining law, to perform the autopsy.

After the interview I discussed the 'new evidence' with Perry, inviting him to come and see it for himself. I described the reporting of medical fact by the Clark panel, then quoted in the death cerificate. He said that if the government could do such things he would be terrified. I told him, 'Then you *should* be terrified' [*Post Mortem,* pages 378–79].

Chapter 19

The President's Clothes—
Or the Emperor's of the Commission

PERHAPS THE BEST SINGLE SUBJECT WITH WHICH TO ILLUSTRATE HOW
utterly the opposite of the truth was *JAMA*'s intent and that of Humes
and Boswell in what they said about the President's clothes:

> It was only during their interviews with Warren Commission
> investigators that Humes and Boswell saw for the first time the
> clothing worn by President Kennedy. Humes says, 'Once we saw
> the holes in the back of the President's suit jacket and shirt and
> the nicks on his shirt collar and the knot of his necktie, the path
> of the second bullet was confirmed. That bullet was traveling very
> fast and it had to go somewhere. I believe in the single-bullet
> theory that it struck Governor Connally immediately after exiting
> the President's throat.' Boswell adds, 'Having seen the clothing I
> now know that I created a terrible problem with my own autopsy
> drawings. My drawings of the bullet holes on the night of the
> autopsy did not precisely match up with the actual holes in the
> clothing, because we were not aware that the President's suit
> jacket had humped up on his back while he waved at the specta-
> tors. These errors were later exploited by the conspiracy crowd
> to fit their premises and purposes.' The clothing was kept in the
> National Archives, along with the rest of the autopsy materials.

There are nine statements of supposed fact in this relatively brief
quotation from *JAMA*. Some are readily and easily dismissed for
their inaccuracy from what is well-known. Others are not easily dismissed. With all the information supposedly coming from Humes and
Boswell, most of it within quotation marks, an immediate question is:
How much did they really know?

The prosectors did not see the President's clothes until "their interviews with Warren Commission's investigators."—*JAMA*

Humes's and Boswell's interviews by the Commission staff, mostly Specter, took place prior to their testimony. Specter wrote memos covering these interviews.

That Humes and Boswell did not see the clothing before then is their fault. As forensic pathologists they had both the need and the right to examine the clothing. They do not even say that they asked to be able to examine it and were denied access to it. But, if this had happened, all they then need have done is tell the truth, that the requirements of forensic pathology could not be met without their examining the clothing, and they therefore could not continue with their examination.

If they had been wiser, they would, to begin with, have told those above them that forensic pathology was required; that they were not experienced in it; and that the autopsy required those who were. They pretended *they* were forensic pathologists to *JAMA,* but they were not.

This one matter, of the truth from the silent clothing, destroys the entire preconceived "solution." Aside from whether or not the prosectors were too timid to take and preserve this proper and principled position, there is reason to wonder whether they really understood that they required access to the clothing to perform a proper, complete autopsy of a gunshot victim.

As we shall see, Finck knew and said that the autopsy was *not* complete. When he did not prevail, he went along with what he knew was a false representation, that they had performed a "complete" autopsy. This, of course, was known to Humes and Boswell, but they did not see fit to let Lundberg, Breo, or the nation in on that secret. The three prosectors were all together when Finck said they should state the autopsy was not complete and gave his reasons.

"The clothing was kept at the National Archives, along with the rest of the autopsy materials."—*JAMA*

The clothing and the autopsy materials were not "kept" at the National Archives until they were transferred there from the Department of Justice and the FBI. I learned this as a result of my 1970 FOIA lawsuit in which I sought to have the archives take meaningful and clear pictures for me of some of the damages to the clothing. (CA 2569–70, *Harold Weisberg* v. *U.S. General Services Administration and U.S. National Archives and Records Services.*)

One of the pictures that I asked to be taken for me, and again we shall see the need of it for serious research and inquiry, was of the knot of the tie. In the official account of the assassination this magical bullet had to have made a hole in it. That no hole is visible in the Commission's picture is a tribute to the FBI's obfuscatory skills.

Until I filed suit, the regulations required that researchers not be allowed to handle the clothing, but that in substitution, pictures be taken for them. The latter provision was eliminated during the lawsuit, leaving a situation in which pictures were to be taken and shown, but not given to me. The archives was to notify me when the pictures were ready for my examination. Many other pictures of the clothing were and remain accessible at the archives. It also makes copies of these pictures, taken for the Commission by the FBI, for those who want them. The sole difference between the available pictures and those I wanted is that what I wanted photographed is evidence.

The archives became a partisan, not the repository of our most precious national documents. It became an adjunct of the FBI in seeking to continue to hide what the FBI hid because the clothing proves Specter's single-bullet theory is impossible. In turn this meant the crime remained unsolved because the Commission's conclusions were based on the Specter theory.

The archives violated its own rules that were in effect at the time I filed my lawsuit for the clothing. What the archives did was an ex post facto rewriting of the provisions of its regulations. It involved making fraudulent misrepresentations to the federal court. If I had been represented by counsel who could have made effective use of what the judge may not have understood as I tried to present it to him, that, too, could have become a real scandal. It would have focused attention on the meaning of the pictures, copies of which were improperly denied me by the fraudulent misrepresentations and related lies to the judge. While I did not lose, this dangerous abuse of the trust of the court make it impossible for me to show others what these pictures mean. The archives was required to take the pictures I was allowed to examine and thus only can report on.

When some time passed and I heard nothing from the archives, I notified the judge and the archives by letter. As soon as I could thereafter, I went to the archives to see these clear pictures. When I got there, I was told that a letter was in the mail to me. This was because they could not take a picture of the knot of the tie—the *knot,* not the tie, being the evidence—because, so sorry, it had been undone!

Marion Johnson, both an archivist and a lawyer, began by being friendly and helpful to me. After the appearance of my first book and particularly after I asked to study the Commission's records relating to the FBI's spectrographic analyses of the bullet, bullet fragments, and objects they struck, this attitude changed.

Before I stopped going to the archives, Johnson began shaking, literally, when we met. There never had been any argument between us, no unpleasantness of any kind, no reason to fear any violence, but he did shake. By then it was well-known that I was critical of the Commission's work and conclusions and that I was suing under the FOIA.

During a lawsuit against the archives I got copies of some of its records relating to me. This included Johnson's memos, anticipating problems and developments in the withholding of information from me as an adversary, not as an archivist.

With regard to the pictures to be taken for me, particularly of the knot of the tie, Johnson told me that he personally had supervised the transfers from the Department of Justice building across Seventh Street from the archives. He said that the clothing had been in a footlocker, and that when he opened the footlocker to remove and store its contents, the knot was untied.

I knew the necktie knot had been used for a propaganda picture the FBI took as an exhibit for its five-volume report it gave the Commission on December 9, 1963. It is Exhibit 60 in that report. What the FBI actually did was take an unclear picture of the knot of the tie as received by the FBI. It then undid the knot and contorted the tie into the semblance of a knot with the damage that had been on the upper left extreme of the knot when worn appearing to be a bullet hole in the center of the pretended knot. Then it reconstituted the knot.

When the tie was displayed to Commission witnesses, it was tied again, as their testimony reflects. Not a word of any of this tampering with and altering of evidence came from either the FBI or the Commission.

But I had no idea that the FBI's tampering with evidence had not stopped with its initial propaganda need, but had continued after the end of the Commission's life.

In the *JAMA* article Humes and Boswell frequently invoked the report of the House Select Committee on Assassinations and of its forensic panel as confirming their autopsy. That panel examined the necktie. By chance, before that report was issued, I met the chief of that panel, Dr. Michael Baden, then chief medical examiner for the city of New York.

It was the very last day of the hearings of the House Committee on Assassinations. Baden and I were both sitting in the audience while the committee took testimony on issues having nothing to do with his work. He appeared to be expecting to be called as a witness. It just happened that he was sitting on my right. We got to talking.

I asked him, "Was the tie knotted when you had it?"

"Yes, it was," he said, and he asked why I asked that question.

"Would you like to see a letter to me from the archives written several years before the committee was appointed, saying that the knot then was untied?" I asked him.

His smiling response was "I suspected as much."

And yet, Baden, as the chief of the committee's forensic panel, reached and stated conclusions, knowing this quintessential evidence had been tampered with, that treated it as pristine and pure evidence. He said not a word about his suspicions.

Baden knew from me that the tie-knot evidence had been tampered with. I had offered to give him a copy of the archive's letter that stated the knot was untied at the time of the lawsuit. How dependable could Baden have been when he was silent in his official role as chairman of the Congressional committee's panel of experts when he knew there had been hanky-panky with some of the most vital evidence in the assassination of a president?

Perhaps the answer is hinted at in a page-one story in *The New York Times* of August 1, 1979, a story to which, in all, it devoted half a page that day.

[Mayor] Koch Removes Baden as the
City's Medical Examiner

[Under a headline four columns wide on the front page, Richard Severo's story begins:]

Mayor Koch, apparently responding to complaints received from one of the city's five District Attorneys and from the Health Commissioner, announced yesterday that he would not make permanent the appointment of Dr. Michael M. Baden as Chief Medical Examiner. Dr. Baden was appointed provisionally a year ago and the appointment would have become permanent yesterday, the job his until he retired from it. He will now revert to deputy chief medical examiner. In a news conference at City Hall, the Mayor declined to discuss specific charges, saying that 'the entire record is what's important—I base my decision upon the entire record.' The complainants against Dr. Baden were Robert M. Morgenthau, District Attorney of Manhatten, and Dr. Reinaldo A. Ferrer, the Health Commissioner. Their criticisms were contained in letters sent to the Mayor after he had requested evaluations of Dr. Baden's work from the District Attorneys. Dr. Ferrer's comments were not sought but he volunteered them. Mr. Morgenthau and Dr. Ferrer generally charged Dr. Baden with sloppy recordkeeping, poor judgment, and a lack of cooperation. Dr. Baden denied the charges.

The FBI report for which it had altered this most basic evidence was delivered to the Commission more than two months before it took any testimony about the clothing. The Commission had FBI Exhibit 60 with the tie pictured unknotted. It also had the tie itself with the knot more or less restored. And it said not a word.

"That bullet was traveling very fast and it had to go somewhere," said Humes in *JAMA*.

These are not the words of anyone with any experience in forensic pathology.

Humes says "that bullet was traveling very fast," but for rifle bullets it was not. Its muzzle velocity was about 2100 feet per second. That is well inside the medium-velocity range (See *Whitewash*, page 171, for the testimony of FBI SA Robert Frazier).

* * *

"That bullet ... had to go somewhere," said Humes in *JAMA*.
Indeed it did.

Establishing *where* that bullet went was Humes's job. Instead, he *presumed* it.

If he had had the clothing, and the clothing had not been toyed with, the direction in which the fibers at the jacket and shirt bullet holes point would have told him that the bullet came from the opposite direction. (again see, *Whitewash,* page 161, for the testimony of FBI SA Robert Frazier). But that required knowledge of, experience in, and concern for forensic pathology. Humes had neither the knowledge nor the experience nor the interest.

"We were not aware that the President's suit jacket had humped up on his back," said Boswell in *JAMA*.

Indeed Boswell and Humes were not aware of it—because it did not happen!

JFK's "humped up" jacket is one of the cock-and-bull stories made up by the Commission's former assistant counsels and apologists in pretended response to damning facts appearing on the Boswell autopsy face sheet or body chart after I published it. Their comments drew even more attention to it.

Neither Breo nor Lundberg asked Boswell, "How do you know the jacket had humped up on his back?" *If* they had, however, Boswell would not have been able to show him any of the many pictures of JFK taken at that time that show any such "hump." As is also alleged in this canard, supposedly the jacket had a horizontal fold on the back, created when JFK raised his arm to wave to the crowd. In fact, as the Zapruder film shows, when he was shot, his arm was not raised. Only his forearm was, and that would not have caused such a fold.

The President, a natty dresser, wore clothes tailored for him. The shirt, for example, was made for him by Charles of New York. His clothing was not off-the-rack, like the jackets and shirts most of us wear.

The "humping up" of his shirt was even less possible because he was sitting on his shirttails.

*　　*　　*

"My drawings of the bullet holes ... did not precisely match up with the actual holes in the clothing," said Boswell in *JAMA*.

Absolutely, positively 100 percent false.

The Commission, the prosecutors, and the other apologists for the official "solution" who agree with Boswell either are not familiar with the Commission's actual testimony on this, or they lie. The testimony of the FBI, which measured the distances from the collars to the holes, placed the holes precisely where Boswell did, as does much more evidence to which we draw closer.

Again it should be emphasized, Boswell *made no drawings*. He *knows* he made no drawings. He used a standard Navy mimeographed form for autopsies with the bodies already represented by the side by side outlines visible on the forms.

All Boswell did was place a dot on the back outline.

He has to know this. Those are, or then were, standard Navy autopsy forms.

Why Boswell keeps repeating that he "drew" the body outline, when he knows very well he did not, provokes suspicion that his misstatement is for a calculated purpose: to give the false impression that he made a mistake in his drawings. It is the falsity he began with his 1966 interview with *Baltimore Sun* reporter Richard Levine. He told Levine that he placed the mark on the body chart incorrectly.

I remind the reader that I sent both Humes and Boswell copies of *Whitewash* in May 1966. Six months later when Levine interviewed Boswell, he was critical of my book. When I learned this from Levine, I wrote Boswell and he did not reply. But he had read my book, and he had criticized it.

Robert A. Frazier was an FBI laboratory ballistics expert, but the Commission and the FBI both used him as an expert witness in other areas, even when he specified he did not have personal knowledge and that he was not competent to testify.

That made it safe for him to testify incompletely or inaccurately without embarrassing the Commission or the FBI.

Frazier testified at length and with the care that is appropriate for an FBI expert (5H9 ff). He identified the point in the President's clothing represented by the President's 'neck' wound at 5⅜ inches below the top of the collar of the jacket (5H59) and at 5¾ inches below the top of the collar on the shirt (5H60). Spectrographic analysis of the margins of these holes showed 'traces of copper,' proved to be foreign to the cloth. This is at least strongly indicative, if not positive proof, that the bullet making this hole was copper-jacketed, and this, in turn, is indicative of the type of the bullet [*Whitewash,* page 160].

Humes was given the President's coat and shirt to examine (2H365). He saw the bullet holes and located them 'approximately six inches below the top of the collar, and two inches to the right of the middle seam ...' A number of others gave approximately this representation of the location of the bullet holes in the President's garments. The location of this bullet hole, according to Humes, 'corresponds essentially with the point of entrance' of that missile. Six inches down from the collar. Not in the neck [*Whitewash,* page 185].

Frazier's measurements were made at the FBI. They are precise. Humes gave an estimate as he held the jacket in his hands and examined it again before the Commission. These and all other locations of that bullet hole are identical with the mark Boswell placed on the Navy autopsy form!

Yet Boswell told Lundberg and Breo, and they quoted him as saying that "my drawings of the bullet holes ... did not precisely match up with the actual holes in the clothing."

When writing in *Whitewash* about the mark Boswell placed on the face sheet, I wrote: It "is not just a haphazard sketch" and noted that "some dimensions are given in millimeters" on it. And continued:

It cannot be brushed off, as so many of the few criticisms of the Report have been.

Nor is it without substantiation, good, solid substantiation.

[Roy] Kellerman, the Secret Service agent in charge, was with the President's body, except for a few brief instances, from the Dallas hospital until it left the Bethesda Naval Hospital. In his testimony, not quoted in the Report, he repeatedly described this as a 'shoulder' wound, just below the 'large muscle between the shoulder and the neck.' In questioning him, Specter did not refer to this as a neck wound but as a shoulder wound (2H81).

Kellerman called Secret Service Agent Clint Hill into the autopsy room to make formal observation of the President's wounds.

This also is not quoted in the Report, but in his statement (18H740–5) Hill declared 'I observed a wound about six inches down from the neckline on the back just to the right of the spinal column,' precisely what the suppressed autopsy note shows.

Secret Service Agent Glen A. Bennett was looking at the President when the bullet 'hit the President about four inches down from the right shoulder' (R111).

In questioning Humes (2H371), Specter referred to 'the wound in the President's back,' in a context that imparts a different significance to the questions asked of all the Parkland medical people, had they raised or turned the President over. [*Whitewash,* page 185].

Chapter 20

Michael Baden

AFTER ADDING TO HIS FAME AS NEW YORK CITY'S CHIEF MEDICAL
examiner by heading the House Committee on Assassinations and
after he was forced out of his cushy New York City position, Michael
Baden wrote a book, with Judith Adler Hennessee, in which he exploited and commercialized his committee role. It is titled *Unnatural
Death: Confessions of a Medical Examiner* (New York: Random
House, 1989). One of its unintended confessions is its thorough condemnation of this very autopsy and protocol that Baden pretended
was a satisfactory and accurate one.

The House Committee confined its whitewashing of the JFK autopsy to one volume of its massive published appendix, Volume III,
where 352 pages are devoted to it. It contains some criticisms. In
Unnatural Death Baden did not find it necessary to conform with
what that committee so obviously wanted of him and his panel. Instead, in his first chapter, titled "Heroes and Conspiracies" subtitled
"The Price of Fame," he mercilessly devastates the official autopsy.
Here are a few of his comments that are particularly worthy of
noting:

> Humes 'had never autopsied anyone with a gunshot wound'
> [page 8].
> Commander Humes didn't know the difference between an en-
> trance and an exit wound. . . . [The others] didn't know the differ-
> ence, either [page 9].
> Humes 'was not sanguine about doing the autopsy. He had
> never done one like it before. Why not request help? I asked him.
> He explained that he couldn't—he was the low man in the hierar-
> chy, and he had to follow orders in the military, you don't tell
> generals and admirals that you are not qualified for the job.'

Humes 'told us that he wasn't supposed to do a full autopsy. He was just supposed to find the bullet' [page 11].

'. . . the autopsy itself was woefully inadequate' [page 12].

'It took Humes about two hours to do the autopsy . . . [it] should reasonably have taken the better part of a day. A complicated one can take eight hours, and this one was complicated. The autopsy is not finished until you work out the bullet track along with the exits and entrances.' [page 13].

'The X rays and photographs show the [rear, nonfatal] wound to be lower on the back and the track slightly upward' [page 14].

[Humes's] 'was an autopsy report filled with errors, sins of commission and omission. Bullets weren't tracked, the brain wasn't sectioned, the measurements were inaccurate, the head wound wasn't described. . . . He didn't shave any hair around the head wounds in order to examine them. The wounds were photographed through the hair' [page 15].

'Perhaps the most egregious error was the four-inch miscalculation. The head is only five inches long from crown to neck, but Humes . . . placed the head wound four inches lower than it actually was, near the neck instead of the cowlick' [page 16].

Humes's mismeasurement was not an error. It was intended to conform to the official story. Before the changes, which Humes testified were directed by Admiral Galloway, his description of the wound is of "a puncture wound tangential to the surface of the scalp . . ." As changed under Galloway's orders, this phrase, visibly corrected by hand, is simplified and radically altered into merely "a lacerated wound." Because "Tangential to the surface of the scalp" cannot possibly be at the level of the occiput, the knob at the back of the head, the "error" of four inches cannot be regarded as a simple error.

Baden also confirms what I wrote years earlier about the design of military ammunition to prevent precisely the kind of damage done to the President:

The bullet was an Italian 6.5 millimeter . . . a military, not a civilian bullet. In conformity with the Geneva Convention rules of civilized war, military ammunition is made with a full metal jacket. The idea is that the bullet will not break up inside the body, but go through it, causing less pain and suffering [pages 17 and 18].

With regard to the official fantasy as it relates to Connally's wounds, Baden asked, "Had the bullet burrowed into Connally's thigh bone? If it had, it couldn't have leaped out and fallen onto the stretcher. . . . A bullet that goes two inches deep and into the bone doesn't suddenly decide to reverse itself" [page 18].

The last few words in Baden's chapter have wide applicability in the JFK assassination and its official investigations: "People went on thinking what they wanted to think" [page 18].

Preeminently, I add, Baden did.

Yet, for his fee and for the responsibilities he accepted for the House of Representatives, Baden sanctified the knowingly false whitewashing of "the crime of the century."

Quoted in this chapter are the words repeating what I, as a layman, wrote years earlier. He is a recognized professional expert, the expert regarded by the House of Representatives as the one above all others it wanted to head its panel on the medical evidence in the JFK assassination. Years later he confirmed my criticisms, in fact presenting them as his own.

Chapter 21

The Commission Deceived Its Own Dissenting Members!

AT THE TIME I RAISED QUESTIONS ABOUT THE SINGLE-BULLET THEORY, really disproving it in my first book, I had not heard the rumor that a member of the Commission, the respected conservative southern Democrat, Senator Richard B. Russell of Georgia, did not believe it himself. Then, as I worked in the archives and through the FOIA sought to compel the disclosure of all the Commission's executive-session transcripts, I made what to me was a shocking discovery: Rankin, probably with Warren's approval, eliminated the record Russell had made of his doubts for our history.

Two other members, Senator John Sherman Cooper, Kentucky Republican, and Congressman Hale Boggs, conservative Louisiana Democrat, shared Russell's disbelief, Boggs reportedly less vigorously than Cooper.

In *Whitewash IV* I went into Russell's refusal to believe the single-bullet theory. I discussed how Rankin and Warren conned him into signing the Report anyway, based on a misrepresentation to him of the compromise they proposed to him, and based on my own relationship with him thereafter. Russell encouraged my efforts to disprove the Warren Report until the day he died. This information, obviously, was readily available to anyone interested in learning the truth about the assassination and its investigations.

Before presenting the official evidence, lied about and suppressed, that both disproves the single-bullet theory and establishes that there had been a conspiracy to assassinate JFK, I will give an abbreviated account of my relationship with Senator Russell. I will confirm it with records from the archive of his papers he left at the University of Georgia at Athens. I will follow this with an account of how I obtained the shirt-collar picture the Commission did not have and

221

Specter should have gotten the moment he first laid eyes on FBI Exhibit 60.

I had given Russell a copy of a phony "stenographic transcript" of the September 18, 1964, executive session, a session he had forced because of his disagreement with the single-bullet conclusion of the Report. There was no court reporter there, contrary to Russell's belief. It also was the one time when all seven members were in attendance. Not a word about what Russell said in objection to the single-bullet theory was mentioned in the phony transcript, a fabrication of which Rankin must be responsible (See *Whitewash IV,* pages 131–32).

Among the questions Russell had never been able to resolve in his own mind were those most significant in my work and in this January 27 transcript. He was satisfied there had been a conspiracy, that no one man could have done the known shooting, and that 'we have not been told the truth about Oswald' by the federal agencies. Russell told me this as we walked from his office toward the Senate floor the morning I met with him [*Whitewash IV,* page 21].

On the day the government's appeals brief was due in my FOIA lawsuit for it, the postman delivered a copy of the transcript of the January 27, 1964, executive-session transcript, mailed to me from the National Archives. The government apparently had decided that, although it had prevailed before the district court through its misrepresentations, it could not expect to prevail before the appeals court.

I printed all eighty-five pages of it in facsimile in *Whitewash IV.* Called to consider what Rankin referred to as the "dirty rumor" that Oswald had worked for the FBI [page 48], some of the members let their hair down. Former CIA Director Allen Dulles told his fellow members that the CIA lied and committed perjury [pages 52–53, 62–66] and that it should. John J. McCloy and Russell said these agencies used some "terribly bad characters" [page 72], "some of very limited mentalities" [page 72]. But the Commission never did investigate these reports, leading to other doubts Russell had:

He was shaken by the proof that he had been imposed upon and history perverted. He asked me to conduct a further investigation to prove whether or not there still existed a transcript of the executive session Russell had forced on September 18, just before publication of the Report, which went to press less than a week later and then was in page proof.

In the quotation that follows, James B. Rhoads was then archivist:

After I gave Russell Rhoads's certification that this is the stupefying fact, that the bureaucrats would destroy the record of disbelief recorded by a member of a presidential commission allegedly investigating the assassination by which that President took power, he broke his long friendship with Lyndon Johnson and resigned his chairmanship of the Military Affairs Committee so important to him and his district, and with that divested himself of "oversight" responsibilities over the CIA [*Whitewash IV,* page 21].

In the *Washington Post* of October 11, 1968, a small item referred to Russell's ending of his long political friendship and relationship with Johnson, confirming what Russell had told me about this. Then:

What did not appear is that to his dying day Russell, the most conservative of the Commissioners, continued to urge me to disprove the Report he had been tricked into agreeing to sign. He had told me, as I recall, that he had told Warren: " 'Just put a little footnote in there at the bottom of the page saying "Senator Russell dissents" ' and that Warren refused, insisting on unanimity. Russell would not agree that there had been a lone assassin and no conspiracy. One change was made to entice him to agree to sign, but the specific language and the thrust of the Report remained unchanged. It says exactly what Russell would not agree to, what Russell did not believe about the shooting and the wounds [as it appears in the Report]:

2. The weight of the evidence indicates that there were three shots fired.

3. Although it is not necessary to any essential findings of the Commission to determine just which shot hit Governor Connally, there is very persuasive evidence from the experts to indicate that the same bullet which pierced the President's throat also caused Governor Connally's wounds. However, Governor Connally's testimony and certain other factors have given rise to some differences of opinion as to this probability, but there is no question in the mind of any member of the Commission that all the shots which caused the President's and Governor Connally's wounds

were fired from the sixth-floor window of the Texas School
Book Depository.

4. The shots which killed President Kennedy and wounded Governor Connally were fired by Lee Harvey Oswald [*Whitewash IV,*
page 21].

[There was *no* such evidence from *any* experts, as the Commission's own testimony proves and as I exposed in the final two
chapters of *Whitewash.*]

What is quoted above is as close as the Commission came to
explaining the single-bullet theory, which never is mentioned as such
in the Report. The quotation within the excerpt is from the Report's
first chapter, "Summary and Conclusions." The massive Report was
so cumbersome that the Associated Press used this chapter as its
main story on the day the Report was released, September 27, 1964.
Whitewash IV continues:

It is in my belief a great tragedy that the sage and wily Russell deceived himself over the reasons Johnson made him a commissioner.
Russell told me he thought it was to keep him too busy to lead the
southern opposition to the then-pending civil-rights legislation.

"But I fooled Lyndon," Russell chortled, adding that he
did lead the fight and neglected his duties as Warren
Commissioner.

At the time Russell and I met, he knew he had emphysema.
Shortly thereafter he was found to have a cancerous lung. When
he knew he was going to die and after I gave him the proofs he
wanted, he recorded his doubts publicly if with some tact and
delicacy in a broadcast for the Cox TV network in his native
Georgia and privately, on January 30, 1970, in his last letter to me:

I am interested that you are continuing your work, and
there are a number of matters in the investigation which
would be of interest to me if I had the time to devote to
them. Unfortunately, my duties here as Chairman of the Ap-
propriations Committee and President Pro Tempore of the
Senate simply preclude me from spending the time that
would be required to do justice to any further inquiry into
this complicated series of events.

Fairness to the dead LBJ requires recording my belief that he had nothing to do with this deception of Russell and the destruction of the record of his doubt he thought he was making for history [*Whitewash IV*, page 22].

The excerpt that follows discusses the faked September transcript. Ward and Paul is the name of the Commission's official court-reporting firm.

The reference to the January 22 transcript requires a comment. It is printed in facsimile in *Post Mortem* (pages 475 ff.). It is the transcript of a Commission executive session withheld from me for years. In it the members stated their intention to discourage any belief in the existence of any conspiracy, confessed their fear of J. Edgar Hoover and their recognition that he and his FBI dominated them and was not investigating as it should have.

The first two pages of this faked transcript of the 'memory-holed' executive session Russell forced are appended. Rankin withheld these from the commissioners until November 5, 1964, long after the Commission expired with the release of its Report on September 27. By November 5 the commissioners had no interest in this supposed transcript. They merely filed it and went about their other business.

Faking extends even to the pagination. The phony transcript has page numbers that appear to be a continuation of the Ward and Paul transcript. But, beginning with the second page, it is no more than a selective paraphrase. From these and all four subsequent pages Russell's record for history has been omitted.

The trickery with these executive-session transcripts began with the very first, after Rankin became the actual head of the Commission, with the nonexisting one of January 22, 1964, referred to by Ford in opening his commercialization. It was repeated with the last, in which Russell was censored out of history.

Rankin, the experienced bureaucrat who had been solicitor general of the United States when Nixon was vice president, was nothing if not consistent [*Whitewash IV*, page 22].

Thanks to my good friend Gerard "Chip" Selby and his research at the University of Georgia at Athens, where Russell's papers are deposited, my account of my relationship with Russell and his disagreement with the conclusions of the Warren Report no longer rest on my word alone. Selby also found at the University of Georgia confirmation of what Russell told me as I accompanied him to the Senate floor. This was ignored by all those writing on the subject, particularly by those who, like the House Committee, argue that although the Commission was wrong in everything it did, it nonetheless managed to reach the correct "solution."

After Russell's death the university interviewed Senator Cooper in his office on April 21, 1971. The interviewer was Hugh Gates. Cooper's most succinct statement was that both he and Russell absolutely disagreed with the single-bullet theory that is basic to the Commission's Report. This doubt was raised after hearing the testimony of Governor Connally, testimony Cooper said they both felt was "strong." Cooper then said, "Senator Russell just said, 'I'll never sign that report if . . . if . . . if this Commission says categorically that the second shot passed through both of them.' I agreed with him."

In a private letter, too, Russell was unequivocal in restating his disagreement with the basis of the Commission's conclusions. He had heard of an article reporting his disagreement with the single-bullet theory and asked a former Commission junior lawyer, Alfredda Scobey, to try to track it down for him. She was then a law assistant on the staff of the court of appeals of the state of Georgia in Atlanta. In her letter to Russell of December 12, 1966, Scobey said the article of which he had heard "apparently appears on page 53 of the November 25, 1966, issue of *Life* magazine." She then quoted the passage she believed Russell had in mind. Addressing her affectionately as Miss Fredda, Russell thanked her in a letter written the day before Christmas. Referring to the *Life* article, he adds: "It is not nearly as strong as the position that Senator Cooper and I took in regard to the single-bullet theory. As I recall, Congressman Boggs had mild doubts, but Senator Cooper and I refused to accept the single-bullet theory."

There is no doubt at all: Two of the Commission's members were without any reservation at all opposed to that part of the Report vital to its conclusion that there was no conspiracy. A third member was also opposed, though not as strongly.

This also confirms the purpose of Rankin's deception of these members in at least two ways at that last-minute executive session

when the presses were about to roll on the Report. One is that their
objections would have been incorporated in the language of the Report, and the other is that a court reporter would have been present
to take down in detail their position for the historical record. Their
objections were not incorporated; a court reporter was not present.
While Rankin is not alive now to register any disagreement with
this, he was when I first exposed his deception of Russell and Cooper
at that executive session in *Whitewash IV*.

I also had several meetings with Russell's young assistant, C. E.
Campbell. He wrote a memorandum to Russell. Selby gave me a
copy of it. After reading *Whitewash* "completely," scanning the
three other books I had given him, and after reminding Russell of
our brief meeting the previous week, Campbell wrote to Russell:

If the copy of the transcript or minutes attached is the only
record in the archives on what transpired at the September 18
meeting, it would appear to be a very serious matter. Clearly there
are verbatim transcripts available for the other sessions of the
Commission. The treatment of your exceptions to the first proposed draft of the report are obviously inadequate since no real
mention is made of them in the attached copy. You will note that
Weisberg has included a copy of the letter to him from the archivist of the United States under date of May 20th of this year and
in the third paragraph of that letter the statement is made: 'No
verbatim transcript of the Executive Session of September 18,
1964, is known to be among the records of the Commission.' The
only explanation of this which I can think of is perhaps the verbatim transcript is still classified and not available at all. Weisberg
requested that if you have sufficient interest in this matter to make
an effort to see the records in the archives, that you let him know
first because he says he has some other information which he
knows you would want to see before going to the trouble of
making a contact at the archives.

With reference to his general criticisms of the Commission, he
left with me four books which he has written and which have
been published critical of the Commission, and I have scanned
them all and completely read the first one which was the only one
that received very wide dissemination. His work is scholarly and
evidences a tremendous amount of research. His basic approach
is not to try to prove that Oswald was innocent although acceptance of his inferences, etc., lead to that conclusion.

His method is to restrict his criticism to the actual information which the Commission had, and he is critical of the Commission only to the degree that it delegated too heavily to the staff. One of his strongest points of departure with the Commission is on the number of shots fired and on which shots hit Connally and/ or the President. He completely agrees with your thesis that no one shot hit both the President and the Governor. He apparently believes that there were at least four shots fired and probably more, thus destroying the possibility that Oswald acted alone and independent.

Two statements in his book which perhaps are of interest to you are on page 188 in his conclusions:

> The Senators who questioned Marina Oswald at that mysterious Sunday night hearing in September, 1964, have serious doubts about the report that were confirmed by her performance.

Also:

> To anyone with any experience in investigation or analysis, the most incredible part of the Commission's inquiry is its complete lack of question or criticism of the police. It just is not possible that the police are as incompetent as this record shows.

Weisberg was at one time a Senate investigator, and through research, he has apparently become very knowledgeable on all aspects of the Kennedy Assassination.

I have any of his books which you may wish to see.

Campbell's reference to the September questioning of Marina Oswald, forced by Russell, is to her admission to Russell that she had lied earlier under FBI pressure but had stopped lying (See *Whitewash*, pages 132–36).

I believe Russell is the only member of the Commission who agreed with and praised the work critical of his own Commission.

Another record from the Russell archive at the University of Georgia that was released by Senator John Glenn in 1992, when he was chairman of the Senate committee considering legislation to require disclosure of the remaining government records relating to the JFK assassination, confirms what Russell told me. Russell's papers include his notes on what he said at that September executive session for which Rankin arranged that there would be no verbatim transcript and a letter of resignation he did not send to President Johnson. He feared the inevitable national scandal that would have been unavoidable. That there was internal Warren Commission disagreement over the most basic of its conclusions no longer rests on my word alone.

The Commission's statement in the Report quoted earlier from *Whitewash IV* and appearing on page 19 of the Report, misrepresents the "compromise" reached with Russell. It boils down to "it is not necessary to any essential findings of the Commission to determine just which shot hit Governor Connally." To refer to this as anything other than as crude and as brazen a lie as the Report could utter would be to praise the Report. It is *absolutely* "necessary" to the *entire* Report.

The shot that in the Commission's account had to hit Connally had to be the first of the three shots. This was the only shot that could be tortured into the pretense that JFK's and Connally's bodies *could have* lined up with that sixth-floor TSBD window to make it seem possible for that one bullet to have inflicted all seven injuries on both men.

After that moment it was entirely impossible to pretend that the single-bullet theory was within a remote possibility. The relationship of the bodies and that window changed too much as the limousine moved away from the window.

The Report states: "There is very persuasive evidence from the experts to indicate that the same bullet which pierced the President also caused Governor Connally's wounds." This even Connally and his wife disputed.

There is no such "evidence," "persuasive" or of any other kind. What actually happened is that in questioning the many doctors, Specter told each, "not this bullet, any bullet," and then followed with his imagined career of his single-bullet theory. What this part of the Report then does is to pretend that the hypothetical responses are addressed to the real bullet, CE 399!

*   *   *

How I got the FBI picture of the front to the President's shirt collar is amusing. If anyone had realized that it is the total destruction of the Warren Report I doubt I'd have gotten it.

When I filed that FOIA request, I had just won a summary judgment against the Department of Justice, not an everyday occurrence in federal courts in those days, in the first of my FOIA cases to reach judicial determination. That case, CA 718–70, serves to provide an insight into the official mind on political assassination and on compliance with the FOIA, the law of the land. I'd taken the case to federal district court in Washington when the government refused to provide *copies* of records it had made public in London, England. The request was limited to the information submitted to the British court to get James Earl Ray extradited to be tried for killing Martin Luther King, Jr. This information had in part been reported around the world, and it was *public* information. Only the department refused to give me copies of it under the law that says the people have a right to know what their government does!

In those days Department of Justice regulations controlling FOIA requests required that they be addressed to the deputy attorney general and submitted on a special DJ–118 form, accompanied by three dollars. My request for this and several other pictures went to deputy Richard Kleindienst, of later Watergate fame and other infamy. He asked the FBI to send him the pictures I'd asked for so he could determine whether or not to disclose them to me.

Kleindienst, apparently unhappy about the reflection on his department by the court's finding against it in CA 718–70, and seeing nothing secret in those pictures, sent them to me without speaking to the FBI about it. As a result I got no copies but FBI file originals! Several were the originals of exhibits it had prepared for the Warren Commission.

This picture of the shirt collar proves two central and controlling evidentiary points without question. One is that the damage to the shirt collar was not and could not have been by any bullet, regardless of its original direction, and the other is that the wound in the front of the President's neck was higher than in any of the official fictions.

*   *   *

As fundamentally important as the single-bullet theory is to the Commission's conclusion and large as its Report is, it is surprising how little there is in the Report about the Commission's nonconspiracy, Oswald-alone, single-bullet theory it dignifies and inflates by referring to it as its "conclusion."

In addition to the scanty mention of it in the Report's "Summary and Conclusions," a single paragraph, quoted earlier from *Whitewash,* the Report admits that the possibility is controlled by the positions of the bodies of the two victims—which was not known. It then refers to one of the several sets of tests made for the Commission at the Army's Edgewood Arsenal at its Aberdeen, Maryland, proving grounds, saying it "suggested" the possibility. That work there was based not on pictures taken during the autopsy, but on crude artist's renditions of them, based on, of all imprecise and dubious information, Humes's verbal description of what he later believed were the locations of the wounds on JFK. The Report's language here is tricky and evasive. It turns out that only two of the four experts considered it likely. The Report makes no mention of a fourth here, referring to three only.

The fourth was Dr. Joseph Dolce (see *Post Mortem,* pages 55–56, 91 and 503–4). Once Specter learned of the strength of Dolce's expert opinion, in disagreement with Specter's indispensible theory, Dolce disappeared entirely from the Commission's records and was no longer one of its consultants. The Report does not mention him.

Dr. F. W. Light was chief of the biophysics division at the Edgewood Arsenal. One of the staff memos I published in *Post Mortem.* quotes Dolce and Light "as being very strongly of the opinion that Connally had been hit by two separate bullets" [page 91]. Farewell, Specter's single-bullet theory. Their belief required at the least a fourth bullet and at least two to have inflicted the injuries on Connally alone that Specter attributed to a single bullet, CE 399.

The Report gives an entirely different version of what Light said (page 109). He is quoted as saying that at Edgewood "the findings were insufficient for him to formulate a firm opinion as to whether the same bullet did or did not pass through the President's neck before inflicting all the wounds on Connally." No mention of Light's strong belief that *two* bullets hit Connally! Impossible for one bullet is not the same as having no opinion because of inadequate data.

The footnote from *Post Mortem* on page 504 discusses one of these staff memos the Commission suppressed. It relates to the memo cited above of Light's and Dolce's strong opinion that two bullets had hit Connally, what Specter does not mention in the Report.

If the conference of April 14 was destructive of the case being fabricated against Oswald, the conference of April 21 was worse, as [Melvin] Eisenberg's memo reveals. (See page 56). Of course it was nothing new that wound ballistics experts could not accept as fact that 399 had struck a wrist; it is common knowledge and experience that even jacketed bullets do not cause such substantial bone damage and suffer no distortion. All the expert testimony before the Commission was to this effect. But consider what this conference says of the Commission's investigation:

> Dr. Dolce, who "was very strongly of the opinion" that 399 "could not have" caused the wrist wound, was never called to testify before the Commission. The Report and the published evidence are silent about his strong dissent from this finding essential to the government's case;
>
> Dr. Light, who agreed with Mr. Dolce, did testify before the Commission but was never asked why he felt 399 could not have wounded the wrist. In response to Specter's hypothetical question, Dr. Light indicated that the passage of a single bullet through the two victims was a possibility based on the circumstances outlined by Specter (e.g., that 399 was found on Connally's stretcher). Specter even had the audacity to ask Light, "And what about that whole bullet [399] leads you to believe that the one bullet caused the President's neck wound and all of the wounds on Governor Connally?" Light's reply was polite but firm: "Nothing about that bullet. Mainly the position in which they were seated in the automobile." Thus Dr. Light's expert opinion was carefully kept out of the record;
>
> Dr. [Alfred G.] Olivier's tests, in anticipation of which he withheld an opinion at this conference, produced nothing but mangled, distorted bullets (CE's 853, 856, 857). Specter never asked Olivier if 399 could have done what the official theory demands and emerged in such perfect condition;
>
> Nothing was done to investigate the suggestion of the wound ballistics experts that Connally might have been hit by two separate bullets, a possibility incompatible with the

lone-assassin finding. Particularly helpful in this area might
have been the spectrographic and NAA [Neutron Activation
Analysis] tests so carefully kept out of the record.

This memo takes criticism of Specter's Commission work out
of the realm of 'Monday morning quarterbacking.' Specter *knew*
the fatal flaws in his theory at the very time he was trying to
build a record in support of that theory; he *knew* what scientific
tests had to be done, which experts had to be called. He ignored
the flaws, ignored the tests, and ignored the experts and devised
a solution to the crime he had to know was impossible.

And can it be regarded as anything less than culpable that,
with a record like this, especially a suppressed memo of a secret
conference like this, the authors of the Report could write: 'All
the evidence indicated that the bullet found on the Governor's
stretcher could have caused all his wounds'? (R95)

Specter slipped around this problem by adding the results from
the three *separate* tests and pretending they were the one test that
was never made. That test that should have been performed would
have determined if one bullet had the penetrating power to inflict all
seven nonfatal wounds that in Specter's single-bullet theory had to
have been inflicted by the one bullet, CE 399.

This is clearly reflected even in the Report's table of contents. In
Appendix X, "Expert Testimony," an appendix of text, not of the
test results, under "Wound Ballistic Experiments" are separate list-
ings of the three body parts of both men with wounds:

"Tests Simulating President Kennedy's Neck Wound," 582
"Tests Simulating Governor Connally's Chest Wounds," 582
"Tests Simulating Governor Connally's Wrist Wounds," 583

And they just left out Connally's thigh wound—a penetration—
completely.

Chapter 22

Pictures Worth More Than Ten Thousand Words

THE MEMBERS OF TWO PANELS, WHO, WITH A SINGLE EXCEPTION, I RE-gard as the dishonor roll, are here listed. The roster of the Department of Justice panel is taken from pages 1 and 2 of its report, and that of the House Committee from its listing on page 5 of Volume VII of its hearings:

The Department of Justice Panel

(1) Carnes, William H., M. D., Professor of Pathology, University of Utah, Salt Lake City, Utah, Member of Medical Examiner's Commission, State of Utah, nominated by Dr. J. E. Wallace Sterling, President of Stanford University.

(2) Fisher, Russell S., M.D., Professor of Forensic Pathology, University of Maryland, and Chief Medical Examiner of the State of Maryland, Baltimore, Maryland, nominated by Dr. Oscar B. Hunter, Jr., President of the College of American Pathologists.

(3) Morgan, Russell H., M.D., Professor of Radiology, School of Medicine, and Professor of Radiological Science, School of Hygiene and Public Health, The Johns Hopkins University, Baltimore, Maryland, nominated by Dr. Lincoln Gordon, President of John Hopkins University.

(4) Moritz, Alan R., M.D., Professor of Pathology, Case Western Reserve University, Cleveland, Ohio and former Professor of Forensic Medicine, Harvard University, nominated by Dr. John A. Hannah, President of Michigan State University.

Bruce Bromley, a member of the New York Bar who had been nominated by the President of the American Bar Association and thereafter requested by the Attorney General to act as legal counsel to The Panel was present throughout The Panel's examination of the exhibits and collaborated with The Panel in the preparation of this report.

235

House Select Committee on Assassinations

(23)Finally, the committee convened a panel of forensic pathologists to address the medical issues relating to the death of President Kennedy and the wounding of Governor Connally and to recommend procedures to be followed in the event of future assassinations.

(24)The panel of forensic pathologists consisted of two subpanels: One of members who had not previously reviewed the autopsy photographs, X rays, and related material, the other of those who had.

Panel members who had not previously reviewed the evidence were:

John I. Coe, M.D., chief medical examiner of Hennepin County, Minn.

Joseph H. Davis, M.D., chief medical examiner of Dade County, Miami, Fla.

George S. Loquvam, M.D., director of the Institute of Forensic Sciences, Oakland, Calif.

Charles S. Petty, M.D. chief medical examiner, Dallas County, Tex.

Earl Rose, M.D., LL.B., professor of pathology, University of Iowa, Iowa City, Iowa.

Panel members who had previously reviewed the evidence were:

Werner V. Spitz, M.D., medical examiner of Detroit, Mich.

Cyril H. Wecht, M.D., J.D., coroner of Allegheny County, Pa.

James T. Weston, M.D., chief medical investigator, University of New Mexico School of Medicine, Albuquerque, N. Mex.

The chairman of the panel was Michael M. Baden, M.D., chief medical examiner of New York City.

In the 1930s Bromley's prestigious law firm, then Cravath, deGersdorff, Swaine and Wood, assigned him to represent a large detective agency with a long history of antilabor violence and spying.

The one dissenter on the House panel was my friend Dr. Cyril H. Wecht, former president of the American Academy of Forensic Sciences, former Allegheny County, Pa. coroner, a doctor, a lawyer, and a longtime professor who teaches forensic scientists of the future. His testimony appears in the committee's Volume I, pages 332–72. Cyril's appeal to the committee to invest a relatively insignificant sum in tests that related to the impossibility of the single-bullet theory was rejected by the committee.

*   *   *

The career Specter gave his magic bullet required the bullet to have entered the back of the President's neck, exiting through the knot of the tie and the shirt collar, and then inflicting the five additional wounds on Governor Connally by entering his chest under his right armpit, exiting under his right nipple after smashing five inches of his fourth rib, and then shattering his right wrist from its upper side before finally coming to rest in his left thigh. Absolutely indispensable in the Commission's theory is that the bullet must have exited JFK's body through his shirt collar and through the knot of the tie at a point coinciding with this point on the collar. Above all else this should be kept in mind.

Magic is not all that the Specter/Commission concoction required of this one bullet. It had to have had remarkable extrasensory perception and in addition, had to have been able to activate Oswald in the tiniest fraction of a second. Literally. Quite literally.

The Zapruder film, the closest thing known to a time clock of the shooting, presented enormous problems to the official preconception of Oswald as the lone assassin. The Commission could not conclude contrary to that movie.

For some time during the assassination, relatively, because time is in seconds and fractions of seconds, a live oak tree blocked the President from the man presumed to have been Oswald in the TSBD window. He had to have sighted and fired the weapon accurately and so fast that nobody, not even the country's best shots, has been able to duplicate the shooting attributed to this one duffer.

The Commission could not say it saw in the Zapruder film what was precluded by the time it permitted. The camera ran at eighteen frames per second. So, if Oswald had aimed and fired with super rapidity, in two and a half seconds, that meant that it must be at least forty-four frames before or after the Commission said it saw a shot.

The Commission said the first shot was at Zapruder frame 210. This meant the next shot could not have been fired until at least forty-four frames later, or after frame 254. However, the movie shows Governor Connally reacting severely at frame 237. How did the Commission handle that? It merely ordained Connally's reaction was not to his being shot, wounded five times in three parts of his body! With five inches of his fourth rib and his right wrist smashed!

The Commission staged a reenactment with a photographic record made by FBI lab photographic expert Lyndal Shaneyfelt situated in the alleged window manning a camera mounted on a rifle. The immediate problem, and there were others for which we do not have the time, is that the camera's first vision of the President was blocked from that nefarious window by a live oak tree, from Zapruder frames 166 to 210. From Zapruder's grassy knoll position, at frame 210, a large road sign blocked the President from Zapruder's camera until he is seen again emerging from behind it, at frame 225. JFK then is seen raising both hands to the front of his neck.

(Some of the many additional problems are presented in *Whitewash II* on pages 169–72 and 207–18. These include the fact that Shaneyfelt's photographed reenactment with a movie camera did not coincide in time with what Zapruder had filmed. Shaneyfelt testified that his motion-picture film took "a shorter time than in the actual [or Zapruder] film," as it turned out, considerably shorter [*Whitewash II,* page 180]. Shaneyfelt told the Commission not to be troubled because he had stained his reenactment film to mark where it should have shown frames from the Zapruder film to be—but it did not!)

So, how was Oswald able to see and fire the first shot at the President?

As the camera moved to keep up with the limousine when it was blocked from the camera by the live oak tree, not until frame 210, for the first time, does the President come into view from that window. So, based on a May 23, 1964, "reenactment" that presumed every leaf on that tree was positioned on May 23 exactly as each had been on November 22, at frame 210, without needing any time to sight the rifle or to squeeze the trigger, the Commission decided that Oswald fired the Commission's first shot with incredible precision.

Specter was a part of the Commission's reenactment. It was then, he told *U.S. News & World Report,* that Secret Service Inspector Tom Kelley showed him one of the autopsy pictures, of the wound in the President's back (*Whitewash II,* pages 93–109; excerpts of the interview on page 109).

When Specter saw this picture, he knew the rear, nonfatal wound was in the President's back—not in his neck! Yet he proceeded to produce a case based on what he knew was not true.

Specter planned to help the reenactment to the degree he could when he deposed Perry and Carrico in Washington on March 30, 1964. Members present were the chairman, Boggs, Ford, McCloy and Allen W. Dulles, formerly director of Central Intelligence (3H357–90). As we have seen, Specter led Perry into the pretense that he had not identified the anterior neck wound as one of entrance.

Specter's approach to questioning Carrico was simple and direct: He did not ask the most important single question needed to be asked of Carrico, "Where was the wound on the front of the President's neck?"

Dulles made the mistake of asking Carrico what Specter avoided, where the neck wound was. From *Post Mortem:* pages 357–58:

Carrico showed by placing his hand on his own throat while speaking, his rejoinder ending, 'this was a small wound here.'

To this demonstration of 'here,' Dulles responded, 'I see. And you put your hand *right above where your tie is*?' (Emphasis added.)

Carrico confirmed with a 'Yes, sir.'

Although those who drafted the Report for the Commission deliberately ignored this, and the members, of whom only five were present to hear this, seem to have forgotten it, the doctor who first saw the President, the *only* one who saw him before the clothes were removed so the President could be treated, placed the front neck wound *above* the knot of the tie.

Perry did not get to the emergency room until the clothing had been removed (3H377).

Again it was a member, McCloy, not Specter, who asked what had to be asked, 'Was he fully clothed?'

'Not at the time I saw him,' Perry testified, adding that Carrico and the nurses had removed the clothes, 'which is standard procedure.'

Carrico had been well briefed on the official problem, and prior to any of this cited testimony, Specter twice tried to lead him around what he really saw and what really happened (3H359). Careful to avoid asking how, a question he never asked, Specter put it this way the second time: 'What action, if any, was taken with respect to the removal of President Kennedy's clothing?'

'As I said,' Carrico responded, 'after I had opened his shirt and coat, I proceeded with the examination, and the nurses removed his clothing as is the usual procedure.'

Prior to this Carrico had volunteered only that 'we' had 'opened his shirt, coat,' to listen 'very briefly to his chest.'

Not until after Dulles blundered into the truth that Specter sought to hide did Specter get a chance again to try and obscure what Carrico's testimony means, that the wound was above the collar and tie. He asked, 'Was the President's clothing ever examined by you, Dr. Carrico?' When the doctor said 'No,' Specter asked, 'What was the reason for no examination of the clothing?'

This was not a stupidity, for Specter well knew that Carrico had been first too busy and then had left the emergency room. Carrico understood what was expected of him and avoided the pitfall, that never-asked, never-answered question, how the clothing was removed:

"Again in the emergency room situation the nurses removed the clothing after we had initially unbuttoned to get a look at him, at his chest, and as the routine is set up, the nurses removed his clothing and we just don't take time to look at it."

All the members of the Commission knew and at this point all the record shows is that the nurses disrobed the President. But earlier, on March 21, in Dallas, with no member of the Commission present, Specter questioned Margaret M. Henchcliffe (6H139 ff.). She was the first medical person to see the President:

"Well, actually I went in ahead of the cart with him and I was the first one in with him, and just in a minute, or seconds, Dr. Carrico came in."

She followed this (6H141), after describing long experience with gunshot wounds in her emergency-room duties, by identifying this front neck wound as one of 'entrance.'

When Specter tried to get her to say it could have been an exit round, she insisted she had never seen an exit bullet hole that looked like this one. When he pressed her further, all he got was her recitation of her expertise with gunshot wounds. Eight of her twelve years of nursing experience had been in emergency rooms in a city were gunshot wounds are common. She is one of the few courageous witnesses.

It is she who made the record of when the President was disrobed, not until after he was pronounced dead, after all the medical procedures had been completed:

Well, "after the last rites were said, we then undressed him and cleaned him up and wrapped him up in sheets ... (6H141)."

Three days later, again with no member of the Commission present, Specter questioned Nurse Diana Hamilton Bowron (6H134 ff). She is one of those who wheeled stretchers out to the limousine, one of the first medical people to see anything (6H136). In fact, in an emotional moment, Mrs. Kennedy pushed Nurse Bowron away when the nurse attempted to assist in getting the President onto the rolling stretcher. She was one of the first three in the emergency room.

Consistently, Specter avoided the question of what happened to the President's clothing. However, she volunteered it in answer to another question, 'Miss Henchcliffe and I *cut off* his clothing' [emphasis added] so treatment could be started.

Specter had not expected to call her as a witness. He improvised this for other reasons, and she agreed to waive the customary written advance notification (6H134–5). He knew what to avoid and tried to. She had, as had other medical personnel, submitted written reports to their superiors (21H203–4). Beginning with 'I was the first person to arrive on the scene with the cart,' she recounted the same explanation of how she and Nurse Henchcliffe removed the President's clothing [*Post Mortem*, pages 357–58].

As promised, I have not changed a word of what I reported of my interview with Carrico which took place just before I interviewed Perry:

The first doctor available was Charles Carrico, by then on the surgery teaching staff. He confirmed all I have written that relates to him and what happened in his presence and added that which Specter did not want and had not asked for.

Carrico was the first doctor to see the President. He saw the anterior neck wound immediately. *It was above the shirt collar.* Carrico was definite on this. The reader will remember that Dulles had blundered into asking Carrico to locate that wound when Specter failed to probe this essential matter. It is not by accident or from stupidity that Specter did not ask this fundamental question. The only qualification Carrico stipulated in my interview is that the President's body was prone when he saw it. However, when I asked if he saw any bullet holes in the shirt or tie, he was definite in saying 'No.' I asked if he recalled Dulles's question and his own pointing to *above* his own shirt collar as the location of the bullet hole. He does remember this, and he does remember confirming that the hole *was* above the collar, a fact hidden with such care from the Report. Although there is nothing to dispute it in any of the evidence and so much that confirms it, this *had* to be ignored for in and of itself it means the total destruction of the lone-assassin prefabrication. So it, too, was 'memory-holed.'

According to Carrico, the doctor who was there and under whose supervision it was done, the clothes were cut exactly as I report. In emergencies, speed is essential. Clothing is cut to save precious split seconds. Practice was not to take time to undo the tie but to grasp it, as he illustrated with his own, and cut it off close to the knot. The knot is not cut. The customary cut is made where there is but a single thickness of necktie. With a right-handed nurse, what happened with the President's tie was inevitable. In this cutting, a minute nick was made at the extreme edge of the knot. Because of the danger of injury to the patient, the collar button and the top of the shirt are unbuttoned. . . . Trained personnel did exactly what they are trained to do, what they do instinctively. Because these medical personnel are trained to do what they automatically did in this case, Specter had no interest in it. His interest was in the case he framed.

I asked Carrico what Specter *did not dare* ask, the simple question of whether, in his opinion and based on his experience in emergencies, the nick on the knot and the slits in the collar were made by the nurses, not by a bullet. Carrico considers it unlikely. He saw neither the nick in the tie nor the cuts in the shirt before the nurses started cutting.

Was any other examination made, I asked him. He said that he followed standard procedure, running his hands down both sides of the back without turning the body over. The purpose is to ascertain if there is a large wound. If there is, it can be felt through clothing.

If Carrico, an honest, straightforward man, spoke so openly with me, I have no doubt that he would have been no less informative with any and all official investigators, had they—*any* of them—truth for their client [*Post Mortem,* pages 375–76].

These quotations from *Post Mortem* explain in advance the quintessential importance of the FBI picture of the President's shirt collar. I believe also that it explains why Specter and the Commission were not interested in having a clear picture of this shirt collar, the existence of which was pointed out to them, as it was to me, in the FBI's Exhibit 60 of CD1, the definitive investigation President Johnson directed it to make the evening of the day of the assassination.

Specter's failure to get and use this picture is consistent with his avoidance in asking Carrico, the only physician in the world who knew, where the anterior-neck wound was on the President before his clothing was removed, and how his clothing was removed.

The caption I placed on it when it was published in *Post Mortem* says enough. Once again I use what was readily available to the House Assassinations Committee, Humes, Boswell, Lundberg, and Breo, in this instance because it encapsulates other relevant information and puts the picture in context. I've also included here the complete FBI Exhibit 60 as published in *Post Mortem*. Again the photo's caption is from *Post Mortem*.

The FBI undid the tie's knot, thus destroying the original character so important in evidence to be used in court, for the sole purpose of making it appear that there was a hole in the center of the knot, which the single-bullet theory required.

Faking this picture also obscured the fact that the actual damage was in the upper left extremity before the FBI took the knot apart for this propagandist purpose. There it obviously could not have been caused by the exiting bullet of Specter's single-bullet theory, and there it also does not coincide with the slits in the front of the shirt collar. Had those slits been caused by a bullet, the tiny nick in the knot would not be located where it is—where it could not have been caused by that same bullet.

In *Post Mortem* I published a FBI laboratory report of December 5, 1963, on the results of scientific examination of articles of evidence. This single page is from the Commission's files where it makes up two pages, 153–54, of CD 205. In publishing them, I eliminated what was not relevant of the top part of page 153 and of the bottom of 154 to form one page.

The Report relates that on spectrographic analysis the FBI detected traces of bullet metal from the back of President Kennedy's jacket and shirt, but it detected no such traces on the front of the shirt

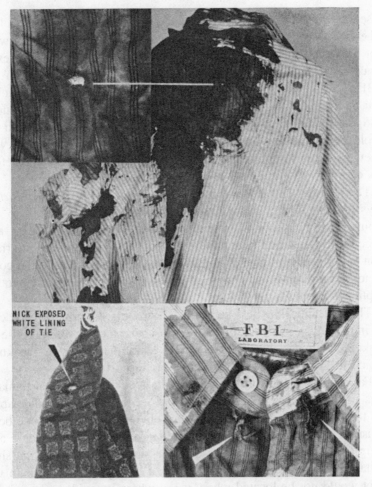

NICK EXPOSED
WHITE LINING
OF TIE

F·B·I
LABORATORY

This is FBI Exhibit 60, which the Commission did not dare print because it contains evidence destructive of its conclusions and its and the FBI's integrity. It is described in chapter 30, beginning on page 328. The enlargement of the bullet hole in the back of the shirt was printed by theFBI upside down. The actual hole coincides exactly with the real location of this wound, which was lied about. The FBI even twisted the tie to make it appear that there was a hole in the center. Actually, this small nick was made with a scalpel and was on the very edge of the knot. It was enlarged with removal of a sample for scientific testing. The tests were suppressed because they proved no bullet hit the tie or shirt front. This combination of suppressed pictures alone proves that the President was not hit in the back of the neck but in the back and that the bullet hole in the front of his neck was above the shirt. Either is total disproof of the entire "solution."

This is an actual FBI print, not from the Warren Commission's files, obtained as described in chapter 30, especially beginning on page 328. It has this caption typed on the back: "Photograph depicting portion of Exhibit 60." It is less clear as part of FBI Exhibit 60 (page 597), but in even that form shows much more than any picture the Commission dared print. In itself this picture, presented here for the first time anywhere, destroys the entire Warren Report and means the falsity could not have been accidental. It shows not bullet holes but slits. It also shows that when the shirt is buttoned they do not coincide and on this added basis could not have been made by a bullet. Note that the slit on the button side is entirely *below* the neckband while that on the buttonhole side extends well up onto it. The FBI and the commission both knew their representations were false. The Commission blundered into the truth separately when Dulles asked Dr. Carrico where the President's front neck wound was and Carrico told him it was *above* the shirt. Carrico confirmed this to me when he also confirmed the obvious, that this damage to the shirt was done when the necktie was cut off by nurses under his supervision during emergency treatment.

This is the official picture of the tie with the knot cutting quite visible, as Dr. Carrico described to me. The skill with which the FBI lab made so poor a picture is apparent by comparing it with the phony picture it made and used in its Exhibit 60. There the pattern is quite visible. In this picture the unaided eye cannot be certain the tie has a pattern. (''C31'' is the FBI lab's identification number, 395 is the Commission's exhibit number.)

This is a digitized and enlarged print of the official picture of the tie knot, Exhibit 395, made for me by my friend John Masland.

It may suggest that, poor as the negative was, the print could have been better. It also established that the pattern is identical with that of the phony tie picture in FBI Exhibit 60.

The digitized print also recaptured some of the color the FBI's science washed out in its photography for the Commission.

collar or the knot of the tie. Attributing still another exploit of sheer magic to this bullet, the FBI's report says that although it deposited detectable metal on the back of the jacket and the shirt, it went through the shirt collar without leaving any such deposits on the collar or on the tie knot. This is additional proof that this damage to the front of the collar and to the tie was not from a bullet because a bullet would have left detectable metallic deposits.

This FBI lab report to the Commission also omits critical information. It does not state that the slits do not coincide with each other and that neither of them coincides with the tiny nick to the knot of the tie.

Referring to the two slits as one, it assigns a single length to both when they are far from the same length and says this single hole "has the characteristics of an exit for a projectile." Of the nick in the knot, it says it "may have been caused by the projectile." The evidence we have seen in this chapter alone leaves it without question that the FBI knew these were false statements when it made and distributed them.

It also says that its "examination of the clothing revealed no additional evidence of value."

In a December 5, 1963, lab report sent to the head of the Secret Service, to the attention of Bouck of the Protective Research Service at the White House, it makes the identical misrepresentations (62–109060–1781).

From the same section of this FBI file, its main HQ file on the JFK assassination, I made an extra copy of three pages of lab examinations also sent to the Secret Service at that time. This report also states that no bullet metal was detected on the front of the shirt collar or on the knot. This is an original lab report, handwritten. The third page tells a big lie, without which no single-bullet theory could have been dared. It has a sketch of the collar and it refers to both slits as overlapping holes. They are neither overlapping nor the same length. They do not overlap! This alone means that no bullet could have made these slits.

Compounding the intent to mislead and misinform, it has a sketch of the shirt that shows only one hole and of the knot of the tie with the nick drawn toward the center so that it can be taken to reflect a bullet hole in about the center of the knot—where the FBI knew there had been none.

That the shot was from the front was reported on TV and radio immediately, and TV at least was monitored at the Naval Hospital from what Humes and Boswell told *JAMA*. It was in the *Washington Post* in the very story Humes quoted in his protocol, as it was in most of the daily papers of the world. It cannot be believed that there was no knowledge at the autopsy and before the protocol was typed that the Dallas medical people had said that wound was an entrance wound.

John F. Gallagher is the FBI lab agent who performed the spectrographic analyses. He was not called to testify to the results by the Commission, and the FBI did not send him to testify to those results. All testimony related to those results was at least secondhand or hearsay.

In CA 78–226 Jim Lesar and I deposed Gallagher. The FBI had signed a receipt for "a missile" recovered from the President's body at the autopsy. There is no such identifiable "missile" in the known evidence. So we asked Gallagher what it was. In the course of his testimony he said that to the FBI a "missile" or a "projectile" is anything that moves, and he actually included a pillow in his responses!

A piece of bone, too, could be a "projectile" as was once theorized with that anterior neck wound. The evidence before the FBI was that no bullet could have caused the damage to the shirt collar. It did not want to state that. So it implied that it was a bullet by referring to it as a "projectile."

Every single, solitary expert who made a professional examination of the clothing and every one who examined the pictures cited earlier and printed in this book, knew that those were not bullet holes and knew whatever had caused the damage to the shirt collar and tie could not have been any bullet or any other kind of "projectile."

With all the official lies that were told to make this theory appear to be possible, it still remains an impossibility, but the government got away with it. It moved the wound that was down on the President's back upward onto his neck. It moved the wound in the front of his neck downward. Both manipulations were to make it appear to be possible that the imagined bullet could have had a downward trajectory so it could perform its magic inside Governor Connally, geeing and hawing all the time. It had to have gotten low enough, upon leaving the front of the President's neck, to make it appear to be possible that it then could dip ever so much lower to enter the governor under his right armpit, so low on his chest that it would hit and wreck five inches of his fourth rib. (There is no need to repeat the rest of the fantasy of this imagined and impossible career of that imagined shot.)

When this was not possible after all the phonying of manufactured evidence that raised the back wound and lowered the front wound, it was much more impossible if these wounds were located accurately.

With the back wound several inches lower and the front correctly an unknown distance higher, nobody would possibly have swallowed and kept down the fiction that the bullet also started more than sixty feet up in the air, at that TSBD window. That would have required it to have come down steeply and then, once inside the President, to have somehow immediately soared steeply upward.

Without bullet holes in the front of the shirt, the single-bullet theory is an absolute impossibility.

Without a hole through the knot of the tie, not merely the tiny nick on it as far away from the center as it could be; and without that hole through the knot coinciding with holes through the center of the shirt collar, which are not holes in any event, on this additional basis the single-bullet theory is an impossibility.

And then the holes through the shirt collar, which are not holes and do not coincide, and the hole through the knot, which does not exist, had to have coincided perfectly with the wound in the front of the President's neck, which none of it does.

Even as baloney it is all phony.

Any departure from the absolute requirements of this single-bullet baloney, at the very least, required an additional shot.

When the best shots in the country could not duplicate the shooting attributed to Oswald in the official three-shots-only scenario, that a fourth shot would be attributed to the duffer Oswald with that rifle known as "Mussolini's contribution to humanitarian warfare" was improbable.

So, at the very least these pictures, each separately and even more, both together, prove that more than three shots were fired. That means no one person could have been shooting at the President.

Chapter 23

Was the FBI Witting? *Yes!*

THE FBI NOT ONLY MOVED INTO THE CASE WHEN IT HAD NO JURISDIC-
tion, before President Johnson told it to; it not only reached the
instant decision Director J. Edgar Hoover boasted about to William
Manchester; it saw to it that the Warren Commission would not dare
disagree with it.

Hoover and the FBI used the report President Johnson had ordered
them to make to intimidate and to box in the Warren Commission
if it gave thought to making a real investigation. This supposedly
definitive FBI report, CD1, is not a report on the assassination at
all. It is a virulent diatribe against Oswald, with so little about the
assassination itself *it does not even account for all the President's
known wounds!* One of the FBI's purposes in this approach was to
make it as unlikely as possible politically for the Commission or any
other body or person to disagree.

In its report the FBI branded Oswald as a "red," the false line
the Commission adopted. Yet the Commission knew that Oswald
hated the USSR and denounced the United States Communist Party.
The former he called "fat, stinking politicians," the latter, "betrayers
of the working class" and stooges for the USSR (*Whitewash,* page
122). He was anti-Soviet while in the USSR. The KGB suspected
he was a United States agent in place or a "sleeper" agent. (See
Whitewash, pages 1, 10, 19, 72, 119–21, 123, 137, and 146, for
Oswald's politics and *Post Mortem,* pages 627–29, for the KGB's
beliefs and suspicions about Oswald.)

Hoover blocked Warren's appointment of his own man, Warren
Olney, as general counsel. He told Warren and the other commissioners all they had to know to understand that he had the power and
that he would use it.

251

When the FBI heard that the Commission was "considering an investigative staff," the FBI went into overdrive to block it. The FBI's liaison with the CIA, Special Agent Sam Papich, learned this from one of his CIA contacts. Papich's contact learned this from Warren commissioner Allen Dulles. As of that minute the FBI started pressuring the Commission by immediately reducing its cooperation. This is recorded in the December 17, 1963, memorandum destined for Hoover through channels, from Alex Rosen, then assistant director of the FBI in charge of its General Investigative Division, to Alan Belmont, second only to Clyde Tolson, Hoover's closest friend and his second in command. This memo is Serial 20 in the FBI's liaison with the Commission main headquarters file, 62–109090.

If Dulles had wanted to keep the Commission from having its own independent investigative staff, he knew there was no better way of accomplishing that then by letting turf-conscious and control-determined Hoover know of the Commission's plans.

The FBI's control over the Commission and its conclusions was virtually guaranteed by its leak of the report Johnson directed it to prepare, numbered Commission Document 1, after it reached the Commission. When Katzenbach appeared at the Commission's first executive session, on December 5, 1963, he told the Commission forthrightly that although the FBI claimed to be moving heaven and earth to discover who did the leaking, only the FBI could have done it since no one else had any copies of that report at the time of the leak. These leaks, according to Assistant Director William Sullivan, in charge of the Domestic Intelligence Division, were ordered by Hoover.

These leaks not only boxed in the Commission—they also terrified its members. In their executive session of January 22, 1964, convoked after the end of the working day to consider reports that Oswald had worked for the FBI, the commissioners spoke of their fear of Hoover, and their acknowledgment that they dared not cross him are explicit in the transcript. (Published in facsimile in *Post Mortem*, pages 475–87.)

On December 9, 1963, never expecting that anyone would ever see his memo, Cartha DeLoach, then assistant director in charge of the Crime Records Division, the division that did the leaking, lobbying, occasional blackmail, and planting of stories, the division that kept a voluminous set of files on the media and persons in it, prepared a memo intended for Hoover, but not addressed to him (62–109090–16). In this case it was addressed to John P. Mohr, assistant to the director.

Clyde Tolson, associate director, was between Mohr and Hoover. Referring to this report, DeLoach was specific, saying it "will be delivered today."

It then lists those to get the eleven copies to be delivered. Eight went to Commission members and their chief counsel, two copies would go to the department and somewhat begrudgingly, the FBI agreed for the Secret Service to get one copy.

As of the time DeLoach wrote this memo, no copies of the report had been given to anyone. So it was impossible for anyone outside the FBI to have leaked it.

On December 5, three days after the first solid leak appeared and the day of the flood in the media, Senator Russell had asked Katzenbach, ". . . How much of their findings does the FBI propose to release to the press before they present their findings to this Commission?"

Katzenbach responded by saying that Hoover and Alan Belmont, "who is the man in charge of this particular investigation, are utterly furious . . . They say they are confident it could not have come from the FBI, and I say with candor to this committee, I can't think of anybody else it could have come from, because I don't know of anybody else that knew that information."

DeLoach knew of this rapidly because as these disclosed FBI records state clearly, member Gerald Ford was an informer for DeLoach inside the Commission.

On December 4 DeLoach's memo to Mohr (62–109090–1901) lists a series of stories of the day before, including one "which states the FBI report will show no conspiracy involved in the assassination of the President." In this case DeLoach said none of them "Is giving any information to the news media," and he hinted that one of those he disliked intensely, Ed Guthman, head of the department's information office, did the leaking through an assistant.

Hoover, as usual making his self-serving record of his innocence and perplexity, wrote in his crabbed hand on the copy of one of the stories; "Again a leak somewhere."

On another he wrote, "I thought no one knew outside the FBI." On its second page he wrote, "Certainly someone is doing too much talking."

On December 5 Courtney A. Evans, an assistant director who handled liaison with the department, wrote Belmont what Katzenbach had told him had transpired when he was before the Commission, what is quoted above not even being hinted at. In it he reported that Katzenbach had just gotten his copy of the FBI report, that he was having his attorneys go over it, and that he would read it that night. This was the first reference to any copy outside the FBI.

In his December 11 memo to Mohr, DeLoach broadened his attack on others for doing what the FBI had done (62–109090–11). Referring to a *Washington Post* story of that day on which Hoover had written: "I just can't understand how some of these details never known before are leaked to the press," DeLoach said, "Since copies of the report have been made available to members of the Commission, there is every indication leaks are coming from the Commission itself."

On December 12 Hoover wrote a memo to eight of his top brass, relating his conversation of that day with Rankin (62–109090–14). In it he said, "I told Mr. Rankin the department held the report about five days and then began to leak items from the department on it . . ." Hoover knew better. He lied. Most of the leaking was when nobody outside the FBI had a copy. One of his notes says this.

On the afternoon of December 17 DeLoach met with Ford at his Capitol Hill office. In that memo he said, "I again went over very carefully with Congressman Ford the fact the FBI had not had any 'leaks' whatsoever. I told him that we were well aware that the department had done considerable talking; furthermore it now appeared somewhat obvious that members of the Commission were beginning to leak the report" (105–82555–NR768[s]).

Ford was pretty cute when it came to leaking, and the FBI remembered his services to them as their informer inside the Commission when Ford wanted to prove later that he had not done any leaking. He asked the FBI to investigate that leak, and he interpreted what the FBI said as "clearing" him. The FBI's total investigation consisted of interviewing Ford—no one else—and getting his denial! (See *Whitewash II,* pages 6–8).

Hoover sent DeLoach to talk to Russell the afternoon of December 20. His memo to Mohr of that afternoon says, "I reiterated that under no circumstances had we 'leaked' any information; however, we certainly knew that it was coming from other sources" (62–109090–38).

Aside from spying on his Commission members for DeLoach and the FBI, Ford was also the point man in serving FBI and CIA interests in secret at the executive sessions. (Copies of all disclosed in the two years since this was written that were taken down by a court reporter are in my files.) Inside the Commission Ford led the fight for the FBI to prevent Warren's appointment of Warren Olney as chief counsel. Ford also led the fight for the CIA to keep the Commission from hearing KGB defectors. It is known that what Ford got for doing the FBI's dirty work on his own Commission and its members was, according to another DeLoach memo, an FBI agent's attaché case with a combination lock.

One of the least inhibited Commission expressions of its fear of the FBI and of being intimidated by it is in the transcript of its January 22, 1964, executive session.

Here are a few of the reflections found in it.

Rankin told the members that although the FBI says it never evaluates, only reports fact, on whether or not there had been a conspiracy, "they are very explicit there was no conspiracy," but "they have not run out all kinds of leads in Mexico and Russia, and so forth, which they could probably [say] "is not our business . . ." Asked to repeat himself by Dulles, Rankin said, "They haven't run out all the leads on the information, and they could probably say—that it isn't our business." Nobody disagreed.

That rushed, unscheduled, after-work session was called to consider reports that Oswald had worked for the FBI. Of this Rankin said, "Reflecting on this, we [Rankin and Warren] said that if it was true and it ever came out and could be established, then you would have people thinking there was a conspiracy to accomplish this assassination that nothing the Commission did nor anybody could dissipate."

After the paragraph from which the above is quoted, Boggs said, "You are so right." Dulles added, "Oh, terrible." Boggs concluded, "Terrific."

After a brief exchange Rankin said, not for the first time, "They

would like to have us fold up and quit.'' Boggs said, ''This closes
the case, you see. Don't you see?'' Dulles said, ''Yes, I see that.''
Rankin added, ''They have found their man. There is nothing more
to do. The Commission supports their conclusions, and we can go
home and that is the end of it.''

After additional observations from Rankin, Boggs, and Dulles,
Dulles said what they agreed to, ''I think this record ought to be
destroyed. Do you think we need a record of this?'' They agreed. It
ended with Boggs and Dulles hoping nobody would ever see their
transcripts, that they ''should be held right here.''

The Ward and Paul court reporter was there, he took it all down
on his stenotype machine, but the Commission decided to ''destroy''
the record. It therefore did not pay for Ward and Paul's services.
Rankin did give them a measly twenty-five dollars for wasting a
night and doing two hours of court reporting.

It happened that the stenotypist's tape, rather than being destroyed,
was given to the Commission. Under the FOIA I compelled its transcription and disclosure.

That the Commission members felt that the FBI could and would
tell it that an investigation of a possible conspiracy was ''not our
business,'' when they were a *presidential* Commission, speaks elo-
quently to fear and intimidation. This was before the Commission
was fully staffed, before it held its first hearing.

It is not easy to believe that the FBI would run the slightest risk of
a perjury charge merely to stonewall, to make the use of the FOIA
costly and prohibitively time consuming. Or, to compile artificial cost
figures to use in seeking amending of the act. Or, to tire out judges
so they would be anxious to end the litigation. There are many reasons the FBI could have had, and it may be that it has little regard for
felonious misconduct or being exposed for it. But it is not possible to
think other than so many collegiate audiences of the 1960s did, when
I was asked almost invariably: ''If they have nothing to hide, why
do they hide so much?''

There was also little prospect of any perjury charges because the
judges I was before, with rare exceptions, had a history of accepting
FBI and CIA perjury. Many judges dislike the FOIA because it

means more work for them. Usually they take it out on the requester of information, not on the law-violating government.

For its part the government went shopping for judges. When the case was before a judge with a record of tolerating official excesses or of tending to favor the government, the government sought to rewrite the act by judicial decisions by encouraging the judges to misinterpret the exemptions. In one of my first cases (CA 2301–70), it actually got a judge to rule that the FBI was for all practical purposes exempt from the act, a provision not legislated and not in the act. That judge had a reputation for being tough. His nickname was "Maximum John." John Sirica was later famous as the Watergate judge.

With the case months old he actually accepted the delivery to him and to us, for the first time in his courtroom, of an "affidavit" that not only was not sworn to—it wasn't even signed. Later investigation disclosed that the original had been executed months earlier.

The affidavit itself stated nothing at all that was relevant. It was a conjectural catalogue of imagined horrors if the FBI were to give up a single piece of paper. Laboratory Special Agent Marion Williams actually claimed that if I was given the results of the *nonsecret* tests in the JFK assassination, the FBI would crumble into ruins. Any records disclosed, he swore, could do "irreparable harm." Although the laboratory records I sought had nothing to do with informers, Williams dumped on Sirica the utterly irrational statement that disclosure of these lab records could "lead, for example, to the exposure of confidential informants" who would be subject to danger as the result (*Whitewash IV,* pages 187–88).

That one kicked back four years later. This decision was cited by the Congress as requiring the 1974 amending of the act's investigative-files exemption, actually restoring the meaning it had in 1966 when Congress enacted it.

Jim Lesar refiled the case for me so early on the morning of the effective date of the amending that it was the first suit filed anywhere under the amended act (CA 75–226). It was assigned to Judge John Pratt. It was not long before he made clear his animosity toward us and his partisanship in favor of the FBI.

As usual the case began with a government lie, its claim to having given me all the relevant FBI records. Lesar responded, "The documents we have been given so far themselves refer to other documents which come within the request, which we have not been given.''

Pratt contented himself with saying that the FBI's affidavits "are made of personal knowledge.'' That was not the problem. The problem was that Lab Special Agent John Kilty swore falsely. So arrogantly falsely that as I pointed out, under oath myself, that he swore in contradiction to himself on what was most material in the lawsuit. In closing the hearing that day and setting a date for the next one, Pratt addressed Lesar this way:

"I presume Mr. Weisberg, at least for the time being has other means of support, doesn't he, Mr. Lesar?''

Lesar responded to that gratuitous nastiness moderately, saying, "Well, his financial circumstances are not good, but that is a situation which I don't expect to change in any event.''

Determined in his irrelevant nastiness and partisanship Pratt then said, "Good enough to hire you.''

Lesar told him, "He has my services without fee.''

Pratt then said only, "All right. Okay.''

Later, embarrassed at having the proof of Kilty's perjury presented to him and in the case record, Pratt told Lesar, "Well, you not only say they lack good faith, but you say the record conclusively demonstrates that both affiants lied.'' (A second agent had filed an affidavit in support of Kilty.) "You and Mr. Weisberg bandy these materials with considerable ease and are very quick to impugn motives.'' He interrupted Jim's response, which began: "Well, I think we have provided the court with considerable—'' Pratt did not want to hear mention of the proof. He thought it best to threaten us, saying, "If you were not in the context of a courtroom, you might get yourself faced with a lawsuit.''

Jim faced the challenge head on, saying, "We will be making the same statements out of court, and I have no fear, there will be no lawsuit.''

Pratt then said, "You mean you have no fear there will be a lawsuit.'' In that he was correct, and there never was one, often as I, under oath and myself subject to the penalties of perjury, attested that the FBI had committed perjury.

Pratt accepted the most unusual defense against a perjury charge.

In a motion submitted before a hearing, the FBI's lawyers explained away the FBI's felony by saying of me:

"In a sense, plaintiff could make such claims ad infinitum since he is perhaps more familiar with events surrounding the investigation of President Kennedy's assassination than anyone now employed by the FBI."

What that did was to give me credentials for my affidavit attributing perjury to the FBI. It did not relieve the perjury. Except that Pratt elected to ignore the official felonies. It certainly did not disprove my statement that the FBI had test-result records it was withholding.

The appeals court directed that we be able to depose the lab agents. We deposed Robert Frazier on February 24, 1977. The purpose was to establish whether or not there remained test results that were withheld.

As Sanford Ungar said in his excellent book *FBI,* the FBI lab agents are trained to confound cross-examination. This was certainly true of those we deposed. They were arrogant, close to insulting, nonresponsive, and in general determined not to testify to what the deposition was to establish one way or the other. Several, Frazier included, demanded in addition to the prescribed witness fees and transportation costs, paid in advance, extra fees for giving "expert testimony."

Despite his practiced skills Frazier did make some admissions that are of interest for the historical record, like never having weighed the specimens he removed from that magic bullet, CE399; that there was a residue that could have been of human tissue on the bullet and that no test was made to determine whether they were such (and if they were not, the entire official "solution" to the assassination is disproved on that basis alone); and that he had seen the JFK autopsy X rays.

When Lesar asked him about bullet fragments in JFK's neck, Frazier admitted he had seen the X rays and said, "I knew there were small fragments." He added that the prosectors had never asked him about them. Fragments in the area, confirmed by the department's panel of experts, destroys the single-bullet theory and with that the nonconspiracy, Oswald as lone nut "solution." If the FBI knew, as Frazier testified it did, that there were bullet fragments in the President's body, it also knew the Warren Report was phony.

Lesar followed this up by showing Frazier the FBI lab's own picture of the front of the neckband of the President's shirt. He asked

Frazier if the slits overlapped. Frazier said, "I wouldn't know." A child would!

As Jim kept after him and ignored his reiterated demand for additional witness fees as an expert, he pointed out the evidence that suggests the slits could not have been made by a bullet, and he asked Frazier if he had made any examination designed to determine that. Frazier admitted that he was aware of the significance and said, "I had it examined by another examiner [i.e., lab agent] for that purpose."

Frazier also testified that Paul M. Stombaugh filed a report on that examination. Frazier assumed that Stombaugh's report had been disclosed to me.

He also assumed that there had been a lab examination "to determine whether the nick in the tie and the damage to the shirt collar were caused by a scalpel." He did acknowledge that the tie had been cut at the point of the knot.

It was agreed that the Stombaugh reports were relevant in this litigation and that they would be provided to me. That never happened. The reason is obvious; any honest test proved that no bullet caused those slits, the inevitable result already forecast by the spectrographic examination, which did not detect any bullet metal.

His testimony before the Commission is published in three of its volumes. He testified extensively to what was outside his expertise. This includes his "expert" testimony on the damage to the President's clothing—in which he made no mention at all of what struck him when he saw the shirt collar and tie, or of the FBI's tampering with that evidence.

It was Frazier who gave the Commission expert testimony on the bullet, CE 399, the most dubious bit of evidence on which the entire official case rested. He knew he had removed much more metal for testing than was required. He knew that there was virtually no metal missing from that bullet, as is confirmed, without the great volume of medical testimony to it, by his weighing of it when it reached the FBI lab the night of November 22, 1963. He required no additional expertise, experienced FBI agent that he was, to know that any bullet fragments in the President's body proved the entire official solution to the crime was a fraud.

Whatever he may have said under oath and otherwise, there is no

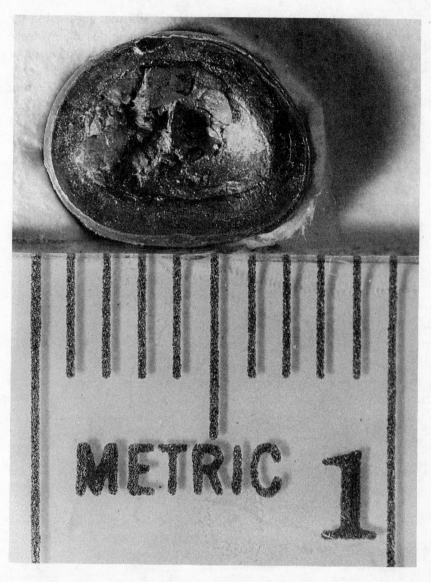

Commission Exhibit 399 is the most dubious piece of evidence in the Warren Commission's case. This photo shows that the bullet's missing metal was cleanly cut out for the FBI's laboratory tests, and was not, as the Commission theorized, deposited on its fantastic journey through Governor Connally's body. The knife's edges are clearly visible.
Credit: The National Archives

question at all that Frazier knew that bullet 399 was not used in the crime as the government said it was, and he knew that the evidence of the front of the shirt collar was separate and of definitive proof of it.

That the FBI still suppresses its testing of the shirt collar, test results that will mean the exposure of the Warren Report as a fraud, has been of no concern to any judge.

Or, to any members of the media.

Chapter 24

Lundberg and *JAMA* as Malice in Blunderland

LUNDBERG OPENED THE OCTOBER 7, 1992, *JAMA* ISSUE, "CLOSING THE Case in JAMA on the John F. Kennedy Autopsy," with these words: "On May 27, 1992, *JAMA* published the detailed and objective recollections of J. T. Boswell, MD, and James J. Humes, MD ..." Detailed, perhaps if we ignore their selectivity and error, but objective? Hardly!

In this issue Lundberg pretended to defend his earlier exploitation and rewriting of the "plain truth" with a belated interview of Pierre Finck. Finck could not and did not prove that *JAMA* had either told "the plain truth" or validated what it had done.

Lundberg sought to use Finck to prove that there were no military intrusions into the autopsy. Finck admitted military control of the autopsy when he appeared as a *defense* witness in the Clay Shaw trial in New Orleans.

The first paragraph of Lundberg's October 7 boast is that Breo's May 27 report "generally supported the findings of the Warren Commission," when in fact, it did not do this with a single one of the Commission's findings. But Lundberg was quite correct in saying that the first article "received worldwide media coverage."

After that issue of *JAMA*, according to Lundberg, only "three legitimate questions remain." This is the beginning of his switching from wholehearted and complete support of the Warren Commission to the pretense that the previous issue referred only to the autopsy. His three questions were: 1.) Why did Finck not participate? 2.) "Was there really a twenty-eight year silence on the part of these physicians ..."; and 3.) "What was the actual status of President Kennedy's adrenal glands at autopsy ... ?"

263

Not one of the contrived "questions" relates in any way to the Lundberg/ *JAMA* initial claim to have once and for all closed the case.

Lundberg, after saying that Finck was interviewed by Breo and that article appears in the issue, thanked Leslie Midgley, without identifying him as the longtime CBS News producer who was a strong and undeviating supporter of the Warren Report, for telling him about Humes's 1967 appearance referred to earlier in this book on a CBS Special. Midgley sent Lundberg a transcript of that interview, and Lundberg published every irrelevant word of it.

Uncritically, too.

What Boswell referred to as his own drawing, that official autopsy face sheet with the body diagram, Humes referred to in that interview as merely "sheets of paper in the autopsy room." Humes told Dan Rather, also always uncritical about the Commission, "They are never meant to be accurate or precisely to scale." In every possible sense this is untrue. Obviously with a murder, in particular.

Instead Humes continued, they made "precise measurements" with "two lines, points of reference from bony points of reference." This, in his concept of forensic pathology and precision in it, meant using "the tip of the right mastoid," which is "the bony prominence just behind the ear," and "the tip of the right acromiom," which is "the extreme outermost portion of the shoulder" as "points of reference"—*which they cannot be!*

The head is movable; the shoulder is movable, each in all directions. So, to pose the question that did not occur to Midgley, Rather, or anyone else at CBS, how can *fixed* measurements be made from two *movable* objects, the positions of which at the time of the assassination or the autopsy, are not known? How can they become "precise measurements"?

It is no trick to get the head or the shoulder to tip much, much closer to or much farther from the other at the autopsy or in real life. That's why the spinal column is the usual point of reference.

After the end of this mishmash of what was far from new or fully accurate when CBS aired it—twenty-eight years ago—Lundberg, without once having mentioned any of the many Boswell interviews some of which here were recounted earlier, apologized for not saying "twenty-five years of silence instead of twenty-eight years." He remains that ignorant or that much a liar.

He then had the effrontery to write that because Humes was interviewed by Rather and said pretty much what for the most part he always has said, that "serves as further validation of the autopsy findings"! This twenty-eight-year-old interview was so vital, so important, in Lundberg's account that he reprinted it "so that it will be available to historians"!

Then Lundberg devoted almost another third of his editorial to what is irrelevant in the assassination: "Solving the Puzzle of Kennedy's Adrenals." What he actually did was to launch an irrelevant sensationalism about the assassination and the Kennedy family. Kennedy's adrenals had nothing at all to do with the cause of his death. Over and over again in the earlier *JAMA* issue, the prosecutors emphasized the untruth, that the sole purpose of the autopsy was to establish the cause of death.

Lundberg said that "John Nichols, MD, of Kansas" [without saying that my friend, the late John Nichols, was a forensic pathologist on the staff of the University of Kansas Medical School] "deduced circumstantially" from medical reports from the Manhattan's Hospital for Special Surgery that Kennedy suffered from Addison's disease. By not referring to all Nichols had said on this, Lundberg wrote that he "stopped short of confirmation." Nichols *was* certain and said so.

There were, from the medical reports Nichols had, several possibilities. What was known without question eliminated the other persons discussed. This left only JFK as the unnamed patient, who had surgery in that New York City hospital in 1954 and was an Addisonian.

Lundberg referred to a July 11, 1967, *Time* magazine report on Nichols's article in *JAMA*. In the "People" section this is what *Time* reported:

Despite vigorous denials by the Kennedy family, medical detectives have long suspected that John F. Kennedy suffered from Addison's disease, a gradual atrophy of the adrenal glands that in its milder stages can be contained by cortisone (which Kennedy took), but in more advanced cases can result in low resistance to infection, chronic backache, and kidney failure. Now a University of Kansas pathologist, Dr. John Nichols, 46, has concluded in the AMA *Journal* that Kennedy did have it, that an infection stemming from it almost killed him after his spinal operation in 1954. Nichols bases his conclusion on an article he came across in the November 1955 *Archives of Surgery,* in which JFK's surgeon, Dr. James A. Nicholas, describes his preparations for an 'Addisonian crisis' in an unnamed 37-year-old man who underwent spinal surgery at Manhattan's Hospital for Special Surgery on Oct. 21, 1954—the same day and the same hospital where 37-year-old John Kennedy underwent the same operation.

Nichols also concluded that the total absence of any mention of the adrenals in the autopsy itself just about proves that Kennedy was an Addisonian.

Lundberg did say, "The claim in a recent book that the autopsy pathologists could not find the adrenals . . . has been independently confirmed on the record" by a pathologist at the autopsy who later became director of the Armed Forces Institute of Pathology, Dr. Robert Karnei.

Harrison Edward Livingstone's *High Treason 2* (New York: Carroll & Graf, 1992) is the "recent book" cited. Lundberg omitted what else is reported at precisely that point in the book, that Dr. Michael Baden, who had been chief of the HSCA forensic panel, identified JFK as an Addisonian in his book *Unnatural Death* (New York: Random House, 1989, page 14; quoted in *High Treason 2* on page 54).

Lundberg treated what was not new as hot news and got attention for it. This scrimshaw of his got two full columns in the "Health" section of the October 6 *Washington Post.* By referring to the established fact that JFK did have Addison's disease as no more than a "rumor," the way he treated it in his editorial, Lundberg was able to get major attention for his editorial and for Breo's interview. He also publicized himself again.

Lundberg next moved on to what he headed "Wrapping up the Medical Aspects of This Case," which he could not do with the wretchedly bad and usually misinformative stuff he published. He began with his usual nonsense, which had nothing to do with the facts of the investigation or with the autopsy, with a condemnation of "conspiracy theorists" and their "growth industry," utterly oblivious of the fact that he, personally, in the course of promoting himself and his previous issue of *JAMA,* admitted that a conspiracy was a likelihood!

And, of course, he and *JAMA* had again done their apples and oranges routine. Whether or not there was a conspiracy is not a matter of theory but of fact. And that there is irrefutable proof that there was a conspiracy does not identify the conspirators.

Lundberg described the prosectors as "the people who best know the truth." He said they "fueled conspiracy theories because of their long silence." But now that they have talked to *JAMA,* this formerly hidden proof is what they told him and he published. Aside from how far from the truth the prosectors were, detailed earlier in this book, how ridiculous it is to pretend that even if they had done the best of possible autopsies they could have told the whole truth when their knowledge was limited to what they observed on their autopsy table.

With nobody to keep his feet on the ground or to tell him how he keeps flaunting his ignorance, Lundberg said, "I can state without reservations that John F. Kennedy was struck *and killed* [emphasis added] by two, and only two, bullets fired from one high-velocity rifle." Each part of this, as we have already seen, is false. That he keeps saying that *two* bullets killed when only can raises questions about how good a pathologist he is. And about common sense. He had no proof that these two bullets were from a single rifle. None at all. And the presumed rifle was not at all "high-velocity." He just does not learn.

For the first time he admitted in the editorial, if only parenthetically and obscured, that the firsthand account of the autopsy he had been touting as enabling him to "close the case," with nothing else, was not really perfect after all, but "was far from perfect." He then listed thirteen omissions in the examination and protocol.

Whether or not these were all the omissions, and I believe they were not, four figure in the protocol. Even as ignorant as his heroes are of forensic pathology, common sense alone should have told them that "dissection of the neck" was indispensable when (contrary to what Perry had told them) they insisted that JFK was not hit in that area. This was also true of the "spinal column," near which Humes and Boswell belatedly admitted there were bullet fragments. Because of the nearness of the conjectured path of the bullet or its impact on them, this was also true of at least the larnyx and the trachea.

Lundberg said the prosecors got all the "salient facts." By saying there were no bullet fragments where there were? By lying?

Like, Humes not asking those present who had been in the Dallas hospital or phoning any Dallas doctor as soon as he examined the body because he believed there had been a tracheotomy?

Seeking to protect these now historical incompetents, Lundberg blamed the Kennedy family for their omissions in contradiction to the limitless autopsy authorization for which Attorney General Robert Kennedy signed on behalf of the widow. There is not even a hint of proof that any Kennedy family member said not to perform a complete and unequivocal autopsy. There is no reason to believe that any one of them did. And that right had already been waived. Not one of these avoided examinations would have been visible after the morticians finished their work. (See the Afterword.)

As Lundberg wound down, he repeated that there was no "government interference" in the autopsy, not quite the same as what had been alleged, *military* interference.

Lundberg pontificated still again against "the myriad of conspiracy theorists" allegedly of "excessive suspiciousness, desire for personal recognition and public visibility and monetary profits."

"We add our voices to those who petition the government to open the Kennedy materials in the National Archives for serious study," he then wrote. He is so ignorant of the matter that he is unaware that only 2 percent of what is in the archives has not long been available. It has been available for "serious study," what he, Breo, Humes, and Boswell eschewed for years. The great bulk of what remain withheld were records of the executive agencies and of the Congress.

This, he says, getting these nonrestricted archive records out and "putting the relevant Kennedy materials on permanent display," would "calm the ardor of honest conspiracy theorists who simply have not had access to the facts."

This is a man who has made a public spectacle of himself and who hasn't the slightest notion of what is fact and isn't, what is real and isn't, yet he undertook to tell the nation, its doctors in particular, what they should understand and believe!

While I have always disagreed with those who espouse conspiracy theories as fact and solutions, what Lundberg said is a bit too much. He has done much more harm than they could. It is difficult to imagine that anyone sought and got more "personal recognition" and "public visibility" than Lundberg with these ignorant, incompetent, and ill-conceived political adventures, particularly at his press conference that got him the maximum, worldwide attention he referred to in his October editorial. No conspiracy theorist ever go that amount of attention and recognition.

His attitude seems to be that those people with whom he does not agree should not be paid for their writings, but it is okay for Breo and himself. They had what no critic had, a job that paid them for what they did, their public visibility, their personal recognition, and their monetary rewards.

As the kids in the neighborhood in which I grew up asked each other when bossed, "Who died and left him king?"

And so they have made their own records for history, demeaning and defaming the AMA and its *Journal* along with themselves. They have added their own names to the long list of tragic figures in the roll call of the great tragedy itself.

Chapter 25

"It Is Over. No More Questions" —Pierre A. Finck

I AM INDEBTED TO THE *JAMA* GANG OF FOUR ENLARGED TO FIVE FOR the timing of their October 7, 1992, assault on truth, on fact, on their own competence and integrity, and on our history. Two days before the issue date I had completed much of this manuscript. I had planned for this to be based on what the May issue said about Finck and about what he had sworn to in New Orleans. That was also the day that *JAMA* made the issue available to the media, the day before a lengthy article limited to the irrelevancy of JFK's adrenals appeared in the *Washington Post*. This gang of five saved me from having to rewrite what follows. It helped materially with its content and with what this book, to this point, has said about them.

The issue, along with letters that Lundberg and Breo ignored, contains an editorial by Editor Lundberg that also characterizes this cabal and *JAMA*'s intentions. If the AMA were innocent in the wretched dishonesty and incompetence of the initial assault on fact, truth, and our history, it could not have been when this repetition magnified its inexcusable misconduct, its misuse of its reputation and prestige in our society for political reasons.

If the only adverse criticisms received were those that Lundberg published, of which there is little probability, some of those letters required an impartial and factual inquiry about the competence, honesty, and purposes of the initial publication. If the AMA made any such inquiry it was not reflected in what its own *Journal* published.

Because they pretended to have drawn on impartial endorsement of their disgraceful original publication with quotation of the supposed public record, they validate the belief with which I began, that

271

their evil should be assessed alongside of the *public record,* available to them.

If they were anything better than literary whores, they knew that my books are based entirely on the official record and official documents. Humes and Boswell did know about them, and did have my first book because I sent it to them and because Boswell, as we have seen, criticized the book and me to *Baltimore Sun* reporter Richard Levine.

Merely seeking to support their May 17 rewriting of our history is not "responsible journalism," and rather than examining the subject "in its entirety" and "seek[ing] out" the "other side," they ignored it and pretended that it did not exist except in what they castigate as "conspiracy theories (and profits)" [Breo's words].

Dr. Gary L. Aguillar of the University of California at San Francisco informed Lundberg: "Neither Humes nor Boswell addressed their critics on contradictory evidence that subsequent government investigations have consistently revealed ...." He also said of the "discrepancies" reported earlier in this book that they "are far from inconsequential clinically, forensically, and evidentially. A 10 cm 'error' just does not occur in a forensic autopsy, and a 6.5 mm bullet fragment simply is not missed" on an X ray. He added that *JAMA,* rather than using Lundberg, with his "well-known military ties," should have chosen a "public representative" for the interviews. Other doctors' letters note other serious factual errors by Humes and Boswell, and *JAMA*'s citing of them alone, "We are asked to believe them simply because they insist it is true."

Lundberg, *JAMA,* and the AMA did not overcome this by interviewing Finck. They magnified it by what they used of that interview and of Finck's earlier statements of which they had copies and used selectively.

Misrepresentation permeates what *JAMA* published earlier. Adding Finck, adds to their misrepresentations. This includes one of Breo's opening misstatements, that "Based upon what follows" in his article "students of the assassination and the conspiracy crowd can now forget the possibility that there was disagreement among the three autopsy pathologists" because and only because "Dr. Finck is again making it unanimous—two bullets, from the rear."

This misrepresents that the two-bullet line is the only matter at issue relating to the assassination and its investigation, the autopsy in particular, and the pretense that there was no other disagreement among them, whether or not there were only the two bullets. Breo's laughable explanation for Finck having not been party to the earlier *JAMA* interviews was that he "does not do phone interviews."

The October issue includes deliberate and dishonest misrepresentation of records Finck made when he was still at AFIP before he retired. He wrote the memo Breo quoted at the request of AFIP's director, Major General J. M. Blumberg, MC, USA. There is the suggestion that there was a struggle for this memo, after which Breo prevailed and these records were disclosed to him and to him alone. But Breo did not force them out of AFIP. They were in fact disclosed to Joseph Scovitch, of College Park, Maryland, whose efforts led to their availability without struggle to all others, including Breo.

Breo also pretended to give his readers the entire contents of those Finck records on file at the AFIP. But he severely limited his use of those sixty-five pages. He limited what he used to a rehash of Finck's published Warren Commission testimony, to which he referred to as "confirmation." It is, of course, no such thing. It remains no more than Finck's saying: "Because I said it in 1964, my repetition of it in 1965 and 1992 proves it was correct in 1964."

JAMA's heading of Breo's quotation of parts of Finck's memo to Blumberg is deceptive: "Finck's notes of the November 22, 1963 autopsy." Finck did make notes, but his memo is not those notes. It is what he wrote in 1965, not what he noted at the autopsy. What he noted at the autopsy or at that time, quite important, has never been seen.

Breo quoted Finck on a remarkable self-indictment. Finck, supposedly experienced in autopsies from his own quoted words and having taken training in, if not practicing, forensic pathology, was the one who saw to it that there could be no meaning at all to the measurements by which the rear, nonfatal wound was located. "I took the measurements," Breo quoted from the memo. But instead of following the normal procedure, measuring from the inflexible backbone, Finck measured from the tip of the very movable shoulder and the also very movable head.

Finck also managed to indict his colleagues, Humes and Boswell, who had started the autopsy before he got there. The autopsy had progressed to where they had opened the body and were examining it before having taken X rays. In Finck's own written account, he put this in capital letters, "I SUGGEST THAT X-RAY FILMS BE TAKEN . . . OF THE ENTIRE BODY BEFORE GOING ANY FURTHER WITH THE AUTOPSY." This was not done.

Breo's direct quotation of what Finck wrote, nothing omitted indicated, continues with this studied and intended deception: "This radiological survey does not reveal any major missiles in the President's cadaver. There are only numerous metallic fragments in the head."

Can it be that the man who headed the AFIP's Wounds Ballistics Branch, who studied the effects of various kinds of wounds on military personnel, was so ignorant or so stupid that he would restrict what he said the X ray of the body showed to only no "major missiles"?

How about "minor missiles," fragments of bullet in the body? The autopsy he signed mentions none and says there were none. This also is true of Humes's Warren Commission testimony that Finck as well as Boswell endorsed as full, complete, and accurate themselves under oath before that Commission. Yet, as we also have seen, those very X rays, the very ones Finck boasted about having had taken so belatedly, reveal bullet fragments in the very area of the body that they were required by Navy regulations to have dissected and that they did not dissect.

As we also have seen, any fragments at all there completely disprove the Warren Report's conclusions, especially that there had been no conspiracy.

It cannot be believed that Finck had risen to his position as head of the AFIP's Wounds Ballistics Branch and been so ignorant he did not know the significance of any "minor missiles" found.

His memo is not much better in its next sentence: "There are only numerous metallic fragments in the head." As we also have seen, this is an inadequate and misleading description of those head fragments. Finck signed the autopsy describing them as "dustlike." He was the Army's expert on wounds caused by military ammunition. The ammunition said to have caused all the President's wounds was military. The alleged bullets were designed and made in accord with international agreements, the philosophy of which goes back to the

Civil War era and the first international agreement to make warfare more humanitarian. In terms of wounds and what causes them, this ammunition was designed not to leave "dustlike" fragments, but to cause through-and-through wounds.

Finck next wrote (still nothing omitted in quotation), "I helped the Navy photographers to take photographs of the occipital wound (external and internal aspects), as well as the wound in the back." He referred to a wound in the back, not in the neck, where the Report and the autopsy protocol he signed places it.

But the more important point here is Finck's lack of reference to what those pictures disclosed. In the section the Department of Justice's panel of experts headed "Examination of photographs of head" (page 8 of the report; reprinted in *Post Mortem* on page 587), they wrote, referring to three of the photographs Finck helped take:

"In the central portion of its base [referring to a "canal" between the front and back of the head], there can be seen a gray-brown rectangular structure measuring approximately 13 x 20 mm. Its identity cannot be established by the panel." Twenty millimeters is about three-quarters of an inch. This obviously is not part of the head. It is a foreign object. Why did the prosectors not refer to this? Can it be that their picture revealed what their eyes did not perceive, especially when it is not the color of the bloodied head?

This is not by any means all the abnormality reflected in the autopsy, but not mentioned in the protocol, the testimony, or here in Finck's memos to his boss and to Breo. On page 11 of this same report (*Post Mortem,* page 590), under the heading, "Examination of X-ray films," the report states, referring to the hole in the back of the head said to be where a bullet entered, "Also there is, embedded in the outer table of the skull close to the lower edge of the hole, a large metallic fragment which on the antero-posterior film (#1) lies 25 mm to the right of the midline. This fragment as seen in the latter film is round and measures 6.5 mm in diameter."

There is no mention of this in any protocol, testimony, or memos. Yet it was so obvious.

"Metallic objects" glow like they are fluorescent in X rays. So here we have Finck belatedly rallying to his own defense and that of his prosector colleagues, their autopsy, their autopsy protocol, and their testimonies without even belated mention of this "structure" in the President's head or—that 6.5 millimeter metallic fragment at the hole in the skull the prosectors themselves said was of entry.

It cannot be believed that Finck helped the photographer take this picture and that neither they nor he saw a foreign object of three-quarters of an inch and a distinctive color. It also cannot be believed that in the prosectors' examination of the X rays during the autopsy or their later examinations of them, when they had plenty of time for careful examination, they did not see this fluorescent metallic fragment so visible to the panel. *It glowed!* They could see "dust-like" fragments in the X rays, some smaller than one millimeter in size, yet they did not see one of 6.5 millimeters?

Appropriate to this chapter, which addresses Breo's October 1992 botching of our history and the truth about the assassination and its investigations, he would fail to notice that Finck's secret records stated that he, on April 14, 1964, "appeared again before the Warren Commission for a hearing. [He] spent five hours at the Veterans of Foreign Wars Building." This is where the Commission had its offices.

But according to the Commission's Report, which lists the witnesses and where their testimony appears in the first fifteen of its twenty-six appended volumes, Finck and the other prosectors were at only a single hearing (R487). Their March 16 testimony appears in Volume 2, pages 348 ff. The table of contents of that volume and the transcript reflect that the three prosectors appeared together, one after the other, on that day, Humes first. His testimony begins on page 348.

Finck's secret AFIP papers also reflect that his memo on their March appearance before the Commission states it lasted *seven hours.* After *seven hours* of testimony, which followed extensive staff interviews and questionings, the Commission had another hearing that Finck said lasted an additional *five hours?* And that previously unknown second hearing of the prosectors was *not* published?

What could have been the purpose of a *secret* hearing after the lengthy hearing that was no secret? And why was the April hearing not published? Even mentioned?

On this Finck's memo is not helpful. It does not even report what that hearing was for.

The memo's second page relates to what followed the appearance of the Report. Aside from identifying those present at the hearing, Finck said nothing at all about it or about what happened there, nor what he, Humes and Boswell did. Here's how the memo reads:

> I saw a copy of the 8 millimeter color motion-picture film taken by an amateur and sold to *Life* magazine for $40,000. I saw the movie several times, at 18 frames per second and at slow motion. I also saw the 35 millimeter color lantern slides made from this movie, frame by frame. The movie and the slides show the President slumping forward after being hit in the back. Then it seems that Governor Connally has a spastic expression on his face, as he had been hit. His thigh is not visible and there is no evidence that blood appeared on his injured right wrist. THEN CAME THE SHOT THROUGH KENNEDY'S HEAD. I had the opportunity to examine the clothing of Governor Connally. The Governor was scheduled to come to Washington during April, we were told. The COAT showed one hole in the back, on the right, at mid-distance between the upper edge and the lower edge of the right shoulder seem [sic], close to the seem [sic], at approximately 20 centimeters from the upper edge of the collar. One hole in the right anterior portion, at approximately 30 centimeters from the collar. One hole in the anterior edge of the right wrist. The TROUSERS revealed one hole in the anterior portion of the knee. The SHIRT disclosed dry brown discoloration, probably blood. We were told that the shirt was sent to a Texan Senator, and had been cleaned and pressed before being submitted to the Investigators. Holes in back and front were larger than in coat. Some holes seemed to have been enlarged by scissors cuts.

Of the mere twenty-one double-spaced typed lines to cover five hours of hearing, only six lines relate to the assassination of President Kennedy. The others relate to Governor Connally.

In his memo, whether or not aware of it, Finck laid a "double-whammy" on the single-bullet theory and thus on the entire Report upon which it is based.

This theory requires that one bullet, CE 399, inflicted all seven nonfatal injuries on both victims by transiting the President's neck, without striking bone, then smashing Connally's rib and wrist before traveling about three inches inside his left thigh to lurk there until deciding the time for its reappearance had come.

Finck's first demolition of this foundation of the entire official solution was in saying he saw Connally hit by a separate bullet, after President Kennedy was hit. His second was in saying that after Connally's right wrist was supposedly smashed by this fantastically capable bullet, there was no sign of this or blood on that wrist at the required point in the Zapruder film which shows Connally and his wrist clearly.

What Finck did not say is also quite visible: *After that wrist was supposedly struck and demolished, Connally's hand was still holding that Texas ten-gallon hat aloft.* Or, Connally was struck by at least *two* bullets!

The most apparent reason for this secret hearing was for indoctrinating the prosecutors, convincing them of the single-bullet theory and reinforcing their confidence in their JFK autopsy testimony. Remember, they all believed and testified that the quintessential single-bullet theory was not possible. (They did not have the transcript of their testimony. That was not published until seven months after this hearing, two months after the Report was published.)

Until this Finck memo was available, there had been no indication of any Commission secret hearings. Its members-only executive sessions were classified TOP SECRET, but their existence was known, and for years all but one of those transcripts have been available. But I recall no record left by the Commission or any I got from the various executive agencies even hinting at any secret hearings held by the Commission.

Breo had some legitimate news, something other than rehash, and he did nothing with it—did not even mention it when quoting from Finck's papers. That the Commission held a secret hearing is news, news that raises troubling questions about the Commission and what it was up to in this unusual secret hearing with the prosecutors, after already having taken their testimony. Ostensibly and from the Commission's published record and its unpublished internal records, their testimony was completed a month earlier, and they were not at any other hearings.

Breo asked Finck nothing about these two refutations of the single-bullet theory and of the official "solution" itself. He blandly quoted Finck in his account of the interview as saying that the single-bullet theory is correct and has been proven to be correct, the opposite of what Finck recorded in this secret memo.

With this sample in mind of what Breo ommitted from the Finck secret AFIP records and his interview with him, about which he wrote so extensively when what he wrote was largely a rehash of no real meaning or significance at all, how about what he did use from his interview with Finck and Finck's papers?

Breo opened with an italicized quotation from the *New York Daily News* of June 9, 1992. It concludes that "if Breo had interviewed Finck, he might have learned that Dr. Finck testified under oath at the 1969 Clay Shaw assassination-conspiracy trial that, 'As I recall I was told not to . . .' track a wound in 'JFK's back for an exit path.' "

Breo's first words of his own in this article are, "Well, this opinion is absolutely wrong. . . . Variations of this theme . . . were the major criticism" of what he wrote for that May issue.

What the *News* published was not opinion, it was fact and contrary to what Breo said about it. In plain English, Breo lied. Finck testified about this matter on both February 24 and 25. His relevant testimony appears in the official February 24 transcript on pages 115–19, 148–49, and 190 and in the next days' transcript on pages 4, 8, and 32–36.

The transcript is available and is quoted extensively in my *Post Mortem.*

Breo pontificated again, with his characteristic disregard for truth or fact: "To be plausible the various conspiracy theories require proof that the bullets came from the front. Otherwise the credible evidence points to Lee Harvey Oswald as the lone assassin."

No part of this is true. If there had been two shooters, both shooting from JFK's back, that, too, would have been a conspiracy. So also would it have been if only one rather than both of the two shots came from the front. Or, from anywhere else. If any other person or persons fired a shot that did not hit either victim, that, too, would have been a conspiracy.

One of Breo's loveliest passages is that previously quoted: "Students of the assassination and the conspiracy crowd can now forget the possibility that there was disagreement among the three patholo-gists." Finck recorded disagreement among them over whether or not the autopsy was complete. He so testified in New Orleans. (See *Post Mortem,* page 236.)

Saying "We got it right in 1963 and it still stands in 1992," Finck told Breo that there was "no evidence for any wounds from the front." There was an abundance of evidence of a shot from the front, and as we have seen, the Dallas doctors said there had been evidence of this three times in their press conference after the Presi-dent was pronounced dead. Their press conference was widely reported.

Finck has a strange habit. For no reason at all he spelled words out. It was silly of Breo to go into this, but he did, where it has no relevance at all, under "Clothing Confirms Autopsy," which it does not in any event. Breo referred to Finck's "habits" that included "spelling out many works [he obviously meant "words"] in mili-tary parlance."

Baloney! The *Post Mortem* chapter on Finck's New Orleans testi-mony is titled "Flatulent Finck and his In-Court Spelling Bee." As I noted from the transcripts of this testimony (*Post Mortem,* pages 231 ff.), "Finck spells out almost everything." Not one word I listed that he spelled out in that courtroom is "military parlance." He spelled out words like crater, cratering, perforating, missile, scheme, cranial, inner, shattering, in, out, and path. Some "military par-lance," too, is in, out, and path!

Breo also referred to Finck as a "perfectionist." Not because he spelled out almost everything, but for other reasons, like his agreeing to less than a complete autopsy because "his impression is that the Kennedy family did not want a complete autopsy." One shudders to consider how much more of a frightful mess that autopsy would have been if Finck was not such a "perfectionist"!

"Flabbergasted" was how Breo described Finck's reaction to a newspaper story referring to the back wound as one of exit for a front entering bullet. Breo said that in addressing this Finck ex-claimed, "The clothing confirmed the neck wound exiting in the front, nicking the necktie." As we have seen, this is not true as is virtually all that Breo quoted Finck as saying about the clothing. Like this:

> Immediately below the upper [collar] button is a bullet hole perforating both flaps of the shirt, right and left. These two anterior holes below the collar button correspond to the exit wound found at Parkland Hospital. . . . The tie shows a tear of the cloth to the left side of the knot and corresponds to the two anterior holes in the shirt. . . . The tie knot was not perforated but GLANCED [Finck's emphasis] by the bullet.

Finck said he and the other prosectors examined the clothing. They therefore should have known that there are no bullet holes in the collarband of the shirt. They are slits; they do not coincide with each other, as the picture makes very clear; and they do not coincide with the cut of the tie. Even the magic attributed to bullet CE 399 by Specter and the Commission would not have enabled it to come through those slits and not make a hole in the middle of the knot of the tie, where there is no hole. Nor could it, as Finck emphasized, "glance" sharply to the left to nick the knot and then resume its imagined flight path by retracing both deviations from it to maneuver its way through Connally.

Actually, not to have made holes through the knot, that bullet would have had to retreat, halting its flight at two thousand feet per second, and then somehow sneak through both the neckband and the shirt's left collar tab at its extreme top.

If Finck did not know the facts he should have kept his mouth shut and not have lied. And that Breo did not know is not surprising. We know that he knew nothing about the facts of the crime and made no effort to learn anything about them. Breo could have called them all perfectionists because the other four are just as wrong, just as uninformed and, like Finck, not on the clothing alone.

In his ecstasy over Finck, Breo pulled out the stops again: "Most importantly, though, he invariably documents the autopsy findings of two bullets from the rear." What Breo considered documentation is, from his own account, what Finck saw at the autopsy, the one he himself described as incomplete, his examination of the clothing, the evidence of which at best he did not understand at all; the Zapruder film; and merely eyeballing the rifle. Incompetent opinion thus became "documentation" to *JAMA*.

Breo ended his account of his interview with Finck quoting him as saying, "It is over. No more questions." In that same issue Lundberg headlined his editorial, "Closing the Case in *JAMA* on the JFK Autopsy."

Both statements are very wrong. It is not over. There now are even more questions.

Chapter 26

Was There a Military Conspiracy?

In his movie JFK Oliver Stone conveyed the idea that there was a military conspiracy to kill JFK. He adopted that from Jim Garrison's book, *On the Trail of the Assassins,* to which he had bought the rights. As with so much in his book Garrison just made that up. I was there, and to a degree, I was aware of what he was doing and perhaps more importantly what he was not doing. I could have said more and in retrospect believe I should have said more. But the trail of assassins is also the trail Garrison refused to take.

I began this book with the intention, consistent with the thrust of my work, of also showing that the basic institutions of our society failed to work at the time of the assassination and since then. The media are one of the our basic institutions. In using nothing new, only what was readily available to the *JAMA* gang, to make the point that the truth, the established fact that is really the *officially* established fact, I used what was readily available to the media, which also had ignored it, and used what *JAMA* should have consulted.

In the course of writing this book, I came to believe that it also should include some of the so-called "new" evidence. That phrase was the irrelevancy employed by the Commission's former member, Gerald Ford, its counsels, it apologists, and its defenders in nonresponse to the criticism of the Report that began with my first book. It was irrelevant because there was nothing wrong with the "old" evidence entirely disproving the Report.

In the course of my investigations I did develop "new" evidence that also bears on whether or not there had been a conspiracy. I turned some of these leads over to Garrison. They did not involve Clay Shaw, so Garrison was not interested in them. My work in New Orleans centered on learning more about Oswald and his efforts to establish what is in police and intelligence work referred to as establishing a cover. He did not, for example, pick up from the printer the handbills he distributed to portray himself as pro-Castro. And, in his distribution of them, he had more than the one assistant identified by the FBI for the Warren Commission.

In support of this I have had and gave Garrison the tape of my first witness interview. When that tape "disappeared" inside Garrison's office, I conducted a second interview, that one in the presence of an assistant district attorney on Garrison's staff. The only two people in the world who had knowledge of it were firm in their independent denials that it was Oswald who picked up that print job from Jones Printing Company, and each, again independently, identified another Warren Commission witness as the one who did.

I displayed about a hundred pictures of men from all around the country. Many were police identification pictures. Several pictures of Oswald were included. Both independently selected four pictures of the same man. Each said it was not Oswald and continued to insist it was not him when I showed them the New Orleans police mug shot of him.

Several years earlier this one man being identified had met Oswald. After the assassination this man sought unsuccessfully to work for the FBI as an informer. Later he lunched at least one time with a Warren Commission counsel. So both the FBI and the Commission knew him.

What was quite shocking to me is that both the FBI and the Commission knew it was not Oswald who picked those handbills—and did nothing at all about it. My leads were the reports the FBI gave to the Commission. What made it even more disturbing to me is that when the New Orleans FBI learned that the New Orleans Secret Service was looking into that print job, it alerted FBIHQ, and in no time at all Secret Service headquarters ordered its New Orleans office to discontinue that investigation.

Garrison could have nailed a Warren Commission witness who was important in pinning the phony "red" label on Oswald. Garrison ignored the airtight, documented case I gave him. (He did file a couple of perjury cases not related to this one.) He could have exposed the related kidnapping of a Warren Commission witness by another Warren Commission witness, who was in one police force, assisted by a member of another police force.

This happened on the day that David Ferrie died. In Garrison's alleged case Ferrie was a conspirator. Ferrie had been active in the Civil Air Patrol, of which Oswald was briefly a member. The evidence I took to Garrison included a taped admission and a description of what had happened to him by the kidnapped Warren Commission witness, supported on that same tape by a family member who was party to the kidnapping. This man had ignored three Garrison grand-jury subpoenaes. For his protection I asked that his lawyer be present, and the lawyer also is on those tapes. These two policemen kept the Commission witness captive for two weeks outside of Garrison's jurisdiction, which was limited to Orleans Parish. They questioned him intensely for those two weeks. He never did understand what they tried to get from him, and they went into so much that was not relevant to it that they left him entirely confused about their purposes in kidnapping him.

If this is not provocative enough, not enough to indicate the sensation Garrison could have brought to light, I add another detail! One of these Warren Commission witnesses arranged with another to be the victim of a gang rape! And I have that on tape, too, from the victim!

These are only a few of the leads I developed in New Orleans as I followed up on *what the FBI and the Commission knew and ignored,* leads the conditions of my life precluded my carrying forward—leads the FBI and the Commission should have followed and would have had either ever intended a real investigation.

Stone made two arguments for a military conspiracy. Garrison's invention of being informed of the Conspiracy was one. The second one Garrison did not make up. It was Finck's sworn testimony in the Clay Shaw trial in which, I repeat for emphasis, he was a *defense* witness, *not* Garrison's, as *JAMA* pretended.

I have the court reporter's transcript of Finck's testimony.

In New Orleans Finck *did* testify to military control over the autopsy examination. As had Boswell and Humes before him, Finck told Breo, "I will repeat this. There was no military interference with the autopsy" [*JAMA,* page 1750].

Finck told Breo, "Except for the comments that I was very 'brass conscious' and that I had 'mistaken perceptions' about an 'alleged military presence in the morgue,' I basically agree with the *JAMA* article. I saw generals, but they did not interfere with the autopsy. There was no military interference." [But see the Afterword.]

There are, however, the AFIP records and Finck's February 1, 1965, memo addressed to Major General Blumberg titled, "Personal Notes on the Assassination of President Kennedy." The second of its three numbered paragraphs reads:

> 2. Before the 'Warren Report' was published, I, in September 1964, received Directives by telephone, from the White House, through your Office and through the Naval Medical School in Bethesda, not to discuss Subject autopsy beyond the contents of the Warren Report.

That they were ordered to silence a second time in 1964, that time by both the White House and by higher military authority, is new to me. Why should the White House have intruded at all? But if it decided it had any such need, why was it not content to have the directive delivered through channels with seeming White House *detachment* from it?

Boswell also had said that the Navy, through its Naval Medical School, ordered him not to talk. How could the *Navy* give any such command to Finck, an *Army* officer, other than through *Army* channels? Finck said that directive also was from the White House!

Why should there have been any need to add to existing regulations, which required privacy and silence? Who in 1964, in the White House or elsewhere, had any reason to believe that Finck would say anything to anybody? This is very improper conduct for the White House. It justifies suspicion about the White House and what it was up to.

The next page of Finck's memo (they are not numbered) says that when Finck got to the autopsy room it was:

> . . . guarded outside by military personnel and inside by Agents of the US Secret Service. Rear Admiral Galloway, Commanding

the Naval Center, CDR Humes and CDR Boswell, MC, USN, Chief of Pathology showed me the wounds in the President's head. The brain, heart and the lungs had been removed shortly before my arrival.

Also present in the autopsy room were: Rear Admiral Kenney, Surgeon General of the Navy; Rear Admiral Burkley, White House Physician; one Army Major General; a Brigadier General, Air Force Aid [sic.] to the President; Captain Stover, MC, USN, Commanding the Naval Medical School; Captain Osborne, MC, USN Chief of Surgery . . .

Finck wrote, "I was denied the opportunity to examine the clothing." This *is* control of the autopsy. It is followed by three lines that were first redacted and then, except for a single word, written in: "One officer who outranked me told me that my request was only of academic interest. The same officer did not agree to state [obliterated] in the autopsy report that the autopsy was incomplete, as I had suggested to indicate."

The Naval officers who outranked Finck, from his own list of them, were the two Naval captains, three admirals, and two generals.

Thus it is apparent that rather than there being no interference or external control over the autopsy and rather than its being a complete autopsy with all the relevant evidence, like clothing being investigated, there was instant control over Finck.

This was not what Finck testified to in New Orleans in 1969. It was what, without pressures of any kind, he wrote only a few months after the Report was issued and when he had no reason to expect that anyone other than his commanding general would see it. In fact, he handlettered the sealed envelope of his copies: "TO BE OPENED ONLY BY GEN BLUMBERG" then a dash and then "FROM: P.A. FINCK." The AFIP got Blumberg's widow to open the envelope in response to Scovitches's request.

Remember, this is one of those Finck/AFIP records that Breo made such a great and phony boast over having gotten when they already had been released.

There was but one military aide there, Brigadier General Godfrey McHugh, air aide and a real pro. The other general was Major General Philip C. Wehle, who commanded the Military District of Washington. I have seen no explanation for his presence inside the autopsy room. That was not some kind of rare show. It was a gruesome moment and one of the saddest moments in our history. It was not an occasion for voyeurism.

Whether or not any of the military had anything at all to do with either the autopsy examination or the protocol on, their presence is extraordinarily important for a number of reasons. These range from the simple impropriety of any intrusion into either the examination of the body or the report on it to the impact on the autopsy and report on the investigation of the crime and any successful effort to solve it to whether or not there had been a military conspiracy.

It is Oliver Stone's movie's account that the military controlled the autopsy. This had supposedly turned on Humes and Boswell after all these years. Stone, taking it from Garrison's book, said that the control was exercised by a general. All the denials we have quoted are in terms of a general controlling the autopsy.

So, along with the substantive changes in the holograph of the report that replaced the one Humes burned, there is no doubt at all that there had been the "interference" all the prosectors denied. This denial is all the more remarkable coming from Finck because his own memos show it to be untrue and because, *under oath,* he had testified to this in New Orleans.

Finck also admitted to Breo: "We did not do everything possible in the way of a complete autopsy . . . did not dissect the organs of the neck." In specifying that he had no personal knowledge of it, he attributed this to the "wishes of the Kennedy family." Of this no proof has ever been offered by any of those who blame their own failings on that family. Finck added what is obviously false, that "it was not necessary to dissect the organs of the neck to determine the cause of death." Cause of death was not the only purpose of the autopsy.

To compound this, Finck also told Breo that they, the "prosectors, complied with the autopsy permit and its restrictions." In plain English, this too, is a lie. *There were no restrictions.*

Another of the palpably false claims made to justify the failings of the autopsy is, as Breo quoted Finck as saying, "the pathologists had no information from Parkland Hospital during the autopsy." They *did* have *important* information, those two of the three missing pieces of the skull and the bullet later identified as CE 399. Moreover what his formulation avoids, as Lundberg and Breo both knew, is that they could have had all the information available by a phone call they did not make. They could have had much of it by merely asking three of those with them in the autopsy room, Burkley, the one physician in both places, and Secret Service Agents Roy Kellerman and William R. Greer. They certainly would have known without question of the tracheotomy. (See Afterword.)

What makes this and more like it unpardonable from Finck is that he, under oath, testified to the Commission that they agreed with Humes's testimony to the extreme unlikelihood that CE 399 could have caused all seven nonfatal wounds. Moreover, Finck testified with regard to only one of these wounds, the smashing of Connally's wrist, that it could not have caused that wound "because there are too many fragments" in the wrist. *Any* fragments in the President's neck area *or* "too many fragments" in Governor Connally's wrist— *either* one—disproves the entire Warren Report—*and we have both!*

Nothing the military could have done could have been more improper and more seriously, more unpardonably wrong. In itself this demands that we at the very least suspect that there might have been a military conspiracy.

Before the autopsy began, several hours before the President's body reached the Bethesda Naval Hospital, beginning at about 2:30 the afternoon of the assassination, Washington time, the Dallas doctors stated in the first press conference of the Lyndon Johnson administration that the President had been shot from the front because the wound in the front was one of entrance.

They repeated this, and the media of the entire world reported it, including radio, which was instantaneous, and TV, which followed only minutes later in reporting it. So, obviously, the military knew it.

But Oswald was well behind the President. He could not have fired the shot that entered the front of the President's neck. This alone meant that with Oswald as assassin there had to be at least one other assassin, shooting from where Oswald was not, from the front. This means there had been a conspiracy. But the military did not want the investigation of a conspiracy to take place.

Chapter 27

The Army Protected the Conspiracy.
Why?

WHAT FOLLOWS IS ANOTHER OF THE MANY PARTS OF THE STORY AS WELL as the history that will never be complete and that could have been used appropriately in several other chapters. I believe that although most of it relates to the Commission, it is of greater significance as it relates to a military conspiracy and to the Army's protection of the conspiracy to kill.

We begin with the first-person account of the most preeminent expert in this field, whom the Commission did not call as a witness, Dr. Joseph Dolce. He was the Army's chief consultant on wound ballistics. His name appears nowhere in the Report or its appended twenty-six volumes of that estimated ten million words. The reason, obviously, is not lack of space.

When a University of Maryland student working on a JFK assassination TV documentary for his master's thesis in communications, Gerard "Chip" Selby, first came to see me for help on it, he asked who I thought he should interview. My first recommendation was Dr. Joseph Dolce. Chip went to West Palm Beach and filmed Dolce. He could use only a short excerpt, about one minute, in his documentary, *Reasonable Doubt,* which has been aired on the A&E cable network innumerable times, each time with a strong and positive reaction. (It has an exceptional record for any documentary, perhaps an unprecedented record for a writer/producer/director's first that is also a university thesis. It won the "Golden Eagle," the highest award in the history division in the 1988 competition of the Council on International Nontheatrical Events (CINE). It is available on a white Star video cassette.)

Dolce is a nonperson in the enormity the Commission published, but he does figure in a staff memorandum that the Commission ignored. All others writing in the field missed it, even after I brought him and what he said that the Commission had found so unwelcome to light in *Post Mortem* (pages 55–56, 91, and 503–5).

In reporting that six months after the assassination, the Commission was still ignoring the missing bullet that wounded Jim Tague slightly while accounting for three shots each impacting, I quoted and reproduced Commission Counsel Melvin Eisenberg's April 22, 1964, "Memorandum for the Record" on the "Conference of April 21, 1964." It was to determine "which frames of the Zapruder film show the impact of the first and second bullets." I wrote that "all participants are not named. Those who are include *five* doctors, *three* FBI agents, *five* Commission lawyers, including Rankin, the Connallys, and Commissioner McCloy. Specter alone dissented from the conclusion that Connally's chest wound could not have been inflicted after frame 236" [*Post Mortem*, page 55].

Frame 236 was but a second and a half after the first shot the Commission said was fired at frame 210—an absolute impossibility with that rifle.

Before quoting the paragraph from Eisenberg's memo that follows, I also wrote in *Post Mortem* that "the single-bullet theory was eliminated while it was being dreamed up":

In a discussion after the conference, Drs. [F. W.] Light and Dolce expressed themselves as being very strongly of the opinion that Connally had been hit by two separate bullets, principally on the ground that the bullet recovered from Connally's stretcher [*sic*] could not have broken his radius [wrist bone] without having suffered more [*sic*] distortion. [The bullet is entirely undeformed. 'More' suggests it had been deformed.] . . . Dr. Dolce, consultant to the Biophysics Division at Edgewood Arsenal, was not called as a witness. Thus his 'very strong' scientific opinion contrary to what the Commission was cooking up is *not* in the evidence [*Post Mortem*, pages 55–56].

In another reference I made more of a point of this:

It is an unusually naive reader who will now be startled to learn that Dr. Dolce was not called as a witness before the Commission and that there was no duplication [in tests] of the history attributed to the heroic bullet of Specter's saga, hence nothing upon which Drs. Light and [Alfred G.] Olivier could base altered testimony. Dr. Dolce's name, in fact, is not mentioned a single time in all the volumes of testimony [*Post Mortem,* page 91.] [Light and Olivier are identified in the transcript of Selby's interview of Dolce that follows.]

Although the file memorandum is a poor and unclear carbon copy, I reproduced it in facsimile, in *Post Mortem,* with a lengthy note. Two excerpts from the note read:

Dr. Dolce, who 'was very strongly of the opinion' that 399 'could not have' caused [Connally's] wrist wound was never called to testify before the Commission. . . . This memorandum takes criticism of Specter's Commission out of the realm of 'Monday morning quarterbacking.' [That was a common Commission counsels' criticism of adverse comment on their work.] Specter *knew* the fatal flaws in his theory at the very time he was trying to build a record in support of that theory; he *knew* what scientific tests had to be done, which experts had to be called. He ignored the flaws, ignored the tests, ignored the experts and devised a solution to the crime he knew had to be impossible. And can it be regarded as anything less than culpable that, with a record like this, especially a suppressed memo of a secret conference like this, the authors of the Report could write: 'All the evidence indicated that the bullet found on the Governor's stretcher could have caused all his wounds'? (R95) . . . [*Post Mortem,* page 504].

The truth is the exact opposite.

This is why I urged Chip Selby to interview Dr. Dolce. It and the Eisenberg memo were the basis for his questioning. The interview was on October 17, 1986, in Dolce's West Palm Beach home.

Of the conference reported in Eisenberg's memo, Selby first asked him, "Why were you asked to participate . . . ?" Dolce's answer is why I use excerpts taken from Selby's transcript of the interview at this point:

That is a very good question. Right after the assassination, the Army and Navy doctors appeared to take over everything. As a

matter of fact, it was in the Army rules that in the event of an
injury, a serious injury to any VIP In Congress in [*sic*], and any
in the administration, that I was to be called in to go over the
case. I was not called. The Army and Navy took over.

Dolce was so preeminent an expert on the medical aspects of
gunshot wounds that "in the event of any injury, serious injury to
any VIP in Congress" or "to any in the administration" he "was
to be called to go over the case." The *President,* certainly, is a VIP.
But, *Dolce was not called.* Instead, as he said twice, "The Army
and the Navy took over."

This, of course, is not in even the secret Commission memo!

When the department's lawyers (he probably meant the Commission's) got "answers" that "did not fit," which Dolce also referred
to disparagingly as "the proper answers," they asked the Army for
"their top ballistics man." The Army sent Dolce:

> I went there with Dr. [F. W.] Light. Dr. Light was the Ph.D.
> in mathematics. He was also a forensic pathologist. To me he was
> a most brilliant man. He did not become Chief of the Wound
> Ballistics Program because he would disagree too often, and in
> conferences you cannot disagree too often. You can disagree if
> you're entirely right, but if you're just a little bit right you
> shouldn't disagree. Especially when you're discussing bullets be-
> fore three- and four-star generals and so on. So Dr. Light never
> became [chief], but Dr. Light and I went along with Dr. [Alfred G.]
> Olivier, who at the time was chief of the Wound Ballistics
> Program.

Of Olivier, Dolce said, he is "a veterinarian doctor, and you might
say why is he a ballistics man . . . I think he should never have been
made chief of ballistics."

They viewed the Zapruder film. Dolce pointed out where the film
shows Connally's rib was smashed:

> The bullet hit his fifth rib, shattering his fifth rib in many places.
> One of the points of a portion of the rib punctured the lung and
> he developed a sudden pneumothorax. And if you look, you can
> see the point . . . That's sudden shortness of breath and sudden
> pain from the collapsed lung. That's where he was hit in the chest.

Where Connally reflects this is clearly visible in the Zapruder film. It is immediately after, as Connally testified, he started to turn to this right after he heard the first shot.

Dolce continued, "I do not remember the number [of the frame] of the film. But you can look at that film, and he does this [demonstrating] with his mouth and that's where he was hit in the chest." This sequence begins where all at the conference, save Specter, said he could not have been struck, later than frame 236.

The relevant still pictures from the Zapruder film (183 ff.) show this clearly. It means that Connally was struck by a separate bullet fired *after* frame 210, the time the Commission claims its first bullet hit both Kennedy and Connally. While the visible impact on Connally is only about a second and a half after frame 210, that is about a quarter of the time permitted for all the shooting by the Zapruder film's recording of the assassination.

What this means is that Connally was not struck by the first bullet that hit Kennedy and that he was struck quite some time before Oswald or anyone else using that rifle could have reloaded, reaimed, and fired again to hit Connally with a separate shot.

It means also that there was at least a second assassin firing away.

Specter's opposition to what the others agreed upon at that conference was rooted in the fact that it proved his single-bullet theory was impossible and that there was a conspiracy to kill the President.

Dolce was called as an expert to consult on the first two shots of the Commission's limit of three, not to testify about the fatal shot to the head. The bullet he referred to, Commission Exhibit 399, is what came to be known as Specter's magic bullet. In his response to Selby's questions, Dolce expressed his opinion about the impossibility of it:

Now this bullet is then supposed to have come to hit Governor Connally in his wrist, shattered the radius. There are two small bones in the wrist—the radius is the thumb bone. The ulna is the little, small finger bone. We have done some experimental work.

The radius, during the Civil War, was noted to be the most difficult bone to break with a bullet. This same bullet now, that has gone through the neck of President Kennedy, through his, through the chest Pr-, of Governor Connally, hit the radius of Governor Connally, shattered it in pieces, and I will show you the diagram in pieces, and came out as a perfectly normal, pristine bullet with just a slight, slight flattening on one side . . .

Uh, now, uh, the disturbing feature at this conference was that the lawyer says, 'Now Doctor, we want you to tell us exactly wh-, how this bullet traveled, the velocity traveled, the velocity lost during the period of travel. And why it came out as a pristine bullet, unmarked bullet.' I said, 'Sorry, it doesn't happen that way. This bullet should have been deformed.' Whereupon they said, 'Well, suppose you do some research at the Edgewood Arsenal. We'll give you the original rifle, Oswald,' rifle, Mannlicher-Carcano, we'll give you the bullets.' We say, 'Good,' We went to Edgewood, carried out these experiments. I will discuss that later. So you go on with your questioning.

Selby then asked him "What was your position at Edgewood Arsenal? What did the position entail? Dolce replied:

At the time I was the chief consultant in wound ballistics for the Army. I was chairman of the Wound Ballistics Board. The Wound Ballistics was made up of professors in the various specialities of surgery. Such as neurosurgey—brain and spinal cord; thoracic surgery—chest surgery; uh, plastic surgery, rectal surgery, orthopedic surgery, general surgery. We had all of these various men to give their, for them to give us their ideas of certain types of damages done by certain types of bullets.

"What exactly was discussed at this conference? What opinions and conclusions were reached, if any?" Selby then asked. Dolce answered:

We discussed at the conference, reviewing the Zapruder film to tell exactly how the shots were fired, what parts of the body were involved. All right. Also, uh, the idea was to prove that the, uh, pristine bullet was the one that did all the damage. The purpose also was to discuss with Governor Connally how he felt during the shooting, what he knew about the shooting. His wife was there and she also brought her thoughts in. Uh, the main thing though was to look at the film and then to discuss with the legal talent

there just why this bullet caused so much damage and was not
deformed. But the disturbing thing was they wanted this to be
the bullet that caused all of the damage and I did not go along
with that. . . .

Uh, I talked to Governor Connally's doctors to explain the
wounds to me. They did not feel that this bullet, as a pristine
bullet, could do all of that damage. So the, uh, legal people were
not too happy with me. I can't help it, but I had to give what I
thought was correct and honest.

As we saw earlier, all the doctors told the commission that the
single-bullet theory was impossible, and the Report merely lied and
said they all agreed that it was possible. Again, that was Specter's
part of the Report. He prepared for it by substituting "not this bullet,
Doctor," referring to Exhibit 399, "any bullet, can any bullet" followed by his conjecture career of that supermagical 399. Dolce confirms that they did not agree and that the lawyers were unhappy
about his strongly expressed disagreement.

Dolce's response to Selby's question of "How many bullets struck
Connally?" came from his extensive experience and personal knowledge of ballistics prior to the assassination and from the tests he and
his associates made at the Aberdeen proving grounds for the
Commission:

I feel Governor Connally was hit by two bullets.' [He referred
to Bullet 399 as "the pristine bullet" because that was how it
was commonly referred to and because it had no deformity, no
visible scratching and only minor flattening at its back end.] 'I
feel also that his fractured wrist was not caused by the pristine
bullet, but was caused by a second assassin, most likely firing
from the grass knoll.' This he said is indicated by the pictures,
referring to the individual frames of Zapruder's film. He added,
'And I also feel, because the experiments we did, in each and
every instance, striking only the bone of the radius, the bullet is
markedly deformed.

At Aberdeen, he said, they shot into the wrists of ten cadavers for
the Commission, and in all instances, true to the medical record he
cited going back to the Civil War, all the bullets were deformed—
from hitting the radius bone only. Dolce repeated this, in summary,

when asked by Selby, "Which wounds it [bullet 399] could have caused and remained in this condition?"

"It could not have caused all the wounds," Dolce responded, "because our experiments have shown beyond any doubt, that merely shooting the wrist deformed the bullet drastically, and yet this bullet came out almost a perfectly normal, pristine bullet," in the Commission and Specter's theory represented as fact.

Then Selby asked, "What was the opinion you expressed during the conference regarding this? What was the reaction to it?" Dolce said:

> I got the, the [sic] opinion, and I've been a doctor fifty-seven years now, I got the impression after looking at these people, and I try to look at people when I talk to them, I got the impression that they wanted this assassination conference and research discussions made shorted [sic] as possible. They did not want to go too much into further research or further conferences, but that they just wanted this bullet to do all the damages. This is what we want you to tell us. And I got that impression immediately. And I even told the, uh, one of the lawyers, I've forgotten his name, as [sic] this is impossible. It does not work this way.
>
> So the impression I got, that they were trying to hide something. What that is, I don't know.

When he continued, Dolce identified this lawyer as Specter.

After saying, "At the conference the group [of Commission lawyers] did not accept" his expert opinion on the absolute impossibility of Specter's single-bullet theory, Dolce added:

> Because they wanted it otherwise and felt that if I went there as a ballistics expert, I think they should listen to me. Otherwise, there's no reason for them calling me. All right. Oh, I'm glad you brought that up. He's a Senator from Pennsylvania.

"What experience did you have with these types of gunshot wounds that enables you to give this opinion," Selby then asked. Dolce certainly had the experience:

> Well, I think I've had a lot of experience. I was a battlefield surgeon in the Pacific war. I was in the combat zone for three

years. I'm a retired full colonel of the Army. I saw many, many of these wounds. Besides that, we did a tremendous amount of research at the Edgewood Arsenal. And I think that's enough evidence. And besides that, in my own private experience as a surgeon, I've seen many bullet wounds.... So I would say my experience is a large one.

By education, training, surgical battlefield experience, and his research for the Army, Dolce was without question the outstanding expert in the field who, like Light, as indicated earlier, did not advance further because he asked questions the generals did not want asked or answered.

After mocking the supposed expertise of a mathematician used by the HSCA as a ballistic expert and saying that the committee did not conduct the tests he had been part of at Aberdeen, this is how he answered Selby's questions: "What, exactly was discussed at this conference forced the Commission to have tests made that it should have had made months earlier:

No definite conclusions were reached as, except that we as ballistics experts did not agree that CE 399, which is the pristine bullet, did all of the damages. When the Ar-legal personnel could get, could not get us to agree with them, they said well, we think you ought to go back to Edgewood and carry out some tests. And so they gave us the original rifle, the Mannlicher-Carcano, plus a hundred bullets, 6.5 millimeters, and we went, and we shot the cadaver wrists, as I've just mentioned, and in every instance the front, or the tip of the bullet was smashed. This was not so [with Bullet 399] ... They did not accept this.

Selby then repeated most of the questions to see if Dolce varied in any way in his responses to them. He did not.

(Selby's files hold his videotape of this interview and the transcript of it. My files hold the transcript only.)

Although Specter and the Commission did not call Dolce, the most important and most highly qualified expert of them all to testify, he did question Light (6H94–7). That testimony Specter kept remarkably brief, and even more remarkable, selective. It is less than four printed pages long.

In his questions of others Specter did not ask a single question about the deformity of all ten of the bullets fired into cadaver wrists. Not one volunteered that information either, although from their employment they were certainly aware of it. This is part of the three-monkeys type of investigating, speak no evil, see no evil, hear no evil, in which, when on the Commission, Specter specialized.

When the President was assassinated, and Dolce was his most authoritative expert witness, Specter did not call him to establish the truth because he did not want the truth that, as we have seen. Dolce would have sworn to.

Without Specter's suppression of what he learned from Dolce, the Report as written would have been impossible.

Specter had practiced his trickery on the Commission. Knowing that all ten of the bullets fired into cadavers' wrists were deformed, where as the single bullet of his impossible theory was unscathed, virtually pristine, Specter asked not a single question about those deformities of his substitutes for Dolce.

Pictures were taken of these test results at Aberdeen, and the Commission had them, but they are not even alluded to in this testimony.

Howard Roffman had a deeper regard for the right of the people to know. In his excellent book, *Presumed Guilty* (New Brunswick: Fairleigh-Dickinson University Press, 1975), Roffman published a Commission photograph of four test bullets, all with seriously deformities. The Commission's identification of this photograph reads, "6.5 MM Mannlicher-Carcano Bullets Recovered after being Fired Through Distal Ends of Radi of Cadaver Wrists" [*Presumed Guilty,* page 141]. Roffman's caption notes that this photograph was withheld from research for eight years. It was actually classified, although there was no legal ground for any classification of any grade.

Because this photograph did not qualify for classification, the only reason it was classified clearly was to be able to deny access to its refutation of the entiré Report and the entire official "solution" to the crime until long after there was any major attention to the controversy over the Report.

The photograph was not disclosed to Roffman until long after the fiasco of Jim Garrison's Mardi Gras-like "solution" to the JFK assassination. His trial of Clay Shaw ended with a "not guilty" verdict reached by the jury in less than an hour. That chilled interest in the assassination and criticism of the Report. As Roffman also noted, the one of these four bullets in this "classified" photograph that was least deformed appears to be the only one of those ten wrist test fired bullets that was entered into the Commission's record. It appears to be Commission Exhibit 856.

From what Dolce told Selby, it was obvious that if Specter had intended honesty he would have introduced those pictures into evidence during Light's testimony—handed them to him and asked him to describe them and what they showed. But that would have aborted his beloved bastard, so Specter did not ask the obvious and required questions.

They danced a stately minute around it, never once getting into the nitty-gritty.

Nor did he ask them of the Olivier, whose testimony preceded Light (5H74–90).

Then there is the testimony of Ronald Simmons. It, too, utterly destroys the fraudulent official "solution" that also served to protect any military conspiracy.

Chief of the Infantry Weapons Evaluation Branch of the Ballistics Research Laboratory at Aberdeen proving grounds, Simmons testified to the results of other and irrelevant shooting tests that in part established the impossibility of Oswald's having fired those three shots in a fraction of more that five seconds, the absolute essentiality of the official "solution." His testimony as published, naturally for this Commission, is separated from that of the others like Light and Olivier. It was published two volumes earlier, in Volume 3, pages 443–51.

Oswald was officially rated by the Marines in its Warren Commission testimony as a duffer, "a rather poor shot." To determine whether he could have performed the superhuman assassination feat attributed to him, the Army used three riflemen all "rated as Master by the National Rifle Association," the most expert of all expert riflemen (3H445). Toward the end of Simmons's testimony, Commission member McCloy, who was also present at the conference at which Dolce had spelled out how completely impossible the Commission's "solution" was, asked Simmons what the "master" rating was. He asked, "Is that a higher grade than sharpshooter in the Army?" Simmons told him that the master rating was the very highest, so high "there is really no comparison between the rating of master in the NRA and the rating of sharpshooter in the Army." Rather than being a sharpshooter, Oswald scored only the minimum required of all in the military. His Marine mates indicated to the Commission that his shooting was so bad even this minimum score was their gift to him.

What Simmons testified to was only the beginning of the Army's stacking of the evidentiary deck.

With the official solution having the shots come from more than sixty feet in the air, from that sixth-floor TSBD window, the Army built a platform at Aberdeen that was only thirty feet high. With Oswald allegedly shooting at a moving target, the Army had fixed targets planted in the ground at the distances the Commission said the limousine was from that window.

While this reduced the serious shooting problems of that steep angle and a moving target, the Army, in its test with "master" riflemen, still encountered a serious problem when the riflemen moved the rifle from one *still* target to the next. This caused misses.

The Mannlicher-Carcano rifle when compared to our rifles is a piece of junk. It was in poor condition when it reached the FBI in Washington. The FBI overhauled it and put it in its best possible condition. But even then the Aberdeen tests required additional improvement. As Simmons testified, his shooters "could not sight the weapon in using the telescopic sight" in some tests. So, "we did adjust the telescopic sight by the addition of two shims," one to adjust it vertically, the other side to side [3H443].

Even then, to begin with, "for the first four attempts the firers [i.e., the best shots in the country] missed the second target" [3H446]. In part this was because they had to reorient the rifle, and at that a to *still target they'd had time to adjust to,* not at a moving target without time to make any adjustment. In part these misses were because "of the amount of effort required to open the bolt" to remove the empty shell after a bullet was fired and close the bolt to chamber another time to be fired and because of "the trigger pull . . . a two-stage operation where the first—in the first stage the trigger is relatively free, and it suddenly required a greater pull to actually fire the weapon" [3H447]. This would "obviously require considerable experience ... because of the amount of effort required to work the bolt'' [3H449].

How serious a problem was this for the country's very best riflemen under the vastly improved and easier conditions?

"In our experiments," Simmons testified, "the pressure to open the bolt was so great we tended to move the rifle off target" [3H449].

With all that shooting expertise, the very greatest in the country, with all that improvement in the rifle and its sight and the shooting conditions, at a distance of 270 feet, the estimated distance of the rifle from the President's head when blown apart by the fatal shot, the country's very best riflemen could not duplicate the shooting attributed to Oswald. Simmons was asked by Melvin Eisenberg, the Commission counsel who questioned him, about an answer he had expressed in a tiny decimal, an evaluation of 0.4, Does 0.4 mean you have four chances in 10 of hitting?'' Simmon said merely, "Yes" [3H449]. This means that unlike the poor shot Oswald, these "masters" missed—under vastly improved conditions—six times out of ten!

And even this is not all. Could they do it in the *time* Oswald had in the official solution? No pun intended, this is the killer! Eisenberg was careful not to ask Simmons for the results on all their shooting, which in this test was of forty-seven bullets (3H449). One series was of twenty-one shots [3H445]. The only test that fairly can be compared to the assassination, in which with the rifle that Oswald was never known to have fired, he allegedly fired the three very accurate shots of the official account, three and no more. No dry runs for him. No practice shots. No shots to set the sight—which according to the FBI would not hold a setting in any event and which Aberdeen had to shim to use at all—the first three and that was it for him, and that was that.

Simmons testified of the three "masters" shooting that "on the first four attempts [all] the firers missed the second target" [3H446].

Of a master rifleman whose name is given only as "Mr. Hendrix" in Simmons's testimony, his "time for the first exercise was 8.25 seconds; the time for the second exercise was 7.0 seconds." The second master rifleman whose name Simmons gave only as "Mr. Staley" did "6 3/4 seconds" on his first try and 6.45 for the second

(3H446). This is 15 percent more time, regardless of his misses, than Oswald had.

The third master rifleman did not use the telescopic sight so that did not count for Simmons (3H446).

Remember that missing of the fatal shot six times out of ten? Here the first four shots at the second target also missed.

And these "masters" could not even approach the extremely rapid shooting attributed to as poor a shot as ever disgraced the Marines, Lee Harvey Oswald, the Commission's and Specter's William Tell.

Conspicuously Commissioner McCloy, the wily, worldly international lawyer, did not ask for a tabulation of the time required by each master for each series of shots. Eisenberg did not even ask if such a tabulation had been prepared or could be prepared.

For all the hemming and hawing, all the discussion of the arcane and irrelevant that could be impressive to the uninformed, the record that between them McCloy and Eisenberg made is that the very best riflemen in the land could not begin to duplicate the shooting performance officially attributed to Oswald.

Shooting is a mechanical skill. Good shooting requires regular practice. Oswald is known to have fired a rifle, a different and a much better weapon, only twice, years earlier, when he was in the Marines. Save for hunting squirrels with his brother, Robert, one time with a boy's .22 caliber rifle—and then he could not hit the side of a barn—Oswald is not known to have ever fired *any* rifle at any other time in his entire life. This includes that Mannlicher-Carcano he supposedly fired in the assassination. There is no evidence that he ever fired it and no reason to believe that he did.

The Army knew its tests proved the official "solution" was impossible. Neither Simmons nor any other witnesses testified to this shocking truth, that they knew the official concoction was an absolute impossibility. They all were careful in their testimony to steer clear of that.

This means that whatever its reason the Army knew there was a conspiracy, and it protected the conspirators. If it did not know earlier, it knew there had to have been a conspiracy because at Aberdeen it proved exactly that.

*   *   *

I include this, the only Dolce interview of which I know, in our consideration of whether or not there had been a military conspiracy for two reasons in particular. One is that the very first thing this retired Army full colonel, a rather high rank for a World War II battlefield surgeon, indicated was that there had been a military conspiracy. He twice said that the military took the autopsy over and then that the Army's own rules were violated in not calling him in immediately: "Right after the assassination the Army and Navy doctors appeared to take over everything," he said first. "The Army and Navy took over." This is what the evidence already showed without any question at all. Dolce's authoritative confirmation of it was suppressed.

Between them, Dolce's and the Simmons's testimonies, correctly understood, twice administer a "double whammy"—to the Commission and to the Army.

There is no apparent definitive answer to the questions I posed earlier: Why should the military have intervened at all and what purpose other than that of protecting the conspiracy could have been served by its gross improprieties?

There also is no answer in any of the evidence to the question: Why in the autopsy under military control were the prescribed rules for autopsies by the Armed Forces Institute of Pathology not followed in the autopsy on the President?

To this Dolce added that it was in the Army's rules that "in the event of injury to any VIP . . . I was to be called in to go over the case. I was not called." yet he was the Army's number one expert in the field.

How many explanations can there be other than that the military wanted to control what the autopsy could disclose and what its report would state about the shooting in the assassination?

Why should it want to control what could be known about the shooting other than to hide the fact that there had been a conspiracy to kill the President?

A second assassin meant there certainly had been a conspiracy.

The shooting was impossible for a single assassin.

Absent any other explanation for the military immediately "taking over" control of the autopsy that was supposed to have been completely independent and uncontrolled in any way and its refusal to call its own preeminent expert, Dolce, "in to go over the case," the only apparent explanation for these gross and incredible improprieties was that the military wanted to hide the fact that there had been a conspiracy. This it began doing immediately.

Does this not suggest that the conspiracy being hidden was a military conspiracy?

What other reasonable explanations *can* there be?

Chapter 28

Finck in New Orleans

APPLAUSE BOOKS PUBLISHED STONE'S *JFK* SCREENPLAY (NEW YORK, 1992). In it Finck takes up but a printed page, much of which is blank (pages 158–59). It is adapted from Garrison's *On the Trail of the Assassins* (pages 246–49). Most of these four pages is a direct quotation of the stenographic transcript of Finck's testimony, but Stone actually understated what Finck had testified to about military control of the autopsy. Finck, recall, testified in Shaw's defense at the trial.

Garrison wrote, referring to Alvin Oser, an assistant district attorney and later a judge, as his father had been:

> Oser greeted Dr. Finck with a warm smile. Within minutes he had the autopsy pathologist backpedaling at a rapid rate. After Dr. Finck committed himself to the proposition that the entry wound was in the back of the neck, Oser quickly moved to the question of whether the neck wound had been probed at the autopsy. This should have been a standard and routine examination to determine the route of the wound. When Dr. Finck's answer was negative, Oser began pressing him:
> **Dr. Finck.** I will remind you that I was not in charge of this autopsy, that I was called—
> **Mr. Oser.** You were a coauthor of the [autopsy] report though, weren't you, doctor?
> **Dr. Finck.** Wait. I was called as a consultant to look at these wounds; that doesn't mean I am running the show.
> **Mr. Oser.** Was Dr. Humes running the show?
> **Dr. Finck.** Well, I heard Dr. Humes stating that—he said, "Who's in charge here?" and I heard an Army general, I don't remember his name, stating, "I am." You must understand that in those circumstances, there were law enforcement officers, military

people with various ranks and you have to coordinate the operation according to directions.

Mr. Oser. Was this Army general a qualified pathologist?

Dr. Finck. No.

Mr. Oser. Was he a doctor?

Dr. Finck. No, not to my knowledge.

Mr. Oser. Can you give me his name, Colonel?

Dr. Finck. No, I can't. I don't remember.

Garrison then made some comments about the autopsy pictures and X rays and resumed quoting the trial transcript:

Mr. Oser. How many other military personnel were present in the autopsy room?

Dr. Finck. That autopsy room was quite crowded. It is a small autopsy room, and when you are called, in circumstances like that to look at the wound of the President of the United States who is dead, you don't look around too much to ask people for their names and take notes on who they are and how many there are. I did not do so. The room was crowded with military and civilian personnel and federal agents, Secret Service agents, FBI agents, for part of the autopsy, but I cannot give you a precise breakdown as regards the attendance of the people in that autopsy room at Bethesda Naval Hospital.

Mr. Oser. Colonel, did you feel that you had to take orders from this Army general that was there directing the autopsy?

Dr. Finck. No, because there were others, there were admirals.

Mr. Oser. There were admirals?

Dr. Finck. Oh, yes, there were admirals, and when you are a lieutenant colonel in the Army you just follow orders, and at the end of the autopsy, we were specifically told—as I recall it, it was by Admiral Kenney, the surgeon of the Navy—this is subject to verification—we were specifically told not to discuss the case.

To appreciate the full impact of what Finck here testified to, it is necessary to remember what Oser was questioning him about, "Who was running the show?" Or, who was in charge at the autopsy. Finck testified that so far as he was concerned, it was the Navy admirals who were in charge.

This is the exact opposite, however it may be interpreted, of what this trio of prosecutors told Lundberg, Breo, and *JAMA*.

Oser turning to JFK's nonfatal wound, continued questioning Finck:,

> **Mr. Oser.** Did you have occasion to dissect the track of that particular bullet in the victim as it lay on the autopsy table?
>
> **Dr. Finck.** I did not dissect the track in the neck.
>
> **Mr. Oser.** Why?
>
> **Dr. Finck.** This leads us into the disclosure of medical records.
>
> **Mr. Oser.** Your Honor, I would like an answer from the colonel and I would ask the Court so to direct.
>
> **The Court.** That is correct, you should answer, doctor.
>
> **Dr. Finck.** We didn't remove the organs of the neck.
>
> **Mr. Oser.** Why not, doctor?
>
> **Dr. Finck.** For the reason that we were told to examine the head wounds and the—
>
> **Mr. Oser.** Are you saying someone told you not to dissect the track?
>
> **The Court.** Let him finish his answer.
>
> **Dr. Finck.** I was told that the family wanted an examination of the head, as I recall, the head and chest, but prosecutors in this autopsy didn't remove the organs of the neck, to my recollections.

Oser was not as willing to be gulled as were Lundberg and Breo. When Finck persisted in evading questions, Oser asked the judge to order him to give a direct answer. It was only then that Finck relented and told the truth: *He was ordered not to trace the path of that nonfatal bullet through JFK's body!*

> **Mr. Oser.** You have said they did not. I want to know why didn't you as an autopsy pathologist attempt to ascertain the track through the body, which you had on the autopsy table, in trying to ascertain the cause or causes of death? Why?
>
> **Dr. Finck.** I had the cause of death.
>
> **Mr. Oser.** Why did you not trace the track of the wound?
>
> **Dr. Finck.** As I recall I didn't remove these organs from the neck.
>
> **Mr. Oser.** I didn't hear you.
>
> **Dr. Finck.** I examined the wounds, but I didn't remove the organs of the neck.
>
> **Mr. Oser.** You said you didn't do this; I am asking you why you didn't do this as a pathologist?

Dr. Finck. From what I recall I looked at the trachea, there was a tracheotomy wound the best I can remember, but I didn't dissect or remove these organs.

Mr. Oser. Your Honor, I would ask Your Honor to direct the witness to answer my question. I will ask you the question one more time: Why did you not dissect the track of the bullet wound that you have described today and you saw at the time of the autopsy at the time you examined the body? Why? I ask you to answer the question.

Dr. Finck. As I recall I was told not to, but I don't remember by whom.

Or, the autopsy was incomplete because it *was ordered not to be complete.* The only persons there who could have given such orders were military persons and of higher rank than Finck. The two Navy captains outranked Finck and so did the three admirals. At least one of these five or Major General Wehle ordered that there not be a complete autopsy on the assassinated President! The reason could not have been cosmetic or in response to imagined family wishes because the torso had been laid open, from the armpits to the groin, but this simple examination, to trace the path of the bullet, was ordered not to be made.

Consistent with this the *rewritten* autopsy, the original having been consigned to the flames after Ruby killed Oswald, makes no reference at all to the bullet fragments in the area of the body that are shown on the X rays taken during the autopsy. These were examined during the autopsy by Finck, Humes, Boswell, and the radiologist, John Ebersole.

The examination ordered not to be made would have made it impossible to get away with that preconceived lone-nut assassin "solution" given to the people.

Without this ordered—*militarily* ordered—gross impropriety, not to perform a real autopsy, the fiction of the Warren Report would have been impossible.

Unlike Humes and Boswell chatting with Lundberg and Breo, Finck was under oath and subject to the penalties of perjury. When he tried to evade, the judge compelled him to be responsive. Humes's account of this incident in *JAMA* is unrecognizable. The one thing they have in common is the word "general." Here is the Humes account.

Humes was in total charge

By 7:30 PM, Humes was in his scrubs in the hospital's new morgue, built only four months earlier. He had selected Dr. Boswell as his assistant. The morgue was at the back of the hospital, and as Dr. Humes stepped *outside* the morgue onto the loading dock, he noticed a crowd milling about and an unknown man carrying a large, old-fashioned 'Speed graphic' camera. Still outside the morgue, the pathologist told the unknown cameraman, 'Get out!' Then Humes asked, 'Who's in charge here?'

The answer was only two feet away, as a man in full military dress answered, 'I am. Who wants to know?' Humes explains, 'The man who said he was in charge outside the morgue was some general representing the military section of the District of Columbia. I told him what my assignment was and asked him about the chap with the camera. Well, seconds later, this chap with the camera was sent away.'

No generals in the morgue

As the general remained *outside* the morgue, Humes stepped back inside to prepare to receive the President's body. He emphasizes, 'Nobody made any decision in the morgue except ME. Nobody distracted or influenced me in any way, shape, or form.'

Following this, the article continues with its account of the motorcade to the hospital from the air base.

JAMA emphasized Humes's untruthfulness with the two subheads; the first, over a single paragraph that has Humes "in total charge" when he wasn't; the second, referring only to the single short paragraph quoted, although in *JAMA* that subhead supposedly relates to what took up the rest of that page and continued onto almost all of the next page. Aside from "no generals in the morgue" being untrue, it has no relationship at all to the rest of this long section of the story.

Humes had no general to explain away until Stone's movie attracted considerable attention. Humes's story in *JAMA* makes no sense at all. He has himself asserting authority and exercising functions he did not have. He was a doctor, not a military policeman. He has himself getting some fresh air at the time he testified he had begun the autopsy examination, about a half-hour after the corpse reached the hospital and some time after it was at that loading dock which is not far from the morgue. He had himself not seeing a general, although he was of comparatively low rank himself. And he refers to the commanding officer of the Military District of Washington as "some general representing the military section of the District of Columbia," which has no "military section."

Humes's account of his alleged stroll to and along the loading dock has him idling with nothing better to do at the time he was, from the account of the two FBI agents, present at the autopsy and in the third car of the motorcade to the hospital, with the corpse after the corpse was there and about thirteen minutes after he began preparations for the autopsy. (FBI 62–109060–2637; their 3/12/64 account of their interview that day by Arlen Specter.) They stated the preparations for the autopsy began at precisely 7:17 P.M. Unless these preparations required only about ten minutes, it appears to be quite unlikely that Humes was not busy in the morgue making and supervising others in the preparations for the autopsy, not leisurely strolling along the loading dock.

It appears that without bothering to check any records, Humes just made up the story to try to offset Finck's testimony—that *there was military control of the autopsy.*

JAMA provided the emphasis within the quoted text with the false statement that Major General Wehle was *"outside"* the morgue.

But it was Humes who had this major general pulling the military-police duty of a private!

And at such a time!

From Humes's careless concoction, Finck had to have been at the Naval Hospital an hour before he got there—and he did not get there until after the body had been opened and some organs removed!

Humes and Finck each referred to but a single general being there. Humes contrived to not have him in the autopsy room, the apparent purpose being to convey the idea that he could not have been in the morgue to tell Humes he was in charge.

Humes told Lundberg and Breo, "Nobody made any decisions in the morgue except ME, [*JAMA's* emphasis]. Nobody distracted or influenced me in any way, shape or form."

We have already seen that this is a lie as it relates to the protocol, which was altered on Admiral Galloway's orders, according to Humes's own sworn testimony.

Finck testified that they were "told not to" trace the path of the bullet through the body, and therefore did not.

And not doing that avoided proof that the crime was beyond the capability of any one man—a conspiracy.

The tiniest fragment of bullet recovered from the body, under spectrographic or neutron-activation analysis, could have been identified as coming from Bullet 399—*or as not coming from it!*

Not making the required examination—*as ordered*—eliminated the possibility of recovering any of the fragments in the track of the untracked bullet.

Finck began with the official obscenity and indecency of pretending that the required examinations were not made because the Kennedy family did not want them made, but when he had no other real choice and had to answer directly, he abandoned that outrage and testified to the autopsy being controlled by the military.

Nothing else explains the gross omissions in the examination. No pathologist would have dared not do what was required on the basis his own authority.

Humes and Boswell portray Finck as a milquetoast, as mild and meek. This one excerpt from his testimony shows he persisted in evading and avoiding answering questions, not a mark of timidity. But this is nothing like the toughness Finck displayed over the two days of his testimony. He even tried to tell the judge how to run the trial!

As the foregoing is limited to citation of what was public and readily available to the quintet, what follows is also limited to what was as readily available to them. It is from the "Flatulent Finck and His In-Court Spelling Bee" chapter of *Post Mortem*.

The opening paragraph of this excerpt, written two decades before it served Humes's and Boswell's selfish interests to portray Finck as meek and mild, is a summary of my impression of him after reading "all 269 pages" of the stenographic transcript of his trial testimony from February 24 and 25, 1969:

Arrogance, self-importance, a determination to be judge, prosecution and defense lawyers, and witness—to ask the ques-

tions he wanted to answer or to answer not the questions asked
of him but those he wanted asked—a scarcely hidden and fierce
partisanship highly improper in a man of science and an expert
witness in forensic medicine in a criminal proceeding—permeate
all 269 pages of [Lieutenant] Colonel Pierre Finck's New Orleans
testimony of February 24 and 25, 1969 [*Post Mortem*, page 230].

This does not describe a man who was either meek or mild. It
does describe him through two days of rough cross-examination.

On the next page I began writing about Finck's evasiveness and
demeanor:

Finck is undisguised in his open, deliberate evading of questions
when those questions called for answers he, from his lofty and
superior position and understanding, just did not want to answer.
Much of his deliberate evasion of response and the clear meaning
of the question asked is undisguised. Oft he is skilled, so smooth
that neither judge nor prosecutor caught him. But, when caught
and *ordered* to respond, he out and out refused to do as directed.
He undertook to give everyone else legal advice from the witness
chair until finally told by patient Judge Edward Haggerty to sus-
pend his legal lectures, that he, Finck was *not* running the show.

Finck's testimony grew increasingly reluctant as Oser questioned him. Finck was a veritable verbal, medical snake, impossible to believe, most of all because of his experience, training,
background, and former use by the Warren Commission as an
expert to authenticate what he had to know was a fake; because
he consciously sought to hide evidence that decency and honor
compelled of him almost as much as did his function as an expert
witness in a criminal proceeding; and because, instead of answering the questions asked of him, he pretended more congenital
questions were asked and to the unasked questions he volunteered
unasked and self-serving answers. His appearance was an unending argument in which usually he was not responsive. Whenever
he could get away with it, it was also volunteered and voluble
propaganda.

One example was his response to a very simple direction, that
he mark on the back of the shirt of one of the defense counsel
the spot that the rear, nonfatal wound entered the President. Not
content with doing as told, as he knew, all he was supposed to
do, Finck then launched into an entire page [page 12] of propaganda, for all the world as though he had been asked a question,

which he had not been, beginning with an orientation of the wound by what his training told him is wrong, only moving parts of the body. This means the wound is not and cannot thus be located, for there is no way of knowing the position of each of the movable parts at the time of measurement.

The verbal torrent gushed out, all improper, all nonresponsive, all propaganda, I think compelled by a guilty conscience, a compulsion for self-justification. One of the gross examples is: 'When examining this wound, I saw the regular edges pushed inward, what we call inverted.' He then repeated this same thing, the second time spelling 'inverted.'

This was deliberate deception.

There was, to Finck's knowledge, an explanation for the condition of the tissues at the edge of this wound and the fact that they were 'pushed inward.' They had, in actuality, been pushed inward at that hospital before his arrival but to his subsequent knowledge. This most unscientific probing was by his Naval colleague, Dr. Humes, who had unnecessarily, having already taken X rays, in which lead glows like fluorescent light, pushed that tissue in with his little finger!

So, Finck's outpouring of the unasked, unsought, and false is not without purpose. It is propaganda, not fact or testimony. It was not in response to the very simple direction, not even a question, that he 'point out on his [Shaw's lawyer's] anatomy the approximate location of the wound,' a request made a page and a half earlier. It is typical of Finck.

Even Dymond [Irving Dymond, one of New Orleans more prominent attorneys, was one of Shaw's lawyers.] thought he had better bring this to an end before the judge did and tried to stop Finck when he interrupted his propagandizing to spell 'inverted' for the blighted judge, lawyers, court stenographer, and world press. Dymond spoke only four words before he, too, was interrupted by his witness, Finck, who was determined to control both defense and prosecution proffers of evidence. The omniscient Finck cut him off after 'Doctor, did you make—' to insist on adding further propaganda, his reiteration in different words of the alleged appearance of the edges of this wound.

This is just for openers [pages 11–13]. It never stopped. It gives the feel of the enormous ego, the man who alone could put it all together, the man who dominated and sought to dominate what evidence could be sought and obtained as it related to the autopsy and its procedures.

And when the defense lawyer, whose witness he was, finally turned him off before there was an eruption from the judge or opposing counsel, Finck returned to his spelling fetish, with words so difficult for lawyers, the judge, and the press to understand, 'abrasion,' 'entry,' and 'entrance' all spelled out on page 13.

But, even in the presentation of the defense side of the case, it was not long before the sneaky Finck, who might better have accomplished his illicit purposes by saying much less and letting the skilled lawyer Dymond run the show, started making the most serious errors in judgment and volunteering what would, in any decent society, be the basis of criminal charges against him and his associates.

For example, he was asked a simple question to which he should—and *knew* he should—have answered merely 'yes' or 'no.' 'Now, Doctor, did you examine on the remains of the late President Kennedy a wound in the frontal neck region?' Finck launched into a combination of futile self-justification and mumbo jumbo of meaningless pontifications, complete with another needless spelling, this time inaccurately, adding a characterization of that wound as one of exit, while also admitting he did not then see it. After a half page of this rambling, he went into a double hearsay, what he knew was improper and incompetent, that on the day after the autopsy, 'Dr. Humes called the surgeons of Dallas.' This is hearsay, for Finck was not there, and an error, for Humes phoned only one doctor. Finck added, 'And he was told that they'—hearsay twice removed, for Finck did not hear what, if anything, was said—before Oser interrupted, 'I object to the hearsay' [page 14].

Then Dymond pretended to caution Finck—a caution *entirely unnecessary* to a man certified in forensic science: 'You may not say what the surgeons of Dallas told Dr. Humes. That would be hearsay.' Finck argued with him, beginning with, 'I have to base my interpretation on all the facts available and not on one fact only . . .' Patently, this is false. The proper and possible answers are 'yes,' 'no,' or 'I am not certain.' If necessary, Finck could then ask permission to amplify his answer. Here it was not necessary except for propaganda, which is not the purpose of a legal proceeding. Dymond, of course, was quite anxious for Finck to load the record with all the propaganda and irrelevancies he could get in and to complicate Oser's already serious problems as much as he could. So, he let Finck carry on without interruption for most of a page [15] until the judge, for the first but no the last time, called Finck to book.

Knowing full well it was entirely improper, Finck argued, 'I insist on that point, and that telephone call to Dallas from Dr. Humes.' Judge Haggerty chided him, 'You may insist on the point, Doctor, but we are going to do it according to the law. If it is legally objectionable, even if you insist, I am going to sustain the objection' [*Post Mortem*, pages 231–33].

This is meek? And it was not even in "reference" to his opponent, Garrison's lawyer. It was when questioned by Shaw's lawyer, the lawyer for whom he was testifying, the lawyer to whom he should have listened and to whose indications of propriety he should have heeded. But Finck did not change throughout his direct testimony.

As neither Garrison nor Stone picked up from Finck's testimony:

But *no general of any* rank controls *any* Naval installation— not normally, anyway. So the next day Finck changed his testimony about the man in charge being a general, saying he was an admiral [*Post Mortem*, page 234].

After a citation from the AFIP manual *The Autopsy, Post Mortem* continues:

Throughout his testimony, reluctant as he was to admit it and hard as Shaw's lawyers tried to testify for him, to come to his rescue when he was pressed and did not want to admit what was damaging to the official account of the presidential assassination, Finck nonetheless was forced to acknowledge that the nature of the examination made and not made was not determined by the requirements of the law or regulation, but by direct orders given on the spot by top brass.

Important as was the tracing of the path of that magical bullet 399 through the President's body to learn if, in fact, there was *any* bullet that did or could have taken this guessed-at path, Finck finally admitted that the doctors were ordered not to do this obviously necessary thing [2/24, pages 115–9, 148–49; 2/25, pages 4, 8, 32–36]. [Reference is to pages of the stenographic transcript holding further testimony relating to this nonfatal shot.] First he tried to blame Robert Kennedy [page 115]. In the end, after what amounts to repeated evading and lying, he admitted the orders were military orders and had nothing to do with the family. Not until the second day of his testimony was the deliberateness of his intended deception and the viciousness of this military effort to blame the family for the gross and shameful deficiencies of the autopsy fully laid bare.

Toward the end of the first day, he acknowledged that this was not 'a complete autopsy under the definition used by the American Board of Pathology' [page 199]. This seemingly full admission is far from it. The military autopsy manual requires examination of the thorax and neck organs. It has special sections describing the incisions, exposure, and inspections to be made. . . .

Yet even into the second day he tried to pretend the required examination, the tracing of the alleged track of the alleged nonfatal bullet through the cadaver, was not done 'not to create unnecessary mutilation of thecadaver' [page 17]. Of course, this was entirely false, the cadaver having been laid open pretty completely, much as he tried to weasel [pages 32–36].

'The chest cavity of the President' was laid open [page 33].

'The usual Y-cut incision' *was* made [page 34].

This lays open the 'rib cage—so you can get the vital organs of the body' [page 34].

[References to transcript pages in what follows are to the second day of Finck's testimony.]

As illustrated in the military autopsy manual, the 'Y'-cut begins above the armpits, into the shoulder joints, is semicircular to below the nipples, and from the center extends to the genitals.

This is not 'mutilation' enough? It was done.

With this much mutilation acknowledged, is it credible that a slightly upward probing would cause objectionable 'mutilation'?

It is a lie. The purpose of the lie is to suppress evidence.

But, regardless, it was an examination required to be made. And it was not made.

The reason had nothing to do with the alleged wish of the family, that unending and shameful effort to blame the bereaved family for the deficiencies of the autopsy.

[Remember Humes's tough talk to Lundberg and Breo, that he alone made decisions and that nobody influenced him in any way?]

Finck admitted that Admiral Galloway *personally* ordered changes in the autopsy report *after* it was drafted [pages 4–5].

The autopsy surgeons were threatened by high authority [page 5] if they said a word. The man in charge was not this unnamed general but 'the Adjutant General' [page 6]. [he meant the Surgeon General] of the Navy, Admiral Kenney [page 6].

[From Finck's testimony, also, we discover that more notes are missing than those missing ones made by Humes!]

When I walked out of that autopsy room I didn't have notes with me, to the best of my recollection. I remember taking measurements and giving them to Dr. Humes and Dr. Boswell [page 96].

What immediately precedes this identifies these as written notes he personally made during the autopsy. They used small pieces of paper besides the autopsy descriptive sheet. Twice on this one page alone Finck admits that both the others also took notes:

'I saw both Dr. Humes and Dr. Boswell taking notes at the time of the autopsy' and 'both of them made notes during the autopsy.'

Among the many impermissible, intolerable facts established beyond doubt by Finck's New Orleans testimony is that, although *all* the medical men knew that the alleged path of the allegedly nonfatal bullet through the President's body *had* to be traced, it was not done; *all* made written notes required to be preserved, and they no longer exist; what he participated in cannot and does not qualify as a full autopsy; top military brass immediately took over the autopsy, severely limiting what the surgeons could do and ordering them not to do what they had to do, what had to be done; the commanding officer of the Naval Medical Center ordered changes in the written autopsy after it was prepared, the most substantive changes; and the autopsy surgeons were threatened with retaliation if they opened their mouths [*Post Mortem*, pages 235–3].

The conclusions of this chapter of two decades ago are appropriate today, after all that time has passed—more appropriate because of the *JAMA*/AMA/prosecutors attempt to rewrite the facts of the autopsy into what, in other societies, would have been called "official propaganda," even if not issued by officialdom.

This much the reluctant Finck did admit. There was much more he did not. For example, all medical personnel present at the autopsy or who merely passed through the room while it was being conducted received the same threat, in writing.

Aside from the grossest improprieties in taking over a medico-legal function required to be completely independent, especially when that is an inquest into how a president was assassinated, can this threatening, this ordering of what must be left out or altered, do other than feed conspiratorial belief about the involvement of the military in some kind of plot?

Why should *any* general, *any* admiral, *any* officer of *any* rank, want to interfere in *any* way with what the autopsy report would say about how the President was killed? Why should *anybody* order that required examinations *not* be made and reported?

Is there any reasonable nonconspiratorial explanation that *can* be made?

Why should anyone in the whole world, assuming there had been no conspiracy of any kind, have wanted anything but the most complete, the most dependable, the most unfettered autopsy examination and report made with total and complete independence?

One that would permit the existence of no unasked or unanswered questions.

Inevitably, this record requires better answers from the military than silence, lies, destructions, and evasions. Something more than the self-serving falsehoods of the TV tube, the evasions and lies of the unpublicized testimony, performances that I believe involve criminal conduct requiring criminal action [*Post Mortem*, page 523–38].

These questions also remain appropriate. How does what is here reported so much of which was reported so long ago not warrant suspecting that there had been a military conspiracy?

How explain what AMA, *JAMA*, Lundberg, Breo, Humes, Boswell, and Finck did rather than let the sleeping dogs of their past transgressions slumber?

Is it possible to give a rational explanation of what Lundberg and Breo did, when, as experienced as they are as an editor and as a medical writer, they have written as they have about what they know nothing at all about, one of the greatest tragedies in our history?

That truly great tragedy about which so many caring Americans remain so deeply troubled.

Among the most deeply troubled, from my mail and phone calls, are so many Americans who had not been born at the time of the tragedy?

How could Lundberg and Breo even think of departing so radically from the accepted standards of responsible journalism? And for a respected, influential publication like *JAMA*?

How could they, in the name of the respected association of the nation's doctors, mislead, misinform, deceive, and, yes, lie to the nation, and to its doctors, in particular?

What Finck actually swore to in New Orleans bears heavily on whether or not there was or could have been a military conspiracy.

This is a matter about which *JAMA* would lie, lie as brazenly as its gang of five would have it lie. And *JAMA* would persist in the lie with Finck, after all the criticism in response to its first articles.

It was Oliver Stone's version of the JFK assassination that triggered the gang of five. Then, obviously, what that movie says is where it all begins. This means that, at the very least, all five had to know what the movie did say before making any comment on it. *Had to,* assuming honesty and responsibility, as we should be able to expect of *JAMA*.

It is because of this that I first quoted the movie script and then Garrison's book, on which Stone based his film, to report what Stone and Garrison said of Finck's testimony. I then quoted what I had written about it, what was readily available to all, a decade and a half earlier. What I quoted from *Post Mortem* is from the official stenographic transcript of the court record. Garrison did not lie about Finck's testimony, he did not exaggerate it, and for once Stone also didn't.

They understated it, as the verbatim record of Finck's testimony establishes beyond any question at all.

Finck did testify to absolute military control over the President's autopsy!

That was very, very wrong, so very wrong it requires that we ask if the military did conspire because, why else would it even think of controlling the autopsy that it supposed to establish truth by recognized and necessary procedures?

Why would *JAMA* and its gang of five not want to report carefully and accurately on this—and why would it lie about so important a matter, one that requires wonder about a military coup d'état?

Al Oser did an excellent, responsible, fair job of cross-examining Finck. No tricks, no dirty stuff at all. He was well prepared, and he had the ability to do it. He and Garrison's other assistants involved in the prosecution had a good understanding of what Sylvia Meagher in her superb *Accessories After the Fact* and I, beginning with and especially in *Whitewash,* had brought to light. They had studied the published Commission transcripts of the medical testimony. Although after agreeing to be what Garrison called his "Dealey Plaza expert" at the trial, I had broken with him when I learned what his supposed case against Shaw was and despite the fact that *The New York Times* reported that I sat at the counsel table with the prosecution, I did not. I was not in the courtroom. I never laid eyes on Shaw. But I did spend most of the Sunday before the first day of the trial, the day selection of the jury began, with Oser and his assistant at Oser's home to help them with the facts of the case to the degree I could. When we parted at suppertime that Sunday, I told Al they would lose the case, and they deserved to because there was no case against Shaw at all, but that was separate and distinct from the medical evidence in the JFK assassination. About that no lawyer could have been better prepared to cross-examine Finck, and the transcript of that testimony attests to Oser's ability, preparation, and responsibility.

The record he made with Finck as a *defense* witness, incredible as that was, is a solid and fair record, one that is of great significance in our history.

It is a truthful record, it is a record that demands concern over whether we suffered a military conspiracy to overthrow the elected and popular President who had, despite the inevitable and profitable revisionist claims of today, turned toward peace in the world.

And it is horrifying—ghastly to me that a publication like *JAMA* would lie about it.

It is no comfort to us that our major media did not tell us the truth when *JAMA* lied about the possibility of a military conspiracy, about a military overthrow of the elected government.

The truth, as this chapter makes clear, was readily available to it.

Terrifying as this truth should be to those who care about the preservation of our system of government, it is not yet all. Our account is not yet finished, thanks to Lundberg and what he admitted in promoting himself and his *JAMA* monstrosity.

Chapter 29

"There May Have Been Other Gunshots"—George D. Lundberg

DEFENSE OF THE WARREN REPORT IS CHARACTERIZED BY IGNORANCE and stupidity. The only other means of defending it is by lies. Indiscriminately and lustily *JAMA* resorts to all these means under Lundberg's spirited and uninhibited leadership.

In one of his little-noticed displays of both ignorance and stupidity, after all that effort in *JAMA* and in his eminently successful press conference, he actually admitted that the Report is unacceptable and wrong beyond repair. And appeared entirely unaware of it!

But the devotion of the media to its own support of the Report as well as media ignorance of the established facts of the assassination, let him get away with it even as he was making his unintended confession or error on *The MacNeil/Lehrer Newshour* of May 20, 1992.

The Warren Report concluded that Oswald alone fired three shots and that no other shots were fired during the assassination. Admitting a single additional shot at the very least was to admit that without possibility of any question at all, there had been a conspiracy. Without enough time for three shots, a fourth was impossible for Oswald with that rifle.

Thus, even without Specter's impossible concoction of that magic bullet having inflicted all seven nonfatal wounds on the President and Connally, on the basis of a fourth shot alone there was a conspiracy. It seems both the FBI and the Secret Service independently determined to deny there had been a conspiracy. Each decided to ignore the shot that was fired during the assassination and missed the car and its occupants widely, by a large margin, if fired from that "Oswald" window.

Throughout all the articles, Lundberg's editorial, and the selection of letters it published, *JAMA* acknowledged only two shots having been fired.

Typical is Lundberg at his press conference quoted in the *Los Angeles Times* of May 20, 1992: "I can state without concern or question that President Kennedy was struck and killed by two, and only two bullets, fired from one high-velocity rifle. No other bullets struck the President. A single assassin fired both."

He amplified this with what is not tainted by a single accuracy: "The main conspiracy theory rests on there being more than one gun and the bullets hitting the President in more than one direction. We can categorically state that to be untrue." If, however, other shots that struck nobody were fired, that means there was a conspiracy.

When the FBI could no longer ignore other shots, it dismissed the bullets forced upon it with the non sequitur that those bullets would not have fit in Oswald's rifle! This, of course, is what an honest investigation would have used as the basis for further investigation.

Jim Lehrer of *The MacNeil/Lehrer Newshour* knew that there had been at least a third shot because he reported it when he worked for the *Dallas Times Herald*. He had interviewed James Tague, who was wounded by a spray of concrete from a curbstone that had been struck by a bullet during the assassination. On the Lundberg broadcast Lehrer made no mention of his personal knowledge of this "missed" shot, which could not have come from where Oswald was allegedly shooting.

MacNeil, saying he would "play devil's advocate," said that *JAMA* was "not capable of saying that those were the only bullets fired at the President."

(On November 11, 1963, MacNeil, then an NBC reporter in the motorcade, heard three shots and said that when he rushed in to the TSBD looking for a phone, *Oswald directed him to one on the first floor* when Oswald was allegedly on the sixth floor. So, naturally, the Commission did not call him to testify. He did not recall this when interviewing Lundberg [See, Manchester's *The Death of a President,* page 229]).

Lundberg's reply was: "No. There may have been many other gunshots . . . But none of them hit the President."

MacNeil then said, "The evidence they've [Humes and Boswell] given you is not conclusive proof that there wasn't somebody firing from other directions who missed.''

Lundberg evaded response by referring to his favorite two-bullets-only theory.

Lundberg's saying that ''there may have been many other gun-shots'' means that the Warren Report is wrong in not eliminating that possibility—which it never addressed despite the ample relevant evidence in its files and testimony.

Lundberg's admission that ''there may have been many other gun-shots,'' entirely missing in anything he published, is also an admis-sion that he had no right to say there had been only Oswald firing or that the Report was correct. Yet this is precisely what he did in *JAMA*.

Lundberg's knowledge that there could have been ''many'' other shots fired during the assassination, while suppressing that from all the many thousands of partisan words he published, is also an admis-sion that he knew before publishing them that he could have been entirely wrong in what he did publish.

The editor of *JAMA*'s deliberate excising of his own knowledge of the possibility of more than three shots from the article, from his press releases, and from his press conference is more than mere blind partisanship, although it is blind and partisan. It raises serious ques-tions about Lundberg's personal and professional integrity and the integrity of the *Journal* of the American Medical Association.

But, if there had been vestige of professionalism in Lundberg, he never would have said what neither he nor the prosectors had any way of knowing, that the two bullets of which he spoke at his press conference were both ''fired from one high-velocity rifle.'' It was impossible for them to know this, and they had no factual basis for assuming it. Yet Lundberg pronounced it ''without concern or question.''

Of all the many indications that there were, and there had to have been more than three shots reported in this book, none is, I believe, more important than Specter's bastard, that impossible single-bullet theory. The *JAMA* gang treated this with ignorance, incompetence, and staggering, overt dishonesty, as we also have seen.

The Commission's own evidence, so openly misrepresented in its Report, disproved the magic-bullet theory long before the Report was written. (For how early this was apparent see *Whitewash*, chapters "The Doctors and the Autopsy" and "The Number of Shots.")

What I did not know when I wrote my first book in which this was brought to light for the first time is that three authorities, who were intimately involved, also did not believe it. They are Richard Russell, Commission member and Senator; Jesse Curry, the Dallas chief of police; and Henry Wade, Dallas district attorney, who would have prosecuted Oswald.

Wade wrote me on October 10, 1968, "I have always felt there was an accomplice of someone else involved in this matter with Oswald . . ." Based on what he had been told by the police, particularly homicide Captain Will Fritz, Wade did believe that Oswald was an assassin. But with an accomplice, that meant there was a conspiracy.

As indicated earlier in this book, Russell was conned into agreeing with what had been misrepresented to him as a compromise to accommodate his position, only to find out that the Commission said exactly what he would not agree to say, but did it by using different words. There was the September 18, 1964, executive session at which this was discussed, the one to which Rankin had seen to it that there would be no record of Russell's disagreement that was reportedly shared by two other members, Senator John Sherman Cooper of Kentucky and Congressman Hale Boggs of Louisiana. (See *Whitewash IV*, pages 21–22 and 132.)

Two days before that executive session Russell prepared what he intended to say there. It was disclosed during the 1992 Congressional consideration of litigation to compel the disclosure of still-withheld official JFK assassination records. It was also ignored by the media. Two brief excerpts from it are unequivocal on Russell's refusal to accept the single-bullet theory:

> I do not share the finding of the Commission to the probability that both President Kennedy and the Governor Connally were struck by the same bullet and my conviction that the bullet that passed through Governor Connally's body was not the same bullet as that which passed through the President's back and neck.

More than two decades earlier in 1968, after reading *Whitewash* and skimming my next three books for Russell, his assistant, C.E.

Campbell, said that my work "is scholarly and evidences a tremendous amount of research. His basic approach is not to try to prove that Oswald was innocent although acceptance of his inferences, etc., lead to that conclusion. His method is to restrict his criticism to the actual information which the Commission had . . . One of his strongest points of departure is on the number of shots fired and on which shots hit Connally and/or the President. He completely agrees with your thesis that no one shot hit both.''

Russell was on the verge of resigning from the Warren Commission several times, but recognized it to be a political impossibility. One of his letters of resignation in his archives is dated early in the Commission's life, February 24, 1964.

Allen Dulles leaked word of Russell's disenchantment. It reached J. Edgar Hoover on June 22, 1964, when Edward A. Tamm, a former assistant who had been appointed to the federal appeals court in Washington, telephoned him. In a memo on the conversation that Hoover sent to only his four top honchos, he said that Tamm had learned from Ernest Cuneo, who was to write a five-thousand-word article about the Warren Commission, that "Senators [Edward V.] Long and Russell and a couple of others were taking a very vigorous stand, and it looked like there was going to be a repudiation of Warren" [FBIHQ 62–109090–176, with four duplicate filings noted].

When Lieutenant Jack Revill headed the Dallas police intelligence unit, he caused the first of several serious flaps when he reported that the FBI knew that Oswald had the capability, but they did not expect him to do it. That was only the first of the major flaps in which FBI Special Agent James P. Hosty, Jr., figured. He then was the Oswald Dallas case agent, and he was Revill's source. Another was in 1975, when after his retirement, Dallas Special Agent-in-Charge Gordon Shanklins was sure someone in the Dallas FBI office leaked to the *Times-Herald* the fact that several weeks before the assassination Oswald had left a note for him threatening violence if Hosty did not stop hassling Oswald's wife. Hosty destroyed this note on orders after Oswald was killed. (There is a separate file of duplicates of all disclosed records relating to this flap and the FBI inspector-general's investigation of it in the author's files.)

Just before that leak was publicly known, Revill needled the FBI again when he bumped into an agent whose name was redacted from the September 4, 1978, record it disclosed to me in CA 78–0322. (The FBI had been disclosing all those agents names, as Hoover had ordered years earlier, and in that lawsuit they even gave me several lists of the Dallas agents complete with their home addresses and telephone numbers, when as a stonewalling trick they started withholding these names alleged to protect "privacy.")

Revill encountered the FBI agent who can, from the unredacted initials on the memo, only have been Charles T. Brown, Jr., who lived at 916 Beechwood Drive in Richardson, a Dallas suburb, and whose phone number was AD5–3016. Revill also told him that Curry had told Revill "that two men were involved in the shooting," [Brown's words]. One of Curry's reasons was something he had been told by his police motorcycle escort of JFK.

So, contrary to the slurs from the depths of their ignorance by *JAMA*'s cabal and equally uniformed Commission apologists as well as the not entirely uniformed staffers who protest their purity and performance when prodded a bit, there are those, other than the critics, who agree with the critics. Actually, it is the other way around. The critics agree with them, like Russell and Curry, who knew before the critics could.

The best known of these other shots is the one the Commission acknowledged missed the motorcade entirely, the one that rushed the gestation of Specter's bastard. Although it was known and reported in the papers, the Commission ignored it, as the FBI and Secret Service still do. Tom Dillard, the *Dallas Morning News* photographer, had photographed it the day after the assassination and had told the local United States attorney, Barefoot Sanders about it. (A longer account appears in *Post Mortem* beginning on page 453. Dillard's photo is on page 609.) Oddly Sanders had said nothing about this when the picture appeared in the paper on November 24 and was on TV the night before. The FBI did not report it either. Dillard gave me a Xerox of the file Xerox in the paper's morgue. The caption says the bullet caused a "hole."

He also printed and gave me a copy of his best remaining negative, those he referred to as the "federales" not having returned the ones they "borrowed."

The spray of concrete from this "hole" in the curbstone on the south side of Main Street about twenty feet east of the Triple Under-

The spray of concrete from this "hole" in the curbstone on the south side of Main Street about twenty feet east of the triple underpass slightly wounded James T. Tague, who was standing there, traffic being blocked solidly. The bullet that caused this "hole" could not have been fired from the Texas School Book Depository.
Credit: Tom Dillard

pass slightly wounded James T. Tague, who was standing there, traffic being blocked solidly. The blood on his face was noticed by Leonard L. Hill, a policeman, and by Eddy H. "Buddy" Walthers, a deputy sheriff. It was broadcast to police headquarters immediately (See *Post Mortem*, page 454). (Walthers was killed—with his own weapon—in a careless moment when making an arrest while I was in Dallas in 1968. He was not a Commission witness. Hill filed no report with the police and he was not even interviewed by anyone from the Warren Commission. My source on Hill is a July 29, 1977, letter to me from then District Attorney Henry Wade.)

James Underwood, KRLD-TV photographer, took pictures of it that were aired on that station on November 23, 1963. The FBI clipped the papers and monitored the police radio. So it knew.

Knowing its meaning full well, the FBI filed no reports on this until a story appeared in a local paper. With Tague seeking and getting anonymity, the FBI referred to him as a publicity seeker. A new kind, that, the anonymous publicity seeker.

(There were efforts to pretend Tague had no credibility by referring to him as "a used car salesman." In fact he was one of the country's leading sellers of large fleets of autos. Witnesses, who said what was not consistent with the official preconception or who disputed it to the various critics, have files in all agencies and in the Commission, abounding in criticisms of them that are not infrequently exaggerated, distorted, or just plain false.)

FBIHQ and its Dallas office also knew about this missed bullet that caused Tague's slight wound from another source. It was reported on the police radio and the Dallas FBI transcribed the recording of those broadcasts for the Commission. Yet it claimed in court throughout the decade of my FOIA lawsuit for all copies of its Dallas JFK assassination records (CA 78–0322) that it did not have these recordings. It persisted in what I charged without even pro forma denial was perjury, even when I provided the FBI and the court with the name of the special agent who dubbed the police recordings and when he did it and even identified the make of the FBI's recording machine, a Wollensak. That judge, John Lewis Smith, for all practical purposes an arm of the FBI, was totally indifferent to this and a number of other undenied felonies before him, perjuries.

The FBi is so corrupt in what it regards as delicate for it and its reputation that it even hides by tricky indexing. I have through that FOIA lawsuit a Xerox of its Dallas JFK assassination index of more than 40 linear feet of 3x5 cards. It holds no reference to the FBI's dubs of the police records or of instructions to get and transcribe them. Yet it does refer to the sending of the transcripts to FBIHQ for forwarding to the Commission—impossible to have done without having the recordings in the first place. Without doubt obtaining of the dubs is indexed, but not under "JFK Assassination." Probably it is under the Dallas police.

The FBI did not want to have to acknowledge that there had been this bullet fired during the assassination. If it did, it acknowledged there had been a conspiracy. So, to the degree possible, it hid the information. (It also had other reasons for not wanting critics to have copies of its tapes of those police broadcasts. One reason is that the FBI did not investigate the fact that at the very moment of the assassination one police radio channel was unusable for five minutes.)

Having hidden all it could hide and having avoided all it could avoid, the FBI then blandly pretended that no bullet fired during the assassination missed.

It had no real choice from the moment Hoover had his instant vision on the day of the assassination of the lone-nut assassin. It knew that the magic-bullet theory was impossible and refused to use it in its own pretended solution. Acknowledging that there had been a bullet that missed would have required admitting that more than three bullets were fired. That would have made it impossible for the FBI to allege that there had not been a conspiracy.

There was constant leaking of what the official conclusions would be. All the traceable leak can be traced to the FBI, which stoutly denied it had leaked anything and blamed others, who it knew could not have made the leaks. Dillard read one of these leaks, accounting for the assassination without any mention of this "missed" shot, when he covered an event in Dallas at which he saw United States Attorney Barefoot Sanders. When he told Sanders that he knew of a shot not accounted for in the leaks, Sanders notified the Commission. At that point Specter's magic bullet neared birth.

"The federales," as Dillard called them, came and took the negatives of the best of the pictures he had taken at the time of the assassination. The paper published the very best on November 24,

1963   ★★★★

—Dallas News Staff Photo.

CONCRETE SCAR

A detective points to a chip in the curb on Houston Street opposite the Texas School· Book Depository. A bullet from the rifle that took President Kennedy's life apparently caused the hole.

Tom Dillard's photo of the curbstone as it appeared in the *Dallas Morning News*. Credit: Courtesy of the *Dallas Morning News*

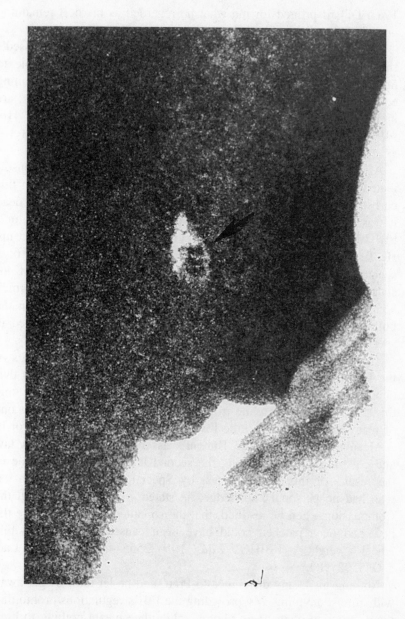

Here is an enlargement of the electrostatic copy of the photo that was printed in the *Dallas Morning News*. Tom Dillard made this for me.
Credit: Tom Dillard

1963. Dillard printed for me what he regarded as his best remaining negative (See *Post Mortem*, page 608).

The entire series of FBI shenanigans relating to this "missed" shot, beginning with its first "explanation" of not being able to find the point of of impact on that curbstone because street-cleaning equipment had washed the hole on the concrete *curbstone* away, are in *Whitewash* (pages 158–60) and *Post Mortem* (pages 57–58, 416, 419–20, 428, 440, 443, 453–61, 618, 623–24). It was no secret—except to *JAMA*'s readers.

As the Special Agent Gemberling synopsis page of a larger consolidated FBI Dallas report reflects, the FBI knew that the hole in this curbstone had been patched. With Oswald in police custody or dead it was not patched by him. (But perhaps was by a nonconspirator?) FBI laboratory Agent Lyndal Shaneyfelt had that curbstone dug up. He flew it to the lab where it was subjected to the charade of a spectrographic analysis, on which the FBI neither made a report nor stated why it did not. According to the handwritten lab notes, which I have, it detected only about a fifth of the elements present in the bullet. It then "memory-holed" the thin photographic plate used in spectrographic analysis.

This became an issue in my CA 75–228, a suit for the results of the FBI's scientific testings. In it Judge John Pratt accepted as evidence the FBI's unsworn presumption by a retired FBI agent that this thin, tiny plate was destroyed to save space. It is the only one of many that according to the FBI created a "space" problem for it.

Meanwhile, covering the Bureau's ass being the FBI's first law and covering your own being the second law, in the notes made of the results of this supposed test by Special Agent Robert Frazier, who had no personal knowledge, he stated what he did not tell the Commission when he testified, that the so-called "smear" where the hole had been patched could have been caused by an automobile wheel weight! (FBIHQ File 105–82555–4668X; FBI Lab. # D455927HO.)

Nothing made any difference to Pratt, and he let the FBI get away with almost anything. My providing the FBI's regulations prohibiting the destruction of that thin photographic plate meant nothing to him. When we proved that the FBI lab witness, John Kilty, had sworn in contradiction to himself about what was material—perjury—Pratt told

James Lesar, my attorney, and me that we would catch more flies with honey than with vinegar. When we persisted in trying to get the FBI to abide by the law and proved that it had not and had in fact committed perjury, Pratt actually threatened us, telling us we could get in trouble that way!

At least in theory this is all preserved in the case record, with all proofs, in the court's and the government's files, but if those copies, too, suffer an unexplained mysterious disappearance, for the historical record, duplicates are in my files and elsewhere.

A fuller account is in "The New 'New Evidence' " in *Post Mortem* on pages 403–66. It includes some of the information I did get in that lengthy and costly lawsuit, including the suppressed results of neutron-activation analysis that proved Oswald had not fired a rifle that day!

The Dallas police made the usual tests to determine whether Oswald's hands and face held traces of the gases that are blown back when a rifle is fired. They are known as paraffin tests because molten paraffin is placed on the hands and face and allowed to harden.

It should be understood that the deposits are of common substances, that are found in such items as soaps and inks. The mere presence of these substances on the casts is, therefore, not incriminating. But their absence is exculpatory.

Traces were detected on Oswald's hands. However, they did not necessarily come from the discharge of a rifle. Of the many materials that leave the same deposits, one was the ink on the books and cartons he handled on the job. Another could have been soap if he had washed his hands.

Traces were not detected on the paraffin casts of his face. This means he did not fire a rifle. It also meant that tests were kept official hush-hush until the very last minute of the Commission's life.

The FBI was forced to have neutron-activation analysis made when, only a few days after the assassination, Paul Aebersold, then in charge of this area of the work of the Energy and Research and Development Administration (ERDA), successor to the Atomic Energy Commission, wrote the Criminal Division of the department

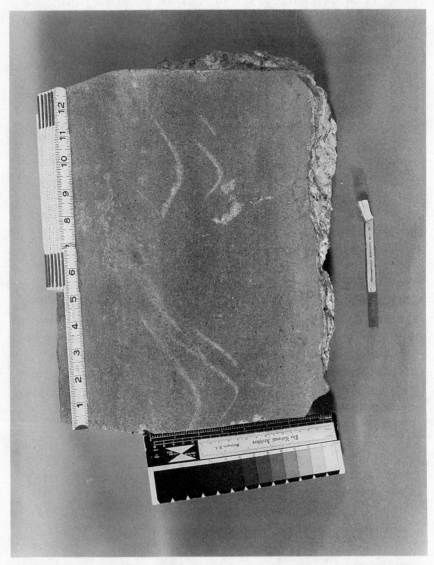

The National Archives supplied me with this photo of Commission Exhibit 34, the curbstone. The arrow locates the quite visible patch that was applied to the "hole" left by the bullet that missed its target. The FBI flew the curbstone to Washington, DC, for tests; they ended up testing the material of the patch, not of the original impact.
Credit: The National Archives

urging that they be done on the bullet and fragments of bullet. He recommended an expert to perform the test.

I learned of this and much else about these tests when ERDA, which I had joined in the lawsuit, CA 75–226, anxious not to be besmirched for noncooperation in the lawsuit that the Department of Justice and the FBI controlled, decided to give me copies of its records. They were delivered to my lawyer, Jim Lesar, at this home by the assistant United States attorney for the District of Columbia who represented the government in the lawsuit. These records included the results of a number of test firings with that rifle and the paraffin tests made on those who fired it. The test firings left heavy deposits on all the shooters' faces, quite the opposite of what the paraffin tests of Oswald's face disclosed. This, of course, was even more exculpatory.

FBI lab agent, John F. Gallagher, the spectrographer who did not testify to any of his spectrographic examinations before the Warren Commission, handled the deal for the FBI. He began by bad-mouthing Aebersold, and then he bad-mouthed Dr. Vincent Guinn, the expert Aebersold recommended. (Guinn was later the HSCA's neutron-activation analysis expert witness.) Gallagher supervised the tests he arranged for at the ERDA installation at Oak Ridge, Tennessee. They were performed by a government contractor already working there.

The transcript of the Warren Commission's executive session of January 27, 1964, classified TOP SECRET until I got it through FOIA action (the subject of *Whitewash IV* and there printed in facsimile, includes discussion of the performance of these tests by Rankin and the Commission members present. After that they all ignored them entirely until the Report was in page proof and the presses were about to roll. Then, almost as an afterthought, on September 15, 1964, Norman Redlich deposed Gallagher.

Like all the Commission testimony, this was in complete secrecy. It remained secret for two months, until the Commission's twenty-six volumes were published. Lost in the mass of those ten million words all dumped on the press at once, it got no attention at all. It is the very last testimony, in the last volume of the testimony, Volume 15 (pages 764–52). The purpose of this afterthought was to get Gallagher to say that paraffin tests are worthless. (No doubt the reason police used them!)

They could have been quite valuable to the defendant and his counsel. As they certainly would have been to Oswald and his lawyer if Oswald had lived to be tried!

Suppose—just suppose—that if for once the media had not failed in their reporting of the JFK assassination and its investigation.

If they had not blindly reported what amounts to the official hand-out on the crime as the unquestionable truth.

If they had checked this Redlich-Gallagher-Commission/FBI trickery out. If they had bothered to learn the truth and had reported it.

Could the Warren Report then have survived the official 1966 reporting of what exculpated Oswald?

And the utter dishonesty with which the results of and the meaning of the results of the paraffin testing were misrepresented?

If the media or any major component had reported that the Commission's own evidence indicated the probability that Oswald had not fired a rifle that day?

With Oswald the only official candidate for assassin!

If the media had reported what they should have reported, the Report would not and could not have been accepted as truth.

At minimum there would have been a major controversy about the Report and its conclusions.

And there is a good probability that with the Report not accepted at least a gesture at a real investigation would have been inevitable.

The press reported nothing at all about that paraffin test, and the Report, the official mythology, as a result, could be and was palmed off on us and on our history.

None of the media mavens knowing anything at all about the established fact of the assassination or its contradictory official "solutions" and none, apparently, being at all curious about this exploit so unusual for the AMA; none caring to follow the traditional standards of responsible journalism stated so clearly and simply in the quoted *Washington Post* editorial and seek the other side, nowhere was it reported that in Lundberg's stout insistence, "I can state without concern or question that President Kennedy was struck and killed by two, only two bullets . . . ," put him, *JAMA*, and the AMA in direct conflict with the FBI, unless among other oversights, the FBI pretended that Governor Connally was not there to receive five wounds from two bullets of which fragments remained in his chest and left thigh. Connally is the missing man in *JAMA*.

As we saw earlier, the FBI's "solution" that so troubled the Commission is limited, in that supposedly definitive report ordered by the new President the evening of the assassination, CD1 in the Commission files, to two sentences—in five volumes. Two sentences in five volumes is all the FBI had to say about all the shooting and all the wounds, so little that it does not account for all the wounds the President suffered or even mentions those the Governor got!

I. *THE ASSASSINATION*

President John Fitzgerald Kennedy was assassinated in Dallas, Texas, at approximately 12:29 P.M. (CST) on November 22, 1963.

....

Two bullets struck President Kennedy, and one wounded Governor Connally.

....

Medical examination of the President's body revealed that one of the bullets had entered just below his shoulder to the right of the spinal column at an angle of 45 to 60 degrees downward, that there was no point of exit, and that the bullet was not in the body.

Commission Document Number 1

The first of these two sentences states that each of the three acknowledged shots impacted, and there is no mention of the bullet known to have missed and to have caused Tague's minor injury: "Two bullets struck President Kennedy, and one wounded Governor Connally." This contradicts the entire Warren Report.

The second says only, "Medical examination of the President's body revealed that one of the bullets had entered just below his shoulder to the right of the spinal column at an angle of 45 to 60 degrees downward, and there was no point of exit, and that the bullet was not in the body." "Below" Kennedy's "shoulder" is *not* in his neck as the Commission and the *JAMA* crew claimed (CD1). (See *Whitewash* page 195, where these excerpts are reproduced in facsimile.) This steep downward angle was consistent with pinning the rap on Oswald if it was not consistent with the known and reported facts.

That the FBI "solved" the crime without mention of the cause of death, without a word about so much of the President's head being blown out, never received any notice in any of the major media of which I am aware. Or in *JAMA*. In all the many FBI records I have examined, I saw none in which it changed this pretended solution. That came into existence the very evening of the crime, as we saw earlier, when FBI Director J. Edgar Hoover, as he boasted to William Manchester, had his instant vision of his lone-nut assassin, the vision Katzenbach put on paper two days later, as soon as Oswald was killed, and he knew there would be no trial.

The FBI's exhibits section, which does magnificent work, particularly in its detailed scale models, made one of Dealey Plaza. In its explanation of this model it states that each of the three bullets "hit the target." These are the words that begin its explanation of each shot as represented on its beautiful scale model.

The Commission was basing its work on this FBI scale model, and the FBI's interpretation of it stated in an FBIHQ internal record of January 23, 1964. That day L. J. Gauthier of the exhibits section spent three hours using this scale model to indoctrinate four of the Commission's counsels with the FBI line on the crime (62–109090, Not Recorded 1/23/94, Gauthier to Callahan memo, copies to all the FBIHQ top brass).

Gauthier was back at the Commission on April 15, almost three months later, to amplify Humes's "leading" Commission staff "discussion" of the shooting (FBIHQ 62–109090–2998). The need for Specter's theory not yet being apparent, the Commission staff disclosed that it had by then adhered to two different explanations of the three shots that it, the FBI, and, the Secret Service admitted were fired during the assassination—without mention of the known "missed" shot:

[L. J. Gauthier to Mr.Callahan. 4–15–64 Letterhead Memo]

Dr. Humes, U.S. Navy Commander, who performed the autopsy on the President, appeared to lead the discussion throughout the 4-hour session. All of his associates were generally in agreement with previous findings of the Commission as to where Shots 1, 2, and 3 approximately occurred.

The most revealing information brought out by the doctor is as follows:

1. That Shot 1 struck the President high in the right shoulder

area, penetrating the torso near the base of the neck damaging the flesh of the throat but not tearing the throat wall. This bullet, according to the doctors, continued and entered Governor Connally's right shoulder, emerging below the right nipple. The velocity of the missile, according to the doctors apparently was snagged in the coat and shirt, eventually falling out on Connally's stretcher. [sic].

2. That Shot 2 struck the wrist of the Governor, continuing on into his thigh.

3. That Shot 3 struck the right side of the President's head, carrying much bone and brain tissue away, leaving a large cavity. There is nothing controversial about where Shot 3 occurred inasmuch as the Zapruder movie indicates with much clarity where this happened.

Heretofore it was the opinion of the Commission that Shot 1 had only hit the President, that Shot 2 had entered the Governor's right shoulder area penetrating his torso through the chest area emerging and again entering the wrist and on into his leg [62–109090–2998].

Contrary to his own representation to Lundberg and Breo, the FBI has Humes taking the lead in "solving" the crime for the Commission.

According to the FBI, he then had a different explanation than what he gave *JAMA*.

How he could possibly know anything about Connally's wounds is not stated in this memo on his four-hour dissertation on the crime to the Commission staff. It is not in anything known that he has ever said. It is not in his Lundberg/Breo interview.

After the appearance of *Whitewash* in 1966 and of the two books that followed it, the controversy escalated. *Life* magazine published a major article urging a "review" of the assassination. Assistant FBI Director Alex Rosen wrote a memo on it to be bucked up to Hoover through DeLoach, as it happened on the third anniversary of the assassination, November 22, 1966 (FBIHQ 62–109090–4267).

Careful to seek to avoid involving the FBI in any of this controversy and forgetting the FBI's own different "solutions," Rosen referred instead to the Commission's conclusion of the single-bullet theory. Rosen, still without mentioning that it was the FBI's solution, concluded his memo saying, "Initially, it was believed that of the

three shots fired, two hit the President and the third Governor Connally.'' He adds that as of the time th FBI filed CD1, "The sequence
of shots was not known.''

In commenting on this report, Hoover drew vertical lines in the
margin for emphasis and added in his unique crabbed hand: "We
don't agree with the Commission as it says one shot missed entirely.
We contend all three shots hit. H''

From the outset the Secret Service agreed with the FBI. Its "solution,'' like the FBI's, was never abandoned. Inspector Tom Kelley
wrote Secret Service Director James Rowley on November 28, 1963,
the day before the Commission was appointed, explaining the same
imagined history of the three shots later stated by the FBI in CD1
(CD 87, #2).

The next day Dallas FBI Special Agents Robert Barrett and Ivan
Lee reported having been told by Secret Service Special Agent John
Howlett of its reconstruction of the crime with a surveyor to pinpoint
the location of the limousine at the time of the impact of each of
the three shots. This Secret Service "solution'' is identical with the
FBI's in CD1. It, too, acknowledges no "missed'' shot.

While neither agency ever abandoned its no-missed-shot "solution,'' once the Warren Report appeared, its "solution'' alone was
what the agencies always cited, *including* the missed shot, even
though the agencies did not agree. For them Jim Tague bled in vain.
But for the FBI this meant that it avoided involving itself in any
unnecessary controversy about the "solution.'' Instead it cited the
Commission's conclusions as authoritative.

All the official "reconstructions'' used the Zapruder film. This
really meant they all *mis*used it. To a degree it can serve as a time
clock, but not to the degree it was stretched by officials to try to
make it conform with and seem to prove the official preconception
of that lone-nut assassin.

In order to be able to pin the rap on Oswald it was necessary for
him to have been able to see the President through the dense foliage
of the live oak tree. Fortuitously, at the later time of the Commission's reconstruction, in May 1964, looking from that "Oswald window there was a gap in the foliage that coincided with frame 210 of
the film in the reconstruction. That "reconstruction,'' as FBI photographic expert Lyndal Shaneyfelt testified, did not coincide with Za-

pruder's film. It was much faster, which meant much less time for the shooting. But not to worry, Shaneyfelt reassured the Commission, he had placed a visible stain on the reconstruction film to make it seem to work out with the Zapruder film. This is strange because they also filmed the reconstruction with *Zapruder's* camera! But from where he stood. (*Whitewash II*, page 180).

Then there was another problem: In the Zapruder film Connally is seen to react violently to a shot before the minimum number of Zapruder frames required for Oswald to get off his second shot. But the Commission had a pretty good formula for such problems: It merely concluded the opposite of its credible testimony! It "concluded" that although its experts told it that the body reacts instantly to a shot that strikes bone, as Connally's bones were *really* struck, Connally had a delayed reaction! And when he is seen receiving a shot, he did not get it then. The Commission actually has him reacting to the bullet that had not yet hit him!

At the same time, with the President reacting visibly at frame 225, the Commission decided that, although in its "solution" none of his bones had been hit, he did have that instant reaction.

This simple formula of "concluding" the exact opposite of the evidence is the means by which the Commission solved another major problem, of Oswald taking the rifle into the TSBD. There, too, *all* the witnesses testified that it was impossible, and the Commission merely ignored 100 percent of its testimony and concluded the opposite (*Whitewash*, pages 15–20).

The Zapruder film presented other problems, but the Commission's simple solution to them was just to ignore them. From issue to issue, the executive agencies were helpful, if only in not leaking contradiction of the Commission. Where it would have been disastrous to the preconception and to the Report, the CIA, which had made its own study of the Zapruder film with its National Photographic Interpretation Center, kept its results secret. Its experts decided that the possibilities for the impact of the first shot, frame 210 in the Report, did not include that frame! (*Photographic Whitewash*, 1976 reprint edition, pages 297–323).

The Zapruder film proves that the President was shot before frame 210 in ways other than those employed by the CIA. The Commission ignored it.

There is universal agreement that an amateur photographer, Phil Willis, snapped a picture of the motorcade before he was ready, before his camera had been readjusted, in reaction to the shot the Commission says was at frame 210. Willis did react involuntarily. Examination of the *original* Zapruder film and the slides made from it show this clearly, but it cannot be seen on projection.

Zapruder's film is moved in the camera by a sprocket gear attached to the motor when its teeth engage the sprocket holes in the film. In the original eight millimeter film, all there was in those days before Super Eight, the sprocket-hole area is about 20 percent of the film. The film of the sprocket hole also takes the picture, but the picture it takes is masked when the film is projected. In this unprojected part of the film, at frame 202, Willis is seen doing exactly what he testified he did, *taking the camera from his face after taking that picture* and stepping from the curb into the street to take another picture of the receding motorcade. Before frame 210 he had taken the camera down from his eye (*Whitewash II*, pages 195 ff.). This means that *before* frame 210—*before* frame 202, Willis took the picture he took *after* the President was struck by a bullet.

The instant official determination, which was based on Hoover's instant non-conspiracy vision, required the Commission to conclude that the President was hit at frame 210 and come hell, high water, or evidence to the contrary, it said he was first shot at frame 210.

The FBI's determination to persist in its imagined "solution," which was not the same as the Commission's, arrived at later, is reflected in the 1966 Hoover note quoted earlier. The FBI just pretended that poor Jim Tague, little as he bled, bled in vain. As Hoover wrote, the FBI just does not admit that it happened. As of the time of this writing, it still does not.

The FBI could not ignore what concerned citizens told it about it or brought it bullets believed to have been fired during the assassination. A few illustrations that follow certify the marvel that can be wrought by secrecy. While far from all the indications of other shots fired during the assassination, these samples do reflect the official determinations, by both the FBI and the Commission, to ignore them or to assign no meaning at all to them so the official preconceptions could appear to be validated.

There was indeed reason for Lundberg to admit that "there may have been other shots'' fired during the assassination, whether or not he knew that there had been. What MacNeil did not ask Lundberg is how *JAMA* could, if more than three shots had been fired, insist that the Warren Report was correct in concluding that *only* three shots were fired. Obviously *JAMA* could not be correct when nobody ever has been able to duplicate the feat attributed to Oswald in either the FBI and Secret Service or the Commission versions. How much more impossible were any of these official ''solutions'' if there was even one of the ''many more'' shots Lundberg told MacNeil could have been fired.

The FBI got away with its obviously false account of the shooting, without mention of the cause of death, because its supposedly definitive five-volume report on the crime was kept secret until long after the Commission's became the official ''solution,'' the ''solution'' behind which the FBI still hides. The FBI could and did pretend that this proof did not exist. But the Commission could not dare ignore Dillard's information given it by Barefoot Sanders.

The Commission adopted Specter's bastard as its own legitimate offspring.

Although neither does, both the Commission and the FBI pretend to have accounted for all the shooting in three shots.

However, with Lundberg's admission to *The MacNeil/Lehrer Newshour* that there could have been ''many'' more shots, he disputed *all* the official versions of the assassination he used *JAMA* to proclaim were true, and he simultaneously admitted that all the many words in support of errant officialdom that he published and propagandized so extensively were false.

This without comment from MacNeil, Lehrer, or anyone, anywhere in the media.

Chapter 30

How Much the FBI Does Not—or Maybe Does—Love Me

WHILE THERE IS NO REASON TO BELIEVE THAT LUNDBERG KNEW WHAT he was talking about in saying "there may have been many other gunshots" during the assassination, and the probability is that he made this response to avoid finding himself in an impossible position on the nationwide telecast, there were a number of reports of varying degrees of credibility about these other shots. When the Commission could not just ignore these reports, those eyewitnesses who claimed sightings were, protected as the Commission was by total secrecy, treated as was Mrs. Virginia Rachley whose story was reported earlier. There were other reports of seeing bullets impact in Dealey Plaza. They were even less welcome to the FBI than to the Commission, and the FBI was the Commission's de facto investigating staff. These reports continued after the Commission's life ended. They then involved the FBI alone.

How the FBI treated those who made these reports requires an understanding of the kind of people those FBI agents were, and how, in general, over the years, the FBI evolved a method of coping with evidence not to its liking through its laboratory.

In his book, *FBI*, Sanford Ungar, experienced reporter, Washington correspondent, and university school of journalism dean, a book in the preparation of which he was assisted by the FBI, reported that laboratory agents are trained to confound defense counsel to the degree that many just stipulate to what these agents would testify to rather than having to try to cross-examine them:

> The agents from the lab who testify in court are permitted to
> do so only after a rigorous training program which includes 'moot

court' rehearsals to prepare them for the tactics of eloquent and experienced defense attorneys and graduate study of forensic science. Once they are experienced, the agents may spend most of their time touring the nation, providing precise and conclusive testimony for the prosecution that impresses juries and sends men and women off to jail. Some agents have appeared in hundreds of cases. 'Many defense attorneys will often stipulate vital information, when they learn that someone from the FBI lab is about to testify,' says Briggs J. White, assistant director for the laboratory'' [Ungar, Sanford. FBI. Boston: Little, Brown, 1976, page 154].

In my experience and from my observation this special and very effective training extends well past the science of the lab and its agents. The ''moot court'' training to which Ungar refers is training to avoid answering questions, the answers to which can be helpful to the opposition; in answering questions not asked, to load the record with partisan and prejudicial information and misinformation and to distract and mislead the questioner; in seeming to answer questions, when in fact they are not answered; to misuse the question to make points against the opposition's interest that the FBI wants to make— in general to make counsel and the record for the other side look bad and to confuse and confound him or her.

We experienced this extensively in the FOIA lawsuits in which, with great difficulty, we were able to depose some of these lab agents who are by training, in fact, professional witnesses.

It was clear that the special training these agents received was adapted to their personalities and that they were trained to accomplish the same ends by sometimes different means.

The spectrographer, John F. Gallagher, for example, appeared to come straight from Hollywood's central casting. I have never seen anyone who could appear to be agonized over a claimed inability to remember what, without reasonable doubt, he remembered very well. One almost expected him to weep over his regretted inability to remember, while he was cunningly getting in the record what the FBI wanted there and frustrating examination at the same time. What he wanted to remember and knew the FBI wanted him to remember was sharp and clear to him.

By contrast, Frazier, Shaneyfelt, and Kilty were insolent, arrogant, disputatious, sometimes insulting and condescending, giving the impression that they could barely tolerate being in the presence of inferiors who lacked understanding. After it became clear that I would seek to depose the lab agents involved with the records sought in CA 75–1996, Gallagher, Frazier, and Shaneyfelt retired. The FBI then argued in court that because they were no longer FBI employees they could not be deposed in a lawsuit in which the FBI was the respondent. This question had to be litigated through the appeals court before we were permitted to depose them. We finally won that.

When witnesses are subpoenaed, prior to their appearance, the court requires that their expenses and witness fees, fixed by the court, be paid in advance.

The sole purpose of deposing these lab agent was to establish whether or not the FBI had records within the litigation that it continued to withhold, a polite way of saying suppressed.

Whenever my lawyer, Jim Lesar, started asking questions relating to the existence of suppressed information, Frazier and sometimes Shaneyfelt chanted, "You are asking me to testify as a professional witness, and you have not paid me for that." They wanted unspecified additional fees prior to responding to questions that were, in not a single case, improper or had any other purpose than to establish the existence or nonexistence of the information called for in the litigation. This prolonged the deposition and meant that costly time was wasted. Each time each raised this spurious objection, it had to be argued, or we just had to forget about it and go on to something else. It was an effective, if dishonest, trick for avoiding responses that their former employer, the FBI, did not want in the record because it could establish that the FBI's response in the litigation was incomplete and/or if dishonest and that it had and suppressed pertinent records.

When these lab agents appeared at the depositions, they were, of course, represented by the government's lawyer, in most instances an assistant United States attorney for the District of Columbia. But the FBI does not trust the Department of Justice. So, in all instances, it also had its own lawyer from its Legal Counsel Division present. The FBI's lawyers were present when the former lab agents, no longer FBI employees, testified.

Shaneyfelt was particularly offensive in his manner. At the end he volunteered that he at one time had considered suing me while he was still an FBI employee.

There was, as I knew, no chance at all that Shaneyfelt would expose himself to informed questioning under oath about his record in the work he did for the Commission. The FBI certainly did not want any attention drawn to it. Like to Tague and that curbstone.

My first exposure of Shaneyfelt's absolutely astounding record in his lab work for the Commission was his failure to inform it that what the Commission itself found to be the key frames of the Zapruder film centering on frame 210 (where the Commission decided that the President was struck by the first shot) no longer existed in the original of that film. Shaneyfelt personally numbered the slides made from the original for the Commission by *Life* magazine. As he testified on deposition, he suggested that the slides be made and *Life* made them (transcript, page 30). In his numbering, he just ignored the fact that these key frames no longer existed, and he made no mention of it in his testimony.

He said nothing about the clearly visible splice in the frame he had numbered 207. He said nothing about the next frame being numbered 212. He said nothing at all about this frame showing a large tree, with its upper half about a quarter of the width of the film, growing without any base in the upper half of the slide and the base growing without any top in the bottom half of the slide, or about people in it who appeared having heads only, with other people having no legs or feet (*Whitewash*, page 206).

So, of course, he made no investigation that he reported to determine just how this single most important photographic evidence of the crime had those crucial frames removed from its original. Aside from the ever present importance of originals, it is only the original that is complete. The mechanical process of making duplicates eliminates the part of what is photographed that is in the area of the sprocket holes by which the film is moved, about a fifth of the picture in the original.

We have seen the importance of this part of that film. It is hardly likely Shaneyfelt would want to be questioned about its proof that the actual timing of the Commission's first shot is before frame 210, when Oswald could not have fired it. As we saw with Phil Willis having taken his picture after the first shot, he took the camera down from his eye and was walking into the street at frame 202, a time at which he Commission itself concluded Oswald could not have fired that shot. Instead of making the obvious and accurate analysis for the Commission and for his testimony to it, he prepared an attractive exhibit consisting of this one of Willis's photographs and the surveyor's plat of Elm Street in support of the Commission's incorrect presumption of when that shot was fired to make it appear that Oswald had fired it, when, in fact, it was fired before Oswald could have fired. The Commission's own reconstruction supported this (*Whitewash II*, page 246).

(There is considerable additional information about Shaneyfelt, his photographic expertise and services to the Commission and his testimony and that of others about the work he did and the interpretations given it throughout *Whitewash II*.)

Associated Press Photographer James "Ike" Altgens took a number of still pictures at the time of the crime, including one taken during the shooting of JFK, of which the Commission made much use. It shows the limousine and its occupants and their positions after at least the first shot was fired. It has many other evidentiary values. It includes the first four cars of the motorcade, the immediate motorcycle escort, innumerable people who were witnesses, including those in the TSBD doorway, in which a man stands who looks like Oswald—who was supposed to be at that very moment six floors higher and shooting at JFK. The FBI never once made a copy of the full negative of this picture for the Commission. Instead it provided several versions of it, all of which were cropped differently so as not to include the entire picture.

After prolonged effort I finally obtained a print made from the full negative from the Associated Press and published it in *Whitewash II* on pages 250–1, along with an enlargement of that part of the photo that shows the man who looks like Oswald and of the shirt he wore. Also shown is a Shaneyfelt print of a Dallas photograph of Oswald wearing the shirt in which he was arrested. The FBI and the Commission held that the man in Altgens's picture was not Oswald, but was Billy Lovelady. At the same point in its text *Whitewash II* contains two FBI photographs of Lovelady in the shirt it said he was wearing. The shirt on the man in the doorway looks remarkably like the Oswald shirt. The shirt the FBI said Lovelady was wearing cannot possibly be the shirt the man had on.

There is no reason to believe that Shaneyfelt would have relished being questioned under oath about his work for and his testimony before the Commission. Most of all he would not want to be queried about what he did not do for the Commission and the errors, gaps, and diversions in his testimony.

Neither the FBI nor Shaneyfelt could have been expected to look forward to the public attention a trial would give his thoroughgoing corruption of the most important evidence and its significance in the official "solution" to the crime. The same is true about those pictures of the President's clothing selectively rendered in the perfection of professional incompetences so that the pattern of the tie and the shirt cannot be made out.

Can anyone believe that Shaneyfelt wanted to testify in public about the "missed" shot and his charade of taking the patched curbstone to the lab for analysis—of the visible patch where the hole or scar had been? Or, that the FBI would have wanted that?

There is more like this. So, when Shaneyfelt tried to poison the record that would be given to the judge—I could not respond because I was not a witness and was not being deposed—I sat quietly in amused silence. When he had finished testifying and had left, I told Assistant United States Attorney Michael Ryan and the FBI's lawyer, Emil Moschella, that although I was confident Shaneyfelt would not sue, I would like him to and would advance the charges he would have to pay to file a lawsuit against me. Before long Moschella was promoted to head the FBI's FOIA section. Whether or not they conveyed my challenge/offer to Shaneyfelt, as I had asked, I received no acceptance of my offer from him.

At the end of the deposition Shaneyfelt said, volunteering, "I had considered bringing suit against Mr. Weisberg for *Photographic Whitewash* because of his remarks that were made in that. I decide I would not."

But he said he made no report to the FBI about it. He did, however, discuss "it with officials of the FBI, including Legal Counsel." He refused to identify which FBI official he had discussed suing me with because I caused him "enough distress already without going any further." [Shaneyfelt deposition of March 28, 1977; transcript prepared by Hoover Reporting Co., Inc., pages 36–37. Copies should be in court and government case files and are in my files.]

Having refused to testify as an expert on what he claimed was outside the purposes of the litigation, Shaneyfelt lost no time in billing me for "professional services in the form of testimony for a deposition . . ." His bill was for three hours of expert-witness testimony, from which he had deducted the court-determined payment I had made in advance. He addressed his bill to my lawyer, Jim Lesar, whose name he misspelled "Levar."

As soon as the bill reached me, I wrote Shaneyfelt in some detail, beginning by castigating him for his "bill for falsely represented expert testimony." I described that as "unspeakably arrogant and indecent," as a "fraudulent misrepresentation" and as "far from your worst offenses against decency."

I also told him that as soon as he left, I had told Moschella that I'd pay Shaneyfelt's filing costs and waive the running of the statute of limitations (after ten years) and told him, "If you want to sue . . . you can accept this letter as that waiver."

I told him that he was afraid to sue me, saying, "You'll do that when shrimps whistle from the backs of cows jumping over a green cheese moon!" And I wound up with the rhetorical question: "Have you no shame?"

In between I ticked off a spontaneous and incomplete critique of his work for the Commission, some of what would figure in the suit I told him he would not dare file.

In more than a decade and a half I heard nothing from him.

Later, in another FOIA action, I obtained, among other records, those relating to his alleged desire to sue me. It turns out that he was looking for Brownie points and had no intention of suing me. The record indicates that he got his Brownie points.

On January 26, 1967, Shaneyfelt wrote the memorandum on suing me to his lab superior to be bucked upward through Ivan Conrad, assistant director in charge of the lab. Along with the stock and baseless FBI slurs about me, he referred to my only recently published *Whitewash II*, not as he testified on deposition, to *Photographic Whitewash*. (Although the FBI is supposed to have given me all its records on me and my books, too, it has not given me any records relating to its analyses of them or of comments by agents like Shaneyfelt who read them.)

He said my books are "highly critical of the Bureau and specifically of the testimony of FBI laboratory examiner Special Agent Lyndal L. Shaneyfelt." He then took out of context direct quotations from my writings and misrepresented them: "a very specific implication that Special Agent Shaneyfelt cut out the much publicized missing frames 208 through 211 of the Zapruder film to conceal from the public what really happened during the assassination." This last of his allegations is entirely false.

The thrust of my writing is not that the professional Shaneyfelt did so amateurish a splicing job, but that he failed to testify to any of this before the Commission, or from the existing record, to have called it to the staff's attention (with or without any explanation and/or investigation).

He offered the opinion: "The allegations of Weisberg would appear to be libelous of both the Bureau and Special Agent Shaneyfelt." So, in "an effort to discourage or stop such irresponsible and unwarranted attacks against the Bureau, [the FBI] may wish to explore the feasibility of having a libel action brought against Weisberg in Special Agent Shaneyfelt's name." He listed some "factors to be weighed" and said that he, "of course, contemplates no action in this matter unless so desired by the Bureau." Shaneyfelt concluded with the "Recommendation" that the memo and the book be referred "to the Legal Research Desk for review and consideration as to whether it might serve as a basis for libel action against Weisberg."

Shaneyfelt's language is specific enough: He was offering to act as a front for the FBI if it wanted to use a suit libel to "stop" me and my writing.

On January 31, J. J. Casper of the Legal Research Unit wrote John P. Mohr*, his channel to Hoover, sending copies to four other assistant directors, plus one to the FBI's most proficient leaker as well as to others. Without checking to determine whether the allegations

---

*After Mohr's retirement from the number 3 position in the FBI, several newspaper accounts reported a Department of Justice internal investigation to determine whether he had "had a $5,000 wine rack built in his home by FBI personnel using government-owned material" (*Washington Post*, Sept. 3, 1976] and other abuses and improprieties if not illegalities [*The New York Times*, Jan. 12, 1976 and Aug. 6, 1976], and among other dubious practices, instructing an FBI secretary to sign "the name of former associate FBI director Clyde A. Tolson to documents giving Mohr control over both Tolson's finances and the estate of J. Edgar Hoover" [*Washington Post*, July 22, 1976].

were factually correct, Casper (who did not write the memo him-self—"DJD" did) concluded that "the statements are libelous and that Special Agent Shaneyfelt has a cause of action against Weis-berg." He concluded that Shaneyfelt was not a "public person in terms of the controlling *New York Times versus Sullivan* decision" and thus was not required to prove that "the utterance was false ... made with malice ... in reckless disregard" of the truth as well as a few other requirements of that decision.

But what Casper's legal memo does not cite is a single proof that a single statement I made was incorrect, libelous, malicious, or wrong in any way. It merely assumed that the few comments Shaneyfelt had made were factually correct when they were not. Because, with-out such proof in hand, merely approving the filing of the suit was quite dangerous and subject to severe internal criticism, it is apparent that Casper knew the intent was to get publicity adverse to me and my book, not to win any lawsuit. If the FBI had lost the lawsuit, it would have been disastrous to all involved it is apparent that nobody believed there was any possibility of any suit being filed, that this was all part of a con job on the aging Hoover, with two purposes: first, to make Shaneyfelt look good the way Hoover liked his agents to look dedicated to him and to his FBI; and second, to deceive him about the quality of the work done for the Commission by his FBI.

Without recommending that the Bureau use Shaneyfelt to front for it, Casper suggested that the memo with his signature "be referred to the FBI laboratory." Period. Not another word.

Before the Casper memo reached Hoover, however, ten of the more important and the very most important FBI officials read and initialled it. Mohr's notation, the first, is: "Suggest we leave it up to Shaneyfelt as to whether he should sue." Next to his note appears the marks of Clyde Tolson, Hoover's next in command and best personal friend, and of Cartha De Loach, the maestro of many deli-cate responsibilities, including lobbying, leaking, and keeping track of the media. Underneath it, with an arrow pointing to it, Hoover wrote, "Yes," and followed with his "H" below that.

When the legal research desk memo reached the lab, it was again Shaneyfelt who wrote his assistant director via his superior. It re-quired but a single sentence for Shaneyfelt to dispose of the matter. "Since there is no assurance that any benefit to the Bureau would be forthcoming if Special Agent Shaneyfelt undertook the civil suit against Weisberg and since Special Agent Shaneyfelt has no desire to obtain a financial advantage therefrom, he contemplates no action.''

All these records have a copy routed to the Personal Records Unit for its Shaneyfelt file. His willingness to front for the FBI in an attempt to ''stop'' me and my writing, a ''benefit to the Bureau'' that he apparently overlooked or forgot once all the top FBI brass were aware of his demonstration of loyalty and self-sacrifice, accumulated Brownie points.

While none of the other FBI agents, with whom I had contact in and out of the courtroom over the years, threatened to sue me and sought to influence the judge in any litigation by such means as Shaneyfelt proposed, most had personalities and attitudes similar to Shaneyfelt.

The innumerable dirty tricks these agents pulled in my FOIA lawsuits are too numerous to list. They were costly in time and money, frustrating compliance, which meant disclosure of what the FBI did not want disclosed. Those who were most successful at this were rewarded by promotions. At least one clerk, who prolonged one case greatly and succeeded in withholding *in toto*, and by excessive ''Swiss-cheesing'' of documents, selectively, was promoted from clerk to agent, a big jump in rank and pay.

Earlier, a few of the FBI's intrusions into my life were mentioned. There are others that may or may not have been by the FBI. Like waking me after 2 A.M. to play the sound track of the movie *Shane* to me. It is not just any Tom, Dick, or Harry who can make a direct feed of a movie soundtrack into a telephone line, and most people wouldn't own this soundtrack to use as a threat in the wee hours.

Because I had no charge accounts and bought nothing for which I could not pay cash when in the earlier stages of my work I was broke and in debt, there was no reason for me to get phone calls from those representing themselves as employees of credit agencies. While speaking to them and saying nothing, I checked the phone book, and the credit agencies did not exist. When I said that to the callers, I was cursed out and the callers hung up. Not many people had any reason for or interest in doing this. Or, in having me asked to complete credit questionnaires.

Or, who knew I was away when it was not known and then phoned threats to my wife.

Or, had any interest in shadowing me when I was out of town, as was observed when a man I was to meet was late, and he saw my shadow following me from the train gate to the phone booths and then onto the subway in New York City.

Or, who could intercept and hold my mail and see to it that some, including offers to publish and returned manuscripts, never reached me.

During the period of this mail interception the Senate Church Committee did establish that the FBI was then doing that for the CIA. Neither the FBI nor the CIA provided me with any records relating to the interception of my mail when nobody else was in a position to do this. What agencies had any interest in seeing to it that offers to publish books abroad do not reach me, and could see to it they did not?

So there are people who through a misguided sense of loyalty, or merely to hold their jobs, do what is wrong, very wrong in a free and democratic society.

All societies have all varieties of people and some agencies, like the FBI, prize employees who do what they are told without asking questions about it.

Another incident reveals other dimensions to the FBI agent profile. The daughter of an FBI agent who testified before the Warren Commission and was also involved in my FOIA lawsuits really surprised me—stunned me would be more like it—with what she said about her father and the offer she made me. I had arrived a little early at the university at which I was to speak and was standing outside the auditorium waiting for the students who had invited me, when this young woman who somehow knew me, although we had never met, came up to me. She introduced herself as that agent's daughter, and said of him, "The only use I have for that son of a bitch is to baby-sit" and volunteered to help me in any way she could.

She told me of gatherings in her home of other FBI agents and people who were not FBI employees when her father displayed official evidence, including the FBI's copy of the Zapruder film.

I asked her no questions, thanked her for her offer, and in order not to offend her, told her we were separated by too much distance for her to offer to be practical. I then referred her to the students at that institution whom I knew were interested in the JFK assassination.

The extreme opposite of Shaneyfelt's attitude toward me—probably—is that of Farris Rookstool III. Without identifying himself as an FBI agent, he phoned me from Dallas, describing himself as my devoted fan who had limitless appreciation for the work I had done and asking if he might visit me when, as happened from time to time, he had business in Washington. I invited him. He also told me that he had what he described as a "rare" picture of me, which he at our meeting would to give me.

His phone call was, according to his March 27 1989, note, on July 7 of the year before. He wrote that he was a "close friend" of a Dallas researcher, said he had visited me in 1988, of which I had no recollection, said he was a student, and ordered a set of books.

In his note to me, he wrote:

> I didn't realize the financial costs of my tuition at the university I am attending. Now thanks to a IRS tax refund I am able to send you my request. I have a great amount of respect for you and the work you have done. You were the first original thinker re: the assassination. You blazed a trail for many. . . . I would love to have an *autographed complete set* of your works [his emphasis]. . . . Do you have a black-and-white photo of yourself you might sign?

And he enclosed payment for the books, which he received. He wrote me on April 5: "I am so grateful to you. I think very highly you [*sic*] and the work you have done. As a historian, I believe in years to come many will say Harold Weisberg was the first original critic who made the greatest impact on how Kennedy assassination material is viewed." He said he would "love the opportunity to meet [me] in person," although nine days earlier he said he had the year before. He also said, "I have located a rare photograph of you I will be sending you to autograph." Without explanation, he added, "I'm sure you see it will bring back memories."

From his forgetting what he had said only a few days earlier and from his effusiveness and his having a "rare" picture, I got suspicious, looked at his return address to which I'd paid no attention before and recognized the street number as that of the Dallas FBI office.

When some time had passed, and he did not send the picture, curious about it, on July 27, 1990, I wrote to remind him. I gave him a hint of my suspicions in referring to my "past that some refer to as 'nefarious.' " This he should have recognized as one of the FBI's favorite characterizations of me.

Two weeks later he sent me a Sony copy of the picture with a note expressing "shock" over my heart surgery of the year before. He wrote, "You are going to be the bionic man." He apologized for not having a better print and said he would soon be sending me "a photo to autograph for my collection." Whether that collection is his or the FBI's he did not indicate.

I wrote him on August 14, 1990, telling him who had taken the pictures, when and where, and asking him how he got it. I've not heard from him since.

The picture was taken by assassination critic Fred Newcomb in his Sherman Oaks, California, backyard in February 1968. I have no reason to believe that Newcomb was an FBI informer. It is possible that he had given the picture to other critics, like the one in Dallas who Rookstool said was his friend and from whom Rookstool could have gotten his copy. But I also knew that the Los Angeles and San Francisco FBI offices had informers reporting on critics, including me, because I have copies of their records reflecting it. So I was curious.

Once I suspected that he might be an FBI agent, I checked and learned that he was. I gave this no more thought when he did not respond to my last letter until I was reminded of it by a 1992 *Los Angeles Daily News* article relating to the number of phone calls the FBI began to get about the JFK assassination after the attention to it generated by the Oliver Stone's *JFK*. That story quotes "Farris L. Rookstool III, an investigative analyst for the FBI in Dallas, who is a Kennedy assassination specialist."

After recognizing his return address, I asked a friend in the Dallas media about him. I was told he was the Dallas FBI's JFK assassination case agent. Rookstool's expression of respect and admiration for me and for my work are not calculated to earn him Brownie points in the FBI hierarchy. Whatever his reason for initiating this contact, representing himself not as the Dallas FBI case agent but as a history student, whether his lengthy phone call of 1988 was personal or official, and whether during that conversation he sought information from me, it was a subterfuge call. Whatever accounts for it, I have no secrets to disclose, and I respond to all reasonable inquiries.

Among the thousands of phone calls I have received, there may well have been other such subterfuge calls, but I doubt if any was as excessive in its praises as Rookstool's.

Whether or not he was genuine, that he is an FBI "Kennedy assassination specialist" and the Dallas case agent in the subject indicates that he should be familiar with the work of the critics of the official "solution."

Save for the special demands of their jobs and the environment in which they have had to survive, FBI agents are pretty much like all other people. In his endorsement of the Warren Report Lundberg was also endorsing the work of some who may have prayed loudest from the front pews on Sundays and were a little less holy at work, on week days.

My first personal experience with FBI agents, not in Washington, associated me with some truly fine men, one of whom became a good friend. In 1938 the Department of Justice borrowed me from to Senate committee, for which I then worked as its editor (earlier I was an investigator), because of my knowledge of that committee's record relating to "Bloody Harlan" County, Kentucky. In the case of *The United States* v. *Mary Helen et al.* (the name of a mine, not a female defendant), the department, having indicted about sixty-five coal operators, their association, and some thirty deputized gun thugs, who had committed of a wide variety of violent crimes including murder, wanted my knowledge for the preparation of subpoena *duces tecum*. These subpoenas required the production of records about which I knew more than anyone in the department or its FBI.

About a half-dozen FBI agents were assigned to the case. Their acting agent in charge was James M. McInerney. There were times when all the other agents were in the field investigating, leaving

McInerney alone when he had to go out. I was the only one who could go with him, and I did, riding shotgun, so to speak, but without a shotgun. I suppose that Hoover would have had conniptions if he had known it. But before McInerney gave me his second weapon, an automatic pistol, and had me crouch behind the passenger-side door to cover him, he made me learn how to take that automatic apart and reassemble it blindfolded so that I would be thoroughly familiar with it.

It was a bit scary for a twenty-five-year-old in those remote and sparsely settled mountains, where violence was endemic and murder was commonplace. McInerney and I developed a friendship based on trust. We remained friends after he became the assistant attorney general in charge of two different department divisions, the second its criminal division.

Another agent, whose name I remember but do not reveal because he may still be alive, came to my room in the New Harlan Hotel in the city of Harlan the first week we were there to caution me that they had to report everything. He also told me he would soon be leaving the FBI for a different kind of life in which he did not have to inform on friends. For four months I lived and worked with them on that important case. We ate and drank together. We had a friendly relationship. They all impressed me as fine men.

(I was the party rumrunner in that dry county. Brien McMahon, then chief of the criminal division and later a United States Senator and author of the atomic-energy act, loaned me the party's official armored Buick for my weekly trips to Lexington, Kentucky, or Jellico, Tennessee, from which I returned with the week's booze for us all. The trip was more than two hours in either direction, mountains all the way, with narrow, twisting roads. The local authorities never caught me. Or, us. On those roads it would have been easy, if the authorities knew or cared.)

Soon after we moved to the seat of the federal court in London, Laurel County, and the national press poured in, there was a persuasive demonstration of the fact that the agents did report to headquarters on what individuals did and said. At one of the drinking parties the *New York Daily News* reporter made some cracks about Hoover being a homosexual. Before the next night fell, he disappeared, and the following day his replacement was there.

I want to make the point that all FBI agents are not alike and do not necessarily behave like those with whom I had relationships and contacts in the FOIA matters and on the assassination cases. When I was able to make investigations in these cases, I was helped by several former FBI agents.

One man risked his job and his future in warning the parent of one of a group of students, who associated with me, that the FBI was keeping tabs on them, that they were included in the FBI's records and that it could interfere with their job opportunities after graduation.

This is police-state practice. So also is the FBI's watching and keeping files on those of us who do not agree with the official assassination mythology.

It actually filed my FOIA requests in its "100" file classification. That classification is, from the FBI's own list of them, marked as a "Security-Related Classification." It is for "Subversive matter [individuals]; Internal Security [Organizations]; Domestic Security Investigations." This should help the reader understand that to the FBI, which supposedly investigated the assassination of the President, those of us who used the law that "guarantees" the people copies of the official records on that assassination and its investigation became "subversive" and, as individuals are under this file classification and/ or become the subject of "security investigations" by the FBI.

Thus my admirer, as he described himself, Dallas FBI JFK assassination case agent, Farris Rookstool III, has a picture of me in a Sherman Oaks, California, backyard, with me holding a duplicate of the Oswald rifle I'd just bought that day in Pasadena. Who can estimate the number of unsolved crimes that could have been solved if not prevented by the enormous amount of time and money the FBI invested in spying on the many of us who questioned the official "solution" to the JFK assassination and its investigations?

Those who did what they did in the various aspects of the JFK assassination investigations made their own records, records Lundberg endorsed in his praising of the Warren Report and in his pronouncing it correct.

What they did and did not do influenced our history and what could be known about it—more, what could *not* be known about it. They, as is Lundberg, are now part of that history, for what they did and for what they did not do in the investigation of "the crime of the century" and for their interference with and prevention of the disclosure of records relating to it. These are records to which under the law all of us are entitled.

In addition to what we have seen, there is more information on some agents and on the lab with regard to the reports of other shots having been fired during the assassination.

Chapter 31

Rosetta Stones

DAVID BELIN, THE "SLACKEST-JAWED," LOUDEST, MOST OFTEN HEARD and least rational of the Commission's former assistant counsels, whose basic argument was that the Commission was right because it and he said so and nothing else mattered, is fond of referring to the murder of Dallas Policeman J. D. Tippit as the "Rosetta stone" of the assassination.

Not surprisingly, the Tippit component was Belin's Commission baby. Not surprisingly, to any impartial examination, it was the biggest of Belin's personal fiascos. And not surprisingly, the major media went for his guff big and gave him and his "Rosetta stone" much attention. (See *Whitewash* pages 52–63 and of the many subsequent references in my books, page 493 of *Post Mortem* in particular.)

In Belin's "Rosetta stone" of the JFK assassination, he could not get Oswald to the scene of the crime until after Tippit was murdered. When a citizen radioed a report of the death to the dispatcher, his periodic announcements of the time clocked it. The citizen's report to the police dispatcher was before Oswald could have reached the scene in Belin's own reconstruction. "Rosetta stone," indeed!

There are aspects of the JFK assassination and its investigations, however, that are real Rosetta stones, not like Belin's fictional one. An honest, unbiased inquiry would have recognized and used them.

One of these is the slight wounding of Jim Tague by the "missed" shot. There is enough information available on it for a book, not a chapter. A real examination of it that does not have the intent of trying to justify the unjustifiable gives us insight into all the official investigations and their ideological soul mates, like the AMA, its

JAMA, and *JAMA*'s gang of five who entirely ignored it, proclaiming that the Report is correct and they have proved it.

From my first treatment in 1965 of this "missed" shot in *Whitewash*, pages 156–59, 165, and 193, to the twenty-four pages cited to it in the index of *Post Mortem*, and including innumerable FBI records the disclosure of which was compelled in CA's 75–226 and 78–0322/0420, the truth about this missed shot has always been available, some only inside the government until I compelled their disclosure, beginning long before this *JAMA* gang began its rewriting of our history.

The truth is, however, that those few drops of blood on Jim Tague's cheek were like a mighty torrent in exposing the official determination not to investigate the crime itself, to avoid all indications or proofs of a conspiracy to blame the crime on Oswald alone, to ignore all that was even publicly known that disputed or disproved the official preconception, and with this shot, to pretend that it had never been fired.

This is the case without any question at all. It is supported by the selection of long-secret official records finally disgorged under FOIA pressure, beginning with J. Edgar Hoover's boast to William Manchester that he made the instant determination, without any investigation at all, to pin the rap on Oswald. In its TOP SECRET executive sessions, from which the Commission excluded all its assistant counsels, the Commission confessed its fear of Hoover, admitted that he dominated it, decided to destroy that record, and then proceeded to record it in its own earliest outline of its work—before making any investigation at all—that it would follow Hoover's line that for all practical purposes was his *dikat*.

Several outlines with related internal memoranda appear in facsimile in *Post Mortem* on pages 494–504. Their reproduction is faithful, the record copies in the Commission's files, from which the author obtained them, are that poor and close to illegible.

The outlines all begin with the assumption of Oswald's sole guilt and do not reflect either the intent or the need of any real investigation.

The Report the Commission evolved is as close to the line Hoover and the FBI laid down in the five-volume report ordered by President

Johnson the night of the assassination as the Commission could hope to be able to get away with.

The Commission hewed to the knowingly false Hoover line that there was no missed shot until that became intolerable, really impossible. By then the Commission was more than halfway through its life. The FBI was content publicly with the Commission's account of the shooting and the wounding and with its treatment of the "missed" bullet invented for Specter and it by the FBI.

Any other course meant official recognition of the fact that there had been a conspiracy to assassinate the President. Of the many known, readily available, and definitive proofs of a conspiracy to kill President Kennedy this "missed" shot is perhaps the most comprehensible. It is simple and straightforward: With nobody in the world able to duplicate the shooting attributed to Oswald in three shots, a fourth shot, which the "missed" one assuredly was, made it impossible to pretend that Oswald had fired a fourth shot, too. (See Chapter 27.)

As we have seen, Tague's wounding, those few drops of blood, and the fresh "hole," "scar," or "mark" on the curbstone as it was variously referred to, was known immediately and reported immediately, first by the police and the sheriff, and during the next two days by the newspapers and TV.

But it was not then reported by the FBI, which did know about it.

This is the same FBI that had the obligation to, in one of those clichés Hoover loved so dearly and the rest of the FBI adopted, "leave no stone unturned." In a week the Commission was in ultimate authority and responsibility, but that did not in any degree at all reduce the obligation of the FBI, which did almost all the Commission's investigating for it.

We have lived so long with the instant official preconception of Oswald's lone guilt that most of us do not realize that the primary obligations of all official investigators were first to identify the killer and prove his guilt and then to determine whether or not there had been a conspiracy, both to the degree humanly possible and both by fact. Each of these basic factors required diligent, competent, and thorough investigation, the the exact opposite of beginning with a hoked-up solution, a political "truth."

Neither the FBI nor the Commission ever made any real investigation in a legitimate effort to prove that Oswald or any other person fired the fatal shot, and neither made an effort to establish whether or not there had been a conspiracy, or any person or persons, whether or not as a shooter, involved with the one who fired the fatal shot. But in spite of themselves and their best efforts, the FBI and the Commission both proved with evidence each ignored that there had been a conspiracy. The simplest proof, and there are others, is that the crime as officially accounted for officially proved to be beyond the capability of any one person.

Many elements of the evidence immediately available were viable, promising leads.

One of these is the impact on the curbstone that caused Tague's minor wound.

To simplify (and it must be simplified because there *is* enough information available for a book-length study, a politically and historically important study of how our basic institutions worked or did not work at the moment of what could have been an unimaginable crisis), a ballistic impact leaves an identifiable and retrievable deposit that can be compared, roughly, with a fingerprint, although it is not that unique. The definitive tests that can be performed, spectrographic and neutron-activation analyses, are finer than in parts *per million!* They require only the minutest specimens, as tiny a piece, if in pieces, as a millimeter in length, and if no piece that small is available, only a minute collection of very small fragments.

There was a very small hole in the windshield of the presidential limousine. The FBI swept up the almost invisible particles *after the limousine was back in Washington* and performed spectrographic analysis with these sweepings. (When it later attempted to subject that specimen to neutron-activation analysis, as I learned in CA 75–226, it no longer existed.)

Each test determines the composition of what is tested and the concentration of each element. This makes it possible to state, with bullet fragments, that they did or did not have a common origin and with whole bullets whether or not they came from the same manufacturer's batch. Neutron-activation analysis, relatively new at the time of the JFK assassination, is the finer test. Spectrographic analyses have been recognized by the courts for about seventy-five years.

All police know these things and what to do to be able to perform them or have them performed. The FBI, which performs this test routinely, certainly knew of the importance in any real investigation of retrieving the ballistic signature, the metallic deposit, on the curbstone at the point of impact, and comparing it with the other specimens it had.

It did not do it. Nor did it recommend this to the Commission a week later, when the Commission was appointed. It was not even attempted for more than eight months, and then it was a farce and a futility, an opportunity that was not missed by ignorance.

There was no question of jurisdiction, either. Nor was there of instructions. The first record placed in the Dallas FBI field office JFK assassination file, Serial 1 in 89–43, was the memorandum to file by Special Agent-in-Charge Gordon Shanklin, dated the day of the assassination and timed in its first sentence:

At approx. 1:25 P.M. I talked to ALAN H. BELMONT, Asst. to the Director, who had just finished talking to the Director ...'
The seventh and last paragraph on this single-page memo begins, 'BELMONT stated again to *offer all possible assistance; that jurisdiction does not matter now—to react as if it were ours* ... [Emphasis added].

And this was within an hour of the shooting.

Shanklin told Belmont that "as many as three shots were fired as they hit three people," that one man had been arrested, and that the shots came from the TSBD.

Unless Shanklin was just running off at the mouth, he then knew that Tague had been wounded, that he was the third man wounded.

With instructions to "offer all possible assistance," told that "jurisdiction" is of no concern, "to react as if it [the case] were ours," the FBI ignored the third wounding, the impact on the curbstone, and did not even report it to FBIHQ, from the records I have, supposedly and attested to as all of the records on the subject.

What did ensue, at no point and in no way, reflects the quintessential importance of a proper and thorough investigation of this curbstone impact, although from time to time the Keystone Kops and the Pink Panther movies are suggested.

Despite public reporting the next day at least on KRLD–TV, and in the *Dallas Morning News,* the following day when it published its Tom Dillard photograph and the immediate police reporting of the hit, the Dallas FBI sent nothing to Washington until after the *News* carried a story headlined: "QUESTIONS RAISED ON MURDER BULLETS." The story's first sentence is "Did a bullet from Lee Harvey Oswald's rifle chip the curb on Main Street near the triple underpass?"

The story appeared Friday, December 13, without naming Tague. The next day two FBI agents interviewed Tague. They did not even dictate their short report (DL 100–10461), less than a page, until Monday, after the weekend. After it was typed, they sent it to FBIHQ. In time FBIHQ gave copies to the Commission, where it is CR 205. (The Commission identified its files CR for Commission Record and later CD for Commission Document.) The report makes no reference to Sheriff's Investigator Buddy Walthers or to Allan Sweatt, chief criminal deputy, both of whom observed the impact and searched the area for a bullet or what remained of one.

The FBI report says much less than was known in its first paragraph. It does not include the observation and search by the police and sheriffs or the recording of the "missed" shot on the police radio.

Its second paragraph, of all things, goes into questioning Tague to learn whether or not he knew Jack Ruby, hardly relevant in any investigation of the shooting. For the next six months there was no further reference to Tague or his wounding or this "missed" shot.

During this time, as we have seen, the Commission was supposedly investigating the crime pretending there was no "missed" shot, when if it knew no other way, it did know from its own file, Number 205, which held the FBI's December report on its Tague interview. It was then proceeding on the assumption that the second shot hit Connally only, inflicting all five of his wounds, tooth fairy stuff. In addition to the staff memos on these sessions previously cited, the FBI had its own memos. One reports a January 28, 1964, session at which Specter and the prosecutors were not listed as present. In addition to a number from the FBI and Secret Service, listed as participating were Rankin's assistant, Norman Redlich, and assistant counsels Belin, Joseph Ball, and Melvin Eisenberg (FBIHQ 62–109060–2366, with copies to the FBI's top echelon).

Jim Lehrer's previously referred to *Dallas Times Herald* story was published June 6. Without naming Tague, who preferred anonymity, it recounts what he and the police and sheriffs said and saw and that Tague was interviewed also at police headquarters. It quotes unnamed Tague as saying, "The FBI talked to me for about fifteen minutes and seemed mainly concerned about whether I knew Jack Ruby," hardly part of a serious investigation of the shooting. Lehrer's story concludes, "What made him finally decide to talk about it again was the revelation last week that the Warren Commission had come around to the belief that only two of the three bullets actually hit President Kennedy and Gov. John Connally."

This, roughly, dates the Commission's decision that it could no longer pretend that all three shots hit the two victims and that there was no missed shot. But it still had not spoken to Tague. With its Report originally planned to have been issued at about that time, this makes it certain that, although the Commission knew about this "missed" shot, it had decided to ignore it, *to lie*.

This also was the Commission's own description of the real character of its "investigation" of the assassination of President Kennedy.

In 1992 all those assistant counsels joined in a coast-to-coast press conference and in a well-publicized statement in reaction to Oliver Stone's movie in which they proclaimed their purity, their personal and professional integrity, and the honesty, soundness and completeness of the Commission's work.

In the Commission's files (CR 1245, pages 32–33) is an undated summary memorandum from the Dallas 100–10461 file referring to this Lehrer story. It bears the initials of the Dallas case agent, Robert P. Gemberling. It belittles Tague as a "used car salesman," a slur false from the Dallas FBI's own records, makes another effort to defame him, quotes Lehrer as saying the story was not at all unusual or "startling," and concludes by referring to the December 13 interview, which was not forwarded from Dallas for ten days after that interview, according to Gemberling himself in this memo. As case agent he put together a miscellaneous collection of reports to which the Commission gave the file number CR205. The Tague interview is page 31 in the FBI's copy of that report.

On June 8 Alex Rosen, assistant director in charge of the FBI's General Investigative Division, took note of the Lehrer interview, which United Press International used. With copies to five of the FBI's top command, among others, he, too, undertook to undermine confidence in Tague and what he said. This memo reports that Tague "asked that his identity be concealed" and simultaneously misrepresents the Lehrer story as "more dramatic" when it says nothing Tague had not said before—all as an excuse for saying that Tague "exaggerated the incident to obtain personal publicity."

Anonymous "personal publicity"?

Covering his own and the FBI's ass, they all having known about this "missed" shot and pretending that it never happened, Rosen said, "Based on information developed recently, it is possible that one of the shots fired by Oswald did go wild; however, efforts to locate the portion of curb where a possible shot might have hit have been negative."

I do not recall any record reflecting any FBI investigation, if that word is appropriate, of this "missed" shot as of that date.

He then concluded that "since this interview has been reported to the Commission and the United Press International release contains substantially the same information developed by our investigation, no further action is recommended." Translated from FBI special uses of language, he was telling the others, "We have not done a damned thing, and I recommend that we not do anything now."

The FBI "investigation" to which he refers was a fiction. It consisted entirely of the December 13 interview that merely repeated what was in the newspaper. But virtually nobody reading Rosen's memo would be in a position even to suspect that. As he knew.

On June 5 Shanklin wrote a garbled memo to file (100–10461–6537). Inspector J. R. Malley phoned him from FBIHQ and quoted the UPI story. Shanklin worked in that KRLD-TV had a copyrighted story the week before quoting "a source close to the Warren Commission" as saying that one shot struck both men. It includes a partial rehash of what Tague had said.

On June 11 Specter sent a short memo to Rankin, covering his ass and the Commission's, but at the same time recording that as of the time the Commission had planned to be filing its Report, it had not investigated the "missed" shots:

> If additional depositions are taken in Dallas, I suggest that Jim Tague, 2424 Inwood, Apartment 253, and Virginia Rachley, 405 Wood Street, be deposed to determine the knowledge of each on where missing bullets struck. These two witnesses were mentioned in the early FBI reports, but they have never been deposed. [This record is from the Commission's "Other Persons" File.]

We have seen how Wesley Liebeler saw to it that when the Commission read Virginia Rachley's testimony they would place no credence in it at all, when in fact it was credible testimony. This was the Commission's practice with all who reported seeing other shots strike near them.

Eleven days after Malley phoned Shanklin, Dallas responded, reporting what it had done on the eleventh, five days earlier. It got copies of Underwood's film of the curbstone. The memo, written by Ivan D. Lee, continues the FBI's line of playing it all down, concluding with what from Underwood's own picture (*Post Mortem*, page 608) is obviously false: "UNDERWOOD stated that the object which struck the curb did not break nor leave a permanent mark" [FBIHQ 105–82555–4295].

The FBI delivered the report to the Commission by courier after waiting four or five more days. It then waited until June 30, according to the July 7 letter from Rankin to Hoover, to send the Commission prints of Underwood's pictures. In no less a great rush, as the urgency of the investigation required, Rankin wrote Hoover asking that "an analysis be made on the curb to determine whether there are any lead deposits there or any other evidence upon which a conclusion can be reached as to whether this mark was caused by the striking of a bullet" [FBIHQ 62–109060–3659].

That Rankin! He sure was a stickler! He wasn't satisfied with mere eyewitness testimony, including that of the sheriffs, the policemen, and others who could have been located. And he certainly was expert on the Commission's own evidence when he expected the impact of a copper-jacketed bullet to deposit lead, not copper.

On July 9 Rankin notified Tague by registered mail that they intended deposing him on the sixteenth and that Specter would do it. Tague notified the U.S. Attorney's Office, as instructed, that he would be out of town that day. (His deposition was rescheduled, Specter was not in Dallas that day, so Liebeler deposed Tague.)

A mere two weeks after Rankin's requests, on July 15, Special Agents Lee and Robert M. Barrett picked up Underwood and Dillard, and by use of their cameras and three reference points, located the point of impact, to within an inch. (DL 100–10461, 7/15/64). Their fourth and concluding paragraph of the report is where the Keystone Kops start sneaking in:

It should be noted that no nick or break in the concrete was observed, in the area checked (i.e. 'ten feet in either direction'), nor was there any mark similar to the one in the photograph taken by Underwood and Dillard observed in the area checked either by Special Agents BARRETT and LEE, not by Mr. UNDERWOOD or Mr. DILLARD. It should be noted that, since this mark was observed on November 23, 1963, there have been numerous rains which could possibly have washed away such a mark and also that the area is cleaned by a street-cleaning machine about once a week, which would also wash away any such mark.

The wonder then is that any of Dallas's paved streets remain when rain and street-cleaning equipment can melt concrete!

As the FBI knew and as its own records show, the impact did leave a hole, also called a ''scar'' and in other ways is described as a visible mechanical damage. Rain and street-cleaning equipment would wash *concrete* away so that the hole no longer existed? And leave the rest of that curbstone intact?

Then there is the reckless driving the FBI attributes to those destructive machines and their operators. Not content to eat up the streets, they mounted the sidewalk to eliminate that hole or scar because it was in the curve of the concrete curbstone, as the Dillard and Underwood pictures show clearly, not in the street, the normal place for *street*-cleaning equipment.

Eight days later FBIHQ told the Dallas office what additional pictures to take. The instructions eliminated all locations other than the TSBD as the source of the shot. The initials on the FBI file copy of this memorandum are those of Lab Agent Lyndal L. Shaneyfelt.

For even this Commission and those derring-do investigation assistant counsels, the FBI's July 15 report was a bit much. On August 4—what a great rush they were all in—FBIHQ teletyped Dallas informing it that:

> PLANS BEING MADE TO REMOVE PORTION OF CURB FOR LABORATORY ANALYSIS. SA LYNDAL SHANEYFELT WILL ARRIVE DALLAS SIX FORTY P.M. TODAY.... MAKE PRELIMINARY ARRANGEMENTS WITH APPROPRIATE OFFICIALS ... SO THAT APPROXIMATELY ONE FOOT OF CURBING CAN BE REMOVED.

Shaneyfelt, aka Inspector Clousseau, using the same two photographs, found the correct spot the next day. The city had the mechanical equipment there to remove that section of curbing and he flew it back for the lab to analyze.

Remember that Gemberling synopsis page on a large collection of Dallas reports (105–82555) sent to Washington August 5? Gemberling covered all asses this way:

> Additional investigation conducted concerning mark on curb on south side of Main Street near triple underpass, which it is alleged was possibly caused by a bullet fired during the assassination. No evidence of mark on nick on curb now visible. Photographs taken of location where mark once appeared ...

Shaneyfelt took other pictures from different positions so he could provide absolutely dependable information. This prepared him to testify with all the haste indicated—on September 1 (15H686–702). Shaneyfelt computed that shot at Zapruder frame 410! That, even for a nutty assassin, is pretty hard to believe. It means that after he fired he hung around as long as all the shooting took, after seeing the President's head explode, not concerned about getting caught, and then, with the victims already fallen over, fired this additional shot that hit the curbstone. Not at them but way over their heads. At what target cannot be guessed. Or, for what purpose, other than perhaps in celebration? Perhaps as a salute? Can *anybody* be *that* crazy?

As we have seen, Frazier, not Shaneyfelt or Gallagher, who performed the spectrographic analysis, made the notes. It is just a few notations and sketch. It is so grossly inadequate and incompetent it does not even list the components known to have been in the imagined bullet. *Only two* of the dozen elements of the bullet are noted as detected in the spectrographic analysis!

Usually all the elements of the bullet are posted. Only those detected and specially noted. This time there is no listing of them all is not surprising.

This means that, as the FBI knew in advance, it was not bullet residues that were being tested in that charade, *it was the patch!*

So, if the lab had done the normal thing and had treated this as all other such examinations are treated, the result would have established that it was not bullet traces that were detected. My, what a scene that would have been!

With the whole farcical pretense going up in smoke!

And so, with the official alchemy made possible by complete secrecy, in the best of possible worlds there was the best of possible solutions—hocus-pocus, hole you became a smear.

Which is precisely what the FBI called it.

When I examined that curbstone in the National Archives, it was very obvious that there had been a hole and that it had been patched. To a degree this is clear in the picture I had taken. The patch is much darker. Because the material used for the patch, which was a relatively small area, prevented the use of coarse aggregates, it is ever so much smoother to the touch as it is visible to the eye.

Shaneyfelt and his laboratory colleagues knew even better than I that they went through the ghastly charade of digging up a curbstone that they knew had been patched and submitted it to "scientific testing" in the vaunted FBI lab, for all the world as though it had not been patched—when Oswald could not have done the patching. And those so pure in heart and clear in mind on the Commission of eminences were all content. And then and since have been silent about this.

When Henry Hurt, a roving editor for *Reader's Digest,* was working on his book, *Reasonable Doubt,* I helped him all I could, mainly with its first half, a recap of the known facts about the JFK assassination. I asked him, for his purposes and mine, the *Digest* having resources I lacked and lack, to have an expert on concrete examine that curbstone. They engaged Construction Environment, Inc., of Alexandria, Virginia. Its chief engineer, Jose T. Fernandez, made that examination on March 10, 1983. He reported it March 17. He found the "dark gray spot" readily, "at the center of the concrete section, on the vertical face, just below the curbed transition between the horizontal and vertical surfaces ... The dark spot had fairly well-defined boundaries, as that it stood out visually from the surrounding concrete surface.... elliptical in shape approximately ½ in. by ¾ in. in principle dimension." He found no other such areas on the curbstone and regarded that as "significant."

The spot also had different characteristics. He attributed the "difference in color" to "the cement paste" that was used. He found a difference in the sand grains because, unlike the rest, the "dark spot" contained only semi-translucent light gray sand grains. He found a flaw on the upper edge of the patch "consistent with the relatively weaker zones that normally occurs in the thin, or feathered edges of surface patch." His summary is: that it was a surface patch.

So, what I could see with the naked eye, feel with my fingers, the FBI could not perceive? With all its science? Of course it could! *It knew what it was doing. It was faking evidence, faking a false "solution" to the assassination of a president of the United States!**

It was another implement of the Katzenbach-Hoover conspiracy to protect President Kennedy's killers by not investigating the crime itself.

With so many knowing it!

So many, too, of those pure in heart, noble in spirit, impeccable in performance Commission assistant counsels.

That this was central in the FOIA lawsuit for the results of the scientific testing caused some problems for the FBI, but nothing that, with the tolerance of Judge John Pratt, they could not overcome with frequent lying that did include perjury.

In that lawsuit I asked Jim Tague to provide an affidavit. I sent him FBI and Commission records that helped him understand what they were up to. He and his wife, Judy, had local clippings. His affidavit, with those attachments, is in all copies of that lawsuit file.

*The full text of the scientific examination of the curbstone, which is permanently in the National Archives, appears in *Case Open* (New York: Carroll & Graf/Richard Gallen, 1994, pages 164–65).

Tague was under oath and subject to the penalties of perjury if he lied because his affidavit was quite material on the legal points at issue.

A few selections from it help make some of the actualities clearer.

Buddy Walthers was thirty to forty feet away when he first saw the damage to the curbstone. Other officers also examined it, including one on a motorcycle who radioed the dispatcher to report it. Oswald was in the next cubicle in the homicide division when Tague's statement was taken.

About an hour and a half after Lehrer left after interviewing Tague, he phoned in great excitement, saying, "They are calling me from all over on the story." This included FBIHQ, to which Lehrer gave Tague's name. (No FBI report on that phone call is in the FBI's files.)

Although Tague's Commission testimony was published (7H552 ff), some transcripts had been altered. I gave him a copy of the typescript. Liebeler, who deposed him because Specter was not in Dallas that day, said, "Now I understand that you went back there subsequently and took some pictures of the area." This surprised Tague because he "didn't know anybody knew about that." Liebeler showed him a picture and asked if it was one Tague had taken. It wasn't.

Tague, planning a trip to visit his folks in Indiana, had taken some movies to show them of where he had become part of the history of the assassination. But he had told nobody about that.

"Was it [the hole] still there?" Liebeler asked. Tague responded that it was not. (Later, when I interviewed him, he told me that was in May.)

Tague was surprised because he had not told any official investigators about those pictures and none had asked him about them. He was also surprised because that roll of film was stolen from his house. Nothing else was taken. And there is no FBI or Commission record reflecting how Liebeler could have known that Tague took those pictures. No report, for example, of anyone telling the FBI that Tague had taken those pictures or that anyone had told the Commission. That Liebeler did know means that, with no FBI or Commission record of how he could have known, there was official knowledge or some sort of clandestine observation of Tague and/or that bullet impact on the curbstone. This is a strange business made stranger because that curbstone had been patched when Oswald could not have done it and the only purpose served was to eliminate the possibility of retrieving deposits from the bullet impact that could be scientifically compared with other bullets fired during the assassination. The only apparent reason for making this impossible appears to be knowledge that the tests would disclose that this was a different bullet, or one that is not what the official "solution" says was the only kind fired. And that would have caused official tizzies, a great commotion, and would have ended the possibility of pinning it all on Oswald.

It is certain that the Commission knew before recognizing that it could no longer avoid taking Tague's testimony that the curbstone had been patched. The FBI, instead of making the tests still possible, went through the unseemly nonsense of pretending that rains and the street-cleaning equipment had washed *concrete* away and wiped out that hole or scar. It did not report the obvious truth, that the hole had been eliminated by patching. It then unashamedly took the curbstone to the FBI lab and made a phony show of performing spectrographic analysis on it. The results establish beyond question, that as Shaneyfelt and the others knew, they were not testing any bullet impact. This one spectrographic plate then allegedly suffered a mysterious disappearance, conjectured as destruction to save space, when any such destruction was strictly prohibited by law as documents in a historic case, a law carefully observed by the FBI in annual inventories and other ways. The space to be saved was a tiny fraction of an inch in those simply enormous files of the Bureau. The FBI also avoided a test it knew it should have made if it intended making a test that could be helpful in the investigation.

When we deposed FBI Lab Agent John Kilty in CA 75–225, he described the proper test as "X-ray fluorescent techniques." He added, and this is the advice I took in asking Henry Hurt to have an expert examination made:

> What you want to do is have a building-materials scientist look at that. Different kinds of concrete are used. They can tell the difference between a patching material and a permanent material. It is not a very difficult thing . . .

The FBI knew what to do—and did not do it.

The FBI treatment of the curbstone damaged during the murder typifies its attitude toward the performance in the investigation of that most subversive of crimes in a society like ours, the assassination of a president.

This is still another part of the voluminous, indeed massive, documentary record which makes clear the one thing the FBI intended not to do was investigate the crime itself.

The Bureau knew the significance of the impact of that bullet, it knew the tests it could still make and what it could learn from those tests, and it knew of that impact from virtually the moment that bullet was fired because it had monitored the police radio. Yet it did nothing but fake and lie, avoiding this quintessential evidence in any *real* and *honest* investigation, and by this means, was able to file a "solution" to the crime in which there is no mention of this "missed" shot at all, or of Tague or of his being wounded during the assassination in the report President Johnson ordered of it..

For its part the Commission also knew; the record was in its files before its staff was fully organized. It knew of the "missed" shot, of Tague's being wounded, and of the FBI's avoidance of that and then of its faking. Yet it joined the FBI in abdicating its responsibilities. The sole purpose was to make it appear to be possible that Oswald was a lone assassin when the evidence to the contrary was so overwhelming. Until the Commission was certain beyond question that it could no longer get away with avoiding this "missed" shot, which Oswald could not possibly have fired, to be able to lie to the nation and to the world about this crime that turned the nation and the world around, it lived a terrible lie. It did that also in the outrageously false and dishonest lie about all of this in its Report.

Aside from how thorough its work and its Report, the Commission treated the proof of this particular missed shot, which alone is proof that there had been a conspiracy to kill President Kennedy, not being able to ignore it and Tague entirely, it included this single paragraph on poor Jim Tague who bled in vain; a paragraph that argues rather than reports fact; a paragraph that twists and distorts facts, and lies; a paragraph in which the Commission carefully selected quotations that would deceive the reader and make a false record for our history:

At a different location in Dealey Plaza, the evidence indicated that a bullet fragment did hit the street. James T. Tague, who got out of his car to watch the motorcade from a position between Commerce and Main streets near the triple underpass, was hit on the cheek by an object during the shooting. Within a few minutes Tague reported this to Deputy Sheriff Eddy Walthers, who was examining the area to see if any bullets had struck the turf. Walthers immediately started to search where Tague had been standing and located a place on the south curb on Main Street where it appeared a bullet had hit the cement. According to Tague, 'There was a mark quite obviously that was a bullet, and it was very fresh.' In Tague's opinion, it was the second shot which caused the mark, since he think he heard the third shot after he was hit in the face. This incident appears to have been recorded in the contemporaneous report of Dallas Patrolmen L. L. Hill, who radioed in around 12:40 P.M.: 'I have one guy that was possibly hit by a ricochet from the bullet off the concrete.' Scientific examination of the mark on the south curb on Main Street by FBI experts disclosed metal smears which 'were spectrographically determined to be essentially lead with a trace of antimony.' The mark on the curb could have originated from the lead core of a bullet, but the absence of copper precluded 'the possibility that the mark on the curbing section was made by an unmutilated military full metal-jacketed bullet such as the bullet from Governor Connally's stretcher.'

But without this, atop all else this chapter discloses, the government could not have lied in saying that it had no evidence of any conspiracy.

This truth about this "missed" shot was known to many in the FBI and on the Commission staff. What they did and did not do represents the grossest of dishonesties in an important investigation, an investigation that also involved the honor and the integrity of the nation. What they did and did not do amounts to an unspeakable obscenity and a betrayal of trust.

This, too, is what the AMA and its gang endorsed and justified in their campaign to have the Warren Report believed and *all criticism* of it not believed.

The FBI, the Commission, and its staff's treatments of the shot that wounded Tague can be likened to the very poor apology for an autopsy that they also went to all that trouble to make believable, where the truth so strongly suggests a conspiracy, really proves it, and a military conspiracy at that.

It was no street punk who was sophisticated enough to know to patch that curbstone to deny the evidence it held, and it was no jerk who did that patching.

That Oswald could not have done it alone shrieks "CONSPIRACY"!

With the *official* record here cited can it be assumed that it was not an *official* conspiracy?

Is not the covering up itself a despicable conspiracy, separate and distinct from the conspiracy that killed President Kennedy?

Lundberg may not have known what he was talking about, may just have been pursuing his propaganda and self-promotion when he said "there may have been many other gunshots" fired in the assassination, but this was not true of the FBI and the Commission staff. They all knew—had guilty knowledge.

For them there is no excuse—no innocence—in perpetuity.

Chapter 32

Waketh the Watchman

THE PRECEDING REVIEW OF THE AVAILABLE OFFICIAL EVIDENCE OF THE Commision-admitted "missed" bullet and of Jim Tague's wounding is necessarily incomplete. The FBI avoided any investigation of it when it cried out for immediate, diligent, and intensive investigation, and in the end, managed to make no investigation of it at all. The FBI still persists in ignoring it in its own pretended "solution." Should one not wonder why?

Why in particular the very day of the assassination, when it was solely in charge of the federal investigation, as it remained for a week, and when knowledge of this bullet and of Tague's wounding were public and when the FBI certainly knew about it.

The preceding glimpse of the FBI's attitude toward critics of the official solutions and its behavior in FOIA litigation seeking JFK assassination records, the merest glimpse to reflect how extreme the opposition sometimes was and something of the personalities of some of the intimately involved, longtime FBI agents, also should prompt wonder. Why indeed should the entire top FBI echelon approve a spurious lawsuit to "stop" a critic and his work, and that without even the most perfunctory inquiry into the facts of the lawsuit they approved?

Both relate to reported missed shots. While these reports, meaning those that are known, which need not be all of them because there is no way of knowing whether any were reported to the Dallas Police or Texas Rangers, the media which did not report them, or to the Secret Service, there is official confirmation of their existence. It was in the area of Shaneyfelt's expert-witness testimony to the Warren Commission. It is in the analysis of the Zapruder film made by

383

the CIA's National Photographic Interpretation Center in the reprints edition of *Photographic Whitewash*, (pages 295 ff.).

I saw no reference to this in the Commission's files. It is not properly subject to classification, and the records ultimately disclosed were not classified. It was disclosed to Commission- and self-defender David Belin, who managed not to include it in the report of the Presidential Rockefeller Commission he headed or even to mention it anywhere else of which I know. Those CIA records dispute, if not disprove, the basic conclusion of the Warren Report. They indicate the impact of shots as reflected in the Zapruder film, a matter to which as the Commission's expert witness on that film, Shaneyfelt did not testify.

In no known instance did the FBI or the Commission have any interest in or initiate any investigation of any bullet other than the three each accounted for differently, the FBI ludicrously in its supposedly definitive report ordered by the new President. In each and every known instance, of which there are more than is reported in what follows, both the FBI and the Commission, when these reports could no longer be entirely ignored, resorted to efforts to deprecate them and those who reported them.

Again, does this not also provide wonder, asking why?

The first known report of any shot that missed made after the Report was out and when the Commission was still functioning was reported to it, albeit incompletely, by the FBI. My first knowledge of it came from the Commission's files (CD 1546). I published that FBI report in *Whitewash II* (pages 37–38).

The concerned and indignant citizen who made that report, Eugene Aldredge, and I were thereafter in contact by phone, letters, and even through a call-in radio talk show. I examined the scar that seemed to have been made by a bullet he reported to the FBI, and I agreed with his comment on it, "this particular marksman was NOT [his emphasis] inside the Depository building."

Aldredge told this to the FBI. It is not reflected in the FBI's first or later reports. (November 16, 1968, letter to author.) He also said that such a shot had to have "come from the direction of the southwest corner of the Depository building." This the FBI did confirm, but in this unique way of dismissing it—because Oswald did not fire it!—and of seeking to put the hat on the Commission. Everybody else is wrong except the FBI. Everybody else is responsible, not the FBI:

Note the effort to deprecate the source of information on the ground that he was in some way derelict for expecting his government to do its job, to have known what was public knowledge:

On September 29, 1964, EUGENE P. ALDREDGE, 9304 Lenel, Dallas, Texas, telephonically advised that he disagreed with the President's Commission report that Oswald did not have help in the assassination.

ALDREDGE stated he saw a television program shortly after the assassination, believed to be on Channel Four, in which a mark on the sidewalk was pointed out.

Approximately three months ago, he stated he viewed such mark, which he is sure was caused by a bullet, and that this mark is approximately six inches long. He described the location of this mark as being in the middle of the sidewalk on the north side of Elm Street, which side is nearest the Texas School Book Depository Building. He stated there is a lamppost near the sidewalk, which is about even with the west end of the Texas School Book Depository Building and that the above-described mark is approximately eight feet east of the lamppost on the sidewalk. He stated that a reporter for "The Dallas Morning News," CARL FREUND, has also stated this is a bullet mark.

When asked as to why he had waited until this time to furnish the foregoing information, he stated he felt that such an important point would be covered in the President's Commission report and did not want to become involved by furnishing the information at this time, but felt that such information, if overlooked, should be made available.

The very next day, September 30, 1964, two FBI agents confirmed this proof of an additional bullet striking in the area. Faced with this, the FBI, in conformity with its employment of language throughout the proceedings, begs the question, blames the Commission, in effect, and defends itself by use of the Report, according to which this bullet '. . . could not have come from the direction of the window the President's Commission . . . has publicly stated was used by Lee Harvey Oswald . . .':

The sidewalk on the east [*sic*] side of Elm Street between the triple underpass and Houston Street was visually checked for any scars which might appear to have been made by a bullet.

The area covered in this inspection was in the general sidewalk area from the first to the second lamppost on the east [*sic*] side of Elm Street and just west of the intersection of Elm and Houston streets. It is noted that the first lamppost is almost directly in line with the west end of the main multistoried building of the Texas School Book Depository Building, while the second lamppost is almost directly in line with the western end of the one story building which is connected to the main Texas School Book Depository Building.

It was noted that the sidewalk is made of concrete and the general texture of the sidewalk is rough.

No mark was located on the sidewalk in the general area of the first lamppost which would appear to have been made by a projectile.

In the area of the second lamppost, approximately thirty-three feet east of the post, in the sixth large cement square, four feet from the street curb, and six feet from the parkside curbing, is an approximately four inches long by one-half-inch-wide dug-out scar, which could possibly have been made by some blunt-end type instrument or projectile. It is noted that this scar lies in such a direction that if it had been made by a bullet, it could not have come from the direction of the window the President's Commission on the Assassination of President KENNEDY has publicly stated was used by LEE HARVEY OSWALD when firing his assassination bullets at the late President.

This particular scar is in line with the western end of the multifloor section of the Texas School Book Depository Building, that is, the opposite end of the building from where OSWALD was shooting at the President.

No other mark was found in the area of the second lamppost which might appear to have been made by a bullet [*Whitewash II*, pages 37–38].

The Dallas FBI regarded Aldredge's phone call with enough seriousness to teletype FBIHQ with the information it later followed up with the report quoted above (FBIHQ 105–82555). The teletype was sent before the FBI examined the scar. In the teletype Dallas told FBIHQ that it would examine "the area," but would make "NO OTHER INVESTIGATION" unless, put in the FBI's abbreviation, "UACB," or "unless advised to the contrary by the Bureau."

The files hold no record of any outraged, indignant, or incredulous phone call or teletype from FBIHQ asking, "What do you mean you are not going to investigate that report?"

Can it be that the Dallas office expected any complaint?

Of course not, or it would not have risked getting chewed out and possibly disciplined. It knew what was wanted and what was not wanted by FBIHQ.

In its airmailed report, it says nothing at all about that.

It did not report what was obvious to Aldredge and to me, that no bullet fired from any elevation could have created that shallow scar.

The FBI's interest was in keeping the possible point of origin inside the TSBD, where it said Oswald was while pretending that the scar Aldredge saw and reported was irrelevant.

It does not, for example, point out that there is another grassy knoll on the other, or south side of, Dealey Plaza and that a bullet that caused that scar could have come from there.

There also is no record indicating that Rankin requested the FBI to make and report on an investigation.

This report's explanation of why Aldredge had not reported the scar earlier, because he believed the Commission would go into it, is not what I remember Aldredge having told me. He was deeply suspicious of the FBI, and in effect, he told it he presumed it knew its business and knew about the scar from the TV report on it.

In a short memo of October 12 FBIHQ told Dallas to investigate and report. It was routed to a surprising number of FBI higher-ups. At the lab it was addressed to Shaneyfelt's attention, to a photographic rather than a ballistics expert (FBIHQ 105–82555–5076).

Four days later Gemberling, in Dallas, reported on the investigation by Special Agents Manning Clements and Richard Burnett (FBIHQ 105–82555–5169). They found the scar, but not exactly where they had understood Aldredge to say it was. It was an "approximately four inches long by one-half-inch-wide dug-out scar, which could possibly have been made by some blunt-end type of instrument or a projectile," but "could not have come from . . . the window . . . used by . . . Oswald," according to the Commission, they said.

"Dug-out" suggests some depth to this scar, and it had no depth at all. I am not an expert, of course, but that scar could not, I believe, have been made by any "blunt-end" kind of instrument and not crack the concrete around its edge, or left so uniform a scar.

There were no cracks.

Dallas collected some scrapings from the edges of the scar and sent them to the lab on October 28 (DL 100–10461–1A470). No hurry, obviously. There are confusing notations of when it was sent to the lab and when the lab returned it, the dates each way contradicting each other, but it was returned to Dallas, which Xeroxed even the envelope that held a "box containing material from sidewalk." The form on which this information is posted, an FD–340, is known as an "evidence envelope." It has blocks indicting whether the lab is to return it or not, Dallas put an "x" in the "No" box, but the lab ignored this and returned it anyway.

With two different dates for the sending and the return, it is possible that the one evidence envelope, without so indicating, held specimens sent on two different occasions.

Something really strange happened, according to Aldredge's November 16, 1968, letter to me. It is included in the FBI's contemporaneous report on it of November 6 of four years earlier (FBIHQ 105–82555–5256). Aldredge wrote me that "less than a week after my telephone report to the FBI concerning an apparent bullet mark at the scene of the John Kennedy assassination, I mentioned about the mark to a friend of mine, Mr. George Booth," who "wanted" to see the mark, "whereupon we went to the cite and found the mark, formerly about ¼ inch deep, had been filled in with what appeared to be a mixture of concrete and asbestos . . . A crude attempt had been made to make the altered mark appear to be weather-worn to match the surrounding concrete."

The Dallas FBI's November 6, 1964, letter to FBIHQ confirms that the scar had been "patched" by the addition of "foreign material." Expressing neither surprise nor wonder over an effort to disguise what might be assassination evidence, it sent the lab "pieces of the unknown material" it "gathered" the day before "from the 'bullet' scar,'' asking the lab to determine what "this foreign matter might be" (FBIHQ 105–82555–5256).

In a longer and earlier letter of the same day reporting that it would be collecting some of this "foreign material" and asking the lab to identify it, the Dallas FBI confirmed what Aldredge said, that this "foreign material" had been added after the FBI had examined that scar and had sent the scrapings to the lab:

> [I]t was was noted that there is now some sort of foreign material partially covering this nick in the sidewalk. . . . It is noted that an inspection of this same mark on 9/30/64 did not disclose such a filling as of that date [FBIHQ 105–82333–5246].

The four-inch-long and half-inch-wide "dug-out scar" is downgraded in importance by being referred to as no more than a "nick," and then as even conspicuous, as no more than a "mark."

The lab returned the specimen on November 17 (FBIHQ 105–82555–5284), describing it as consisting "of a number of fragmented white cotton yarns that appear to have originated from a piece of fabric. The cotton fibers of the yarns have become a little brittle indicating possible exposure to the elements for a period of time." That "period of time" was less than a week.

Of all the people of varying rank in the FBI who were aware of this strange business of the ignored scar that could have been caused by a bullet fired during the assassination and then of the amateurish effort to obliterate it *after* the FBI examined it, not one suggested that an effort be made to determine who would have made such an effort or why. Not one referred to the patching and obliterating of the evidence of the bullet impact on the curbstone not far away on the opposite side of Dealey Plaza.

The obliterating of assassination evidence was treated as an everyday event, save for the efforts to make Aldredge appear to be unreliable and to pretend that this scar and the gesture at hiding it had no significance at all.

For almost a year this scar was ignored by those who, whether seriously or as a provocation, added that "foreign material" to it. This did not happen until *after* so belatedly the FBI had examined it. And not a single person in the FBI found this to be in any way unusual? Not in any way provocative? No suggestion, perhaps, of needling or taunting the FBI?

Is it not to wonder why and why, despite the many different personalities and kinds of people, as addressed in the previous chapter, the FBI, like all agencies has, *not one* had anything at all to say about this at the very least strange business of patching the scar in the concrete that could have been made during the assassination of a president?

The matter bears a strong resemblance to the FBI's ignoring of the Commission-acknowledged "missed" shot that had wounded Tague slightly, even though it, too, had been publicly reported.

That "scar" or "hole" was patched more skillfully, although it was very obvious. With it the FBI went through the charade of pretending it had not been altered by patching. It then tested the patch and palmed it off as a "mark" left by the led core of a bullet even though its spectrographic analysis proved that it could not have been made by a bullet core.

The grim and deeply disturbing truth is that the FBI was professionally unprofessional in its obdurate determination to make no real investigation at all of the many reports of other shots having been fired during the assassination. It adhered to a preconceived position unaltered by any consideration, whether of evidence or honesty or integrity.

Any other shot meant that there had been a conspiracy, and Hoover had decided the evening of the assassination that there had been no conspiracy. So all the efforts the FBI made relating to these other shots from places other than—it was alleged with no proof of it at all—where Oswald was perched doing all the shooting was to dismiss them all as irrelevant.

After the Commission ceased to exist, with the FBI alone sitting in judgment on itself, the FBI shamelessly dismissed all such reports as irrelevant because Oswald could not have fired those shots!

Here are a few of the reflections of this in its records that were secret until I sued it and forced incomplete, but nonetheless extensive, disclosure of what it had kept secret for all those years.

There are other reportings of shots and finding of bullets. These are presented as illustrative and to establish that it did not happen just once, that the FBI held that if Oswald could not have fired the shot, it had no relevance to the assassination or in any investigation of it.

In 1966, when I wrote *Whitewash II*, this was obvious even without access to the FBI's then still-secret records. The available Commission records proved it. As I then wrote of Dallas FBI Case Agent Robert P. Gemberling's large collections of individual reports given to the Commission as a single document, "Two other of Gemberlings' reports reveal the refusal of the FBI to really search the area at the time of the assassination for real clues or at any time for any other clues not consistent with Oswald as the lone assassin. The Commission adopted the same attitude. Numerous witnesses reported bullets striking the street and sidewalks in the vicinity" [*Whitewash II*, page 36]. Many ran up on the grassy knoll, believing shots came from there.

A little later in the same book, I wrote, "Specter concedes that 'there were reports that objects did strike in other parts of Dealey Plaza,' a rather understated version . . ." [*Whitewash II*, page 106].

"Objects"? *Could* there have been any other type than bullets?

And it was neither then nor later, only *in* Dealey Plaza.

In July or August 1967, William Barbee was working on the roof of a building on the Stemmons Freeway, slightly to the west of the scene of the crime. He found a cartridge imbedded in the roof. A recent magazine article prompted him to give it to the Dallas FBI, which sent it to the lab. The lab's reports state that the bullet "is entirely different from any ammunition specimens examined in connection with the assassination evidence. It could not have been fired in the assassination rifle owed by Oswald" [62–109060–5908].

While the probability is that that particular bullet had been fired during the assassination is not high, the Dallas FBI's reason for rejecting it after receiving a phone call from FBIHQ, "requesting further clarification concerning the location of the found cartridge," is, "the building at 1615 Stemmons Freeway would not be in any way in the line of fire" from the TSBD window from which allegedly Oswald fired.

Finding the *cartridge* on the roof, *not* a bullet, indicates a shot fired from there, not ending there, as certainly these experienced FBI agents knew. So whether it could have been fired from the so-called

Oswald window is an irrelevant contrivance (FBIHQ 62–109060–5908, 5987).

Rex Olivier was working with a Texas highway department crew slightly to the west of the scene of the crime, near the Commerce Street exit of the Stemmons Freeway, in the fall of 1969, when he found a weathered, corroded bullet. The engineer on the job, in the words of the Dallas letter to FBIHQ, "suggested it may be the 'third bullet,' which he had heard about in connection with the assassination" [DL 89–43–8869]. Five days later Dallas sent this bullet to the lab (FBIHQ 62–109060–6787), for no apparent reason because its report concludes "that this bullet is different from any ammunition examined in the assassination case and could not have been fired from the assassination rifle." With this the preordained conclusion, and I known of no exception, why do all the work, and go to the time and expense to make any lab study anything but the caliber? That alone precluded its being "fired from the assassination rifle." But, of course, the more work of this kind the FBI did, the more it artificially inflated its statistics, which are its traditional response to almost any criticism.

Wayne Hartman, a manufacturer's representative, and his wife Edna, were far from alone in reporting bullet impacts in Dealey Plaza. They were in the Plaza moments after the assassination and reported seeing a gouged-out place in the grass south of Elm Street, a point identified in the FBI FD302 interview reports only in terms of pictures not attached to it, and thus not in the hands of anyone reading the report. The pictures also are not described. This can have significance because news photographers took pictures of Deputy Sheriff Buddy Walthers and an unidentified man in the Ivy League-style suit Hoover preferred for FBI men then picking something up from the grass not far from the Elm Street south curb.

There also were eyewitness reports of seeing bullet impacts on the manhole cover at that point and near it. These are not mentioned in the records relating to the Hartmans (FBIHQ 105–82555–4877, pages 42–46).

More than a month after the Dallas FBI interviewed the Hartmans, it took a metal detector to the area (DL 100–10461–8027, 8028). It reported finding no bullet or fragments of bullet, only "one bottle cap and one aluminum plug," of which it gave the dimensions.

The FBI resorted to other means to deprecate what both Hartmans reported seeing, that has some confirmation in the pictures and reports of others. It proceeded to do no more about it, having made it appear that what the Hartmans said was false. But the very next pages in this sequence from one of those volumes of collected individual reports (in FBIHQ 105–82555–Section 207, pages 42–45), an insert, numbered page 46 from Dallas, points relevance out in stating that a piece of President Kennedy's skull had been found near the spot where the Hartmans saw this gouged-out area of turf; that this spot pointed out by the Hartmans was "in line with the shot that struck President Kennedy in the head" and that it is "not in a direct line with the mark on the curb," where that acknowledged "missed" bullet hit, causing Tague's wound, a polite way of saying it could not be associated with that impact.

The initials of the agent who dictated this report, "ARS," are not the initials of any agent assigned to the Dallas office the day of the assassination.

But, if ARS had been in Dallas the day of the assassination, he might have known of some newspaper pictures taken, as the Dallas office would have known if it had not ignored all the pictures it could avoid, of a group of four men close to the curb on the grass on the south side of Elm Street, who were photographed in a manner coinciding almost perfectly with, ARS's words, "in line with the shot that struck President Kennedy in the head."

These pictures were taken soon after backed-up traffic again was permitted to use Elm Street. And that, almost certainly, eliminated any evidence, like bullets, that may have been in the street.

The Hertz clock on the TSBD roof shows it was before 1 P.M. That picture, in which Deputy Sheriff Buddy Walthers is seen lighting a cigarette, appears to have been the last in this series because the others show him with an unlit cigarette. There are four men in focus. In addition to Walthers there is a uniformed Dallas policeman whose badge number cannot be made out because he does not face the camera; a man who in one picture is holding a light-weight topcoat (it had rained that morning) and who is in a suit that appears to be rather Ivy League; and a man wearing a light-weight waist-length pale zippered jacket.

First Walthers and then the man dressed as if for his office reach down for an object that this man picks up from the grass not much more than a foot from the curb. It cannot be identified. He appears to have left with it. When only Walthers and the policeman remain in the camera's view, facing each other, in line between the lens and that easternmost sixth-floor TSBD window is what appears to be a clump of sod of about two inches on the side facing the camera. It is midway between Walther's right shoe as he lights his cigarette and the policeman's left shoe, no more than a foot from either.

Whoever the suited man was, he had to have been someone with some kind of authority in order for the policeman and the deputy sheriff to permit him to pick up whatever had interested them and go off with it. The most perfunctory investigation by the FBI or the local police would have determined what this object was and what connection it could have had with the assassination. This is consistent with the Hartmans' account of what they saw at about that time— the account the FBI undertook to discredit.

If two additional shots were not reported by the best eyewitnesses, then they each gave solid, dependable eyewitness accounts to disprove that impossible single-bullet theory. Each of these eyewitnesses should have been interviewed by Specter, or he should have had then interviewed. It did not happen.

Of the four Dallas motorcycle policemen flanking the President, the two on his right were Jim Chaney and Douglas Jackson. All investigations studiously avoided both of them.

My interest in Chaney came from what Specter and the Commission knew when they flumed up their "solution." My source is their testimony. It has been publicly available since my first book, *Whitewash*, the book of which I gave copies to Humes and Boswell and to all members of the Commission. Referring to the Commission testimony of Marrion Baker, the motorcycle policeman who had that dramatic confrontation with Oswald in the TSBD second-floor lunch room at the Coke machine after the assassination, the confrontation in which Baker had his revolver or pistol in Oswald's stomach, that is what *Whitewash* says:

Unsolicitedly, Baker also offered the Commission unwelcome evidence of the invalidity of its conclusions that a single bullet hit both the President and the Governor. He quoted Officer Jim Chaney, one of the four flanking the presidential car. *Chaney said he saw a separate bullet hit the Governor* and that he had so informed the chief of police [emphasis added]. [*Whitewash*, page 38]

With this testimony from a policeman, the Commission did not call Chaney as a witness or ask the FBI to interview him.

In November 1968, when I was in Dallas and learned that Chaney had been interviewed by radio station KLIF, I spoke to the man who owned it, Gordon McClendon, and asked him if would be kind enough to let me have a dub of that Chaney interview. McClendon told me that was impossible because all the station's tapes had disappeared. However, he said, he could provide me with at least some of what Chaney said because before the tapes disappeared, he had produced a phonograph record using those assassination-day tapes. He said he thought he might still be able to find one. He did and he mailed it to me.

Chaney is the first of the eyewitnesses interviewed on this record. He said he had thought the first shot was a backfire, had turned in the direction from which he thought it had come, and had just turned back to look at the limousine when he saw the second shot hit the President. His words are: "It struck him in the face." He clearly meant the front. But, even if he did not mean that, his recorded account, recorded as soon as the reporter could reach him after the shooting, disputes the official solutions. Because what he said was known, it is a reasonable presumption he was not interviewed because the FBI did not want it on file and did not want to contend with what he would say that would refute the official story. (From the phonograph record, "The Fateful Hour.")

Earlier we quoted a September 4, 1975, letterhead memorandum (DL 89–43–9614) to the Dallas special agent in charge from an agent whose name was obliterated by the FBI in processing the Dallas records for disclosure to me in CA 78–0322, later consolidated with

CA 78–0420, for disclosure of the similar New Orleans records. The spurious reason claimed was to protect the privacy of the FBI's agents, but in fact, there was no privacy to protect. Remember, the FBI had given me lists of all the Dallas agents, complete with their home addresses and even private home telephones. Aside from harassment, delaying the litigation and disclosures, and making use of the FOIA cumbersome, time-consuming, and costly for requesters and the courts, there was no reason for these withholdings after the disclosure of the lists of names and addresses. In addition, for the first half of the records disclosed, these names had not been withheld. So the purpose of withholding, if there was one other than those above, could have been to make it difficult in the future to correlate poor or bad or dishonest performances by agents with their names.

This is the memorandum in which that agent reported that Dallas Chief of Police Jesse Curry believed that "two men were involved in the shooting" [DL 89–43–9614].

In eliminating the name, the FBI failed to withhold the initials. "CTB" can be only Charles T. Brown, Jr. (He then lived at 916 Beechwood Drive in the Dallas suburb of Richardson. His phone was Ad5–3016.)

In this memo Brown unbagged other cats.

He recounted bumping into Dallas Police Lieutenant Jack Revill. His first reference to what Revill said required translation from FBI circumlocution into plain English because, as Brown formulated it, only a few of the very few authentic subject experts would have the remotest notion of what was being talked about. Few would know either that it reflects Revill's revenge, sticking his needle in the FBI's arm in return for the problems it had caused him and the police, when Revill had told the truth, one Hoover did not like:

"LT. REVILL expressed sympathy for Special Agent JIM HOSTY and his present publicity in the press concerning the assassination of President Kennedy."

Hosty, the Dallas Oswald case agent, had blurted out to Revill only moments after Oswald was arrested "at about 2:50 P.M." that the FBI "had information that this Subject was capable of committing the assassination of President Kennedy" [November 22, 1963, letter from Revill to Captain W. P. Gannaway, Special Services Bureau, executed as an affidavit April 7, 1964]. Revill was then Lieutenant, Criminal Intelligence Section. On March 1, 1980, the *Dallas Morning News* reported his promotion from captain to assistant chief of police.

When the police disclosed this information to protect itself from criticism for not having had Oswald under surveillance, Hoover had ordered Shanklin to force Curry to get on nationwide TV and apologize and retract his truthful statement as untruthful. After Curry did that, Hoover broke off all relations with the Dallas police. Proof was leaked to the *Dallas Times Herald* from inside the Dallas FBI office as soon as Shanklin's retirement was secure. It is the publicity relating to this leak that Revill, to whom it all traces, was really talking about.

The essence of the leak was that two weeks or so before the assassination Oswald left a threatening note for Hosty with the office receptionist, Nannie Lee Fenner. It was in an unsealed envelope, and several FBI employees read it. Oswald believed that Hosty was giving his wife, Marina, a rough time. This was his complaint over which he made threats.

During the FBI inspector general's investigation forced by the leak, Fenner signed three affidavits.* She consistently attested that Oswald's note to Hosty said: "Let this be a warning to you. I will blow up the FBI and the Dallas Police Department if you don't stop bothering my wife." [FBIHQ 62–109060 7229X, 7314X, Part 2, and 7407X].(The "X" number indicates a later insertion into a report already serialized whose number precedes the "X".)

The leak to the paper forced an FBI investigation of the FBI by its inspector general. This self-investigation, hard as it tried, could not avoid confirming that Oswald had threatened to blow up the FBI office or police headquarters, or both. Recollections differed after a dozen years. As soon as Oswald was killed, Shanklin ordered Hosty to destroy the note, and although neither the FBI's investigation of itself nor one by the House Judiciary Committee's FBI subcommittee

---

*The author has made duplicate copies of all the records of this investigation he obtained in the FOIA lawsuit and placed them in his "subject" file, so in the future it will be necessary to examine the great volume of records in which those on any one subject may be scattered. This file includes a separate file on each of the persons who were interviewed and signed statements or affidavits and separate files on all the principals.

established it, the untitled tickler disclosed by the FBI to my friend Mark Allen, that I describe as a damage-control tickler in "Dirty Linen" is explicit: "Hosty note destruction: handled by Bureau [i.e., FBIHQ] on Nov 24 and effect subsequent days."

This is what Brown referred to as *Hosty's* "present publicity"!

Revill's revenge continued, in Brown's formulation of it, with his having told Brown that he had just spoken to Chaney and that Chaney told him "that he had never been interviewed by anyone following the assassination to obtain his observations as a witness." Brown checked the indices. They confirmed that the FBI had never interviewed Chaney.

Brown also checked the list of Warren Commission witnesses. Chaney was not one. Brown then provided the references to Chaney in the Warren Commission's testimony. There are four. Of one, to Volume III, page 161. What Brown reported motorcycle policeman Marrion Baker had testified to is that Chaney " 'was on the right rear of the car or to the side.' " Reference is to the President's limousine. Chaney and Douglas Jackson were the closest police escorts on the President's right, B. J. Martin and Billy Hargis were on his left.

Brown's quotation is correct, but entirely out of context. It was in response to the question about Chaney, "Where was he?" by David Belin, after Baker had testified to what Chaney had told him the afternoon of the assassination, quoted earlier from *Whitewash*. Baker quoted Chaney as telling him "that the two shots hit Kennedy first, and then the other one hit the Governor." Brown could not have missed reading this, yet he omitted it in his answer to Belin. This, of course, refutes the official explanation of the shots and at the same time refutes Specter's single-bullet theory.

Belin, he of the St. Vitus mouth in self- and Commission defense, asked for not a word of further information from Baker about Chaney's *observation* of the impact of the shots that disputes the official theories, and neither he nor any of the Commission's stalwart assistant counsels demanded that Chaney be called as a witness.

Brown's memo was rushed to Deputy Associate Director James Adams, reaching him late that afternoon. Adams was then the FBI's number three man. Further exchanges ensued, including long-distance phone calls. (All the relevant records are not used or cited here.

Those desiring a fuller account are referred to the FBIHQ "Oswald" file 105–82555, in which the next record to be cited is Serial 5736 and the Dallas "Oswald" file 100–10461 and its JFK assassination file 89–43. The FBI does not file is records chronologically. They are filed as they are processed for filing by the clerks. And records that were delayed in reaching the files would thus appear later than their dates. See also my subject file under "Hosty Flap".)

At 6:43 P.M., four days later, on September 8, slugged "urgent," Dallas teletyped FBIHQ a report on its Chaney interview. In seven pages it makes no mention of Chaney's observations that dispute the FBI's and the Commission's theorized "solutions" of the crime. It omits nothing that supports those theories presented as facts.

Brown did provide the names of other policemen in the President's motorcycle escort.

Not one of the eighteen was interviewed by the FBI! (FBIHQ 62–109060–7256)

Chaney also told Brown that Jackson had never been interviewed. Brown confirmed this from the Dallas files and the Warren Commission's list of witnesses. He also said in this teletype, that "Chaney stated that Jackson has retained notes made by him following the assassination as to his observations." Dallas recommended that Chaney be interviewed. In the FBI that remains Byzantine after Hoover's death, this means that Dallas actually wanted FBIHQ approval to interview Chaney, one of the ignored witnesses—twelve years after it should have interviewed all eighteen!

In the General Investigative Division at FBIHQ this and other related communications led to a four-page memo to be bucked upward. (FBIHQ 62–109060–7256). It continues the cover-the-ass nature of these records in attempting to justify the neglect of the Dallas FBI in not interviewing the policemen who observed the crime. With no inhibitions coming from truth, it says, "The Dallas Office interviewed numerous people who were in the immediate vicinity on foot and had a better view of the area." The "view" of the "area" has nothing at all to do with the impact of the shots as seen by those closest of all to JFK. Chaney was only a few feet from him, with nothing between them to block his vision. Jackson was on Chaney's right. As it relates to any view of the impact and on the victims, this memo disgresses and is irrelevant, as it avoids the relevant truth without technically lying.

In seeking to justify Dallas's avoidance of all eighteen police eye-witnesses, this memo reflects that, in the JFK assassination case, "specific instructions were issued from FBIHQ regarding certain aspects of the investigation, but none have been located relating directly to interviews of assassination witnesses."

Dallas FBI said that FBIHQ gave no written instructions on interviewing any or all assassination witnesses to its office in charge of the field investigations, and that it required instruction before interviewing witnesses!

At FBIHQ the actual author of this memo was Special Agent W. E. Nettles. He prepared another one September 16, 1975, for the same routing and bucking (FBIHQ 62–109060–7345). Whether or not the other records of this series reached him, this memo of the sixteenth led the new FBI Director, Clarence Kelley, to ask in a handwritten note at the bottom of the record copy, "How many such officers are there?" or, how many did you not interview?

In this memo Nettles recounted that FBIHQ had received the Dallas teletype of its Jackson interview (62–109060–7344) and included the briefest summary of it. The summary includes reference to Jackson's "notes" and repeats he had not been interviewed by the FBI or Commission (FBIHQ 62–109060–7345). The next day, the seventeenth, Brown filed an FD302 report on his Chaney interview he said was nine days earlier, on the eighth. Again, he includes only what can be interpreted as supporting the official theories (FBIHQ 62–109060–7369). Part of the same serial at FBIHQ is the Dallas Jackson interview of the fifteenth dictated on the sixteenth.

It was by two agents, names obliterated, the one who dictated having initials not of any agent assigned to the Dallas office on November 22, "DHI." While this report is also intended to support the official theories as much as possible, it does attribute to Jackson several statements about the shots that can have the opposite effect. This report again reflects that the FBI avoided getting the available copy of Jackson's long memoirs the FBI describes as "notes."

One of Jackson's statements was that Connally reacted to the first shot by turning to his right, and with the second shot, Jackson "saw CONNALLY jerk to his right." This can be interpreted as confirming

Connally's testimony that he heard the first shot, which did not hit him, and was struck by the second shot.

Jackson saw "President KENNEDY struck in the head above his right ear, and the impact of the bullet exploded the top portion of his head, toward the left side of the presidential vehicle." There is no attempt to reconcile how a shot to the head above the right ear could explode all the brain matter and tissue of the head, spreading out to the left, as seen so graphically in the Zapruder film, if that shot had come from straight in back of the President, where it had to have originated if Oswald fired it.

At the hospital, to which Jackson and Chaney led the motorcade, he helped place Connally on a stretcher. By then Mrs. Kennedy had stopped refusing to permit the removal of the President. Jackson then did that with a Secret Service agent who "observed a massive wound of the President's left forehead and used his coat to cover the President's head as he was being transported into the hospital."

This, too, is inconsistent with the official account of the wounds and with the available leaked autopsy photographs and the medical artist's rendition of them for the HSCA.

Kelley was placated by that FBI's account of these two policemen confirming the official story, when in fact they did not. No additional policemen in the escort were interviewed. It all just dropped dead in the FBI's files. The FBI believed it could get away with this most deliberate and grossest of negligence, and it did.

While being careful not to obtain Jackson's memoirs, Dallas was also careful to cover its own ass. It did this in the penultimate sentence of the report: "Jackson advised immediately following his release from duty on November 22, 1963, he prepared a detailed written account of the above incident and had maintained it in his possession since that time."

As this quotation indicates, I found quite provocative the failure of all the agencies to interview the best of witnesses, the eighteen professional police of the presidential escort, except for two, who so belatedly could not be avoided. I found it even more provocative in reading FBI records, in which with Jackson all but thrusting his memoir on them, they refused to get, read, and send it to FBIHQ. So I asked my friend Henry Wade, then Dallas district attorney and a former FBI agent, if he would please ask Jackson to let me have a copy. Instead of Xeroxing a copy, Henry thoughtfully had his secretary type it. Jackson had a limited education. He made some spelling and grammatical errors that I correct in quoting it. It is a warm, quietly emotional, detailed, and precise account of his day that began with his pride at being called upon for the second time to escort his President (the first was when Kennedy was there for the 1961 burial of former House Majority Leader Sam Rayburn) and that concludes with his unexpected, additional honoring by the Secret Service which asked him to improvise and lead the escort of the procession with the corpse from the hospital to *Air Force One* and the sad flight to Bethesda, the additional tragedy of the incompetent, inadequate, and military dominated and controlled autopsy.

Five years after the FBI interviewed Jackson (twelve years after it should have), he told Wade that it had read his memoirs, but did not keep it or make a copy of it. (Wade's letter is in author's files.)

Jackson describes the police plan for the escort, the landing of the planes, of which there were three, and referring to the motorcycle policemen, himself included, as "Motor Jockeys," gives a more detailed and precise account of the trip into town and through the crowds, asking JFK to stop, than I have seen anywhere. Although the FBI's versions of what he said has him never closer than twelve feet to limousine, his own account has Chaney on his left almost touching it, he almost touching Chaney, with his right handlebars "hitting people in the stomach," in places the crowds were that dense.

After they had turned onto Elm Street, he heard the first shot while not looking at the limousine. He turned to look at it "and saw Mr. Connally jerk back to his right . . . I could see a shocked expression on his face." After seeing President Kennedy's head explode, he and Chaney led the limousine to Parkland Memorial Hospital.

Jackson's own and detailed account of getting the victims into the hospital does not include seeing any "massive wound" of the left forehead of the FBI report of his interview with them—no wound is mentioned at all, but it says that the left eye "bulged" out.

He helped place both victims on stretchers, and thus had a good look at them. When they reached the door to the emergency room, the Secret Service asked him to stand guard there "and not to let anybody but doctors and nurses in."

For what he there saw, heard, and did he should on that basis alone have been used as a witness because of events in controversy and for the historical record.

Access to the halls and the immediate area was not denied. People walked up and spoke to him until the hospital security chief, O. P. Wright, a former Dallas chief of police to whom Jackson refers as "Pokey," asked him not to do that.

Jackson even provided the mayor with radio communications with his motorcycle radio.

He was a good, caring, conscientious, and competent cop, who performed well under the extraordinary emergency conditions, and he was a witness to much. In anything that could be considered a real investigation he was an important witness.

But nobody wanted any real witnesses. Distressed that his own police department had no interest in asking him anything at all when there was but one other person closer to the President when he was assassinated, Jackson wrote his memoir out that night at home.

His account does have Connally hit by the second bullet, not the first. Chaney, as quoted by Baker, had Connally hit by the third, not the first bullet.

Whether or not these were among Lundberg's "many other shots" that he told *The MacNeil/Lehrer Newshour* could have been fired that day, all the evidence, save for some mistaken ear witnesses, is that there had to have been.

Lundberg apparently is so ignorant he was unaware of his own assault on their personal and professional integrity, on that of his gang, particular the prosecutors, on the *Journal* he edits, and on its parent, the AMA. He did this in his admission of more shots on that telecast. There are many simple disproofs of the official solutions that his gang endorsed. One is more than three shots. So here Lundberg said there very well could have been more shots, "many" more than three shots, while he simultaneously insists the Warren Report is correct.

Under oath the prosectors, along with just about all the other doctors, testified that the single-bullet theory is impossible, yet they, too, insisted in *JAMA* that the Report, which without the single-bullet theory *is* impossible, is correct, and they lustily endorse it.

There were reports of additional bullets being fired, but not a single one of these reports was ever really investigated. They were deprecated when they could not be ignored, and those who made the reports were made to appear irresponsible, or as fabricators of false reports.

The FBI's dismissal of other bullets merely because they would not fit in the rifle they said Oswald used would be ludicrous if it were not that the FBI refused to make the investigation obviously required at the outset and thereafter.

In a sense the Commission is even more guilty than the FBI because it was supposedly in charge. It had the legal authority to be in charge. It also knew about the other shots and treated them as the FBI did, as irrelevant, not on the basis of evidence, but on the simple basis they would, any one, destroy the Report designed to meet the demands of the initial preconception, of Oswald's lone guilt. This was the intent of the Katzenbach-Hoover conspiracy.

How can Specter be excused for having the Report state that all the doctors said his single-bullet theory was possible, when they all said the exact opposite? The officially admitted shooting alone required as an absolute minimum at least one additional shot because all the experts who tried found it impossible to duplicate the shooting attributed to Oswald by Specter's theory with the time limit imposed by the Zapruder film.

How can Belin be excused for ignoring the testimony he personally took that Connally was not struck by the first bullet, indispensable in the single-bullet theory that is indispensable in the Report?

There is no point in asking how the FBI can justify the negligence reflected in its own records, when its record in obfuscating and misrepresenting what happened in the JFK assassination in its massive cover-up is proof of Lord Acton's wisdom when he said that power corrupts; absolute power corrupts absolutely.

For all practical purposes the FBI is a law unto itself, answerable to nobody and immune in all offenses.

From the record Lundberg made with these two issues of *JAMA*, he also is a law unto himself, and he, too, is immune in all offenses. Witness the fact that he remained editor after the first disgraceful issue to produce the second one.

For this the American Medical Association is responsible. And for that being possible, the major media are responsible. They abdicated their critical responsibilities in a society like ours.

Or, as my work in this field now for more than three decades has shown over and over again, in times of crisis and thereafter, all the basic institutions of our society have failed us and our system of freedom through self-government.

In Orwellian fashion the Katzenbach-Hoover conspiracy protected the conspiracy to kill President Kennedy by lying about the number of shots that were fired during the assassination. With the official solution impossible in its three-shots-only scenario, it was even more impossible, if that can be, with any more than three shots being fired or with the official explanation of its three-shot limit having caused all the wounds officially admitted, and there is the most probative evidence that even that is not true.

There is nothing secret in this chapter. *All the FBI records I used are those I obtained by those many FOIA lawsuits. They were the records of the FBI itself. They were all available to the Commission. It had many of them. All those with FBIHQ file identifications were available to the major media before I obtained copies of them. All of those of the Dallas FBI office became accessible to others, the major media in particular, once the FOIA was amended in 1974.*

But nobody cared enough to examine carefully and critically all that were available, or to make the effort to force the disclosure of and obtain the FBI's Dallas and New Orleans records that I could not make for four years until 1978.

After I made those records available to all beginning in 1978, nobody really gave a damn about them, the major media especially having no interest in them at all. All failed to see what was right there in the open to be seen and understood, and as in Stevenson's tale, up became down and in became out. All the many evidences of the firing of more than the three shots stand outside the official account of how the Kennedy administration came to its end.

Nobody wanted the professional observations of the many police who the FBI and Commission ignored because they condemned the official "solution" to its much deserved hell in proving the account of the shooting to be false and dishonest—official lies.

This is what prescient Orwell told us, that in rewriting history, rewriting the past, Big Brother controlled the future.

This was the effect of the conspiracy not to solve the crime or make it solvable that protected the conspiracy to kill.

Whatever may be thought of the many officially ignored shots reported by others, beginning in this chapter with Aldredge, whose observations were confirmed by the FBI itself, Chaney and Jackson were experienced, professional policemen, or professional criminal observers. They were also physically closer to the victims of the assassination than anyone else. This fact was known immediately to all the official so-called investigators. Without exception, beginning as Jackson recorded so dolefully, with his own Dallas police superiors, not a single one gave a damn—not a single one wanted to know the truth about the assassination.

Jackson did everything he could to get the FBI to accept his touching, detailed, and informative memoir he wrote out that very evening so there would be a record of what he knew, saw, and did. The FBI refused to have a copy of it.

Had a single reporter who covered the assassination had the slightest interest in learning the truth, in obtaining fact from other than official handouts, the eighteen motorcycle policemen in the motorcade were obviously the best sources for them. None were more obvious or better than the four flanking the presidential limousine.

Of them, the most obviously best were Chaney and Jackson.

KLIF alone interviewed Chaney and reported what he saw and said.

Not a single one spoke to sorrowing Jackson.

Had the major media met their traditional responsibilities and interviewed Chaney and Jackson and published their eyewitness accounts, it would have been difficult if not impossible for the conspiracy not to investigate the crime to succeed. And if the reporting had been done in the traditional way, immediately, the day of the assassination, it might have been possible for the actual conspirators to be identified and apprehended.

Throughout this book there are many redundant proofs of the fact that there was a conspiracy to kill President Kennedy—which automatically would mean changing his policies.

None is more comprehensible than the impossibility of the official description of the effects of the three shots officially admitted to have been fired, or than the proof that more than three shots were fired because the official "death rifle" could not have fired the three admitted shots, thus it could not have fired any more than three in the time permitted. Each proved that there was a conspiracy to kill.

And all of this was right out in the open—unseen by the investigators or the major media.

The institutions to protect us failed us. They failed themselves, too.

These failures made it possible for the conspiracies to succeed.

To paraphrase the old saying, lest our institutions guard us, the watchman waketh in vain.

Except to shine a light into the future, a light of knowledge and of understanding, so that those who failed, fail not in the future.

Chapter 33

Never Again!

HOW TO CONCLUDE A BOOK LIKE THIS?

Never Again! states its conclusions at the very outset: A government conspiracy saw to it that the crime was not investigated, that there would be no leads to be followed later by others, and thus that the crime would never be solved.

Never Again! then shows how this was done, and to a degree, by whom.

Never Again! reports who lied, misrepresented, ignored, and invented evidence so that the scheme would succeed. (It does not discuss all those who did, of course; there were too many.) In doing this, it reports a great volume of the misrepresented truth and the lies.

In doing this, *Never Again!* proves, with official evidence only, that the crime was the end product of a conspiracy, establishing beyond a question of doubt at the same time that those who foisted off the knowingly false solution to President John F. Kennedy's assassination were well aware of the official evidence that proved theirs was a false solution, one they invented that conforms with the conspiracy.

In reporting some of the misrepresented, distorted, and lied-about official evidence, *Never Again!* explains what that evidence means.

Never Again! exposes the American Medical Association's politicizing of the tragedy through its *JAMA*, with contemptuous disregard for the established, publicly available fact, without regard for any professional responsibilities, while pretending that this fact did not exist. It says and it proves that the AMA had become a partisan, a propagandist.

Never Again! uses this *JAMA* misrepresentation of the fact and

409

reality as illustrative of the major media and their failings in reporting and nonreporting on the assassination and on its investigations.

Never Again! states and shows how all the basic institutions of our society failed us in that time of great crisis and ever since then. And that all of this combines to be a threat to our society.

There is much, much more than can be included in any one book, even one as large as this one, which is limited to addressing as fully as possible what was raised so dishonestly by *JAMA* and publicized so unquestioningly and extensively by the major media. One of these matters is the reaction to the truth when first brought to light in my first books and the first few of those that followed it, before the conspiracy theorizers preempted the field in all the media and in public appearances. There is no way in which straightforward fact can compete in exciting audiences with those who, in making their theories up, could make them as attractive and as exciting as novels.

Which, in fact, is what most were.

In pretended response to the earliest and factual criticism of the Report, then necessarily limited to the Report and its twenty-six volumes of appendix, the Commission's members, staff, apologists, and sycophants demanded that "new evidence" be produced. Prominent in making this demand was Commission member Gerald Ford.

Inherent in this phony demand for new evidence when faced with criticism of the Report was the assumption that the "old" evidence supported the Commission's conclusions when it was in fact this very "old" evidence—the Commission's own evidence—that proved its Report to be wrong. To make this clear is one of my reasons for the verbatim extensive use of what was publicly known, this "old" evidence, instead of rewriting it.

The media played this phony nonresponse as legitimate for all the world, as though there was something wrong with the "old" evidence that was officially misrepresented, ignored, hidden, or lied about.

All the initial criticism of the official "solution" was based on the available official evidence. There was no need for any new evidence at all. There was not a thing wrong with this "old" evidence except that it disproved the official solution. Thus there was no other response the Commission, members, staff, and their supporters and apologists could make other than to pretend that its conclusions were fairly and honestly based on all the official evidence. This was a very big lie. They got away with it because the media accepted it, and for no other reason.

There was nonetheless an abundance of "new" evidence. It was new in the sense of existing in official hands and files and being officially ignored, misused, or misrepresented. *Never Again!* makes this obvious by being restricted to the official evidence, particularly what I had already made publicly available. All of that was based on and contained quotes from the ignored or misrepresented "old" evidence. That it had been ignored or misrepresented made it the "new evidence" the Commission members, staff, and apologists demanded.

The pretense that the Report was supported by all the official evidence and that new evidence was required even to question it was baloney, and even as baloney it was phony.

None of what the government perpetrated would have been possible without that great curse to freedom and the proper functioning of representative society: secrecy. Where secrecy was neither justified nor necessary. It was invoked for improper purposes. *All* of the Commission's testimony and *all* of its exhibits were kept entirely secret until they were all published at one time in a massive indigestable lump, first of the 912-page Report and then of the estimated 10,000,000 words in its 26 appended volumes. If the hearings had not been held entirely in secret, the Report as issued would not have been possible because the underlying testimony would have been reported and so severely criticized that what I first understated by describing as the "whitewash" and then as the "cover-up" would have been exposed enough to prevent publication of anything like the Report.

Just imagine: the Commission even classified as TOP SECRET the testimony it was to publish!

The use of that classification is limited to what can lead to war and similar disasters!

Moreover, *the Commission lacked the legal authority to classify anything!*

Without secrecy, excessive, entirely unnecessary, and unjustifiable secrecy, the government conspiracy could not have succeeded. It thus seems reasonable to believe that those who cooked up the scheme expected to be protected by secrecy.

What a scandal it would have been if it had been known that before the victim was in his grave the government—what had been his government—plotted to see to it that his assassination would not be investigated, would be whitewashed and covered up, and would be impossible to investigate and solve later!

At the least that would have had multitudes protesting in the streets.

While from extensive personal experience in writing *Post Mortem*, I disagreed with some of what Meg Greenfield had written about secrecy in the *Washington Post* of August 13, 1975, there was much truth in her article. I emphasize the last sentence in this excerpt:

> What has come to be the way of life in government and come to be accepted by the courts was later neatly summarized by Meg Greenfield of the *Washington Post*'s editorial staff. In an article dealing with the excesses of intelligence agencies (CIA: Reality vs. Romance,) she addressed the fact and the consequences of official secrecy. One may or may not agree with her opinion, 'I do not think that excessive secrecy in these matters represents nearly so great a threat to the public's right to know as it does to the perspective and judgment of those who live in the world of secrets.' Long experience, more than a decade of it on this subject alone, leaves no doubt that this 'excessive secrecy' has been a constant 'threat to the public's right to know.' This same experience is, however, affirmation of her observation, 'the first and foremost danger of excessive secrecy is that it corrupts the people who hold the secrets' [*Post Mortem*, page 409].

[N.B. As of this writing Greenfield is the *Post*'s editorial page editor and a *Newsweek* Washington columnist.]

It is without question that "excessive secrecy corrupts the people who hold the secrets," as Meg Greenfield wrote.

This, too, is repetitiously proven throughout this book.

All of the doctors whose testimony Arlen Specter took testified that his single-bullet theory, without which a nonconspiracy report was unthinkable, was not possible. Can it be believed that *this* part of the Report would have dared say the exact opposite, that all the doctors testified it was possible, if their testimony had not been kept secret?

Does anyone believe that if the hearings had been in public the Commission, again in Specter's part of its hearings and Report, would have dared ignore Admiral Burkley's official certificate of death? Keeping it secret also made the noconspiracy Report—the intent of the government conspiracy—possible.

Only excessive secrecy made this and many other individual offenses possible. Secrecy enabled the conspiracy to succeed.

But at the time of the hearings as well as since, not one major-media component protested this unjustified and unnecessary secrecy. Not one campaigned for the hearings to be open to the media and to the public.

Would Hoover and Katzenbach have dared articulate their conspiracy if they had any reason to believe that there would be any public inquiry at all? Obviously not. This means that, based on their extensive experience in Washington, they knew they could depend on complete secrecy. Without secrecy, even that past master of both secrecy and deceit, Hoover, would have been pilloried.

The media's failure to insist that all proceedings be open and public made this corrupting secrecy possible.

Yet the fact that all on their own fell into lockstep with this inappropriate and unnecessary secrecy is more of a danger to our constitutional democracy than if they had gotten together and agreed to that major departure from the usual media attitude toward denying the press access.

Major-media attitudes protected the conspiracy from the outset, without the media's even knowing there was a conspiracy. Later the major media ridiculed factual criticisms of the Report. The result is that the impossible official theory, presented as fact, was protected. This, too, is the exact opposite of the traditional role of the media in our society.

The major media's unquestioning acceptance of and praise for *JAMA*'s propaganda reflect their continuing failure.

Quietly, without attracting much attention or comment, the *Post* had reported that there had been a conspiracy to kill the President. Yet its only article in the massive Sunday edition of the day of the twenty-ninth anniversary of the assassination was a snide, smartalekey piece by its Charles Paul Freund. It appeared in the Sunday editorial section, "Outlook."

His "The Crowd on the Grassy Knoll," with the subhead "The JFK Assassination Raising Stakes in the Contest of Confession and Conspiracy," was given about seventy-five cubic inches of space, beginning on the first page. It ridiculed and belittled all criticism as nutty, as nothing but a weird assortment of "confessions" and theories presented as fact in which the claimed assassins were virtually standing in line on the grassy knoll.

While Freund did not exaggerate the number, the zaniness, the impossibility, the irrationality, or the unreasonableness of all the amateur, childlike, would-be Perry Masons, he nonetheless did mislead readers into believing that his selection of the far-outs represents all those working in the field, and all that has been written about the assassination and its investigations.

This was the best treatment of the tragedy's anniversary one of the nation's most important newspapers could give its readers? Given the importance and impact of the *Post*, especially in the nation's capital and elsewhere in syndication, this snotty and essentially dishonest article constituted a stout endorsement of the official assassination mythology, particularly inside the government and in the Congress and the courts.

While this is not, and is not presented as, typical of the *Post*'s reporting and articles, it is a fair representation of the major media's attitude and of their abdications and unthinking, unquestioning acceptance of the official assassination mythology. With this lingering attitude after thirty plus years and after so much had been published in the *Post*, it is apparent that Katzenbach, Hoover et al., from their own experiences and observations, had every reason to believe that they would have no problems from the major media they could not handle. Hoover had had many experiences in managing the press. He had even succeeded, as reported in this book, in persuading the *Post* through DeLoach to abandon its editorial endorsement of the appointment of a presidential commission. This is only one example of many.

While Freund's smart-aleck indulgence to commemorate so great a national tragedy is not the most extreme by any means, it is extreme and inappropriate for the *Post*, which has reported the best of all major media on the assassination and its investigations.

That began in its December 18, 1963, issue when its then-medical reporter, the much honored Nate Haseltine, reported that the President's rear nonfatal wounds were "five to seven inches below the collar line" [*Post Mortem*, pages 65–66.] Haseltine gave as his source the report of the Naval Hospital pathologists.

Beginning early in 1967 when news of Jim Garrison's adventuring with the JFK assassination broke, George Lardner became the *Post*'s assassination reporter. He also became by far the best-informed reporter on the subject. He wrote more stories about the JFK assassination than any other reporter. I was often his source when he brought new information to public attention. His reporting of the transgressions of the HSCA, which also began under a general counsel and staff director with his own agenda and preconceptions, was by far the best. It made these official failings a matter of public record and knowledge.

There is only one professional bibliography on the JFK assassination. (Guth and Wrone. *The Assassination of President John F. Kennedy*, Westport, CT: Greenwood Press, 1980) It also evaluates the *Post*'s reporting on the assassination as the country's best.

The *JAMA* spectaculars are closer to typical of the major media, for most of which, as or and in JAMA, there was nothing other than the official assassination party line.

Most of the papers and magazines, all of the TV "specials" and virtually all TV and radio reporting was, for all practical purposes, indistinguishable from official handouts. Without this the official conspiracy could not have succeeded.

Over the years my books have reported the failure of our basic institutions at the time of the assassination and thereafter. With most of the media reporting the official assassination line only and debunking all else, because there is no government control over it as there was in foreign dictatorships, the failings of the major media are more serious. This is because, while not under government control the media voluntarily performed as though they were. Under dictatorships the people know their media are the official mouthpiece and suspect them. In this country the people have no reason for any such suspicions because they know the media are not under the government's control. They therefore assumed at the time of the assassination that the major media's rubber-stamping of the official assassination line was impartial and independent, that it was fair and honest reporting, when in fact most often it was not. There were a few rare exceptions, like Lardner's reporting.

While there was and there remains widespread popular distrust of and disbelief in the official assassination party line, the major media also conditioned themselves to believe this party line by what it did and did not report and how it reported. In its superficiality and snottiness Freund's cheap shot is not atypical of the major media so long after that assassination.

Some of the major media's attitude can be justified by the character of the proliferation of conspiracy-theory books, once publishers learned that books inventing an unproven or untenable theory sold well. Even if they were ignored by the major media, as most were, the TV and radio talk shows loved them and aired their authors extensively and uncritically for the most part. This sold books, books that misinform and mislead, books that turned the major media off, and led younger reporters and editors who were not adults at the time of the assassination to believe that these commercializing and exploiting conspiracy-theory books are all there is on the subject.

This contributed to the major problem faced by serious writers who restricted themselves to fact. We had the need to compete with the proliferating conspiracy-theory books and lecturers who, making it up, could and did make their inventions exciting and attractive.

Caught between both extremes, the people, while never really swallowing the official line, were confused and became more confused as more confusing books appeared to exploit the ready market created by those who wanted information and had no other source for it.

From the first not a single publisher commissioned a single responsible, factual book on the assassination. In more recent years there was nothing too trashy, too obviously fictional, too irresponsible, or impossible to be published. Even a supposedly scholarly publisher, after soliciting two readings by subject experts, both of whom devastated a cheap, fanciful, grossly inaccurate book, published it nonetheless.

At the time of the *JAMA* desecrations of truth and of our history, all sorts of really bad books were hastily reprinted. There was nothing too deplorably bad for greedy publishers to peddle to the American people interested in the assassination of the President and its investigations.

The major media, most minor media, and those conspiracy-theory books all failed, along with all the basic institutions of our society— and that with regard to the crime of the greatest magnitude!

Publishers never had any real interest in factual books on the subject. The few that were published had great difficulty being published, and those few publishers made no real promotional efforts at all. There was one exception. Holt, Reinhart and Winston, after it had been contracted in England by the Bodley Head, published Mark Lane's *Rush to Judgment* with a large and successful promotional campaign. But, by then Lane's book, already dated, held nothing new and was angled to blame Warren and Rankin. It obscured the identities of the counsel, even in supposedly verbatim repetition of the transcripts of testimony. It focused on these two who Lane regarded as his enemies, and thus tended to exculpate staff counsel.

With my earlier publishing of *Whitewash*, I broke the ice for Lane and others.

When, as soon happened, I was alone in publishing factual books based on the official evidence, and for a long time, alone in seeking to compel the disclosure of JFK assassination records that had been kept secret, the middle, in which I was and have always been, was a very lonely place. With no funds for advertising and promotion it was lonelier still.

Those of us who write nonfiction are expected to be dispassionate and neutral, or at least to be or to appear to be, dispassionate and neutral in our writing—unless we are revisionists. Revising the popular conception of John Kennedy, his administration, and where he was seeking to lead us and the world when he was assassinated has been profitable for those who built and are building careers from the effort. They are not expected to be neutral and impartial, and that they are not is accepted.

What I write is not dispassionate, and I am not neutral. What I write is not exaggerated, it is factual and it comes from official records. Some of these records might not have existed if those who created them knew there would be a Freedom of Information Act that would require their disclosure.

For these many years I have been dealing intimately and intensely, with the record and the records of the most incredible, and I do hope never to be repeated, official corruption that permeated our government. Who could possibly believe that an American president could be gunned down on the streets of a large and modern American city in broad daylight, and then be consigned to history with the dubious epitaph of an official conspiracy to ensure that the crime would not be investigated?

A conspiracy that ensured the crime could not be later investigated because it would have and leave no legitimate leads to be followed?

A conspiracy that would be protected and sanctified by a presidential commission of the eminent and the prominent, who had support in all the country's political strata?

Or, that the conspiracy would be further protected and sanctified by the major media that instantly abandoned all their critical faculties, asked no questions at all about the preconceived and preordained official "solution," and fell all over themselves in adulation of a report that cannot be read with an open mind, and then believed?

About all of this and much more, in a country like ours, a writer is to be dispassionate and neutral, to have no strong feelings? To be an emotional, an intellectual, and a literary eunuch?

And still meet his responsibilities in a society like ours, the responsibility of informing the people?

Neutrality and blind compliance is the lot and the role of writers in dictatorships, but it should not be in this country, the very first to ensure a writer's complete freedom under its Constitution's First Amendment, that glorious charter that also imposes obligations on writers, in return for this marvellous freedom.

My writing is factual. It is accurate. It is fair.

But it is not dispassionate. I am not dispassionate, and I believe that those writers with the information I have to take to the people need not and cannot be dispassionate. I cannot be.

All eight of my earlier books are intensely controversial. I name names, without circumlocutions or evasions, but with pointedness and directness. In all the many years since the first of my books appeared, not a single person has written or phoned me to complain about being treated unfairly in any degree, no matter how slight.

The very concept of our precious First Amendment is that writers will not be neutral and dispassionate. It was conceived to protect those who are not. In this our Founding Fathers knew that American writers had not been and would not be neutral and without feelings. They intended licensing, protecting, and encouraging writing that comes from the strongest feelings.

Yet, despite my strong feelings, feelings I believe we all should have about the assassination of a president, a crime that nullifies our entire system of society, and about its official whitewashing and cover-up that we now know were the successful intent of an official conspiracy on the highest level, in all my earlier books in which I documented endless official mendacity, I do not recall using the word "liar" once. And, my! the number of lies and the liars about whom I wrote! Without, I repeat, a peep of complaint from any one of that multitude.

A writer who is not a neuter and does not pretend to be, need not be, and in our country, ought not be or pretend to be a neuter, to have no feelings, or to be required to sublimate them. An American writer should write, I believe, in accord with how he feels about the material about which he writes.

So I have no apologies for not hiding my emotions, or for the first time calling a liar a liar—in each case proving it from the official records I have compiled and leave as a permanent and free public archive.

I am not an apologist for errant government, obviously, and thanks to their great passion and shunning of neutrality, our Founding Fathers gave all writers this right, simultaneously protecting them in asserting this right for themselves and for the people.

I have sought to meet the obligation imposed on writers by this unprecedented charter.

And in going where nobody had gone, the fine and simple, but expressive words of the poet, to leave a path for others—from what I have written and in the massive archive of some sixty file cabinets, most full, and innumerable boxes of once-secret official records.

All writers will forever have free access to all of this. And, I add, all have always had.

*   *   *

When I had almost completed the draft of this book, my dear friend, history professor Dave Wrone, told me, "You must tell the people what they can do!"

I had just begun to think about how to conclude this book when a mature woman friend, who had returned to college when her family was grown and had attended my dear friend Jerry McKnight's "The Politics of Assassinations" course at local Hood College, phoned me on the last day of classes. "What am I to take from this?" she asked, meaning not from her course, but from what she had learned in it.

I think I know: All the major institutions of our society did fail us, and they continue to fail us.

This official conspiracy also saw to it that the crime cannot be solved because, in not investigating the crime itself in 1963 and 1964, it ensured there would be no leads, I fear, forever.

To suggest that based on what I now know the crime can be solved in the future, the longing of so many who have written me over the years, is to deceive and raise false hopes.

What can I tell people to do? Erect and mount barricades? No.

Futilities breed disillusionment and depression, and individually and collectively we need no more of that.

It is possible to give my student friend a partial answer to her question.

Our society, and with it, the world has changed very much since that other day that will long live in infamy, Franklin Delano Roosevelt's characterization of the Japanese attack on Pearl Harbor and elsewhere.

It has not, I hope, changed to the point where a book like this can be accepted with equanimity.

When what this book states and proves, largely with formerly secret official proofs, can happen—and it did happen—in our country, are we any better, except in some degree, than the military dictatorships of my lifetime that we have abhorred, some even when we were helping them establish themselves and survive?

Knowing of these events that I earlier described as only a "whitewash" and a "cover-up," are we now much more than the world's largest "banana republic"?

For good or ill, as one of our most eminent Supreme Court justices, Louis Brandeis, wrote in his landmark case of *Olmstead versus U.S.* (1928), the government is our teacher. For perspective and understanding, a fuller quotation is helpful:

> Decency, security, and liberty alike demand that government officials shall be subject to the same rules of conduct that commands the citizen. In a government of laws, the existence of the government will be imperilled if it fails to observe the law scrupulously. Our government is the potent, the omnipresent teacher. For good or ill, it teaches the whole people by its example. Crime is contagious. If the government becomes a law breaker, it breeds contempt of the law; it invites every man to become a law unto himself; it invites anarchy.

He also wrote that the end justifying the means is a "pernicious doctrine," to which the Supreme Court "should resolutely set its face." Much like this is pertinent in the wisdom of the ages.

In the *Federalist Papers*, a collection of essays written by Alexander Hamilton, James Madison, and John Jay in the 1780s in defense of the new Constitution, in Number Twenty-five Hamilton wrote, "For it is a truth, which the experience of all the ages has attested, that the people are commonly in most danger when the means of injuring their rights are in the possession of those of whom they entertain the least suspicion" [*Mentor* edition. New York: New American Library, 1961, page 164]. Hamilton was writing about the military, but these words, with the passing of time, apply to all branches of the government today.

In a partial answer to the student's question, we can refer to Thomas Jefferson's formulation of the obligation of the press (which includes writers) and the consequences of press failure when he wrote:

> A popular government without popular information or the means of acquiring it is but a prologue to a farce or a tragedy or perhaps both. Knowledge will forever govern ignorance, and a people who mean to be their own government must arm themselves with the power which knowledge gives.

Jefferson also wrote that "no government ought to be without censors, and where the press is free none ever will. The only security of us all is a free press. The agitation it produces must be submitted to. It is necessary to keep the waters pure."

Still another applicable quotation of Jefferson is:

> The great principles of right and wrong are legible to every reader. To pursue them requires not the aid of many counselors. The whole art of government consists of the art of being honest.

We can also cite St. Jerome: "If an offense comes out of the truth, better is it that the offense come than that the truth be concealed."

Of all that is so quotable from Shakespeare, think of the government in the words he wrote for Macbeth's question: "Will all great Neptune's ocean wash this blood clean from my hands?" [Act II, Scene II]

While the government is the most potent and omnipotent teacher, writers also teach, and some of what is here quoted applies also to those of us who seek to provide the "popular information" Jefferson told us the people need to "arm themselves" if they are to be "their own government."

Winston Churchill said what is applicable to governments and addresses that which writers write: "A nation without conscience is a nation without a soul. A nation without a soul is a nation that cannot live."

We have been considering what, in a different context, Tom Paine referred to as "a time that try men's souls." He meant the Revolution: we mean the assassination of our President and the government's conspiracy not to solve it, to keep it from being solved, and to do all that was so wrong to make those wrongs succeed.

In his *Requiem for a Nun* William Faulkner, quoting Gavin Stevens, gives us an epigram that describes the past and forecasts the future of this lingering assassination controversy: "The past is never dead. It is not even past."

In ending these invocations of the wisdom of the ages, two of our most respected presidents stated what I felt and feel in the decades of my work and my writing. The first is:

If the end brings me out all right, what is said against me won't amount to anything. If the end brings me out wrong, ten angels swearing I was right would make no difference.

These words of Abe Lincoln also apply, of course, to the government.

How a writer does hope that Andrew Jackson is again right, as he was proven to be in the 1974 amending of the Freedom of Information Act, in saying that "one determined man becomes a majority."

Armed with this quoted wisdom and with the content of this book, we can ask ourselves questions, and we can answer some with ease, if not with joy or satisfaction. We can, each of us, make an independent assessment of the consequences of the successful government conspiracy, beginning perhaps with the statement by Brandeis and what the government taught with the end product of its successful conspiracy.

Did it not teach dishonesty as a way of life and that dishonesty can succeed?

If only subliminally, is this not in the back of the minds of those who are a large majority, those who do not believe the official "solution" to this great crime?

Has it not also taught by its example that lying, cheating, fraud, and not caring are the way to live—even that you can sometimes get away with murder?

The assassination of John Kennedy did turn this country around. It did turn the world around at the same time. From crime in the streets to the vast self-destructiveness of drugs; to the economy and the national debt and the loss, really the exportation of so many hundreds of thousands of our best jobs probably forever; and with this the simply enormous losses and increased costs and indebtedness from the loss of those industries and the loss of the profits from them, do we not see great change in our country in the wake of the assassination of President Kennedy?

There were, in the aborted Kennedy administration, two separate and distinct Kennedy presidencies. The change came with the Cuba Missile Crisis of October 1962, a frightful confrontation between the superpowers involving the possibility of nuclear war. [N.B. not the *Cuban* Missile Crisis as conventionally held for this formulation prej-

udices the presumption of the nature of the crisis. It had to do with
a Soviet-American policy question, not a Cuban one.] After it Kennedy and Khrushchev began groping toward peace.

In this aftermath Kennedy said in a memorable speech, ''Mankind
must put an end to war, or war will put an end to mankind.''

He undertook to bring this end-to-the-war policy about, and he
stated this to be his policy. In his efforts to reduce the national
treasure wasted in war and in preparation for war, he took a number
of politically dangerous steps. These are reported in the earliest of
the books of those close to him in his White House, particularly
Arthur Schlesinger's *One Thousand Days* (Boston: Houghton Mifflin
Co., 1965) and Theodore Sorensen's *Kennedy* (New York: Harper &
Row, 1965). Kennedy's most forceful restatement of his policy, of
working toward the end of the war that could mean the end of
mankind of not heeded, is in the eloquence of his June 1963 speech
at the American University in Washington. It was, unfortunately, his
last great speech.

Schlesinger reports Kennedy's ideas and thinking that led to this
speech and what it said, and he quotes from it to reflect Kennedy's
thinking and objectives and how he hoped to enlist popular support
by making his effort comprehensible to the people:

'World Peace' is 'the most important topic on earth': Peace
does not mean 'a pax American enforced on the world by American weapons of war': 'We must reexamine our own attitude [to-
ward the USSR]—as individuals and as a Nation—for our attitude
is as essential as theirs' [of this Schlesinger said it is ''a sentence
capable of revolutionizing the whole American view of the cold
war'']: While 'peace would not end all quarrels' it 'does not require that each man love his neighbor—it requires that they live
together in mutual tolerance.' In history 'enmity between states
did not last forever' and 'the tide of time and events will often
bring surprising changes in the relations between the nations.' (He
repeated this before the Irish Parliament, to which he said, 'Across
the gulfs and barriers that now divide us we must remember that
there are no permanent enemies.' He there also referred to 'our
common vulnerability on this planet.' If there is another war 'all
we have worked for would be destroyed in the first twenty-four
hours.' Nonetheless 'we are both caught up in a vicious and dangerous cycle in which suspicion on one side breeds suspicion on

the other and new weapons beget counterweapons.' '... if we cannot end all differences now at least we can make the world safe for diversity' for 'we all inhabit this small planet. We all breathe the same air.... And we are all mortal.' Thus John F. Kennedy believed that the USSR and this country both had 'a mutually deep interest in a just and genuine peace and in halting the arms race' [*One Thousand Days*. Boston: Houghton Mifflin Co., 1965, pages 900-2].

Even though he feared the reaction of his military, a fear of a military revolt, to paraphrase the words of the President's brother Robert, he did try to reduce spending on military extravagance. Even though he feared and had reason to fear that those of opposite view and belief in the Senate would defeat the effort, he did dispatch Averill Harriman to negotiate the first of the efforts to control the nuclear Frankenstein with his limited test-ban agreement.

In sending the experienced diplomat Harriman on his mission to formalize that first halting step toward peace in the world and reducing the mutual emnity of the major powers, Kennedy told him, "regarding possible concessions [Schlesinger's words], I have some cash in the bank in West Germany and am prepared to draw on it if you think I should."

Pulitzer Prize-winning Schlesinger did not translate this so cryptic and so meaningful an empowerment to make it understandable to the average reader.

(Does not this suggest that as war is too important to trust to the general, so also is history too important to entrust to our professional historians? Does not the record of the professional historians and of their prestigious professional journals with regard to the assassination and in its wake also justify the belief?)

Kennedy had no personal bank accounts in Berlin. So, what could he have been telling Harriman to feel free to spend? Is there much else he could have had in mind other than with a reciprocal action he was willing to end NATO if he could end the need for it? However this is interpreted, it cannot mean spending that capital for war and it can only mean spend it if that can bring us meaningful peace.

As Julius Caesar was a fop and a spendthrift at twenty-eight and controlled most of the known world at twenty-nine, in an entirely different sense did John F. Kennedy grow after that October, 1962, missile crisis that could have incinerated the world, when what he was before it is compared with what he became and sought after it. That crisis could have incinerated the world

He had entered office as a cold warrior. Although in "The Torch has been passed to a new generation of Americans" inaugural address he spoke frequently of peace, in practice he initiated no meaningful steps toward it. And his inaugural address also challenged Khrushchev with a "pay any price" theme. He inherited what came to be known as "The Bay of Pigs" fiasco from the Eisenhower-Nixon administration. He did not cancel it. He assumed full responsibility for it when it failed, and that was the beginning of his ever increasing popularity.

But he could earlier have ended that violation of international law, of our United Nations obligations and of so many of our treaties, especially in our hemisphere.

Whatever may be the reason, he did not end it, and he did allow the CIA to proceed with it. (Haynes Johnson's *The Bay of Pigs* is the earliest of a nonrevisionist dependable source on it). [New York: Dell Publishing Co., 1964]

But before he was assassinated he was seeking an end to that conflict on the official level at the United Nations, with our ambassador to it, William Attwood, negotiating with the Cuban ambassador. On the unofficial level, before JFK left on the trip to Dallas where his life ended, he met with the French correspondent, Jean Daniel, and he asked Daniel, to more or less act as an unofficial emissary, feel Castro out on negotiating differences and to report back to him. Daniel was with Castro when Castro learned of the assassination. He wrote movingly about it, published in the United States by *The New Republic*.

There are many other ways in which the basic changes in Kennedy and in his policies can be evaluated. One of his steps toward peace that was fraught with and met with the most serious international consequences was his cancellation of our contract to manufacture "Blue Streak" missiles for Great Britain.

Those who were not his partisans—and I did not being as one— may dispute the basic changes in him. This is not the place to argue that.

It is the place and the point at which to return to what Dave Wrone told me and the student asked me.

It is true, as the earliest calloused, unthinking, and uncaring defenders of the Warren Report actually argued in trying to end criticism of it, that Kennedy is dead and cannot be brought back to life.

That cannot be changed.

It is also true, and I believe this more than all my earlier books show, that there is no real possibility of solving the crime.

So, why not forget it? Why not consign it to history's scrap heap?

Why, in my advanced years and impaired health, have I kept working? And why did I write this book and hope yet to write others?

Three or more of those wise statements of the past provide a means of addressing these interrelated questions.

Oft repeated is the quote: "The past is prologue."

The words of the American philosopher George Santayana, who was also a poet, have been confirmed painfully often: "He who does not learn from the past is doomed to relive it."

And British Lord Acton's "Power corrupts; absolute power corrupts absolutely" so often has been validated by so many demonstrations of such enormous disaster in the world's history since he uttered them, as it had been throughout recorded history.

So we cannot recover the assassinated President. But do we want *this* past to be prologue? Do we want to relive this great national trauma? Would not the nation relive it were another president or other prominent leader assassinated? Do we want to continue to accept the corruption by the absolute power that corrupted so absolutely, beginning almost with the first shot fired in Dealey Plaza? Should those in government of whatever station or agency live and work as all now do, without facing the rebuke of a national refusal to accept the successful conspiracy's abuse of power? Would a national and ongoing condemnation, as much as can be mustered, be a warning for the future?

When I completed my first book in mid-February, 1965, I was naive and optimistic. I believed then, when all the records since rescued and made available were secret, that the crime should and could be solved. I then believed it could be done by the Congress. That belief came from personal experience in working for a Senate investigation and from my wife's on working for two Senate investi-

gations, all three important and somewhat sensational in those effer-
vescent New Deal days. I worked for the Senate Civil Liberties
Committee, my wife for the Senate's Munitions and Railroad Investigating Committee.

It was wrong for me to believe that the members of either House
and their staffs of three decades later would be as determined to
conduct as vigorous and as definitive of investigations as in my day
on Capitol Hill.

How sadly mistaken I was indeed.

My experience with just two Congressional efforts, one in each
house, dispelled this idealistic illusion from my past.

The JFK assassination subcommittee of the Senate's first intelligence committee, known after its chairman as the (Frank) Church
Committee, was under Pennsylvania Senator Richard Schweiker, who
was Ronald Reagan's running mate in 1976, when Reagan ran for
president and was defeated by Jimmy Carter. Schweiker became an
afficionado of conspiracy theories and his subcommittee was a joke,
its slim report deservedly ignored. (Senator Gary Hart, the other
subcommittee member, was inactive on it and later ridiculed that
report.)

I spent the physically most painful morning of my life with the
pleasant and intendedly serious Schweiker and his assistant Dave
Marsden in Schweiker's office en route to the hospital with a venous
thrombosis. Schweiker was addicted to four of the least credible
assassination conspiracy theories. I debunked all four for him with
extensive factual and document data, and left with the impression he
had recognized they had no validity at all. But then the thin report
was issued, and he was still gung-ho for all four. If he had not been,
however, he would have had no report at all.

Two years after the Schweiker disaster, thanks largely to the showing of a very clear pirated copy of the Zapruder film on nationwide
TV and to members of the House of Representatives and their staffs,
the House created its special Committee on Assassinations. Its chief
counsel and staff director was Richard Sprague, former Philadelphia
district attorney. He asked me to confer with him. When I detected
his Perry Mason self-concept, I warned him that from having worked
there I knew the Hill was a different world from the one he envi-

sioned, and that if he conducted himself there as he did as district
attorney, he would find himself "cut off at the knees."

That very evening it happened. Ken Brooten, an assistant who
succeeded Sprague briefly, phoned me to tell me that Sprague had
been fired, that I was "Merlin, remembering the future," and that
he had been a witness to it.

Sprague's permanent replacement was Robert Blakey. He had in-
oculated himself with the mafia-did-it bug, having been on the Department of Justice's organized-crime staff. Blakey could not make
that case, could not include it in his report, but with Richard Billings
of his staff he did write a book alleging it.

Blakey began each hearing with a narration of what would be
developed at it. Each narration was aimed at critics Blakey named
and whose work he cited. All but one. He never once mentioned me.
Debunking criticism of the Warren Report was hardly the way to
run a Congressional investigation of the assassination of President
Kennedy. As a result the committee's own work yielded no new
information at all. The FBI was so openly contemptuous of it that
some FBI records I obtained reveal its plan to at best permit Blakey
to have only some of what had already been disclosed to me. It did,
of course, give him more in response to his specific requests, but
when they were centered around his personal mafia-did-it preconception, what he got was trash.

Blakey had saved for the last what he anticipated would be the
putdown of putdowns of the critics. He had had the tapes of the
Dallas police radio broadcasts analyzed scientifically. That analysis
reported there had been a fourth shot. But because he had saved this
for last, his committee by then had wasted the largest appropriation
in history and was not able to pay for any further investigation.

In seeking to refute all criticism of the official solutions and in
not conducting any real investigation, Blakey had no support for the
scientists' conclusions that a fourth shot had been fired. If he had
not investigated the critics instead of the crime, "Flat-World" Blakey
would have had abundant confirmation of the scientists' conclusion.
He would have had that proven before he could no longer avoid the
tapes of the police broadcasts that were forced on him.

So Blakey was reduced to trying to save face by alleging there
had been a conspiracy, the very thing he had devoted all that staff,

hearings, time, and money to disproving. Broke from his misspent extravagances, he asked the FBI to carry that work forward. The FBI would not; it had it referred to the National Academy of Science, and the academy disputed the interpretations Blakey had gotten from respected authentic experts.

There were these two supposed assassination investigations by the Congress, one by each house, and each failed to accomplish anything worthwhile. Each also made it more than apparent that my 1965 belief that Congress alone could be expected to conduct a real investigation was naive and without recognition of the change that had taken place on the Hill and in our national life.

So, what can be done, what can be expected or hoped for? Could another Congressional investigation do the job that has never been done officially? Sadly, the answer is ''no.''

The major reason, in its simplest form, is that any real investigation of the assassination means a real investigation of the FBI, and no political figure can hope to politically survive the FBI's enmity. The one example, already given, of its lies to the White House about my wife and me, one of many really dirty things it did, and prejudicial lies it told itself and others, illustrates what any political figure can expect of the FBI if it has motive for doing him harm. The slightest criticism of it, from many of its records I have, the FBI does regard as ample motive.

There is no reason to expect any major media interest in seeing to it that they report as much of the unquestionable fact as is possible. They have not in the past. There is no reason to expect that interest now, and there is even less reason to expect it to develop in the future, absent the kind of unexpectable development that demands their interest and involvement. Should that happen, the media's record indicates that the interest and attention will be short-lived. That is all it was when the FBI's general releases were available to it in December 1977 and January 1978. Even then it had so little interest, that in all, the FBI sold only eight sets, at the nominal price of ten cents a page.

What remains are only concerned, caring people, Americans who care about their nation, its honor and its integrity; who care about their basic institutions and their integrity.

There is no glowing promise in preserving interest and continuing to direct attention to this official conspiracy and what its success cost us in self-respect and national integrity, but we owe the effort, whatever forms it may take, to ourselves and to our country.

Not in the sense that it is for some, who have every right to see and to think of that one brief moment that was Camelot.

Not in the hope that we may yet solve the crime.

Not in the expectation that in the disclosure of still-secret records there may be any smoking gun, for there is no reason to believe there is a smoking gun other than of official embarrassment.

Not in any kind of a storybook concept.

Unpleasant as it is, shame of the nation that it is, much as it caused us to lose the decent concern and respect of so many abroad, from pride, national and personal, in our glorious traditions, we must still make the efforts now possible. We must call all the responsible attention we can to the fact that is now established. We must apply any pressure we can on the many official miscreants with public attention to what they did and to what they did not do.

Above all we do not want any repetition of any such conspiracy in the wake of any such crime in the future.

Our presidents, whether we like them or approve of their policies or not, must be free of the fear of a Damoclean sword dangling over their heads—another national inheritance of the unsolved assassination of President Kennedy.

The agencies that failed themselves and all of us so shamefully at the time of that great crisis, and ever since then, most of all the FBI, on whom all of us depend, must be made to see that this once was much too much and that it should never again intend and execute such monumental failures as when President Kennedy was assassinated.

The nation in varying degrees depends on all the agencies that failed, that were dishonest, and they must come to see that they must, for their own self-respect and that of the rest of us, that for them it will be, *"Never Again!"*

Our honor, our self-respect, how the rest of mankind regards us, personally and as a nation, demands of each of us, to the degree possible that we not let this most enormous of national disgraces die of the atrophy of disinterest; that we do whatever may be possible at any time and in any way to see to it that it does not; and that more of us learn and understand the grim truth, and with that resolutely decide that for us and for our government and its agencies and employees the determination will be *Never Again!*

Especially the younger ones among us can learn and understand much of the great cost we all bear if they compare us as a people and our country and its administrations now with then. The changes are great, as the costs have been and will be.

Of what we have lost we can yet regain our self-respect, our personal and national honor, and our integrity. We should long for it, strive for it, recruit others for it, and glory in it as we can even if all we have is the effort itself.

That everlasting flame should not be on the grave alone. It should be in the heart and soul of each of us.

We cannot—we must not—let this invidious government conspiracy succeed any more than it has, and we must hope that we can and do what we can to recover what it cost us and undo what it may be possible to undo of its success, and that of the conspiracy to assassinate that it protected.

Personally and as a nation, this should be a hope and a goal.

NEVER AGAIN!

Epilogue

Nicholas Katzenbach, former deputy attorney general, acting attorney general, and attorney general of the United States, conceived and recorded the conspiracy this book begins by reporting. Thanks to the Freedom of Information Act, which did not exist at the time he connived with J. Edgar Hoover, the record he made is no longer secret.

Not intending anything at all like it, Katzenbach also provides an appropriate epilogue with which we end the book that began with him and his conspiracy.

On February 2, 1993, he wrote an op-ed article for the *Washington Post*. It is titled "No More Independent Counsel." That captures the essence of what Katzenbach wrote at the time Congress was about to consider renewing that function.

The Independent Counsel was enacted during the Nixon Watergate scandals. Nixon had fired several of his attorneys general because they would not ignore the law, whitewash and cover up for him and the crimes against our system for which he and those around him were responsible.

The act requires that the attorney general take the initiative and recommend a special counsel's appointment to a panel of federal judges. They select the special counsel, who is also known as an independent prosecutor.

Thus any administration can prevent the appointment of a special prosecutor by refusing to ask the judges to appoint one. In its last days the Bush administration refused to request an independent prosecutor.

While Katzenbach avoids the direct statement, the thrust of his argument is that "we give the next attorney general a chance to prove that he or she can faithfully and impartially enforce the laws of the United States.'' He did not say ''will enforce.'' They ''can'' enforce the laws but they do not all do that. Witness Katzenbach himself, or before him John Mitchell and a number of others.

With attorneys general going to jail as felons and with others being convicted but escaping jail—true of Mitchell's successor, Richard Kleindienst—and others not enforcing some laws, recent history makes it clear that the nation and its integrity do require that these independent prosecutors be appointed. We can then hope they are not necessary.

But Katzenbach, with that part of his record herein recorded alone, can hardly give us a credible assurance that we can trust all our attorneys general to see to it that the laws are faithfully enforced or to take steps to prevent the kinds of criminality and other serious official misconduct of some recent administrators.

This book does show, as do all my books, that at the time of the assassination of President Kennedy and ever since then, our basic institutions failed us.

In addition to the government conspiracy not to investigate the crime itself, a determination not to solve the crime and not to punish those those who perpetrated it, a major failure came from the major media. *JAMA* is the prime example in this book. But all the major media failed to meet their traditional and essential obligations, to inform the people fully and fairly about major issues.

While we devoted less space and attention to the courts, they also failed. That is the only real reason so many JFK assassination records remained unnecessarily and improperly secret after three decades.

In this the courts not only tolerated but also accepted and rewarded perjury—a serious crime, a felony. Those innumerable perjuries were by those under the attorneys general, mostly by the FBI. These perjuries were presented to the courts by Department of Justice lawyers, some of whom may well have been guilty of the added felony of suborning perjury. There can be no honest government, no justice, when perjury and other serious governmental offenses are unpunished and are disregarded.

Had the major media not protected these serious offenses by not reporting them, they could not have continued succeeding; and after the first few were reported, many fewer would have been dared—if any.

As a result, today government lawyers, especially Department of Justice prosecutors, are immune from the normal disciplining procedures.

There is little doubt that had it not been for the assassination of President Kennedy those who followed him would not have been president. But those who followed him, especially Reagan and Bush, packed the courts with judges who were hardly the best available, who shared their political bent and who could be expected to—and who did—interpret the laws in accord with those political views.

The courts dominated or controlled by these Reagan-Bush political rather than the traditional best-possible appointees have already immunized government prosecutors for anti-American abuses, for violation of rights long established and respected.

Beginning with its January 10, 1993, issue the *Washington Post* published a series of lengthy articles detailing the expansion of the powers of these prosecutors and their immunity from very serious offenses unless the Department of Justice punished them. Which it never did.

Federal judges who were aghast at some of these abuses, dishonesties, and corruptions of our system of justice were overruled by the appointees of those who succeeded Kennedy, particularly those appointed by Reagan and Bush.

By those who were and who could be appointed only because Kennedy was assassinated.

As the *Post* reporter Jim McGee details, this most serious and deeply offensive prosecutorial misbehavior was immunized by the Supreme Court, most of whose justices and its dominating chief justice were appointed by Nixon, Ford, Reagan, and Bush.

Some of those overruled traditional judges were traditional Republicans. But then the prosecutorial abuses were under Republican administrations. Not traditional Republican; postassassination Republican.

Bar association protests were unheeded.

"An eleventh-hour effort to cement" some of these immunities, as *The New York Law Review* reported on February 1, 1993, failed in the very last minute, the last day of the Bush administration only because of an unexpected "slip-up." Proposed originally by then-Attorney General Richard Thornburgh was a change in rules, which "would have had the status of a formal regulation," according to the *Law Journal*. It was published in the *Federal Register* November 20, 1992. After the required public comments the "final rule" was drafted by Attorney General William P. Barr when he had less than six days remaining in office, on January 14. Only by a slip-up was it not formalized the last day of the Bush administration, on January 19, 1993.

The *Law Review* reports that it, along with one hundred other Bush administration regulations that had not yet taken effect, were rescinded by the new Clinton administration.

Remember all that Reagan and Bush incantation that they would give us less government interference in our lives? In addition to all the new rules they promulgated were these one hundred that had not yet taken effect and were killed.

These postassassination administrations were revolutionizing our traditional concepts and standards, even of ethics. As one prominent defense lawyer, quoted in the *Law Review* on what Thornburg and Bush almost got away with, said:

> At a minimum, the rescission of the regulation will allow the organized bar a second chance to make its case to the Clinton administration that the proper course is for the Justice Department to seek desired exceptions from ethical restrictions rather than attempting to write them itself.

The former vice chairman of the American Bar Association's Criminal Justice Section said:

> What was so infuriating about the Thornburgh memorandum [was the assumption that the Justice Department] can determine what's proper conduct and tell its lawyers that they don't have to comply with state ethics rules when there is a conflict.

And as the McGee *Post* series reports, innocent men are in jail merely because of a variety of official abuses, including prosecutors lying to judges.

This already in-place radicalization of traditional American concepts of justice and of legal ethics is a revolution from the right, a revolution possible only because President Kennedy was assassinated.

When the outgoing attorney general of that *Federal Register* revision of our legal ethics and traditions launched a last-minute attack on the FBI director who had sought to end racism and sexism in the FBI, another prominent Republican lawyer, Whitney North Seymour, a former Manhattan district attorney, wrote in *The New York Times*, of February 5, 1993, that it was "Time to Get Politics Out of Justice."

Remembering Watergate days, of which Barr reminded him, Seymour described Barr's attack on Sessions as "a chilling reminder of the need for constant vigilance to protect the independence of the FBI from interference by political appointees." He described Barr's criticism of the FBI director as "almost ludicrous." Remembering also that he had "served" with Mr. Sessions when we were both United States attorneys in the early 1970s, Seymour described him as "an honest public servant in a tough job."

It was the Democrat, Katzenbach, who joined the right-wing Republican campaign against renewal of the special-counsel act and against the current Republican special prosecutor, Lawrence E. Walsh. Walsh was investigating the Iran/Contra scandal of the Reagan administration when President Bush pardoned Reagan's Secretary of Defense Caspar Weinberger at the end of his administration after Weinberger's indictment but before his trial.

Bush had claimed steadfastly that as vice president he had no knowledge of those matters until they were public, that he was "out of the loop" on them. But as Walsh disclosed, had Weinberger gone to trial after having denied under oath that But had any such knowledge, former Secretary of State George P. Shultz and former Reagan White House chief of staff Donald T. Regan were prepared to testify to what would have made liars of Reagan and Bush, that they had knowledge of their administration's illegalities about which Weinberger was accused of lying to the Congress.

According to *The New York Times* February 9, 1993, account of Walsh's indignant reaction to the rushed pardoning of Weinberger before trial and to vilification of him by the Reagan-Bush supporters, "Mr. Shultz would have expressed his concern that the White House had tried to 'rearrange the record' to shield Reagan from the possible legal consequences'' because he had lied.

Can it be believed, that Attorneys General Thornburgh or Barr, to name only two, would have investigated the truly scandalous behavior of the president who had made Bush president by selecting him as his vice president or that with Bush as president his Department of Justice even would have dreamed of any such investigation—of crimes punishment which Bush aborted by his end-of-the-term and exceptional *pretrial* pardon?

That "rearranging" of White House records to wipe them out was another last-minute Bush administration scandal made possible by the rulings of the Department of Justice. What did happen is what Katzenbach said would not happen.

On the very last day he was in office, January 20, 1993, the man Bush appointed to be the archivist of the United States, Don W. Wilson, approved what George Lardner, writing in the February 17, 1993, *Washington Post* referred to as the "controversial arrangement" that gave Bush, rather than the government, control over his computer and other records and then accepted appointment as executive director of the George Bush Center for Presidential Studies at Texas A & M University.

A number of members of the Congress found it improper that Wilson had any involvement in any negotiations or agreements involving the Bush records when he was going to go to work at the Bush library.

The Wilson-Bush deal, signed the last morning Bush was in office, as Lardner reported the next day, gave out-of-office Bush "exclusive legal control of all presidential information" on the computer tapes. This, as the *Post*'s editorial of February 18 states, "circumvents the Federal Records Act," which the archivist "is charged with enforcing." It also was accused of flouting "the landmark ruling of [traditionally Republican] U.S. District Court Judge Charles Richey that blocked the Bush White House from destroying computer tapes and records during the waning days of that defeated presidency."

And who told Archivist Wilson that it was perfectly all right to engage in such a dubious arrangement with Bush, who has so much to hide, to violate Judge Richey's decision and several laws, as a number of members of Congress charged? Wilson issued a statement through his spokeswoman, Susan Cooper, who stated, as quoted by Lardner on February 17, 1993, that it was all "drawn up" by " 'attorneys for the various agencies involved,' " including the National Security Council, the White House counsel's office, and Justice Department, and the National Archives.

All under Bush and in particular his Justice Department, that Katzenbach had said should be trusted to see to it that its own administration does not violate the laws.

These post-Kennedy assassination scandals, so many of which are a revolution from the right, are strange to those of my age who lived through earlier years of our history, when they were without precedent.

Without the assassination of President Kennedy and without the failure of the basic institutions of our society then and since then, none of these things would have happened, *could* have happened because those who as president made them possible or saw to it that they came to pass would not have been president and able to.

On the opposite extreme from these subversions, which is what these assorted abuses mentioned earlier really are, there is the cheap pettiness of the hacks. As Bill McAllister reported in the February 18 *Post*, "In his last days as head of the Federal Emergency Management Agency, Wallace E. Stickney "approved a distinguished service medal" for "Marilyn Quayle, wife of the former vice president, and nineteen Bush political appointees at the agency which enjoyed anything but a good reputation or one for 'distinguished service' of any kind." Stickney also lavished financial rewards on some of his aides—with federal money.

What did Mrs. Quayle do to earn her medal for "distinguished service?" She spent a week in Florida "sometimes working with hurricane relief teams," as Stickney said, "in a dirty T-shirt and dungarees." If *that* deserves a distinguished service medal, is not an appreciable percentage of Florida's population even more entitled to such a medal?

They did not get themselves dirty for only a few days in real relief efforts. This disgusting sycophancy and the hack who did it are direct consequences of the assassination of President Kennedy and the subsequent institutional failures that alone gave us such officials.

At both extremes it is a radical change in our country, a revolution in law and concepts of law, both relating to freedom and to justice, as well as to ethics and to concepts of public service.

The Kennedy assassination gave us Richard Nixon with his assortment of felons from his attorneys general down to and including staff members inside the White House. That was our first need for a special counsel to take decisions on and investigations of administration criminality out of the hands of those administrations. It was a new need, a need that developed because of the assassination of President Kennedy. Until after that, until what that made possible, we had no such need. Nor did we have felons for attorneys general.

Taking a leading role in the campaign to end the special prosecutors—who are not appointed by the attorneys general—and to leave all such matters to the attorneys general themselves is former Attorney General Nicholas Katzenbach—the originator of the government conspiracy to see to it that the assassination of President Kennedy was not officially investigated. Which meant that it would not and could not be solved, and the guilty would go punished.

How many of these attorneys general can we believe would be equal to the responsibility of investigation themselves or their own administrations, from John Mitchell and Richard Kleindienst, both found guilty, to Richard Thornburg and William Barr and their efforts to revolutionize our standards and concepts of law and justice.

Or, would seek the freedom for so many who lost their freedom even though innocent?

Those who have difficulty attributing the radical changes in our country since the assassination of President Kennedy may see and understand more if they compare crime, from crime in the streets to crime in the government and the White House, then and now. Or compare our economy and national debt and multitudinous other problems then and now. Almost anything in all aspects of our national life, then and now.

There were radical changes, all toward authoritarianism.

This was not the Kennedy belief.

It was made possible by his assassination—and by the man who saw to it that his assassination would not be investigated then took the lead in seeing to it that the crimes in its wake also would not be investigated.

Nicholas Katzenbach did give us an appropriate epilogue.

So also did *JAMA* editor George Lundberg.

I began this book using his total abandonment of all our traditional journalistic standards of decency and honesty as the skeleton for this assassination and assassination investigations overview. I conclude it with the personal self-condemnation that he did not recognize for what it was when he spoke to the Midwest Conference on Assassination in Chicago, Illinois, on April 3, 1993. He was a member of the panel on the medical evidence.

Without knowing it, and certainly without intending it, Lundberg validated the criticisms of him that I made throughout this book, the most basic of which was that Humes was right because he said he was right. As an American editor, that is all that Lundberg needed to launch the largest single unofficial campaign to support and defend the official JFK assassination mythology until then.

This excerpt from pages 2 and 3 of the typescript of Lundberg's seven-page prepared statement, which was provided by Dr. Gary Aguillar of San Francisco, one of a number of doctors whose complaints to the AMA about Lundberg and his misuse of his position as *JAMA*'s editor were to no avail, can be read as Lundberg's unintended confession of guilt to the charges I make:

I am really not much of an expert at this thing at all. It has never been all that interesting to me until the last year or so. My role in that and in this whole thing is that of a journalist along with Mr. Dennis Breo of our own *JAMA* staff. I have essentially no primary source of information to share with you nor do I plan to achieve any. It's really not my main interest. I am a journalist. What then and whom then do I trust? I have known Dr. James Humes, the principal autopsy pathologist, personally since 1957. To paraphrase, Ronald Reagan who was paraphrasing Lloyd Bensen [*sic*], 'I know Jim Humes. He is a friend of mine. I would trust him with my life.' Dr. Humes is an outstanding general pathologist before and after 1963, acclaimed by his peers for thirty years, forty years perhaps; but never was before, during, or after an equally trained forensic pathologist and never claimed to be. He did not volunteer to do that job, he was assigned. Moving from 1963 to 1968, the United States attorney general appointed a four-person blue-ribbon panel to study and reevaluate the JFK autopsy.... This four-member panel had developed unanimous support for the autopsy work, results and interpretation. A team member of that panel was the late Dr. Russell Fisher, chief medical examiner for the state of Maryland and probably the world's top-ranking pathologist of his time. I knew Russell Fisher. He is [*sic*] a friend of mine. I would trust him with my life. . . .

Lundberg is indeed fortunate that in fact, rather than in rhetoric, he did not trust his life to Humes or to Fisher. Or, to any of the others.

Our history is less fortunate. So also are all those, especially doctors, who were so thoroughly deceived and misled by the Lundberg who didn't give a damn about the JFK assassination until Oliver Stone's movie got all that attention. Millions, uncountable millions, more were misinformed by the massive campaign of propaganda in AMA's name when the May 27, 1992, *JAMA* stories were promoted so effectively and extensively by Lundberg in the AMA's name. Virtually every American was grossly misinformed. Perhaps the most serious consequence was that virtually all in the major media had their brains washed by the AMA as propagandist in support of errant officialdom, and that on a political rather than a medical matter.

Throughout the world Lundberg's misuses of the *JAMA* influenced what most people could and did believe about our "crime of the century."

Lundberg even makes himself out to be a liar—unless he beseeched Humes to be interviewed almost daily. In his articles he says his efforts were over a considerable period of time. Yet, eleven months after that *JAMA* issue appeared, he said that he had no interest in the subject at all "until the last year or so."

Forgetting his responsibilities to the AMA and its members, Lundberg said, "My role in this whole thing is that of a journalist, along with Mr. Dennis Breo of our own *JAMA* staff."

This more than validates my frequent statement about and quotation of the standards of journalistic responsibility in that excellent *Washington Post* editorial. As journalists, Lundberg and Breo did not meet their traditional and essential responsibilities.

Nor did they ever intend to! In Lundberg's own words, "I have essentially no primary source of information" and worse, that long after all the criticism of what he published, "nor do I plan to achieve any."

There is now and there was then a superabundance of "primary" sources in the official records to which he had unrestricted access. He could easily have learned what and where they are. That was more than adequately laid out for him in my published work. It was available to him from any local bookstore.

Lundberg simplified it, as I did in different words. He based all of what he published in that monumental deceit of so many millions and millions of people on this unquestioned trust of those who were *parti pris* in the ongoing controversy, those whose well-publicized failings contributed so much to that controversy and to criticism of the government and of them personally:

> What then and whom do I trust? I have known Dr. James Humes, the principal autopsy pathologist, personally since 1957. . . . He is a friend of mine. I would trust him with my life. Dr. Humes is an outstanding general pathologist . . . [but was never] an equally trained forensic pathologist and never claimed to be.

Under oath, Humes and Boswell both testified to the Warren Commission that they were trained in forensic pathology and were qualified in it.

Referring to the Department of Justice panel, Lundberg said it "developed unanimous support for the autopsy work, the results and interpretations." This is false.

It is apparent that trusting one's life to Lundberg is a risky business.

While that panel did say it *supported* the autopsy *report*, neither it nor any other body supported "the autopsy work, results and interpretation." As the reader learned in this book, that panel found the autopsy very wrong on the location of the wounds, that alone disproving the conclusion of the autopsy report, and found it additionally wrong in saying that the so-called "magic bullet" did not strike bone in the President's body, another total disproof of the Humes-Boswell-Finck conclusions.

Lundberg refers to the late Dr. Russell Fisher of that panel saying he was "the chief medical examiner for the state of Maryland, probably the world's top-ranking pathologist of the time. I knew Dr. Fisher. He is [*sic*] a friend of mine. I would trust him with my life."

Would the reader trust his or her life to a world-famous pathologist who found that the wound of entry in the President's head was four inches higher than the Humes gang placed it, that the wound on his back was lower than they placed it, and that there were bone fragments where they said there were none, and who nonetheless said their autopsy report was correct?

And that on the autopsy of a president?

Lundberg, months after I criticized him in the draft of this book, months after the draft was complete, said more or less as a boast and as proof of his personal and professional integrity that what I had charged was his abdication of all his many responsibilities, particularly as *JAMA*'s editor: that Humes and Boswell were right in their autopsy report because, and only because, they said they were right and nothing else matters.

Now that Lundberg, without any external pressure, validated all that I said in criticism of him, of *JAMA*, and of the AMA, it is time, actually well past time, given the many doctors who complained about Lundberg's adventure into political propaganda in the AMA's name, for the AMA not to be silent on any of this. And that includes paying the costs of Lundberg's Broadway/Madison Avenue press conference that was the largest by far of the propagandist efforts in support of the official mythology, the official "solution" to the President's assassination that, then and now, has been solved.

It is also time for the doctors in whose name *JAMA* speaks for the AMA to ask if that is what their dues go for, the most irresponsible and boastedly irresponsible propaganda foisted off as a scientific perfection in the name of all the doctors who are members of the AMA. Is *this* what their organization exists for? Is this what they want done with their money they pay to the AMA?

If the Lundberg/*JAMA* crew had been a conscious part of the Katzenbach-Hoover conspiracy, they could not have served it any better or any more effectively. Nor could they more effectively have served those who conspired to kill the President.

That "primary source" information of which Lundberg is so contemptuous, *the official evidence*, when not lied about, proves that there was a conspiracy.

So Lundberg did *not* have it, did not want it, and boasted that he was going to continue to be ignorant of it.

This in the name of the nation's doctors and their medical association.

If the AMA remains silent, it accepts Lundberg's outrages in its name.

The AMA and its members, too, should at long last insist, *Never Again!*

If they do not they continue their support and protection of the government's JFK assassination conspiracy by Lundberg in their name.

Whether spying or analysis provides most or the best intelligence is and has been debated for years. My own service in intelligence was fifty years ago. Fifty years without any direct connection with intelligence and the fact that I was never in spooking—I was an analyst—may prejudice my belief that most and the best intelligence is produced by analysis of what is readily available without any spying.

In the late 1960s I planned a book, *Tiger to Ride*, in which I intended to analyze, first, the changes in President Kennedy and in his policies after the October 1962 Cuba Missile Crisis and then President Johnson's changes in Kennedy's policies. I collected information for *Tiger to Ride* at the same time that I was continuing my work on the assassination and its investigations. The process included making contemporaneous analyses of significant events, sometimes before they had run their course. This is what professional analysts do.

The Gulf of Tonkin incident, the direct cause of our open military involvement in Vietnam, was one such significant event. In preparing my analysis of it, the only information available to me was the information available to all—the public press.

Years later, my analysis that the entire incident was a fake created to lead to our fighting inside Vietnam was proven to be correct by others who had come to have access to official records. The first of the books that I recall confirming my spot analysis was Joseph Goulden's *The Gulf of Tonkin Incident*. (Goulden, then a reporter for the *Philadelphia Inquirer*, was also one of the first to publish the unconfirmed report that Oswald had been connected with the FBI. He appears in the FBI's and the Commission's records.)

Eventually it became clear to me that my other work would preclude my writing *Tiger to Ride* for quite some time. I loaned that research, including copies of my several contemporaneous analyses of ongoing and potentially the most serious of events, to a young friend. As it turned out, he, too, did not have the time to do a book. He returned the material to me with a separate comment on how unusual it was to find so accurate an analysis of such significant events prepared at the very time those events were going on. That, however, is the norm in intelligence. Two historians who later read the material still recall my analysis, but its accuracy is not in fact any special tribute to me. Rather is it commentary on the failure of the media to make their independent assessments and analyses for fear of the political consequences should they not agree with the official line. The media largely restricted themselves to official handouts.

In essence, my analysis states that the events described by the military never happened, that they would have been senseless for the North Vietnamese who had nothing to gain from firing torpedoes at those two American destroyers without hitting either of them, and that the stories released by the military were not even credible. They were also contradictory. My analysis went further and said that the reason for the military making up those hasty stories was to provide an excuse for American involvement in land fighting in Vietnam in support of the imposed government American military operations were to keep in power. Thus, there was a military conspiracy to get us in a land war in Vietnam. (In one of history's quirks, only two in the Congress opposed Johnson's Gulf of Tonkin resolution. In the House it was the most liberal member, Vito Marcantonio of New York: in the Senate it was "Mr. Conservative," Robert Taft of Ohio. Both voted against the resolution; both held it violated the Constitution.)

This book makes a prima facie case of a military conspiracy in the JFK assassination. While it was being edited for publication Professor David Wrone of Wisconsin, one of the historians who read my Tonkin Golf analysis, sent me a copy of the 110 pages of an oral history he had obtained from the Lyndon Johnson Library, in Austin, Texas. The interviewee was the late Kenneth O'Donnell. What is captioned a "legal agreement" by the National Archives, Lyndon Baines Johnson Library, was signed jointly by O'Donnell's widow, Justine, and by the national archivist. O'Donnell had, among other JFK White House responsibilities, that of appointments secretary. That is the one who grants and denies appointments to see the presidents. He was also one of the top echelon of the JFK White House staff who accepted President Johnson's request to continue to serve under him. O'Donnell had a number of the highest responsibilities under Johnson, with whom he was and had been friends. He thus was in an official position of trust, high up in the Johnson White House, although he remained a Kennedyite.

His statements in the oral history are in this sense official statements.

On pages 84 and 85 of the official transcript of the oral history conducted by Dr. Paige E. Mullhollan on July 23, 1969, at what was then O'Donnell's office in the Park Square Building in Boston, Massachusetts, Mullhollan led O'Donnell into remembering Johnson's campaign in the 1964 election. What follows is O'Donnell's entirely different version of Johnson and Vietnam and how he got us fighting there, on land. It is also an account of how the military created and used that "Tonkin Gulf Incident," as it is known, although there were two allegedly involving two different destroyers on two different occasions:

A. The only other part of the [1964] campaign that I think was of any significance—there are two parts. Number one, which is coming back to haunt him, is the Vietnam thing.

Q. Was that even considered much? Was that just crept into the speeches without much consideration at the time?

A. No. You see, what happened Vietnam had become pretty hot now. Tonkin Gulf has now come, which again the poor guy is maligned about—Senator Fullbright is not correct—but it was not his [LBJ's] fault, nobody had ever told him the truth. [Senator William Fullbright of Arkansas at the time was chairman of the Senate Foreign Relations Committee. He criticized Johnson for getting us into a land war in Vietnam.] I was there when the thing broke. Lyndon Johnson no more wanted Vietnam in his pocket than he wanted anything in the world. The military men may have told him fibs. I don't know. But he took it as a test, and he and I talked about it that night, of whether he has got any guts or not, that's all. They're just testing him, why would you do something like that doesn't make any sense? A provocation which has no military significance to it. They're going to test him to see if he has got enough backbone, or whether in a political campaign he dared do anything about it, and then they'd go further maybe next time. So he asked for the resolution and then they retaliated, but it was perfectly on the up and up—there was no thought of troops, no nothing. But Dick Goodwin [also of Kennedy's staff] was writing his stuff on Vietnam. I'm as sure as I'm sitting here Lyndon Johnson was as sincere as he possible [*sic*] could be about Vietnam and getting out of there. That comes really to fruition in 1964 and then in early 1965 when the military situation changed rather drastically. But I think he was as straight as a string on his speeches. He gets a little flamboyant and he says things maybe a little more than he should have, but basically that is what he meant. I know that. I talked to him about it many, many times. I was for getting out of Vietnam totally from 1961 on, and he and I used to talk about it. There was no problem on that until late in 1964.

As the professional interrogator, Mullhollan should have seen to it that when the oral history was typed there would be no confusion, but he did not. What is more surprising is that when O'Donnell recorded this definitive and startlingly different account of how we got into that terrible and very costly war in Vietnam, Mullhollan did not ask a single question about it. He asked only the single quoted question about the campaign speeches!

It is astounding that an expert would not ask a *single* question, or ask for any specifics or added details or for names or for more information about the military lying to the President and keeping him ignorant. Or, of course, about the fabrication of an incident that, as O'Donnell says, was designed to get us into a land war in Vietnam by giving Johnson no political alternative to the Tonkin Gulf resolution, which bypassed the Constitutional requirement that the Congress, and only the Congress, declare war.

As O'Donnell said, what the Navy attributed to the North Vietnamese "doesn't make any sense." He described it as "provocation which has no military significance to it."

That the Tonkin Gulf incident was made up by our military is not new. That fact no longer rests on analysis, mine or anyone else's; it is now clear. What is new in O'Donnell's statements is that it was not Johnson's desire or intention to get us into that war and that the military timed this adventure in the Gulf of Tonkin to coincide with the political campaign in which the militarist Goldwater was LBJ's opponent. (These were not the only military provocations of that era and it was Goldwater who sensationalized one of them. There were at least two such contrived incidents involving Cuba, the Cuba our military wanted to attack and invade at the time of the 1962 Cuba Missile Crisis. One involved our Naval base at Guantanamo, for which there has been no military need at all since World War II. The other involved capturing Cuban fishing boats on the high seas. But Castro did not take either bait.)

The military understood Johnson very well. They knew he would regard it as "a test" of "whether he has got any guts or not" to "see if he has got enough backbone."

O'Donnell is correct on all points, as I recall from that period. Any such pipsqueak attack by the North Vietnamese served no military purpose for them at all. But, given the nature of Goldwater's campaign, if Johnson did nothing in reaction to those invented incidents, he would then have been ruined politically. A man who had no "guts" or "not enough backbone," a man who might be a coward, could ever be elected president, and that is what gave Johnson no real choice, no matter how much he opposed it.

Fairness also requires, Johnson being Johnson, that the opposite evidence not be ignored.

In his extraordinarily fine, definitive and fair book, *JFK and Vietnam* (New York: Warner Books, 1992) John M. Newman presents evidence to the contrary, that Johnson did want us in a ground war in Southeast Asia. Newman retired as an Army major after eighteen years in intelligence. He served in Southeast Asia, in Thailand, the Philippines, Japan, and China. On the University of Maryland, College Park, faculty, he has taught courses in Soviet, Chinese Communist, East Asia, and Vietnam war history.

In November 1993 testimony before the House of Representatives Government Operations Oversight Committee, presided over by Michigan Democrat John Conyers, Newman expressed what is the thrust of my work in testifying that "a great deal more is at stake than who killed President Kennedy. What is at stake is nothing less than the faith of the people in our institutions." The *Washington Post* headlined a more than full-page article by Jefferson Morley on

Newman and his testimony in its "Style" rather than main news section of November 18 with "DID DEMOCRACY DIE IN DALLAS?" The subhead read "John Newman says the government's lies about JFK's assassination are tearing America apart."

In *JFK and Vietnam*, in the chapter titled "Webs of Deception" (referring to those spun by the military), Newman cited "incontrovertible proof" that Johnson knew that the military was lying. (See chapter section titled "Back Channel to the Vice President," pages 225 ff.)

Of Johnson's desire not to get involved in a ground war in Vietnam, as reported by O'Donnell, Newman began to make the very persuasive opposite case in the chapter "The Drums after Dallas" (pages 438 ff). In the section titled "NSAM-273—The Dam Breaks" he cited a National Security Action Memorandum (NSAM) that had been drafted in accord with Kennedy's instructions for his approval when he returned from his Texas trip. As soon as Kennedy was killed it was revised immediately, Newman said, and "*significantly* [his emphasis]" in accord with "directives that Johnson gave on Sunday, November 24. . . . These revisions were uniformly escalatory." Newman's source is the version of *The Pentagon Papers* edited by then Senator Mike, Gravel, volume 3, Document 156, pages 494-96. Newman continued, "The truly important change in NSAM-273 . . . was the authorization for plans to widen the war against Vietnam." Kennedy had permitted only "advisers" in Southeast Asia. The military, however, soon expanded their function, but *within* South Vietnam. As these military operations against North Vietnam were expanded, the Navy was authorized to use "destroyers in the Gulf of Tonkin to 'acquire visual, electronic, and photographic intelligence on infiltration activities and coastal navigation." Referring to the second of these operations, Newman said "The [destroyer] *Maddox* was authorized to go within eight nautical miles of the coast [within what North Vietnam regarded as its territorial waters], leading to the incident with North Vietnam on August 2—the match that lit the tinderbox."

Later it became clear that there had not been any attack on the *Maddox*. Nor had there been a second provocation involving the destroyer the *C. Turner Joy*. But these pretended attacks were used by Johnson to get Congress to enact a simple resolution rather than the declaration of war required by the Constitution for the United States to engage in that war.

On Johnson's intentions, Newman quoted former *Washington Post* reporter Stanley Karnow's 1983 book, *Vietnam* (New York: Viking, page 326): "At a White House reception on Christmas Eve, a month after he succeeded to the presidency, Lyndon Johnson told the Joint Chiefs [of Staff], 'Just get me elected, and then you can have your war.' "

It never ceases to amaze me how the most competent reporters miss significant information despite their expertise, knowledge, and questioning instincts. The military intent to get us involved in a war on the Asian mainland was brought to light by Pulitzer Prize historian Arthur Schlesinger, who was also on JFK's White House staff, in his 1965 book *One Thousand Days* (Boston: Houghton Mifflin & Co., page 338).

Even as sharp a reporter as my conservative friend the late Stephen Barber, then the Washington correspondent of the conservative *London Standard*, missed this. Steve covered the war in Vietnam. He knew and told me that the military was lying its head off, particularly about its claimed successes and enemy body-counts. Yet he read Schlesinger's definitive book without understanding that, referring to the Kennedy presidency:

> The Pentagon was developing what would become its standard line in Southeast Asia—unrelenting opposition to limited intervention except on the impossible condition that the President agree in advance to every further step they deemed sequential, including, on occasion, nuclear bombing of Hanoi and even Peking. At one National Security Council meeting General Lemnitzer outlined the processes by which each American action would provoke a Chinese counteraction, provoking in turn an even more drastic American response. He concluded: "If we are given the right to use nuclear weapons, we can guarantee victory." The President sat glumly rubbing his upper molar, saying nothing. After a moment someone said, "Mr. President, perhaps you would have the General explain to us what he means by victory." Kennedy grunted and dismissed the meeting. Later he said, "Since he couldn't think of any further escalation, he would have to promise us victory."

In this country, policy is set by the president under the Constitution, not by the military. JFK's clear policy was not to get involved in such a war, but the military was nonetheless set upon a course of its own, one opposite the President's, as Newman in particular documented with painstaking and overwhelming detail. Was that not a military conspiracy?

The danger of military conspiracy was foreseen by our Founding Fathers, and they drafted the Constitution with the intent of precluding it by vesting policy in the presidency. Judicious, explanatory essays written in support of the pending Constitution by Alexander Hamilton, James Madison, and John Jay were later collected and published in book form as *The Federalist Papers*. In the twenty-fifth paper, speaking of the military, Hamilton wrote, ''For it is a truth, which the experience of all ages has attested, that the people are more commonly in danger when the means of injuring their rights are in the possession of those of whom they entertain the least suspicion.''

Whether O'Donnell's opinion that LBJ wanted not to get involved in a war in Vietnam but was manipulated into it by the military is correct or not, it is a fact that Johnson did order the change in policy that did involve us in that war, and he did it before Kennedy's body was in its grave.

While such things are never adjudicated, Newman made an irrefutable case for a military conspiracy to get us involved in that war—a military conspiracy that did indeed succeed.

This is why there have been those who from the time those shots were fired in Dallas suspected that Kennedy was killed as the end product of a military conspiracy engineered by those who wanted to change policy.

That policy was changed—immediately. And with the most disastrous consequences.

Bibliography

and
Bibliographical Essay

The two most serious problems in preparing this bibliography are, I believe, unusual in nonfiction. One is the absence of relevant publications by other authors. The other is giving the reader a meaningful, comprehensible description of the simply enormous volume of the information drawn upon in writing this book.

Almost all of the considerable volume of pretendedly serious books ostensibly on the assassination of President John F. Kennedy have lengthy lists of other books. Those lists usually are largely unrelated to the contents of the books listing them. They are compiled to appeal to those who believe all nonfiction books have such bibliographies. They amount to false advertising. In these books that in fact do not use all the listed books—if any—most of these bibliographies are sucker-bait, intended to give the impression that these listed books are scholarly.

They are not.

With the exception of two other writers whose books are excellent, Sylvia Meagher's *Accessories After the Fact* (Indianapolis: Bobbs-Merrill, 1967) and Howard Roffman's *Presumed Guilty* (New Brunswick: Associated University Presses, 1975), mine are the only books coming from the center, a position in which for years I have been very lonely.

All other books on both sides are foisted off as fact but in fact are works of theory.

It is little recognized, but the Warren Report itself is only a theory. It is a theory that, as this book shows, the Commission, meaning both its members and staff, knew was impossible. Thus, inevitably, all books in support of the official theory of the Warren Commission are also works of theory only, regardless of the claims of their authors.

These two contending extremes of theoreticians confuse the people, the nonconspiracy theory of the official mythology and its innumerable defenders, and the conspiracy theories of those who do not accept the official mythology.

Books of both extremes claim to be truthful and factual, but are neither.

The new kick in support of the official mythology is that while the Commission was wrong in everything it did, it nonetheless reached the right conclusion. With nothing but failures to face, these sycophants simply declare victory for the Commission over those who, with varying degrees of accuracy and inaccuracy, rendered it unacceptable to any fair and impartial reading.

Some authors simultaneously espouse with equanimity contradictory theories in separate writings. This is particularly true of those that enjoyed the largest sales and profited most. A case in point is David Lifton's *Best Evidence* (New York: Macmillan, 1982). It is not his evidence, when he presents evidence, and it is best only in the success of the fraud of a theory he perpetrated as evidence. Another instance is Harry Livingstone's first two books, *High Treason* (Baltimore: Conservatory 1989) and *High Treason 2* (New York: Carroll & Graf, 1992). If those who created and not infrequently profited greatly from their inventions come to believe in them implicitly, the inventions are nonetheless no better than mythologies. Some are knowing frauds.

We, thus, save for me alone today, have two contending mythologies to which the people have access. Whatever the intent of the authors, whether or not they or their writings are even rational, whether or not they believe in their work without reservation, they are mythologists, and they all exploit and commercialize the assassination of the President. Including them in this bibliography would deceive, mislead, and confuse the reader.

To list the work of these mythologists in a bibliography could be interpreted as an endorsement of them as works of fact, of information in which the people can believe, and that would be wrong. It would be wrong, too, because they are not in any way used in this book. They are worthless—worse than worthless, precisely because they deceive and mislead.

The center between these competing mythologies is a lonely place, but it is the only place for fact and established fact alone in dealing with the deeply subversive and most important domestic crime possible in a country like ours.

This book has only five sources. All are indicated in the text.

Five is a small number but it is the only small number in my actual sources. The total pages in these five sources run well into the millions. The number of words is so large it is incalculable.

These five sources are the published and unpublished work of the Warren Commission; the previously withheld records of the executive agencies of the government relating to the assassination and its official investigations; the records generated, mostly by me, in my thirteen Freedom of Information lawsuits for this suppressed information; the records I obtained in that litigation, about .33 million pages; and my own publication of the information that I obtained by these other four sources in my seven published books. (But see page 464.)

After the Commission's records were transferred to the National Archives, I drove there, a hundred miles daily, for weeks on end. The staff there was quite helpful—for about eight months. The records I requested would be awaiting me when I got to the guarded reading room at its opening time. That was the usual practice, until it was understood that my work was critical of the Commission. Then I began encountering unusual delays, often of several hours, as I waited for records I had requested the day before to come from the locked area in which they were kept. The open stonewalling, the visible connivance with the FBI to withhold Bureau documents and thus protect the FBI from its omissions in the records it gave the Commission, the inappropriate opposition to what I was doing, finally made my use of those records much too costly in the time it took; so I turned to other work. This included writing and publishing. By the middle of 1967 I had completed writing my fourth book and the third, which I had published myself, was in distribution.

While I have no way of evaluating the amount of material studied by other writers in the preparation of their books, throughout history,

I believe, only those scholars who have spent long and intense lifetimes researching can appreciate the actual volume of records reflected in this bibliography and the time required for examining them.

The Warren Report itself is 912 printed pages. The twenty-six-volume appendix it published is officially estimated as ten million words. In the first fifteen of those volumes is testimony. In the other eleven volumes are the facsimile reproductions of exhibits, often with two pages of a document printed on a single page. When the Commission files were deposited in the National Archives their volume was officially estimated to be of two hundred cubic feet.

The .33 million pages of previously withheld official records that I obtained through lawsuits take up most of sixty file cabinets. Those cabinets have four drawers each, and each drawer is either twenty-four inches or twenty-six inches in length; almost all of them are filled tightly. About .25 million pages of this staggering volume of once-secret records relate to the JFK assassination and its investigations.

My copies of the records of my FOIA lawsuits, housed in file cabinets and overflowing into storage cartons, alone measure about twenty solid linear feet. Most of them I prepared myself, largely in the form of affidavits. I was under no obligation either to file all that information or to state it under oath. I decided to do it in order to perfect the record for our history. I voluntarily placed myself under oath—which means that I am subject to the penalties of the felony of perjury if I lied to anything at all that was material in those lawsuits—to challenge the government. For in these lawsuits my agency opponents were represented by the very officials who file and prosecute such felonies. And all the judges before whom I swore that the government committed perjury tolerated it—or worse—actually consciously protected it.

FBI perjury was omnipresent in the field offices' combined cases before Judge Lewis Smith. The most persistent of those FBI perjurers was Special Agent John Phillips. In each and every instance proving that he had perjured himself, with his perjuries actually or in effect suborned by the Department of Justice lawyers, Smith made not a single comment, took not a single act; and when I repeatedly alleged and proved those perjuries to the federal appeals court, it merely ignored those felonies. And held against me.

My CA 75–226 was made possible by Congress's 1974 amending of the act's investigative-files exemption. It was official mendacity in the earlier form of that case that led to this amending. Nonetheless FBI Laboratory Agent John W. Kilty proved my allegation of his perjury by a swearing in contradiction to himself about what is most material in the FOIA litigation, whether the records sought exist and were searched for.

When my attorney, Jim Lesar, called my attestation of Kilty's perjury to the attention of Judge John Pratt, Pratt remonstrated, saying you can catch more flies with honey than with vinegar. When Lesar brought the renewed perjury up at a subsequent court session, Pratt told him that if we made such allegations outside the courtroom, in which what is said is privileged, we could bet on trouble. Without waiting a second, Lesar replied, "We are prepared to leave this courtroom right now and repeat those same charges."

Pratt dropped it, but did not forget it. He was in effect on the government's side thereafter. And like all the others, he said not a word about the felonies thrown into his face by the government. That means he did nothing to preserve the supposed Constitutional independence of the judiciary. It cannot be independent if it bows to and immunizes official perjuries.

The files on my litigation as well as those of the court, the Justice Department, and the FBI include copies of all these proceedings. My files and Lesar's also hold verbatim transcripts of the hearings, which should stand forever as an official recording of the repeated felonies by the government and the fact that not a single court ever did a thing about them or charged me with perjury—because I created the legal situation in which one side was perjurious.

This was not daring. There was no risk in it at all, the false swearing was that thoroughly proven. It also was not in any sense wrongfully dramatic. Its sole purpose and the purpose in which it succeeded was to make an unequivocal record for out history that when the President of the United States was killed, the government he had headed—a government that was then led by his automatic successor—was guilty of repeated serious crimes by withholding records relating to the official investigations of that serious crime it did not want the people to know about.

In an effort to perfect this record for history, I undertook to inform the courts as fully as I could and with extensive documentation. A number of those affidavits are book length.

. My lawyer, Jim Lesar, once told me the following story to illustrate how well known among the clerks in the office of the clerk of the federal district court in Washington this unusual if not unprecedented thing I was doing was.

One morning when he drew up to the counter for the filing of pleadings, he told the clerk who handled the file, "I have an affidavit by Mr. Weisberg to file."

"Long and detailed," the clerk said.

"Yes," Jim responded.

"And extensively documented," the clerk said with a broad smile.

The administrative appeals relating to this litigation, also thoroughly documented and filed by the subject matter of those appeals, is fourteen feet in depth. Most of those files were filed with the Department of Justice and by far most relate to the FBI's withholdings and to other noncompliances with the law.

The working files in my office require three dozen file drawers. I have no more space there. The overflow takes up ten file drawers in the basement as well as innumerable boxes.

If it were physically possible to stack the contents of all these file cabinets and many boxes in a single pile they would extend up into the air about a tenth of a mile! Which is more than most city blocks.

And all of this, it should be clearly understood, I have always made freely available to anyone else writing in the field and to students. By "freely available" I mean I have never made any charge for the use of this material and never supervised the searches of all these records by anyone. I have no idea what was read or copied on our copier, which was also accessible without supervision. Despite this absolutely free access, few of those specialists in the invention of untenable cockamamie theories came to use these records.

All except my current working files are in our basement. My ability to use those stairs and to stand at file cabinets began to be limited in 1975; in ensuing years it grew continuously more limited. So I could not have supervised the access I gave to others even if I had wanted to. And I did not want to. To facilitate work in the archive in our basement, I set up a very sturdy table there and got a Hermes portable typewriter. Also, I have always kept a supply of paper, clips, tape, pens, and pencils there, exclusively for the use of others.

That not a single one of the small army of those who would have the public believe that they are authentic assassination scholars engaged in legitimate research has ever made any real use of what is by any reasonable standard an unimaginably vast amount of information for which there has never been any charge for admission or use is a disappointment to me. Their books of course make evident that these authors had no interest in or use for either certifiably factual official information or by far the largest portion of the lawsuit files—what is critical of officially alleged fact and the manner in which it was obtained, used, and misused.

This unscholarly attitude toward ''scholarship'' applies to the other side as well. In this book the most conspicuous insistence upon remaining ignorant of the established fact of the assassination is *JAMA*'s. That is the reason I quoted so extensively from my earlier books, particularly from *Whitewash* and *Post Mortem*, both of which have detailed name and subject indexes to make the point that what is officially said to be fact was readily available to those who found it easier to engage in their propaganda by perserving a condition of the most determined and profound ignorance.

For all the many self-conceived supersleuths of both extremes, ignorance was indeed bliss. Their minds untroubled by fact, they were without restraint in inventing their imagined ''solutions.'' From this studied ignorance came freedom—freedom from the restraint that most of them evolved as taint—the taint of fact.

Only those who have examined my archive can understand how available the information is despite its vastness. Each and every file drawer has its contents identified by the file and files in it, by their official designations of the sections, or volumes, and the serial numbers within each section. They are like page numbers, but relate to documents, not pages. There is also a card index by subject indicating the file drawers holding records relating to each subject.

One of the most comprehensive means of locating most of the information about persons and major events required months and months of arduous, extremely diligent in-court pressure before the government was compelled to disclose to me a large index it strove to keep secret. Its existence was denied by numerous FBI lies that in context are felonious; perjury. (This was not in any sense unusual. It often required month after month of repeated briefings, arguments, and documentations to compel the disclosure of countless records that were improperly withheld—many thousands of them. It actually was not unusual for some of these efforts to require years during which there were appeals to the appeals court, an additional time-consuming and costly effort. Only those who have been rubbed by it can appreciate the harsh grinding of the omnipresent official mill-stone when the government did not want to disclose what the law required it to disclose, wanted to hide what could be embarrassing to it, or just wanted to wear me down in that litigation. This matter of that index is but one of innumerable illustrations.)

But, after all those months of efforts, copies of the secret Dallas FBI office special subject index—42 linear feet of 3 × 5 cards—were given to me. This index identifies each reference by file and serial number. This index is not limited to records originated in Dallas, known as the Office of Origin, because, consistent with FBI practice, the information developed by the FBI's other offices was funneled to FBIHQ through Dallas.

The number of court appearances in all this litigation is well over one hundred, perhaps closer to two hundred. Only those who have litigated can begin to appreciate the amount of time and effort this represents. And it does not include what was and usually is much more common, the filing of pleadings by both litigants.

Some of the lawsuits in the following list set precedents. After all these years I no longer recall all of them. In retrospect I believe the one that means most to me—distinguished as it is from precedents that required that the records I sought be searched for with due diligence and then disclosed to me and the case that got me the records sought without charge—is the suit that established that one cannot copyright the nation's history and then deny access to it. As a result, the FBI was required to print and give me copies of more than one hundred photographs that were taken by Joseph Louw, the only photographer on the scene when Martin Luther King, Jr., was killed. They were copyrighted, with fewer than 10 percent of them ever used in public. The property right of the copyright holder was preserved for him. I may not publish those photographs without per-mission to do so. But the effect of that decision was to hold that copies of copyrighted information must be made available for research, for the private study of the scholar.

In each of these exceptionally successful cases it was Jim Lesar who did the work and to whom we are all indebted for its success.

In this sense, of what is success, I lost in the case over which the law was amended in 1974. It went all the way to the Supreme Court, which refused to take the case. That was clearly a failure. Yet it was also the greatest success of all because it did open to the FOIA requesters the relevant records of the FBI, the CIA, and similar agencies when Congress noted it in amending the act. The case cited in the Senate as requiring the 1974 amending of the FOIA's investigative files exemption was only the second suit I filed. It is CA 2301–70.

"CA" denotes "civil action," to distinguish such cases from criminal cases. That federal district court then listed the case number first, 2301, then the year, 70, for 1970. In later years the court reversed the order.

Other abbreviations used include the following:

"J" after the names identify the judges.

"D. C. Cir." denotes the United States Court of Appeals for the District of Columbia. Where I have the citation of the decisions as printed in the law books, this is the last entry under each appeal.

Jim Lesar prepared this list. While not 100 percent complete, the list does identify the cases and their ultimate disposition.

These cases also represent a simply enormous labor by Jim Lesar and the sacrifices made by him and his family when I was not able to pay him.

FOIA Lawsuits

CA 718–70, *Harold Weisberg* v. *United States Department of Justice* (Edward Curran, J.).

CA 2301–70, *Harold Weisberg* v. *United States Department of Justice* (John Sirica, J.).

D. C. Cir. 71–1026, *Harold Weisberg* v. *U.S. Department of Justice*, 160 U. S. App. D. C. 71, 489 F. 2d 1195 (*en banc*), *certiorari denied* 416 U. S. 993 (1974).

CA 2052–73, *Harold Weisberg* v. *General Services Administration* (Gerhard Gesell, J.).

CA 75–0226, *Harold Weisberg* v. *United States Department of Justice, United States Energy Research and Development Administration* (John H. Pratt, J.).

Weisberg v. *Department of Justice*, 177 U. S. App. D. C. 161, 543 F. 2d 308 (1976) (Spottswood Robinson III, Malcolm Wilkey, William Jameson, J.)

Weisberg v. *United States Department of Justice*, 438 F. Supp. 492 (D. D. C. 1977)

Weisberg v. *United States Department of Justice*, 627 F. 2d 365, 200 U. S. D. C. 312 (1980).

D. C. Cir. 82–1072, *Weisberg* v. *U. S. Department of Justice*, 227 U. S. App. D. C. 253, 705 F. 2d 1344 (1983).

CA 75–1448, *Harold Weisberg* v. *General Services Administration* (Robinson, J.).

D. C. Cir. 77–1831 (David L. Bazelon, Spottswood Robinson III, and Edward Tamm, J.).

D. C. Cir. 78–1731 (Bazelon, Robinson, and Tamm, J.).

D. C. Cir. 81–1009, *Weisberg* v. *General Services Administration.*

CA 75–1996, *Weisberg* v. *U. S. Department of Justice*, (June L. Green, J.). [King Assassination records case.]

D. C. Cir. 78–1641, *Weisberg* v. *U. S. Department of Justice*, 203 U. S. App. D. C. 242, 631 F. 2d 824 (1980) (Bazelon, J.).

D. C. Cir. 82–1229, 82–1274, 83–1722, and 83–1476, *Weisberg* v. *U. S. Department of Justice*, 745 F. 2d 1476 (D. C. Cir. 1984); 764 F. 2d 1436 (D. C. Cir. 1985).

D. C. Cir. 82–1229, 82–1274, 83–1722, and 83–1476, *Weisberg* v. *U. S. Department of Justice*, 763 F. 2d 1436 (D. C. Cir. 1985) (per curiam; dissent by Bork, J.).

D. C. Cir. 87–5302, *Weisberg* v. *U. S. Department*, 848 F. 2d 1245 (D. C. Cir. 1988).

D. C. Cir. 89–5410 (appeal dismissed 2/15/90).

CA 77–1997, *Harold Weisberg* v. *Central Intelligence Agency, National Security Agency* (John Lewis Smith, J.), D. C. Cir. 79-1729.

CA 77–2155, *Harold Weisberg* v. *Griffin Bell, et al.,* (Gesell, J.).

CA 78–0249, *Harold Weisberg* v. *Clarence M. Kelley, Griffin Bell, and U. S. Department of Justice* (Smith, J.).

CA 78–0322 and 78–0420, Combined *Harold Weisberg* v. *Federal Bureau of Investigation, William H. Webster, United States Department of Justice, and Griffin Bell* (Smith, J.) (originally assigned to Aubrey Robinson, J.). [Combined after filing with CA 78–0322.]

CA 81–0023, *Harold Weisberg* v. *United States Department of Justice*, (Green, J.).

The Most Important Records Obtained by Litigation
Listed by File Classifications

The Assassination of President John F. Kennedy: Headquarters 62–109060; Dallas 89–43; New Orleans 89–69.

Lee Harvey Oswald: FBIHQ 105–82555; Dallas 100–10461; New Orleans 100–16601; Mexico City 105–3702.

Liaison with the Warren Commission: FBIHQ 62–109090; Dallas 62–35888.

Jack Leon Ruby: FBIHQ 44–24016; Dallas 44–1639; New Orleans 44–2064; Dallas Special Index of letters to Ruby, 44–1639A.

Marina Oswald: FBIHQ 105–126032; New Orleans 100–16926; Dallas 105–1435; 66–1313, 66–1313A.

George DeMohrenschildt: Dallas 105–632.

Including most other files disclosed by the FBI would be merely padding because they lack real significance. An example is the Dallas Field Office file 9–1984, an "Extortion" file on Oswald.

However, the special Dallas indexes are important. One is its index of case communication, the other its vast subject index of the 122 sections totaling 42 linear feet of 3 × 5 cards.

One Department of Justice file released to me by the Criminal Division, 129–11, is important. It contains much information not in any disclosed FBI files. This is its assassination file.

The FBI's and the department's files are not integrated. They do not have the same titles or classification systems.

Of the FBI files listed above, these are their official titles: "44" is "Civil Rights," with three additional titles relating to voting and elections; "62" is "Miscellaneous—including Administrative Inquiry"; "89" is "Assaulting or Killing a Federal Officer; Congressional Assassination Statute." (The assassination of a president was not then a federal offense. Lacking any appropriate file classification because the assassination was not a federal offense, these field offices used the "89" classifications for those records.)

"One hundred" and "105" are "Subversive" files used so inclu-

sively that my earlier FOIA requests were filed in the "100" "sub-
versive" file! Their official titles are, "100. Subversive Matter
[Individuals]; Internal Security [Organizations]; Domestic Security
Investigations." The "105" official description is, "Foreign
Counterintelligence-Russia [formerly Internal Security] [Nationalis-
tic Tendency-Foriegn Intelligence] [Individuals and Organizations by
Country].[1] Both files are listed with **. This indicates they are
"Security-related Classifications."

When the deterioration of my health and physical capabilities prevented my prosecuting any additional FOIA lawsuits to bring suppressed assassination records to light, Mark Allen, my friend from
his undergraduate days of two decades earlier, with Lesar as his
lawyer, carried on with considerable success. As of this writing they
compelled the disclosure of withheld records numbering well into
the six figures of pages.

In each and every instance in this book all the information cited
is in my files, as it will be when they are transferred to Hood College
in Frederick, Maryland.

While most of the usual kinds of footnotes exceeded my capabilities when writing this book, all the required information not in such
notes is in the text.

I used no secret information, therefore no citation needed to be
withheld.

I hope readers and professional historians will understand my reasons for not listing as sources meretricious works that I do not use
as sources and that ought not be used as such by professional scholars. Those sources mislead.

This is not self-praise. It is condemnation of the others for their
failings.

That is still another of the many tragedies in the wake of our
political assassinations of the 1960s.

As written, this Bibliography and Bibloiographical Essay applied to
what by then I had written, before I wrote the Epilogue and
Afterword. In those late writings, all sources are identified.

Afterword

This book begins by bringing to light, and documenting with official documents that were officially suppressed, the fact that there was an official conspiracy to see to it that the assassination of President John F. Kennedy was never officially investigated.

Once this agreement was reached, on the highest official levels, it was also officially decided that Oswald was the lone assassin. These official decisions were reached as soon as Oswald was dead. That meant there would be no trial since he was the only official candidate for assassin. With no trial, there would be no independent examination of the alleged evidence of this lone guilt.

As we have also seen, the alleged official evidence does not convict him.

And that means that the most subversive crime in a country like ours, a crime that has the effect of a coup d' etat, is without any solution. It was immediately decided, as we have seen, on the very highest official levels, to ordain Oswald the lone assassin. That was before any real investigation was possible. It also meant that there would be no leads from the official "investigation" for private persons to follow in any effort to learn what really did happen.

For all of this to be pulled off successfully, official suppression was the first requirement. To meet this basic need, there then was official suppression, to the degree that was politically possible. There, therefore, was suppression from the outset of what could endanger the success of this conspiracy, not to investigate the crime itself, and of the coexisting need to have it believe that Oswald was the lone assassin and that the crime itself has been officially solved when in fact it was never officially investigated—the need to have it believed that Oswald alone was responsible for the assassination.

When there was absolutely no need for it and every legitimate and American belief that the official hearings, the closest thing there would be to a trial, and would be public, the Commission held all its hearings in tightest secrecy. When it did not have the authority to classify anything at all, the Commission classified all its proceedings as TOP SECRET or SECRET. All that it would publish thus was classified illegally. Once illegally classified, all access to it was denied any of the media who might demand access to it. Not that there was any record of which even one lone reporter made any such demand, or that any media component did.

As a direct and obviously intended result when the Commission's massive Report of 912 pages was released, there was no independent information with which it could be compared—had any of the media had such interest.

As the intended result, all the media and private persons could do was evaluate what the Report says and concludes against the so-called evidence published with it. That evidence was carefully culled from the Commission's files of some two hundred cubic feet in extent to make the Report, its conclusions—its "solution" to what was correctly called the "crime of the century"—seem credible.

The fact is, however, that despite the best efforts of its staff of more than merely competent lawyers, their Report itself, without access to anything else at all, cannot survive critical examination.

This is the kind of examination that in our system of justice is made *in public* by defense counsel. Only with no live accused, there was no such defense. And thus the official "solution" was ordained. It was not established in the traditional American way, at a public trial.

And because for all its boasts of freedom and independence the media did not critically examine that Report at all, officialdom got away with this intended success of the conspiracy to see to it that the crime itself was never officially investigated.

Two months after the report was issued, the Commission published its twenty-six volumes of evidence. Fifteen volumes are of the transcripts of the testimony it took, and eleven volumes are what it said was the other evidentiary basis for its Report. While that great volume of words, officially estimated at ten million words, in itself defied immediate access to all of it, the media made no such examination.

Making any such evaluation fell to private citizens like me. My *Whitewash: The Report on the Warren Report*, was the first critical examination of that Report. It proved overwhelmingly that the conclusions of the Report were not justified by its alleged official backstopping.

But the major media ignored it.

And, save for some reviewers, the major media also ignored those books that followed my first book. As it also almost entirely ignored all my books that followed, all based on the official evidence itself. The very evidence that the Commission and the executive agencies of the government said established Oswald's lone guilt.

That official evidence in fact established the exact opposite.

And, as my books established, that official evidence in fact proved that there had been a conspiracy to kill the President.

Even though all polls and other reflections of opinion disclosed that the official "solution" was never accepted by most of the people, the government got away with it in the absence of any real media interest in bringing the truth to light. The media, in fact, acted as an arm of government. Its efforts were directed at having the Report that cannot survive critical examination believed.

When, as was true at the time of the thirtieth anniversary of this assassination, a poll taken for CBS News showed that nine out of ten Americans did not believe what long before then I referred to as the "official mythology," there was no major media change. They still, uncritically, supported the official mythology.

But public dissatisfaction did in the 1970s force the Congress to hold hearings on the assassination. A special "select" committee of the House of Representatives was created to make that investigation. Because of my own contacts with it in its earliest days, I knew that it also began with the determination not to investigate the crime itself, and so I decided to have nothing to do with it. Although it did hold public hearings, they also were rigged. This in fact was unhidden, but that, too, was ignored by most of the major media. I was the source of most of the few criticisms it faced during its lifetime.

Although that committee did hold those public hearings, it also proceeded in secrecy. Much of its work was done in secret hearings and staff inquiries. They were not public save for a few the committee believed buttressed its conclusions, which endorsed the official mythology. Much of the committee's work was recorded in staff reports and memoranda that were not published. They were kept secret when that committee published its conclusions.

Under the standing rules of the House of Representatives, the unpublished records of its committees are kept secret for fifty years. That rule protects the innocent from hearsay and other character assassination; the Congress is not required to observe the rules of evidence. But this perfectly proper, indeed, necessary rule, also permitted the suppression of evidence that the committee itself had not published.

There was also the extensive records of many executive agencies of the government.

Under the Freedom of Information Act of 1966, those records under that law became accessible on July 4, 1967. I then began to seek from the FBI this withheld evidence—evidence that by its nature is not secret, the kind of evidence that the prosecution is required to make public at trials. By mendacity that was shocking to me, the FBI actually rewrote that law before the compliant courts. The Congress cited that lawsuit in its 1974 amending of FOIA to restore its original meaning and intent. Thus the FBI's shocking mendacity kicked back on it because those 1974 amendments to the act opened all such records to access under the act.

As a result, some of those records were forced into disclosure. Through a dozen FOIA lawsuits I alone obtained about .3 million pages of withheld official records.

But vast quantities of official records remained suppressed.

These were records of the executive agencies and of the Congress.

The House of Representatives by a simple resolution could have ordered all the records of its Select Committee on Assassinations to be made accessible. It passed no such resolution, and they remained suppressed.

While there remained diligent efforts by private persons, mostly my friends Mark Allen, Kevin Walsh, and Jim Lesar, to have these withheld records disclosed, they did not succeed.

Oliver Stone's very successful movie, *JFK*, added enormously to the demand for disclosure of what remained withheld. The Congress decided in 1992 to make those withheld records accessible under the act.

First the administration of President George Bush and then that of President Clinton stonewalled implementing the law. But finally, toward the end of 1993, an estimated million pages were made accessible.

Even this large number of pages of official records does not include all of them!

A volume of information in itself denies meaningful access. Nobody can afford the cost of paying for it, about .25 million dollars, and the cost of the hundreds of file cabinets in which to hold those records or to buy or rent space in which to keep them. And were this not true, working a lifetime would be required for any meaningful examination of them.

This does reflect the vast volume of information that for thirty years had been suppressed, the obvious need and intent of the official conspiracy not to investigate the crime itself.

Because I was by then eighty years old and in failing health that precluded my going to the National Archives in Washington to examine these records, the relatively few copies I obtained were sent to me by friends. The most significant of these few records that were given to me were some of those of the HSCA that I had, since my first contact with it, referred to as "the House Assassins." After this book was written, I was given copies of some of its unpublished records relating to the utterly incompetent autopsy performed on the President's body at the Bethesda, Maryland Naval Hospital.

It was five months after those records were first made accessible that Dr. Gary L. Aguillar, a San Francisco ophthalmologist, sent me some of those he had obtained. They had been sent to him by Anna Marie Kuhns Walko, who was working in those newly released records in Washington. As far as I know, others had made no use of them. Others, too, had special interests in what records they could get. Over the years pursuing their special interests has blinded some researchers to what does not relate to their theories, blurring the meaning of these records.

One example of these special interests that I do not and never have shared is proving that the pictures and X rays said to be of the autopsy have been faked, doctored, or substituted for the originals. This is why:

Because my own work, beginning with my first book, which was completed in mid-February 1965, and particularly in detail in *Post Mortem*, which was published in 1975, proved that this official autopsy film destroys the official mythology, I did not and do not share these conspiracy theorists' view. It made no sense to me that anyone would run the great risk involved in faking such pictures and X rays, only to create fakes that destroy the official "solution" they allegedly were faked to support.

Officialdom would create fakes to disprove what officialdom was determined to say?

No such risk dared be taken when the autopsy film was certain to be used in Oswald's trial.

And then there is the fact that the original autopsy was burned and a new one was written as soon as it was known that with Oswald's murder there would be no such trial.

That destruction as we have seen coincides with the beginning of this governmental conspiracy not to investigate the crime itself.

As of that time the Navy medical people did not have either the autopsy photographs or X rays. The Secret Service did. The photographs had not yet been developed and printed. Creating fake X rays would have entailed insurmountable problems. Among these are that when for the first time faking of any kind could have been considered, there was no way of knowing whether there would be any other official proceedings. In the murder case only Texas had jurisdiction. There was no way of knowing if through blundering evidence it would point to other assassins. Another is that several committees of each house of the Congress with proper jurisdiction would decide to hold hearings. Any such hearings meant a public investigation.

Moreover, as officialdom knew very well, at the very least the Zapruder film captured the known shooting. Any doctoring could be exposed by it.

The most common allegation of film fakery alleges that the back of the President's head had been blown out. The Zapruder film proves that did not happen. The back of the head is quite clear in a number of frames that follow those recording the fatal shot to the head. They show that the back of the head is intact and that there is not even the suggestion of any blood on it, or on what else is quite clear in those frames immediately following the fatal shot, the back of his shirt collar and his jacket in that area. And, with all the duplicates of the original of Zapruder's film known to have been made, any faking of that film would require that the original and all prints also would have to be changed identically. Not only was that impossible, but by then many people had already examined the film closely.

While this belatedly disclosed new evidence from the secret records of the HSCA does not address any faking, it does bear on the impossibility of it and it does provide explanations for what was so widely interpreted as a faking of the possible autopsy X rays.

This "new" evidence was suppressed as part of the government's conspiracy not to investigate the crime itself, whether or not that was the intent of any of the members of that committee. It was suppressed for fifteen years of the most intense controversy. No member of the staff, all of whom had been required to sign pledges of eternal secrecy, leaked any of this information. While there is no way of knowing all the staff members who had this information, there is the certainty that those I will name did have it.

And as will become clear, despite Blakey's sanctimony and endless assurances of his purest of motives and factual accuracy in the official report for which he was responsible and over which he exercised the tightest of control, had he not suppressed this information, he would not have dared issue that report.

It was not consideration of space that caused him to keep this information secret. His report is as bulky as that of the Commission. His appendix runs twelve volumes. Five are of transcripts of testimony, seven are of exhibits.

His report concludes other than this suppressed evidence says and means. This new information destroys much of his report in any impartial examination of it.

Blakey was more careful than the Commission's counsel in avoiding publication of what he had that contradicted his report.

The nature of this evidence makes it apparent that whether or not it is worthwhile is not a legitimate consideration. All information is worthwhile in any quest for truth.

What Gary sent me is the stenographic transcript of one day of sworn testimony taken by the HSCA's medical panel plus a number of staff memoranda on their investigations, several accompanied by affidavits. All of it relates to the medical evidence.

The day of this testimony was Saturday, March 11, 1978. It was in room 503 of the National Archives, which is the repository of the autopsy pictures and X rays. The witnesses were Dr. John Ebersole, the radiologist at the Naval Hospital who took the autopsy X rays, and Dr. Pierre Finck, who was, as we have seen, one of the autopsy prosectors. From the transcript, those also present at 10:20 A.M. when the questioning began were: "Marion Johnson, Archivist; D.A. [Andy] Purdy and F. Mark Flanagan, Staff; Michael Baden, M.D., Charles S. Petty, M.D., Werner U. Spitz, M.D., George L. Loquvam, M.D., Cyril H. Wecht, M.D., John I. Coe, M.D., Earl F. Rose, M.D., James T. Weston, M.D., and Joseph H. Davis, M.D.''

Blakey's committee called not a single one of the people, whose testimony and what they told the committee staff are included in the records that Gary sent to me. Finck, as we have seen, testified to the Warren Commission and was a defense witness in the Clay Shaw trial.

Ebersole, the autopsy radiologist, was never a witness whose testimony should have been taken in public and published? Or, in private by the Commission to be published later? He should have been.

The photographers, John T. Stringer and Floyd Riebe, neither a witness, in secret or published?

Important as the X rays and pictures are and always have been?

Blakey, it is appropriate to remember, is a professor of law at Notre Dame University after the committee's life ended. What kind of lawyers does he turn out when this is his practice—suppression at all levels? Not taking the only possible firsthand testimony, important as the autopsy film is in any investigation?

There should be no misunderstanding of my purposes in this Afterword. I am bringing guilty knowledge to light. Guilty knowledge and the deliberate suppression of vital evidence in the assassination. This official suppression is what absolutely destroys the official mythology that was palmed off on the people of this country and of the world.

As we shall see, that guilty knowledge was not limited to Blakey. In addition to those of Blakey's staff identified above, other names appear in these records.

There also should be no misunderstanding of the magnitude of what was not done.

Both the presidential Commission and the specially empowered committee of the House of Representatives had the neigh to sacred responsibility of fully investigating that most subversive of crimes, the assassination of a President. Important the X rays and photographs taken during the autopsy are, in any such inquiries neither the Commission nor the committee heard any testimony from the radiologist or the photographers. Where the committee's medical panel of outside experts did take the radiologist's testimony, the questioning was much too limited and was not in that committee's report. Along with the information that follows, which was obtained from others who should have been witnesses and were not, this new information invalidates all official "solutions."

This book also raises the question; was there a military conspiracy?

Some of this new information does bear on that. It strengthens that belief.

The autopsy was entirely a military matter, from the moment on the sorrowful return trip of *Air Force One* that Admiral Burkley gave the widow the choice between two military hospitals, the Army's Walter Reed and the Navy's Bethesda. Both are fine institutions as hospitals, but neither offered what is the prime consideration in an autopsy—the best possible *forensic* pathology, this being the most serious murder possible in our country. Even the Armed Forces Institute of Pathology could not provide this, as we have seen from its expert, Pierre Finck. What was needed was the best forensic pathologists available. The military did not have them. And it did not get them.

At least two such eminent experts, had there been the desire, could have been at Bethesda by the time the body was there for examination. Dr. Russell Fisher, Maryland's chief medical examiner and the author of texts used in the field, was only minutes away by helicopter. Dr. Cyril Wecht, former head of the American Academy of Forensic Sciences, could have reached Bethesda from Pittsburgh in plenty of time, if the military had desired that. By the time Finck got to the autopsy room, a large number of other forensic pathologists could easily have arrived. *If* the military had wanted it.

Instead the military at Bethesda, as one of its first acts, removed all but military personnel from the autopsy room and then mounted a guard to prevent any civilians or unauthorized military personnel from entering (*Post Mortem*, pages 532-33).

Then, as soon as the autopsy was completed, all the military personnel present were ordered into perpetual silence about it. First this was verbal and then it was given to each one present in written form (*Post Mortem*, page 303).

Anyone who ever opened his mouth would be court-martialed, that notice warned, really threatened.

The military, which had complete control, not only did not see to it that the best forensic pathologists performed the autopsy—it is not really unfair to say that they saw to it that the best forensic pathologists did *not*. They also failed, which again can be interpreted as meaning saw to it, that the autopsy prosectors would not have the best assistance in the other areas of expertise required for the best autopsy examination.

One of the innocent victims, of whom more was asked than he could deliver, is the fine radiologist Dr. John Ebersole. Asked at the very end of his testimony to the HSCA's medical panel what they ought recommend for the future, his advice was that the government "have a team of forensic pathologists when this happens again, God help us" [transcript, page 65].

In the absence of the hospital's chief radiologist, Ebersole that night was the acting chief.

They asked the extent of his experience, "How many gunshot cases" he had X-rayed or read the X rays. He replied that in his entire professional life, "during my residency and subsequent to that, in perhaps twenty to twenty-five cases," and they were largely "shotgun wounds to self-inflicted revolver wounds and so on" [transcript, page 15].

His understanding of the forensic requirements was so limited he wanted to "emphasize ... these X rays were taken solely for the purpose of finding what at that time was thought to be a bullet that had entered the body and had not exited. If we were looking for fine bone detail, the type of diagnostic exquisite detail we want in life, we'd have taken the pictures in the X-ray department, made the films there, but we felt that the portable X-ray equipment was adequate for the purpose, i.e., locating a metallic fragment'' [transcript, pages 6-7].

At several points Ebersole emphasized that their sole purpose in taking the X rays was to locate the bullet he said the prosectors believed had entered the back or neck.

(At one of these points, not referring to the use of less than the best X-ray equipment there and available for use, he refers to his qualifications for this particular job of X-raying, ''As far as my expertise that night, I don't think it should be questioned because what was asked of my expertise was, is there a slug in the body'' [transcript, page 28].

When no bullet or fragment was found, it was not a doctor who asked them to try again. When no bullet showed ''we were asked by the Secret Service agents present to repeat the film, and we did so'' [transcript pages 4, 51, and elsewhere].

Throughout Ebersole's so long delayed and then kept secret testimony, he refers to other consequences of use of other than the best available X-ray equipment, inferior X rays that had ''artifacts'' of various kinds distorting them and their meaning.

There is much else in Ebersole's testimony that can explain Arlen Specter's keeping him away from the Warren Commission and Blakey's keeping him away from his committee's members.

Where both locate the rear, nonfatal wound the President had at his neck, an indispensibility for that single-bullet fraud to have been tried to be perpetrated, Ebersole testified it was ever so much lower, in the ''back to the right of the midline, three or four centimeters to the right of the midline, just perhaps inside the medial board to the upper scapula'' [transcript, page 3].

The scapula is the shoulder bone, and as nobody ever testified anywhere that very moveable bone, depending on the position of the body and arms when X-rayed, could have placed that wound as much as two inches higher than it was as inflicted on the sitting President. (He was X-rayed and photographed prone, his hands placed upward, which has the effect automatically, of moving the seeming location of the wound higher than it was. Yet Ebersole even then testified that it was in the back, not as Specter stated so misleadingly, in the neck.

Ebersole also gave an entirely different point of entry of a bullet

in the President's head. With what he had not said asked of him as
a question by Dr. Weston, Ebersole corrected Weston, saying "that
the wound of entrance was somewhere to the side or to the posterior
quadrant" of the head [transcript, page 28].

Medical panel chairman Baden, at whom we earlier took a look,
had asked Ebersole, "where the wound of entrance was in the head
radiologically." Ebersole's reply was, "In my opinion it would have
come from the side . . ." [transcript, page 18].

Thus, Ebersole, one of the doctors closest to the corpse, the working radiologist at the autopsy, under oath, testified contrary to what
the government says and has always said about both of the President's admitted wounds. He saw both and for his X-raying *had* to
examine them. His testimony contradicts what the government says
about both. He placed the back wound much lower. That creates a
number of questions never asked. With regard to the official mythology, it eliminates any possibility at all of the single-bullet theory on
which the Report is based. That also precludes any exit where the
bullet hole in the front of the neck was. In short, this refutes the
Report entirely. (As we see below, so did FBI Special Agent Francis
X. O'Neill.)

The government says the entrance of the only officially admitted
head wound was in the back of the head. Its "solution requires this.
Ebersole's testimony does exactly the same with the bullet said to
have caused death: he says it was of side entrance, not a bullet that
entered the back of the head. And that, too, destroys the official
"solution."

As we have seen, some of the unofficial evidence makes a liar of
Humes in his fanciful account of not knowing there had been a bullet
wound in the President's anterior neck. Humes both read and quoted
the newspapers which reported on the Perry news conference, at
which, shortly after the President was pronounced dead, he said three
different times in response to reporters' questions that the bullet impacting there was from the front. Yet Humes's sworn-to account is
that he had no knowledge of this until the next morning he phoned
Perry. Humes swore that was the earliest he ever spoke to Perry,
during the *morning* of the day after the assassination.

We also recalled Dr. Clark's testimony, that because Humes had told Perry what the autopsy report would say, Perry asked Clark to handle that day's scheduled news conference for him.

At several points Ebersole attested that *in his presence Humes phoned Perry during the autopsy!* His first of these several references to this is: "I believe by 10, to 10:30, approximately a communication was established with Dallas . . ." [transcript, page 5].

Baden hoisted himself and his committee on their own petard in questioning Ebersole about this, saying, "and it was your impression that before the autopsy was finished, at 10:30 at night, contact had been made between Dr. Humes and—" Here Ebersole interrupted, saying, "I must say these times are approximate, but I would say in the range of 10 to 11 P.M., Dr. Humes had determined that a procedure had been carried out in the anterior neck covering the wound of exit" [transcript, page 20].

Humes had "determined" nothing. The best that it can be called is a conjecture. Closer to the truth is that he just made up that it was an exit wound because that was wanted of him, because that made it possible for the government to claim there had been only the one assassin, Oswald.

But Ebersole insisted that Humes phoned Perry *during* the autopsy. *And he was there!*

Dr. Weston returned to this later, when he correctly cited what Ebersole had testified to and Ebersole gave him the same answer [transcript, page 47].

If we assume that all the other members of the HSCA's medical panel were asleep or daydreaming, without question its chairman, Baden, and the prestigious Weston, author of a JFK assassination book, knew the truth, knew very well what Ebersole swore to repeatedly and of personal knowledge and with that destroyed Humes's integrity, if he did not also prove that Humes had sworn falsely, a felony. Ebersole's testimony also proved the official "solution" was impossible and was known to be impossible.

But they preserved in that awful crime of silence when men should speak out, should be heard, and should demand to be heard.

As we have seen, because no proof was ever offered of it and because it makes the Kennedy family responsible for the awful mess of that autopsy, it was from the first—and often thereafter—the official party line that what was wrong with the autopsy, what was not done in it that should have been done, was in response to alleged family demands. Finck pulled it off often enough in New Orleans.

Ebersole, who testified that he was almost always in that autopsy room and after the autopsy was with the prosectors and the body until 3 A.M. the next morning, testified that no such thing ever happened. He attested to this over and over again. Baden tried to put these words in Ebersole's mouth when arguing with him:

> **Dr. Baden.** 'But there was no clear implication you had that somebody in that [autopsy] room was giving orders as to how the autopsy should be done?'

Ebersole's response was "absolutely not" [transcript, page 15].

Knowing full well what was expected of them, as professional experts usually do, Baden and Weston returned to this at the end of that morning session. It is, I believe, explicit and important enough to be quoted at length.

> **Dr. Baden.** 'Some question has been raised to the autopsy personnel being aware of and perhaps concerned about the wishes of the family as to rapidity in which the autopsy would be done and as to the extent of the autopsy. Was the impression you had at the time of the autopsy that there was any such consideration?'
> **Dr. Ebersole.** 'I had no contact with the family nor did I hear the family mention that that night.'
> **Dr. Baden.** 'More specifically do you think in any way, shape or form there was any specific consideration given to the wishes of the family in any manner in which the autopsy was conducted, both as to the extent and as to rapidity of being performed?'
> **Dr. Ebersole.** 'I am aware of no such strictures on the autopsy protocol.'
> **Dr. Weston.** 'I would like to be more specific. Did the President's personal physician actually indicate any instructions to either Dr. Humes or—'
> **Dr. Ebersole.** 'Not that I heard, no, sir.'
> **Dr. Weston.** 'And you were there about 80 to 90 percent of the time, would you say?'
> **Dr. Ebersole.** 'Yes, sir.'
> **Dr. Weston.** 'And you never heard him say that you ought to do this or you ought not do that?'

Dr. Ebersole. 'No, sir.'

Dr. Weston. 'You didn't?'

Dr. Ebersole. 'No.'

Dr. Wecht. 'Jim, are you referring to Admiral Berkley [*sic*]?'

Dr. Weston. 'Yes . . .'

Dr. Wecht. 'I think Dr. Ebersole's answer makes it clear, but I just wanted to complete it as a corollary to Jim's question.'

Dr. Ebersole. 'You don't recall them, I assume, from what you have already said having heard any other admiral or general or Secret Service or FBI agent to any of the three autopsy physicians or to anybody else in the autopsy room that because of requests or instructions from the family or from somebody else that any particular procedure will or will not be done or that the autopsy will in any way be limited? Is that what you have said?'

Dr. Ebersole. 'That is correct. I was not aware of any limitations that we were held to. . . .'

Dr. Baden. 'Now relative to the other discussion about perceived pressures or potential perceived pressures by the prosectors, we have all here been in the position of doing official autopsies where for one reason or another we are aware of desires by family members (a) not to do an autopsy or (b) to do it rapidly or to do it partially, and we have all been in that position.'

Dr. Ebersole. 'Yes.'

Dr. Baden. 'Often this kind of awareness can't be pinpointed to one person telling another person but just to a general behavior pattern. Apart from that did anybody say anything to anybody? Is it your impression as a physician your role was different from Dr. Humes and Dr. Boswell or Dr. Finck, that there was a perception, for whatever the reason, real or imaginary, on the part of anybody doing the autopsy, especially in the light of what you raised about the adrenal glands in particular and other considerations about rapidity in which the examination would be done that have not been raised here that there was any feeling from your impression on any of your four doctors' parts that any part of the body should not be examined or it should be done quickly or it should be limited in any way, shape or form?'

Dr. Ebersole. 'I was not then aware of any such pressures. I am aware that they can occur in the course of an autopsy.'

Dr. Baden. 'But to the best of your recollection—'

Dr. Ebersole. 'But to the best of my recollection there was no such pressure on us' [transcript, pages 42–45].

Still again, this is not in the Warren Report or that of the HSCA.

But both bodies knew these truths kept secret, until a law was finally passed requiring its disclosure.

And now, as we see still again, those upon whom we depend for the information our society requires in order to function as it should, have failed us and themselves with their total silence.

This was obviously more accessible to the media than to immobile me.

The papers and TV abounded in pictures of reporters going over the boxes of these belatedly disclosed official records.

But what I here report, in a book so long in the writing and so delayed in its being published, is reported for the very first time!

While the same media with the same bent seeks to contrive criticisms of another supposedly liberal White House and in doing that ignores so much that requires public attention and understanding.

There is no need at this point in so long and detailed a book to repeat what can be said about that atrocity of a phony autopsy and what it says about the government's responsibility for it, particularly that part played by the military.

But I think that it was just plain ugliness that the government blamed the President's family for what the government itself conspired to do as soon as Oswald was dead and it was known there would be no trial. In many ways this is the greatest indecency and outrage of all.

That afternoon Finck was the only witness. He had learned in New Orleans that a witness, no matter how highly he may think of himself and how little he may think of the judge and all others in a lawsuit, does not run the proceedings and does not lecture all, including the judge.

He also learned that the safest responses were those he used most often: "I do not remember" or "I do not know."

But when he got to the very end, after jockeying and parrying about it, this is what he testified to about the source of that pressure applied with such care that Ebersole did not detect it. It is the very last thing before the panel bid him adieu with the words, "You are among lots of good friends. It is good to see you again." In reading this testimony, Finck has testified throughout that the Kennedy family prevented a complete autopsy, to which Ebersole had just sworn to the exact opposite, not a member of the panel noted this contradiction, nor did any one of them ask Finck to justify his statement that is so obviously self-serving when the panel had just heard testimony to the contrary:

Dr. Weston. 'I just wanted to ask a final question, Pierre. At the time this examination was done, there was a possibility that there was going to be a criminal prosecution. What is your practice as a forensic pathologist to stop short of doing a medical legal autopsy in face of criminal prosecution notwithstanding the wishes of anybody else?'

Dr. Finck. 'What you are saying, we should not have listened to the recommendations—'

Dr. Weston. 'No, I am not saying anything. I am asking you if it is not accepted medical legal practice when you anticipate a criminal prosecution to do a complete examination?'

Dr. Finck. 'Yes.'

Dr. Weston. 'Okay. Then the reason that you did not do a complete examination was that you were ordered not to, is that correct?'

Dr. Finck. 'Yes, restrictions from the family as the reason for limiting our actions.'

Dr. Weston. 'But do you really believe that the family has— is this not physical evidence which belongs to the state notwithstanding the wishes of the family when there is a suspected criminal prosecution?'

Dr. Finck. 'Of course it is ideal. In those circumstances you are told to do certain things. There are people telling you to do certain things. It is unfortunate.'

Dr. Weston. 'The last question. What do you consider would be the personal consequences of you or any of the other members of the team had you chosen to withdraw from the examination and not complete the examination or sign your name to it in view of the restrictions placed upon you? Did you consider that at that time?'

Dr. Finck. 'No. It is a delicate situation to say the least.'

Dr. Weston. 'I understand that, but it is still a delicate situation.'

Dr. Finck. 'We were handicapped by those restrictions.'

Dr. Weston. 'Okay. Those restrictions you mentioned were, as you remember now, Admiral Galloway?'

Dr. Finck. 'Who passed them on to us as I remember, so he should be consulted and asked who asked to have those restrictions.'

Dr. Petty. 'Pierre, we want to thank you so very much for coming by. You are among lots of good friends. It is good to see you again.'

Mr. Flanagan. 'Concluding this tape at 3:24' [transcript, pages 128-129].

And so it was Admiral Calvin B. Galloway who gave the restrictive orders to the autopsy prosectors. Finck also got away with the lie that Humes did not speak to Perry until the next day rather than during the autopsy. The records given me include an unsigned staff interview of Galloway three double-spaced pages long only. That he and Finck were not in the same world, let alone the same morgue, raised no recorded committee hackles.

This interview was so important to that committee it was conducted by phone rather than in person with Galloway only located less than an hour away, in Annapolis. Of what the unnamed staffer put on paper, this alone is what is new, that the committee got from the admiral who was in charge of that entire Navy operation of which the hospital is only part:

"Galloway said he was present throughout the autopsy," and "during the autopsy Galloway said that no orders were being sent in from outside the autopsy room either by phone or by person."

He was there the entire time and no word came in from outside!

Yet, without any doubt at all, this autopsy was entirely incomplete at the very best.

This is what the sworn testimony is:

The autopsy was inadequate and incomplete because it was ordered to be inadequate and incomplete.

Admiral Galloway was there all the time, and no order to do anything other than a full and the best possible autopsy came into the autopsy room from the outside.

And Finck said that the orders to the pathologists not to do what they knew they should do were from Galloway himself.

So Galloway gave the orders, and he got no orders to do that.

This means the military, and it alone, saw to it that the autopsy was a very bad one, to quote myself—one unfit for a Bowery bum.

And it was the military itself that blamed the family for what it ordered and did!

The task of the House committee was to investigate the "crime of the century" and the earlier official investigations of it. This is a fair sample of how under the pious and sanctimonious Blakey, who insisted upon being referred to as "professor," as he is in the committee's own secret hearings transcripts, the HSCA really set about its "investigations." Blakey and his committee suppressed all I here report!

It is also a fine example of why I always referred to it as "the House assassins committee."

In this testimony and in the dozen and a half staff reports and memos Gary gave me, Andy Purdy is Blakey's honcho most of the time. I first knew Andy when he was a student at the University of Virginia at Charlottesville. He and others of a group there, who professed the strongest disagreement with the official mythology, drove up to the Washington area to meet with friends of mine who were students at the University of Maryland at College Park, a Washington suburb. He had hardly had time to do more than graduate from law school before he was Blakey's boy, one of his assistant counsels on that committee. His lust to support the official mythology we have seen in small part in the testimony of Ebersole and Finck, where he was in charge. He also was pretty much in charge of one of the remaining items of special interest and importance in the assassination and all its investigations. This is the presence of those, the words of the autopsy protocol, "forty dustlike fragments" of bullet metal in the President's head.

As we have seen, it is a physical impossibility for that so-called Oswald ammunition, made under the provisions of the Geneva Convention, to do that. Hardened, jacketed military ammunition is designed, under the provisions of that Geneva Convention, not to be able to do just that.

It is possible for one familiar with the evidence to write a book about just this one of the innumerable travesties, Blakey's control of the committee so that it would not make the required investigations and what that yielded. But at this point in this book, there is no need for all of that. What Blakey led that committee into doing is what it would have done if it had been party to that government conspiracy not to investigate the crime itself. Because there is no such need in this book, I restrict what follows to these dustlike fragments impossible for the imputed Oswald bullet to have deposited in the President's head.

That was not matter pursued by the autopsy panel, the Warren Commission in this part of its testimony, of which Arlen Specter was in charge, or in its Report, in the Blakey committee's so-called investigation or in its report, or as we just have seen, in the deliberations of that committee's panel of medical experts or in its report, to which the committee devoted an entire volume.

This was, however, of great interest to both the Secret Service men present and the FBI agents sent to remain throughout the autopsy and to report on it. Roy Kellerman was the Secret Service agent in charge of the presidential escort that day. Francis X. O'Neill and James W. Sibert were the two FBI agents. Sibert in particular was very interested in the unusual fragmentation.

My first knowledge of this was in about May, 1966, when in the Commission's records I found the Sibert-O'Neill report on what they observed at that autopsy. I later published it in facsimile in *Post Mortem*:

"The Chief Pathologist [Humes] advised approximately forty particles of disintegrated bullet and smudges indicated that the projectile had fragmented while passing through the skull region."

Sibert's interest did not begin when he wrote this report. It galvanized him during the autopsy. If the committee did not know this earlier, as it must have, it did know not later that August 25, 1977, when Purdy, accompanied by Jim Kelley of the staff, interviewed Sibert at the Sheraton Motor Inn, in Fort Myer, Florida. In their report on their Sibert interview, this is some of what they said:

Sibert recalls the X rays of the head being shown in the room. He said the X ray had many ... flecks like the Milky Way ... part of the bullet has fragmentized or disintegrated. Sibert said a lot of the metal fragments were tiny and all that were removed from the body were put in a little jar with a black top. Sibert said that before they left the morgue they signed a receipt for the metal fragments.

Sibert was questioned further about his call to [FBI lab firearms expert Charles L.] Killion and what prompted it. Sibert said the doctors were at a loss as to where the bullet went. He said nothing was ever mentioned about the anterior neck wound being a possible exit bullet wound. Sibert said the doctors were discussing the amount of fragmentation of the bullet and the fact that they couldn't find a large piece. They were wondering if it was a kind of bullet which "fragmentizes" completely. This is why Sibert left the room to call the lab, to find out about that type of bullet.

These long-suppressed records make clear what is not in a word of any testimony anywhere or in any of their many public statements by the prosecutors, that they wondered "if it was the kind of bullet which 'fragmentized' completely. That is why Sibert left the room to call the lab, to find out about that type of bullet."

This is to say, *not* the "type" of bullet allegedly fired by Oswald!

Certainly this is the most important kind of information in any real investigation. The Blakey bunch regarded it as so important they waited for more than a year to get back to Sibert!

And from the record, no other official investigation even did that little.

They sent Sibert a draft of an affidavit for him to sign under the date of October 18, 1978. Sibert spoke to them by phone a week to the day later, according to his letter of October 24, with which he sent them the affidavit that he rewrote and executed. In the committee-prepared affidavit draft there is passing mention of this bullet "which fragments completely." In the affidavit that Sibert himself wrote and executed October 24, 1978, he attested to this, following his statement that he left the autopsy room to phone the FBI lab:

". . . and spoke to Agent Chuck Killion. I asked him if he could furnish any information regarding a type of bullet that would almost completely fragmentize. Agent Killion then asked if we knew about a bullet which had been found on a stretcher at Parkland Hospital and had been received at the laboratory from a Secret Service agent."

And with this it all just drops dead!

The committee had no interest in the "type of bullet that would almost completely fragmentize" and ignored this entirely, as all earlier official bodies and all the many who write in support of the official mythology also have always done.

Sibert's partner that night, Francis X. O'Neill, was also interviewed by the committee. For some reason, not immediately apparent, the names of the committee people are ommitted from their
lengthy report. They also sent O'Neill the draft of an affidavit, and
like Sibert, he also rewrote it. While the interview was on January
10, 1978, it was not for over nine months before O'Neill was sent
a draft to sign. O'Neill then signed the affidavit he had prepared on
November 8. Because the investigative report includes what was
omitted from the affidavit, the omission serving the committee's interest, I quote from the unsigned statement that emerged from
O'Neill's letter. It was again Purdy and Flanagan, along with James
Kelly of the committee staff who worked on this.

One of these omissions would have been another *coup de grâce* for
the committee's Oswald as the lone-assassin theory and conclusion:

"O'Neill mentioned that he does not see how the bullets entered
below the shoulder in the back 'could have come out of the throat.' "

That means the end of Arlen Specter's and the entire government's
single-bullet theory. Thus there was even more reason for O'Neill
having not been a witness, although he and Sibert, both FBI special
agents, were the most trained and experienced of all those who saw
the body with regard to bullets and their effects. This was not lost
on O'Neill:

"Although O'Neill was interviewed at length by Arlen Specter,
he felt it was odd that he was not called to give testimony."

So the Blakey committee did not call him to testify either!

O'Neill would have added to what Sibert said about the cause-of-
death bullet, the supposed major autopsy interest:

"O'Neill stated that some discussion did occur concerning the
disintegration of the bullet. A 'general feeling' existed that a soft-
nosed bullet struck JFK." Some of the bottom of page 6 is omitted
from the copy given me. On the top of the next page this resumes
by describing this soft-nosed or a different bullet as one that "disolves after contact." Then: "There was no real sense that either of
the wounds were caused by the same kind of bullet."

In the affidavit he wrote himself, O'Neill added additional information about both wounds and bullets. On page 2 he referred in general
to his discussions during the autopsy as "lengthy conversations with

Greer and Kellerman.'' On page 8 he indicated that those discussions were even wider:

"Some discussion did occur concerning the disintegration of the bullet. A general feeling existed during the autopsy that a soft-nosed bullet struck JFK. There was discussion concerning the back wound that the bullet could have been a 'plastic' type or an 'ice' bullet, one which disolves after contact.''

This does not seem to limit the discussions of the kinds of bullet *other than the hardened military-type* bullet Oswald alone allegedly used, and it does not seem to limit O'Neill's discussions to those two Secret Service agents only.

In all the records created about this and all those I have studied about it, which includes all in the Commission's files and all the FBI provided among those many thousands of pages and in all the testimony there are no other mentions of any bullets other than the one attributed to Oswald, hardened, full-jacketed military ammo. There is no other mention of any other possibility and no mention of any autopsy or discussions about it.

This, too, reflects the effectiveness of the government's conspiracy not to investigate the crime itself.

But in the mythology successfully foisted off on us as the conclusions of a genuine investigation, which there never was, it made no difference. It was well known that the supposed Oswald bullet could not do what was done by a bullet or bullets in the President's head, "disintegrate," the word O'Neill used, or Sibert's "fragmentize," leaving what the autopsy describes as "forty dustlike fragments," while an unknown part exploded out of the head. It made no difference because as this book began by proving, the "solution" was decided upon before any real investigation could have been made. All official parties nominated Oswald as the lone assassin, and they elected him unanimously, untroubled by the evidence they had and could not avoid which, like this fragmentation of a bullet into "forty dustlike fragments," proves it was not possible.

If Blakey, Purdy, and company had any interest in what, if anything, the FBI's lab told Sibert in response to his question, there is no known reflection of it.

As Sibert rewrote what Purdy sent to him to swear to, Sibert's choice of words is more than merely interesting. It is provocative.

In one sentence he stated that he had asked Killion for "information regarding the type of bullet that would almost completely fragmentize," and in the next sentence he said that Killion did not answers this important question, but asked if they "knew about a bullet" found at Parkland Hospital.

Not only in Sibert's own account did the lab tell him nothing in response to the question on which the solution to that most serious crime hung, it warned him that a bullet, of a particular type, had been connected to the assassination.

Killion was warning Sibert to drop the whole thing because of the bullet found at the hospital!

If it was not the kind that could so completely fragment, then there were real problems the FBI did not want to face.

It required no laboratory examination for the FBI to know that the bullet from the hospital was hardened, full-jacketed military ammunition and what that meant. Merely looking at that bullet is all that was necessary for the truth to be known: that kind of bullet could not have fragmented that way and proved fatal.

Or, *Oswald did not assassinate the President!*

Which gets back still again to the conspiracy engaged in by Katzenbach and Hoover as soon as they knew Oswald was dead and that there would be no trial at which any evidence would have to be made public to convict him and then be examined by his lawyer.

There is no question at all about it, all the officials involved in all these official investigations knew that it was not possible that Oswald fired what in their official account of the assassination was the one shot that killed the President.

They all knew, and they all suppressed it.

And these records, which reflect that guilty knowledge from the time the first autopsy X rays were taken and looked at, was suppressed for a decade and a half—until a law required their disclosure.

Once disclosed, they were totally ignored by everybody in the sense of giving them this meaning, which they do have, for the half-year between their disclosure and this writing.

This was ignored not only throughout all the official investigations, when all those investigations reflected this knowledge.

It continued to be ignored after I published the proof in 1975.

It was ignored insofar as any investigation of it was concerned by that committee after, according to a Purdy memo dated August 17, 1977, "I urged him to study what I had written and they had." That was *before* he first spoke to Sibert from these records so long suppressed.

It was ignored in terms of doing anything at all with it when Sibert then confirmed to Purdy and Klein what I had published of what he had written in 1963.

It was ignored by all the media when so belatedly these records were made available toward the end of 1993.

And it was then also ignored by all those working in those records in the uses I here make of those records.

The major media have never sought or been at all interested in the truth, in fact.

And the critics pursue theories, so many of them like apprentice Keystone Kops—and junior grade at that.

This is but another proof of the success of the government conspiracy to see to it that the crime was not investigated.

It also is a proof that the Katzenbach memo intended for the President with which this book begins was false: the evidence then in hand *did not prove Oswald guilty—it proved he was not the assassin.*

And that alone explains the total suppression for fifteen years of the records here used for the first time.

When this can happen—*and it did happen*—it says more about our country and our government than anyone should want to spell out, more than in asking are we more than or better than a "banana republic," the largest of them all?

There lingers the question: Was there a military conspiracy to assassinate the President?

Are our admirals and generals fools and incompetents with this their record?

Especially when a President—their commander in chief—is assassinated?

This may not be the full and complete record of the military in the assassination.

But it is that part of the record that is established by fact—mostly long-suppressed fact—and the rest universally ignored.

It is a record that cannot be ignored. Not safely!

Is this a time, despite our wealth and power, in those simple yet moving words so important in the beginning of our history, that tries men's souls?

If it is, do we have in our political leadership today, again the moving words from our very beginnings, only summer soldiers, no winter soldiers?

This long-overdue focus on the military should not exclude consideration again of co-conspirator J. Edgar Hoover and the FBI, which he cloned in his image and which he dominated so completely there has been not a word from any of the multitude in it who were witting and participated as in effect co-conspirators. Many of them are still alive.

It is not necessary to repeat the catalogue of the FBI's horrors. Recalling a few, however, provides perspective for this newest addition to that unprecedented catalogue.

Like that horror of digging up that Dallas curbstone struck by a bullet during the assassination after it was patched, with the full knowledge that it was patched, as was so obvious, then flying it to the fabled FBI laboratory at Washington headquarters, and testing the patch before all the world as though it was the original deposit from the bullet impact that was being tested. And then palming that off as the actual results of the test of that bullet impact!

Without, of course, seeking to learn who patched that curbstone in order to deny forever the bullet-metal evidence buried forever by the patch, the only purpose of the patching.

And then, shamelessly, pretending that "lead with a trace of antimony" was said to have been determined by that test, which is fine to parts per million, disclosed a bullet's impact. How many hundreds knew that bullets are made of more than lead and antimony—and were and remain silent?

Without their silence this conspiracy could not have succeeded.

So those many hundreds were and remain silent.

Lyndal Shaneyfelt knew when he had that curbstone dug up and took it for that horror of "testing." So did the Dallas case agent, Robert Gemberling. While not using the word "patch," he covered his own ass by saying there was the patch, but without using the word "patch."

So did Robert Frazier. He provided most of the FBI's secondhand testimony to the Warren Commission when those who could give firsthand information were unavailable. Frazier covered his ass with the ignored comment on a lab report that the impact could have been by an automobile wheel's weight.

Frazier and two others who had firsthand knowledge retired from the FBI when I sought to depose them in the lawsuit for the results of the FBI's testings. The FBI pretended unsuccessfully that because they were no longer employed by the FBI they could not be deposed. For that litigation the lab agent John Kilty replaced Frazier. When I proved in court that Kilty committed perjury in the FBI's never ending effort to preserve secrets that should not be secret, the judge in that case, John Pratt, threatened my lawyer, Jim Lesar, and me— and accepted that perjury. With that Pratt surrendered the Constitutional independence of the judiciary.

And the thin photographic plate, which is the basis of that spectrographic test remains withheld. The FBI told the court and me that it was probably discarded to save space! A minute fraction of an inch is space to save in the unimaginable enormity of the FBI's files?

That one plate of all the many exposed in the JFK assassination testing was gotten rid of to save *space?*

While the FBI's files on a Republican-owned magazine, for which I was its Washington correspondent, from its founding in the 1930s— its life ended in the 1940s—were not discarded to save space. And so much other trash the FBI had no proper business collecting still cluttered its files in the 1980s when I got copies.

Like that fabulous FBI report on the assassination ordered by President Johnson before he appointed his Commission—those beautifully gotten-up five volumes that told all, that solved the crime—without accounting for all the known shooting of even the official account of the shooting and without even stating the cause of death! This I exposed, with facsimiles of its account, before any other book on the Warren Report was published.

That FBI report did not fail in its purpose. It was a diatribe against Oswald that extended even to its index. And it scared the hell out of the Warren Commission, as it confessed to itself in the expectation of permanent TOP SECRET protection that it further protected by having the stenographic transcript destroyed. Until I was able to compel, under the FOIA, the transcription of the stenotypist's tape.

Speaking of the FBI, at that emergency, nighttime executive session, the Commission's general counsel, the former solicitor general of the United States, J. Lee Rankin, wailed, "They would like us to fold up and quit." Member Hale Boggs rejoined, again speaking of the FBI report, "This closes the case, you see. Don't you see?" Rankin added, "They found the man. There is nothing more to do. The Commission supports their conclusions, and we can go home, and that is the end of it" [*Post Mortem*, pages 486-87].

My, *were* they scared!

Or, what I was not able to publish but is no longer secret, thanks to the FOIA, that the FBI prepared "dossiers" on the Commission members! On its staff *twice*! And on the "critics," "sex dossiers!"

For what purpose other than to blackmail?

Tax money is spent for this police-statism in a free country? And with impunity?

There is no need for a longer cataloguing when a full cataloguing is impossible. The name of the FBI's game is control, and by that control it saw to the success of its sainted Director's conspiracy, extending that control even into the courts.

With this reminder, let us look again at what Sibert and O'Neill and Killion and who knows how many more in the FBI have been publicly silent about because each, separately, destroys the official "solution" to the crime and protects both this government conspiracy not to investigate the crime itself and the conspiracy to kill itself.

Sibert knew that full-jacketed, hardened, military ammunition could not "fragmentize" in the President's head, that it had to be other and "soft" ammunition—not Oswald's.

O'Neill, who at the autopsy "stated" there then was "discussion" of this and that there was "a 'general feeling' " that the "disintegration" came from "soft-nosed" ammunition.

They all knew this could not have been the ammunition the government said Oswald used!

O'Neill, who examined the body, not pictures of it, told the HSCA fellow suppressors "that he does not see how the bullets entered below the shoulder in the back and 'could have come out the back of the throat.' "

The President, in all the official "solutions," was struck by these two bullets only.

These two FBI agents said that neither bullet was Oswald's.

And they and all others who knew, of whom inside the FBI alone there were many, very many, said nothing.

Not during the "investigation" and not when and after the Warren Report was issued, and they knew what it said: what they knew was not possible.

And so both conspiracies were protected, the conspiracy not to investigate the crime itself and the conspiracy to kill.

How much longer can Hoover's ghost continue to control the FBI as in life he did so completely?

There must be thousands in the FBI as well as in other agencies and throughout the military who knew that the ammunition attributed to Oswald could not have caused the fatal shot and who knew that the shooting attributed to Oswald was impossible.

They all kept their silence—and their jobs and their futures.

That is how the conspiracy to kill succeeded.

Its success was possible only because the government conspiracy not to investigate the crime itself succeeded.

If there had not been this conspiracy not to investigate the crime itself, while that would not have prevented the President's killing, it might have made possible the capture of those who were the assassins.

After this Afterword was completed, there was another of those releases of what had been kept secret for three decades for the sole purpose of avoiding official embarrassment. What then was released, additional tapes of Johnson's phone conversations, did not qualify for classification. It did not involve even the most convoluted concept of "national security." They were suppressed by every administration after JFK, beginning with Johnson's.

It made the news, all right. It was on TV and radio and it was in the newspapers.

But not in any meaningful way did any element of the media address the actual significance of some of the more important content.

Johnson did not believe Castro had anything to do with the assassination, as there never had been any rational reason even to suspect.

That phony line was long misused by those of the right political extreme for their own political purposes. So, radio and TV aired them, and the people could hear Johnson discussing this with his then attorney general, Ramsey Clark.

To the *Washington Post* the only newsworthy content of these released tapes was a question: Had Johnson really referred to the widow Kennedy as "honey"? Reflecting the importance the *Post* saw in all those disclosed taped conversations, this one juicy bit of gossip was a small item in a tidbit column in its "Style" section.

While I have no way of knowing whether it was reported elsewhere, of all I saw and read of these disclosures that I regard as of great significance I saw only in the Associated Press story that appeared in the *Los Angeles Times* of April 16, 1994, from which I quote below and the Sunday *New York Times* of the next day. It was not in the story the Associated Press put on its Maryland wire for its Maryland papers.

As the story appeared in the *Times*, it did not convey to its readers the significance of what I here quote, what followed Johnson's reference to that Castro-did-it theory as "preposterous."

Even the date of a conversation Johnson had with Senator and Warren commissioner Richard B. Russell had an unreported significance. But the likelihood is that few if any reporters or their editors knew or could know of that significance. It was the very day Russell believed he had made a record of his resolute refusal to agree with the single-bullet theory without which that single-assassin Report could not have been issued, without which the canard that Oswald was the lone assassin could not have been gotten away with. So, it was much on Russell's mind. The two versions are not identical. This was in the *Los Angeles Times*:

> Johnson's conversation with Russell, about the bullet that hit Connally, occurred on Sept. 18, 1964. They discussed progress in preparing the report on Kennedy's slaying
>
> The senator noted some members of the Commission headed by Chief Justice Earl Warren believed that 'the same bullet that hit Kennedy first is the one that hit Connally.'
>
> Responding to Johnson's musing, Russell said, 'Well, it don't make much difference.' He added, 'Well, I don't believe it . . .'
>
> 'I don't either,' Johnson responded.

The New York Times version includes what was very much on Russell's mind that day when he believed the record of his doubts was made and preserved for history:

> Russell said the report would note disagreement on the panel over whether Connally had been struck by a bullet that had already hit Kennedy or by a separate one. . . .
>
> Many people who see a conspiracy contend that if the same bullet could not have wounded both men, there had to have been a second bullet, and therefore a second gunman.

Of all the accounts of that conversation sent me it was only the New Zealand Sunday *Star-Times* of April 17 that told its readers the truth about hemming and hawing as the Associated Press and its member papers did. Its story, sent me by my dear friend, Auckland history professor Dal McGuirk, rewrote the Reuters wire service copy to report correctly and without any equivocation the precise and unquestionable truth:

"If the same bullet could not have wounded both men, there had to have been a second gunman."

As none of our papers told their readers, the Report does not note any such disagreement at all. The Commission knew very well that if both men were not wounded by that one bullet there had been the conspiracy it was determined at the outset to report there had not been.

Nor is it only as the Associated Press's second-day version that *The New York Times* rubber-stamped, that only those it has always castigated as conspiracy theorists "see a conspiracy" and "contend that it, the same bullet," did not inflict all nonfatal wounds, there was "therefore a second gunman."

Nothing in this world is more certain that that from the official evidence itself!

And the long-kept secret is that the President of the United States himself believed that this proved there had been a conspiracy. Despite what his Commission's Report said. And that means it was a conspiracy that made him President of the United States of America!

Let us not treat this as some kind of game of Monopoly as the major media and major publishers have come to do, where the real importance is who is going to get to Boardwalk. Let us remember that this is that most deeply subversive of crimes in a country like ours, the crime that had the effect of a coup d'état, the assassination of any president inevitably having that effect.

Lyndon Johnson became President by that assassination, which is to say in that coup d'état. It was he who decided to have the crime investigated and reported on by a presidential commission, and it was he who selected those commissioners and in some instances coerced them to serve when they objected strongly, as Russell did. In a very real sense, Johnson co-opted the state of Texas, which alone had legal criminal jurisdiction, and saw to it that Texas would not consider the possibility that anyone other than Oswald had been involved in the assassination. The killing of a president not then being a federal crime, Johnson also coopted both houses of the Congress, either of which could have conducted an investigation. Both were considering holding investigations.

In a very real sense, although it received no attention at all, *Johnson's* Commission of *his* commissioners was to certify to *his* legitimacy, for there were many who believed and said that somehow Johnson was involved, that the assassination was to make him the President.

So on the very day that Johnson's Commission saw to it that the determined refusal of two of its members to agree with its most basic conclusion, and that is what disagreeing with Arlen Specter's single-bullet theory does mean, on that very day less than a week before that ponderous Report was handed to him, Johnson also was in secret recorded as also believing that the Report his commissioners issued for him was one with which he, too, could not agree!

Six days later all the media showed Johnson accepting that Report which, among other things, certified to the legitimacy of his presidency. It is no exaggeration to say that he, as far as its reflection in the media is concerned, greeted that Report warmly. In effect, he endorsed it. As then and since then, the unquestioning media also has.

Johnson, who became President of the United States by the assassination of President John F. Kennedy actually believed that the Report on that assassination by his own Commission was a lie and in advance of its release said so!

This does mean that from the official evidence alone and on this basis alone Johnson was made president by a conspiracy—and that he knew he confirmed later, as we have seen in the Cartha DeLoach memo quoted earlier in this book.

This was not worth being pointed out to the people by any element of the media, from the least to the most important?

Wasn't it news?

Hell, man, that was thirty years ago, wasn't it? Nah, no news in it.

But to one of the most important media components, the *Washington Post*, the paper that is most influential in Washington, particularly in all parts of the government, there was that one thing that was worthy of mention, to titillate: Had Johnson really referred to Jackie Kennedy as "honey"?

(This matter of state it left unresolved.)

There was no editorial, no op-ed piece in the majestic paper of record, *The New York Times*. Which had only recently extended itself to propagandize for the most dishonest of all books ostensibly on the JFK assassination, the knowingly mistitled *Case Closed* by Gerald Posner. (The *Post* did not go along with that one, however.)

The major media have for thirty years been critical and ridiculed those of us who wrote books critical of the Report of Johnson's Commission when all the time its most severe critics in terms of their authority were the President who appointed that Commission and its most conservative member, Richard Russell.

It was no secret that Russell disagreed with the Report, although there was virtually no reporting of it when commission staff members leaked it.

It was not worth any media attention when I published the fact that Russell's disagreement was fatal to that Report and that to his dying day he encouraged me to expose his own commission. In my *Whitewash IV* (1974) I reported that, along with the details of how the Commission contrived to wipe out the record of his disagreement, shared by Kentucky's respected Republican Senator John Sherman Cooper. Russell wanted to make known his disagreement that he and Cooper believed they were making for our history.

My first book on the Warren Report, which dates to mid-February 1965, was not the first criticism of it. As Russell's assistant, in a memo prepared for Russell after he read my first four books said correctly, *I* agreed with *Russell*.

Newsworthy? Hell, no, man. The cat's dead thirty years, ain't he?

And so, when after thirty years it was no longer suppressed by all the governments in power, it was no longer secret that the President of the United States himself did not believe his own Commission's "solution" to the crime that alone made him president, that also was not news.

Naturally, therefore, the legitimacy given to all my books and to a few others by no less a person than the President made president by that assassination was not worthy of any mention, either.

This is a true reflection of some of what has happened to us in the wake of that assassination. It is a gruesomely accurate reflection of what has become of our major media.

And it is why this book is titled as it is.

"Never Again!" is what Jews—and not Jews alone—have been saying ever since the unprecedented atrocities of Hitler's Holocaust became known. Secretary of State George Shulz was in the USSR on April, 19 1988, after the belated dedication of a monument at Babi Yar, what he referred to as "among the first places where we saw the Holocaust, the slaughter of Jews." He also said, as I quote from William J. Korey's contribution to *The Holocaust in the Soviet Union* (New York and London: M. E. Sharp, 1993, page 75), "We have to say to ourselves, always, 'Never Again.' "

If our politicians and major media continue to persist in refusing to acknowledge what they did and did not do at the time of and following this great tragedy and refuse to utter these words; if our government does not repent and speak them; we must seek to see it however we can that there never be such an authentic subversion as we had from all those lies, sworn and unsworn; from all those deceptions of the people, calculated or not; from such a corruption of our history; from such abdication of our national honor and integrity; from such failures of all our basic institutions; from such a monolithic lack of responsibility, of any concept of decency; from such a total disregard for the decent concern of mankind—nothing like what this book brings to light about these and so many terrible things without precedent in our history at the time of and after the JFK assassination—

NEVER AGAIN!